THE SELECTED SHORT STORIES OF EDITH WHARTON

THE SELECTED
SHORT STORIES
OF
Edith Wharton

Introduced and edited by

R.W.B. LEWIS

CHARLES SCRIBNER'S SONS
NEW YORK

MAXWELL MACMILLAN CANADA
Toronto
MAXWELL MACMILLAN INTERNATIONAL
New York   Oxford   Singapore   Sydney

Copyright © 1991 by Charles Scribner's Sons

Introduction and notes copyright © 1991 by R. W. B. Lewis

Charles Scribner's Sons
Macmillan Publishing Company
866 Third Avenue, New York, NY 10022

Maxwell Macmillan Canada, Inc.
1200 Eglinton Avenue East, Suite 200
Don Mills, Ontario M3C 3N1

Macmillan Publishing Company is part of the Maxwell Communication Group of Companies.

Library of Congress Cataloging-in-Publication Data

Wharton, Edith, 1862–1937.
    [Short stories. Selections]
    The selected short stories of Edith Wharton / introduced and edited by R.W.B. Lewis.
        p.   cm.
    ISBN 0-684-19304-3
    I. Lewis, R. W. B.   II. Title.
    PS3545.H16A6   1991   91-11433   CIP
    813'.52—dc20

Design by Ellen R. Sasahara

Printed in the United States of America

CONTENTS

INTRODUCTION

EDITH WHARTON was a relatively late starter as a writer of fiction. When her first short story appeared in July 1891, she was twenty-nine years old, married, the owner of a small expensive house on Park Avenue (near 78th Street), and a visible if restive member of the upper-middle-class New York society into which she was born. She had been married since 1885 to Edward Robbins Wharton, an affable, somewhat aimless Boston gentleman; her domestic situation was already proving unsatisfactory, both sexually and, so to say, intellectually, and would lead before long to a serious breakdown, of which the symptoms were exhaustion, nausea, and melancholy. Her material condition, otherwise, was comfortable enough. She was independently wealthy: she had inherited a sturdy trust fund upon her father's death; and in 1888 she came into a legacy of $120,000 from an eccentric and reclusive New York cousin. It was with this latter sum that she bought the Park Avenue home, and soon afterward an estate at Newport, Rhode Island, overlooking the Atlantic Ocean.

In these early literary days, accordingly, Edith Wharton was far from having to "live by her pen," in her own phrase. It would take a good deal of time and practice, indeed, and the experience of dealing with editors and publishers, and puzzling over the practices of book advertising, before she became a professional writer and recognized herself as such: a professional, that is, rather than a wife and homemaker with a busy social calendar. In the eight years after her first publication, though she wrote a dozen stories, she later repudiated a number of them, and held back others until her first collection of short fiction, *The Greater Inclination,* in 1899, which contained some expert tales (three of them are in the present volume).

But in 1900 alone, Edith Wharton brought out seven stories. It is fair to say that after that, except during the formidably distracting interlude of the First World War, her fiction-writing energy never let up. A couple more statistics may be added. Between 1900 and the outbreak of the war in 1914, Edith Wharton produced almost fifty short stories, an average of three or four a year. And this during a period in her private life which saw the abandonment and sales of her American homes, her permanent expatriation to France and a Faubourg St. Germain apartment, the end of her marriage in a painful divorce, and a passionate, disturbing love affair with Morton Fullerton, an American journalist based in Paris—all elements one can find reflected overtly or obscurely in the stories produced. Between the end of the war and her death in 1937, Edith Wharton wrote twenty-four stories, one or two a year; but in those same years, it should be remembered, she brought out nine novels (*The Age of Innocence* and *A Mother's Recompense* among them), four novellas (the splendid durable *Old New York* foursome), a book of poems, a collection of critical essays, and an autobiography. "You are a wonder," her editor once said to her. "Do you marvel that I bow low before such energy?"

In the prewar years, Edith Wharton's stories were published in the influentially genteel magazines, with their appeal to cultivated upper-class taste and their solid if limited readership: the excellent *Scribner's Magazine* for the most part; the *Century* or *Harper's* if *Scribner's* was booked up. Financial figures are more readily available for Mrs. Wharton's novels than for her stories, but it is a reasonable guess that she received about $300 per story in the early 1900s. Her wares increased steadily in value. After the success of her first novel, *The Valley of Decision* in 1902, which brought in $10,000 in royalties in a matter of months, the Scribners publishing house willingly gave her a $5,000 advance on her next novel, *The House of Mirth*. This became the fastest-selling novel in the history of Scribners and earned its author $30,000 in sixty days. (It is safe to multiply any of these figures by ten to get a sense of the contemporary equivalent.) Edith Wharton was now getting $700 and more for a short story. The sum would be more like $1,500 by 1913; and in 1925, to glance forward, a mild little anecdote called "Miss Mary Pask," which Edith Wharton wrote in a single afternoon on the terrace of her Riviera winter home while recovering from the grippe, netted her $1,800.

That story appeared in the up-and-coming monthly, the *Pictorial Review*; and in fact, by this stage Edith Wharton had moved from what would later be called "quality publishing" into the world of (relatively) big literary money. She had shifted over from Scribners to Appleton & Company in 1912 for her novel *The Reef*, in response to Appleton's offer of a $15,000 advance; and for stories and serials, she turned to magazines of large, even mass circulation: the *Pictorial Review*, the *Saturday Evening Post,* and *Hearst's International-Cosmopolitan*. In 1920 the *Pictorial Review* paid $18,000 for magazine rights to *The Age of Innocence*. Edith Wharton belatedly realized what she had let herself in for when she discovered the first installment flanked by advertisements for soap flakes and Sani-Flush, a detergent for cleaning toilet bowls. She understood further when the editor notified her casually that several installments would have to be trimmed to make space for illustrations and further ads. "I cannot consent to have my work treated as prose by the yard," she declared wrathfully.

She won that particular case, but there is no doubt that Edith Wharton after 1920 wrote and sold a number of flimsy fictional concoctions for large sums of money—to pay the expenses of her elegant manner of life, her travels, her lavishly hospitable homes in southern France and outside of Paris, and her many private charities. Even during the depths of the Depression, though she had trouble placing her more serious work, she received $2,000 from the *Saturday Evening Post* for the forgettable "A Glimpse," and $5,000 from *Hearst's* for the negligable if likable "Charm Incorporated" (neither of these is in this volume). When in 1934 Edith Wharton flew into a temper with Appleton-Century (as it had been renamed) over its allegedly poor advertising and generally inadequate treatment of her books, the senior editor replied with a long financial statement demonstrating that the house had paid her almost $580,000—for royalites on novels, serial rights, short stories, motion picture and dramatic rights—over the last fourteen years of their association. In present terms the amount would be reckoned in millions.

But the creative picture must not be falsified. It is true that Edith Wharton's only collection of stories in the 1920s, *Here and Beyond* in 1926, contained nothing but potboilers, to borrow the title of one of her own early tales (though the story "Bewitched" had a second life on television not long ago). But of her short stories in the 1930s, no less than seven, one-third of the total, find their place in this book, beginning with the strange masterpiece "A Bottle of Perrier" in 1930 and continuing through "After Holbein," "Roman Fever" and others. Almost literally to the day she died—she sent on her story "All Souls' " to her agent only a few months before her death in the summer of 1937—Edith Wharton maintained the high level and the remarkable variety that had characterized her achievement in the writing of short stories for forty-six years.

Edith Wharton's earliest story, "Mrs. Manstey's View," is a touching little sketch of an elderly widow living out her days in a shabby New York boardinghouse. "All Souls'," the last of her tales, deals with the walking dead and witches' covens. Edith Wharton's story-writing imagination habitually ranged and roamed between these generic extremes, between the social realism of the former and the ritualistic and quasi-mythic atmosphere of the latter, with excursions into social and cultural satire along the way. If the present commentary favors a little the transrealistic phases, so to call them, it is because Whartonian criticism in most quarters of late has sufficiently emphasized the social realist.

The dramatic rise in Edith Wharton's literary standing in the past decade or so—it is an extraordinary and ongoing phenomenon—has been both cause and consequence of innumerable books and articles and conferences (with an invaluable newsletter to keep one abreast of it all), exploring almost every conceivable aspect of her work. (This writer heard recently of an apparently well-executed dissertation which argues that Edith was incestuously violated by her father and older brother, and tried to commit suicide because of it, the evidence being discoverable in her fiction when properly decoded. The example of Virginia Woolf, along with Edith Wharton's fascination with the incest motif, makes one hesitate to dismiss even this otherwise outré theory.) The expanded attention to Edith Wharton, as it happens, coincided with a marked increase of stress in American criticism at large on the historically and socially conditioned. Among the several Edith Whartons that have come into view, perhaps the most visible at the moment is the delineator as well as the victim of class distinctions, the analyst of a marketplace culture, and the historian of women as social beings in modern America.

As to the validity of this profile, one need look no further than "The Other Two," the best story of its kind that Edith Wharton ever wrote, and one made to order for the social or even sociological critic. It comes to us through the fluctuating and maturing consciousness of a New York investment broker, Waythorn, his wife's third husband. The first husband, Haskett, is a lower-class figure; he looks like a piano tuner, has an "over-the-counter politeness," and an uncultivated manner of speech, and worst of all, for Waythorn, he wears a made-up tie with an elastic. The second husband, Gus Varick, a florid man-about-town, is, in Waythorn's reflection and "whatever his faults," "a gentleman, in the conventional, traditional sense of the term." Varick visits Waythorn's Wall Street office to consult about a $100,000 investment, and the two men establish affable business relations.

But Waythorn comes to realize Varick's essential crudity of character and social manner, even as he grows aware of Haskett's probity and humanity. His social education completes itself in his understanding of his wife Alice and her curious pliancy toward both her former husbands. In an idiom nicely blending the financial with the erotic, he muses that "He held so many shares in his wife's personality, and his predecessors were his partners in the business." But a larger proposition (though of course it conveys Waythorn's way of thinking not less than an insight into his wife) is carried in an astonishing, evolving figure that draws upon consumer tactics, sexual innuendo, and the psychology of personality to move into the realm of the mythopoetic:

She was "as easy as an old shoe"—a shoe that too many feet had worn. Her elasticity was the result of tension in too many directions. Alice Haskett—Alice Varick—Alice Waythorn—she had been each in turn, and had left hanging to each name a little of her privacy, a little of her personality, a little of the inmost self where the unknown gods abide.

With "The Other Two," as luminous exercises in social realism, we can place "Souls Belated," "The Dilettante," "Autres Temps . . . ," "The Long Run," and "Roman Fever." Each has its particular attractions. "Souls Belated" is an early enactment of one of Edith Wharton's darkest themes: the absence of any truly satisfying alternative to life within conventional society (something writ painfully large in *The Age of Innocence* and, as it were, countrified, in *Ethan Frome*). "The Dilettante," a model of brevity, dramatizes an ironic inversion of attitudes toward the extramarital relationship. "Autres Temps . . ." in 1911 draws upon and, as a note will explain, suggestively transforms an episode out of Boston's social history in the 1890s. The softly spoken but breathtaking last line of "Roman Fever" (in Edith Wharton's final collection *The World Over* in 1936) discloses with a kind of formal perfection a situation that has silently endured for more than two decades.

"The Long Run" of 1912 is an archetypal story, what the great critic Kenneth Burke might call a representative anecdote: representative in this case of so many stories inherent in the aborted impulses and inadequate passions of the very well-to-do in the American society of several generations past. Halston Merrick thinks himself chivalrous, at the time, to turn back Paulina Trant's brave offer of herself; but as he later acknowledges, he was only being fatuous and self-protective, and there followed a ruined life for both of them. F. Scott Fitzgerald almost certainly had "The Long Run" in mind when he wrote "The Rich Boy," one of the finest of all his tales, in 1926. Even the names seem to echo: the very wealthy Anson Hunter, New Yorker and Yale graduate, holds back from marrying Paula Legendre, and is never thereafter a quite complete human being, a paradigm of what Fitzgerald meant when he said there are no second acts in American lives. He can merely repeat himself in later relations, as when he turns back the passionate appeal of Dolly Karger, a scene that leads to the memorable little passage:

For a long time afterward Anson believed that a protective God sometimes interfered in human affairs. But Dolly Karger, lying awake and staring at the ceiling, never again believed in anything at all.

Of Edith Wharton's social and cultural satires, "The Mission of Jane" is exemplary. The satirical eye is that of the elegant and sophisticated Lethbury, who is given to witty but coolly detached inward aphorisms about his wife's response to a domestic challenge: "She was like a dried sponge put in water; she expanded, but she did not change her shape." Against every rational instinct, he agrees to his wife's suggestion that they adopt a baby. The infant, Jane, develops into an impossible teenage girl bent on reforming the whole household, and Lethbury's satirizing turns fearfully from wife to daughter: her young mind, he reflects, "remained . . . a kind of cold storage from which anything which had been put there could be taken out at a moment's notice, intact but congealed." Jane is asked in marriage by a young man named Budd, and Lethbury expresses a frantic hope that the engagement will be a short one. The dialogue that follows may be matched with Jack Benny's famous exchange with the gunman:

> "Engagement!" said his wife solemnly. "There is no engagement."
> Lethbury dropped his cigar. "What on earth do you mean?"
> "Jane is thinking it over."
> "*Thinking it over?*"
> . . . Lethbury fell back with a gasp.*

After hair-raising hesitation, Jane marries and departs. Her parents come together on the common ground of relief as they had not done in all the years of marriage; and thus is Jane's mission fulfilled. Lethbury at the end, chastened and contrite, has emerged from his satirically envisioned world into that of the inescapably real.

"Duration" (1936) would seem to derive its best effects from the techniques of contemporary film comedy, though it has yet to be proven that Edith Wharton ever attended the cinema. Two centenarians, Martha Little of Boston and a remote cousin, Syngleton Perch from Newport, are being prepared for a celebration of their fabulous longevity. For the rhetorically and visually antic, the pivotal scene would not be easy to match. Cousin Syngleton is to be moved from his armchair into another room in Martha Little's house, and a younger relative is needed to assist:

> for extricating Syngleton from the armchair was like hooking up a broken cork which, at each prod, slips down farther into the neck of the bottle. Once on his legs he goose-stepped valiantly forward; but until he had been balanced on them he tended to fold up at the very

---

*Gunman: "Your money or your life."
Benny (after a long pause): "I'm thinking it over."

moment when his supporters thought they could prudently release him.

That moment and the final one—which could be titled Martha Little's Revenge—are the high points of Wharton's physiological comedy.

Edith Wharton had an acute eye for the folly, pretentiousness, and vulgarization to which the American cultural scene was vulnerable, and her authorial being rejoiced in the depiction of it. In "The Pelican," the fuzzy-minded, tenacious Mrs. Amyot lectures on alleged philosophical and literary subjects across the land, to meet the needs of her young son, as she explains; and continues to do so long after the son has grown up, made his own life, and paid her back in full. The narrator, taken by Mrs. Amyot's "dear contradictions and irrelevancies," consents to help her prepare a talk on Plato. "If she wanted to lecture on Plato, she should!—Plato must take his chance like the rest of us." Edith Wharton sums up an entire modern phase of pseudoerudition when she explains that Mrs. Amyot's talks on literary influences had fallen into disfavor, since her "too-sophisticated audiences . . . now demanded either that the influence or the influenced should be quite unknown, or that there should be no perceptible connection between the two." (Again to speak personally, I recall a learned talk at a distinguished American university on the subject of Arnold and the Celtish Renaissance, in which it was demonstrated beyond question that Arnold had not the slightest connection with the Celtish Renaissance. I thought then—it was long before I read "The Pelican" or anything else by Edith Wharton—that this opened up new vistas of scholarship.)

The satirical tone grows harsher in "The Descent of Man," as though more were at stake. The narrative begins in light-hearted play about the gullibility of the reading public and the earnest idiocy of (some) publishers; but it goes on to portray, subtly and knowingly, the corruption of the intellectual (how familiar this has become) by enormous popular and financial success. The story "Xingu" shapes up as a beautifully managed hoax, with the members of a ladies' club being led adroitly up the garden path by a playful associate. Two genuine cultural monuments lie behind these two tales: Charles Darwin's *Descent of Man* of 1871 behind the first of them, and probably Sir James Frazer's epochal inquiry into the origins of myth, *The Golden Bough* of 1890, behind the second.

Edith Wharton's imagination tended persistently toward the mythic: toward an enlargement, even a mystifying of the human, through suggestions of the ritualistic and the ancient in common human experience. "The

Legend," in 1910, provides a fascinating and problematic instance of the tendency.

John Pellerin, a philosopher of great if unspecified visionary power, reappears in New York after having been thought dead for twenty-five years. He returns bearing the name Winterman, and reveals himself only to a youthful disciple, to whom he explains that years before he had vanished and allowed himself to be assumed dead because his writings, so urgent and ambitious, had been grossly misunderstood or simply disregarded. During his absence a wealthy idler, Howland Wade, has earned a national reputation offering explanatory lectures on Pellerinism, with particularly enthusiastic audiences at the local Uplift Club. It is news of his own fame that has brought Pellerin back. As Winterman, he shows Wade his new philosophical manuscript; Wade dismisses it as pure nonsense and a crude plagiarism of Pellerin. Winterman thereupon takes himself off and is never heard of again. The last thing he was heard to say was that he was "going home."

The range of elements in this still relatively little-known tale is astonishing even for Edith Wharton. On one level the story partakes of cultural satire. One may easily see Mrs. Amyot in "The Pelican" holding forth on Plato at the Uplift Club; and Wade's obviously mindless gabbing about Pellerinism and its profundities seems akin to Mrs. Roby's spurious allusions in "Xingu" to the nonexistent occult doctrine. But a deeper current runs through "The Legend," via the twice-blighted intellectual career of Pellerin-Winterman.

In the presentation of her protagonist, Edith Wharton had in mind Henry James, as she informed her friend and lover Morton Fullerton in March 1910, after a visit with the then suicidally depressed James in London. "[I] thought of him when I described the man in 'The Legend,' " she said, "as so sensitive to human contacts and yet so *secure* from them." The connection was closer than that, was indeed in a collapse of security: Winterman, talking to his young friend about the failure of his early work, recalls the sneers and silence that greeted it; Henry James in the winter of 1910 was brought to the verge of suicide by the failure of the Collective Edition of *his* work. Edith Wharton had intuited the Jamesian collapse: in "The Legend," written some months before the London visit, she has Pellerin tell how near he had come to killing himself—"I felt that the easiest thing would be to lie down and go to sleep in the snow."

There is yet a dimension beyond that, and it is suggested by the two names Pellerin and Winterman. Pellerin, of course, in its Gallic form of Pélérin, is the French word for pilgrim, and the person so named is nothing other than a pilgrim, a seeker, a wanderer after truth, arriving at last, for the unheeding public, with a "message," a "cry," a "revelation." His disappearance had been a kind of death, and when, in his own phrasing, he "came to life again," it was "on the underside of the world," a phrase it is next to impossible not to compress into the single word "underworld." He reenters the human landscape as Winterman: the man (may it not be surmised) from the winter-world; and it is there that he is returning, as autumn settles in, back to his dark kingdom, when he goes home.

The mythic aspect of "The Legend" lurks in the narrative as a possibility of meaning, a matter of names and rhythms, and a title that may or may not point beyond the legendary philosopher himself to some ancient seasonal rite. In "Pomegranate Seed" of 1931, the myth encloses the tale.

Kenneth Ashby, after the death of his first wife, is happily married to Charlotte Gorse, the two of them occupying a comfortable old-fashioned house in New York. But soon after their honeymoon, there begin to arrive in the dusk of winter days letters addressed to Ashby in a nearly illegible but visibly feminine hand. The letters have a disintegrating effect on Ashby, though he will say nothing about them. In the wake of one of them, he disappears; and it is conjectured by Charlotte and her mother-in-law, amid frissons of terror and disbelief, that the letters have been summonses from the dead wife, and that Ashby has gone to join her.

When asked about the story's title, Edith Wharton told her editor that it came from "classical mythology," and explained: "When Persephone left the under-world to re-visit her mother Demeter, her husband Hades, lord of the infernal regions, gave her a pomegranate seed to eat, because he knew that if he did so she would never be able to remain among the living, but would be drawn back to the company of the dead." In the opening section of the old legend, in Ovid's *Metamorphoses* and elsewhere, the maiden Persephone is espied by Hades, who abducts her, carries her down to the world below, and there makes her his queen. Her mother Demeter, the earth-goddess, searches the world for her, and eventually secures her release—but only for half of each year. More than likely, the myth was a narrative working-out of the death, or ground-burial, of the corn seed in one season and birth or growth in another.

Edith Wharton was obsessed by the Persephone myth throughout her literary life. References to it, and the Eleusinian mysteries associated with it, turn up in her letters, notebooks, and stories. In two of her early tales, *The Touchstone* and "Copy," novels entitled *Pomegranate Seed* are attributed to the women writers involved; and Edith Wharton herself wrote a short poetic drama of that name published in *Scribner's* in 1912. In this interesting, modest effort, chiefly a dialogue between the temporarily reunited Demeter and Persephone, the daughter, who bears an "estranging darkness" on her brow, declares forthrightly:

> I, that have eaten of the seed of death,
> And with the dead die daily, am become
> Of their undying kindred.

She announces her preference for that dark world over the sunlit earth-world of her mother. Her last words are: "Free me. I hear the voices of my dead."*

The pomegranate seeds in the Whartonian story appear to be the letters from the former Mrs. Ashby; by consuming them, that is by reading them, Kenneth Ashby has made it imperative, even irresistible for him to spend a portion of his time in the dead woman's company. Part of the story's technical brilliance is that we know about that wife, as we know everything else, only through the disturbed consciousness of Charlotte, for whom she is simply "a distant, self-centered woman." The reader is invited to partici-pate in the serious game of interpretation. For this reader, we have a ghostly metaphor of masculine yielding, of masochistic submission to female power of the sexual and psychological variety.

Such a reading has, in any case, the advantage of bringing "Pomegranate Seed" in line with other Edith Wharton ghost stories: "The Lady's Maid's Bell," "Kerfol," "Mr. Jones," "The Eyes," "All Souls'." The mythic is quiescent in some of these stories, which may be seen rather as fictional strategies—something Edith Wharton shared with other writers in the Anglo-American Victorian age—for dealing with intensities of sexual behavior by distancing them into the spectral and legendary. So distanced, the behavior could be dealt with more freely than the proprieties normally allowed. In "The Lady's Maid's Bell," the brutish physical demands made by one Brampton upon his frail fastidious wife (and with which the maid, the bell, and the ghostliness are implicated) can be referred to, in tight-lipped fashion, by the servant Hartley: "I turned sick," she remembers, peering back into the far past, "to think what some ladies have to endure and hold their tongues about." In "Kerfol," an American visitor, puzzled by a cluster of silent small dogs he encounters in the courtyard of an old

---

*Taking these allusions, with some others, as seminal clues, Candace Waid has written a compelling and handsomely argued study called *Edith Wharton's Letters from the Underworld: Fictions of Women and Writing* (University of North Carolina Press, 1991). "Persephone," writes Professor Waid, "is Wharton's figure for the woman writer," the person who metaphorically "chooses to leave the world of the mother and dwell in the underworld of experience," there "savoring the supernatural fruit of letters and books."

Professor Waid hears the very voice of Edith Wharton the writer in the quotation from Apuleius (*The Golden Ass*, Book XI), which Wharton inscribed in a 1914 notebook: "I trod the confines of death and the threshold of Proserpine [the Latin name for Persephone]; I was swept all around the elements and back again; I saw the sun shining at midnight in purest radiance; Gods of heaven and Gods of hell I saw face to face and adored them."

house in Brittany, is led to discover the seventeenth-century drama of the house, a drama of sexual torment, monstrous revenge, and madness. In "Mr. Jones," an Englishwoman, taking possession through inheritance of a six-hundred-year-old country mansion, ferrets out the poignant tale, dating back to the 1820s, of its former mistress: the deaf-and-dumb heiress Juliana, whom her heartless husband kept in solitary confinement under the iron guard of his caretaker Mr. Jones. For permitting this secret history to be known, the present-day housekeeper, Mrs. Clemm, is strangled to death by the ghost of Mr. Jones.

The housekeeper's name, incidentally, is the same as that of Edgar Allan Poe's housekeeper in Baltimore, after Poe had married *that* Mrs. Clemm's daughter Virginia. The use of it is no doubt Edith Wharton's gesture of kinship to one of the two American writers (Hawthorne was the other) whom she acknowledged as her precursors in what (in her 1925 essay "Telling a Short Story") she called "the peculiar category of the eerie."

"All Souls' " of 1937 is another exceedingly well-wrought ghost story enhanced by ritual association. The feast itself, a time of solemn prayers for the dead in the Roman Catholic and Anglican calendar and usually cele-brated on November 2, was always a moment of special significance for Edith Wharton. Regularly, on this date, she listed and murmured to herself the names of all the dear deceased she could remember, back to her childhood days. To her imagining, All Souls' was a moment when the dead could be conversed with, and warmed by love. Such is the burden of her poem "All Souls'," in the winter of 1909 and set on "All Souls' Night, / When the dead can hear and the dead have sight." A lover tells his beloved that they should walk among the graves, and as the dead folk

> rise and walk in the cold,
> Let us warm their blood and give youth to the old.

The dead can be heard speaking to the lovers:

> "Ah thus
> In the prime of the year it was with us!"
> Till their lips drawn close, and so long unkist,
> Forget they are mist that mingles with mist.

The love motif has become an unbridled eroticism in the story "All Souls' " that Edith Wharton wrote almost thirty years later, and the experience thoroughly unnerving for the unfortunate protagonist. At dusk, on the last day of October, Sara Clayburn, a middle-aged widow living in a somewhat remote old house overlooking the Connecticut River, meets a strange woman approaching her home and wanting "to see one of the girls." Moments later Mrs. Clayburn slips and sprains her ankle and is forced to bed. Next morning her Scottish personal maid fails to appear, and after waiting in vain Mrs. Clayburn hobbles downstairs in great pain, searching for help. The house is entirely empty, not a servant to be seen; telephone and electricity have been cut off; and worst of all is an absolute deathly silence. Mrs. Clayburn spends the day and night in panic-stricken solitude. On the second morning the servants are at their appointed tasks, all insisting that nothing unusual has happened, it must be a bad dream.

Exactly one year later, Mrs. Clayburn sees the same strange woman coming up to her house, and she flees in hysterics to her cousin in New York. Between them they conjecture that the woman was a dead woman, a "fetch," come to escort the servants to a witches' coven; or possibly and even more alarmingly a living woman inhabited by a witch and arriving on the same errand. For as the narrator-cousin says, a few people can probably still remember that All Souls' is a time when the dead can walk, and when other spirits, "piteous or malevolent," are also freed to roam the earth. As to the coven, she continues, those who take part in one are said to be seized by a fierce desire that increases to "uncontrollable longing," and all inhibitions break down.

It should be noted that Edith Wharton's lifelong sense of the potential vitality or mobility of the dead found expression in several tales that are not ghost stories, strictly speaking, though they might well be included in any collection of her stories of the uncanny. In "A Journey," seemingly the earliest of the tales she thought worth gathering into a volume, a young woman traveling by train from Colorado to New York with her fatally ill husband discovers that her husband has died, his corpse stiffening in the berth adjacent. In a terrified half-dream, she feels that she too has died, has plunged into "a black whirlwind on which they were both spinning like leaves, in wild uncoiling spirals, with millions and millions of the dead." In the much later "A Bottle of Perrier"—a saga of murder and derangement in an African desert fortress, and with a thematic richness all its own—the hectic cross-purpose talk of servant and guest implies that the dead archeologist Almodham (his body at the foot of the well, polluting its contents) can walk the night and even kill.

Rarest of all in this cluster is "After Holbein" (1930), in which Anson Warley, the aging but tireless New York diner-outer, his memory failing him one evening, turns up uninvited at the home of Mrs. Jaspar. She was once the city's leading hostess, but is now reduced in her senility to coming down every evening "to her great shrouded drawing-rooms . . . to receive a stream of imaginary guests." Warley arrives and is shown in; the footman George announces dinner; and the couple, in the fixed hallucination of some far-gone social event, proceed slowly to the empty dining room. Here is the visual image:

> The couple continued to advance, with rigid smiles and eyes staring straight ahead. Neither turned to the other, neither spoke. All their attention was concentrated on the immense, the almost unachievable effort of reaching the point halfway down the long dinner table, opposite the Dubarry dish, where George was drawing back a gilt armchair for Mrs. Jaspar.

The title, "After Holbein," directs us to the legend somewhere at work in this story, to the sixteenth-century woodcuts of Hans Holbein the Younger taken from the medieval theme of "the Dance of Death." One may think in particular of the engraving of a lavishly dressed lady and gentleman being led away by Death as a drum-beating skeleton. Like Kenneth Ashby in "Pomegranate Seed," Warley and Mrs. Jaspar are responding to a summons from the land of the dead; they engage in a slow-motion dance toward it; and quite literally, as he is leaving the house after dinner, Warley loses consciousness and falls dead on the pavement.

In her short introduction to *Ghosts*, the posthumous collection of her ghost stories, Edith Wharton spoke fondly of the genre, of the two conditions indispensable for its working (silence and continuity, or time for reappearances), and of a few of its expert practitioners: Stevenson, Le Fanu, Walter de la Mare, and Henry James. She ended by laying it down that "the teller of supernatural tales should be well-frightened in the telling." The *un*frightened teller, she suggests, could scarcely achieve the scarifying effect required. We may perhaps suppose that, as the teller, she was frightened in the telling of some of these tales by the account—even if on the remote and mythicized levels where she set it—of sexual violence. We know that she was not alarmed by the sexual impulse itself; far from it. But a few of these cases (stories written, say, before 1913) may be extreme versions, as of a condition carried to the nearly unthinkable, of her personal experiences: her disastrously unhappy marriage to Teddy Wharton, her eventually debilitating love affair with the bisexual Morton Fullerton.*

*See R.W.B. Lewis, *Edith Wharton: a Biography* (1975).

"The Eyes" is her masterwork in the genre, and one can envision her shuddering inwardly as she wrote it, in Paris, in the winter of 1910. It has no little in common with Henry James's *The Turn of the Screw*, the story Edith Wharton regarded as unmatched for its "imaginative handling of the supernatural"; and in particular, in its shared insistence on a ghostly *doubling*. To his guests seated about the coal fire in his library one evening, the dilettantish Andrew Culwin tells of a pair of spectral eyes that visited him at two successive epochs. The first experience followed what Culwin recalled as an act of spontaneous generosity, his proposal of marriage, out of pure kindness, to his timid cousin Alice Nowell. The second, some months later in Rome, came after he had pretended immense enthusiasm for the hopelessly inept writings of young Gilbert Noyes, simply because he couldn't bear to hurt the boy. In both cases Culwin was confronted the same night by a pair of ugly red sneering eyes, hovering before him in his bedroom. The eyes continued to appear night after night, glaring derisively, until Culwin, exhausted, took flight, abandoning first his fiancée and then his protégé. In the denouement Culwin and his current disciple, Phil Frenham, come simultaneously to a paralyzing recognition of the eyes' owner.

The pattern of sexual inclination and recoil in this story is almost beyond admiration, as it is almost beyond sorting out. One could well say of a real-life Culwin that he was homoerotic by nature, and that he had sought to repress or to flee the consequences thereof in the two episodes. (Morton Fullerton, seen in a disenchanted perspective, with a touch of the prophetic, seems to be the prototype here.) But this does not explain the eyes. What Culwin really is by nature is a *devourer*; a feeder *on* others and *for* the satisfactions of the self. He "liked 'em juicy," an associate says about him; and Culwin, during the Rome visitation, says in as yet unknowing recognition that the eyes reminded him of "vampires with a taste for young flesh." His taste no doubt is especially for young men, but he can feed on a young woman like poor Alice Nowell as well. He is appalling not because he is a latent homosexual (Edith Wharton was anything but put off by the phenomenon), but because he is pure self. His gestures of compassion—like Herrick's "chivalry" in the fatal interview of "The Long Run" (the two stories are realistic and ghostly versions of each other)—are willful indulgences of the devouring ego. This is what the eyes know; it is what they are: Culwin's true self sneering at his falsifying self.

There is in this narrative a special, palpable intellectual and imaginative power, a metaphysical force. It derives, I would venture, from a certain American cultural tradition, which we can call Jamesian. The reference first of all is to the elder Henry James and his view that the greatest spiritual evil in the universe was "selfhood"; or, as he variously labeled it, egotism, selfishness, self-righteousness; in general, the self-satisfied conscience. It was, as James recognized and as we can recognize, the repellent consequence of Puritan doctrine, one of the recurring fatalities of our culture. And it is just in his "glow of self-righteousness" after the proposal, and his feeling of "good conscience" after the spurious literary praise, that Culwin is the exact embodiment of the old condition and of the Jamesian evil; and it is then that the eyes appear, to devastate him.

Edith Wharton had an intuitive affinity with the Jamesian vision of evil. But she came upon it as a literary resource in the narrative forms given it by Henry James, Junior: in the withering figure of Gilbert Osmond in *The Portrait of a Lady*, and even more in the character of John Marcher in "The Beast in the Jungle," where again we witness one human being destroying another in the self-deluding guise of being kind, Andrew Culwin is a more sinister John Marcher, and "The Eyes," as one rereads and absorbs it and thinks about it, can chill one to the bone. Like so many other stories by Edith Wharton, it can also delight the mind and heart of anyone who finds pleasure in the narrative art at its best.

THE SELECTED SHORT STORIES OF EDITH WHARTON

A JOURNEY

AS SHE LAY in her berth, staring at the shadows overhead, the rush of the wheels was in her brain, driving her deeper and deeper into circles of wakeful lucidity. The sleeping car had sunk into its night silence. Through the wet windowpane she watched the sudden lights, the long stretches of hurrying blackness. Now and then she turned her head and looked through the opening in the hangings at her husband's curtains across the aisle. . . .

She wondered restlessly if he wanted anything and if she could hear him if he called. His voice had grown very weak within the last months and it irritated him when she did not hear. This irritability, this increasing childish petulance seemed to give expression to their imperceptible estrangement. Like two faces looking at one another through a sheet of glass they were close together, almost touching, but they could not hear or feel each other: the conductivity between them was broken. She, at least, had this sense of separation, and she fancied sometimes that she saw it reflected in the look with which he supplemented his failing words. Doubtless the fault was hers. She was too impenetrably healthy to be touched by the irrelevancies of disease. Her self-reproachful tenderness was tinged with the sense of his irrationality: she had a vague feeling that there was a purpose in his helpless tyrannies. The suddenness of the change had found her so unprepared. A year ago their pulses had beat to one robust measure; both had the same prodigal confidence in an exhaustless future. Now their energies no longer kept step: hers still bounded ahead of life, pre-empting unclaimed regions of hope and activity, while his lagged behind, vainly struggling to overtake her.

When they married, she had such arrears of living to make up: her days had been as bare as the whitewashed schoolroom where she forced innutritious facts upon reluctant children. His coming had broken in on the

1

slumber of circumstance, widening the present till it became the encloser of remotest chances. But imperceptibly the horizon narrowed. Life had a grudge against her: she was never to be allowed to spread her wings.

At first the doctors had said that six weeks of mild air would set him right; but when he came back this assurance was explained as having of course included a winter in a dry climate. They gave up their pretty house, storing the wedding presents and new furniture, and went to Colorado. She had hated it there from the first. Nobody knew her or cared about her; there was no one to wonder at the good match she had made, or to envy her the new dresses and the visiting cards which were still a surprise to her. And he kept growing worse. She felt herself beset with difficulties too evasive to be fought by so direct a temperament. She still loved him, of course; but he was gradually, undefinably ceasing to be himself. The man she had married had been strong, active, gently masterful: the male whose pleasure it is to clear a way through the material obstructions of life; but now it was she who was the protector, he who must be shielded from importunities and given his drops or his beef juice though the skies were falling. The routine of the sickroom bewildered her; this punctual administering of medicine seemed as idle as some uncomprehended religious mummery.

There were moments, indeed, when warm gushes of pity swept away her instinctive resentment of his condition, when she still found his old self in his eyes as they groped for each other through the dense medium of his weakness. But these moments had grown rare. Sometimes he frightened her: his sunken expressionless face seemed that of a stranger; his voice was weak and hoarse; his thin-lipped smile a mere muscular contraction. Her hand avoided his damp soft skin, which had lost the familiar roughness of health: she caught herself furtively watching him as she might have watched a strange animal. It frightened her to feel that this was the man she loved; there were hours when to tell him what she suffered seemed the one escape from her fears. But in general she judged herself more leniently, reflecting that she had perhaps been too long alone with him, and that she would feel differently when they were at home again, surrounded by her robust and buoyant family. How she had rejoiced when the doctors at last gave their consent to his going home! She knew, of course, what the decision meant; they both knew. It meant that he was to die; but they dressed the truth in hopeful euphemisms, and at times, in the joy of preparation, she really forgot the purpose of their journey, and slipped into an eager allusion to next year's plans.

At last the day of leaving came. She had a dreadful fear that they would never get away; that somehow at the last moment he would fail her; that the doctors held one of their accustomed treacheries in reserve; but nothing happened. They drove to the station, he was installed in a seat with a rug over his knees and a cushion at his back, and she hung out of the window waving unregretful farewells to the acquaintances she had really never liked till then.

The first twenty-four hours had passed off well. He revived a little and it amused him to look out of the window and to observe the humors of the car. The second day he began to grow weary and to chafe under the dispassionate stare of the freckled child with the lump of chewing gum. She had to explain to the child's mother that her husband was too ill to be disturbed: a statement received by that lady with a resentment visibly supported by the maternal sentiment of the whole car. . . .

That night he slept badly and the next morning his temperature frightened her: she was sure he was growing worse. The day passed slowly, punctuated by the small irritations of travel. Watching his tired face, she traced in its contractions every rattle and jolt of the train, till her own body vibrated with sympathetic fatigue. She felt the others observing him too, and hovered restlessly between him and the line of interrogative eyes. The freckled child hung about him like a fly; offers of candy and picture books failed to dislodge her: she twisted one leg around the other and watched him imperturbably. The porter, as he passed, lingered with vague proffers of help, probably inspired by philanthropic passengers swelling with the sense that "something ought to be done"; and one nervous man in a skull cap was audibly concerned as to the possible effect on his wife's health.

The hours dragged on in a dreary inoccupation. Towards dusk she sat down beside him and he laid his hand on hers. The touch startled her. He seemed to be calling her from far off. She looked at him helplessly and his smile went through her like a physical pang.

"Are you very tired?" she asked.

"No, not very."

"We'll be there soon now."

"Yes, very soon."

"This time tomorrow—"

He nodded and they sat silent. When she had put him to bed and crawled into her own berth she tried to cheer herself with the thought that in less than twenty-four hours they would be in New York. Her people would all be at the station to meet her—she pictured their round unanxious faces pressing through the crowd. She only hoped they would not tell him too loudly that he was looking splendidly and would be all right in no time: the subtler sympathies developed by long contact with suffering were making her aware of a certain coarseness of texture in the family sensibilities.

Suddenly she thought she heard him call. She parted the curtains and listened. No, it was only a man snoring at the other end of the car. His snores had a greasy sound, as though they passed through tallow. She lay down and tried to sleep. . . . Had she not heard him move? She started up trembling. . . . The silence frightened her more than any sound. He might not be able to make her hear—he might be calling her now. . . . What made her think of such things? It was merely the familiar tendency of an overtired mind to fasten itself on the most intolerable chance within the range of its forebodings. . . . Putting her head out, she listened: but she could not distinguish his breathing from that of the other pairs of lungs about her. She longed to get up and look at him, but she knew the impulse was a mere vent for her restlessness, and the fear of disturbing him restrained her. . . . The regular movement of his curtain reassured her, she knew not why; she remembered that he had wished her a cheerful good night; and the sheer inability to endure her fears a moment longer made her put them from her with an effort of her whole sound-tired body. She turned on her side and slept.

She sat up stiffly, staring out at the dawn. The train was rushing through a region of bare hillocks huddled against a lifeless sky. It looked like the first day of creation. The air of the car was close, and she pushed up her window to let in the keen wind. Then she looked at her watch: it was seven o'clock, and soon the people about her would be stirring. She slipped into her clothes, smoothed her disheveled hair and crept to the dressing room. When she had washed her face and adjusted her dress she felt more hopeful. It was always a struggle for her not to be cheerful in the morning. Her cheeks burned deliciously under the coarse towel and the wet hair about her temples broke into strong upward tendrils. Every inch of her was full of life and elasticity. And in ten hours they would be at home!

She stepped to her husband's berth: it was time for him to take his early glass of milk. The window shade was down, and in the dusk of the curtained enclosure she could just see that he lay sideways, with his face away from her. She leaned over him and drew up the shade. As she did so she touched one of his hands. It felt cold. . . .

She bent closer, laying her hand on his arm and calling him by name. He did not move. She spoke again more loudly; she grasped his shoulder and gently shook it. He lay motionless. She caught hold of his hand again: it slipped from her limply, like a dead thing. A dead thing?

Her breath caught. She must see his face. She leaned forward, and hurriedly, shrinkingly, with a sickening reluctance of the flesh, laid her hands on his shoulders and turned him over. His head fell back; his face looked small and smooth; he gazed at her with steady eyes.

She remained motionless for a long time, holding him thus; and they looked at each other. Suddenly she shrank back: the longing to scream, to call out, to fly from him, had almost overpowered her. But a strong hand arrested her. Good God! If it were known that he was dead they would be put off the train at the next station—

In a terrifying flash of remembrance there arose before her a scene she had once witnessed in traveling, when a husband and wife, whose child had died in the train, had been thrust out at some chance station. She saw them standing on the platform with the child's body between them; she had never forgotten the dazed look with which they followed the receding train. And this was what would happen to her. Within the next hour she might find herself on the platform of some strange station, alone with her husband's body. . . . Anything but that! It was too horrible— She quivered like a creature at bay.

As she cowered there, she felt the train moving more slowly. It was coming then—they were approaching a station! She saw again the husband and wife standing on the lonely platform; and with a violent gesture she drew down the shade to hide her husband's face.

Feeling dizzy, she sank down on the edge of the berth, keeping away from his outstretched body, and pulling the curtains close, so that he and she were shut into a kind of sepulchral twilight. She tried to think. At all costs she must conceal the fact that he was dead. But how? Her mind refused to act: she could not plan, combine. She could think of no way but to sit there, clutching the curtains, all day long. . . .

She heard the porter making up her bed; people were beginning to move about the car; the dressing-room door was being opened and shut. She tried to rouse herself. At length with a supreme effort she rose to her feet, stepping into the aisle of the car and drawing the curtains tight behind her. She noticed that they still parted slightly with the motion of the car, and finding a pin in her dress she fastened them together. Now she was safe. She looked round and saw the porter. She fancied he was watching her.

"Ain't he awake yet?" he inquired.

"No," she faltered.

"I got his milk all ready when he wants it. You know you told me to have it for him by seven."

She nodded silently and crept into her seat.

At half-past eight the train reached Buffalo. By this time the other passengers were dressed and the berths had been folded back for the day. The porter, moving to and fro under his burden of sheets and pillows, glanced at her as he passed. At length he said: "Ain't he going to get up? You know we're ordered to make up the berths as early as we can."

She turned cold with fear. They were just entering the station.

"Oh, not yet," she stammered. "Not till he's had his milk. Won't you get it, please?"

"All right. Soon as we start again."

When the train moved on he reappeared with the milk. She took it from him and sat vaguely looking at it: her brain moved slowly from one idea to another, as though they were steppingstones set far apart across a whirling flood. At length she became aware that the porter still hovered expectantly.

"Will I give it to him?" he suggested.

"Oh, no," she cried, rising. "He—he's asleep yet, I think—"

She waited till the porter had passed on; then she unpinned the curtains and slipped behind them. In the semiobscurity her husband's face stared up at her like a marble mask with agate eyes. The eyes were dreadful. She put out her hand and drew down the lids. Then she remembered the glass of milk in her other hand: what was she to do with it? She thought of raising the window and throwing it out; but to do so she would have to lean across his body and bring her face close to his. She decided to drink the milk.

She returned to her seat with the empty glass and after a while the porter came back to get it.

"When'll I fold up his bed?" he asked.

"Oh, not now—not yet; he's ill—he's very ill. Can't you let him stay as he is? The doctor wants him to lie down as much as possible."

He scratched his head. "Well, if he's *really* sick—"

He took the empty glass and walked away, explaining to the passengers that the party behind the curtains was too sick to get up just yet.

She found herself the center of sympathetic eyes. A motherly woman with an intimate smile sat down beside her.

"I'm real sorry to hear your husband's sick. I've had a remarkable amount of sickness in my family and maybe I could assist you. Can I take a look at him?"

"Oh, no—no, please! He mustn't be disturbed."

The lady accepted the rebuff indulgently.

"Well, it's just as you say, of course, but you don't look to me as if you'd had much experience in sickness and I'd have been glad to assist you. What do you generally do when your husband's taken this way?"

"I—I let him sleep."

"Too much sleep ain't any too healthful either. Don't you give him any medicine?"

"Y—yes."

"Don't you wake him to take it?"

"Yes."

"When does he take the next dose?"

"Not for—two hours—"

The lady looked disappointed. "Well, if I was you I'd try giving it oftener. That's what I do with my folks."

After that many faces seemed to press upon her. The passengers were on their way to the dining car, and she was conscious that as they passed down the aisle they glanced curiously at the closed curtains. One lantern-jawed man with prominent eyes stood still and tried to shoot his projecting glance through the division between the folds. The freckled child, returning from breakfast, waylaid the passers with a buttery clutch, saying in a loud whisper, "He's sick"; and once the conductor came by, asking for tickets. She shrank into her corner and looked out of the window at the flying trees and houses, meaningless hieroglyphs of an endlessly unrolled papyrus.

Now and then the train stopped, and the newcomers on entering the car stared in turn at the closed curtains. More and more people seemed to pass—their faces began to blend fantastically with the images surging in her brain. . . .

Later in the day a fat man detached himself from the mist of faces. He had a creased stomach and soft pale lips. As he pressed himself into the seat facing her she noticed that he was dressed in black broadcloth, with a soiled white tie.

"Husband's pretty bad this morning, is he?"

"Yes."

"Dear, dear! Now that's terribly distressing, ain't it?" An apostolic smile revealed his gold-filled teeth. "Of course you know there's no such thing as sickness. Ain't that a lovely thought? Death itself is but a deloosion of our grosser senses. On'y lay yourself open to the influx of the sperrit, submit yourself passively to the action of the divine force, and disease and dissolution will cease to exist for you. If you could indooce your husband to read this little pamphlet—"

The faces about her again grew indistinct. She had a vague recollection of hearing the motherly lady and the parent of the freckled child ardently disputing the relative advantages of trying several medicines at once, or of taking each in turn; the motherly lady maintaining that the competitive system saved time; the other objecting that you couldn't tell which remedy had effected the cure; their voices went on and on, like bell buoys droning through a fog. . . . The porter came up now and then with questions that she did not understand, but somehow she must have answered since he went away again without repeating them; every two hours the motherly lady reminded her that her husband ought to have his drops; people left the car and others replaced them. . . .

Her head was spinning and she tried to steady herself by clutching at her thoughts as they swept by, but they slipped away from her like bushes on the side of a sheer precipice down which she seemed to be falling. Suddenly her mind grew clear again and she found herself vividly picturing what would happen when the train reached New York. She shuddered as it occurred to her that he would be quite cold and that someone might perceive he had been dead since morning.

She thought hurriedly: "If they see I am not surprised they will suspect something. They will ask questions, and if I tell them the truth they won't believe me—no one would believe me! It will be terrible"—and she kept repeating to herself—"I must pretend I don't know. I must pretend I don't know. When they open the curtains I must go up to him quite naturally—and then I must scream!" She had an idea that the scream would be very hard to do.

Gradually new thoughts crowded upon her, vivid and urgent: she tried to separate and restrain them, but they beset her clamorously, like her school children at the end of a hot day, when she was too tired to silence them. Her head grew confused, and she felt a sick fear of forgetting her part, of betraying herself by some unguarded word or look.

"I must pretend I don't know," she went on murmuring. The words had lost their significance, but she repeated them mechanically, as though they had been a magic formula, until suddenly she heard herself saying: "I can't remember, I can't remember!"

Her voice sounded very loud, and she looked about her in terror; but no one seemed to notice that she had spoken.

As she glanced down the car her eye caught the curtains of her husband's berth, and she began to examine the monotonous arabesques woven through their heavy folds. The pattern was intricate and difficult to trace; she gazed fixedly at the curtains and as she did so the thick stuff grew transparent and through it she saw her husband's face—his dead face. She struggled to avert her look, but her eyes refused to move and her head seemed to be held in a vice. At last, with an effort that left her weak and shaking, she turned away; but it was of no use; close in front of her, small and smooth, was her husband's face. It seemed to be suspended in the air between her and the false braids of the woman who sat in front of her. With an uncontrollable gesture she stretched out her hand to push the face away, and suddenly she felt the touch of his smooth skin. She repressed a cry and half started from her seat. The woman with the false braids looked around, and feeling that she must justify her movement in some way she rose and lifted her traveling bag from the opposite seat. She unlocked the bag and looked into it; but the first object her hand met was a small flask of her husband's, thrust there at the last moment, in the haste of departure. She locked the bag and closed her eyes . . . his face was there again, hanging between her eyeballs and lids like a waxen mask against a red curtain. . . .

She roused herself with a shiver. Had she fainted or slept? Hours seemed to have elapsed; but it was still broad day, and the people about her were sitting in the same attitudes as before.

A sudden sense of hunger made her aware that she had eaten nothing since morning. The thought of food filled her with disgust, but she dreaded a return of faintness, and remembering that she had some biscuits in her bag she took one out and ate it. The dry crumbs choked her, and she hastily swallowed a little brandy from her husband's flask. The burning sensation in her throat acted as a counterirritant, momentarily relieving the dull ache of her nerves. Then she felt a gently-stealing warmth, as though a soft air fanned her, and the swarming fears relaxed their clutch, receding through the stillness that enclosed her, a stillness soothing as the spacious quietude of a summer day. She slept.

Through her sleep she felt the impetuous rush of the train. It seemed to be life itself that was sweeping her on with headlong inexorable force— sweeping her into darkness and terror, and the awe of unknown days. —Now all at once everything was still—not a sound, not a pulsation. . . . She was dead in her turn, and lay beside him with smooth upstaring face. How quiet it was!—and yet she heard feet coming, the feet of the men who were to carry them away. . . . She could feel too—she felt a sudden prolonged vibration, a series of hard shocks, and then another plunge into darkness: the darkness of death this time—a black whirlwind on which they were both spinning like leaves, in wild uncoiling spirals, with millions and millions of the dead. . . .

She sprang up in terror. Her sleep must have lasted a long time, for the winter day had paled and the lights had been lit. The car was in confusion, and as she regained her self-possession she saw that the passengers were gathering up their wraps and bags. The woman with the false braids had brought from the dressing room a sickly ivy plant in a bottle, and the Christian Scientist was reversing his cuffs. The porter passed down the aisle with his impartial brush. An impersonal figure with a gold-banded cap asked for her husband's ticket. A voice shouted "Baiggage express!" and she heard the clicking of metal as the passengers handed over their checks.

Presently her window was blocked by an expanse of sooty wall, and the train passed into the Harlem tunnel. The journey was over; in a few minutes she would see her family pushing their joyous way through the throng at the station. Her heart dilated. The worst terror was past. . . .

"We'd better get him up now, hadn't we?" asked the porter, touching her arm.

He had her husband's hat in his hand and was meditatively revolving it under his brush.

She looked at the hat and tried to speak; but suddenly the car grew dark. She flung up her arms, struggling to catch at something, and fell face downward, striking her head against the dead man's berth.

THE PELICAN

SHE WAS very pretty when I first knew her, with the sweet straight nose and short upper lip of the cameo-brooch divinity, humanized by a dimple that flowered in her cheek whenever anything was said possessing the outward attributes of humor without its intrinsic quality. For the dear lady was providentially deficient in humor: the least hint of the real thing clouded her lovely eye like the hovering shadow of an algebraic problem.

I don't think nature had meant her to be "intellectual"; but what can a poor thing do, whose husband has died of drink when her baby is hardly six months old, and who finds her coral necklace and her grandfather's edition of the British Dramatists inadequate to the demands of the creditors?

Her mother, the celebrated Irene Astarte Pratt, had written a poem in blank verse on "The Fall of Man"; one of her aunts was dean of a girls' college; another had translated Euripides—with such a family, the poor child's fate was sealed in advance. The only way of paying her husband's debts and keeping the baby clothed was to be intellectual; and, after some hesitation as to the form her mental activity was to take, it was unanimously decided that she was to give lectures.

They began by being drawing-room lectures. The first time I saw her she was standing by the piano, against the flippant background of Dresden china and photographs, telling a roomful of women preoccupied with their spring bonnets all she thought she knew about Greek art. The ladies assembled to hear her had given me to understand that she was "doing it for the baby," and this fact, together with the shortness of her upper lip and the bewildering cooperation of her dimple, disposed me to listen leniently to her dissertation. Happily, at that time Greek art was still, if I may use the phrase, easily handled: it was as simple as walking down a museum gallery lined with pleasant familiar Venuses and Apollos. All the

10

later complications—the archaic and archaistic conundrums; the influences
of Assyria and Asia Minor; the conflicting attributions and the wrangles of
the erudite—still slumbered in the bosom of the future "scientific critic."
Greek art in those days began with Phidias and ended with the Apollo
Belvedere; and a child could travel from one to the other without danger of
losing his way.

Mrs. Amyot had two fatal gifts: a capacious but inaccurate memory, and
an extraordinary fluency of speech. There was nothing she did not remember—
wrongly; but her halting facts were swathed in so many layers of rhetoric
that their infirmities were imperceptible to her friendly critics. Besides, she
had been taught Greek by the aunt who had translated Euripides; and the
mere sound of the αἰς and οἰς that she now and then not unskillfully let slip
(correcting herself, of course, with a start, and indulgently mistranslating
the phrase), struck awe to the hearts of ladies whose only "accomplish-
ment" was French—if you didn't speak too quickly.

I had then but a momentary glimpse of Mrs. Amyot, but a few months
later I came upon her again in the New England university town where the
celebrated Irene Astarte Pratt lived on the summit of a local Parnassus,
with lesser muses and college professors respectfully grouped on the lower
ledges of the sacred declivity. Mrs. Amyot, who, after her husband's death,
had returned to the maternal roof (even during her father's lifetime the roof
had been distinctively maternal); Mrs. Amyot, thanks to her upper lip, her
dimple and her Greek, was already ensconced in a snug hollow of the
Parnassian slope.

After the lecture was over it happened that I walked home with Mrs.
Amyot. From the incensed glances of two or three learned gentlemen who
were hovering on the doorstep when we emerged, I inferred that Mrs.
Amyot, at that period, did not often walk home alone; but I doubt whether
any of my discomfited rivals, whatever his claims to favor, was ever treated
to so ravishing a mixture of shyness and self-abandonment, of sham
erudition and real teeth and hair, as it was my privilege to enjoy. Even at
the opening of her public career Mrs. Amyot had a tender eye for strangers,
as possible links with successive centers of culture to which in due course
the torch of Greek art might be handed on.

She began by telling me that she had never been so frightened in her
life. She knew, of course, how dreadfully learned I was, and when, just as
she was going to begin, her hostess had whispered to her that I was in the
room, she had felt ready to sink through the floor. Then (with a flying
dimple) she had remembered Emerson's line—wasn't it Emerson's?—that
beauty is its own excuse for *seeing,* and that had made her feel a little more
confident, since she was sure that no one saw beauty more vividly than
she—as a child she used to sit for hours gazing at an Etruscan vase on the

bookcase in the library, while her sisters played with their dolls—and if *seeing* beauty was the only excuse one needed for talking about it, why, she was sure I would make allowances and not be *too* critical and sarcastic, especially if, as she thought probable, I had heard of her having lost her poor husband, and how she had to do it for the baby.

Being abundantly assured of my sympathy on these points, she went on to say that she had always wanted so much to consult me about her lectures. Of course, one subject wasn't enough (this view of the limitations of Greek art as a "subject" gave me a startling idea of the rate at which a successful lecturer might exhaust the universe); she must find others; she had not ventured on any as yet, but she had thought of Tennyson—didn't I *love* Tennyson? She *worshiped* him so that she was sure she could help others to understand him; or what did I think of a "course" on Raphael or Michelangelo—or on the heroines of Shakespeare? There were some fine steel engravings of Raphael's Madonnas and of the Sistine ceiling in her mother's library, and she had seen Miss Cushman in several Shakespearian roles, so that on these subjects also she felt qualified to speak with authority.

When we reached her mother's door she begged me to come in and talk the matter over; she wanted me to see the baby—she felt as though I should understand her better if I saw the baby—and the dimple flashed through a tear.

The fear of encountering the author of "The Fall of Man," combined with the opportune recollection of a dinner engagement, made me evade this appeal with the promise of returning on the morrow. On the morrow, I left too early to redeem my promise; and for several years afterwards I saw no more of Mrs. Amyot.

My calling at that time took me at irregular intervals from one to another of our larger cities, and as Mrs. Amyot was also peripatetic it was inevitable that sooner or later we should cross each other's path. It was therefore without surprise that, one snowy afternoon in Boston, I learned from the lady with whom I chanced to be lunching that, as soon as the meal was over, I was to be taken to hear Mrs. Amyot lecture.

"On Greek art?" I suggested.

"Oh, you've heard her then? No, this is one of the series called 'Homes and Haunts of the Poets.' Last week we had Wordsworth and the Lake Poets, today we are to have Goethe and Weimar. She is a wonderful creature—all the women of her family are geniuses. You know, of course, that her mother was Irene Astarte Pratt, who wrote a poem on 'The Fall of Man'; N. P. Willis called her the female Milton of America. One of Mrs. Amyot's aunts has translated Eurip—"

"And is she as pretty as ever?" I irrelevantly interposed.

My hostess looked shocked. "She is excessively modest and retiring. She says it is actual suffering for her to speak in public. You know she only does it for the baby."

Punctually at the hour appointed, we took our seats in a lecture hall full of strenuous females in ulsters. Mrs. Amyot was evidently a favorite with these austere sisters, for every corner was crowded, and as we entered a pale usher with an educated mispronunciation was setting forth to several dejected applicants the impossibility of supplying them with seats.

Our own were happily so near the front that when the curtains at the back of the platform parted, and Mrs. Amyot appeared, I was at once able to establish a comparison between the lady placidly dimpling to the applause of her public and the shrinking drawing-room orator of my earlier recollections.

Mrs. Amyot was as pretty as ever, and there was the same curious discrepancy between the freshness of her aspect and the staleness of her theme, but something was gone of the blushing unsteadiness with which she had fired her first random shots at Greek art. It was not that the shots were less uncertain, but that she now had an air of assuming that, for her purpose, the bull's-eye was everywhere, so that there was no need to be flustered in taking aim. This assurance had so facilitated the flow of her eloquence that she seemed to be performing a trick analogous to that of the conjurer who pulls hundreds of yards of white paper out of his mouth. From a large assortment of stock adjectives she chose, with unerring deftness and rapidity, the one that taste and discrimination would most surely have rejected, fitting out her subject with a whole wardrobe of slop-shop epithets irrelevant in cut and size. To the invaluable knack of not disturbing the association of ideas in her audience, she added the gift of what may be called a confidential manner—so that her fluent generalizations about Goethe and his place in literature (the lecture was, of course, manufactured out of Lewes's book) had the flavor of personal experience, of views sympathetically exchanged with her audience on the best way of knitting children's socks, or of putting up preserves for the winter. It was, I am sure, to this personal accent—the moral equivalent of her dimple— that Mrs. Amyot owed her prodigious, her irrational success. It was her art of transposing secondhand ideas into firsthand emotions that so endeared her to her feminine listeners.

To anyone not in search of "documents" Mrs. Amyot's success was hardly of a kind to make her more interesting, and my curiosity flagged with the growing conviction that the "suffering" entailed on her by public speaking was at most a retrospective pang. I was sure that she had reached the point of measuring and enjoying her effects, of deliberately manipulating her public; and there must indeed have been a certain exhilaration in attaining results so considerable by means involving so little conscious effort. Mrs. Amyot's art was simply an extension of coquetry: she flirted with her audience.

In this mood of enlightened skepticism I responded but languidly to my hostess' suggestion that I should go with her that evening to see Mrs. Amyot. The aunt who had translated Euripides was at home on Saturday evenings, and one met "thoughtful" people there, my hostess explained: it was one of the intellectual centers of Boston. My mood remained distinctly resentful of any connection between Mrs. Amyot and intellectuality, and I declined to go; but the next day I met Mrs. Amyot in the street.

She stopped me reproachfully. She had heard I was in Boston; why had I not come last night? She had been told that I was at her lecture, and it had frightened her—yes, really, almost as much as years ago in Hillbridge. She never *could* get over that stupid shyness, and the whole business was as distasteful to her as ever; but what could she do? There was the baby—he was a big boy now, and boys were so expensive! But did I really think she had improved the least little bit? And why wouldn't I come home with her now, and see the boy, and tell her frankly what I had thought of the lecture? She had plenty of flattery—people were so kind, and everyone knew that she did it for the baby—but what she felt the need of was criticism, severe, discriminating criticism like mine—oh, she knew that I was dreadfully discriminating!

I went home with her and saw the boy. In the early heat of her Tennyson worship Mrs. Amyot had christened him Lancelot, and he looked it. Perhaps, however, it was his black velvet dress and the exasperating length of his yellow curls, together with the fact of his having been taught to recite Browning to visitors, that raised to fever heat the itching of my palms in his Infant Samuel-like presence. I have since had reason to think that he would have preferred to be called Billy, and to hunt cats with the other boys in the block: his curls and his poetry were simply another outlet for Mrs. Amyot's irrepressible coquetry.

But if Lancelot was not genuine, his mother's love for him was. It justified everything—the lectures *were* for the baby, after all. I had not been ten minutes in the room before I was pledged to help Mrs. Amyot carry out her triumphant fraud. If she wanted to lecture on Plato she should—Plato must take his chance like the rest of us! There was no use, of course, in being "discriminating." I preserved sufficient reason to avoid that pitfall, but I suggested "subjects" and made lists of books for her with a fatuity that became more obvious as time attenuated the remembrance of her smile; I even remember thinking that some men might have cut the knot by marrying her, but I handed over Plato as a hostage and escaped by the afternoon train.

The next time I saw her was in New York, when she had become so fashionable that it was a part of the whole duty of woman to be seen at her lectures. The lady who suggested that of course I ought to go and hear Mrs. Amyot, was not very clear about anything except that she was perfectly lovely, and had had a horrid husband, and was doing it to support her boy. The subject of the discourse (I think it was on Ruskin) was clearly of minor importance, not only to my friend, but to the throng of well-dressed and absent-minded ladies who rustled in late, dropped their muffs, and pocketbooks, and undisguisedly lost themselves in the study of each other's apparel. They received Mrs. Amyot with warmth, but she evidently represented a social obligation like going to church, rather than any more personal interest; in fact, I suspect that every one of the ladies would have remained away, had they been sure that none of the others were coming.

Whether Mrs. Amyot was disheartened by the lack of sympathy between herself and her hearers, or whether the sport of arousing it had become a task, she certainly imparted her platitudes with less convincing warmth than of old. Her voice had the same confidential inflections, but it was like a voice reproduced by a gramophone: the real woman seemed far away. She had grown stouter without losing her dewy freshness, and her smart gown might have been taken to show either the potentialities of a settled income, or a politic concession to the taste of her hearers. As I listened I reproached myself for ever having suspected her of self-deception in saying that she took no pleasure in her work. I was sure now that she did it only for Lancelot, and judging from the size of her audience and the price of the tickets I concluded that Lancelot must be receiving a liberal education.

I was living in New York that winter, and in the rotation of dinners I found myself one evening at Mrs. Amyot's side. The dimple came out at my greeting as punctually as a cuckoo in a Swiss clock, and I detected the same automatic quality in the tone in which she made her usual pretty demand for advice. She was like a musical box charged with popular airs. They succeeded one another with breathless rapidity, but there was a moment after each when the cylinders scraped and whizzed.

Mrs. Amyot, as I found when I called on her, was living in a sunny flat, with a sitting room of flowers and a tea table that had the air of expecting visitors. She owned that she had been ridiculously successful. It was delightful, of course, on Lancelot's account. Lancelot had been sent to the best school in the country, and if things went well and people didn't tire of his silly mother he was to go to Harvard afterwards. During the next two or three years Mrs. Amyot kept her flat in New York, and radiated art and literature upon the suburbs. I saw her now and then, always stouter, better dressed, more successful and more automatic: she had become a lecturing machine.

I went abroad for a year or two and when I came back she had disappeared. I asked several people about her, but life had closed over her. She had been last heard of as lecturing—still lecturing—but no one seemed to know when or where.

It was in Boston that I found her at last, forlornly swaying to the oscillations of an overhead strap in a crowded trolley car. Her face had so changed that I lost myself in a startled reckoning of the time that had elapsed since our parting. She spoke to me shyly, as though aware of my hurried calculation, and conscious that in five years she ought not to have altered so much as to upset my notion of time. Then she seemed to set it down to her dress, for she nervously gathered her cloak over a gown that asked only to he concealed, and shrank into a seat behind the line of prehensile bipeds blocking the aisle of the car.

It was perhaps because she so obviously avoided me that I felt for the first time that I might be of use to her; and when she left the car I made no excuse for following her.

She said nothing of needing advice and did not ask me to walk home with her, concealing, as we talked, her transparent preoccupations under the guise of a sudden interest in all I had been doing since she had last seen me. Of what concerned her, I learned only that Lancelot was well and that for the present, she was not lecturing—she was tired and her doctor had ordered her to rest. On the doorstep of a shabby house she paused and held out her hand. She had been so glad to see me and perhaps if I were in Boston again—the tired dimple, as it were, bowed me out and closed the door on the conclusion of the phrase.

Two or three weeks later, at my club in New York, I found a letter from her. In it she owned that she was troubled, that of late she had been unsuccessful, and that, if I chanced to be coming back to Boston, and could spare her a little of that invaluable advice which—. A few days later the advice was at her disposal. She told me frankly what had happened. Her public had grown tired of her. She had seen it coming on for some time, and was shrewd enough in detecting the causes. She had more rivals than formerly—younger women, she admitted, with a smile that could still afford to be generous—and then her audiences had grown more critical and consequently more exacting. Lecturing—as she understood it—used to be simple enough. You chose your topic—Raphael, Shakespeare, Gothic Architecture, or some such big familiar "subject"—and read up about it for a week or so at the Athenaeum or the Astor Library, and then told your audience what you had read. Now, it appeared, that simple process was no longer adequate. People had tired of familiar "subjects"; it was the fashion to be interested in things that one hadn't always known about—natural selection, animal magnetism, sociology and comparative folklore; while, in literature, the demand had become equally difficult to meet, since Matthew Arnold had introduced the habit of studying the "influence" of one author on another. She had tried lecturing on influences, and had done very well as long as the public was satisfied with the tracing of such obvious influences as that of Turner on Ruskin, of Schiller on Goethe, of Shakespeare on English literature; but such investigations had soon lost all charm for her too-sophisticated audiences, who now demanded either that the influence or the influenced should be quite unknown, or that there should be no perceptible connection between the two. The zest of the performance lay in the measure of ingenuity with which the lecturer established a relation between two people who had probably never heard of each other, much less read each other's works. A pretty Miss Williams with red hair had, for instance, been lecturing with great success on the influence of the Rosicrucians upon the poetry of Keats, while somebody else had given a "course" on the influence of St. Thomas Aquinas upon Professor Huxley.

Mrs. Amyot, warmed by my participation in her distress, went on to say that the growing demand for evolution was what most troubled her. Her grandfather had been a pillar of the Presbyterian ministry, and the idea of her lecturing on Darwin or Herbert Spencer was deeply shocking to her mother and aunts. In one sense the family had staked its literary as well as its spiritual hopes on the literal inspiration of Genesis: what became of "The Fall of Man" in the light of modern exegesis?

The upshot of it was that she had ceased to lecture because she could no longer sell tickets enough to pay for the hire of a lecture hall; and as for the managers, they wouldn't look at her. She had tried her luck all through the Eastern States and as far south as Washington; but it was of no use, and unless she could get hold of some new subjects—or, better still, of some new audiences—she must simply go out of the business. That would mean the failure of all she had worked for, since Lancelot would have to leave Harvard. She paused, and wept some of the unbecoming tears that spring from real grief. Lancelot, it appeared, was to be a genius. He had passed his opening examinations brilliantly; he had "literary gifts"; he had written beautiful poetry, much of which his mother had copied out, in reverentially slanting characters, in a velvet-bound volume which she drew from a locked drawer.

Lancelot's verse struck me as nothing more alarming than growing pains; but it was not to learn this that she had summoned me. What she wanted was to be assured that he was worth working for, an assurance which I managed to convey by the simple stratagem of remarking that the poems reminded me of Swinburne—and so they did, as well as of Browning, Tennyson, Rossetti, and all the other poets who supply young authors with original inspirations.

This point being established, it remained to be decided by what means his mother was, in the French phrase, to pay herself the luxury of a poet. It was clear that this indulgence could be bought only with counterfeit coin, and that the one way of helping Mrs. Amyot was to become a party to the circulation of such currency. My fetish of intellectual integrity went down like a ninepin before the appeal of a woman no longer young and distinctly foolish, but full of those dear contradictions and irrelevancies that will always make flesh and blood prevail against a syllogism. When I took leave of Mrs. Amyot I had promised her a dozen letters to Western universities and had half pledged myself to sketch out a lecture on the reconciliation of science and religion.

In the West she achieved a success which for a year or more embittered my perusal of the morning papers. The fascination that lures the murderer back to the scene of his crime drew my eye to every paragraph celebrating Mrs. Amyot's last brilliant lecture on the influence of something upon somebody; and her own letters—she overwhelmed me with them—spared me no detail of the entertainment given in her honor by the Palimpsest Club of Omaha or of her reception at the University of Leadville. The college professors were especially kind: she assured me that she had never before met with such discriminating sympathy. I winced at the adjective, which cast a sudden light on the vast machinery of fraud that I had set in motion. All over my native land, men of hitherto unblemished integrity were conniving with me in urging their friends to go and hear Mrs. Amyot lecture on the reconciliation of science and religion! My only hope was that, somewhere among the number of my accomplices, Mrs. Amyot might find one who would marry her in the defense of his convictions.

None, apparently, resorted to such heroic measures; for about two years later I was startled by the announcement that Mrs. Amyot was lecturing in Trenton, New Jersey, on modern theosophy in the light of the Vedas. The following week she was at Newark, discussing Schopenhauer in the light of recent psychology. The week after that I was on the deck of an ocean steamer, reconsidering my share in Mrs. Amyot's triumphs with the impartiality with which one views an episode that is being left behind at the rate of twenty knots an hour. After all, I had been helping a mother to educate her son.

The next ten years of my life were spent in Europe, and when I came home the recollection of Mrs. Amyot had become as inoffensive as one of those pathetic ghosts who are said to strive in vain to make themselves visible to the living. I did not even notice the fact that I no longer heard her spoken of; she had dropped like a dead leaf from the bough of memory.

A year or two after my return I was condemned to one of the worst punishments a worker can undergo—an enforced holiday. The doctors who pronounced the inhuman sentence decreed that it should be worked out in the South, and for a whole winter I carried my cough, my thermometer and my idleness from one fashionable orange grove to another. In the vast and melancholy sea of my disoccupation I clutched like a drowning man at any human driftwood within reach. I took a critical and depreciatory interest in the coughs, the thermometers and the idleness of my fellow sufferers; but to the healthy, the occupied, the transient I clung with undiscriminating enthusiasm.

In no other way can I explain, as I look back on it, the importance I attached to the leisurely confidences of a new arrival with a brown beard who, tilted back at my side on a hotel veranda hung with roses, imparted to me one afternoon the simple annals of his past. There was nothing in the tale to kindle the most inflammable imagination, and though the man had a pleasant frank face and a voice differing agreeably from the shrill inflections of our fellow lodgers, it is probable that under different conditions his discursive history of successful business ventures in a Western city would have affected me somewhat in the manner of a lullaby.

Even at the time I was not sure I liked his agreeable voice: it had a self-importance out of keeping with the humdrum nature of his story, as though a breeze engaged in shaking out a tablecloth should have fancied itself inflating a banner. But this criticism may have been a mere mark of my own fastidiousness, for the man seemed a simple fellow, satisfied with his middling fortunes, and already (he was not much past thirty) deep sunk in conjugal content.

He had just started on an anecdote connected with the cutting of his eldest boy's teeth, when a lady I knew, returning from her late drive, paused before us for a moment in the twilight, with the smile which is the feminine equivalent of beads to savages.

"Won't you take a ticket?" she said sweetly.

Of course I would take a ticket—but for what? I ventured to inquire.

"Oh, that's *so* good of you—for the lecture this evening. You needn't go, you know; we're none of us going; most of us have been through it already at Aiken and at Saint Augustine and at Palm Beach. I've given away my tickets to some new people who've just come from the North, and some of us are going to send our maids, just to fill up the room."

"And may I ask to whom you are going to pay this delicate attention?"

"Oh, I thought you knew—to poor Mrs. Amyot. She's been lecturing all over the South this winter; she's simply *haunted* me ever since I left New York—and we had six weeks of her at Bar Harbor last summer! One has to take tickets, you know, because she's a widow and does it for her son—to pay for his education. She's so plucky and nice about it, and talks about him in such a touching unaffected way, that everybody is sorry for her, and we all simply ruin ourselves in tickets. I do hope that boy's nearly educated!"

"Mrs. Amyot? Mrs. Amyot?" I repeated. "It she *still* educating her son?"

"Oh, do you know about her? Has she been at it long? There's some comfort in that, for I suppose when the boy's provided for the poor thing will be able to take a rest—and give us one!"

She laughed and held out her hand.

"Here's your ticket. Did you say *tickets*—two? Oh, thanks. Of course you needn't go."

"But I mean to go. Mrs. Amyot is an old friend of mine."

"Do you really? That's awfully good of you. Perhaps I'll go too if I can persuade Charlie and the others to come. And I wonder"—in a well-directed aside—"if your friend—?"

I telegraphed her under cover of the dusk that my friend was of too recent standing to be drawn into her charitable toils, and she masked her mistake under a rattle of friendly adjurations not to be late, and to be sure to keep a seat for her, as she had quite made up her mind to go even if Charlie and the others wouldn't.

The flutter of her skirts subsided in the distance, and my neighbor, who had half turned away to light a cigar, made no effort to reopen the conversation. At length, fearing he might have overheard the allusion to himself, I ventured to ask if he were going to the lecture that evening.

"Much obliged—I have a ticket," he said abruptly.

This struck me as in such bad taste that I made no answer; and it was he who spoke next.

"Did I understand you to say that you were an old friend of Mrs. Amyot's?"

"I think I may claim to be, if it is the same Mrs. Amyot I had the pleasure of knowing many years ago. My Mrs. Amyot used to lecture too—"

"To pay for her son's education?"

"I believe so."

"Well—see you later."

He got up and walked into the house.

In the hotel drawing room that evening there was but a meager sprinkling of guests, among whom I saw my brown-bearded friend sitting alone on a sofa, with his head against the wall. It could not have been curiosity to see Mrs. Amyot that had impelled him to attend the performance, for it would have been impossible for him, without changing his place, to command the improvised platform at the end of the room. When I looked at him he seemed lost in contemplation of the chandelier.

The lady from whom I had bought my tickets fluttered in late, unattended by Charlie and the others, and assuring me that she would *scream* if we had the lecture on Ibsen—she had heard it three times already that winter. A glance at the program reassured her: it informed us (in the lecturer's own slanting hand) that Mrs. Amyot was to lecture on the Cosmogony.

After a long pause, during which the small audience coughed and moved its chairs and showed signs of regretting that it had come, the door opened, and Mrs. Amyot stepped upon the platform. Ah, poor lady!

Someone said "Hush!" The coughing and chair shifting subsided, and she began.

It was like looking at one's self early in the morning in a cracked mirror. I had no idea I had grown so old. As for Lancelot, he must have a beard. A beard? The word struck me, and without knowing why I glanced across the room at my bearded friend on the sofa. Oddly enough he was looking at me, with a half-defiant, half-sullen expression; and as our glances crossed, and his fell, the conviction came to me that *he was Lancelot.*

I don't remember a word of the lecture; and yet there were enough of them to have filled a good-sized dictionary. The stream of Mrs. Amyot's eloquence had become a flood: one had the despairing sense that she had sprung a leak, and that until the plumber came there was nothing to be done about it.

The plumber came at length, in the shape of a clock striking ten; my companion, with a sigh of relief, drifted away in search of Charlie and the others; the audience scattered with the precipitation of people who had discharged a duty; and, without surprise, I found the brown-bearded stranger at my elbow.

He stood alone in the bare-floored room, under the flaring chandelier.

"I think you told me this afternoon that you were an old friend of Mrs. Amyot's?" he began awkwardly.

I assented.

"Will you come in and see her?"

"Now? I shall be very glad to, if—"

"She's ready; she's expecting you," he interposed.

He offered no further explanation, and I followed him in silence. He led me down the long corridor, and pushed open the door of a sitting room.

"Mother," he said, closing the door after we had entered, "here's the gentleman who says he used to know you."

Mrs. Amyot, who sat in an easy chair stirring a cup of bouillon, looked up with a start. She had evidently not seen me in the audience, and her son's description had failed to convey my identity. I saw a frightened look in her eyes; then, like a frost flower on a windowpane, the dimple expanded on her wrinkled cheek, and she held out her hand.

"I'm so glad," she said, "so glad!"

She turned to her son, who stood watching us. "You must have told Lancelot all about me—you've known me so long!"

"I haven't had time to talk to your son—since I knew he was your son," I explained.

Her brow cleared. "Then you haven't had time to say anything very dreadful?" she said with a laugh.

"It is he who has been saying dreadful things," I returned, trying to fall in with her tone.

I saw my mistake. "What things?" she faltered.

"Making me feel how old I am by telling me about his children."

"My grandchildren!" she exclaimed with a blush.

"Well, if you choose to put it so."

She laughed again, vaguely, and was silent. I hesitated a moment and then put out my hand.

"I see you are tired. I shouldn't have ventured to come in at this hour if your son—"

The son stepped between us. "Yes, I asked him to come," he said to his mother, in his clear self-assertive voice. "*I* haven't told him anything yet; but you've got to—now. That's what I brought him for."

His mother straightened herself, but I saw her eye waver.

"Lancelot—" she began.

"Mr. Amyot," I said, turning to the young man, "if your mother will let me come back tomorrow, I shall be very glad—"

He struck his hand hard against the table on which he was leaning.

"No, sir! It won't take long, but it's got to be said now."

He moved nearer to his mother, and I saw his lip twitch under his beard. After all, he was younger and less sure of himself than I had fancied.

"See here, Mother," he went on, "there's something here that's got to be cleared up, and as you say this gentleman is an old friend of yours it had better be cleared up in his presence. Maybe he can help explain it—and if he can't, it's got to be explained to *him*."

Mrs. Amyot's lips moved, but she made no sound. She glanced at me helplessly and sat down. My early inclination to thrash Lancelot was beginning to reassert itself. I took up my hat and moved toward the door.

"Mrs. Amyot is under no obligation to explain anything whatever to me," I said curtly.

"Well! She's under an obligation to me, then—to explain something in your presence." He turned to her again. "Do you know what the people in this hotel are saying? Do you know what he thinks—what they all think? That you're doing this lecturing to support me—to pay for my education! They say you go round telling them so. That's what they buy the tickets for—they do it out of charity. Ask him if it isn't what they say—ask him if they weren't joking about it on the piazza before dinner. The others think I'm a little boy, but he's known you for years, and he must have known how old I was. *He* must have known it wasn't to pay for my education!"

He stood before her with his hands clenched, the veins beating in his temples. She had grown very pale, and her cheeks looked hollow. When she spoke her voice had an odd click in it.

"If—if these ladies and gentlemen have been coming to my lectures out of charity, I see nothing to be ashamed of in that—" she faltered.

"If they've been coming out of charity to *me*," he retorted, "don't you see you've been making me a party to a fraud? Isn't there any shame in that?" His forehead reddened. "Mother! Can't you see the shame of letting people think I was a deadbeat, who sponged on you for my keep? Let alone making us both the laughingstock of every place you go to!"

"I never did that, Lancelot!"

"Did what?"

"Made you a laughingstock—"

He stepped close to her and caught her wrist.

"Will you look me in the face and swear you never told people you were doing this lecturing business to support me?"

There was a long silence. He dropped her wrists and she lifted a limp handkerchief to her frightened eyes. "I did do it—to support you—to educate you—" she sobbed.

"We're not talking about what you did when I was a boy. Everybody who knows me knows I've been a grateful son. Have I ever taken a penny from you since I left college ten years ago?"

"I never said you had! How can you accuse your mother of such wickedness, Lancelot?"

"Have you never told anybody in this hotel—or anywhere else in the last ten years—that you were lecturing to support me? Answer me that!"

"How can you," she wept, "before a stranger?"

"Haven't you said such things about *me* to strangers?" he retorted.

"Lancelot!"

"Well—answer me, then. Say you haven't, Mother!" His voice broke unexpectedly and he took her hand with a gentler touch. "I'll believe anything you tell me," he said almost humbly.

She mistook his tone and raised her head with a rash clutch at dignity.

"I think you'd better ask this gentleman to excuse you first."

"No, by God, I won't!" he cried. "This gentleman says he knows all about you and I mean him to know all about me, too. I don't mean that he or anybody else under this roof shall go on thinking for another twenty-four hours that a cent of their money has ever gone into my pockets since I was old enough to shift for myself. And he shan't leave this room till you've made that clear to him."

He stepped back as he spoke and put his shoulders against the door.

"My dear young gentleman," I said politely, "I shall leave this room exactly when I see fit to do so—and that is now. I have already told you that Mrs. Amyot owes me no explanation of her conduct."

"But I owe you an explanation of mine—you and everyone who has bought a single one of her lecture tickets. Do you suppose a man who's been through what I went through while that woman was talking to you in the porch before dinner is going to hold his tongue, and not attempt to justify himself? No decent man is going to sit down under that sort of thing. It's enough to ruin his character. If you're my mother's friend, you owe it to me to hear what I've got to say."

He pulled out his handkerchief and wiped his forehead.

"Good God, Mother!" he burst out suddenly, "what did you do it for? Haven't you had everything you wanted ever since I was able to pay for it? Haven't I paid you back every cent you spent on me when I was in college? Have I ever gone back on you since I was big enough to work?" He turned to me with a laugh. "I thought she did it to amuse herself—and because there was such a demand for her lectures. *Such a demand!* That's what she always told me. When we asked her to come out and spend this winter with us in Minneapolis, she wrote back that she couldn't because she had engagements all through the South, and her manager wouldn't let her off. That's the reason why I came all the way on here to see her. We thought she was the most popular lecturer in the United States, my wife and I did! We were awfully proud of it too, I can tell you." He dropped into a chair, still laughing.

"How can you, Lancelot, how can you!" His mother, forgetful of my presence, was clinging to him with tentative caresses. "When you didn't need the money any longer I spent it all on the children—you know I did."

"Yes, on lace christening dresses and life-size rocking horses with real manes! The kind of thing children can't do without."

"Oh, Lancelot, Lancelot—I loved them so! How can you believe such falsehoods about me?"

"What falsehoods about you?"

"That I ever told anybody such dreadful things?"

He put her back gently, keeping his eyes on hers. "Did you never tell anybody in this house that you were lecturing to support your son?"

Her hands dropped from his shoulders and she flashed round on me in sudden anger.

"I know what I think of people who call themselves friends and who come between a mother and her son!"

"Oh, Mother, Mother!" he groaned.

I went up to him and laid my hand on his shoulder.

"My dear man," I said "don't you see the uselessness of prolonging this?"

"Yes, I do," he answered abruptly; and before I could forestall his movement he rose and walked out of the room.

There was a long silence, measured by the lessening reverberations of his footsteps down the wooden floor of the corridor.

When they ceased I approached Mrs. Amyot, who had sunk into her chair. I held out my hand and she took it without a trace of resentment on her ravaged face.

"I sent his wife a sealskin jacket at Christmas!" she said, with the tears running down her cheeks.

SOULS BELATED

THEIR RAILWAY carriage had been full when the train left Bologna; but at the first station beyond Milan their only remaining companion—a courtly person who ate garlic out of a carpetbag—had left his crumb-strewn seat with a bow.

Lydia's eye regretfully followed the shiny broadcloth of his retreating back till it lost itself in the cloud of touts and cab drivers hanging about the station; then she glanced across at Gannett and caught the same regret in his look. They were both sorry to be alone.

"Par-ten-za!" shouted the guard. The train vibrated to a sudden slamming of doors; a waiter ran along the platform with a tray of fossilized sandwiches; a belated porter flung a bundle of shawls and band-boxes into a third-class carriage; the guard snapped out a brief *Partenza!* which indicated the purely ornamental nature of his first shout; and the train swung out of the station.

The direction of the road had changed, and a shaft of sunlight struck across the dusty red-velvet seats into Lydia's corner. Gannett did not notice it. He had returned to his *Revue de Paris,* and she had to rise and lower the shade of the farther window. Against the vast horizon of their leisure such incidents stood out sharply.

Having lowered the shade, Lydia sat down, leaving the length of the carriage between herself and Gannett. At length he missed her and looked up.

"I moved out of the sun," she hastily explained.

He looked at her curiously: the sun was beating on her through the shade.

"Very well," he said pleasantly; adding, "You don't mind?" as he drew a cigarette case from his pocket.

It was a refreshing touch, relieving the tension of her spirit with the suggestion that, after all, if he could *smoke*—! The relief was only momentary. Her experience of smokers was limited (her husband had disapproved of the use of tobacco) but she knew from hearsay that men sometimes smoked to get away from things; that a cigar might be the masculine equivalent of darkened windows and a headache. Gannett, after a puff or two, returned to his review.

It was just as she had foreseen; he feared to speak as much as she did. It was one of the misfortunes of their situation that they were never busy enough to necessitate, or even to justify, the postponement of unpleasant discussions. If they avoided a question it was obviously, unconcealably because the question was disagreeable. They had unlimited leisure and an accumulation of mental energy to devote to any subject that presented itself; new topics were in fact at a premium. Lydia sometimes had premonitions of a famine-stricken period when there would be nothing left to talk about, and she had already caught herself doling out piecemeal what, in the first prodigality of their confidences, she would have flung to him in a breath. Their silence therefore might simply mean that they had nothing to say; but it was another disadvantage of their position that it allowed infinite opportunity for the classification of minute differences. Lydia had learned to distinguish between real and factitious silences; and under Gannett's she now detected a hum of speech to which her own thoughts made breathless answer.

How could it be otherwise, with that thing between them? She glanced up at the rack overhead. The *thing* was there, in her dressing bag, symbolically suspended over her head and his. He was thinking of it now, just as she was; they had been thinking of it in unison ever since they had entered the train. While the carriage had held other travelers they had screened her from his thoughts; but now that he and she were alone she knew exactly what was passing through his mind; she could almost hear him asking himself what he should say to her.

The thing had come that morning, brought up to her in an innocent-looking envelope with the rest of their letters, as they were leaving the hotel at Bologna. As she tore it open, she and Gannett were laughing over some ineptitude of the local guidebook—they had been driven, of late, to make the most of such incidental humors of travel. Even when she had unfolded the document she took it for some unimportant business paper sent abroad for her signature, and her eye traveled inattentively over the curly *Whereases* of the preamble until a word arrested her: Divorce. There it stood, an impassable barrier, between her husband's name and hers.

She had been prepared for it, of course, as healthy people are said to be prepared for death, in the sense of knowing it must come without in the least expecting that it will. She had known from the first that Tillotson meant to divorce her—but what did it matter? Nothing mattered, in those first days of supreme deliverance, but the fact that she was free; and not so much (she had begun to be aware) that freedom had released her from Tillotson as that it had given her to Gannett. This discovery had not been agreeable to her self-esteem. She had preferred to think that Tillotson had himself embodied all her reasons for leaving him; and those he represented had seemed cogent enough to stand in no need of reinforcement. Yet she had not left him till she met Gannett. It was her love for Gannett that had made life with Tillotson so poor and incomplete a business. If she had never, from the first, regarded her marriage as a full canceling of her claims upon life, she had at least, for a number of years, accepted it as a provisional compensation,—she had made it "do." Existence in the commodious Tillotson mansion in Fifth Avenue—with Mrs. Tillotson senior commanding the approaches from the second-story front windows—had been reduced to a series of purely automatic acts. The moral atmosphere of the Tillotson interior was as carefully screened and curtained as the house itself: Mrs. Tillotson senior dreaded ideas as much as a draft in her back. Prudent people liked an even temperature; and to do anything unexpected was as foolish as going out in the rain. One of the chief advantages of being rich was that one need not be exposed to unforeseen contingencies: by the use of ordinary firmness and common sense one could make sure of doing exactly the same thing every day at the same hour. These doctrines, reverentially imbibed with his mother's milk, Tillotson (a model son who had never given his parents an hour's anxiety) complacently expounded to his wife, testifying to his sense of their importance by the regularity with which he wore galoshes on damp days, his punctuality at meals, and his elaborate precautions against burglars and contagious diseases. Lydia, coming from a smaller town, and entering New York life through the portals of the Tillotson mansion, had mechanically accepted this point of view as inseparable from having a front pew in church and a parterre box at the opera. All the people who came to the house revolved in the same small circle of prejudices. It was the kind of society in which, after dinner, the ladies compared the exorbitant charges of their children's teachers, and agreed that, even with the new duties on French clothes, it was cheaper in the end to get everything from Worth; while the husbands, over their cigars, lamented municipal corruption, and decided that the men to start a reform were those who had no private interests at stake.

To Lydia this view of life had become a matter of course, just as lumbering about in her mother-in-law's landau had come to seem the only possible means of locomotion, and listening every Sunday to a fashionable Presbyterian divine the inevitable atonement for having thought oneself bored on the other six days of the week. Before she met Gannett her life had seemed merely dull; his coming made it appear like one of those dismal Cruikshank prints in which the people are all ugly and all engaged in occupations that are either vulgar or stupid.

It was natural that Tillotson should be the chief sufferer from this readjustment of focus. Gannett's nearness had made her husband ridiculous, and a part of the ridicule had been reflected on herself. Her tolerance laid her open to a suspicion of obtuseness from which she must, at all costs, clear herself in Gannett's eyes.

She did not understand this until afterwards. At the time she fancied that she had merely reached the limits of endurance. In so large a charter of liberties as the mere act of leaving Tillotson seemed to confer, the small question of divorce or no divorce did not count. It was when she saw that she had left her husband only to be with Gannett that she perceived the significance of anything affecting their relations. Her husband, in casting her off, had virtually flung her at Gannett: it was thus that the world viewed it. The measure of alacrity with which Gannett would receive her would be the subject of curious speculation over afternoon tea tables and in club corners. She knew what would be said—she had heard it so often of others! The recollection bathed her in misery. The men would probably back Gannett to "do the decent thing"; but the ladies' eyebrows would emphasize the worthlessness of such enforced fidelity; and after all, they would be right. She had put herself in a position where Gannett "owed" her something; where, as a gentleman, he was bound to "stand the damage." The idea of accepting such compensation had never crossed her mind; the so-called rehabilitation of such a marriage had always seemed to her the only real disgrace. What she dreaded was the necessity of having to explain herself; of having to combat his arguments; of calculating, in spite of herself, the exact measure of insistence with which he pressed them. She knew not whether she most shrank from his insisting too much or too little. In such a case the nicest sense of proportion might be at fault; and how easily to fall into the error of taking her resistance for a test of his sincerity! Whichever way she turned, an ironical implication confronted her: she had the exasperated sense of having walked into the trap of some stupid practical joke.

Beneath all these preoccupations lurked the dread of what he was thinking. Sooner or later, of course, he would have to speak; but that, in the meantime, he should think, even for a moment, that there was any use in speaking, seemed to her simply unendurable. Her sensitiveness on this point was aggravated by another fear, as yet barely on the level of consciousness; the fear of unwillingly involving Gannett in the trammels of her dependence. To look upon him as the instrument of her liberation; to resist in herself the least tendency to a wifely taking possession of his future; had seemed to Lydia the one way of maintaining the dignity of their relation. Her view had not changed, but she was aware of a growing inability to keep her thoughts fixed on the essential point—the point of parting with Gannett. It was easy to face as long as she kept it sufficiently far off: but what was this act of mental postponement but a gradual encroachment on his future? What was needful was the courage to recognize the moment when, by some word or look, their voluntary fellowship should be transformed into a bondage the more wearing that it was based on none of those common obligations which make the most imperfect marriage in some sort a center of gravity.

When the porter, at the next station, threw the door open, Lydia drew back, making way for the hoped-for intruder; but none came, and the train took up its leisurely progress through the spring wheat fields and budding copses. She now began to hope that Gannett would speak before the next station. She watched him furtively, half-disposed to return to the seat opposite his, but there was an artificiality about his absorption that restrained her. She had never before seen him read with so conspicuous an air of warding off interruption. What could he be thinking of? Why should he be afraid to speak? Or was it her answer that he dreaded?

The train paused for the passing of an express, and he put down his book and leaned out of the window. Presently he turned to her with a smile.

"There's a jolly old villa out here," he said.

His easy tone relieved her, and she smiled back at him as she crossed over to his corner.

Beyond the embankment, through the opening in a mossy wall, she caught sight of the villa, with its broken balustrades, its stagnant fountains, and the stone satyr closing the perspective of a dusky grass walk.

"How should you like to live there?" he asked as the train moved on.

"There?"

"In some such place, I mean. One might do worse, don't you think so? There must be at least two centuries of solitude under those yew trees. Shouldn't you like it?"

"I—I don't know," she faltered. She knew now that he meant to speak.

He lit another cigarette. "We shall have to live somewhere, you know," he said as he bent above the match.

Lydia tried to speak carelessly. *"Je n'en vois pas la nécessité!* Why not live everywhere, as we have been doing?"

"But we can't travel forever, can we?"

"Oh, forever's a long word," she objected, picking up the review he had thrown aside.

"For the rest of our lives then," he said, moving nearer.

She made a slight gesture which caused his hand to slip from hers.

"Why should we make plans? I thought you agreed with me that it's pleasanter to drift."

He looked at her hesitatingly. "It's been pleasant, certainly; but I suppose I shall have to get at my work again some day. You know I haven't written a line since—all this time," he hastily amended.

She flamed with sympathy and self-reproach. "Oh, if you mean *that*—if you want to write—of course we must settle down. How stupid of me not to have thought of it sooner! Where shall we go? Where do you think you could work best? We oughtn't to lose any more time."

He hesitated again. "I had thought of a villa in these parts. It's quiet; we shouldn't be bothered. Should you like it?"

"Of course I should like it." She paused and looked away. "But I thought—I remember your telling me once that your best work had been done in a crowd—in big cities. Why should you shut yourself up in a desert?"

Gannett, for a moment, made no reply. At length he said, avoiding her eye as carefully as she avoided his: "It might be different now; I can't tell, of course, till I try. A writer ought not to be dependent on his *milieu;* it's a mistake to humor oneself in that way; and I thought that just at first you might prefer to be—"

She faced him. "To be what?"

"Well—quiet. I mean—"

"What do you mean by 'at first'?" she interrupted.

He paused again. "I mean after we are married."

She thrust up her chin and turned toward the window. "Thank you!" she tossed back at him.

"Lydia!" he exclaimed blankly; and she felt in every fiber of her averted person that he had made the inconceivable, the unpardonable mistake of anticipating her acquiescence.

The train rattled on and he groped for a third cigarette. Lydia remained silent.

"I haven't offended you?" he ventured at length, in the tone of a man who feels his way.

She shook her head with a sigh. "I thought you understood," she moaned. Their eyes met and she moved back to his side.

"Do you want to know how not to offend me? By taking it for granted, once for all, that you've said your say on the odious question and that I've said mine, and that we stand just where we did this morning before that—that hateful paper came to spoil everything between us!"

"To spoil everything between us? What on earth do you mean? Aren't you glad to be free?"

"I was free before."

"Not to marry me," he suggested.

"But I don't *want* to marry you!" she cried.

She saw that he turned pale. "I'm obtuse, I suppose," he said slowly. "I confess I don't see what you're driving at. Are you tired of the whole business? Or was I simply a—an excuse for getting away? Perhaps you didn't care to travel alone? Was that it? And now you want to chuck me?" His voice had grown harsh. "You owe me a straight answer, you know; don't be tenderhearted!"

Her eyes swam as she leaned to him. "Don't you see it's because I care—because I care so much? Oh, Ralph! Can't you see how it would humiliate me? Try to feel it as a woman would! Don't you see the misery of being made your wife in this way? If I'd known you as a girl—that would have been a real marriage! But now—this vulgar fraud upon society—and upon a society we despised and laughed at—this sneaking back into a position that we've voluntarily forfeited: don't you see what a cheap compromise it is? We neither of us believe in the abstract 'sacredness' of marriage; we both know that no ceremony is needed to consecrate our love for each other; what object can we have in marrying, except the secret fear of each that the other may escape, or the secret longing to work our way back gradually—oh, very gradually—into the esteem of the people whose conventional morality we have always ridiculed and hated? And the very fact that, after a decent interval, these same people would come and dine with us—the women who talk about the indissolubility of marriage, and who would let me die in a gutter today because I am 'leading a life of sin'—doesn't that disgust you more than their turning their backs on us now? I can stand being cut by them, but I couldn't stand their coming to call and asking what I meant to do about visiting that unfortunate Mrs. So-and-so!"

She paused, and Gannett maintained a perplexed silence.

"You judge things too theoretically," he said at length, slowly. "Life is made up of compromises."

"The life we ran away from—yes! If we had been willing to accept them"—she flushed—"we might have gone on meeting each other at Mrs. Tillotson's dinners."

He smiled slightly. "I didn't know that we ran away to found a new system of ethics. I supposed it was because we loved each other."

"Life is complex, of course; isn't it the very recognition of that fact that separates us from the people who see it *tout d'une pièce?* If *they* are right—if marriage is sacred in itself and the individual must always be sacrificed to the family—then there can be no real marriage between us, since our—our being together is a protest against the sacrifice of the individual to the family." She interrupted herself with a laugh. "You'll say now that I'm giving you a lecture on sociology! Of course one acts as one can—as one must, perhaps—pulled by all sorts of invisible threads; but at least one needn't pretend, for social advantages, to subscribe to a creed that ignores the complexity of human motives—that classifies people by arbitrary signs, and puts it in everybody's reach to be on Mrs. Tillotson's visiting list. It may be necessary that the world should be ruled by conventions—but if we believed in them, why did we break through them? And if we don't believe in them, is it honest to take advantage of the protection they afford?"

Gannett hesitated. "One may believe in them or not; but as long as they do rule the world it is only by taking advantage of their protection that one can find a *modus vivendi.*"

"Do outlaws need a *modus vivendi?*"

He looked at her hopelessly. Nothing is more perplexing to man than the mental process of a woman who reasons her emotions.

She thought she had scored a point and followed it up passionately. "You do understand, don't you? You see how the very thought of the thing humiliates me! We are together today because we choose to be—don't let us look any farther than that!" She caught his hands. *"Promise* me you'll never speak of it again; promise me you'll never *think* of it even," she implored, with a tearful prodigality of italics.

Through what followed—his protests, his arguments, his final un-convinced submission to her wishes—she had a sense of his but half-discerning all that, for her, had made the moment so tumultuous. They had reached that memorable point in every heart history when, for the first time, the man seems obtuse and the woman irrational. It was the abundance of his intentions that consoled her, on reflection, for what they lacked in quality. After all, it would have been worse, incalculably worse, to have detected any overreadiness to understand her.

* II *

When the train at nightfall brought them to their journey's end at the edge of one of the lakes, Lydia was glad that they were not, as usual, to pass from one solitude to another. Their wanderings during the year had indeed been like the flight of outlaws: through Sicily, Dalmatia, Transylvania and Southern Italy they had persisted in their tacit avoidance of their kind. Isolation, at first, had deepened the flavor of their happiness, as night intensifies the scent of certain flowers; but in the new phase on which they were entering, Lydia's chief wish was that they should be less abnormally exposed to the action of each other's thoughts.

She shrank, nevertheless, as the brightly-looming bulk of the fashionable Anglo-American hotel on the water's brink began to radiate toward their advancing boat its vivid suggestion of social order, visitors, lists, Church services, and the bland inquisition of the *table d'hôte*. The mere fact that in a moment or two she must take her place on the hotel register as Mrs. Gannett seemed to weaken the springs of her resistance.

They had meant to stay for a night only, on their way to a lofty village among the glaciers of Monte Rosa; but after the first plunge into publicity, when they entered the dining room, Lydia felt the relief of being lost in a crowd, of ceasing for a moment to be the center of Gannett's scrutiny; and in his face she caught the reflection of her feeling. After dinner, when she went upstairs, he strolled into the smoking room, and an hour or two later, sitting in the darkness of her window, she heard his voice below and saw him walking up and down the terrace with a companion cigar at his side. When he came up he told her he had been talking to the hotel chaplain—a very good sort of fellow.

"Queer little microcosms, these hotels! Most of these people live here all summer and then migrate to Italy or the Riviera. The English are the only people who can lead that kind of life with dignity—those soft-voiced old ladies in Shetland shawls somehow carry the British Empire under their caps. *Civis Romanus sum*. It's a curious study—there might be some good things to work up here."

He stood before her with the vivid preoccupied stare of the novelist on the trail of a "subject." With a relief that was half painful she noticed that, for the first time since they had been together, he was hardly aware of her presence.

"Do you think you could write here?"

"Here? I don't know." His stare dropped. "After being out of things so long one's first impressions are bound to be tremendously vivid, you know. I see a dozen threads already that one might follow—"

He broke off with a touch of embarrassment.

"Then follow them. We'll stay," she said with sudden decision.

"Stay here?" He glanced at her in surprise, and then, walking to the window, looked out upon the dusky slumber of the garden.

"Why not?" she said at length, in a tone of veiled irritation.

"The place is full of old cats in caps who gossip with the chaplain. Shall you like—I mean, it would be different if—"

She flamed up.

"Do you suppose I care? It's none of their business."

"Of course not; but you won't get them to think so."

"They may think what they please."

He looked at her doubtfully.

"It's for you to decide."

"We'll stay," she repeated.

Gannett, before they met, had made himself known as a successful writer of short stories and of a novel which had achieved the distinction of being widely discussed. The reviewers called him "promising," and Lydia now accused herself of having too long interfered with the fulfilment of his promise. There was a special irony in the fact, since his passionate assurances that only the stimulus of her companionship could bring out his latent faculty had almost given the dignity of a "vocation" to her course: there had been moments when she had felt unable to assume, before posterity, the responsibility of thwarting his career. And, after all, he had not written a line since they had been together: his first desire to write had come from renewed contact with the world! Was it all a mistake then? Must the most intelligent choice work more disastrously than the blundering combinations of chance? Or was there a still more humiliating answer to her perplexities? His sudden impulse of activity so exactly coincided with her own wish to withdraw, for a time, from the range of his observation, that she wondered if he too were not seeking sanctuary from intolerable problems.

"You must begin tomorrow!" she cried, hiding a tremor under the laugh with which she added, "I wonder if there's any ink in the inkstand?"

Whatever else they had at the Hotel Bellosguardo, they had, as Miss Pinsent said, "a certain tone." It was to Lady Susan Condit that they owed this inestimable benefit; an advantage ranking in Miss Pinsent's opinion above even the lawn tennis courts and the resident chaplain. It was the fact of Lady Susan's annual visit that made the hotel what it was. Miss Pinsent was certainly the last to underrate such a privilege: "It's so important, my dear, forming as we do a little family, that there should be someone to give *the tone;* and no one could do it better than Lady Susan—an earl's daughter and a person of such determination. Dear Mrs. Ainger now—who really *ought,* you know, when Lady Susan's away—absolutely refuses to assert herself." Miss Pinsent sniffed derisively. "A bishop's niece!—my dear, I saw her once actually give in to some South Americans—and before us all. She gave up her seat at table to oblige them—such a lack of dignity! Lady Susan spoke to her very plainly about it afterwards."

Miss Pinsent glanced across the lake and adjusted her auburn front.

"But of course I don't deny that the stand Lady Susan takes is not always easy to live up to—for the rest of us, I mean. Monsieur Grossart, our good proprietor, finds it trying at times, I know—he has said as much, privately, to Mrs. Ainger and me. After all, the poor man is not to blame for wanting to fill his hotel, is he? And Lady Susan is so difficult—so very difficult—about new people. One might almost say that she disapproves of them beforehand, on principle. And yet she's had warnings—she very nearly made a dreadful mistake once with the Duchess of Levens, who dyed her hair and—well, swore and smoked. One would have thought that might have been a lesson to Lady Susan." Miss Pinsent resumed her knitting with a sigh. "There are exceptions, of course. She took at once to you and Mr. Gannett—it was quite remarkable, really. Oh, I don't mean that either—of course not! It was perfectly natural—we *all* thought you so charming and interesting from the first day—we knew at once that Mr. Gannett was intellectual, by the magazines you took in; but you know what I mean. Lady Susan is so very—well, I won't say prejudiced, as Mrs. Ainger does—but so prepared *not* to like new people, that her taking to you in that way was a surprise to us all, I confess."

Miss Pinsent sent a significant glance down the long laurustinus alley from the other end of which two people—a lady and gentleman—were strolling toward them through the smiling neglect of the garden.

"In this case, of course, it's very different; that I'm willing to admit. Their looks are against them; but, as Mrs. Ainger says, one can't exactly tell them so."

"She's very handsome," Lydia ventured, with her eyes on the lady, who showed, under the dome of a vivid sunshade, the hourglass figure and superlative coloring of a Christmas chromo.

"That's the worst of it. She's too handsome."

"Well, after all, she can't help that."

"Other people manage to," said Miss Pinsent skeptically.

"But isn't it rather unfair of Lady Susan—considering that nothing is known about them?"

"But, my dear, that's the very thing that's against them. It's infinitely worse than any actual knowledge."

Lydia mentally agreed that, in the case of Mrs. Linton, it possibly might be.

"I wonder why they came here?" she mused.

"That's against them too. It's always a bad sign when loud people come to a quiet place. And they've brought van loads of boxes—her maid told Mrs. Ainger's that they meant to stop indefinitely."

"And Lady Susan actually turned her back on her in the salon?"

"My dear, she said it was for our sakes: that makes it so unanswerable! But poor Grossart *is* in a way! The Lintons have taken his most expensive suite, you know—the yellow damask drawing room above the portico—and they have champagne with every meal!"

They were silent as Mr. and Mrs. Linton sauntered by; the lady with tempestuous brows and challenging chin; the gentleman, a blond stripling, trailing after her, head downward, like a reluctant child dragged by his nurse.

"What does your husband think of them, my dear?" Miss Pinsent whispered as they passed out of earshot.

Lydia stooped to pick a violet in the border.

"He hasn't told me."

"Of your speaking to them, I mean. Would he approve of that? I know how very particular nice Americans are. I think your action might make a difference; it would certainly carry weight with Lady Susan."

"Dear Miss Pinsent, you flatter me!"

Lydia rose and gathered up her book and sunshade.

"Well, if you're asked for an opinion—if Lady Susan asks you for one—I think you ought to be prepared," Miss Pinsent admonished her as she moved away.

* III *

Lady Susan held her own. She ignored the Lintons, and her little family, as Miss Pinsent phrased it, followed suit. Even Mrs. Ainger agreed that it was obligatory. If Lady Susan owed it to the others not to speak to the Lintons, the others clearly owed it to Lady Susan to back her up. It was generally found expedient, at the Hotel Bellosguardo, to adopt this form of reasoning.

Whatever effect this combined action may have had upon the Lintons, it did not at least have that of driving them away. Monsieur Grossart, after a few days of suspense, had the satisfaction of seeing them settle down in his yellow damask *premier* with what looked like a permanent installation of palm trees and silk cushions, and a gratifying continuance in the consumption of champagne. Mrs. Linton trailed her Doucet draperies up and down the garden with the same challenging air, while her husband, smoking innumerable cigarettes, dragged himself dejectedly in her wake; but neither of them, after the first encounter with Lady Susan, made any attempt to extend their acquaintance. They simply ignored their ignorers. As Miss Pinsent resentfully observed, they behaved exactly as though the hotel were empty.

It was therefore a matter of surprise, as well as of displeasure, to Lydia, to find, on glancing up one day from her seat in the garden, that the shadow which had fallen across her book was that of the enigmatic Mrs. Linton.

"I want to speak to you," that lady said, in a rich hard voice that seemed the audible expression of her gown and her complexion.

Lydia started. She certainly did not want to speak to Mrs. Linton.

"Shall I sit down here?" the latter continued, fixing her intensely-shaded eyes on Lydia's face, "or are you afraid of being seen with me?"

"Afraid?" Lydia colored. "Sit down, please. What is it that you wish to say?"

Mrs. Linton, with a smile, drew up a garden chair and crossed one openwork ankle above the other.

"I want you to tell me what my husband said to your husband last night."

Lydia turned pale.

"My husband—to yours?" she faltered, staring at the other.

"Didn't you know they were closeted together for hours in the smoking room after you went upstairs? My man didn't get to bed until nearly two o'clock and when he did I couldn't get a word out of him. When he wants to be aggravating I'll back him against anybody living!" Her teeth and eyes flashed persuasively upon Lydia. "But you'll tell me what they were talking about, won't you? I know I can trust you—you look so awfully kind. And it's for his own good. He's such a precious donkey and I'm so afraid he's got into some beastly scrape or other. If he'd only trust his own old woman! But they're always writing to him and setting him against me. And I've got nobody to turn to." She laid her hand on Lydia's with a rattle of bracelets. "You'll help me, won't you?"

Lydia drew back from the smiling fierceness of her brows.

"I'm sorry—but I don't think I understand. My husband has said nothing to me of—of yours."

The great black crescents above Mrs. Linton's eyes met angrily.

"I say—is that true?" she demanded.

Lydia rose from her seat.

"Oh, look here, I didn't mean that, you know—you mustn't take one up so! Can't you see how rattled I am?"

Lydia saw that, in fact, her beautiful mouth was quivering beneath softened eyes.

"I'm beside myself!" the splendid creature wailed, dropping into her seat.

"I'm so sorry," Lydia repeated, forcing herself to speak kindly; "but how can I help you?"

Mrs. Linton raised her head sharply.

"By finding out—there's a darling!"

"Finding what out?"

"What Trevenna told him."

"Trevenna—?" Lydia echoed in bewilderment.

Mrs. Linton clapped her hand to her mouth.

"Oh, Lord—there, it's out! What a fool I am! But I supposed of course you knew; I supposed everybody knew." She dried her eyes and bridled. "Didn't you know that he's Lord Trevenna? I'm Mrs. Cope."

Lydia recognized the names. They had figured in a flamboyant elopement which had thrilled fashionable London some six months earlier.

"Now you see how it is—you understand, don't you?" Mrs. Cope continued on a note of appeal. "I knew you would—that's the reason I came to you. I suppose *he* felt the same thing about your husband; he's not spoken to another soul in the place." Her face grew anxious again. "He's awfully sensitive, generally—he feels our position, he says—as if it wasn't *my* place to feel that! But when he does get talking there's no knowing what he'll say. I know he's been brooding over something lately, and I *must* find out what it is—it's to his interest that I should. I always tell him that I think only of his interest; if he'd only trust me! But he's been so odd lately—I can't think what he's plotting. You will help me, dear?"

Lydia, who had remained standing, looked away uncomfortably.

"If you mean by finding out what Lord Trevenna has told my husband, I'm afraid it's impossible."

"Why impossible?"

"Because I infer that it was told in confidence."

Mrs. Cope stared incredulously.

"Well, what of that? Your husband looks such a dear—anyone can see he's awfully gone on you. What's to prevent your getting it out of him?"

Lydia flushed.

"I'm not a spy!" she exclaimed.

"A spy—a spy? How dare you?" Mrs. Cope flamed out. "Oh, I don't mean that either! Don't be angry with me—I'm so miserable." She essayed a softer note. "Do you call that spying—for one woman to help out another? I do need help so dreadfully! I'm at my wits' end with Trevenna, I am indeed. He's such a boy—a mere baby, you know; he's only two-and-twenty." She dropped her orbed lids. "He's younger than me—only fancy, a few months younger. I tell him he ought to listen to me as if I was his mother; oughtn't he now? But he won't, he won't! All his people are at him, you see—oh, I know *their* little game! Trying to get him away from me before I can get my divorce—that's what they're up to. At first he wouldn't listen to them; he used to toss their letters over to me to read; but now he reads them himself, and answers 'em too, I fancy; he's always shut up in his room, writing. If I only knew what his plan is I could stop him fast enough—he's such a simpleton. But he's dreadfully deep too—at times I can't make him out. But I know he's told your husband everything—I knew that last night the minute I laid eyes on him. And I *must* find out—you must help me—I've got no one else to turn to!"

She caught Lydia's fingers in a stormy pressure.

"Say you'll help me—you and your husband."

Lydia tried to free herself.

"What you ask is impossible; you must see that it is. No one could interfere in—in the way you ask."

Mrs. Cope's clutch tightened.

"You won't, then? You won't?"

"Certainly not. Let me go, please."

Mrs. Cope released her with a laugh.

"Oh, go by all means—pray don't let me detain you! Shall you go and tell Lady Susan Condit that there's a pair of us—or shall I save you the trouble of enlightening her?"

Lydia stood still in the middle of the path, seeing her antagonist through a mist of terror. Mrs. Cope was still laughing.

"Oh, I'm not spiteful by nature, my dear; but you're a little more than flesh and blood can stand! It's impossible, is it? Let you go, indeed! You're too good to be mixed up in my affairs, are you? Why, you little fool, the first day I laid eyes on you I saw that you and I were both in the same box—that's the reason I spoke to you."

She stepped nearer, her smile dilating on Lydia like a lamp through a fog.

"You can take your choice, you know; I always play fair. If you'll tell I'll promise not to. Now then, which is it to be?"

Lydia, involuntarily, had begun to move away from the pelting storm of words; but at this she turned and sat down again.

"You may go," she said simply. "I shall stay here."

* IV *

She stayed there for a long time, in the hypnotized contemplation, not of Mrs. Cope's present, but of her own past. Gannett, early that morning, had gone off on a long walk—he had fallen into the habit of taking these mountain tramps with various fellow lodgers; but even had he been within reach she could not have gone to him just then. She had to deal with herself first. She was surprised to find how, in the last months, she had lost the habit of introspection. Since their coming to the Hotel Bellosguardo she and Gannett had tacitly avoided themselves and each other.

She was aroused by the whistle of the three o'clock steamboat as it neared the landing just beyond the hotel gates. Three o'clock! Then Gannett would soon be back—he had told her to expect him before four. She rose hurriedly, her face averted from the inquisitorial façade of the hotel. She could not see him just yet; she could not go indoors. She slipped through one of the overgrown garden alleys and climbed a steep path to the hills.

It was dark when she opened their sitting-room door. Gannett was sitting on the window ledge smoking a cigarette. Cigarettes were now his chief resource: he had not written a line during the two months they had spent at the Hotel Bellosguardo. In that respect, it had turned out not to be the right *milieu* after all.

He started up at Lydia's entrance.

"Where have you been? I was getting anxious."

She sat down in a chair near the door.

"Up the mountain," she said wearily.

"Alone?"

"Yes."

Gannett threw away his cigarette: the sound of her voice made him want to see her face.

"Shall we have a little light?" he suggested.

She made no answer and he lifted the globe from the lamp and put a match to the wick. Then he looked at her.

"Anything wrong? You look done up."

She sat glancing vaguely about the little sitting room, dimly lit by the pallid-globed lamp, which left in twilight the outlines of the furniture, of his writing table heaped with books and papers, of the tea roses and jasmine drooping on the mantelpiece. How like home it had all grown—how like home!

"Lydia, what is wrong?" he repeated.

She moved away from him, feeling for her hatpins and turning to lay her hat and sunshade on the table.

Suddenly she said: "That woman has been talking to me."

Gannett stared.

"That woman? What woman?"

"Mrs. Linton—Mrs. Cope."

He gave a start of annoyance, still, as she perceived, not grasping the full import of her words.

"The deuce! She told you—?"

"She told me everything."

Gannett looked at her anxiously.

"What impudence! I'm so sorry that you should have been exposed to this, dear."

"Exposed!" Lydia laughed.

Gannett's brow clouded and they looked away from each other.

"Do you know *why* she told me? She had the best of reasons. The first time she laid eyes on me she saw that we were both in the same box."

"Lydia!"

"So it was natural, of course, that she should turn to me in a difficulty."

"What difficulty?"

"It seems she has reason to think that Lord Trevenna's people are trying to get him away from her before she gets her divorce—"

"Well?"

"And she fancied he had been consulting with you last night as to—as to the best way of escaping from her."

Gannett stood up with an angry forehead.

"Well—what concern of yours was all this dirty business? Why should she go to you?"

"Don't you see? It's so simple. I was to wheedle his secret out of you."

"To oblige that woman?"

"Yes; or, if I was unwilling to oblige her, then to protect myself."

"To protect yourself? Against whom?"

"Against her telling everyone in the hotel that she and I are in the same box."

"She threatened that?"

"She left me the choice of telling it myself or of doing it for me."

"The beast!"

There was a long silence. Lydia had seated herself on the sofa, beyond the radius of the lamp, and he leaned against the window. His next question surprised her.

"When did this happen? At what time, I mean?"

She looked at him vaguely.

"I don't know—after luncheon, I think. Yes, I remember; it must have been at about three o'clock."

He stepped into the middle of the room and as he approached the light she saw that his brow had cleared.

"Why do you ask?" she said.

"Because when I came in, at about half-past three, the mail was just being distributed, and Mrs. Cope was waiting as usual to pounce on her letters; you know she was always watching for the postman. She was standing so close to me that I couldn't help seeing a big official-looking envelope that was handed to her. She tore it open, gave one look at the inside, and rushed off upstairs like a whirlwind, with the director shouting after her that she had left all her other letters behind. I don't believe she ever thought of you again after that paper was put into her hand."

"Why?"

"Because she was too busy. I was sitting in the window, watching for you, when the five o'clock boat left, and who should go on board, bag and baggage, valet and maid, dressing bags and poodle, but Mrs. Cope and Trevenna. Just an hour and a half to pack up in! And you should have seen her when they started. She was radiant—shaking hands with everybody—waving her handkerchief from the deck—distributing bows and smiles like an empress. If ever a woman got what she wanted just in the nick of time that woman did. She'll be Lady Trevenna within a week, I'll wager."

"You think she has her divorce?"

"I'm sure of it. And she must have got it just after her talk with you."

Lydia was silent.

At length she said, with a kind of reluctance, "She was horribly angry when she left me. It wouldn't have taken long to tell Lady Susan Condit."

"Lady Susan Condit has not been told."

"How do you know?"

"Because when I went downstairs half an hour ago I met Lady Susan on the way—"

He stopped, half smiling.

"Well?"

"And she stopped to ask if I thought you would act as patroness to a charity concert she is getting up."

In spite of themselves they both broke into a laugh. Lydia's ended in sobs and she sank down with her face hidden. Gannett bent over her, seeking her hands.

"That vile woman—I ought to have warned you to keep away from her; I can't forgive myself! But he spoke to me in confidence; and I never dreamed—well, it's all over now."

Lydia lifted her head.

"Not for me. It's only just beginning."

"What do you mean?"

She put him gently aside and moved in her turn to the window. Then she went on, with her face turned toward the shimmering blackness of the lake, "You see of course that it might happen again at any moment."

"What?"

"This—this risk of being found out. And we could hardly count again on such a lucky combination of chances, could we?"

He sat down with a groan.

Still keeping her face toward the darkness, she said, "I want you to go and tell Lady Susan—and the others."

Gannett, who had moved towards her, paused a few feet off.

"Why do you wish me to do this?" he said at length, with less surprise in his voice than she had been prepared for.

"Because I've behaved basely, abominably, since we came here: letting these people believe we were married—lying with every breath I drew—"

"Yes, I've felt that too," Gannett exclaimed with sudden energy.

The words shook her like a tempest: all her thoughts seemed to fall about her in ruins.

"You—you've felt so?"

"Of course I have." He spoke with low-voiced vehemence. "Do you suppose I like playing the sneak any better than you do? It's damnable."

He had dropped on the arm of a chair, and they stared at each other like blind people who suddenly see.

"But you have liked it here," she faltered.

"Oh, I've liked it—I've liked it." He moved impatiently. "Haven't you?"

"Yes," she burst out; "that's the worst of it—that's what I can't bear. I fancied it was for your sake that I insisted on staying—because you thought you could write here; and perhaps just at first that really was the reason. But afterwards I wanted to stay myself—I loved it." She broke into a laugh. "Oh, do you see the full derision of it? These people—the very prototypes of the bores you took me away from, with the same fenced-in view of life, the same keep-off-the-grass morality, the same little cautious virtues and the same little frightened vices—well, I've clung to them, I've delighted in them, I've done my best to please them. I've toadied Lady Susan, I've gossiped with Miss Pinsent, I've pretended to be shocked with Mrs. Ainger. Respectability! It was the one thing in life that I was sure I didn't care about, and it's grown so precious to me that I've stolen it because I couldn't get it in any other way."

She moved across the room and returned to his side with another laugh.

"I who used to fancy myself unconventional! I must have been born with a cardcase in my hand. You should have seen me with that poor woman in the garden. She came to me for help, poor creature, because she fancied that, having 'sinned,' as they call it, I might feel some pity for others who had been tempted in the same way. Not I! She didn't know me. Lady Susan would have been kinder, because Lady Susan wouldn't have been afraid. I hated the woman—my one thought was not to be seen with her—I could have killed her for guessing my secret. The one thing that mattered to me at that moment was my standing with Lady Susan!"

Gannett did not speak.

"And you—you've felt it too!" she broke out accusingly. "You've enjoyed being with these people as much as I have; you've let the chaplain talk to you by the hour about The Reign of Law and Professor Drummond. When they asked you to hand the plate in church I was watching you—*you wanted to accept.*"

She stepped close, laying her hand on his arm.

"Do you know, I begin to see what marriage is for. It's to keep people away from each other. Sometimes I think that two people who love each other can be saved from madness only by the things that come between them—children, duties, visits, bores, relations—the things that protect married people from each other. We've been too close together—that has been our sin. We've seen the nakedness of each other's souls."

She sank again on the sofa, hiding her face in her hands.

Gannett stood above her perplexedly: he felt as though she were being swept away by some implacable current while he stood helpless on its bank.

At length he said, "Lydia, don't think me a brute—but don't you see yourself that it won't do?"

"Yes, I see it won't do," she said without raising her head.

His face cleared.

"Then we'll go tomorrow."

"Go—where?"

"To Paris; to be married."

For a long time she made no answer; then she asked slowly, "Would they have us here if we were married?"

"Have us here?"

"I mean Lady Susan—and the others."

"Have us here? Of course they would."

"Not if they knew—at least, not unless they could pretend not to know."

He made an impatient gesture.

"We shouldn't come back here, of course; and other people needn't know—no one need know."

She sighed. "Then it's only another form of deception and a meaner one. Don't you see that?"

"I see that we're not accountable to any Lady Susans on earth!"

"Then why are you ashamed of what we are doing here?"

"Because I'm sick of pretending that you're my wife when you're not—when you won't be."

She looked at him sadly.

"If I were your wife you'd have to go on pretending. You'd have to pretend that I'd never been—anything else. And our friends would have to pretend that they believed what you pretended."

Gannett pulled off the sofa tassel and flung it away.

"You're impossible," he groaned.

"It's not I—it's our being together that's impossible. I only want you to see that marriage won't help it."

"What will help it then?"

She raised her head.

"My leaving you."

"Your leaving me?" He sat motionless, staring at the tassel which lay at the other end of the room. At length some impulse of retaliation for the pain she was inflicting made him say deliberately:

"And where would you go if you left me?"

"Oh!" she cried.

He was at her side in an instant.

"Lydia—Lydia—you know I didn't mean it; I couldn't mean it! But you've driven me out of my senses; I don't know what I'm saying. Can't you get out of this labyrinth of self-torture? It's destroying us both."

"That's why I must leave you."

"How easily you say it!" He drew her hands down and made her face him. "You're very scrupulous about yourself—and others. But have you thought of me? You have no right to leave me unless you've ceased to care—"

"It's because I care—"

"Then I have a right to be heard. If you love me you can't leave me."

Her eyes defied him.

"Why not?"

He dropped her hands and rose from her side.

"Can you?" he said sadly.

The hour was late and the lamp flickered and sank. She stood up with a shiver and turned toward the door of her room.

* V *

At daylight a sound in Lydia's room woke Gannett from a troubled sleep. He sat up and listened. She was moving about softly, as though fearful of disturbing him. He heard her push back one of the creaking shutters; then there was a moment's silence, which seemed to indicate that she was waiting to see if the noise had roused him.

Presently she began to move again. She had spent a sleepless night, probably, and was dressing to go down to the garden for a breath of air. Gannett rose also; but some undefinable instinct made his movements as cautious as hers. He stole to his window and looked out through the slats of the shutter.

It had rained in the night and the dawn was gray and lifeless. The cloud-muffled hills across the lake were reflected in its surface as in a tarnished mirror. In the garden, the birds were beginning to shake the drops from the motionless laurustinus boughs.

An immense pity for Lydia filled Gannett's soul. Her seeming intellectual independence had blinded him for a time to the feminine cast of her mind. He had never thought of her as a woman who wept and clung: there was a lucidity in her intuitions that made them appear to be the result of reasoning. Now he saw the cruelty he had committed in detaching her from the normal conditions of life; he felt, too, the insight with which she had hit upon the real cause of their suffering. Their life was "impossible," as she had said—and its worst penalty was that it had made any other life impossible for them. Even had his love lessened, he was bound to her now by a hundred ties of pity and self-reproach; and she, poor child, must turn back to him as Latude returned to his cell.

A new sound startled him: it was the stealthy closing of Lydia's door. He crept to his own and heard her footsteps passing down the corridor. Then he went back to the window and looked out.

A minute or two later he saw her go down the steps of the porch and enter the garden. From his post of observation her face was invisible, but something about her appearance struck him. She wore a long traveling cloak and under its folds he detected the outline of a bag or bundle. He drew a deep breath and stood watching her.

She walked quickly down the laurustinus alley toward the gate; there she paused a moment, glancing about the little shady square. The stone benches under the trees were empty, and she seemed to gather resolution from the solitude about her, for she crossed the square to the steamboat landing, and he saw her pause before the ticket office at the head of the wharf. Now she was buying her ticket. Gannett turned his head a moment to look at the clock: the boat was due in five minutes. He had time to jump into his clothes and overtake her—

He made no attempt to move; an obscure reluctance restrained him. If any thought emerged from the tumult of his sensations, it was that he must let her go if she wished it. He had spoken last night of his rights: what were they? At the last issue, he and she were two separate beings, not made one by the miracle of common forbearances, duties, abnegations, but bound together in a *noyade* of passion that left them resisting yet clinging as they went down.

After buying her ticket, Lydia had stood for a moment looking out across the lake; then he saw her seat herself on one of the benches near the landing. He and she, at that moment, were both listening for the same sound: the whistle of the boat as it rounded the nearest promontory. Gannett turned again to glance at the clock: the boat was due now.

Where would she go? What would her life be when she had left him? She had no near relations and few friends. There was money enough . . . but she asked so much of life, in ways so complex and immaterial. He thought of her as walking barefooted through a stony waste. No one would understand her—no one would pity her—and he, who did both, was powerless to come to her aid.

He saw that she had risen from the bench and walked toward the edge of the lake. She stood looking in the direction from which the steamboat was to come; then she turned to the ticket office, doubtless to ask the cause of the delay. After that she went back to the bench and sat down with bent head. What was she thinking of?

The whistle sounded; she started up, and Gannett involuntarily made a movement toward the door. But he turned back and continued to watch her. She stood motionless, her eyes on the trail of smoke that preceded the appearance of the boat. Then the little craft rounded the point, a dead white object on the leaden water: a minute later it was puffing and backing at the wharf.

The few passengers who were waiting—two or three peasants and a snuffy priest—were clustered near the ticket office. Lydia stood apart under the trees.

The boat lay alongside now; the gangplank was run out and the peasants went on board with their baskets of vegetables, followed by the priest. Still Lydia did not move. A bell began to ring querulously; there was a shriek of steam, and someone must have called to her that she would be late, for she started forward, as though in answer to a summons. She moved waveringly, and at the edge of the wharf she paused. Gannett saw a sailor beckon to her; the bell rang again and she stepped upon the gangplank.

Halfway down the short incline to the deck she stopped again; then she turned and ran back to the land. The gangplank was drawn in, the bell ceased to ring, and the boat backed out into the lake. Lydia, with slow steps, was walking toward the garden.

As she approached the hotel she looked up furtively and Gannett drew back into the room. He sat down beside a table; a Bradshaw lay at his elbow, and mechanically, without knowing what he did, he began looking out the trains to Paris.

THE DESCENT
OF MAN

WHEN PROFESSOR LINYARD came back from his holiday in the Maine woods the air of rejuvenation he brought with him was due less to the influences of the climate than to the companionship he had enjoyed on his travels. To Mrs. Linyard's observant eye he had appeared to set out alone; but an invisible traveler had in fact accompanied him, and if his heart beat high it was simply at the pitch of his adventure: for the professor had eloped with an idea.

No one who has not tried the experiment can divine its exhilaration. Professor Linyard would not have changed places with any hero of romance pledged to a flesh-and-blood abduction. The most fascinating female is apt to be encumbered with luggage and scruples: to take up a good deal of room in the present and overlap inconveniently into the future; whereas an idea can accommodate itself to a single molecule of the brain or expand to the circumference of the horizon. The Professor's companion had to the utmost this quality of adaptability. As the express train whirled him away from the somewhat inelastic circle of Mrs. Linyard's affections, his idea seemed to be sitting opposite him, and their eyes met every moment or two in a glance of joyous complicity; yet when a friend of the family presently joined him and began to talk about college matters, the idea slipped out of sight in a flash, and the Professor would have had no difficulty in proving that he was alone.

But if, from the outset, he found his idea the most agreeable of fellow travelers, it was only in the aromatic solitude of the woods that he tasted the full savor of his adventure. There, during the long cool August days, lying full length on the pine needles and gazing up into the sky, he would meet the eyes of his companion bending over him like a nearer heaven. And what eyes they were!—clear yet unfathomable, bubbling with inexhaustible laughter, yet drawing their freshness and sparkle from the central depths of thought! To a man who for twenty years had faced an eye reflecting the commonplace with perfect accuracy, these escapes into the inscrutable had always been peculiarly inviting; but hitherto the Professor's mental infidelities had been restricted by an unbroken and relentless domesticity. Now, for the first time since his marriage, chance had given him six weeks to himself, and he was coming home with his lungs full of liberty.

It must not be inferred that the Professor's domestic relations were defective: they were in fact so complete that it was almost impossible to get away from them. It is the happy husbands who are really in bondage; the little rift within the lute is often a passage to freedom. Marriage had given the Professor exactly what he had sought in it: a comfortable lining to life. The impossibility of rising to sentimental crises had made him scrupulously careful not to shirk the practical obligations of the bond. He took as it were a sociological view of his case, and modestly regarded himself as a brick in that foundation on which the state is supposed to rest. Perhaps if Mrs. Linyard had cared about entomology, or had taken sides in the war over the transmission of acquired characteristics, he might have had a less impersonal notion of marriage; but he was unconscious of any deficiency in their relation, and if consulted would probably have declared that he didn't want any woman bothering with his beetles. His real life had always lain in the universe of thought, in that enchanted region which, to those who have lingered there, comes to have so much more color and substance than the painted curtain hanging before it. The Professor's particular veil of Maia was a narrow strip of homespun woven in a monotonous pattern; but he had only to lift it to step into an empire.

This unseen universe was thronged with the most seductive shapes: the Professor moved Sultan-like through a seraglio of ideas. But of all the lovely apparitions that wove their spells about him, none had ever worn quite so persuasive an aspect as this latest favorite. For the others were mostly rather grave companions, serious-minded and elevating enough to have passed muster in a Ladies' Debating Club; but this new fancy of the Professor's was simply one embodied laugh. It was, in other words, the smile of relaxation at the end of a long day's toil: the flash of irony which the laborious mind projects, irresistibly, over labor conscientiously performed. The Professor had always been a hard worker. If he was an indulgent friend to his ideas he was also a stern taskmaster to them. For, in addition to their other duties, they had to support his family: to pay the butcher and baker, and provide for Jack's schooling and Millicent's dresses. The Professor's household was a modest one, yet it tasked his ideas to keep it up to his wife's standard. Mrs. Linyard was not an exacting wife, and she took enough pride in her husband's attainments to pay for her honors by turning Millicent's dress and darning Jack's socks and going to the College receptions year after year in the same black silk with shiny seams. It consoled her to see an occasional mention of Professor Linyard's remarkable monograph on the Ethical Reactions of the Infusoria, or an allusion to his investigations into the Unconscious Cerebration of the Amoeba.

Still there were moments when the healthy indifference of Jack and Millicent reacted on the maternal sympathies; when Mrs. Linyard would have made her husband a railway director, if by this transformation she might have increased her boy's allowance and given her daughter a new hat, or a set of furs such as the other girls were wearing. Of such moments of rebellion the Professor himself was not wholly unconscious. He could not indeed understand why anyone should want a new hat; and as to an allowance, he had had much less money at college than Jack, and had yet managed to buy a microscope and collect a few "specimens"; while Jack was free from such expensive tastes! But the Professor did not let his want of sympathy interfere with the discharge of his paternal obligations. He worked hard to keep the wants of his family gratified, and it was precisely in the endeavor to attain this end that he at length broke down and had to cease from work altogether.

To cease from work was not to cease from thought of it; and in the unwonted pause from effort the Professor found himself taking a general survey of the field he had traveled. At last it was possible to lift his nose from the loom, to step a moment in front of the tapestry he had been weaving. From this first inspection of the pattern so long wrought over from behind, it was natural to glance a little farther and seek its reflection in the public eye. It was not indeed of his special task that he thought in this connection. He was but one of the great army of weavers at work among the threads of that cosmic woof; and what he sought was the general impression their labor had produced.

When Professor Linyard first plied his microscope, the audience of the man of science had been composed of a few fellow students, sympathetic or hostile as their habits of mind predetermined, but versed in the jargon of the profession and familiar with the point of departure. In the intervening quarter of a century, however, this little group had been swallowed up in a larger public. Everyone now read scientific books and expressed an opinion on them. The ladies and the clergy had taken them up first; now they had passed to the schoolroom and the kindergarten. Daily life was regulated on scientific principles; the daily papers had their "Scientific Jottings"; nurses passed examinations in hygienic science, and babies were fed and dandled according to the new psychology.

The very fact that scientific investigation still•had, to some minds, the flavor of heterodoxy, gave it a perennial interest. The mob had broken down the walls of tradition to batten in the orchard of forbidden knowledge. The inaccessible goddess whom the Professor had served in his youth now offered her charms in the market place. And yet it was not the same goddess, after all, but a pseudo-science masquerading in the garb of the real divinity. This false goddess had her ritual and her literature. She had her sacred books, written by false priests and sold by millions to the faithful. In the most successful of these works, ancient dogma and modern discovery were depicted in a close embrace under the limelights of a hazy transcendentalism; and the tableau never failed of its effect. Some of the books designed on this popular model had lately fallen into the Professor's hands, and they filled him with mingled rage and hilarity. The rage soon died: he came to regard this mass of pseudo-literature as protecting the truth from desecration. But the hilarity remained, and flowed into the form of his idea. And the idea—the divine incomparable idea—was simply that he should avenge his goddess by satirizing her false interpreters. He would write a skit on the "popular" scientific book; he would so heap platitude on platitude, fallacy on fallacy, false analogy on false analogy, so use his superior knowledge to abound in the sense of the ignorant, that even the gross crowd would join in the laugh against its augurs. And the laugh should be something more than the distention of mental muscles; it should be the trumpet blast bringing down the walls of ignorance, or at least the little stone striking the giant between the eyes.

* II *

The Professor, on presenting his card, had imagined that it would command prompt access to the publisher's sanctuary; but the young man who read his name was not moved to immediate action. It was clear that Professor Linyard of Hillbridge University was not a specific figure to the purveyors of popular literature. But the publisher was an old friend; and when the card had finally drifted to his office on the languid tide of routine he came forth at once to greet his visitor.

The warmth of his welcome convinced the Professor that he had been right in bringing his manuscript to Ned Harviss. He and Harviss had been at Hillbridge together, and the future publisher had been one of the wildest spirits in that band of college outlaws which yearly turns out so many inoffensive citizens and kind husbands and fathers. The Professor knew the taming qualities of life. He was aware that many of his most reckless comrades had been transformed into prudent capitalists or cowed wage earners; but he was almost sure that he could count on Harviss. So rare a sense of irony, so keen a perception of relative values, could hardly have been blunted even by twenty years' intercourse with the obvious.

The publisher's appearance was a little disconcerting. He looked as if he had been fattened on popular fiction; and his fat was full of optimistic creases. The Professor seemed to see him bowing into the office a long train of spotless heroines laden with the maiden tribute of the hundred-thousandth volume.

Nevertheless, his welcome was reassuring. He did not disown his early enormities, and capped his visitor's tentative allusions by such flagrant references to the past that the Professor produced his manuscript without a scruple.

"What—you don't mean to say you've been doing something in our line?"

The Professor smiled. "You publish scientific books sometimes, don't you?"

The publisher's optimistic creases relaxed a little. "H'm—it all depends—I'm afraid you're a little *too* scientific for us. We have a big sale for scientific breakfast foods, but not for the concentrated essences. In your case, of course, I should be delighted to stretch a point; but in your own interest I ought to tell you that perhaps one of the educational houses would do you better."

The Professor leaned back, still smiling luxuriously.

"Well, look it over—I rather think you'll take it."

"Oh, we'll *take* it, as I say; but the terms might not—"

"No matter about the terms—"

The publisher threw his head back with a laugh. "I had no idea that science was so profitable; we find our popular novelists are the hardest hands at a bargain."

"Science is disinterested," the Professor corrected him. "And I have a fancy to have you publish this thing."

"That's immensely good of you, my dear fellow. Of course your name goes with a certain public—and I rather like the originality of our bringing out a work so out of our line. I dare say it may boom us both." His creases deepened at the thought, and he shone encouragingly on the Professor's leave-taking.

Within a fortnight, a line from Harviss recalled the Professor to town. He had been looking forward with immense zest to this second meeting; Harviss' college roar was in his tympanum, and he could already hear the protracted chuckle which would follow his friend's progress through the manuscript. He was proud of the adroitness with which he had kept his secret from Harviss, had maintained to the last the pretense of a serious work, in order to give the keener edge to his reader's enjoyment. Not since undergraduate days had the Professor tasted such a draught of pure fun as his anticipations now poured for him.

This time his card brought instant admission. He was bowed into the office like a successful novelist, and Harviss grasped him with both hands.

"Well—do you mean to take it?" he asked with a lingering coquetry.

"Take it? Take it, my dear fellow? It's in press already—you'll excuse my not waiting to consult you? There will be no difficulty about terms, I assure you, and we had barely time to catch the autumn market. My dear Linyard, why didn't you *tell* me?" His voice sank to a reproachful solemnity, and he pushed forward his own armchair.

The Professor dropped into it with a chuckle. "And miss the joy of letting you find out?"

"Well—it *was* a joy." Harviss held out a box of his best cigars. "I don't know when I've had a bigger sensation. It was so deucedly unexpected— and, my dear fellow, you've brought it so exactly to the right shop."

"I'm glad to hear you say so," said the Professor modestly.

Harviss laughed in rich appreciation. "I don't suppose you had a doubt of it; but of course I was quite unprepared. And it's so extraordinarily out of your line—"

The Professor took off his glasses and rubbed them with a slow smile.

"Would you have thought it so—at college?"

Harviss stared. "At college? Why, you were the most iconoclastic devil—"

There was a perceptible pause. The Professor restored his glasses and looked at his friend. "Well—?" he said simply.

"Well—?" echoed the other, still staring. "Ah—I see; you mean that that's what explains it. The swing of the pendulum, and so forth. Well, I admit it's not an uncommon phenomenon. I've conformed myself, for example; most of our crowd have, I believe; but somehow I hadn't expected it of you."

The close observer might have detected a faint sadness under the official congratulation of his tone; but the Professor was too amazed to have an ear for such fine shades.

"Expected it of me? Expected what of me?" he gasped. "What in heaven do you think this thing is?" And he struck his fist on the manuscript which lay between them.

Harviss had recovered his optimistic creases. He rested a benevolent eye on the document.

"Why, your apologia—your confession of faith, I should call it. You surely must have seen which way you were going? You can't have written it in your sleep?"

"Oh, no, I was wide awake enough," said the Professor faintly.

"Well, then, why are you staring at me as if I were *not?*" Harviss leaned forward to lay a reassuring hand on his visitor's worn coat sleeve. "Don't mistake me, my dear Linyard. Don't fancy there was the least unkindness in my allusion to your change of front. What is growth but the shifting of the standpoint? Why should a man be expected to look at life with the same eyes at twenty and—at our age? It never occurred to me that you could feel the least delicacy in admitting that you have come round a little—have fallen into line, so to speak."

But the Professor had sprung up as if to give his lungs more room to expand; and from them there issued a laugh which shook the editorial rafters.

"Oh, Lord, oh, Lord—is it really as good as that?"

Harviss had glanced instinctively toward the electric bell on his desk; he was evidently prepared for an emergency.

"My dear fellow—" he began in a soothing tone.

"Oh, let me have my laugh out, do," implored the Professor. "I'll—I'll quiet down in a minute; you needn't ring for the young man." He dropped into his chair again and grasped its arms to steady his shaking. "This is the best laugh I've had since college," he brought out between his paroxysms. And then, suddenly, he sat up with a groan. "But if it's as good as that it's a failure!" he exclaimed.

Harviss, stiffening a little, examined the tip of his cigar. "My dear Linyard," he said at length. "I don't understand a word you're saying."

The Professor succumbed to a fresh access, from the vortex of which he managed to fling out, "But that's the very core of the joke!"

Harviss looked at him resignedly. "What is?"

"Why, your not seeing—your not understanding—"

"Not understanding *what?*"

"Why, what the book is meant to be." His laughter subsided again and he sat gazing thoughtfully at the publisher. "Unless it means," he wound up, "that I've overshot the mark."

"If I am the mark, you certainly have," said Harviss, with a glance at the clock.

The Professor caught the glance and interpreted it. "The book is a skit," he said, rising.

The other stared. "A skit? It's not serious, you mean?"

"Not to me—but it seems you've taken it so."

"You never told me—" began the publisher in a ruffled tone.

"No, I never told you," said the Professor.

Harviss sat staring at the manuscript between them. "I don't pretend to be up on such recondite forms of humor," he said still stiffly. "Of course you address yourself to a very small class of readers."

"Oh, infinitely small," admitted the Professor, extending his hand toward the manuscript.

Harviss appeared to be pursuing his own train of thought. "That is," he continued, "if you insist on an ironical interpretation."

"If I insist on it—what do you mean?"

The publisher smiled faintly. "Well—isn't the book susceptible of another? If *I* read it without seeing—"

"Well?" murmured the other, fascinated.

"—Why shouldn't the rest of the world?" declared Harviss boldly. "I represent the Average Reader—that's my business, that's what I've been training myself to do for the last twenty years. It's a mission like another —the thing is to do it thoroughly; not to cheat and compromise. I know fellows who are publishers in business hours and dilettantes the rest of the time. Well, they never succeed: convictions are just as necessary in business as in religion. But that's not the point—I was going to say that if you'll let me handle this book as a genuine thing I'll guarantee to make it go."

The Professor stood motionless, his hand still on the manuscript.

"A genuine thing?" he echoed.

"A serious piece of work—the expression of your convictions. I tell you there's nothing the public likes as much as convictions—they'll always follow a man who believes in his own ideas. And this book is just on the line on popular interest. You've got hold of a big thing. It's full of hope and enthusiasm: it's written in the religious key. There are passages in it that would do splendidly in a Birthday Book—things that popular preachers would quote in their sermons. If you'd wanted to catch a big public you couldn't have gone about it in a better way. The thing's perfect for my purpose—I wouldn't let you alter a word of it. It will sell like a popular novel if you'll let me handle it in the right way."

* III *

When the Professor left Harviss' office the manuscript remained behind. He thought he had been taken by the huge irony of the situation—by the enlarged circumference of the joke. In its original form, as Harviss had said, the book would have addressed itself to a very limited circle: now it would include the world. The elect would understand; the crowd would not; and his work would thus serve a double purpose. And, after all, nothing was changed in the situation; not a word of the book was to be altered. The change was merely in the publisher's point of view, and in the "tip" he was to give the reviewers. The professor had only to hold his tongue and look serious.

These arguments found a strong reinforcement in the large premium which expressed Harviss' sense of his opportunity. As a satire the book would have brought its author nothing; in fact, its cost would have come out of his own pocket, since, as Harviss assured him, no publisher would have risked taking it. But as a profession of faith, as the recantation of an eminent biologist, whose leanings had hitherto been supposed to be toward a cold determinism, it would bring in a steady income to author and publisher. The offer found the Professor in a moment of financial perplexity. His illness, his unwonted holiday, the necessity of postponing a course of well-paid lectures, had combined to diminish his resources; and when Harviss offered him an advance of a thousand dollars the esoteric savor of the joke became irresistible. It was still as a joke that he persisted in regarding the transaction; and though he had pledged himself not to betray the real intent of the book, he held *in petto* the notion of some day being able to take the public into his confidence. As for the initiated, they would know at once: and however long a face he pulled his colleagues would see the tongue in his cheek. Meanwhile it fortunately happened that, even if the book should achieve the kind of triumph prophesied by Harviss, it would not appreciably injure its author's professional standing. Professor Linyard was known chiefly as a microscopist. On the structure and habits of a certain class of coleoptera he was the most distinguished living authority; but none save his intimate friends knew what generalizations on the destiny of man he had drawn from these special studies. He might have published a treatise on the Filioque without shaking the confidence of those on whose approval his reputation rested; and moreover he was sustained by the thought that one glance at his book would let them into its secret. In fact, so sure was he of this that he wondered the astute Harviss had cared to risk such speedy exposure. But Harviss had probably reflected that even in this reverberating age the opinions of the laboratory do not easily reach the street; and the Professor, at any rate, was not bound to offer advice on this point.

The determining cause of his consent was the fact that the book was already in press. The Professor knew little about the workings of the press, but the phrase gave him a sense of finality, of having been caught himself in the toils of that mysterious engine. If he had had time to think the matter over his scruples might have dragged him back; but his conscience was eased by the futility of resistance.

* IV *

Mrs. Linyard did not often read the papers; and there was therefore a special significance in her approaching her husband one evening after dinner with a copy of the *New York Investigator* in her hand. Her expression lent solemnity to the act: Mrs. Linyard had a limited but distinctive set of expressions, and she now looked as she did when the President of the University came to dine.

"You didn't tell me of this, Samuel," she said in a slightly tremulous voice.

"Tell you of what?" returned the Professor, reddening to the margin of his baldness.

"That you had published a book—I might never have heard of it if Mrs. Pease hadn't brought me the paper."

Her husband rubbed his eyeglasses and groaned. "Oh, you would have heard of it," he said gloomily.

Mrs. Linyard stared. "Did you wish to keep it from me, Samuel?" And as he made no answer, she added with irresistible pride: "Perhaps you don't know what beautiful things have been said about it."

He took the paper with a reluctant hand. "Has Pease been saying beautiful things about it?"

"The Professor? Mrs. Pease didn't say he had mentioned it."

The author heaved a sigh of relief. His book, as Harviss had prophesied, had caught the autumn market: had caught and captured it. The publisher had conducted the campaign like an experienced strategist. He had completely surrounded the enemy. Every newspaper, every periodical, held in ambush an advertisement of *The Vital Thing*. Weeks in advance the great commander had begun to form his lines of attack. Allusions to the remarkable significance of the coming work had appeared first in the scientific and literary reviews, spreading thence to the supplements of the daily journals. Not a moment passed without a quickening touch to the public consciousness: seventy millions of people were forced to remember at least once a day that Professor Linyard's book was on the verge of appearing. Slips emblazoned with the question: *Have you read "The Vital Thing"?* fell from the pages of popular novels and whitened the floors of crowded streetcars. The query, in large lettering, assaulted the traveler at the railway bookstall, confronted him on the walls of elevated stations, and seemed, in its ascending scale, about to supplant the interrogations as to sapolio and stove polish which animate our rural scenery.

On the day of publication the Professor had withdrawn to his laboratory. The shriek of the advertisements was in his ears and his one desire was to avoid all knowledge of the event they heralded. A reaction of self-consciousness had set in, and if Harviss' check had sufficed to buy up the first edition of *The Vital Thing* the Professor would gladly have devoted it to that purpose. But the sense of inevitableness gradually subdued him, and he received his wife's copy of the *Investigator* with a kind of impersonal curiosity. The review was a long one, full of extracts: he saw, as he glanced over the latter, how well they would look in a volume of "Selections." The reviewer began by thanking his author "for sounding with no uncertain voice that note of ringing optimism, of faith in man's destiny and the supremacy of good, which has too long been silenced by the whining chorus of a decadent nihilism. . . . It is well," the writer continued, "when such reminders come to us not from the moralist but from the man of science—when from the desiccating atmosphere of the laboratory there rises this glorious cry of faith and reconstruction."

The review was minute and exhaustive. Thanks no doubt to Harviss' diplomacy, it had been given to the *Investigator's* "best man," and the Professor was startled by the bold eye with which his emancipated fallacies confronted him. Under the reviewer's handling they made up admirably as truths, and their author began to understand Harviss' regret that they should be used for any less profitable purpose.

The *Investigator,* as Harviss phrased it, "set the pace," and the other journals followed, finding it easier to let their critical man-of-all-work play a variation on the first reviewer's theme than to secure an expert to "do" the book afresh. But it was evident that the Professor had captured his public, for all the resources of the profession could not, as Harviss gleefully pointed out, have carried the book so straight to the heart of the nation. There was something noble in the way in which Harviss belittled his own share in the achievement, and insisted on the inutility of shoving a book which had started with such headway on.

"All I ask you is to admit that I saw what would happen," he said with a touch of professional pride. "I knew you'd struck the right note—I knew they'd be quoting you from Maine to San Francisco. Good as fiction? It's better—it'll keep going longer."

"Will it?" said the Professor with a slight shudder. He was resigned to an ephemeral triumph, but the thought of the book's persistency frightened him.

"I should say so! Why, you fit in everywhere—science, theology, natural history—and then the all-for-the-best element which is so popular just now. Why, you come right in with the How-to-Relax series, and they sell way up in the millions. And then the book's so full of tenderness—there are such lovely things in it about flowers and children. I didn't know an old Dryasdust like you could have such a lot of sentiment in him. Why, I actually caught myself sniveling over that passage about the snowdrops piercing the frozen earth; and my wife was saying the other day that, since she's read *The Vital Thing,* she begins to think you must write the 'What-Cheer Column,' in the *Inglenook.*" He threw back his head with a laugh which ended in the inspired cry: "And, by George, sir, when the thing begins to slow off we'll start somebody writing against it, and that will run us straight up into another hundred thousand."

And as earnest of this belief he drew the Professor a supplementary check.

* V *

Mrs. Linyard's knock cut short the importunities of the lady who had been trying to persuade the Professor to be taken by flashlight at his study table for the Christmas number of the *Inglenook*. On this point the Professor had fancied himself impregnable; but the unwonted smile with which he welcomed his wife's intrusion showed that his defences were weakening.

The lady from the *Inglenook* took the hint with professional promptness, but said brightly, as she snapped the elastic around her notebook: "I shan't let you forget me, Professor."

The groan with which he followed her retreat was interrupted by his wife's question: "Do they pay you for these interviews, Samuel?"

The Professor looked at her with sudden attention. "Not directly," he said, wondering at her expression.

She sank down with a sigh. "Indirectly, then?"

"What is the matter, my dear? I gave you Harviss' second check the other day—"

Her tears arrested him. "Don't be hard on the boy, Samuel! I really believe your success has turned his head."

"The boy—what boy? My success—? Explain yourself, Susan!"

"It's only that Jack has—has borrowed some money—which he can't repay. But you mustn't think him altogether to blame, Samuel. Since the success of your book he has been asked about so much—it's given the children quite a different position. Millicent says that wherever they go the first question asked is, 'Are you any relation to the author of *The Vital Thing?*' Of course we're all very proud of the book; but it entails obligations which you may not have thought of in writing it."

The Professor sat gazing at the letters and newspaper clippings on the study table which he had just successfully defended from the camera of the *Inglenook*. He took up an envelope bearing the name of a popular weekly paper.

"I don't know that the *Inglenook* would help much," he said, "but I suppose this might."

Mrs. Linyard's eyes glowed with maternal avidity.

"What is it, Samuel?"

"A series of 'Scientific Sermons' for the Round-the-Gas-Log column of *The Woman's World*. I believe that journal has a larger circulation than any other weekly, and they pay in proportion."

He had not even asked the extent of Jack's indebtedness. It had been so easy to relieve recent domestic difficulties by the timely production of Harviss' two checks that it now seemed natural to get Mrs. Linyard out of the room by promising further reinforcements. The Professor had indignantly rejected Harviss' suggestion that he should follow up his success by a second volume on the same lines. He had sworn not to lend more than a passive support to the fraud of *The Vital Thing;* but the temptation to free himself from Mrs. Linyard prevailed over his last scruples, and within an hour he was at work on the "Scientific Sermons."

The Professor was not an unkind man. He really enjoyed making his family happy; and it was his own business if his reward for so doing was that it kept them out of his way. But the success of *The Vital Thing* gave him more than this negative satisfaction. It enlarged his own existence and opened new doors into other lives. The Professor, during fifty virtuous years, had been cognizant of only two types of women: the fond and foolish, whom one married, and the earnest and intellectual, whom one did not. Of the two, he infinitely preferred the former, even for conversational purposes. But as a social instrument woman was unknown to him; and it was not till he was drawn into the world on the tide of his literary success that he discovered the deficiencies in his classification of the sex. Then he learned with astonishment of the existence of a third type: the woman who is fond without foolishness and intellectual without earnestness. Not that the Professor inspired, or sought to inspire, sentimental emotions; but he expanded in the warm atmosphere of personal interest which some of his new acquaintances contrived to create about him. It was delightful to talk of serious things in a setting of frivolity, and to be personal without being domestic.

Even in this new world, where all subjects were touched on lightly, and emphasis was the only indelicacy, the Professor found himself constrained to endure an occasional reference to his book. It was unpleasant at first; but gradually he slipped into the habit of hearing it talked of, and grew accustomed to telling pretty women just how "it had first come to him."

Meanwhile the success of the "Scientific Sermons" was facilitating his family relations. His photograph in the *Inglenook,* to which the lady of the notebook had succeeded in appending a vivid interview, carried his fame to circles inaccessible even to *The Vital Thing;* and the Professor found himself the man of the hour. He soon grew used to the functions of the office, and gave out hundred-dollar interviews on every subject, from labor strikes to Babism, with a frequency which reacted agreeably on the domestic exchequer. Presently his head began to figure in the advertising pages of the magazines. Admiring readers learned the name of the only breakfast food in use at his table, of the ink with which "The Vital Thing" had been written, the soap with which the author's hands were washed, and the tissue builder which fortified him for further effort. These confidences endeared the Professor to millions of readers, and his head passed in due course from the magazine and the newspaper to the biscuit tin and the chocolate box.

* VI *

The Professor, all the while, was leading a double life. While the author of *The Vital Thing* reaped the fruits of popular approval, the distinguished microscopist continued his laboratory work unheeded save by the few who were engaged in the same line of investigations. His divided allegiance had not hitherto affected the quality of his work: it seemed to him that he returned to the laboratory with greater zest after an afternoon in a drawing room where readings from "The Vital Thing" had alternated with plantation melodies and tea. He had long ceased to concern himself with what his colleagues thought of his literary career. Of the few whom he frequented, none had referred to *The Vital Thing;* and he knew enough of their lives to guess that their silence might as fairly be attributed to indifference as to disapproval. They were intensely interested in the Professor's views on beetles but they really cared very little what he thought of the Almighty.

The Professor entirely shared their feelings, and one of his chief reasons for cultivating the success which accident had bestowed on him, was that it enabled him to command a greater range of appliances for his real work. He had known what it was to lack books and instruments; and *The Vital Thing* was the magic wand which summoned them to his aid. For some time he had been feeling his way along the edge of a discovery: balancing himself with professional skill on a plank of hypothesis flung across an abyss of uncertainty. The conjecture was the result of years of patient gathering of facts: its corroboration would take months more of comparison and classification. But at the end of the vista victory loomed. The Professor felt within himself that assurance of ultimate justification which, to the man of science, makes a lifetime seem the mere comma between premise and deduction. But he had reached the point where his conjectures required formulation. It was only by giving them expression, by exposing them to the comment and criticism of his associates, that he could test their final value; and this inner assurance was confirmed by the only friend whose confidence he invited.

Professor Pease, the husband of the lady who had opened Mrs. Linyard's eyes to the triumph of *The Vital Thing,* was the repository of her husband's scientific experiences. What he thought of *The Vital Thing* had never been divulged; and he was capable of such vast exclusions that it was quite possible that pervasive work had not yet reached him. In any case, it was not likely to affect his judgment of the author's professional capacity.

"You want to put that all in a book, Linyard," was Professor Pease's conclusion, after listening to the summary of his friend's projected work. "I'm sure you've got hold of something big; but to see it clearly yourself you ought to outline it for others. Take my advice—chuck everything else and get to work tomorrow. It's time you wrote a book, anyhow."

It's time you wrote a book, anyhow! The words smote the Professor with mingled pain and ecstasy: he could have wept over their significance. But his friend's other phrase reminded him with a start of Harviss. "You have got hold of a big thing—" it had been the publisher's first comment on "The Vital Thing." But what a world of meaning lay between the two phrases! It was the world in which the powers who fought for the Professor were destined to wage their final battle; and for the moment he had no doubt of the outcome.

"By George, I'll do it, Pease!" he said, stretching his hand to his friend.

The next day he went to town to see Harviss. He wanted to ask for an advance on the new popular edition of *The Vital Thing.* He had determined to drop a course of supplementary lectures at the University and to give himself up for a year to his book. To do this additional funds were necessary; but thanks to *The Vital Thing* they would be forthcoming.

The publisher received him as cordially as usual; but the response to his demand was not as prompt as his previous experience had entitled him to expect.

"Of course we'll be glad to do what we can for you, Linyard; but the fact is we've decided to give up the idea of the new edition for the present."

"You've given up the new edition?"

"Why, yes—we've done pretty well by *The Vital Thing,* and we're inclined to think it's *your* turn to do something for it now."

The Professor looked at him blankly. "What can I do for it?" he asked—"what *more*" his accent added.

"Why, put a little new life in it by writing something else. The secret of perpetual motion hasn't yet been discovered, you know, and it's one of the laws of literature that books which start with a rush are apt to slow down sooner than the crawlers. We've kept *The Vital Thing* going for eighteen months—but, hang it, it ain't so vital any more. We simply couldn't see our way to a new edition. Oh, I don't say it's dead yet—but it's moribund, and you're the only man who can resuscitate it."

The Professor continued to stare. "I—what can I do about it?" he stammered.

"Do? Why, write another like it—go it one better: you know the trick.

The public isn't tired of you by any means; but you want to make yourself heard again before anybody else cuts in. Write another book—write two, and we'll sell them in sets in a box: 'The Vital Thing Series.' That will take tremendously in the holidays. Try and let us have a new volume by October—I'll be glad to give you a big advance if you'll sign a contract on that."

The Professor sat silent: there was too cruel an irony in the coincidence.

Harviss looked up at him in surprise.

"Well, what's the matter with taking my advice—you're not going out of literature, are you?"

The Professor rose from his chair. "No—I'm going into it," he said simply.

"Going into it?"

"I'm going to write a real book—a serious one."

"Good Lord! Most people think *The Vital Thing* is serious."

"Yes—but I mean something different."

"In your old line—beetles and so forth?"

"Yes," said the Professor solemnly.

Harviss looked at him with equal gravity. "Well, I'm sorry for that," he said, "because it takes you out of our bailiwick. But I suppose you've made enough money out of *The Vital Thing* to permit yourself a little harmless amusement. When you want more cash come back to us—only don't put it off too long, or some other fellow will have stepped into your shoes. Popularity don't keep, you know; and the hotter the success the quicker the commodity perishes."

He leaned back, cheerful and sententious, delivering his axioms with conscious kindliness.

The Professor, who had risen and moved to the door, turned back with a wavering step.

"When did you say another volume would have to be ready?" he faltered.

"I said October—but call it a month later. You don't need any pushing nowadays."

"And—you'd have no objection to letting me have a little advance now? I need some new instruments for my real work."

Harviss extended a cordial hand. "My dear fellow, that's talking—I'll write the check while you wait; and I dare say we can start up the cheap edition of *The Vital Thing* at the same time, if you'll pledge yourself to give us the book by November. How much?" he asked, poised above his checkbook.

In the street, the Professor stood staring about him, uncertain and a little dazed.

"After all, it's only putting it off for six months," he said to himself; "and I can do better work when I get my new instruments."

He smiled and raised his hat to the passing victoria of a lady in whose copy of *The Vital Thing* he had recently written:

Labor est etiam ipsa voluptas.

THE MISSION
OF JANE

LETHBURY, surveying his wife across the dinner table, found his transient glance arrested by an indefinable change in her appearance.

"How smart you look! Is that a new gown?" he asked.

Her answering look seemed to deprecate his charging her with the extravagance of wasting a new gown on him, and he now perceived that the change lay deeper than any accident of dress. At the same time, he noticed that she betrayed her consciousness of it by a delicate, almost frightened blush. It was one of the compensations of Mrs. Lethbury's protracted childishness that she still blushed as prettily as at eighteen. Her body had been privileged not to outstrip her mind, and the two, as it seemed to Lethbury, were destined to travel together through an eternity of girlishness.

"I don't know what you mean," she said.

Since she never did, he always wondered at her bringing this out as a fresh grievance against him; but his wonder was unresentful, and he said good-humoredly: "You sparkle so that I thought you had on your diamonds."

She sighed and blushed again.

"It must be," he continued, "that you've been to a dressmaker's opening. You're absolutely brimming with illicit enjoyment."

She stared again, this time at the adjective. His adjectives always embarrassed her: their unintelligibleness savored of impropriety.

"In short," he summed up, "you've been doing something that you're thoroughly ashamed of."

To his surprise she retorted: "I don't see why I should be ashamed of it!"

Lethbury leaned back with a smile of enjoyment. When there was nothing better going he always liked to listen to her explanations.

"Well—?" he said.

She was becoming breathless and ejaculatory. "Of course you'll laugh—you laugh at everything!"

"That rather blunts the point of my derision, doesn't it?" he interjected; but she pushed on without noticing:

"It's so easy to laugh at things."

"Ah," murmured Lethbury with relish, "that's Aunt Sophronia's, isn't it?"

Most of his wife's opinions were heirlooms, and he took a quaint pleasure in tracing their descent. She was proud of their age, and saw no reason for discarding them while they were still serviceable. Some, of course, were so fine that she kept them for state occasions, like her great-grandmother's Crown Derby; but from the lady known as Aunt Sophronia she had inherited a stout set of everyday prejudices that were practically as good as new; whereas her husband's, as she noticed, were always having to be replaced. In the early days she had fancied there might be a certain satisfaction in taxing him with the fact; but she had long since been silenced by the reply: "My dear, I'm not a rich man, but I never use an opinion twice if I can help it."

She was reduced, therefore, to dwelling on his moral deficiencies; and one of the most obvious of these was his refusal to take things seriously. On this occasion, however, some ulterior purpose kept her from taking up his taunt.

"I'm not in the least ashamed!" she repeated, with the air of shaking a banner to the wind; but the domestic atmosphere being calm, the banner drooped unheroically.

"That," said Lethbury judicially, "encourages me to infer that you ought to be, and that, consequently, you've been giving yourself the unusual pleasure of doing something I shouldn't approve of."

She met this with an almost solemn directness.

"No," she said. "You won't approve of it. I've allowed for that."

"Ah," he exclaimed, setting down his liqueur glass. "You've worked out the whole problem, eh?"

"I believe so."

"That's uncommonly interesting. And what is it?"

She looked at him quietly. "A baby."

If it was seldom given her to surprise him, she had attained the distinction for once.

"A baby?"

"Yes."

"A—human baby?"

"Of course!" she cried, with the virtuous resentment of the woman who has never allowed dogs in the house.

Lethbury's puzzled stare broke into a fresh smile. "A baby I shan't approve of? Well, in the abstract I don't think much of them, I admit. Is this an abstract baby?"

Again she frowned at the adjective; but she had reached a pitch of exaltation at which such obstacles could not deter her.

"It's the loveliest baby—" she murmured.

"Ah, then it's concrete. It exists. In this harsh world it draws its breath in pain—"

"It's the healthiest child I ever saw!" she indignantly corrected.

"You've seen it, then?"

Again the accusing blush suffused her. "Yes—I've seen it."

"And to whom does the paragon belong?"

And here indeed she confounded him. "To me—I hope," she declared.

He pushed his chair back with an articulate murmur. "To you—?"

"To *us,*" she corrected.

"Good Lord!" he said. If there had been the least hint of hallucination in her transparent gaze—but no; it was as clear, as shallow, as easily fathomable as when he had first suffered the sharp surprise of striking bottom in it.

It occurred to him that perhaps she was trying to be funny: he knew that there is nothing more cryptic than the humor of the unhumorous.

"Is it a joke?" he faltered.

"Oh, I hope not. I want it so much to be a reality—"

He paused to smile at the limitations of a world in which jokes were not realities, and continued gently: "But since it is one already—"

"To us, I mean: to you and me. I want—" her voice wavered, and her eyes with it. "I have always wanted so dreadfully . . . it has been such a disappointment . . . not to . . ."

"I see," said Lethbury slowly.

But he had not seen before. It seemed curious now that he had never thought of her taking it in that way, had never surmised any hidden depths beneath her outspread obviousness. He felt as though he had touched a secret spring in her mind.

There was a moment's silence, moist and tremulous on her part, awkward and slightly irritated on his.

"You've been lonely, I suppose?" he began. It was odd, having suddenly to reckon with the stranger who gazed at him out of her trivial eyes.

"At times," she said.

"I'm sorry."

"It was not your fault. A man has so many occupations; and women who are clever—or very handsome—I suppose that's an occupation too. Sometimes I've felt that when dinner was ordered I had nothing to do till the next day."

"Oh," he groaned.

"It wasn't your fault," she insisted. "I never told you—but when I chose that rosebud paper for the front room upstairs, I always thought—"

"Well—?"

"It would be such a pretty paper—for a baby—to wake up in. That was years ago, of course; but it was rather an expensive paper . . . and it hasn't faded in the least . . ." she broke off incoherently.

"It hasn't faded?"

"No—and so I thought . . . as we don't use the room for anything . . . now that Aunt Sophronia is dead . . . I thought I might . . . you might . . . oh, Julian, if you could only have seen it just waking up in its crib!"

"Seen what—where? You haven't got a baby upstairs?"

"Oh, no—not *yet*," she said, with her rare laugh—the girlish bubbling of merriment that had seemed one of her chief graces in the early days. It occurred to him that he had not given her enough things to laugh about lately. But then she needed such very elementary things: she was as difficult to amuse as a savage. He concluded that he was not sufficiently simple.

"Alice," he said almost solemnly, "what *do* you mean?"

She hesitated a moment: he saw her gather her courage for a supreme effort. Then she said slowly, gravely, as though she were pronouncing a sacramental phrase:

"I'm so lonely without a little child—and I thought perhaps you'd let me adopt one. . . . It's at the hospital . . . its mother is dead . . . and I could . . . pet it, and dress it, and do things for it . . . and it's such a good baby . . . you can ask any of the nurses . . . it would never, *never* bother you by crying. . . ."

* II *

Lethbury accompanied his wife to the hospital in a mood of chastened wonder. It did not occur to him to oppose her wish. He knew, of course, that he would have to bear the brunt of the situation: the jokes at the club, the inquiries, the explanations. He saw himself in the comic role of the adopted father and welcomed it as an expiation. For in his rapid reconstruction of the past he found himself cutting a shabbier figure than he cared to admit. He had always been intolerant of stupid people, and it was his punishment to be convicted of stupidity. As his mind traversed the years between his marriage and this unexpected assumption of paternity, he saw, in the light of an overheated imagination, many signs of unwonted crassness. It was not that he had ceased to think his wife stupid: she *was* stupid, limited, inflexible; but there was a pathos in the struggles of her swaddled mind, in its blind reachings toward the primal emotions. He had always thought she would have been happier with a child; but he had thought it mechanically, because it had so often been thought before, because it was in the nature of things to think it of every woman, because his wife was so eminently one of a species that she fitted into all the generalizations of the sex. But he had regarded this generalization as merely typical of the triumph of tradition over experience. Maternity was no doubt the supreme function of primitive woman, the one end to which her whole organism tended; but the law of increasing complexity had operated in both sexes, and he had not seriously supposed that, outside the world of Christmas fiction and anecdotic art, such truisms had any special hold on the feminine imagination. Now he saw that the arts in question were kept alive by the vitality of the sentiments they appealed to.

Lethbury was in fact going through a rapid process of readjustment. His marriage had been a failure, but he had preserved toward his wife the exact fidelity of act that is sometimes supposed to excuse any divagation of feeling; so that, for years, the tie between them had consisted mainly in his abstaining from making love to other women. The abstention had not always been easy, for the world is surprisingly well stocked with the kind of woman one ought to have married but did not; and Lethbury had not escaped the solicitation of such alternatives. His immunity had been purchased at the cost of taking refuge in the somewhat rarefied atmosphere of his perceptions; and his world being thus limited, he had given unusual care to its details, compensating himself for the narrowness of his horizon by the minute finish of his foreground. It was a world of fine shadings and the nicest proportions, where impulse seldom set a blundering foot, and the feast of reason was undisturbed by an intemperate flow of soul. To such a banquet his wife naturally remained uninvited. The diet would have disagreed with her, and she would probably have objected to the other guests. But Lethbury, miscalculating her needs, had hitherto supposed that he had made ample provision for them, and was consequently at liberty to enjoy his own fare without any reproach of mendicancy at his gates. Now he beheld her pressing a starved face against the windows of his life, and in his imaginative reaction he invested her with a pathos borrowed from the sense of his own shortcomings.

In the hospital the imaginative process continued with increasing force. He looked at his wife with new eyes. Formerly she had been to him a mere bundle of negations, a labyrinth of dead walls and bolted doors. There was nothing behind the walls, and the doors led no whither: he had sounded and listened often enough to be sure of that. Now he felt like a traveler who, exploring some ancient ruin, comes on an inner cell, intact amid the general dilapidation, and painted with images which reveal the forgotten uses of the building.

His wife stood by a white crib in one of the wards. In the crib lay a child, a year old, the nurse affirmed, but to Lethbury's eye a mere dateless fragment of humanity projected against a background of conjecture. Over this anonymous particle of life Mrs. Lethbury leaned, such ecstasy reflected in her face as strikes up, in Correggio's "Nightpiece," from the child's body to the mother's countenance. It was a light that irradiated and dazzled her. She looked up at an inquiry of Lethbury's, but as their glances met he perceived that she no longer saw him, that he had become as invisible to her as she had long been to him. He had to transfer his question to the nurse.

"What is the child's name?" he asked.

"We call her Jane," said the nurse.

* III *

Lethbury, at first, had resisted the idea of a legal adoption; but when he found that his wife could not be brought to regard the child as hers till it had been made so by process of law, he promptly withdrew his objection. On one point only he remained inflexible; and that was the changing of the waif's name. Mrs. Lethbury, almost at once, had expressed a wish to rechristen it: she fluctuated between Muriel and Gladys, deferring the moment of decision like a lady wavering between two bonnets. But Lethbury was unyielding. In the general surrender of his prejudices this one alone held out.

"But Jane is so dreadful," Mrs. Lethbury protested.

"Well, we don't know that *she* won't be dreadful. She may grow up a Jane."

His wife exclaimed reproachfully. "The nurse says she's the loveliest—"

"Don't they always say that?" asked Lethbury patiently. He was prepared to be inexhaustibly patient now that he had reached a firm foothold of opposition.

"It's cruel to call her Jane," Mrs. Lethbury pleaded.

"It's ridiculous to call her Muriel."

"The nurse is *sure* she must be a lady's child."

Lethbury winced: he had tried, all along, to keep his mind off the question of antecedents.

"Well, let her prove it," he said, with a rising sense of exasperation. He wondered how he could ever have allowed himself to be drawn into such a ridiculous business; for the first time he felt the full irony of it. He had visions of coming home in the afternoon to a house smelling of linseed and paregoric, and of being greeted by a chronic howl as he went upstairs to dress for dinner. He had never been a club man, but he saw himself becoming one now.

The worst of his anticipations were unfulfilled. The baby was surprisingly well and surprisingly quiet. Such infantile remedies as she absorbed were not potent enough to be perceived beyond the nursery; and when Lethbury could be induced to enter that sanctuary, there was nothing to jar his nerves in the mild pink presence of his adopted daughter. Jars there were, indeed: they were probably inevitable in the disturbed routine of the household; but they occurred between Mrs. Lethbury and the nurses, and Jane contributed to them only a placid stare which might have served as a rebuke to the combatants.

In the reaction from his first impulse of atonement, Lethbury noted with sharpened perceptions the effect of the change on his wife's character. He saw already the error of supposing that it could work any transformation in her. It simply magnified her existing qualities. She was like a dried sponge put in water: she expanded, but she did not change her shape. From the standpoint of scientific observation it was curious to see how her stored instincts responded to the pseudo-maternal call. She overflowed with the petty maxims of the occasion. One felt in her the epitome, the consummation, of centuries of animal maternity, so that this little woman, who screamed at a mouse and was nervous about burglars, came to typify the cave mother rending her prey for her young.

It was less easy to regard philosophically the practical effects of her borrowed motherhood. Lethbury found with surprise that she was becoming assertive and definite. She no longer represented the negative side of his life; she showed, indeed, a tendency to inconvenient affirmations. She had gradually expanded her assumption of motherhood till it included his own share in the relation, and he suddenly found himself regarded as the father of Jane. This was a contingency he had not foreseen, and it took all his philosophy to accept it; but there were moments of compensation. For Mrs. Lethbury was undoubtedly happy for the first time in years; and the thought that he had tardily contributed to this end reconciled him to the irony of the means.

At first he was inclined to reproach himself for still viewing the situation from the outside, for remaining a spectator instead of a participant. He had been allured, for a moment, by the vision of severed hands meeting over a cradle, as the whole body of domestic fiction bears witness to their doing; and the fact that no such conjunction took place he could explain only on the ground that it was a borrowed cradle. He did not dislike the little girl. She still remained to him a hypothetical presence, a query rather than a fact; but her nearness was not unpleasant, and there were moments when her tentative utterances, her groping steps, seemed to loosen the dry accretions enveloping his inner self. But even at such moments—moments which he invited and caressed—she did not bring him nearer to his wife. He now perceived that he had made a certain place in his life for Mrs. Lethbury, and that she no longer fitted into it. It was too late to enlarge the space, and so she overflowed and encroached. Lethbury struggled against the sense of submergence. He let down barrier after barrier, yielding privacy after privacy; but his wife's personality continued to dilate. She was no longer herself alone: she was herself and Jane. Gradually, a monstrous fusion of identity, she became herself, himself and Jane; and instead of trying to adapt her to a spare crevice of his character, he found himself carelessly squeezed into the smallest compartment of the domestic economy.

* IV *

He continued to tell himself that he was satisfied if his wife was happy; and it was not till the child's tenth year that he felt a doubt of her happiness.

Jane had been a preternaturally good child. During the eight years of her adoption she had caused her foster parents no anxiety beyond those connected with the usual succession of youthful diseases. But her unknown progenitors had given her a robust constitution, and she passed unperturbed through measles, chicken pox and whooping cough. If there was any suffering it was endured vicariously by Mrs. Lethbury, whose temperature rose and fell with the patient's, and who could not hear Jane sneeze without visions of a marble angel weeping over a broken column. But though Jane's prompt recoveries continued to belie such premonitions, though her existence continued to move forward on an even keel of good health and good conduct, Mrs. Lethbury's satisfaction showed no corresponding advance. Lethbury, at first, was disposed to add her disappointment to the long list of feminine inconsistencies with which the sententious observer of life builds up his favorable induction; but circumstances presently led him to take a kindlier view of the case.

Hitherto his wife had regarded him as a negligible factor in Jane's evolution. Beyond providing for his adopted daughter, and effacing himself before her, he was not expected to contribute to her well-being. But as time passed he appeared to his wife in a new light. It was he who was to educate Jane. In matters of the intellect, Mrs. Lethbury was the first to declare her deficiencies—to proclaim them, even, with a certain virtuous superiority. She said she did not pretend to be clever, and there was no denying the truth of the assertion. Now, however, she seemed less ready, not to own her limitations, but to glory in them. Confronted with the problem of Jane's instruction she stood in awe of the child.

"I have always been stupid, you know," she said to Lethbury with a new humility, "and I'm afraid I shan't know what is best for Jane. I'm sure she has a wonderfully good mind, and I should reproach myself if I didn't give her every opportunity." She looked at him helplessly. "You must tell me what ought to be done."

Lethbury was not unwilling to oblige her. Somewhere in his mental lumber room there rusted a theory of education such as usually lingers among the impedimenta of the childless. He brought this out, refurbished it, and applied it to Jane. At first he thought his wife had not overrated the quality of the child's mind. Jane seemed extraordinarily intelligent. Her precocious definiteness of mind was encouraging to her inexperienced preceptor. She had no difficulty in fixing her attention, and he felt that every fact he imparted was being etched in metal. He helped his wife to engage the best teachers, and for a while continued to take an ex-official interest in his adopted daughter's studies. But gradually his interest waned. Jane's ideas did not increase with her acquisitions. Her young mind remained a mere receptacle for facts: a kind of cold storage from which anything which had been put there could be taken out at a moment's notice, intact but congealed. She developed, moreover, an inordinate pride in the capacity of her mental storehouse, and a tendency to pelt her public with its contents. She was overheard to jeer at her nurse for not knowing when the Saxon Heptarchy had fallen, and she alternately dazzled and depressed Mrs. Lethbury by the wealth of her chronological allusions. She showed no interest in the significance of the facts she amassed: she simply collected dates as another child might have collected stamps or marbles. To her foster mother she seemed a prodigy of wisdom; but Lethbury saw, with a secret movement of sympathy, how the aptitudes in which Mrs. Lethbury gloried were slowly estranging her from her child.

"She is getting too clever for me," his wife said to him, after one of Jane's historical flights, "but I am so glad that she will be a companion to you."

Lethbury groaned in spirit. He did not look forward to Jane's companionship. She was still a good little girl: but there was something automatic and formal in her goodness, as though it were a kind of moral calisthenics which she went through for the sake of showing her agility. An early consciousness of virtue had moreover constituted her the natural guardian and adviser of her elders. Before she was fifteen she had set about reforming the household. She took Mrs. Lethbury in hand first; then she extended her efforts to the servants, with consequences more disastrous to the domestic harmony; and lastly she applied herself to Lethbury. She proved to him by statistics that he smoked too much, and that it was injurious to the optic nerve to read in bed. She took him to task for not going to church more regularly, and pointed out to him the evils of desultory reading. She suggested that a regular course of study encourages mental concentration, and hinted that inconsecutiveness of thought is a sign of approaching age.

To her adopted mother her suggestions were equally pertinent. She instructed Mrs. Lethbury in an improved way of making beef stock, and called her attention to the unhygienic qualities of carpets. She poured out distracting facts about bacilli and vegetable mold, and demonstrated that curtains and picture frames are a hotbed of animal organisms. She learned by heart the nutritive ingredients of the principal articles of diet, and revolutionized the cuisine by an attempt to establish a scientific average between starch and phosphates. Four cooks left during this experiment, and Lethbury fell into the habit of dining at the club.

Once or twice, at the outset, he had tried to check Jane's ardor; but his efforts resulted only in hurting his wife's feelings. Jane remained impervious, and Mrs. Lethbury resented any attempt to protect her from her daughter. Lethbury saw that she was consoled for the sense of her own inferiority by the thought of what Jane's intellectual companionship must be to him; and he tried to keep up the illusion by enduring with what grace he might the blighting edification of Jane's discourse.

* V *

As Jane grew up he sometimes avenged himself by wondering if his wife was still sorry that they had not called her Muriel. Jane was not ugly; she developed, indeed, a kind of categorical prettiness which might have been a projection of her mind. She had a creditable collection of features, but one had to take an inventory of them to find out that she was good-looking. The fusing grace had been omitted.

Mrs. Lethbury took a touching pride in her daughter's first steps in the world. She expected Jane to take by her complexion those whom she did not capture by her learning. But Jane's rosy freshness did not work any perceptible ravages. Whether the young men guessed the axioms on her lips and detected the encyclopedia in her eye, or whether they simply found no intrinsic interest in these features, certain it is, that, in spite of her mother's heroic efforts, and of incessant calls on Lethbury's purse, Jane, at the end of her first season, had dropped hopelessly out of the running. A few duller girls found her interesting, and one or two young men came to the house with the object of meeting other young women; but she was rapidly becoming one of the social supernumeraries who are asked out only because they are on people's lists.

The blow was bitter to Mrs. Lethbury; but she consoled herself with the idea that Jane had failed because she was too clever. Jane probably shared this conviction; at all events she betrayed no consciousness of failure. She had developed a pronounced taste for society, and went out, unweariedly and obstinately, winter after winter, while Mrs. Lethbury toiled in her wake, showering attentions on oblivious hostesses. To Lethbury there was something at once tragic and exasperating in the sight of their two figures, the one conciliatory, the other dogged, both pursuing with unabated zeal the elusive prize of popularity. He even began to feel a personal stake in the pursuit, not as it concerned Jane but as it affected his wife. He saw that the latter was the victim of Jane's disappointment: that Jane was not above the crude satisfaction of "taking it out" of her mother. Experience checked the impulse to come to his wife's defence; and when his resentment was at its height, Jane disarmed him by giving up the struggle.

Nothing was said to mark her capitulation; but Lethbury noticed that the visiting ceased and that the dressmaker's bills diminished. At the same time Mrs. Lethbury made it known that Jane had taken up charities; and before long Jane's conversation confirmed this announcement. At first Lethbury congratulated himself on the change; but Jane's domesticity soon began to weigh on him. During the day she was sometimes absent on errands of mercy; but in the evening she was always there. At first she and Mrs. Lethbury sat in the drawing room together, and Lethbury smoked in the library; but presently Jane formed the habit of joining him there, and he began to suspect that he was included among the objects of her philanthropy.

Mrs. Lethbury confirmed the suspicion. "Jane has grown very serious-minded lately," she said. "She imagines that she used to neglect you and she is trying to make up for it. Don't discourage her," she added innocently.

Such a plea delivered Lethbury helpless to his daughter's ministrations; and he found himself measuring the hours he spent with her by the amount of relief they must be affording her mother. There were even moments when he read a furtive gratitude in Mrs. Lethbury's eye.

But Lethbury was no hero, and he had nearly reached the limit of vicarious endurance when something wonderful happened. They never quite knew afterward how it had come about, or who first perceived it; but Mrs. Lethbury one day gave tremulous voice to their discovery.

"Of course," she said, "he comes here because of Elise." The young lady in question, a friend of Jane's, was possessed of attractions which had already been found to explain the presence of masculine visitors.

Lethbury risked a denial. "I don't think he does," he declared.

"But Elise is thought very pretty," Mrs. Lethbury insisted.

"I can't help that," said Lethbury doggedly.

He saw a faint light in his wife's eyes; but she remarked carelessly: "Mr. Budd would be a very good match for Elise."

Lethbury could hardly repress a chuckle: he was so exquisitely aware that she was trying to propitiate the gods.

For a few weeks neither said a word; then Mrs. Lethbury once more reverted to the subject.

"It is a month since Elise went abroad," she said.

"Is it?"

"And Mr. Budd seems to come here just as often—"

"Ah," said Lethbury with heroic indifference; and his wife hastily changed the subject.

Mr. Winstanley Budd was a young man who suffered from an excess of manner. Politeness gushed from him in the driest seasons. He was always performing feats of drawing-room chivalry, and the approach of the most unobtrusive female threw him into attitudes which endangered the furniture. His features, being of the cherubic order, did not lend themselves to this role; but there were moments when he appeared to dominate them, to force them into compliance with an aquiline ideal. The range of Mr. Budd's social benevolence made its object hard to distinguish. He spread his cloak so indiscriminately that one could not always interpret the gesture, and Jane's impassive manner had the effect of increasing his demonstrations: she threw him into paroxysms of politeness.

At first he filled the house with his amenities; but gradually it became apparent that his most dazzling effects were directed exclusively to Jane. Lethbury and his wife held their breath and looked away from each other. They pretended not to notice the frequency of Mr. Budd's visits, they struggled against an imprudent inclination to leave the young people too much alone. Their conclusions were the result of indirect observation, for neither of them dared to be caught watching Mr. Budd: they behaved like naturalists on the trail of a rare butterfly.

In his efforts not to notice Mr. Budd, Lethbury centered his attentions on Jane; and Jane, at this crucial moment, wrung from him a reluctant admiration. While her parents went about dissembling their emotions, she seemed to have none to conceal. She betrayed neither eagerness nor surprise; so complete was her unconcern that there were moments when Lethbury feared it was obtuseness, when he could hardly help whispering to her that now was the moment to lower the net.

Meanwhile the velocity of Mr. Budd's gyrations increased with the ardor of courtship; his politeness became incandescent, and Jane found herself the center of a pyrotechnical display culminating in the "set piece" of an offer of marriage.

Mrs. Lethbury imparted the news to her husband one evening after their daughter had gone to bed. The announcement was made and received with an air of detachment, as though both feared to be betrayed into unseemly exultation; but Lethbury, as his wife ended, could not repress the inquiry, "Have they decided on a day?"

Mrs. Lethbury's superior command of her features enabled her to look shocked. "What can you be thinking of? He only offered himself at five!"

"Of course—of course—" stammered Lethbury "—but nowadays people marry after such short engagements—"

"Engagement!" said his wife solemnly. "There is no engagement."

Lethbury dropped his cigar. "What on earth do you mean?"

"Jane is thinking it over."

"*Thinking it over?*"

"She has asked for a month before deciding."

Lethbury sank back with a gasp. Was it genius or was it madness? He felt incompetent to decide; and Mrs. Lethbury's next words showed that she shared his difficulty.

"Of course I don't want to hurry Jane—"

"Of course not," he acquiesced.

"But I pointed out to her that a young man of Mr. Budd's impulsive temperament might—might be easily discouraged—"

"Yes; and what did she say?"

"She said that if she was worth winning she was worth waiting for."

* VI *

The period of Mr. Budd's probation could scarcely have cost him as much mental anguish as it caused his would-be parents-in-law.

Mrs. Lethbury, by various ruses, tried to shorten the ordeal, but Jane remained inexorable; and each morning Lethbury came down to breakfast with the certainty of finding a letter of withdrawal from her discouraged suitor.

When at length the decisive day came, and Mrs. Lethbury, at its close, stole into the library with an air of chastened joy, they stood for a moment without speaking; then Mrs. Lethbury paid a fitting tribute to the proprieties by faltering out: "It will be dreadful to have to give her up—"

Lethbury could not repress a warning gesture; but even as it escaped him he realized that his wife's grief was genuine.

"Of course, of course," he said, vainly sounding his own emotional shallows for an answering regret. And yet it was his wife who had suffered most from Jane!

He had fancied that these sufferings would be effaced by the milder atmosphere of their last weeks together; but felicity did not soften Jane. Not for a moment did she relax her dominion: she simply widened it to include a new subject. Mr. Budd found himself under orders with the others; and a new fear assailed Lethbury as he saw Jane assume prenuptial control of her betrothed. Lethbury had never felt any strong personal interest in Mr. Budd; but as Jane's prospective husband the young man excited his sympathy. To his surprise he found that Mrs. Lethbury shared the feeling.

"I'm afraid he may find Jane a little exacting," she said, after an evening dedicated to a stormy discussion of the wedding arrangements. "She really ought to make some concessions. If he *wants* to be married in a black frock coat instead of a dark gray one—" She paused and looked doubtfully at Lethbury.

"What can I do about it?" he said.

"You might explain to him—tell him that Jane isn't always—"

Lethbury made an impatient gesture. "What are you afraid of? His finding her out or his not finding her out?"

Mrs. Lethbury flushed. "You put it so dreadfully!"

Her husband mused for a moment; then he said with an air of cheerful hypocrisy: "After all, Budd is old enough to take care of himself."

But the next day Mrs. Lethbury surprised him. Late in the afternoon she entered the library, so breathless and inarticulate that he scented a catastrophe.

"I've done it!" she cried.

"Done what?"

"Told him." She nodded toward the door. "He's just gone. Jane is out, and I had a chance to talk to him alone."

Lethbury pushed a chair forward and she sank into it.

"What did you tell him? That she is *not* always—"

Mrs. Lethbury lifted a tragic eye. "No; I told him that she always *is*—"

"Always *is*—?"

"Yes."

There was a pause. Lethbury made a call on his hoarded philosophy. He saw Jane suddenly reinstated in her evening seat by the library fire; but an answering chord in him thrilled at his wife's heroism.

"Well—what did he say?"

Mrs. Lethbury's agitation deepened. It was clear that the blow had fallen.

"He . . . he said . . . that we . . . had never understood Jane . . . or appreciated her . . . ." The final syllables were lost in her handkerchief, and she left him marveling at the mechanism of woman.

After that, Lethbury faced the future with an undaunted eye. They had done their duty—at least his wife had done hers—and they were reaping the usual harvest of ingratitude with a zest seldom accorded to such reaping. There was a marked change in Mr. Budd's manner, and his increasing coldness sent a genial glow through Lethbury's system. It was easy to bear with Jane in the light of Mr. Budd's disapproval.

There was a good deal to be borne in the last days, and the brunt of it fell on Mrs. Lethbury. Jane marked her transition to the married state by a seasonable but incongruous display of nerves. She became sentimental, hysterical and reluctant. She quarreled with her betrothed and threatened to return the ring. Mrs. Lethbury had to intervene, and Lethbury felt the hovering sword of destiny. But the blow was suspended. Mr. Budd's chivalry was proof against all his bride's caprices and his devotion throve on her cruelty. Lethbury feared that he was too faithful, too enduring, and longed to urge him to vary his tactics. Jane presently reappeared with the ring on her finger, and consented to try on the wedding dress; but her uncertainties, her reactions, were prolonged till the final day.

When it dawned, Lethbury was still in an ecstasy of apprehension. Feeling reasonably sure of the principal actors he had centered his fears on incidental possibilities. The clergyman might have a stroke, or the church might burn down, or there might be something wrong with the license. He did all that was humanly possible to avert such contingencies, but there remained that incalculable factor known as the hand of God. Lethbury seemed to feel it groping for him.

At the altar it almost had him by the nape. Mr. Budd was late; and for five immeasurable minutes Lethbury and Jane faced a churchful of conjecture. Then the bridegroom appeared, flushed but chivalrous, and explaining to his father-in-law under cover of the ritual that he had torn his glove and had to go back for another.

"You'll be losing the ring next," muttered Lethbury; but Mr. Budd produced this article punctually, and a moment or two later was bearing its wearer captive down the aisle.

At the wedding breakfast Lethbury caught his wife's eye fixed on him in mild disapproval, and understood that his hilarity was exceeding the bounds of fitness. He pulled himself together and tried to subdue his tone; but his jubilation bubbled over like a champagne glass perpetually refilled. The deeper his draughts the higher it rose.

It was at the brim when, in the wake of the dispersing guests, Jane came down in her traveling dress and fell on her mother's neck.

"I can't leave you!" she wailed, and Lethbury felt as suddenly sobered as a man under a shower. But if the bride was reluctant her captor was relentless. Never had Mr. Budd been more dominant, more aquiline.

Lethbury's last fears were dissipated as the young man snatched Jane from her mother's bosom and bore her off to the brougham.

The brougham rolled away, the last milliner's girl forsook her post by the awning, the red carpet was folded up, and the house door closed. Lethbury stood alone in the hall with his wife. As he turned toward her, he noticed the look of tired heroism in her eyes, the deepened lines of her face. They reflected his own symptoms too accurately not to appeal to him. The nervous tension had been horrible. He went up to her, and an answering impulse made her lay a hand on his arm. He held it there a moment.

"Let us go off and have a jolly little dinner at a restaurant," he proposed.

There had been a time when such a suggestion would have surprised her to the verge of disapproval; but now she agreed to it at once.

"Oh, that would be so nice," she murmured with a great sigh of relief and assuagement.

Jane had fulfilled her mission after all: she had drawn them together at last.

THE OTHER
TWO

WAYTHORN, on the drawing-room hearth, waited for his wife to come down to dinner.

It was their first night under his own roof, and he was surprised at his thrill of boyish agitation. He was not so old, to be sure—his glass gave him little more than the five-and-thirty years to which his wife confessed— but he had fancied himself already in the temperate zone; yet here he was listening for her step with a tender sense of all it symbolized, with some old trail of verse about the garlanded nuptial doorposts floating through his enjoyment of the pleasant room and the good dinner just beyond it.

They had been hastily recalled from their honeymoon by the illness of Lily Haskett, the child of Mrs. Waythorn's first marriage. The little girl, at Waythorn's desire, had been transferred to his house on the day of her mother's wedding, and the doctor, on their arrival, broke the news that she was ill with typhoid, but declared that all the symptoms were favorable. Lily could show twelve years of unblemished health, and the case promised to be a light one. The nurse spoke as reassuringly, and after a moment of alarm Mrs. Waythorn had adjusted herself to the situation. She was very fond of Lily—her affection for the child had perhaps been her decisive charm in Waythorn's eyes—but she had the perfectly balanced nerves which her little girl had inherited, and no woman ever wasted less tissue in unproductive worry. Waythorn was therefore quite prepared to see her come in presently, a little late because of a last look at Lily, but as serene and well-appointed as if her goodnight kiss had been laid on the brow of health. Her composure was restful to him; it acted as ballast to his somewhat unstable sensibilities. As he pictured her bending over the child's bed he thought how soothing her presence must be in illness: her very step would prognosticate recovery.

His own life had been a gray one, from temperament rather than circumstance, and he had been drawn to her by the unperturbed gaiety which kept her fresh and elastic at an age when most women's activities are growing either slack or febrile. He knew what was said about her; for, popular as she was, there had always been a faint undercurrent of detraction. When she had appeared in New York, nine or ten years earlier, as the pretty Mrs. Haskett whom Gus Varick had unearthed somewhere—was it in Pittsburg or Utica?—society, while promptly accepting her, had reserved the right to cast a doubt on its own indiscrimination. Inquiry, however, established her undoubted connection with a socially reigning family, and explained her recent divorce as the natural result of a runaway match at seventeen; and as nothing was known of Mr. Haskett it was easy to believe the worst of him.

Alice Haskett's remarriage with Gus Varick was a passport to the set whose recognition she coveted, and for a few years the Varicks were the most popular couple in town. Unfortunately the alliance was brief and stormy, and this time the husband had his champions. Still, even Varick's stanchest supporters admitted that he was not meant for matrimony, and Mrs. Varick's grievances were of a nature to bear the inspection of the New York courts. A New York divorce is in itself a diploma of virtue, and in the semiwidowhood of this second separation Mrs. Varick took on an air of sanctity, and was allowed to confide her wrongs to some of the most scrupulous ears in town. But when it was known that she was to marry Waythorn there was a momentary reaction. Her best friends would have preferred to see her remain in the role of the injured wife, which was as becoming to her as crepe to a rosy complexion. True, a decent time had elapsed, and it was not even suggested that Waythorn had supplanted his predecessor. People shook their heads over him, however, and one grudging friend, to whom he affirmed that he took the step with his eyes open, replied oracularly: "Yes—and with your ears shut."

Waythorn could afford to smile at these innuendoes. In the Wall Street phrase, he had "discounted" them. He knew that society has not yet adapted itself to the consequences of divorce, and that till the adaptation takes place every woman who uses the freedom the law accords her must be her own social justification. Waythorn had an amused confidence in his wife's ability to justify herself. His expectations were fulfilled, and before the wedding took place Alice Varick's group had rallied openly to her support. She took it all imperturbably: she had a way of surmounting obstacles without seeming to be aware of them, and Waythorn looked back with wonder at the trivialities over which he had worn his nerves thin. He had the sense of having found refuge in a richer, warmer nature than his own, and his satisfaction, at the moment, was humorously summed up in the thought that his wife, when she had done all she could for Lily, would not be ashamed to come down and enjoy a good dinner.

The anticipation of such enjoyment was not, however, the sentiment expressed by Mrs. Waythorn's charming face when she presently joined him. Though she had put on her most engaging tea gown she had neglected to assume the smile that went with it, and Waythorn thought he had never seen her look so nearly worried.

"What is it?" he asked. "Is anything wrong with Lily?"

"No; I've just been in and she's still sleeping." Mrs. Waythorn hesitated. "But something tiresome has happened."

He had taken her two hands, and now perceived that he was crushing a paper between them.

"This letter?"

"Yes—Mr. Haskett has written—I mean his lawyer has written."

Waythorn felt himself flush uncomfortably. He dropped his wife's hands. "What about?"

"About seeing Lily. You know the courts—"

"Yes, yes," he interrupted nervously.

Nothing was known about Haskett in New York. He was vaguely supposed to have remained in the outer darkness from which his wife had been rescued, and Waythorn was one of the few who were aware that he had given up his business in Utica and followed her to New York in order to be near his little girl. In the days of his wooing, Waythorn had often met Lily on the doorstep, rosy and smiling, on her way "to see papa."

"I am so sorry," Mrs. Waythorn murmured.

He roused himself. "What does he want?"

"He wants to see her. You know she goes to him once a week."

"Well—he doesn't expect her to go to him now, does he?"

"No—he has heard of her illness; but he expects to come here."

"*Here?*"

Mrs. Waythorn reddened under his gaze. They looked away from each other.

"I'm afraid he has the right. . . . You'll see. . . ." She made a proffer of the letter.

Waythorn moved away with a gesture of refusal. He stood staring about the softly-lighted room, which a moment before had seemed so full of bridal intimacy.

"I'm so sorry," she repeated. "If Lily could have been moved—"

"That's out of the question," he returned impatiently.

"I suppose so."

Her lip was beginning to tremble, and he felt himself a brute.

"He must come, of course," he said. "When is—his day?"

"I'm afraid—tomorrow."

"Very well. Send a note in the morning."

The butler entered to announce dinner.

Waythorn turned to his wife. "Come—you must be tired. It's beastly, but try to forget about it," he said, drawing her hand through his arm.

"You're so good, dear. I'll try," she whispered back.

Her face cleared at once, and as she looked at him across the flowers, between the rosy candleshades, he saw her lips waver back into a smile.

"How pretty everything is!" she sighed luxuriously.

He turned to the butler. "The champagne at once, please. Mrs. Waythorn is tired."

In a moment or two their eyes met above the sparkling glasses. Her own were quite clear and untroubled: he saw that she had obeyed his injunction and forgotten.

* II *

Waythorn, the next morning, went downtown earlier than usual. Haskett was not likely to come till the afternoon, but the instinct of flight drove him forth. He meant to stay away all day—he had thoughts of dining at his club. As his door closed behind him he reflected that before he opened it again it would have admitted another man who had as much right to enter it as himself, and the thought filled him with a physical repugnance.

He caught the elevated at the employees' hour, and found himself crushed between two layers of pendulous humanity. At Eighth Street the man facing him wriggled out, and another took his place. Waythorn glanced up and saw that it was Gus Varick. The men were so close together that it was impossible to ignore the smile of recognition on Varick's handsome overblown face. And after all—why not? They had always been on good terms, and Varick had been divorced before Waythorn's attentions to his wife began. The two exchanged a word on the perennial grievance of the congested trains, and when a seat at their side was miraculously left empty the instinct of self-preservation made Waythorn slip into it after Varick.

The latter drew the stout man's breath of relief. "Lord—I was beginning to feel like a pressed flower." He leaned back, looking unconcernedly at Waythorn. "Sorry to hear that Sellers is knocked out again."

"Sellers?" echoed Waythorn, starting at his partner's name.

Varick looked surprised. "You didn't know he was laid up with the gout?"

"No. I've been away—I only got back last night." Waythorn felt himself reddening in anticipation of the other's smile.

"Ah—yes; to be sure. And Sellers' attack came on two days ago. I'm afraid he's pretty bad. Very awkward for me, as it happens, because he was just putting through a rather important thing for me."

"Ah?" Waythorn wondered vaguely since when Varick had been dealing in "important things." Hitherto he had dabbled only in the shallow pools of speculation, with which Waythorn's office did not usually concern itself.

It occurred to him that Varick might be talking at random, to relieve the strain of their propinquity. That strain was becoming momentarily more apparent to Waythorn, and when, at Cortlandt Street, he caught sight of an acquaintance and had a sudden vision of the picture he and Varick must present to an initiated eye, he jumped up with a muttered excuse.

"I hope you'll find Sellers better," said Varick civilly, and he stammered back: "If I can be of any use to you—" and let the departing crowd sweep him to the platform.

At his office he heard that Sellers was in fact ill with the gout, and would probably not be able to leave the house for some weeks.

"I'm sorry it should have happened so, Mr. Waythorn," the senior clerk said with affable significance. "Mr. Sellers was very much upset at the idea of giving you such a lot of extra work just now."

"Oh, that's no matter," said Waythorn hastily. He secretly welcomed the pressure of additional business, and was glad to think that, when the day's work was over, he would have to call at his partner's on the way home.

He was late for luncheon, and turned in at the nearest restaurant instead of going to his club. The place was full, and the waiter hurried him to the back of the room to capture the only vacant table. In the cloud of cigar smoke Waythorn did not at once distinguish his neighbors: but presently, looking about him, he saw Varick seated a few feet off. This time, luckily, they were too far apart for conversation, and Varick, who faced another way, had probably not even seen him; but there was an irony in their renewed nearness.

Varick was said to be fond of good living, and as Waythorn sat dispatching his hurried luncheon he looked across half enviously at the other's leisurely degustation of his meal. When Waythorn first saw him he had been helping himself with critical deliberation to a bit of Camembert at the ideal point of liquefaction, and now, the cheese removed, he was just pouring his *café double* from its little two-storied earthen pot. He poured slowly, his ruddy profile bent over the task, and one beringed white hand steadying the lid of the coffeepot; then he stretched his other hand to the decanter of cognac at his elbow, filled a liqueur glass, took a tentative sip, and poured the brandy into his coffee cup.

Waythorn watched him in a kind of fascination. What was he thinking of—only of the flavor of the coffee and the liqueur? Had the morning's meeting left no more trace in his thoughts than on his face? Had his wife so completely passed out of his life that even this odd encounter with her present husband, within a week after her remarriage, was no more than an incident in his day? And as Waythorn mused, another idea struck him: had Haskett ever met Varick as Varick and he had just met? The recollection of Haskett perturbed him, and he rose and left the restaurant, taking a circuitous way out to escape the placid irony of Varick's nod.

It was after seven when Waythorn reached home. He thought the footman who opened the door looked at him oddly.

"How is Miss Lily?" he asked in haste.

"Doing very well, sir. A gentleman—"

"Tell Barlow to put off dinner for half an hour," Waythorn cut him off, hurrying upstairs.

He went straight to his room and dressed without seeing his wife. When he reached the drawing room she was there, fresh and radiant. Lily's day had been good; the doctor was not coming back that evening.

At dinner Waythorn told her of Sellers' illness and of the resulting complications. She listened sympathetically, adjuring him not to let himself be overworked, and asking vague feminine questions about the routine of the office. Then she gave him the chronicle of Lily's day; quoted the nurse and doctor, and told him who had called to inquire. He had never seen her more serene and unruffled. It struck him, with a curious pang, that she was very happy in being with him, so happy that she found a childish pleasure in rehearsing the trivial incidents of her day.

After dinner they went to the library, and the servant put the coffee and liqueurs on a low table before her and left the room. She looked singularly soft and girlish in her rosy-pale dress, against the dark leather of one of his bachelor armchairs. A day earlier the contrast would have charmed him.

He turned away now, choosing a cigar with affected deliberation.

"Did Haskett come?" he asked, with his back to her.

"Oh, yes—he came."

"You didn't see him, of course?"

She hesitated a moment. "I let the nurse see him."

That was all. There was nothing more to ask. He swung round toward her, applying a match to his cigar. Well, the thing was over for a week, at any rate. He would try not to think of it. She looked up at him, a trifle rosier than usual, with a smile in her eyes.

"Ready for your coffee, dear?"

He leaned against the mantelpiece, watching her as she lifted the coffeepot. The lamplight struck a gleam from her bracelets and tipped her soft hair with brightness. How light and slender she was, and how each gesture flowed into the next! She seemed a creature all compact of harmonies. As the thought of Haskett receded, Waythorn felt himself yielding again to the joy of possessorship. They were his, those white hands with their flitting motions, his the light haze of hair, the lips and eyes. . . .

She set down the coffeepot, and reaching for the decanter of cognac, measured off a liqueur glass and poured it into his cup.

Waythorn uttered a sudden exclamation.

"What is the matter?" she said, startled.

"Nothing; only—I don't take cognac in my coffee."

"Oh, how stupid of me," she cried.

Their eyes met, and she blushed a sudden agonized red.

* III *

Ten days later, Mr. Sellers, still housebound, asked Waythorn to call on his way downtown.

The senior partner, with his swaddled foot propped up by the fire, greeted his associate with an air of embarrassment.

"I'm sorry, my dear fellow; I've got to ask you to do an awkward thing for me."

Waythorn waited, and the other went on, after a pause apparently given to the arrangement of his phrases: "The fact is, when I was knocked out I had just gone into a rather complicated piece of business for—Gus Varick."

"Well?" said Waythorn, with an attempt to put him at his ease.

"Well—it's this way: Varick came to me the day before my attack. He had evidently had an inside tip from somebody, and had made about a hundred thousand. He came to me for advice, and I suggested his going in with Vanderlyn."

"Oh, the deuce!" Waythorn exclaimed. He saw in a flash what had happened. The investment was an alluring one, but required negotiation. He listened quietly while Sellers put the case before him, and, the statement ended, he said: "You think I ought to see Varick?"

"I'm afraid I can't as yet. The doctor is obdurate. And this thing can't wait. I hate to ask you, but no one else in the office knows the ins and outs of it."

Waythorn stood silent. He did not care a farthing for the success of Varick's venture, but the honor of the office was to be considered, and he could hardly refuse to oblige his partner.

"Very well," he said, "I'll do it."

That afternoon, apprised by telephone, Varick called at the office.

Waythorn, waiting in his private room, wondered what the others thought of it. The newspapers, at the time of Mrs. Waythorn's marriage, had acquainted their readers with every detail of her previous matrimonial ventures, and Waythorn could fancy the clerks smiling behind Varick's back as he was ushered in.

Varick bore himself admirably. He was easy without being undignified, and Waythorn was conscious of cutting a much less impressive figure. Varick had no experience of business, and the talk prolonged itself for nearly an hour while Waythorn set forth with scrupulous precision the details of the proposed transaction.

"I'm awfully obliged to you," Varick said as he rose. "The fact is I'm not used to having much money to look after, and I don't want to make an ass of myself—" He smiled, and Waythorn could not help noticing that there was something pleasant about his smile. "It feels uncommonly queer to have enough cash to pay one's bills. I'd have sold my soul for it a few years ago!"

Waythorn winced at the allusion. He had heard it rumored that a lack of funds had been one of the determining causes of the Varick separation, but it did not occur to him that Varick's words were intentional. It seemed more likely that the desire to keep clear of embarrassing topics had fatally drawn him into one. Waythorn did not wish to be outdone in civility.

"We'll do the best we can for you," he said. "I think this is a good thing you're in."

"Oh, I'm sure it's immense. It's awfully good of you—" Varick broke off, embarrassed. "I suppose the thing's settled now—but if—"

"If anything happens before Sellers is about, I'll see you again," said Waythorn quietly. He was glad, in the end, to appear the more self-possessed of the two.

The course of Lily's illness ran smooth, and as the days passed Waythorn grew used to the idea of Haskett's weekly visit. The first time the day came round, he stayed out late, and questioned his wife as to the visit on his return. She replied at once that Haskett had merely seen the nurse downstairs, as the doctor did not wish anyone in the child's sickroom till after the crisis.

The following week Waythorn was again conscious of the recurrence of the day, but had forgotten it by the time he came home to dinner. The crisis of the disease came a few days later, with a rapid decline of fever, and the little girl was pronounced out of danger. In the rejoicing which ensued the thought of Haskett passed out of Waythorn's mind, and one afternoon, letting himself into the house with a latchkey, he went straight to his library without noticing a shabby hat and umbrella in the hall.

In the library he found a small effaced-looking man with a thinnish gray beard sitting on the edge of a chair. The stranger might have been a piano tuner, or one of those mysteriously efficient persons who are summoned in emergencies to adjust some detail of the domestic machinery. He blinked at Waythorn through a pair of gold-rimmed spectacles and said mildly: "Mr. Waythorn, I presume? I am Lily's father."

Waythorn flushed. "Oh—" he stammered uncomfortably. He broke off, disliking to appear rude. Inwardly he was trying to adjust the actual Haskett to the image of him projected by his wife's reminiscences. Waythorn had been allowed to infer that Alice's first husband was a brute.

"I am sorry to intrude," said Haskett, with his over-the-counter politeness.

"Don't mention it," returned Waythorn, collecting himself. "I suppose the nurse has been told?"

"I presume so. I can wait," said Haskett. He had a resigned way of speaking, as though life had worn down his natural powers of resistance.

Waythorn stood on the threshold, nervously pulling off his gloves.

"I'm sorry you've been detained. I will send for the nurse," he said; and as he opened the door he added with an effort: "I'm glad we can give you a good report of Lily." He winced as the *we* slipped out, but Haskett seemed not to notice it.

"Thank you, Mr. Waythorn. It's been an anxious time for me."

"Ah, well, that's past. Soon she'll be able to go to you." Waythorn nodded and passed out.

In his own room he flung himself down with a groan. He hated the womanish sensibility which made him suffer so acutely from the grotesque chances of life. He had known when he married that his wife's former husbands were both living, and that amid the multiplied contacts of modern existence there were a thousand chances to one that he would run against one or the other, yet he found himself as much disturbed by his brief encounter with Haskett as though the law had not obligingly removed all difficulties in the way of their meeting.

Waythorn sprang up and began to pace the room nervously. He had not suffered half as much from his two meetings with Varick. It was Haskett's presence in his own house that made the situation so intolerable. He stood still, hearing steps in the passage.

"This way, please," he heard the nurse say. Haskett was being taken upstairs, then: not a corner of the house but was open to him. Waythorn dropped into another chair, staring vaguely ahead of him. On his dressing table stood a photograph of Alice, taken when he had first known her. She was Alice Varick then—how fine and exquisite he had thought her! Those were Varick's pearls about her neck. At Waythorn's instance they had been returned before her marriage. Had Haskett ever given her any trinkets—and what had become of them, Waythorn wondered? He realized suddenly that he knew very little of Haskett's past or present situation; but from the man's appearance and manner of speech he could reconstruct with curious precision the surroundings of Alice's first marriage. And it startled him to think that she had, in the background of her life, a phase of existence so different from anything with which he had connected her. Varick, whatever his faults, was a gentleman, in the conventional, traditional sense of the term: the sense which at that moment seemed, oddly enough, to have most meaning to Waythorn. He and Varick had the same social habits, spoke the same language, understood the same allusions. But this other man . . . it was grotesquely uppermost in Waythorn's mind that Haskett had worn a made-up tie attached with an elastic. Why should that ridiculous detail symbolize the whole man? Waythorn was exasperated by his own paltriness, but the fact of the tie expanded, forced itself on him, became as it were the key to Alice's past. He could see her, as Mrs. Haskett, sitting in a "front parlor" furnished in plush, with a pianola, and copy of *Ben Hur* on the center table. He could see her going to the theater with Haskett—or perhaps even to a "Church Sociable"—she in a "picture hat" and Haskett in a black frock coat, a little creased, with the made-up tie on an elastic. On the way home they would stop and look at the illuminated shop windows, lingering over the photographs of New York actresses. On Sunday afternoons Haskett would take her for a walk, pushing Lily ahead of them in a white enameled perambulator, and Waythorn had a vision of the people they would stop and talk to. He could fancy how pretty Alice must have looked, in a dress adroitly constructed from the hints of a New York fashion paper, and how she must have looked down on the other women, chafing at her life, and secretly feeling that she belonged in a bigger place.

For the moment his foremost thought was one of wonder at the way in which she had shed the phase of existence which her marriage with Haskett implied. It was as if her whole aspect, every gesture, every inflection, every allusion, were a studied negation of that period of her life. If she had denied being married to Haskett she could hardly have stood more convicted of duplicity than in his obliteration of the self which had been his wife.

Waythorn started up, checking himself in the analysis of her motives. What right had he to create a fantastic effigy of her and then pass judgment on it? She had spoken vaguely of her first marriage as unhappy, had hinted, with becoming reticence, that Haskett had wrought havoc among her young illusions. . . . It was a pity for Waythorn's peace of mind that Haskett's very inoffensiveness shed a new light on the nature of those illusions. A man would rather think that his wife has been brutalized by her first husband than that the process has been reversed.

* IV *

"Mr. Waythorn, I don't like that French governess of Lily's."

Haskett, subdued and apologetic, stood before Waythorn in the library, revolving his shabby hat in his hand.

Waythorn, surprised in his armchair over the evening paper, stared back perplexedly at his visitor.

"You'll excuse my asking to see you," Haskett continued. "But this is my last visit, and I thought if I could have a word with you it would be a better way than writing to Mrs. Waythorn's lawyer."

Waythorn rose uneasily. He did not like the French governess either; but that was irrelevant.

"I am not so sure of that," he returned stiffly; "but since you wish it I will give your message to—my wife." He always hesitated over the possessive pronoun in addressing Haskett.

The latter sighed. "I don't know as that will help much. She didn't like it when I spoke to her."

Waythorn turned red. "When did you see her?" he asked.

"Not since the first day I came to see Lily—right after she was taken sick. I remarked to her then that I didn't like the governess."

Waythorn made no answer. He remembered distinctly that, after that first visit, he had asked his wife if she had seen Haskett. She had lied to him then, but she had respected his wishes since; and the incident cast a curious light on her character. He was sure she would not have seen Haskett that first day if she had divined that Waythorn would object, and the fact that she did not divine it was almost as disagreeable to the latter as the discovery that she had lied to him.

"I don't like the woman," Haskett was repeating with mild persistency. "She ain't straight, Mr. Waythorn—she'll teach the child to be underhand. I've noticed a change in Lily—she's too anxious to please—and she don't always tell the truth. She used to be the straightest child, Mr. Waythorn—" He broke off, his voice a little thick. "Not but what I want her to have a stylish education," he ended.

Waythorn was touched. "I'm sorry, Mr. Haskett; but frankly, I don't quite see what I can do."

Haskett hesitated. Then he laid his hat on the table, and advanced to the hearthrug, on which Waythorn was standing. There was nothing aggressive in his manner, but he had the solemnity of a timid man resolved on a decisive measure.

"There's just one thing you can do, Mr. Waythorn," he said. "You can remind Mrs. Waythorn that, by the decree of the courts, I am entitled to have a voice in Lily's bringing-up." He paused, and went on more deprecatingly: "I'm not the kind to talk about enforcing my rights, Mr. Waythorn. I don't know as I think a man is entitled to rights he hasn't known how to hold on to; but this business of the child is different. I've never let go there—and I never mean to."

The scene left Waythorn deeply shaken. Shamefacedly, in indirect ways, he had been finding out about Haskett; and all that he had learned was favorable. The little man, in order to be near his daughter, had sold out his share in a profitable business in Utica, and accepted a modest clerkship in a New York manufacturing house. He boarded in a shabby street and had few acquaintances. His passion for Lily filled his life. Waythorn felt that this exploration of Haskett was like groping about with a dark lantern in his wife's past; but he saw now that there were recesses his lantern had not explored. He had never inquired into the exact circumstances of his wife's first matrimonial rupture. On the surface all had been fair. It was she who had obtained the divorce, and the court had given her the child. But Waythorn knew how many ambiguities such a verdict might cover. The mere fact that Haskett retained a right over his daughter implied an unsuspected compromise. Waythorn was an idealist. He always refused to recognize unpleasant contingencies till he found himself confronted with them, and then he saw them followed by a spectral train of consequences. His next days were thus haunted, and he determined to try to lay the ghosts by conjuring them up in his wife's presence.

When he repeated Haskett's request a flame of anger passed over her face; but she subdued it instantly and spoke with a slight quiver of outraged motherhood.

"It is very ungentlemanly of him," she said.

The word grated on Waythorn. "That is neither here nor there. It's a bare question of rights."

She murmured: "It's not as if he could ever be a help to Lily—"

Waythorn flushed. This was even less to his taste. "The question is," he repeated, "what authority has he over her?"

She looked downward, twisting herself a little in her seat. "I am willing to see him—I thought you objected," she faltered.

In a flash he understood that she knew the extent of Haskett's claims. Perhaps it was not the first time she had resisted them.

"My objecting has nothing to do with it," he said coldly; "if Haskett has a right to be consulted you must consult him."

She burst into tears, and he saw that she expected him to regard her as a victim.

Haskett did not abuse his rights. Waythorn had felt miserably sure that he would not. But the governess was dismissed, and from time to time the little man demanded an interview with Alice. After the first outburst she accepted the situation with her usual adaptability. Haskett had once reminded Waythorn of the piano tuner, and Mrs. Waythorn, after a month or two, appeared to class him with that domestic familiar. Waythorn could not but respect the father's tenacity. At first he had tried to cultivate the suspicion that Haskett might be "up to" something, that he had an object in securing a foothold in the house. But in his heart Waythorn was sure of Haskett's single-mindedness; he even guessed in the latter a mild contempt for such advantages as his relation with the Waythorns might offer. Haskett's sincerity of purpose made him invulnerable, and his successor had to accept him as a lien on the property.

Mr. Sellers was sent to Europe to recover from his gout, and Varick's affairs hung on Waythorn's hands. The negotiations were prolonged and complicated; they necessitated frequent conferences between the two men, and the interests of the firm forbade Waythorn's suggesting that his client should transfer his business to another office.

Varick appeared well in the transaction. In moments of relaxation his coarse streak appeared, and Waythorn dreaded his geniality; but in the office he was concise and clear-headed, with a flattering deference to Waythorn's judgment. Their business relations being so affably established, it would have been absurd for the two men to ignore each other in society. The first time they met in a drawing room, Varick took up their intercourse in the same easy key, and his hostess' grateful glance obliged Waythorn to respond to it. After that they ran across each other frequently, and one evening at a ball Waythorn, wandering through the remoter rooms, came upon Varick seated beside his wife. She colored a little, and faltered in what she was saying; but Varick nodded to Waythorn without rising, and the latter strolled on.

In the carriage, on the way home, he broke out nervously: "I didn't know you spoke to Varick."

Her voice trembled a little. "It's the first time—he happened to be standing near me; I didn't know what to do. It's so awkward, meeting everywhere—and he said you had been very kind about some business."

"That's different," said Waythorn.

She paused a moment. "I'll do just as you wish," she returned pliantly. "I thought it would be less awkward to speak to him when we meet."

Her pliancy was beginning to sicken him. Had she really no will of her own—no theory about her relation to these men? She had accepted Haskett—did she mean to accept Varick? It was "less awkward," as she had said, and her instinct was to evade difficulties or to circumvent them. With sudden vividness Waythorn saw how the instinct had developed. She was "as easy as an old shoe"—a shoe that too many feet had worn. Her elasticity was the result of tension in too many different directions. Alice Haskett—Alice Varick—Alice Waythorn—she had been each in turn, and had left hanging to each name a little of her privacy, a little of her personality, a little of the inmost self where the unknown god abides.

"Yes—it's better to speak to Varick," said Waythorn wearily.

* V *

The winter wore on, and society took advantage of the Waythorns' acceptance of Varick. Harassed hostesses were grateful to them for bridging over a social difficulty, and Mrs. Waythorn was held up as a miracle of good taste. Some experimental spirits could not resist the diversion of throwing Varick and his former wife together, and there were those who thought he found a zest in the propinquity. But Mrs. Waythorn's conduct remained irreproachable. She neither avoided Varick nor sought him out. Even Waythorn could not but admit that she had discovered the solution of the newest social problem.

He had married her without giving much thought to that problem. He had fancied that a woman can shed her past like a man. But now he saw that Alice was bound to hers both by the circumstances which forced her into continued relation with it, and by the traces it had left on her nature. With grim irony Waythorn compared himself to a member of a syndicate. He held so many shares in his wife's personality and his predecessors were his partners in the business. If there had been any element of passion in the transaction he would have felt less deteriorated by it. The fact that Alice took her change of husbands like a change of weather reduced the situation to mediocrity. He could have forgiven her for blunders, for excesses; for resisting Haskett, for yielding to Varick; for anything but her acquiescence and her tact. She reminded him of a juggler tossing knives; but the knives were blunt and she knew they would never cut her.

And then, gradually, habit formed a protecting surface for his sensibilities. If he paid for each day's comfort with the small change of his illusions, he grew daily to value the comfort more and set less store upon the coin. He had drifted into a dulling propinquity with Haskett and Varick and he took refuge in the cheap revenge of satirizing the situation. He even began to reckon up the advantages which accrued from it, to ask himself if it were not better to own a third of a wife who knew how to make a man happy than a whole one who had lacked opportunity to acquire the art. For it *was* an art, and made up, like all others, of concessions, eliminations and embellishments; of lights judiciously thrown and shadows skillfully softened. His wife knew exactly how to manage the lights, and he knew exactly to what training she owed her skill. He even tried to trace the source of his obligations, to discriminate between the influences which had combined to produce his domestic happiness: he perceived that Haskett's commonness had made Alice worship good breeding, while Varick's liberal construction of the marriage bond had taught her to value the conjugal virtues; so that he was directly indebted to his predecessors for the devotion which made his life easy if not inspiring.

From this phase he passed into that of complete acceptance. He ceased to satirize himself because time dulled the irony of the situation and the joke lost its humor with its sting. Even the sight of Haskett's hat on the hall table had ceased to touch the springs of epigram. The hat was often seen there now, for it had been decided that it was better for Lily's father to visit her than for the little girl to go to his boardinghouse. Waythorn, having acquiesced in this arrangement, had been surprised to find how little difference it made. Haskett was never obtrusive, and the few visitors who met him on the stairs were unaware of his identity. Waythorn did not know how often he saw Alice, but with himself Haskett was seldom in contact.

One afternoon, however, he learned on entering that Lily's father was waiting to see him. In the library he found Haskett occupying a chair in his usual provisional way. Waythorn always felt grateful to him for not leaning back.

"I hope you'll excuse me, Mr. Waythorn," he said rising. "I wanted to see Mrs. Waythorn about Lily, and your man asked me to wait here till she came in."

"Of course," said Waythorn, remembering that a sudden leak had that morning given over the drawing room to the plumbers.

He opened his cigar case and held it out to his visitor, and Haskett's acceptance seemed to mark a fresh stage in their intercourse. The spring evening was chilly, and Waythorn invited his guest to draw up his chair to the fire. He meant to find an excuse to leave Haskett in a moment;

but he was tired and cold, and after all the little man no longer jarred on him.

The two were enclosed in the intimacy of their blended cigar smoke when the door opened and Varick walked into the room. Waythorn rose abruptly. It was the first time that Varick had come to the house, and the surprise of seeing him, combined with the singular inopportuneness of his arrival, gave a new edge to Waythorn's blunted sensibilities. He stared at his visitor without speaking.

Varick seemed too preoccupied to notice his host's embarrassment.

"My dear fellow," he exclaimed in his most expansive tone, "I must apologize for tumbling in on you in this way, but I was too late to catch you downtown, and so I thought—"

He stopped short, catching sight of Haskett, and his sanguine color deepened to a flush which spread vividly under his scant blond hair. But in a moment he recovered himself and nodded slightly. Haskett returned the bow in silence, and Waythorn was still groping for speech when the footman came in carrying a tea table.

The intrusion offered a welcome vent to Waythorn's nerves. "What the deuce are you bringing this here for?" he said sharply.

"I beg your pardon, sir, but the plumbers are still in the drawing room, and Mrs. Waythorn said she would have tea in the library." The footman's perfectly respectful tone implied a reflection on Waythorn's reasonableness.

"Oh, very well," said the latter resignedly, and the footman proceeded to open the folding tea table and set out its complicated appointments. While this interminable process continued the three men stood motionless, watching it with a fascinated stare, till Waythorn, to break the silence, said to Varick, "Won't you have a cigar?"

He held out the case he had just tendered to Haskett, and Varick helped himself with a smile. Waythorn looked about for a match, and finding none, proffered a light from his own cigar. Haskett, in the background, held his ground mildly, examining his cigar tip now and then, and stepping forward at the right moment to knock its ashes into the fire.

The footman at last withdrew, and Varick immediately began: "If I could just say half a word to you about this business—"

"Certainly," stammered Waythorn; "in the dining room—"

But as he placed his hand on the door it opened from without, and his wife appeared on the threshold.

She came in fresh and smiling, in her street dress and hat, shedding a fragrance from the boa which she loosened in advancing.

"Shall we have tea in here, dear?" she began; and then she caught sight of Varick. Her smile deepened, veiling a slight tremor of surprise.

"Why, how do you do?" she said with a distinct note of pleasure.

As she shook hands with Varick she saw Haskett standing behind him. Her smile faded for a moment, but she recalled it quickly, with a scarcely perceptible side glance at Waythorn.

"How do you do, Mr. Haskett?" she said, and shook hands with him a shade less cordially.

The three men stood awkwardly before her, till Varick, always the most self-possessed, dashed into an explanatory phrase.

"We—I had to see Waythorn a moment on business," he stammered, brick-red from chin to nape.

Haskett stepped forward with his air of mild obstinacy. "I am sorry to intrude; but you appointed five o'clock—" he directed his resigned glance to the timepiece on the mantel.

She swept aside their embarrassment with a charming gesture of hospitality.

"I'm so sorry—I'm always late; but the afternoon was so lovely." She stood drawing off her gloves, propitiatory and graceful, diffusing about her a sense of ease and familiarity in which the situation lost its grotesqueness. "But before talking business," she added brightly, "I'm sure everyone wants a cup of tea."

She dropped into her low chair by the tea table, and the two visitors, as if drawn by her smile, advanced to receive the cups she held out.

She glanced about for Waythorn, and he took the third cup with a laugh.

THE DILETTANTE

IT WAS on an impulse hardly needing the arguments he found himself advancing in its favor, that Thursdale, on his way to the club, turned as usual into Mrs. Vervain's street.

The "as usual" was his own qualification of the act; a convenient way of bridging the interval—in days and other sequences—that lay between this visit and the last. It was characteristic of him that he instinctively excluded his call two days earlier, with Ruth Gaynor, from the list of his visits to Mrs. Vervain: the special conditions attending it had made it no more like a visit to Mrs. Vervain than an engraved dinner invitation is like a personal letter. Yet it was to talk over his call with Miss Gaynor that he was now returning to the scene of that episode; and it was because Mrs. Vervain could be trusted to handle the talking over as skillfully as the interview itself that, at her corner, he had felt the dilettante's irresistible craving to take a last look at a work of art that was passing out of his possession.

On the whole, he knew no one better fitted to deal with the unexpected than Mrs. Vervain. She excelled in the rare art of taking things for granted, and Thursdale felt a pardonable pride in the thought that she owed her excellence to his training. Early in his career Thursdale had made the mistake, at the outset of his acquaintance with a lady, of telling her that he loved her, and exacting the same avowal in return. The latter part of that episode had been like the long walk back from a picnic, when one has to carry all the crockery one has finished using: it was the last time Thursdale ever allowed himself to be encumbered with the debris of a feast. He thus incidentally learned that the privilege of loving her is one of the least favors that a charming woman can accord; and in seeking to avoid the pitfalls of sentiment he had developed a science of evasion in which the woman of the moment became a mere implement of the game. He owed a great deal of delicate enjoyment to the cultivation of this art. The perils from which it had been his refuge became naïvely harmless: was it possible that he who now took his easy way along the levels had once preferred to gasp on the raw heights of emotion? Youth is a high-colored season; but he had the satisfacion of feeling that he had entered earlier than most into that chiaroscuro of sensation where every halftone has its value.

As a promoter of this pleasure no one he had known was comparable to Mrs. Vervain. He had taught a good many women not to betray their feelings, but he had never before had such fine material to work with. She had been surprisingly crude when he first knew her; capable of making the most awkward inferences, of plunging through thin ice, of recklessly undressing her emotions; but she had acquired, under the discipline of his reticences and evasions, a skill almost equal to his own, and perhaps more remarkable in that it involved keeping time with any tune he played and reading at sight some uncommonly difficult passages.

It had taken Thursdale seven years to form this fine talent; but the result justified the effort. At the crucial moment she had been perfect: her way of greeting Miss Gaynor had made him regret that he had announced his engagement by letter. It was an evasion that confessed a difficulty; a deviation implying an obstacle, where, by common consent, it was agreed to see none; it betrayed, in short, a lack of confidence in the completeness of his method. It had been his pride never to put himself in a position which had to be quitted, as it were, by the back door; but here, as he perceived, the main portals would have opened for him of their own accord. All this, and much more, he read in the finished naturalness with which Mrs. Vervain had met Miss Gaynor. He had never seen a better piece of work: there was no overeagerness, no suspicious warmth, above all (and this gave her art the grace of a natural quality) there were none of those damnable implications whereby a woman, in welcoming her friend's betrothed, may keep him on pins and needles while she laps the lady in complacency. So masterly a performance, indeed, hardly needed the offset of Miss Gaynor's doorstep words—"To be so kind to me, how she must have liked you!"—though he caught himself wishing it lay within the bounds of fitness to transmit them, as a final tribute, to the one woman he knew who was unfailingly certain to enjoy a good thing. It was perhaps the one drawback to his new situation that it might develop good things which it would be impossible to hand on to Margaret Vervain.

The fact that he had made the mistake of underrating his friend's powers, the consciousness that his writing must have betrayed his distrust of her efficiency, seemed an added reason for turning down her street instead of going on to the club. He would show her that he knew how to value her; he would ask her to achieve with him a feat infinitely rarer and

more delicate than the one he had appeared to avoid. Incidentally, he
would also dispose of the interval of time before dinner: ever since he had
seen Miss Gaynor off, an hour earlier, on her return journey to Buffalo, he
had been wondering how he should put in the rest of the afternoon. It was
absurd, how he missed the girl. . . . Yes, that was it: the desire to talk
about her was, after all, at the bottom of his impulse to call on Mrs.
Vervain! It was absurd, if you like—but it was delightfully rejuvenating.
He could recall the time when he had been afraid of being obvious: now he
felt that this return to the primitive emotions might be as restorative as a
holiday in the Canadian woods. And it was precisely by the girl's candor,
her directness, her lack of complications, that he was taken. The sense that
she might say something rash at any moment was positively exhilarating: if
she had thrown her arms about him at the station he would not have given
a thought to his crumpled dignity. It surprised Thursdale to find what
freshness of heart he brought to the adventure; and though his sense of
irony prevented his ascribing his intactness to any conscious purpose, he
could but rejoice in the fact that his sentimental economies had left him
such a large surplus to draw upon.

Mrs. Vervain was at home—as usual. When one visits the cemetery one
expects to find the angel on the tombstone, and it struck Thursdale as
another proof of his friend's good taste that she had been in no undue haste
to change her habits. The whole house appeared to count on his coming;
the footman took his hat and overcoat as naturally as though there had been
no lapse in his visits; and the drawing room at once enveloped him in that
atmosphere of tacit intelligence which Mrs. Vervain imparted to her very
furniture.

It was a surprise that, in this general harmony of circumstances, Mrs.
Vervain should herself sound the first false note.

"You?" she exclaimed; and the book she held slipped from her hand.

It was crude, certainly; unless it were a touch of the finest art. The
difficulty of classifying it disturbed Thursdale's balance.

"Why not?" he said, restoring the book. "Isn't it my hour?" And as she
made no answer, he added gently, "Unless it's someone else's?"

She laid the book aside and sank back into her chair. "Mine, merely,"
she said.

"I hope that doesn't mean that you're unwilling to share it?"

"With you? By no means. You're welcome to my last crust."

He looked at her reproachfully. "Do you call this the last?"

She smiled as he dropped into the seat across the hearth. "It's a way of
giving it more flavor!"

He returned the smile. "A visit to you doesn't need such condiments."

She took this with just the right measure of retrospective amusement.

"Ah, but I want to put into this one a very special taste," she confessed.

Her smile was so confident, so reassuring, that it lulled him into the imprudence of saying: "Why should you want it to be different from what was always so perfectly right?"

She hesitated. "Doesn't the fact that it's the last constitute a difference?"

"The last—my last visit to you?"

"Oh, metaphorically, I mean—there's a break in the continuity."

Decidedly, she was pressing too hard: unlearning his arts already!

"I don't recognize it," he said. "Unless you make me—" he added, with a note that slightly stirred her attitude of languid attention.

She turned to him with grave eyes. "You recognize no difference whatever?"

"None—except an added link in the chain."

"An added link?"

"In having one more thing to like you for—your letting Miss Gaynor see why I had already so many." He flattered himself that this turn had taken the least hint of fatuity from the phrase.

Mrs. Vervain sank into her former easy pose. "Was it that you came for?" she asked, almost gaily.

"If it is necessary to have a reason—that was one."

"To talk to me about Miss Gaynor?"

"To tell you how she talks about you."

"That will be very interesting—especially if you have seen her since her second visit to me."

"Her second visit?" Thursdale pushed his chair back with a start and moved to another. "She came to see you again?"

"This morning, yes—by appointment."

He continued to look at her blankly. "You sent for her?"

"I didn't have to—she wrote and asked me last night. But no doubt you have seen her since."

Thursdale sat silent. He was trying to separate his words from his thoughts, but they still clung together inextricably. "I saw her off just now at the station."

"And she didn't tell you that she had been here again?"

"There was hardly time, I suppose—there were people about—" he floundered.

"Ah, she'll write, then."

He regained his composure. "Of course she'll write: very often, I hope. You know I'm absurdly in love," he cried audaciously.

She tilted her head back, looking up at him as he leaned against the chimney piece. He had leaned there so often that the attitude touched a pulse which set up a throbbing in her throat. "Oh, my poor Thursdale!" she murmured.

"I suppose it's rather ridiculous," he owned; and as she remained silent, he added, with a sudden break—"Or have you another reason for pitying me?"

Her answer was another question. "Have you been back to your rooms since you left her?"

"Since I left her at the station? I came straight here."

"Ah, yes—you *could:* there was no reason—" Her words passed into a silent musing.

Thursdale moved nervously nearer. "You said you had something to tell me?"

"Perhaps I had better let her do so. There may be a letter at your rooms."

"A letter? What do you mean? A letter from *her?* What has happened?"

His paleness shook her, and she raised a hand of reassurance. "Nothing has happened—perhaps that is just the worst of it. You always *hated,* you know," she added incoherently, "to have things happen: you never would let them."

"And now—"

"Well, that was what she came here for: I supposed you had guessed. To know if anything had happened."

"Had happened?" He gazed at her slowly. "Between you and me?" he said with a rush of light.

The words were so much cruder than any that had ever passed between them, that the color rose to her face; but she held his startled gaze.

"You know girls are not quite as unsophisticated as they used to be. Are you surprised that such an idea should occur to her?"

His own color answered hers: it was the only reply that came to him.

Mrs. Vervain went on smoothly: "I supposed it might have struck you that there were times when we presented that appearance."

He made an impatient gesture. "A man's past is his own!"

"Perhaps—it certainly never belongs to the woman who has shared it. But one learns such truths only by experience; and Miss Gaynor is naturally inexperienced."

"Of course—but—supposing her act a natural one—" he floundered lamentably among his innuendoes "—I still don't see—how there was anything—"

"Anything to take hold of? There wasn't—"

"Well, then—?" escaped him, in undisguised satisfaction; but as she did not complete the sentence he went on with a faltering laugh: "She can hardly object to the existence of a mere friendship between us!"

"But she does," said Mrs. Vervain.

Thursdale stood perplexed. He had seen, on the previous day, no trace of jealousy or resentment in his betrothed: he could still hear the candid ring of the girl's praise of Mrs. Vervain. If she were such an abyss of insincerity as to dissemble distrust under such frankness, she must at least be more subtle than to bring her doubts to her rival for solution. The situation seemed one through which one could no longer move in a penumbra, and he let in a burst of light with the direct query: "Won't you explain what you mean?"

Mrs. Vervain sat silent, not provokingly, as though to prolong his distress, but as if, in the attenuated phraseology he had taught her, it was difficult to find words robust enough to meet his challenge. It was the first time he had ever asked her to explain anything; and she had lived so long in dread of offering elucidations which were not wanted, that she seemed unable to produce one on the spot.

At last she said slowly: "She came to find out if you were really free."

Thursdale colored again. "Free?" he stammered, with a sense of physical disgust at contact with such crassness.

"Yes—if I had quite done with you." She smiled in recovered security. "It seems she likes clear outlines; she has a passion for definitions."

"Yes—well?" he said, wincing at the echo of his own subtlety.

"Well—and when I told her that you had never belonged to me, she wanted me to define *my* status—to know exactly where I had stood all along."

Thursdale sat gazing at her intently; his hand was not yet on the clue. "And even when you had told her that—"

"Even when I had told her that I had had no status—that I had never stood anywhere, in any sense she meant," said Mrs. Vervain, slowly, "even then she wasn't satisfied, it seems."

He uttered an uneasy exclamation. "She didn't believe you, you mean?"

"I mean that she *did* believe me: too thoroughly."

"Well, then—in God's name, what did she want?"

"Something more—those were the words she used."

"Something more? Between—between you and me? Is it a conundrum?" He laughed awkwardly.

"Girls are not what they were in my day; they are no longer forbidden to contemplate the relation of the sexes."

"So it seems!" he commented. "But since, in this case, there wasn't any—" he broke off, catching the dawn of a revelation in her gaze.

"That's just it. The unpardonable offence has been—in our not offending."

He flung himself down despairingly. "I give up! What did you tell her?" he burst out with sudden crudeness.

"The exact truth. If I had only known," she broke off with a beseeching tenderness, "won't you believe that I would still have lied for you?"

"Lied for me? Why on earth should you have lied for either of us?"

"To save you—to hide you from her to the last! As I've hidden you from myself all these years!" She stood up with a sudden tragic import in her movement. "You believe me capable of that, don't you? If I had only guessed—but I have never known a girl like her; she had the truth out of me with a spring."

"The truth that you and I had never—"

"Had never—never in all these years! Oh, she knew why—she measured us both in a flash. She didn't suspect me of having haggled with you—her words pelted me like hail. 'He just took what he wanted—sifted and sorted you to suit his taste. Burnt out the gold and left a heap of cinders. And you let him—you let yourself be cut in bits'—she mixed her metaphors a little—'be cut in bits, and used or discarded, while all the while every drop of blood in you belonged to him! But he's Shylock—he's Shylock—and you have bled to death of the pound of flesh he has cut off you.' But she despises me the most, you know—far, far the most—" Mrs. Vervain ended.

The words fell strangely on the scented stillness of the room: they seemed out of harmony with its setting of afternoon intimacy, the kind of intimacy on which, at any moment, a visitor might intrude without perceptibly lowering the atmosphere. It was as though a grand opera singer had strained the acoustics of a private music room.

Thursdale stood up, facing his hostess. Half the room was between them, but they seemed to stare close at each other now that the veils of reticence and ambiguity had fallen.

His first words were characteristic: "She *does* despise me, then?" he exclaimed.

"She thinks the pound of flesh you took was a little too near the heart."

He was excessively pale. "Please tell me exactly what she said of me."

"She did not speak much of you: she is proud. But I gather that while she understands love or indifference, her eyes have never been opened to the many intermediate shades of feeling. At any rate, she expressed an unwillingness to be taken with reservations—she thinks you would have loved her better if you had loved someone else first. The point of view is original—she insists on a man with a past!"

"Oh, a past—if she's serious—I could rake up a past!" he said with a laugh.

"So I suggested: but she has her eyes on this particular portion of it. She insists on making it a test case. She wanted to know what you had done to me; and before I could guess her drift I blundered into telling her."

Thursdale drew a difficult breath. "I never supposed—your revenge is complete," he said slowly.

He heard a little gasp in her throat. "My revenge? When I sent for you to warn you—to save you from being surprised as *I* was surprised?"

"You're very good—but it's rather late to talk of saving me." He held out his hand in the mechanical gesture of leave-taking.

"How you must care!—for I never saw you so dull," was her answer. "Don't you see that it's not too late for me to help you?" And as he continued to stare, she brought out sublimely: "Take the rest—in imagination! Let it at least be of that much use to you. Tell her I lied to her—she's too ready to believe it! And so, after all, in a sense, I shan't have been wasted."

His stare hung on her, widening to a kind of wonder. She gave the look back brightly, unblushingly, as though the expedient were too simple to need oblique approaches. It was extraordinary how a few words had swept them from an atmosphere of the most complex dissimulations to this contact of naked souls.

It was not in Thursdale to expand with the pressure of fate; but something in him cracked with it, and the rift let in new light. He went up to his friend and took her hand.

"You would do it—you would do it!"

She looked at him, smiling, but her hand shook.

"Good-bye," he said, kissing it.

"Good-bye? You are going—?"

"To get my letter."

"Your letter? The letter won't matter, if you will only do what I ask."

He returned her gaze. "I might, I suppose, without being out of character. Only, don't you see that if your plan helped me it could only harm her?"

"Harm *her?*"

"To sacrifice you wouldn't make me different. I shall go on being what I have always been—sifting and sorting, as she calls it. Do you want my punishment to fall on *her?*"

She looked at him long and deeply. "Ah, if I had to choose between you—!"

"You would let her take her chance? But I can't, you see. I must take my punishment alone."

She drew her hand away, sighing. "Oh, there will be no punishment for either of you."

"For either of us? There will be the reading of her letter for me."

She shook her head with a slight laugh. "There will be no letter."

Thursdale faced about from the threshold with fresh life in his look. "No letter? You don't mean—"

"I mean that she's been with you since I saw her—she's seen you and heard your voice. If there *is* a letter, she has recalled it—from the first station, by telegraph."

He turned back to the door, forcing an answer to her smile. "But in the meanwhile I shall have read it," he said.

The door closed on him, and she hid her eyes from the dreadful emptiness of the room.

The Lady's Maid's Bell

IT WAS the autumn after I had the typhoid. I'd been three months in hospital, and when I came out I looked so weak and tottery that the two or three ladies I applied to were afraid to engage me. Most of my money was gone, and after I'd boarded for two months, hanging about the employment agencies, and answering any advertisement that looked any way respectable, I pretty nearly lost heart, for fretting hadn't made me fatter, and I didn't see why my luck should ever turn. It did though—or I thought so at the time. A Mrs. Railton, a friend of the lady that first brought me out to the States, met me one day and stopped to speak to me: she was one that had always a friendly way with her. She asked me what ailed me to look so white, and when I told her, "Why, Hartley," says she, "I believe I've got the very place for you. Come in tomorrow and we'll talk about it."

The next day, when I called, she told me the lady she'd in mind was a niece of hers, a Mrs. Brympton, a youngish lady, but something of an invalid, who lived all the year round at her country place on the Hudson, owing to not being able to stand the fatigue of town life.

"Now, Hartley," Mrs. Railton said, in that cheery way that always made me feel things must be going to take a turn for the better—"now understand me; it's not a cheerful place I'm sending you to. The house is big and gloomy; my niece is nervous, vaporish; her husband—well, he's generally away; and the two children are dead. A year ago I would as soon have thought of shutting a rosy active girl like you into a vault; but you're not particularly brisk yourself just now, are you? and a quiet place, with country air and wholesome food and early hours, ought to be the very thing for you. Don't mistake me," she added, for I suppose I looked a trifle downcast; "you may find it dull but you won't be unhappy. My niece is an angel. Her former maid, who died last spring, had been with her twenty years and worshiped the ground she walked on. She's a kind mistress to all, and where the mistress is kind, as you know, the servants are generally good-humored, so you'll probably get on well enough with the rest of the household. And you're the very woman I want for my niece: quiet, well-mannered, and educated above your station. You read aloud well, I think? That's a good thing; my niece likes to be read to. She wants a maid that can be something of a companion: her last was, and I can't say how she misses her. It's a lonely life. . . . Well, have you decided?"

"Why, ma'am," I said, "I'm not afraid of solitude."

"Well, then, go; my niece will take you on my recommendation. I'll telegraph her at once and you can take the afternoon train. She has no one to wait on her at present, and I don't want you to lose any time."

I was ready enough to start, yet something in me hung back; and to gain time I asked, "And the gentleman, ma'am?"

"The gentleman's almost always away, I tell you," said Mrs. Railton, quicklike—"and when he's there," says she suddenly, "you've only to keep out of his way."

I took the afternoon train and got to the station at about four o'clock. A groom in a dogcart was waiting, and we drove off at a smart pace. It was a dull October day, with rain hanging close overhead, and by the time we turned into Brympton Place woods the daylight was almost gone. The drive wound through the woods for a mile or two, and came out on a gravel court shut in with thickets of tall black-looking shrubs. There were no lights in the windows, and the house *did* look a bit gloomy.

I had asked no questions of the groom, for I never was one to get my notion of new masters from their other servants: I prefer to wait and see for myself. But I could tell by the look of everything that I had got into the right kind of house, and that things were done handsomely. A pleasant-faced cook met me at the back door and called the housemaid to show me up to my room. "You'll see madam later," she said. "Mrs. Brympton has a visitor."

I hadn't fancied Mrs. Brympton was a lady to have many visitors, and somehow the words cheered me. I followed the housemaid upstairs, and saw, through a door on the upper landing, that the main part of the house seemed well furnished, with dark paneling and a number of old portraits. Another flight of stairs led up up to the servants' wing. It was almost dark now, and the housemaid excused herself for not having brought a light. "But there's matches in your room," she said, "and if you go careful you'll be all right. Mind the step at the end of the passage. Your room is just beyond."

I looked ahead as she spoke, and halfway down the passage I saw a woman standing. She drew back into a doorway as we passed and the housemaid didn't appear to notice her. She was a thin woman with a white face, and a dark gown and apron. I took her for the housekeeper and thought it odd that she didn't speak, but just gave me a long look as she went by. My room opened into a square hall at the end of the passage. Facing my door was another which stood open: the housemaid exclaimed when she saw it:

"There—Mrs. Blinder's left that door open again!" said she, closing it.

"Is Mrs. Blinder the housekeeper?"

"There's no housekeeper: Mrs. Blinder's the cook."

"And is that her room?"

"Laws, no," said the housemaid, crosslike. "That's nobody's room. It's empty, I mean, and the door hadn't ought to be open. Mrs. Brympton wants it kept locked."

She opened my door and led me into a neat room, nicely furnished, with a picture or two on the walls; and having lit a candle she took leave, telling me that the servants' hall tea was at six, and that Mrs. Brympton would see me afterward.

I found them a pleasant-spoken set in the servants' hall, and by what they let fall I gathered that, as Mrs. Railton had said, Mrs. Brympton was the kindest of ladies; but I didn't take much notice of their talk, for I was watching to see the pale woman in the dark gown come in. She didn't show herself, however, and I wondered if she ate apart; but if she wasn't the housekeeper, why should she? Suddenly it struck me that she might be a trained nurse, and in that case her meals would of course be served in her room. If Mrs. Brympton was an invalid it was likely enough she had a nurse. The idea annoyed me, I own, for they're not always the easiest to get on with, and if I'd known I shouldn't have taken the place. But there I was and there was no use pulling a long face over it; and not being one to ask questions I waited to see what would turn up.

When tea was over the housemaid said to the footman: "Has Mr. Ranford gone?" and when he said yes, she told me to come up with her to Mrs. Brympton.

Mrs. Brympton was lying down in her bedroom. Her lounge stood near the fire and beside it was a shaded lamp. She was a delicate-looking lady, but when she smiled I felt there was nothing I wouldn't do for her. She spoke very pleasantly, in a low voice, asking me my name and age and so on, and if I had everything I wanted, and if I wasn't afraid of feeling lonely in the country.

"Not with you I wouldn't be, madam," I said, and the words surprised me when I'd spoken them, for I'm not an impulsive person; but it was just as if I'd thought aloud.

She seemed pleased at that, and said she hoped I'd continue in the same mind; then she gave me a few directions about her toilet, and said Agnes the housemaid would show me next morning where things were kept.

"I am tired tonight, and shall dine upstairs," she said. "Agnes will bring me my tray, so that you may have time to unpack and settle yourself; and later you may come and undress me."

"Very well, ma'am," I said. "You'll ring, I suppose?"

I thought she looked odd.

"No—Agnes will fetch you," says she quickly, and took up her book again.

Well—that was certainly strange: a lady's maid having to be fetched by the housemaid whenever her lady wanted her! I wondered if there were no bells in the house; but the next day I satisfied myself that there was one in every room, and a special one ringing from my mistress's room to mine; and after that it did strike me as queer that, whenever Mrs. Brympton wanted anything, she rang for Agnes, who had to walk the whole length of the servants' wing to call me.

But that wasn't the only queer thing in the house. The very next day I found out that Mrs. Brympton had no nurse; and then I asked Agnes about the woman I had seen in the passage the afternoon before. Agnes said she had seen no one, and I saw that she thought I was dreaming. To be sure, it was dusk when we went down the passage, and she had excused herself for not bringing a light; but I had seen the woman plain enough to know her again if we should meet. I decided that she must have been a friend of the cook's, or of one of the other women servants; perhaps she had come down from town for a night's visit, and the servants wanted it kept secret. Some ladies are very stiff about having their servants' friends in the house overnight. At any rate, I made up my mind to ask no more questions.

In a day or two another odd thing happened. I was chatting one afternoon with Mrs. Blinder, who was a friendly-disposed woman, and had been longer in the house than the other servants, and she asked me if I was quite comfortable and had everything I needed. I said I had no fault to find with my place or with my mistress, but I thought it odd that in so large a house there was no sewing room for the lady's maid.

"Why," says she, "there *is* one: the room you're in is the old sewing room."

"Oh," said I; "and where did the other lady's maid sleep?"

At that she grew confused, and said hurriedly that the servants' rooms had all been changed about last year, and she didn't rightly remember.

That struck me as peculiar, but I went on as if I hadn't noticed: "Well, there's a vacant room opposite mine, and I mean to ask Mrs. Brympton if I mayn't use that as a sewing room."

To my astonishment, Mrs. Blinder went white, and gave my hand a kind of squeeze. "Don't do that, my dear," said she, trembling-like. "To tell you the truth, that was Emma Saxon's room, and my mistress has kept it closed ever since her death."

"And who was Emma Saxon?"

"Mrs. Brympton's former maid."

"The one that was with her so many years?" said I, remembering what Mrs. Railton had told me.

Mrs. Blinder nodded.

"What sort of woman was she?"

"No better walked the earth," said Mrs. Blinder. "My mistress loved her like a sister."

"But I mean—what did she look like?"

Mrs. Blinder got up and gave me a kind of angry stare. "I'm no great hand at describing," she said; "and I believe my pastry's rising." And she walked off into the kitchen and shut the door after her.

* II *

I had been near a week at Brympton before I saw my master. Word came that he was arriving one afternoon, and a change passed over the whole household. It was plain that nobody loved him below stairs. Mrs. Blinder took uncommon care with the dinner that night, but she snapped at the kitchenmaid in a way quite unusual with her; and Mr. Wace, the butler, a serious, slow-spoken man, went about his duties as if he'd been getting ready for a funeral. He was a great Bible reader, Mr. Wace was, and had a beautiful assortment of texts at his command; but that day he used such dreadful language, that I was about to leave the table, when he assured me it was all out of Isaiah; and I noticed that whenever the master came Mr. Wace took to the prophets.

About seven, Agnes called me to my mistress' room; and there I found Mr. Brympton. He was standing on the hearth; a big fair bull-necked man, with a red face and little bad-tempered blue eyes: the kind of man a young simpleton might have thought handsome, and would have been like to pay dear for thinking it.

He swung about when I came in, and looked me over in a trice. I knew what the look meant, from having experienced it once or twice in my former places. Then he turned his back on me, and went on talking to his wife; and I knew what *that* meant, too. I was not the kind of morsel he was after. The typhoid had served me well enough in one way: it kept that kind of gentleman at arm's length.

"This is my new maid, Hartley," says Mrs. Brympton in her kind voice; and he nodded and went on with what he was saying.

In a minute or two he went off, and left my mistress to dress for dinner, and I noticed as I waited on her that she was white, and chill to the touch.

Mr. Brympton took himself off the next morning, and the whole house drew a long breath when he drove away. As for my mistress, she put on her hat and furs (for it was a fine winter morning) and went out for a walk in the gardens, coming back quite fresh and rosy, so that for a minute, before her color faded, I could guess what a pretty young lady she must have been, and not so long ago, either.

She had met Mr. Ranford in the grounds, and the two came back together, I remember, smiling and talking as they walked along the terrace under my window. That was the first time I saw Mr. Ranford, though I had often heard his name mentioned in the hall. He was a neighbor, it appeared, living a mile or two beyond Brympton, at the end of the village; and as he was in the habit of spending his winters in the country he was almost the only company my mistress had at that season. He was a slight tall gentleman of about thirty, and I thought him rather melancholy looking till I saw his smile, which had a kind of surprise in it, like the first warm day in spring. He was a great reader, I heard, like my mistress, and the two were forever borrowing books of one another, and sometimes (Mr. Wace told me) he would read aloud to Mrs. Brympton by the hour, in the big dark library where she sat in the winter afternoons. The servants all liked him, and perhaps that's more of a compliment than the masters suspect. He had a friendly word for every one of us, and we were all glad to think that Mrs. Brympton had a pleasant companionable gentleman like that to keep her company when the master was away. Mr. Ranford seemed on excellent terms with Mr. Brympton too; though I couldn't but wonder that two gentlemen so unlike each other should be so friendly. But then I knew how the real quality can keep their feelings to themselves.

As for Mr. Brympton, he came and went, never staying more than a day or two, cursing the dullness and the solitude, grumbling at everything, and (as I soon found out) drinking a deal more than was good for him. After Mrs. Brympton left the table he would sit half the night over the old Brympton port and madeira, and once, as I was leaving my mistress's room rather later than usual, I met him coming up the stairs in such a state that I turned sick to think of what some ladies have to endure and hold their tongues about.

The servants said very little about their master; but from what they let drop I could see it had been an unhappy match from the beginning. Mr. Brympton was coarse, loud and pleasure-loving; my mistress quiet, retiring, and perhaps a trifle cold. Not that she was not always pleasant-spoken to him: I thought her wonderfully forbearing; but to a gentleman as free as Mr. Brympton I dare say she seemed a little offish.

Well, things went on quietly for several weeks. My mistress was kind, my duties were light, and I got on well with the other servants. In short, I had nothing to complain of; yet there was always a weight on me. I can't say why it was so, but I know it was not the loneliness that I felt. I soon got used to that; and being still languid from the fever, I was thankful for the quiet and the good country air. Nevertheless, I was never quite easy in my mind. My mistress, knowing I had been ill, insisted that I should take my walk regularly, and often invented errands for me: a yard of ribbon to be fetched from the village, a letter posted, or a book returned to Mr. Ranford. As soon as I was out of doors my spirits rose, and I looked forward to my walks through the bare moist-smelling woods; but the moment I caught sight of the house again my heart dropped down like a stone in a well. It was not a gloomy house exactly, yet I never entered it but a feeling of gloom came over me.

Mrs. Brympton seldom went out in winter; only on the finest days did she walk an hour at noon on the south terrace. Excepting Mr. Ranford, we had no visitors but the doctor, who drove over from town about once a week. He sent for me once or twice to give me some trifling direction about my mistress, and though he never told me what her illness was, I thought, from a waxy look she had now and then of a morning, that it might be the heart that ailed her. The season was soft and unwholesome, and in January we had a long spell of rain. That was a sore trial to me, I own, for I couldn't go out, and sitting over my sewing all day, listening to the drip, drip of the eaves, I grew so nervous that the least sound made me jump. Somehow, the thought of that locked room across the passage began to weigh on me. Once or twice, in the long rainy nights, I fancied I heard noises there; but that was nonsense, of course, and the daylight drove such notions out of my head. Well, one morning Mrs. Brympton gave me quite a start of pleasure by telling me she wished me to go to town for some shopping. I hadn't known till then how low my spirits had fallen. I set off in high glee, and my first sight of the crowded streets and the cheerful-looking shops quite took me out of myself. Toward afternoon, however, the noise and confusion began to tire me, and I was actually looking forward to the quiet of Brympton, and thinking how I should enjoy the drive home through the dark woods, when I ran across an old acquaintance, a maid I had once been in service with. We had lost sight of each other for a number of years, and I had to stop and tell her what had happened to me in the interval. When I mentioned where I was living she rolled up her eyes and pulled a long face.

"What! The Mrs. Brympton that lives all the year at her place on the Hudson? My dear, you won't stay there three months."

"Oh, but I don't mind the country," says I, offended somehow at her tone. "Since the fever I'm glad to be quiet."

She shook her head. "It's not the country I'm thinking of. All I know is she's had four maids in the last six months, and the last one, who was a friend of mine, told me nobody could stay in the house."

"Did she say why?" I asked.

"No—she wouldn't give me her reason. But she says to me, 'Mrs. Ansey,' she says, 'if ever a young woman as you know of thinks of going there, you tell her it's not worth-while to unpack her boxes.'"

"Is she young and handsome?" said I, thinking of Mr. Brympton.

"Not her! She's the kind that mothers engage when they've gay young gentlemen at college."

Well, though I knew the woman was an idle gossip, the words stuck in my head, and my heart sank lower than ever as I drove up to Brympton in the dusk. There *was* something about the house—I was sure of it now. . . .

When I went in to tea I heard that Mr. Brympton had arrived, and I saw at a glance that there had been a disturbance of some kind. Mrs. Blinder's hand shook so that she could hardly pour the tea, and Mr. Wace quoted the most dreadful texts full of brimstone. Nobody said a word to me then, but when I went up to my room Mrs. Blinder followed me.

"Oh, my dear," says she, taking my hand, "I'm so glad and thankful you've come back to us!"

That struck me, as you may imagine. "Why," said I, "did you think I was leaving for good?"

"No, no, to be sure," said she, a little confused, "but I can't a-bear to have madam left alone for a day even." She pressed my hand hard, and, "Oh, Miss Hartley," says she, "be good to your mistress, as you're a Christian woman." And with that she hurried away, and left me staring.

A moment later Agnes called me to Mrs. Brympton. Hearing Mr. Brympton's voice in her room, I went round by the dressing room, thinking I would lay out her dinner gown before going in. The dressing room is a large room with a window over the portico that looks toward the gardens. Mr. Brympton's apartments are beyond. When I went in, the door into the bedroom was ajar, and I heard Mr. Brympton saying angrily: "One would suppose he was the only person fit for you to talk to."

"I don't have many visitors in winter," Mrs. Brympton answered quietly.

"You have *me!*" he flung at her, sneeringly.

"You are here so seldom," said she.

"Well—whose fault is that? You make the place about as lively as the family vault."

With that I rattled the toilet things, to give my mistress warning, and she rose and called me in.

The two dined alone, as usual, and I knew by Mr. Wace's manner at supper that things must be going badly. He quoted the prophets something terrible, and worked on the kitchenmaid so that she declared she wouldn't go down alone to put the cold meat in the icebox. I felt nervous myself, and after I had put my mistress to bed I was half tempted to go down again and persuade Mrs. Blinder to sit up awhile over a game of cards. But I heard her door closing for the night and so I went on to my own room. The rain had begun again, and the drip, drip, drip seemed to be dropping into my brain. I lay awake listening to it, and turning over what my friend in town had said. What puzzled me was that it was always the maids who left. . . .

After a while I slept; but suddenly a loud noise wakened me. My bell had rung. I sat up, terrified by the unusual sound, which seemed to go on jangling through the darkness. My hands shook so that I couldn't find the matches. At length I struck a light and jumped out of bed. I began to think I must have been dreaming; but I looked at the bell against the wall, and there was the little hammer still quivering.

I was just beginning to huddle on my clothes when I heard another sound. This time it was the door of the locked room opposite mine softly opening and closing. I heard the sound distinctly, and it frightened me so that I stood stock still. Then I heard a footstep hurrying down the passage toward the main house. The floor being carpeted, the sound was very faint, but I was quite sure it was a woman's step. I turned cold with the thought of it, and for a minute or two I dursn't breathe or move. Then I came to my senses.

"Alice Hartley," says I to myself, "someone left that room just now and ran down the passage ahead of you. The idea isn't pleasant, but you may as well face it. Your mistress has rung for you, and to answer her bell you've got to go the way that other woman has gone."

Well—I did it. I never walked faster in my life, yet I thought I should never get to the end of the passage or reach Mrs. Brympton's room. On the way I heard nothing and saw nothing: all was dark and quiet as the grave. When I reached my mistress' door the silence was so deep that I began to think I must be dreaming, and was half minded to turn back. Then a panic seized me, and I knocked.

There was no answer, and I knocked again, loudly. To my astonishment the door was opened by Mr. Brympton. He started back when he saw me, and in the light of my candle his face looked red and savage.

"*You?*" he said, in a queer voice. "*How many of you are there, in God's name?*"

At that I felt the ground give under me; but I said to myself that he had been drinking, and answered as steadily as I could: "May I go in, sir? Mrs. Brympton has rung for me."

"You may all go in, for what I care," says he, and, pushing by me, walked down the hall to his own bedroom. I looked after him as he went, and to my surprise I saw that he walked as straight as a sober man.

I found my mistress lying very weak and still, but she forced a smile when she saw me, and signed to me to pour out some drops for her. After that she lay without speaking, her breath coming quick, and her eyes closed. Suddenly she groped out with her hand, and *"Emma,"* says she, faintly.

"It's Hartley, madam," I said. "Do you want anything?"

She opened her eyes wide and gave me a startled look.

"I was dreaming," she said. "You may go, now, Hartley, and thank you kindly. I'm quite well again, you see." And she turned her face away from me.

* III *

There was no more sleep for me that night, and I was thankful when daylight came.

Soon afterward, Agnes called me to Mrs. Brympton. I was afraid she was ill again, for she seldom sent for me before nine, but I found her sitting up in bed, pale and drawn-looking, but quite herself.

"Hartley," says she quickly, "will you put on your things at once and go down to the village for me? I want this prescription made up—" here she hesitated a minute and blushed "—and I should like you to be back again before Mr. Brympton is up."

"Certainly, madam," I said.

"And—stay a moment—" she called me back as if an idea had just struck her "—while you're waiting for the mixture, you'll have time to go on to Mr. Ranford's with this note."

It was a two mile walk to the village, and on my way I had time to turn things over in my mind. It struck me as peculiar that my mistress should wish the prescription made up without Mr. Brympton's knowledge; and, putting this together with the scene of the night before, and with much else that I had noticed and suspected, I began to wonder if the poor lady was weary of her life, and had come to the mad resolve of ending it. The idea took such hold on me that I reached the village on a run, and dropped breathless into a chair before the chemist's counter. The good man, who was just taking down his shutters, stared at me so hard that it brought me to myself.

"Mr. Limmel," I says, trying to speak indifferently, "will you run your eye over this, and tell me if it's quite right?"

He put on his spectacles and studied the prescription.

"Why, it's one of Dr. Walton's," says he. "What should be wrong with it?"

"Well—is it dangerous to take?"

"Dangerous—how do you mean?"

I could have shaken the man for his stupidity.

"I mean—if a person was to take too much of it—by mistake of course—" says I, my heart in my throat.

"Lord bless you, no. It's only lime water. You might feed it to a baby by the bottleful."

I gave a great sigh of relief and hurried on to Mr. Ranford's. But on the way another thought struck me. If there was nothing to conceal about my visit to the chemist's, was it my other errand that Mrs. Brympton wished me to keep private? Somehow, that thought frightened me worse than the other. Yet the two gentlemen seemed fast friends, and I would have staked my head on my mistress' goodness. I felt ashamed of my suspicions, and concluded that I was still disturbed by the strange events of the night. I left the note at Mr. Ranford's, and hurrying back to Brympton, slipped in by a side door without being seen, as I thought.

An hour later, however, as I was carrying in my mistress's breakfast, I was stopped in the hall by Mr. Brympton.

"What were you doing out so early?" he says, looking hard at me.

"Early—me, sir?" I said, in a tremble.

"Come, come," he says, an angry red spot coming out on his forehead, "didn't I see you scuttling home through the shrubbery an hour or more ago?"

I'm a truthful woman by nature, but at that a lie popped out ready-made. "No, sir, you didn't," said I and looked straight back at him.

He shrugged his shoulders and gave a sullen laugh. "I suppose you think I was drunk last night?" he asked suddenly.

"No, sir, I don't," I answered, this time truthfully enough.

He turned away with another shrug. "A pretty notion my servants have of me!" I heard him mutter as he walked off.

Not till I had settled down to my afternoon's sewing did I realize how the events of the night had shaken me. I couldn't pass that locked door without a shiver. I knew I had heard someone come out of it, and walk down the passage ahead of me. I thought of speaking to Mrs. Blinder or to Mr. Wace, the only two in the house who appeared to have an inkling of what was going on, but I had a feeling that if I questioned them they would deny everything, and that I might learn more by holding my tongue and keeping my eyes open. The idea of spending another night opposite the locked room sickened me, and once I was seized with the notion of packing my trunk and taking the first train to town; but it wasn't in me to throw over a kind mistress in that manner, and I tried to go on with my sewing as if nothing had happened. I hadn't worked ten minutes before the sewing machine broke down. It was one I had found in the house, a good machine but a trifle out of order: Mrs. Blinder said it had never been used since Emma Saxon's death. I stopped to see what was wrong, and as I was working at the machine a drawer which I had never been able to open slid forward and a photograph fell out. I picked it up and sat looking at it in a maze. It was a woman's likeness, and I knew I had seen the face somewhere—the eyes had an asking look that I had felt on me before. And suddenly I remembered the pale woman in the passage.

I stood up, cold all over, and ran out of the room. My heart seemed to be thumping in the top of my head, and I felt as if I should never get away from the look in those eyes. I went straight to Mrs. Blinder. She was taking her afternoon nap, and sat up with a jump when I came in.

"Mrs. Blinder," said I, "who is that?" And I held out the photograph.

She rubbed her eyes and stared.

"Why, Emma Saxon," says she. "Where did you find it?"

I looked hard at her for a minute. "Mrs. Blinder," I said, "I've seen that face before."

Mrs. Blinder got up and walked over to the looking glass. "Dear me! I must have been asleep," she says. "My front is all over one ear. And now do run along, Miss Hartley, dear, for I hear the clock striking four, and I must go down this very minute and put on the Virginia ham for Mr. Brympton's dinner."

* IV *

To all appearances, things went on as usual for a week or two. The only difference was that Mr. Brympton stayed on, instead of going off as he usually did, and that Mr. Ranford never showed himself. I heard Mr. Brympton remark on this one afternoon when he was sitting in my mistress' room before dinner:

"Where's Ranford?" says he. "He hasn't been near the house for a week. Does he keep away because I'm here?"

Mrs. Brympton spoke so low that I couldn't catch her answer.

"Well," he went on, "two's company and three's trumpery; I'm sorry to be in Ranford's way, and I suppose I shall have to take myself off again in a day or two and give him a show." And he laughed at his own joke.

The very next day, as it happened, Mr. Ranford called. The footman said the three were very merry over their tea in the library, and Mr. Brympton strolled down to the gate with Mr. Ranford when he left.

I have said that things went on as usual; and so they did with the rest of the household; but as for myself, I had never been the same since the night my bell had rung. Night after night I used to lie awake, listening for it to ring again, and for the door of the locked room to open stealthily. But the bell never rang, and I heard no sound across the passage. At last the silence began to be more dreadful to me than the most mysterious sounds. I felt that *someone* was cowering there, behind the locked door, watching and listening as I watched and listened, and I could almost have cried out, "Whoever you are, come out and let me see you face to face, but don't lurk there and spy on me in the darkness!"

Feeling as I did, you may wonder I didn't give warning. Once I very nearly did so; but at the last moment something held me back. Whether it was compassion for my mistress, who had grown more and more dependent on me, or unwillingness to try a new place, or some other feeling that I couldn't put a name to, I lingered on as if spellbound, though every night was dreadful to me, and the days but little better.

For one thing, I didn't like Mrs. Brympton's looks. She had never been the same since that night, no more than I had. I thought she would brighten up after Mr. Brympton left, but though she seemed easier in her mind, her spirits didn't revive, nor her strength either. She had grown attached to me, and seemed to like to have me about; and Agnes told me one day that, since Emma Saxon's death, I was the only maid her mistress had taken to. This gave me a warm feeling for the poor lady, though after all there was little I could do to help her.

After Mr. Brympton's departure, Mr. Ranford took to coming again, though less often than formerly. I met him once or twice in the grounds, or in the village, and I couldn't but think there was a change in him too; but I set it down to my disordered fancy.

The weeks passed, and Mr. Brympton had now been a month absent. We heard he was cruising with a friend in the West Indies, and Mr. Wace said that was a long way off, but though you had the wings of a dove and went to the uttermost parts of the earth, you couldn't get away from the Almighty. Agnes said that as long as he stayed away from Brympton the Almighty might have him and welcome; and this raised a laugh, though Mrs. Blinder tried to look shocked, and Mr. Wace said the bears would eat us.

We were all glad to hear that the West Indies were a long way off, and I remember that, in spite of Mr. Wace's solemn looks, we had a very merry dinner that day in the hall. I don't know if it was because of my being in better spirits, but I fancied Mrs. Brympton looked better too, and seemed more cheerful in her manner. She had been for a walk in the morning, and after luncheon she lay down in her room, and I read aloud to her. When she dismissed me I went to my own room feeling quite bright and happy, and for first time in weeks walked past the locked door without thinking of it. As I sat down to my work I looked out and saw a few snowflakes falling. The sight was pleasanter than the eternal rain, and I pictured to myself how pretty the bare gardens would look in their white mantle. It seemed to me as if the snow would cover up all the dreariness, indoors as well as out.

The fancy had hardly crossed my mind when I heard a step at my side. I looked up, thinking it was Agnes.

"Well, Agnes—" said I, and the words froze on my tongue; for there, in the door, stood *Emma Saxon*.

I don't know how long she stood there. I only know I couldn't stir or take my eyes from her. Afterward I was terribly frightened, but at the time it wasn't fear I felt, but something deeper and quieter. She looked at me long and hard, and her face was just one dumb prayer to me—but how in the world was I to help her? Suddenly she turned, and I heard her walk down the passage. This time I wasn't afraid to follow—I felt that I must know what she wanted. I sprang up and ran out. She was at the other end of the passage, and I expected her to take the turn toward my mistress' room; but instead of that she pushed open the door that led to the backstairs. I followed her down the stairs, and across the passageway to the back door. The kitchen and hall were empty at that hour, the servants being off duty, except for the footman, who was in the pantry. At the door she stood still a moment, with another look at me; then she turned the handle, and stepped out. For a minute I hesitated. Where was she leading me to? The door had closed softly after her, and I opened it and looked out, half-expecting to find that she had disappeared. But I saw her a few yards off hurrying across the courtyard to the path through the woods. Her figure looked black and lonely in the snow, and for a second my heart failed me and I thought of turning back. But all the while she was drawing me after her; and catching up an old shawl of Mrs. Blinder's I ran out into the open.

Emma Saxon was in the wood path now. She walked on steadily, and I followed at the same pace, till we passed out of the gates and reached the highroad. Then she struck across the open fields to the village. By this time the ground was white, and as she climbed the slope of a bare hill ahead of me I noticed that she left no footprints behind her. At sight of that my heart shriveled up within me, and my knees were water. Somehow, it was worse here than indoors. She made the whole countryside seem lonely as the grave, with none but us two in it, and no help in the wide world.

Once I tried to go back; but she turned and looked at me, and it was as if she had dragged me with ropes. After that I followed her like a dog. We came to the village and she led me through it, past the church and the blacksmith's shop, and down the lane to Mr. Ranford's. Mr. Ranford's house stands close to the road: a plain old-fashioned building, with a flagged path leading to the door between box borders. The lane was deserted, and as I turned into it I saw Emma Saxon pause under the old elm by the gate. And now another fear came over me. I saw that we had reached the end of our journey, and that it was my turn to act. All the way from Brympton I had been asking myself what she wanted of me, but I had followed in a trance, as it were, and not till I saw her stop at Mr. Ranford's gate did my brain begin to clear itself. I stood a little way off in the snow, my heart beating fit to strangle me, and my feet frozen to the ground; and she stood under the elm and watched me.

I knew well enough that she hadn't led me there for nothing. I felt there was something I ought to say or do—but how was I to guess what it was? I had never thought harm of my mistress and Mr. Ranford, but I was sure now that, from one cause or another, some dreadful thing hung over them. *She* knew what it was; she would tell me if she could; perhaps she would answer if I questioned her.

It turned me faint to think of speaking to her; but I plucked up heart and dragged myself across the few yards between us. As I did so, I heard the house door open and saw Mr. Ranford approaching. He looked handsome and cheerful, as my mistress had looked that morning, and at sight of him the blood began to flow again in my veins.

"Why, Hartley," said he, "what's the matter? I saw you coming down the lane just now, and came out to see if you had taken root in the snow." He stopped and stared at me. "What are you looking at?" he says.

I turned toward the elm as he spoke, and his eyes followed me; but there was no one there. The lane was empty as far as the eye could reach.

A sense of helplessness came over me. She was gone, and I had not been able to guess what she wanted. Her last look had pierced me to the marrow; and yet it had not told me! All at once, I felt more desolate than when she had stood there watching me. It seemed as if she had left me all alone to carry the weight of the secret I couldn't guess. The snow went round me in great circles, and the ground fell away from me. . . .

A drop of brandy and the warmth of Mr. Ranford's fire soon brought me to, and I insisted on being driven back at once to Brympton. It was nearly dark, and I was afraid my mistress might be wanting me. I explained to Mr. Ranford that I had been out for a walk and had been taken with a fit of giddiness as I passed his gate. This was true enough; yet I never felt more like a liar than when I said it.

When I dressed Mrs. Brympton for dinner she remarked on my pale looks and asked what ailed me. I told her I had a headache, and she said she would not require me again that evening, and advised me to go to bed.

It was a fact that I could scarcely keep on my feet; yet I had no fancy to spend a solitary evening in my room. I sat downstairs in the hall as long as I could hold my head up; but by nine I crept upstairs, too weary to care what happened if I could but get my head on a pillow. The rest of the household went to bed soon afterward; they kept early hours when the master was away, and before ten I heard Mrs. Blinder's door close, and Mr. Wace's soon after.

It was a very still night, earth and air all muffled in snow. Once in bed I felt easier, and lay quiet, listening to the strange noises that come out in a house after dark. Once I thought I heard a door open and close again below: it might have been the glass door that led to the gardens. I got up and peered out of the window; but it was in the dark of the moon, and nothing visible outside but the streaking of snow against the panes.

I went back to bed and must have dozed, for I jumped awake to the furious ringing of my bell. Before my head was clear I had sprung out of bed, and was dragging on my clothes. *It is going to happen now,* I heard myself saying; but what I meant I had no notion. My hands seemed to be covered with glue—I thought I should never get into my clothes. At last I opened my door and peered down the passage. As far as my candle flame carried, I could see nothing unusual ahead of me. I hurried on, breathless; but as I pushed open the baize door leading to the main hall my heart stood still, for there at the head of the stairs was Emma Saxon, peering dreadfully down into the darkness.

For a second I couldn't stir; but my hand slipped from the door, and as it swung shut the figure vanished. At the same instant there came another sound from below stairs—a stealthy mysterious sound, as of a latchkey turning in the house door. I ran to Mrs. Brympton's room and knocked.

There was no answer, and I knocked again. This time I heard someone moving in the room; the bolt slipped back and my mistress stood before me. To my surprise I saw that she had not undressed for the night. She gave me a startled look.

"What is this, Hartley?" she says in a whisper. "Are you ill? What are you doing here at this hour?"

"I am not ill, madam; but my bell rang."

At that she turned pale, and seemed about to fall.

"You are mistaken," she said harshly; "I didn't ring. You must have been dreaming." I had never heard her speak in such a tone. "Go back to bed," she said, closing the door on me.

But as she spoke I heard sounds again in the hall below: a man's step this time; and the truth leaped out on me.

"Madam," I said, pushing past her, "there is someone in the house—"

"Someone—?"

"Mr. Brympton, I think—I hear his step below—"

A dreadful look came over her, and without a word, she dropped flat at my feet. I fell on my knees and tried to lift her: by the way she breathed I saw it was no common faint. But as I raised her head there came quick steps on the stairs and across the hall: the door was flung open, and there stood Mr. Brympton, in his traveling clothes, the snow dripping from him. He drew back with a start as he saw me kneeling by my mistress.

"What the devil is this?" he shouted. He was less high-colored than usual, and the red spot came out on his forehead.

"Mrs. Brympton has fainted, sir," said I.

He laughed unsteadily and pushed by me. "It's a pity she didn't choose a more convenient moment. I'm sorry to disturb her, but—"

I raised myself up aghast at the man's action.

"Sir," said I, "are you mad? What are you doing?"

"Going to meet a friend," said he, and seemed to make for the dressing room.

At that my heart turned over. I don't know what I thought or feared; but I sprang up and caught him by the sleeve.

"Sir, sir," said I, "for pity's sake look at your wife!"

He shook me off furiously.

"It seems that's done for me," says he, and caught hold of the dressing room door.

At that moment I heard a slight noise inside. Slight as it was, he heard it too, and tore the door open; but as he did so he dropped back. On the threshold stood Emma Saxon. All was dark behind her, but I saw her plainly, and so did he. He threw up his hands as if to hide his face from her; and when I looked again she was gone.

He stood motionless, as if the strength had run out of him; and in the stillness my mistress suddenly raised herself, and opening her eyes fixed a look on him. Then she fell back, and I saw the death flutter pass over her face. . . .

We buried her on the third day, in a driving snowstorm. There were few people in the church, for it was bad weather to come from town, and I've a notion my mistress was one that hadn't many near friends. Mr. Ranford was among the last to come, just before they carried her up the aisle. He was in black, of course, being such a friend of the family, and I never saw a gentleman so pale. As he passed me, I noticed that he leaned a trifle on a stick he carried; and I fancy Mr. Brympton noticed it too, for the red spot came out sharp on his forehead, and all through the service he kept staring across the church at Mr. Ranford, instead of following the prayers as a mourner should.

When it was over and we went out to the graveyard, Mr. Ranford had disappeared, and as soon as my poor mistress's body was underground, Mr. Brympton jumped into the carriage nearest the gate and drove off without a word to any of us. I heard him call out, "To the station," and we servants went back alone to the house.

THE LEGEND

ARTHUR BERNALD could never afterward recall just when the first conjecture flashed on him: oddly enough, there was no record of it in the agitated jottings of his diary. But, as it seemed to him in retrospect, he had always felt that the queer man at the Wades' must be John Pellerin, if only for the negative reason that he couldn't imaginably be anyone else. It was impossible, in the confused pattern of the century's intellectual life, to fit the stranger in anywhere, save in the big gap which, some five and twenty years earlier, had been left by Pellerin's disappearance; and conversely, such a man as the Wades' visitor couldn't have lived for sixty years without filling, somewhere in space, a nearly equivalent void.

At all events, it was certainly not to Doctor Wade or to his mother that Bernald owed the hint: the good unconscious Wades, one of whose chief charms in the young man's eyes was that they remained so robustly untainted by Pellerinism, in spite of the fact that Doctor Wade's younger brother, Howland, was among its most impudently flourishing high priests.

The incident had begun by Bernald's running across Doctor Robert Wade one hot summer night at the University Club, and by Wade's saying, in the tone of unprofessional laxity which the shadowy stillness of the place invited: "I got hold of a queer fish at St. Martin's the other day—case of heat prostration picked up in Central Park. When we'd patched him up I found he had nowhere to go, and not a dollar in his pocket, and I sent him down to our place at Portchester to rebuild."

The opening roused his hearer's attention. Bob Wade had an instinctive sense of values that Bernald had learned to trust.

"What sort of chap? Young or old?"

"Oh, every age—full of years, and yet with a lot left. He called himself sixty on the books."

"Sixty's a good age for some kinds of living. And age is purely subjective. How has he used his sixty years?"

"Well—part of them in educating himself, apparently. He's a scholar—humanities, languages, and so forth."

"Oh—decayed gentleman," Bernald murmured, disappointed.

"Decayed? Not much!" cried the doctor with his accustomed literalness. "I only mentioned that side of Winterman—his name's Winterman—because it was the side my mother noticed first. I suppose women generally do. But it's only a part—a small part. The man's the big thing."

"Really big?"

"Well—there again. . . . When I took him down to the country, looking rather like a tramp from a 'Shelter,' with an untrimmed beard, and a suit of reach-me-downs he'd slept round the Park in for a week, I felt sure my mother'd carry the silver up to her room, and send for the gardener's dog to sleep in the hall. But she didn't."

"I see. 'Women and children love him.' Oh, Wade!" Bernald groaned.

"Not a bit of it! You're out again. We don't love him, either of us. But we *feel* him—the air's charged with him. You'll see."

And Bernald agreed that he *would* see, the following Sunday. Wade's inarticulate attempts to characterize the stranger had struck his friend. The human revelation had for Bernald a poignant and ever-renewed interest, which his trade, as the dramatic critic of a daily paper, had hitherto failed to diminish. And he knew that Bob Wade, simple and undefiled by literature—Bernald's specific affliction—had a free and personal way of judging men, and the diviner's knack of reaching their hidden springs. During the days that followed, the young doctor gave Bernald further details about John Winterman: details not of fact—for in that respect the stranger's reticence was baffling—but of impression. It appeared that Winterman, while lying insensible in the Park, had been robbed of the few dollars he possessed; and on leaving the hospital still weak and half-blind, he had quite simply and unprotestingly accepted the Wades' offer to give him shelter till such time as he should be strong enough to work.

"But what's his work?" Bernald interjected. "Hasn't he at least told you that?"

"Well, writing. Some kind of writing." Doctor Bob always became vague when he approached the confines of literature. "He means to take it up again as soon as his eyes get right."

Bernald groaned again. "Oh, Lord—that finishes him; and *me!* He's looking for a publisher, of course—he wants a 'favorable notice.' I won't come!"

"He hasn't written a line for twenty years."

"A line of *what?* What kind of literature can one keep corked up for twenty years?"

Wade surprised him. "The real kind, I should say. But I don't know Winterman's line," the doctor added. "He speaks of the things he used to write as merely as 'stuff that wouldn't sell.' He has a wonderful confidential way of *not* telling one things. But he says he'll have to do something for his living as soon as his eyes are patched up, and that writing is the only trade he knows. The queer thing is that he seems pretty sure of selling *now*. He even talked of buying the bungalow off us, with an acre or two about it."

"The bungalow? What's that?"

"The studio down by the shore that we built for Howland when he thought he meant to paint." (Howland Wade, as Bernald knew, had experienced various "calls.") "Since he's taken to writing nobody's been near the place. I offered it to Winterman, and he camps there—cooks his meals, does his own housekeeping, and never comes up to the house except in the evenings, when he joins us on the verandah, in the dark, and smokes while my mother knits."

"A discreet visitor, eh?"

"More than he need be. My mother actually wanted him to stay on in the house—in her pink chintz room. Think of it! But he says houses smother him. I take it he's lived for years in the open."

"In the open where?"

"I can't make out, except that it was somewhere in the east. 'East of everything—beyond the day spring. In places not on the map.' That's the way he put it; and when I said: 'You've been an explorer, then?' he smiled in his beard, and answered: 'Yes; that's it—an explorer.' Yet he doesn't strike me as a man of action: hasn't the hands or the eyes."

"What sort of hands and eyes has he?"

Wade reflected. His range of observation was not large, but within its limits, it was exact and could give an account of itself.

"He's worked a lot with his hands, but that's not what they were made for. I should say they were extraordinarily delicate conductors of sensation. And his eye—his eye too. He hasn't used it to dominate people: he didn't care to. He simply looks through 'em all like windows. Makes them feel like the fellows who think they're made of glass. The mitigating circumstance is that he seems to see such a glorious landscape through me." Wade grinned at the thought of serving such a purpose.

"I see. I'll come on Sunday and be looked through!" Bernald cried.

* II *

Bernald came on two successive Sundays; and the second time he lingered till the Tuesday.

"Here he comes!" Wade had said, the first evening, as the two young men, with Wade's mother, sat on the verandah, with the Virginia creeper drawing, between the arches, its black arabesques against a moon-lined sky.

Bernald heard a step on the gravel, and saw the red flit of a cigar through the shrubs. Then a loosely-moving figure obscured the patch of sky between the creepers, and the spark became the center of a dim bearded face, in which Bernald, through the darkness, discerned only a broad white gleam of forehead.

It was the young man's subsequent impression that Winterman had not spoken much that first evening; at any rate, Bernald himself remembered chiefly what the Wades had said. And this was the more curious because he had come for the purpose of studying their visitor, and because there was nothing to distract his attention in Wade's slow phrases or his mother's artless comments. He reflected afterward that there must have been a mysteriously fertilizing quality in the stranger's silence: it had brooded over their talk like a rain cloud over a dry country.

Mrs. Wade, apparently fearing that her son might have given Bernald an exaggerated notion of their visitor's importance, had hastened to qualify it before the latter appeared.

"He's not what you or Howland would call intellectual—" (Bernald winced at the coupling of the names) "—not in the least *literary;* though he told Bob he used to write. I don't think, though, it could have been what Howland would call writing." Mrs. Wade always named her younger son with a reverential drop of the voice. She viewed literature much as she did Providence, as an inscrutable mystery; and she spoke of Howland as a dedicated being, set apart to perform secret rites within the veil of the sanctuary.

"I shouldn't say he had a quick mind," she continued, reverting to Winterman. "Sometimes he hardly seems to follow what we're saying. But he's got such sound ideas—when he does speak he's never silly. And clever people sometimes *are,* don't you think so?" Bernald sighed an unqualified assent. "And he's so capable. The other day something went wrong with the kitchen range, just as I was expecting some friends of Bob's for dinner; and do you know, when Mr. Winterman heard we were in trouble, he came and took a look, and knew at once what to do? I told him it was a dreadful pity he wasn't married!"

*   *   *

Close on midnight, when the session on the verandah ended, and the two young men were strolling down to the bungalow at Winterman's side, Bernald's mind reverted to the image of the fertilizing cloud. There was something brooding, pregnant, in the silent presence beside him: he had, in place of any circumscribing personal impression, a large hovering sense of manifold latent meanings. And he felt a thrill of relief when, halfway down the lawn, Doctor Bob was checked by a voice that called him back to the telephone.

"Now I'll be with him alone!" thought Bernald, with a throb like a lover's.

Under the low rafters of the bungalow Winterman had to grope for the lamp on his desk, and as its light struck up into his face Bernald's sense of the rareness of the opportunity increased. He couldn't have said why, for the face, with its bossed forehead, its shabby greyish beard and blunt Socratic nose, made no direct appeal to the eye. It seemed rather like a stage on which remarkable things might be enacted, like some shaggy moorland landscape dependent for form and expression on the clouds rolling over it, and the bursts of light between; and one of these flashed out in the smile with which Winterman, as if in answer to his companion's thought, said simply, as he turned to fill his pipe: "Now we'll talk."

So he'd known all along that they hadn't yet—and had guessed that, with Bernald, one might!

The young man's sudden glow of pleasure left him for a moment unable to meet the challenge; and in that moment he felt the sweep of something winged and summoning. His spirit rose to it with a rush, but just as he felt himself poised between the ascending pinions, the door opened and Bob Wade reappeared.

"Too bad! I'm sorry! It was from Howland, to say he can't come tomorrow after all." The doctor panted out his news with honest grief.

"I tried my best to pull it off for you, Winterman: and my brother *wants* to come—he's keen to talk to you and see what he can do. But you see he's so tremendously in demand. He'll try for another Sunday later on."

Winterman gave an untroubled nod. "Oh, he'll find me here. I shall work my time out slowly." He waved his hand toward the scattered sheets on the kitchen table which formed his desk.

"Not slowly enough to suit us," Wade answered hospitably. "Only, if Howland could have come he might have given you a tip or two—put you on the right track—shown you how to get in touch with the public."

Winterman, his hands in his pockets, lounged against the bare pine walls, twisting his pipe under his beard. "Does your brother enjoy the privilege of that contact?" he questioned gravely.

Wade stared a little. "Oh, of course Howland's not what you'd call a *popular* writer; he despises that kind of thing. But whatever he says goes with—well, with the chaps who count; and everyone tells me he's written *the* book on Pellerin. You must read it when you get back your eyes." He paused, as if to let the name sink in, but Winterman drew at his pipe with a blank face. "You must have heard of Pellerin, I suppose?" the doctor continued. "I've never read a word of him myself: he's too big a proposition for *me*. But one can't escape the talk about him. I have him crammed down my throat even in the hospital. The interns read him at the clinics. He tumbles out of the nurses' pockets. The patients keep him under their pillows. Oh, with most of them, of course, it's just a craze, like the last new game or puzzle: they don't understand him in the least. Howland says that even now, twenty-five years after his death, and with his books in everybody's hands, there are not twenty people who really understand Pellerin; and Howland ought to know, if anybody does. He's—what's their great word?—*interpreted* him. You must get Howland to put you through a course of Pellerin."

And as the young men, having taken leave of Winterman, retraced their way across the lawn, Wade continued to develop the theme of his brother's accomplishments.

"I wish I *could* get Howland to take an interest in Winterman: this is the third Sunday he's chucked us. Of course he does get bored with people consulting him about their writings—but I believe if he could only talk to Winterman he'd see something in him, as we do. And it would be such a godsend to the poor devil to have someone to advise him about his work. I'm going to make a desperate effort to get Howland here next Sunday."

It was then that Bernald vowed to himself that he would return the next Sunday at all costs. He hardly knew whether he was prompted by the impulse to shield Winterman from Howland Wade's ineptitude, or by the desire to see the latter abandon himself to the full shamelessness of its display; but of one fact he was assured—and that was of the existence in Winterman of some quality which would provoke Howland to the amplest exercise of his fatuity. "How he'll draw him—how he'll draw him!" Bernald chuckled, with a security the more unaccountable that his one glimpse of Winterman had shown the latter only as a passive subject for observation; and he felt himself avenged in advance for the injury of Howland Wade's existence.

* III *

That this hope was to be frustrated Bernald learned from Howland Wade's own lips, the day before the two young men were to have met at Portchester.

"I can't really, my dear fellow," the Interpreter lisped, passing a polished hand over the faded smoothness of his face. "Oh, an authentic engagement, I assure you: otherwise, to oblige old Bob I'd submit cheerfully to looking over his foundling's literature. But I'm pledged this week to the Pellerin Society of Kenosha: I had a hand in founding it, and for two years now they've been patiently waiting for a word from me—the *Fiat Lux*, so to speak. You see it's a ministry, Bernald—I assure you, I look upon my calling quite religiously."

As Bernald listened, his disappointment gradually changed to relief. Howland, on trial, always turned out to be too insufferable, and the pleasure of watching his antics was invariably lost in the impulse to put a sanguinary end to them.

"If he'd only kept his beastly pink hands off Pellerin," Bernald sighed, thinking for the hundredth time of the thick manuscript condemned to perpetual incarceration in his own desk by the publication of Howland's "definitive" work on the great man. One couldn't, *after* Howland Wade, expose one's self to the derision of writing about Pellerin: the eagerness with which Wade's book had been devoured proved, not that the public had enough appetite for another, but simply that, for a stomach so undiscriminating, anything better than Wade had given it would be too good. And Bernald, in the confidence that his own work was open to this objection, had stoically locked it up. Yet if he had resigned himself to the fact that Wade's book existed, and was already passing into the immortality of perpetual republication, he could not, after repeated trials, adjust himself to the author's talk about Pellerin. When Wade wrote of the great dead he was egregious, but in conversation he was familiar and fond. It might have been supposed that one of the beauties of Pellerin's hidden life and mysterious taking off would have been to guard him from the fingering of anecdote; but biographers like Howland Wade are born to rise above such obstacles. He might be vague or inaccurate in dealing with the few recorded events of his subject's life; but when he left fact for conjecture no one had a firmer footing. Whole chapters in his volume were constructed in the conditional mood and made up of hypothetical detail; and in talk, by the very law of the process, hypothesis became affirmation, and he was ready to tell you confidentially the exact circumstances of Pellerin's death, and of the "distressing incident" leading up to it. Bernald himself not only questioned the form under which this incident was shaping itself before posterity, but the very fact of its occurrence: he had never been able to discover any break in the dense cloud enveloping Pellerin's end. He had gone away—that was all that any of them knew: he who had so little, at any time, been with them or of them; and his going had so slightly stirred the public consciousness that the news of his death, laconically imparted from afar, had dropped unheeded into the universal scrap basket, to be long afterward fished out, with all its details missing, when some inquiring spirit first became aware, by chance encounter with a volume in a London bookstall, not only that such a man as John Pellerin had died, but that he had ever lived, or written.

It need hardly be noted that Howland Wade had not been the pioneer in question: his had been the safer part of swelling the chorus when it rose, and gradually drowning the other voices by his own. He had pitched his note so screamingly, and held it so long, that he was now the accepted authority on Pellerin, not only in the land which had given birth to his genius but in the Europe which had first acclaimed it; and it was the central point of pain in Bernald's sense of the situation that a man who had so yearned for silence should have his grave piped over by such a voice as Wade's.

Bernald's talk with the Interpreter had revived this ache to the momentary exclusion of other sensations; and he was still sore with it when, the next afternoon, he arrived at Portchester for his second Sunday with the Wades.

At the station he had the surprise of seeing Winterman's face on the platform, and of hearing from him that Doctor Bob had been called away to assist at an operation in a distant town.

"Mrs. Wade wanted to put you off, but I believe the message came too late; so she sent me down to break the news to you," said Winterman, holding out his hand.

Perhaps because they were the first conventional words that Bernald had heard him speak, the young man was struck by the quality his intonation gave them.

"She wanted to send a carriage," Winterman added, "but I told her we'd walk back through the woods." He looked at Bernald with a kindliness that flushed the young man with pleasure.

"Are you strong enough? It's not too far?"

"Oh, no. I'm pulling myself together. Getting back to work is the slowest part of the business: not on account of my eyes—I can use them now, though not for reading; but some of the links between things are missing. It's a kind of broken spectrum . . . here, that boy will look after your bag."

The walk through the woods remained in Bernald's memory as an enchanted hour. He used the word literally, as descriptive of the way in which Winterman's contact changed the face of things, or perhaps restored them to their deeper meanings. And the scene they traversed—one of those little untended woods that still, in America, fringe the tawdry skirts of civilization—acquired, as a background to Winterman, the hush of a spot aware of transcendent visitings. Did he talk, or did he make Bernald talk? The young man never knew. He recalled only a sense of lightness and liberation, as if the hard walls of individuality had melted, and he were merged in the poet's deeper interfusion, yet without losing the least sharp edge of self. This general impression resolved itself afterward into the sense of Winterman's wide elemental range. His thought encircled things like the horizon at sea. He didn't, as it happened, touch on lofty themes— Bernald was gleefully aware that, to Howland Wade, their talk would hardly have been Talk at all—but Winterman's mind, applied to lowly topics, was like a lens that brought out microscopic delicacies and differences.

The lack of Sunday trains kept Doctor Bob for two days on the scene of his surgical duties, and during those two days Bernald seized every moment of communion with his friend's guest. Winterman, as Wade had said, was reticent concerning his personal affairs, or rather concerning the practical and material questions to which the term is generally applied. But it was evident that, in Winterman's case, the usual classification must be reversed, and that the discussion of ideas carried one much further into his intimacy than familiarity with the incidents of his life.

"That's exactly what Howland Wade and his tribe have never understood about Pellerin: that it's much less important to know how, or even why, he disapp—"

Bernald pulled himself up with a jerk, and turned to look full at his companion. It was late on the Monday evening, and the two men, after an hour's chat on the verandah to the tune of Mrs. Wade's knitting needles, had bidden their hostess good night and strolled back to the bungalow together.

"Come and have a pipe before you turn in," Winterman had said; and they had sat on together till midnight, with the door of the bungalow open on the heaving moonlit bay, and summer insects bumping against the chimney of the lamp. Winterman had just bent down to refill his pipe from the jar on the table, and Bernald, jerking about to catch him in the circle of lamplight, sat speechless, staring at a face that seemed suddenly to have substituted itself for Winterman's face, or rather to have taken on its features.

"No, they never saw that Pellerin's ideas *were* Pellerin. . . ." He continued to stare at Winterman. "Just as this man's ideas are—why, *are* Pellerin!"

The thought uttered itself in a kind of inner shout, and Bernald started upright with the violent impact of his conclusion. Again and again in the last forty-eight hours he had exclaimed to himself: "This is as good as Pellerin." Why hadn't he said till now: "This *is* Pellerin"? . . . Surprising as the answer was, he had no choice but to take it. He hadn't said so simply because Winterman was *better than Pellerin*—that there was so much more of him, so to speak. Yes; but—it came to Bernald in a flash—wouldn't there by this time have been any amount more of Pellerin? . . . The young man felt actually dizzy with the thought. That was it—there was the solution of the problem! This man was Pellerin, and more than Pellerin! It was so fantastic and yet so unanswerable that he burst into a sudden laugh.

Winterman, at the same moment, brought his palm down with a crash on the pile of manuscript covering the desk.

"What's the matter?" Bernald cried.

"My match wasn't out. In another minute the destruction of the library of Alexandria would have been a trifle compared to what you'd have seen." Winterman, with his large deep laugh, shook out the smoldering sheets. "And I should have been a pensioner on Doctor Bob the Lord knows how much longer!"

Bernald looked at him intently. "You've really got going again? The thing's actually getting into shape?"

"This particular thing is in shape. I drove at it hard all last week, thinking our friend's brother would be down on Sunday, and might look it over."

Bernald had to repress the tendency to another wild laugh.

"Howland—you meant to show *Howland* what you've done?"

Winterman, looming against the moonlight, slowly turned a dusky shaggy head toward him.

"Isn't it a good thing to do?"

Bernald wavered, torn between loyalty to his friends and the grotesqueness of answering in the affirmative. After all, it was none of his business to furnish Winterman with an estimate of Howland Wade.

"Well, you see, you've never told me what your line is," he answered, temporizing.

"No, because nobody's ever told *me*. It's exactly what I want to find out," said the other genially.

"And you expect Wade—?"

"Why, I gathered from our good Doctor that it's his trade. Doesn't he explain—interpret?"

"In his own domain—which is Pellerinism."

Winterman gazed out musingly upon the moon-touched dusk of waters. "And what *is* Pellerinism?" he asked.

Bernald sprang to his feet with a cry. "Ah, I don't know—but you're Pellerin!"

They stood for a minute facing each other, among the uncertain swaying shadows of the room, with the sea breathing through it as something immense and inarticulate breathed through young Bernald's thoughts; then Winterman threw up his arms with a humorous gesture.

"Don't shoot!" he said.

* IV *

Dawn found them there, and the sun laid its beams on the rough floor of the bungalow, before either of the men was conscious of the passage of time. Bernald, vaguely trying to define his own state in retrospect, could only phrase it: "I floated . . . floated. . . ."

The gist of fact at the core of the extraordinary experience was simply that John Pellerin, twenty-five years earlier, had voluntarily disappeared, causing the rumor of his death to be reported to an inattentive world; and that now he had come back to see what the world had made of him.

"You'll hardly believe it of me; I hardly believe it of myself; but I went away in a rage of disappointment, of wounded pride—no, vanity! I don't know which cut deepest—the sneers or the silence—but between them, there wasn't an inch of me that wasn't raw. I had just the one thing in me: the message, the cry, the revelation. But nobody saw and nobody listened. Nobody wanted what I had to give. I was like a poor devil of a tramp looking for shelter on a bitter night, in a town with every door bolted and all the windows dark. And suddenly I felt that the easiest thing would be to lie down and go to sleep in the snow. Perhaps I'd a vague notion that if they found me there at daylight, frozen stiff, the pathetic spectacle might produce a reaction, a feeling of remorse. . . . So I took care to be found! Well, a good many thousand people die every day on the face of the globe; and I soon discovered that I was simply one of the thousands; and when I made that discovery I really died—and stayed dead a year or two. . . . When I came to life again I was off on the underside of the world, in regions unaware of what we know as 'the public.' Have you any notion how it shifts the point of view to wake under new constellations? I advise any man who's been in love with a woman under Cassiopeia to go and think about her under the Southern Cross. . . . It's the only way to tell the pivotal truths from the others. . . . I didn't believe in my theory any less—there was my triumph and my vindication! It held out, resisted, measured itself with the stars. But I didn't care a snap of my finger whether anybody else believed in it, or even knew it had been formulated. It escaped out of my books—my poor stillborn books—like Psyche from the chrysalis, and soared away into the blue, and lived there. I knew then how it frees an idea to be ignored; how apprehension circumscribes and deforms it. . . . Once I'd learned that, it was easy enough to turn to and shift for myself. I was sure now that my idea would live: the good ones are self-supporting. And meanwhile I had to learn to be so; and I tried my hand at a number of things . . . adventurous, menial, commercial. . . . It's not a bad thing for a man to have to live his life—and we nearly all manage to dodge it. Our first round with the Sphinx may strike something out of us—a book or a picture or a symphony; and we're amazed at our feat, and go on letting that first work breed others, as some animal forms reproduce each other without renewed fertilization. So there we are, committed to our first guess at the riddle; and our works look as like as successive impressions of the same plate, each with the lines a little fainter; whereas they ought to be—if we touch earth between times—as different from each other as those other creatures—jellyfish, aren't they, of a kind?—where successive generations produce new forms, and it takes a zoologist to see the hidden likeness. . . .

"Well, I proved my first guess, off there in the wilds, and it lived, and grew, and took care of itself. And I said, 'Someday it will make itself heard; but by that time my atoms will have waltzed into a new pattern.' Then, in Cashmere one day, I met a fellow in a caravan, with a dog-eared book in his pocket. He said he never stirred without it—wanted to know where I'd been, never to have heard of it. It was *my guess*—in its twentieth edition! . . . The globe spun round at that, and all of a sudden I was under the old stars. That's the way it happens when the ballast of vanity shifts! I'd lived a third of a life out there, unconscious of human opinion— because I supposed it was unconscious of *me*. But now—now! Oh, it was different. I wanted to know what they said. . . . Not exactly that, either: I wanted to know *what I'd made them say*. There's a difference. . . . And here I am," said John Pellerin, with a pull at his pipe.

So much Bernald retained of his companion's actual narrative; the rest was swept away under the tide of wonder that rose and submerged him as Pellerin—at some indefinitely later stage of their talk—picked up his manuscript and began to read. Bernald sat opposite, his elbows propped on the table, his eyes fixed on the swaying waters outside, from which the moon gradually faded, leaving them to make a denser blackness in the night. As Pellerin read, this density of blackness—which never for a moment seemed inert or unalive—was attenuated by imperceptible degrees, till a greyish pallor replaced it; then the pallor breathed and brightened, and suddenly dawn was on the sea.

Something of the same nature went on in the young man's mind while he watched and listened. He was conscious of a gradually withdrawing light, of an interval of obscurity full of the stir of invisible forces, and then of the victorious flush of day. And as the light rose, he saw how far he had traveled and what wonders the night had prepared. Pellerin had been right in saying that his first idea had survived, had borne the test of time; but he had given his hearer no hint of the extent to which it had been enlarged and modified, of the fresh implications it now unfolded. In a brief flash of retrospection Bernald saw the earlier books dwindle and fall into their place as mere precursors of this fuller revelation; then, with a leap of rage, he pictured Howland Wade's pink hands on the new treasure, and his prophetic feet upon the lecture platform.

* V *

"It won't do—oh, he let him down as gently as possible; but it appears it simply won't do."

Doctor Bob imparted the ineluctable fact to Bernald while the two men, accidentally meeting at their club a few nights later, sat together over the dinner they had immediately agreed to share.

Bernald had left Portchester the morning after his strange discovery, and he and Bob Wade had not seen each other since. And now Bernald, moved by an irresistible instinct of postponement, had waited for his companion to bring up Winterman's name, and had even executed several conversational diversions in the hope of delaying its mention. For how could one talk of Winterman with the thought of Pellerin swelling one's breast?

"Yes; the very day Howland got back from Kenosha I brought the manuscript to town, and got him to read it. And yesterday evening I nailed him, and dragged an answer out of him."

"Then Howland hasn't seen Winterman yet?"

"No. He said: 'Before you let him loose on me I'll go over the stuff, and see if it's at all worth-while.'"

Bernald drew a freer breath. "And he found it wasn't?"

"Between ourselves, he found it was of no account at all. Queer, isn't it, when the *man* . . . but of course literature's another proposition. Howland says it's one of the cases where an idea might seem original and striking if one didn't happen to be able to trace its descent. And this is straight out of bosh—by Pellerin. . . . Yes: Pellerin. It seems that everything in the article that isn't pure nonsense is just Pellerinism. Howland thinks Winterman must have been tremendously struck by Pellerin's writings, and have lived too much out of the world to know that they've become the textbooks of modern thought. Otherwise, of course, he'd have taken more trouble to disguise his plagiarisms."

"I see," Bernald mused. "Yet you say there *is* an original element?"

"Yes; but unluckily it's no good."

"It's not—conceivably—in any sense a development of Pellerin's idea: a logical step farther?"

"*Logical?* Howland says it's twaddle at white heat."

Bernald sat silent, divided between the satisfaction of seeing the Interpreter rush upon his fate, and the despair of knowing that the state of mind he represented was indestructible. Then both emotions were swept away on a wave of pure joy, as he reflected that now, at last, Howland Wade had given him back John Pellerin.

The possession was one he did not mean to part with lightly; and the dread of its being torn from him constrained him to extraordinary precautions.

"You've told Winterman, I suppose? How did he take it?"

"Why, unexpectedly, as he does most things. You can never tell which way he'll jump. I thought he'd take a high tone, or else laugh it off; but he did neither. He seemed awfully cast down. I wished myself well out of the job when I saw how cut up he was."

Bernald thrilled at the words. Pellerin had shared his own pang, then— the "old woe of the world" at the perpetuity of human dullness!

"But what did he say to the charge of plagiarism—if you made it?"

"Oh, I told him straight out what Howland said. I thought it fairer. And his answer to that was the rummest part of all."

"What was it?" Bernald questioned, with a tremor.

"He said: 'That's queer, for I've never read Pellerin.' "

Bernald drew a deep breath. "Well—and I suppose you believed him?"

"I believed him, because I know him. But the public won't—the critics won't. And if the plagiarism is a pure coincidence it's just as bad for him as if it were a straight steal—isn't it?"

Bernald sighed his acquiescence.

"It bothers me awfully," Wade continued, knitting his kindly brows, "because I could see what a blow it was to him. He's got to earn his living, and I don't suppose he knows how to do anything but write. At his age it's hard to start fresh. I put that to Howland—asked him if there wasn't a chance he might do better if he only had a little encouragement. I can't help feeling he's got the essential thing in him. But of course I'm no judge when it comes to books. And Howland says it would be cruel to give him any hope." Wade paused, turned his wineglass about under a meditative stare, and then leaned across the table toward Bernald. "Look here—do you know what I've proposed to Winterman? That he should come to town with me tomorrow and go in the evening to hear Howland lecture to the Uplift Club. They're to meet at Mrs. Beecher Bain's, and Howland is to repeat the lecture that he gave the other day before the Pellerin Society at

Kenosha. It will give Winterman a chance to get some notion of what Pellerin *was:* he'll get it much straighter from Howland than if he tried to plough through Pellerin's books. And then afterward—as if accidentally—I thought I might bring him and Howland together. If Howland could only see him and hear him talk, there's no knowing what might come of it. He couldn't help feeling the man's force, as we do; and he might give him a pointer—tell him what line to take. Anyhow, it would please Winterman, and take the edge off his disappointment. I saw that as soon as I proposed it."

"Someone who's never heard of Pellerin?"

Mrs. Beecher Bain, large, smiling, diffuse, reached out through the incoming throng on her threshold to detain Bernald with the question as he was about to move past her in the wake of his companion.

"Oh, keep straight on, Mr. Winterman!" she interrupted herself to call after the latter. "Into the back drawing room, please! And remember, you're to sit next to me—in the corner on the left, close under the platform."

She renewed her interrogative clutch on Bernald's sleeve. "Most curious! Doctor Wade has been telling me all about your friend—how remarkable you all think him. And it's actually true that he's never heard of Pellerin? Of course as soon as Doctor Wade told me *that,* I said 'Bring him!' It will be so extraordinarily interesting to watch the first impression. Yes, do follow him, dear Mr. Bernald, and be sure that you and he secure the seats next to me. Of course Alice Fosdick insists on being with us. She was wild with excitement when I told her she was to meet someone who'd never heard of Pellerin!"

On the indulgent lips of Mrs. Beecher Bain conjecture speedily passed into affirmation; and as Bernald's companion, broad and shaggy in his visible new evening clothes, moved down the length of the crowded rooms, he was already, to the ladies drawing aside their skirts to let him pass, the interesting Huron of the fable.

How far he was aware of the character ascribed to him it was impossible for Bernald to discover. He was as unconscious as a tree or a cloud, and his observer had never known anyone so alive to human contacts and yet so secure from them. But the scene was playing such a lively tune on Bernald's own sensibilities that for the moment he could not adjust himself to the probable effect it produced on his companion. The young man, of late, had made but rare appearances in the group of which Mrs. Beecher Bain was one of the most indefatigable hostesses, and the Uplift Club the chief medium of expression. To a critic, obliged by his trade to cultivate convictions, it was the essence of luxury to leave them at home in his hours of ease; and Bernald gave his preference to circles in which less finality of judgment prevailed, and it was consequently less embarrassing to be caught without an opinion.

But in his fresher days he had known the spell of the Uplift Club and the thrill of moving among the Emancipated; and he felt an odd sense of rejuvenation as he looked at the rows of faces packed about the enbowered platform from which Howland Wade was presently to hand down the eternal verities. Many of these countenances belonged to the old days, when the gospel of Pellerin was unknown, and it had required considerable intellectual courage to avow one's acceptance of the very doctrines he had since demolished. The latter moral revolution seemed to have been accepted as submissively as a change in hairdressing; and it even struck Bernald that, in the case of many of the assembled ladies, their convictions were rather newer than their clothes.

One of the most interesting examples of this readiness of adaptation was actually, in the person of Miss Alice Fosdick, brushing his elbow with exotic amulets, and enveloping him in Arabian odors, as she leaned forward to murmur her sympathetic sense of the situation. Miss Fosdick, who was one of the most advanced exponents of Pellerinism, had large eyes and a plaintive mouth, and Bernald had always fancied that she might have been pretty if she had not been perpetually explaining things.

"Yes, I know—Isabella Bain told me all about him. (He can't hear us, can he?) And I wonder if you realize how remarkably interesting it is that we should have such an opportunity *now*—I mean the opportunity to see the impression of Pellerinism on a perfectly fresh mind. (You must introduce him as soon as the lecture's over.) I explained that to Isabella as soon as she showed me Doctor Wade's note. Of course you see why, don't you?" Bernald made a faint motion of acquiescence, which she instantly swept aside. "At least I think I can *make you see why*. (If you're sure he can't hear?) Why, it's just this—Pellerinism is in danger of becoming a truism. Oh, it's an awful thing to say! But then I'm not afraid of saying awful things! I rather believe it's my mission. What I mean is, that we're getting into the way of taking Pellerin for granted—as we do the air we breathe. We don't sufficiently lead our *conscious life* in him—we're gradually letting him become subliminal." She swayed closer to the young man, and he saw that she was making a graceful attempt to throw her explanatory net over his companion, who, evading Mrs. Bain's hospitable signal, had cautiously wedged himself into a seat between Bernald and the wall.

"*Did* you hear what I was saying, Mr. Winterman? (Yes, I know who you are, of course!) Oh, well, I don't really mind if you did. I was talking about you—about you and Pellerin. I was explaining to Mr. Bernald that what we need at this very minute is a Pellerin revival; and we need someone like you—to whom his message comes as a wonderful new interpretation of life—to lead the revival, and rouse us out of our apathy. . . .

"You see," she went on winningly, "it's not only the big public that needs it (of course *their* Pellerin isn't ours!). It's we, his disciples, his interpreters, we who discovered him and gave him to the world—we, the chosen people, the Custodians of the Sacred Books, as Howland calls us—it's *we* who are in perpetual danger of sinking back into the old stagnant ideals, and practicing the Seven Deadly Virtues; it's *we* who need to count our mercies, and realize anew what he's done for us, and what we ought to do for him! And it's for that reason that I urged Mr. Wade to speak here, in the very inner sanctuary of Pellerinism, exactly as he would speak to the uninitiated—to repeat, simply, his Kenosha lecture, 'What Pellerinism Means' and we ought all, I think, to listen to him with the hearts of little children—just as *you* will, Mr. Winterman—as if he were telling us new things, and we—"

"Alice, *dear*—" Mrs. Bain murmured with a warning gesture; and Howland Wade, emerging between the palms, took the center of the platform.

A pang of commiseration shot through Bernald as he saw him there, so innocent and so exposed. His plump pulpy body, which made his evening dress fall into intimate and wrapper-like folds, was like a wide surface spread to the shafts of irony; and the ripples of his voice seemed to enlarge the vulnerable area as he leaned forward, poised on confidential finger tips, to say persuasively: "Let me try to tell you what Pellerinism means."

Bernald moved restlessly in his seat. He had the sense of being a party to something not wholly honorable. He ought not to have come; he ought not to have let his companion come. Yet how could he have done otherwise? John Pellerin's secret was his own. As long as he chose to remain John Winterman it was no one's business to gainsay him; and Bernald's scruples were really justifiable only in respect of his own presence on the scene. But even in this respect he ceased to feel them as soon as Howland Wade began to speak.

* VI *

It had been arranged that Pellerin, after the meeting of the Uplift Club, should join Bernald at his rooms and spend the night there, instead of returning to Portchester. The plan had been eagerly elaborated by the young man, but he had been unprepared for the alacrity with which his wonderful friend accepted it. He was beginning to see that it was a part of Pellerin's wonderfulness to fall in, quite simply and naturally, with any arrangements made for his convenience, or tending to promote the convenience of others. Bernald perceived that his docility in such matters was proportioned to the force of resistance which, for nearly half a lifetime, had kept him, with his back to the wall, fighting alone against the powers of darkness. In such a scale of values how little the small daily alternatives must weigh!

At the close of Howland Wade's discourse, Bernald, charged with his prodigious secret, had felt the need to escape for an instant from the liberated rush of talk. The interest of watching Pellerin was so perilously great that the watcher felt it might, at any moment, betray him. He lingered in the drawing room long enough to see his friend enclosed in a mounting tide, above which Mrs. Beecher Bain and Miss Fosdick actively waved their conversational tridents; then he took refuge, at the back of the house, in a small dim library where, in his younger days, he had discussed personal immortality and the problem of consciousness with beautiful girls whose names he could not remember.

In this retreat he surprised Mr. Beecher Bain, a quiet man with a mild brow, who was smoking a surreptitious cigar over the last number of the *Strand*. Mr. Bain, at Bernald's approach, dissembled the *Strand* under a copy of the *Hibbert Journal,* but tendered his cigar case with the remark that stocks were heavy again; and Bernald blissfully abandoned himself to this unexpected contact with reality.

On his return to the drawing rooms he found that the tide had set toward the supper table, and when it finally carried him thither it was to land him in the welcoming arms of Bob Wade.

"Hullo, old man! Where have you been all this time? Winterman? Oh, *he's* talking to Howland: yes, I managed it finally. I believe Mrs. Bain has steered them into the library, so that they shan't be disturbed. I gave her an idea of the situation, and she was awfully kind. We'd better leave them alone, don't you think? I'm trying to get a croquette for Miss Fosdick."

Bernald's secret leapt in his bosom, and he devoted himself to the task of distributing sandwiches and champagne while his pulses danced to the tune of the cosmic laughter. The vision of Pellerin and his Interpreter, face to face at last, had a Titanic grandeur that dwarfed all other comedy. "And I shall hear of it presently; in an hour or two he'll be telling me about it. And that hour will be all mine—mine and his!" The dizziness of the thought made it difficult for Bernald to preserve the balance of the supper plates he was distributing. Life had for him at that moment the completeness which seems to defy disintegration.

The throng in the dining room was thickening, and Bernald's efforts as purveyor were interrupted by frequent appeals, from ladies who had reached repleteness, that he should sit down and tell them all about his interesting friend. Winterman's fame, trumpeted abroad by Miss Fosdick, had reached the four corners of the Uplift Club, and Bernald found himself fabricating *de toutes pièces* a Winterman legend which should in some degree respond to the Club's demand for the human document. When at length he had acquitted himself of this obligation, and was free to work his way back through the lessening groups into the drawing room, he was at last rewarded by a glimpse of his friend, who, still densely encompassed, towered in the center of the room in all his sovereign ugliness.

Their eyes met across the crowd; but Bernald gathered only perplexity from the encounter. What were Pellerin's eyes saying to him? What orders, what confidences, what indefinable apprehension did their long look impart? The young man was still trying to decipher their message when he felt a tap on the arm, and turned to meet the rueful gaze of Bob Wade, whose meaning lay clearly enough on the surface of his good blue stare.

"Well, it won't work—it won't work," the doctor groaned.

"What won't?"

"I mean with Howland. Winterman won't. Howland doesn't take to him. Says he's crude—frightfully crude. And you know Howland hates crudeness."

"Oh, I know," Bernald exulted. It was the word he had waited for—he saw it now! Once more he was lost in wonder at Howland's miraculous faculty for always, as the naturalists said, being true to type.

"So I'm afraid it's all up with his chance of writing. At least *I* can do no more," said Wade, discouraged.

Bernald pressed him for further details. "Does Winterman seem to mind much? Did you hear his version?"

"His version?"

"I mean what he said to Howland."

"Why, no. What the deuce was there for him to say?"

"What indeed? I think I'll take him home," said Bernald gaily.

He turned away to join the circle from which a few minutes before, Pellerin's eyes had vainly and enigmatically signaled to him; but the circle had dispersed, and Pellerin himself was not in sight.

Bernald, looking about him, saw that during his brief aside with Wade tbe party had passed into the final phase of dissolution. People still delayed, in diminishing groups, but the current had set toward the doors, and every moment or two it bore away a few more lingerers. Bernald, from his post, commanded the clearing perspective of the two drawing rooms, and a rapid survey of their length sufficed to assure him that Pellerin was not in either. Taking leave of Wade, the young man made his way back to the drawing room, where only a few hardened feasters remained, and then passed on to the library which had been the scene of the late momentous colloquy. But the library too was empty, and drifting back to the inner drawing room Bernald found Mrs. Beecher Bain domestically putting out the candles on the mantelpiece.

"Dear Mr. Bernald! Do sit down and have a little chat. What a wonderful privilege it has been! I don't know when I've had such an intense impression."

She made way for him, in a corner of the sofa to which she had sunk; and he echoed her vaguely: "You *were* impressed, then?"

"I can't express to you how it affected me! As Alice said, it was a resurrection—it was as if John Pellerin were actually here in the room with us!"

Bernald turned on her with a half audible gasp. "You felt that, dear Mrs. Bain?"

"We all felt it—everyone of us; I don't wonder the Greeks—it *was* the Greeks?—regarded eloquence as a supernatural power. As Alice says, when one looked at Howland Wade one understood what they meant by the Afflatus."

Bernald rose and held out his hand. "Oh, I see—it was Howland who made you feel as if Pellerin were in the room? And he made Miss Fosdick feel so too?"

"Why, of course. But why are you rushing off?"

"Because I must hunt up my friend, who's not used to such late hours."

"Your friend?" Mrs. Bain had to collect her thoughts. "Oh, Mr. Winterman, you mean? But he's gone already."

"Gone?" Bernald exclaimed, with an odd twinge of foreboding. Remembering Pellerin's signal across the crowd, he reproached himself for not having answered it more promptly. There had been a summons in the look—and it was certainly strange that his friend should have left the house without him.

"Are you quite sure?" he asked, with a startled glance at the clock.

"Oh, perfectly. He went half an hour ago. But you needn't hurry away on his account, for Alice Fosdick carried him off with her. I saw them leave together."

"Carried him off? She took him home with her, you mean?"

"Yes. You know what strange hours she keeps. She told me she was going to give him a Welsh rabbit, and explain Pellerinism to him."

"Oh, if she's going to explain—" Bernald murmured. But his amazement at the news struggled with a confused impatience to reach his rooms in time to be there for his friend's arrival. There could be no stranger spectacle beneath the stars than that of John Pellerin carried off by Miss

Fosdick, and listening, in the small hours, to her elucidation of his doctrines; but Bernald knew enough of his sex to be aware that such an experiment may appear less humorous to its subject than to the detached observer. Even the Uplift Club and its connotations might benefit by the attraction of the unknown; and it was conceivable that to a traveler from Mesopotamia Miss Fosdick might present elements of interest which she had lost for the frequenters of Fifth Avenue. There was, at any rate, no denying that the affair had become unexpectedly complex, and that its further development promised to be rich in comedy.

In the contemplation of these possibilities Bernald sat over his fire, listening for Pellerin's ring. He had arranged his modest quarters with the reverent care of a celebrant awaiting the descent of his deity. He guessed Pellerin to be careless of visual detail, but sensitive to the happy blending of sensuous impressions: to the spell of lamplight on books, and of a deep chair placed where one could watch the fire. The chair was there, and Bernald, facing it across the hearth, already saw it filled by Pellerin's lounging figure. The autumn dawn came late, and even now they had before them the promise of some untroubled hours. Bernald, sitting there alone in the warm stillness of his room, and in the profounder hush of his expectancy, was conscious of gathering up all his sensibilities and percepions into one exquisitely adjusted instrument of notation. Until now he had tasted Pellerin's society only in unpremeditated snatches and had always left him with a sense, on his own part, of waste and shortcoming. Now, in the lull of this dedicated hour, he felt that he should miss nothing, and forget nothing, of the initiation that awaited him. And catching sight of Pellerin's pipe, he rose and laid it carefully on a table by the armchair. . . .

"No. I've never had any news of him," Bernald heard himself repeating. He spoke in a low tone, and with the automatic utterance that alone made it possible to say the words.

They were addressed to Miss Fosdick, into whose neighborhood chance had thrown him at a dinner, a year or so later than their encounter at the Uplift Club. Hitherto he had successfully, and intentionally, avoided Miss Fosdick, not from any animosity toward that unconscious instrument of fate, but from an intense reluctance to pronounce the words which he knew he should have to speak if they met.

Now, as it turned out, his chief surprise was that she should wait so long to make him speak them. All through the dinner she had swept him along on a rapid current of talk which showed no tendency to linger or turn back upon the past. At first he ascribed her reserve to a sense of delicacy with

which he reproached himself for not having credited her; then he saw that
she had been carried so far beyond the point at which they had last faced
each other, that she was finally borne back to it only by the merest hazard
of associated ideas. For it appeared that the very next evening, at Mrs.
Beecher Bain's, a Hindu Mahatma was to lecture to the Uplift Club on the
Limits of the Subliminal; and it was owing to no less a person than
Howland Wade that this exceptional privilege had been obtained.

"Of course Howland's known all over the world as the interpreter of
Pellerinism, and the Aga Gautch, who had absolutely declined to speak
anywhere in public, wrote to Isabella that he could not refuse anything that
Mr. Wade asked. Did you know that Howland's lecture, 'What Pellerinism
Means,' has been translated into twenty-two languages, and gone into a
fifth edition in Icelandic? Why, that reminds me," Miss Fosdick broke
off—"I've never heard what became of your queer friend—what was his
name?—whom you and Bob Wade accused me of spiriting away the night
that Howland gave that very lecture at Hatty Bain's. And I've never seen
you since you rushed into the house the next morning, and dragged me out
of bed to know what I'd done with him!"

With sharp effort Bernald gathered himself together to have it out.
"Well, what *did* you do with him?" he retorted.

She laughed her appreciation of his humor. "Just what I told you, of
course. I said good-bye to him on Isabella's doorstep."

Bernald looked at her. "It's really true, then, that he didn't go home
with you?"

She bantered back: "Have you suspected me, all this time, of hiding his
remains in the cellar?" And with a droop of her fine lids she added: "I wish
he *had* come home with me, for he was rather interesting, and there were
things about Pellerinism that I think I could have explained to him."

Bernald helped himself to a nectarine, and Miss Fosdick continued on a
note of amused curiosity: "So you've really never had any news of him since
that night?"

"No—I've never had any news of him."

"Not the least little message?"

"Not the least little message."

"Or a rumor or report of any kind?"

"Or a rumor or report of any kind."

Miss Fosdick's interest seemed to be revived by the undeniable strangeness of the case. "It's rather creepy, isn't it? What *could* have happened?
You don't suppose he could have been waylaid and murdered?" she asked
with brightening eyes.

Bernald shook his head serenely. "No. I'm sure he's safe—quite safe."

"But if you're sure, you must know something."

"No. I know nothing," he repeated.

She scanned him incredulously. "But what's your theory—for you must have a theory? What in the world can have become of him?"

Bernald returned her look and hesitated. "Do you happen to remember the last thing he said to you—the very last, on the doorstep, when he left you?"

"The last thing?" She poised her fork above the peach on her plate. "I don't think he said anything. Oh, yes—when I reminded him that he'd solemnly promised to come back with me and have a little talk he said he couldn't because he was going home."

"Well, then, I suppose," said Bernald, "he went home."

She glanced at him as if suspecting a trap. "Dear me, how flat! I always inclined to a mysterious murder. But of course you know more of him than you say."

She began to cut her peach, but paused above a lifted bit to ask, with a renewal of animation in her expressive eyes: "By the way, had you heard that Howland Wade has been gradually getting farther and farther away from Pellerinism? It seems he's begun to feel that there's a Positivist element in it which is narrowing to anyone who has gone at all deeply into the Wisdom of the East. He was intensely interesting about it the other day, and of course I *do* see what he feels. . . . Oh, it's too long to tell you now; but if you could manage to come in to tea some afternoon soon—any day but Wednesday—I should so like to explain. . . ."

THE EYES

WE HAD BEEN PUT in the mood for ghosts, that evening, after an excellent dinner at our old friend Culwin's, by a tale of Fred Murchard's—the narrative of a strange personal visitation.

Seen through the haze of our cigars, and by the drowsy gleam of a coal fire, Culwin's library, with its oak walls and dark old bindings, made a good setting for such evocations; and ghostly experiences at first hand being, after Murchard's opening, the only kind acceptable to us, we proceeded to take stock of our group and tax each member for a contribution. There were eight of us, and seven contrived, in a manner more or less adequate, to fulfill the condition imposed. It surprised us all to find that we could muster such a show of supernatural impressions, for none of us, excepting Murchard himself and young Phil Frenham—whose story was the slightest of the lot—had the habit of sending our souls into the invisible. So that, on the whole, we had every reason to be proud of our seven "exhibits," and none of us would have dreamed of expecting an eighth from our host.

Our old friend, Mr. Andrew Culwin, who had sat back in his armchair, listening and blinking through the smoke circles with the cheerful tolerance of a wise old idol, was not the kind of man likely to be favored with such contacts, though he had imagination enough to enjoy, without envying, the superior privileges of his guests. By age and by education he belonged to the stout Positivist tradition, and his habit of thought had been formed in the days of the epic struggle between physics and metaphysics. But he had been, then and always, essentially a spectator, a humorous detached observer of the immense muddled variety show of life, slipping out of his seat now and then for a brief dip into the convivialities at the back of the house, but never, as far as one knew, showing the least desire to jump on the stage and do a "turn."

Among his contemporaries there lingered a vague tradition of his having, at a remote period, and in a romantic crime, been wounded in a duel; but this legend no more tallied with what we younger men knew of his character than my mother's assertion that he had once been "a charming little man with nice eyes" corresponded to any possible reconstitution of his physiognomy.

"He never can have looked like anything but a bundle of sticks," Murchard had once said of him. "Or a phosphorescent log, rather," some one else amended; and we recognized the happiness of this description of his small squat trunk, with the red blink of the eyes in a face like mottled bark. He had always been possessed of a leisure which he had nursed and protected, instead of squandering it in vain activities. His carefully guarded hours had been devoted to the cultivation of a fine intelligence and a few judiciously chosen habits; and none of the disturbances common to human experience seemed to have crossed his sky. Nevertheless, his dispassionate survey of the universe had not raised his opinion of that costly experiment, and his study of the human race seemed to have resulted in the conclusion that all men were superfluous, and women necessary only because someone had to do the cooking. On the importance of this point his convictions were absolute, and gastronomy was the only science which he revered as a dogma. It must be owned that his little dinners were a strong argument in favor of this view, besides being a reason—though not the main one—for the fidelity of his friends.

Mentally he exercised a hospitality less seductive but no less stimulating. His mind was like a forum, or some open meeting place for the exchange of ideas: somewhat cold and drafty, but light, spacious and orderly—a kind of academic grove from which all the leaves have fallen. In this privileged area a dozen of us were wont to stretch our muscles and expand our lungs; and, as if to prolong as much as possible the tradition of what we felt to be a vanishing institution, one or two neophytes were now and then added to our band.

Young Phil Frenham was the last, and the most interesting, of these recruits, and a good example of Murchard's somewhat morbid assertion that our old friend "liked 'em juicy." It was indeed a fact that Culwin, for all his dryness, specially tasted the lyric qualities in youth. As he was far too good an Epicurean to nip the flowers of soul which he gathered for his garden, his friendship was not a disintegrating influence: on the contrary, it forced the young idea to robuster bloom. And in Phil Frenham he had a good subject for experimentation. The boy was really intelligent, and the soundness of his nature was like the pure paste under a fine glaze. Culwin had fished him out of a fog of family dullness, and pulled him up to a peak in Darien; and the adventure hadn't hurt him a bit. Indeed, the skill with which Culwin had contrived to stimulate his curiosities without robbing them of their bloom of awe seemed to me a sufficient answer to Murchard's ogreish metaphor. There was nothing hectic in Frenham's efflorescence, and his old friend had not laid even a finger tip on the sacred stupidities. One wanted no better proof of that than the fact that Frenham still reverenced them in Culwin.

"There's a side of him you fellows don't see. *I* believe that story about the duel!" he declared; and it was of the very essence of this belief that it should impel him—just as our little party was dispersing—to turn back to our host with the joking demand: "And now you've got to tell us about *your* ghost!"

The outer door had closed on Murchard and the others; only Frenham and I remained; and the devoted servant who presided over Culwin's destinies, having brought a fresh supply of soda water, had been laconically ordered to bed.

Culwin's sociability was a night-blooming flower, and we knew that he expected the nucleus of his group to tighten around him after midnight. But Frenham's appeal seemed to disconcert him comically, and he rose from the chair in which he had just reseated himself after his farewells in the hall.

"*My* ghost? Do you suppose I'm fool enough to go to the expense of keeping one of my own, when there are so many charming ones in my friends' closets? Take another cigar," he said, revolving toward me with a laugh.

Frenham laughed too, pulling up his slender height before the chimney piece as he turned to face his short bristling friend.

"Oh," he said, "you'd never be content to share if you met one you really liked."

Culwin had dropped back into his armchair, his shock head embedded in the hollow of worn leather, his little eyes glimmering over a fresh cigar.

"Liked—*liked?* Good Lord!" he growled.

"Ah, you *have,* then!" Frenham pounced on him in the same instant, with a side glance of victory at me; but Culwin cowered gnomelike among his cushions, dissembling himself in a protective cloud of smoke.

"What's the use of denying it? You've seen everything, so of course you've seen a ghost!" his young friend persisted, talking intrepidly into the cloud. "Or, if you haven't seen one, it's only because you've seen two!"

The form of the challenge seemed to strike our host. He shot his head out of the mist with a queer tortoise-like motion he sometimes had, and blinked approvingly at Frenham.

"That's it," he flung at us on a shrill jerk of laughter; "it's only because I've seen two!"

The words were so unexpected that they dropped down and down into a deep silence, while we continued to stare at each other over Culwin's head, and Culwin stared at his ghosts. At length Frenham, without speaking, threw himself into the chair on the other side of the hearth, and leaned forward with his listening smile. . . .

* II *

"Oh, of course they're not show ghosts—a collector wouldn't think anything of them. . . . Don't let me raise your hopes . . . their one merit is their numerical strength: the exceptional fact of their being *two*. But, as against this, I'm bound to admit that at any moment I could probably have exorcised them both by asking my doctor for a prescription, or my oculist for a pair of spectacles. Only, as I never could make up my mind whether to go to the doctor or the oculist—whether I was afflicted by an optical or a digestive delusion—I left them to pursue their interesting double life, though at times they made mine exceedingly uncomfortable. . . .

"Yes—uncomfortable; and you know how I hate to be uncomfortable! But it was part of my stupid pride, when the thing began, not to admit that I could be disturbed by the trifling matter of seeing two.

"And then I'd no reason, really, to suppose I was ill. As far as I knew I was simply bored—horribly bored. But it was part of my boredom—I remember—that I was feeling so uncommonly well, and didn't know how on earth to work off my surplus energy. I had come back from a long journey—down in South America and Mexico—and had settled down for the winter near New York with an old aunt who had known Washington Irving and corresponded with N. P. Willis. She lived, not far from Irvington, in a damp Gothic villa overhung by Norway spruces and looking exactly like a memorial emblem done in hair. Her personal appearance was in keeping with this image, and her own hair—of which there was little left—might have been sacrificed to the manufacture of the emblem.

"I had just reached the end of an agitated year, with considerable arrears to make up in money and emotion; and theoretically it seemed as though my aunt's mild hospitality would be as beneficial to my nerves as to my purse. But the deuce of it was that as soon as I felt myself safe and sheltered my energy began to revive; and how was I to work it off inside of a memorial emblem? I had, at that time, the illusion that sustained intellectual effort could engage a man's whole activity; and I decided to write a great book—I forget about what. My aunt, impressed by my plan, gave up to me her Gothic library, filled with classics bound in black cloth and daguerreotypes of faded celebrities; and I sat down at my desk to win myself a place among their number. And to facilitate my task she lent me a cousin to copy my manuscript.

"The cousin was a nice girl, and I had an idea that a nice girl was just what I needed to restore my faith in human nature, and principally in myself. She was neither beautiful nor intelligent—poor Alice Nowell! —but it interested me to see any woman content to be so uninteresting, and I wanted to find out the secret of her content. In doing this I handled it rather rashly, and put it out of joint—oh, just for a moment! There's no fatuity in telling you this, for the poor girl had never seen anyone but cousins. . . .

"Well, I was sorry for what I'd done, of course, and confoundedly bothered as to how I should put it straight. She was staying in the house, and one evening, after my aunt had gone to bed, she came down to the library to fetch a book she'd mislaid, like any artless heroine, on the shelves behind us. She was pink-nosed and flustered, and it suddenly occurred to me that her hair, though it was fairly thick and pretty, would look exactly like my aunt's when she grew older. I was glad I had noticed this, for it made it easier for me to decide to do what was right; and when I had found the book she hadn't lost I told her I was leaving for Europe that week.

"Europe was terribly far off in those days, and Alice knew at once what I meant. She didn't take it in the least as I'd expected—it would have been easier if she had. She held her book very tight, and turned away a moment to wind up the lamp on my desk—it had a ground-glass shade with vine leaves, and glass drops around the edge, I remember. Then she came back, held out her hand, and said: 'Good-bye.' And as she said it she looked straight at me and kissed me. I had never felt anything as fresh and shy and brave as her kiss. It was worse than any reproach, and it made me ashamed to deserve a reproach from her. I said to myself: 'I'll marry her, and when my aunt dies she'll leave us this house, and I'll sit here at the desk and go on with my book; and Alice will sit over there with her embroidery and look at me as she's looking now. And life will go on like that for any number of years.' The prospect frightened me a little, but at the time it didn't frighten me as much as doing anything to hurt her; and ten minutes later she had my seal ring on her finger, and my promise that when I went abroad she should go with me.

"You'll wonder why I'm enlarging on this incident. It's because the evening on which it took place was the very evening on which I first saw the queer sight I've spoken of. Being at that time an ardent believer in a necessary sequence between cause and effect, I naturally tried to trace some kind of link between what had just happened to me in my aunt's library, and what was to happen a few hours later on the same night; and so the coincidence between the two events always remained in my mind.

"I went up to bed with rather a heavy heart, for I was bowed under the weight of the first good action I had ever consciously committed; and young as I was, I saw the gravity of my situation. Don't imagine from this that I had hitherto been an instrument of destruction. I had been merely a harmless young man, who had followed his bent and declined all collaboration with Providence. Now I had suddenly undertaken to promote the moral order of the world, and I felt a good deal like the trustful spectator who has given his gold watch to the conjurer, and doesn't know in what shape he'll get it back when the trick is over. . . . Still, a glow of self-righteousness tempered my fears, and I said to myself as I undressed that when I got used to being good it probably wouldn't make me as nervous as it did at the start. And by the time I was in bed, and had blown out my candle, I felt that I really *was* getting used to it, and that, as far as I'd got, it was not unlike sinking down into one of my aunt's very softest wool mattresses.

"I closed my eyes on this image, and when I opened them it must have been a good deal later, for my room had grown cold, and intensely still. I was waked by the queer feeling we all know—the feeling that there was something in the room that hadn't been there when I fell asleep. I sat up and strained my eyes into the darkness. The room was pitch black, and at first I saw nothing; but gradually a vague glimmer at the foot of the bed turned into two eyes staring back at me. I couldn't distinguish the features attached to them, but as I looked the eyes grew more and more distinct: they gave out a light of their own.

"The sensation of being thus gazed at was far from pleasant, and you might suppose that my first impulse would have been to jump out of bed and hurl myself on the invisible figure attached to the eyes. But it wasn't—my impulse was simply to lie still. . . . I can't say whether this was due to an immediate sense of the uncanny nature of the apparition—to the certainty that if I did jump out of bed I should hurl myself on nothing—or merely to the benumbing effect of the eyes themselves. They were the very worst eyes I've ever seen: a man's eyes—but what a man! My first thought was that he must be frightfully old. The orbits were sunk, and the thick red-lined lids hung over the eyeballs like blinds of which the cords are broken. One lid drooped a little lower than the other, with the effect of a crooked leer; and between these folds of flesh, with their scant bristle of lashes, the eyes themselves, small glassy disks with an agate-like rim, looked like sea pebbles in the grip of a starfish.

"But the age of the eyes was not the most unpleasant thing about them. What turned me sick was their expression of vicious security. I don't know how else to describe the fact that they seemed to belong to a man who had done a lot of harm in his life, but had always kept just inside the danger lines. They were not the eyes of a coward, but of someone much too clever to take risks; and my gorge rose at their look of base astuteness. Yet even that wasn't the worst; for as we continued to scan each other I saw in them a tinge of derision, and felt myself to be its object.

"At that I was seized by an impulse of rage that jerked me to my feet and pitched me straight at the unseen figure. But of course there wasn't any figure there, and my fists struck at emptiness. Ashamed and cold, I groped about for a match and lit the candles. The room looked just as usual—as I had known it would; and I crawled back to bed, and blew out the lights.

"As soon as the room was dark again the eyes reappeared; and I now applied myself to explaining them on scientific principles. At first I thought the illusion might have been caused by the glow of the last embers in the chimney; but the fireplace was on the other side of my bed, and so placed that the fire could not be reflected in my toilet glass, which was the only mirror in the room. Then it struck me that I might have been tricked by the reflection of the embers in some polished bit of wood or metal; and though I couldn't discover any object of the sort in my line of vision, I got up again, groped my way to the hearth, and covered what was left of the fire. But as soon as I was back in bed the eyes were back at its foot.

"They were an hallucination, then: that was plain. But the fact that they were not due to any external dupery didn't make them a bit pleasanter. For if they were a projection of my inner consciousness, what the deuce was the matter with that organ? I had gone deeply enough into the mystery of morbid pathological states to picture the conditions under which an exploring mind might lay itself open to such a midnight admonition; but I couldn't fit it to my present case. I had never felt more normal, mentally and physically; and the only unusual fact in my situation—that of having assured the happiness of an amiable girl—did not seem of a kind to summon unclean spirits about my pillow. But there were the eyes still looking at me.

"I shut mine, and tried to evoke a vision of Alice Nowell's. They were not remarkable eyes, but they were as wholesome as fresh water, and if she had had more imagination—or longer lashes—their expression might have been interesting. As it was, they did not prove very efficacious, and in a few moments I perceived that they had mysteriously changed into the eyes at the foot of the bed. It exasperated me more to feel these glaring at me through my shut lids than to see them, and I opened my eyes again and looked straight into their hateful stare. . . .

"And so it went on all night. I can't tell you what that night was like, nor how long it lasted. Have you ever lain in bed, hopelessly wide awake, and tried to keep your eyes shut, knowing that if you opened 'em you'd see something you dreaded and loathed? It sounds easy, but it's devilishly hard. Those eyes hung there and drew me. I had the *vertige de l'abîme*, and their red lids were the edge of my abyss. . . . I had known nervous hours before: hours when I'd felt the wind of danger in my neck; but never this kind of strain. It wasn't that the eyes were awful; they hadn't the majesty of the powers of darkness. But they had—how shall I say?—a physical effect that was the equivalent of a bad smell: their look left a smear like a snail's. And I didn't see what business they had with me, anyhow—and I stared and stared, trying to find out.

"I don't know what effect they were trying to produce; but the effect they *did* produce was that of making me pack my portmanteau and bolt to town early the next morning. I left a note for my aunt, explaining that I was ill and had gone to see my doctor; and as a matter of fact I did feel uncommonly ill—the night seemed to have pumped all the blood out of me. But when I reached town I didn't go to the doctor's. I went to a friend's rooms, and threw myself on a bed, and slept for ten heavenly hours. When I woke it was the middle of the night, and I turned cold at the thought of what might be waiting for me. I sat up, shaking, and stared into the darkness; but there wasn't a break in its blessed surface, and when I saw that the eyes were not there I dropped back into another long sleep.

"I had left no word for Alice when I fled, because I meant to go back the next morning. But the next morning I was too exhausted to stir. As the day went on the exhaustion increased, instead of wearing off like the fatigue left by an ordinary night of insomnia: the effect of the eyes seemed to be cumulative, and the thought of seeing them again grew intolerable. For two days I fought my dread; and on the third evening I pulled myself together and decided to go back the next morning. I felt a good deal happier as soon as I'd decided, for I knew that my abrupt disappearance, and the strangeness of my not writing, must have been very distressing to poor Alice. I went to bed with an easy mind, and fell asleep at once; but in the middle of the night I woke, and there were the eyes. . . .

"Well, I simply couldn't face them; and instead of going back to my aunt's I bundled a few things into a trunk and jumped aboard the first steamer for England. I was so dead tired when I got on board that I crawled straight into my berth, and slept most of the way over; and I can't tell you the bliss it was to wake from those long dreamless stretches and look fearlessly into the dark, *knowing* that I shouldn't see the eyes. . . .

"I stayed abroad for a year, and then I stayed for another: and during that time I never had a glimpse of them. That was enough reason for prolonging my stay if I'd been on a desert island. Another was, of course, that I had perfectly come to see, on the voyage over, the complete impossibility of my marrying Alice Nowell. The fact that I had been so slow in making this discovery annoyed me, and made me want to avoid explanations. The bliss of escaping at one stroke from the eyes, and from this other embarrassment, gave my freedom an extraordinary zest; and the longer I savored it the better I liked its taste.

"The eyes had burned such a hole in my consciousness that for a long time I went on puzzling over the nature of the apparition, and wondering if it would ever come back. But as time passed I lost this dread, and retained only the precision of the image. Then that faded in its turn.

"The second year found me settled in Rome, where I was planning, I believe, to write another great book—a definitive work on Etruscan influences in Italian art. At any rate, I'd found some pretext of the kind for taking a sunny apartment in the Piazza di Spagna and dabbling about in the Forum; and there, one morning, a charming youth came to me. As he stood there in the warm light, slender and smooth and hyacinthine, he might have stepped from a ruined altar—one to Antinous, say; but he'd come instead from New York, with a letter from (of all people) Alice Nowell. The letter—the first I'd had from her since our break—was simply a line introducing her young cousin, Gilbert Noyes, and appealing to me to befriend him. It appeared, poor lad, that he 'had talent,' and 'wanted to write'; and, an obdurate family having insisted that his calligraphy should take the form of double entry, Alice had intervened to win him six months' respite, during which he was to travel abroad on a meager pittance, and somehow prove his ability to increase it by his pen. The quaint conditions of the test struck me first: it seemed about as conclusive as a medieval 'ordeal.' Then I was touched by her having sent him to me. I had always wanted to do her some service, to justify myself in my own eyes rather than hers; and here was a beautiful occasion.

"I imagine it's safe to lay down the general principle that predestined geniuses don't, as a rule, appear before one in the spring sunshine of the Forum looking like one of its banished gods. At any rate, poor Noyes wasn't a predestined genius. But he *was* beautiful to see, and charming as a comrade. It was only when he began to talk literature that my heart failed me. I knew all the symptoms so well—the things he had 'in him,' and the things outside him that impinged! There's the real test, after all. It was always—punctually, inevitably, with the inexorableness of a mechanical law—it was *always* the wrong thing that struck him. I grew to find a certain fascination in deciding in advance exactly which wrong thing he'd select; and I acquired an astonishing skill at the game. . . .

"The worst of it was that his *bêtise* wasn't of the too obvious sort. Ladies who met him at picnics thought him intellectual; and even at dinners he passed for clever. I, who had him under the microscope, fancied now and then that he might develop some kind of a slim talent, something that he could make 'do' and be happy on; and wasn't that, after all, what I was concerned with? He was so charming—he continued to be so charming—that he called forth all my charity in support of this argument; and for the first few months I really believed there was a chance for him. . . .

"Those months were delightful. Noyes was constantly with me, and the more I saw of him the better I liked him. His stupidity was a natural grace—it was as beautiful, really, as his eyelashes. And he was so gay, so affectionate, and so happy with me, that telling him the truth would have been about as pleasant as slitting the throat of some gentle animal. At first I used to wonder what had put into that radiant head the detestable delusion that it held a brain. Then I began to see that it was simply protective mimicry—an instinctive ruse to get away from family life and an office desk. Not that Gilbert didn't—dear lad!—believe in himself. There wasn't a trace of hypocrisy in him. He was sure that his 'call' was irresistible, while to me it was the saving grace of his situation that it *wasn't,* and that a little money, a little leisure, a little pleasure would have turned him into an inoffensive idler. Unluckily, however, there was no hope of money, and with the alternative of the office desk before him he couldn't postpone his attempt at literature. The stuff he turned out was deplorable, and I see now that I knew it from the first. Still, the absurdity of deciding a man's whole future on a first trial seemed to justify me in withholding my verdict, and perhaps even in encouraging him a little, on the ground that the human plant generally needs warmth to flower.

"At any rate, I proceeded on that principle, and carried it to the point of getting his term of probation extended. When I left Rome he went with me, and we idled away a delicious summer between Capri and Venice. I said to myself: 'If he has anything in him, it will come out now,' and it *did.* He was never more enchanting and enchanted. There were moments of our pilgrimage when beauty born of murmuring sound seemed actually to pass into his face—but only to issue forth in a flood of the palest ink. . . .

"Well, the time came to turn off the tap; and I knew there was no hand but mine to do it. We were back in Rome, and I had taken him to stay with me, not wanting him to be alone in his *pension* when he had to face the necessity of renouncing his ambition. I hadn't, of course, relied solely on my own judgment in deciding to advise him to drop literature. I had sent his stuff to various people—editors and critics—and they had always sent it back with the same chilling lack of comment. Really there was nothing on earth to say.

"I confess I never felt more shabby than I did on the day when I decided to have it out with Gilbert. It was well enough to tell myself that it was my duty to knock the poor boy's hopes into splinters—but I'd like to know what act of gratuitous cruelty hasn't been justified on that plea? I've always shrunk from usurping the functions of Providence, and when I have to exercise them I decidedly prefer that it shouldn't be on an errand of destruction. Besides, in the last issue, who was I to decide, even after a year's trial, if poor Gilbert had it in him or not?

"The more I looked at the part I'd resolved to play, the less I liked it; and I liked it still less when Gilbert sat opposite me, with his head thrown back in the lamplight, just as Phil's is now. . . . I'd been going over his last manuscript, and he knew it, and he knew that his future hung on my verdict—we'd tacitly agreed to that. The manuscript lay between us, on my table—a novel, his first novel, if you please!—and he reached over and laid his hand on it, and looked up at me with all his life in the look.

"I stood up and cleared my throat, trying to keep my eyes away from his face and on the manuscript.

" 'The fact is, my dear Gilbert,' I began—

"I saw him turn pale, but he was up and facing me in an instant.

" 'Oh, look here, don't take on so, my dear fellow! I'm not so awfully cut up as all that!' His hands were on my shoulders, and he was laughing down on me from his full height, with a kind of mortally stricken gaiety that drove the knife into my side.

"He was too beautifully brave for me to keep up any humbug about my duty. And it came over me suddenly how I should hurt others in hurting him: myself first, since sending him home meant losing him; but more particularly poor Alice Nowell, to whom I had so longed to prove my good faith and my desire to serve her. It really seemed like failing her twice to fail Gilbert.

"But my intuition was like one of those lightning flashes that encircle the whole horizon, and in the same instant I saw what I might be letting myself in for if I didn't tell the truth. I said to myself: 'I shall have him for life'—and I'd never yet seen anyone, man or woman, whom I was quite sure of wanting on those terms. Well, this impulse of egotism decided me. I was ashamed of it, and to get away from it I took a leap that landed me straight in Gilbert's arms.

" 'The thing's all right, and you're all wrong!' I shouted up at him; and as he hugged me, and I laughed and shook in his clutch, I had for a minute the sense of self-complacency that is supposed to attend the footsteps of the just. Hang it all, making people happy *has* its charms.

"Gilbert, of course, was for celebrating his emancipation in some spectacular manner; but I sent him away alone to explode his emotions, and went to bed to sleep off mine. As I undressed I began to wonder what their aftertaste would be—so many of the finest don't keep! Still, I wasn't sorry, and I meant to empty the bottle, even if it *did* turn a trifle flat.

"After I got into bed I lay for a long time smiling at the memory of his eyes—his blissful eyes. . . . Then I fell asleep, and when I woke the room was deathly cold, and I sat up with a jerk—and there were *the other eyes*. . . .

"It was three years since I'd seen them, but I'd thought of them so often that I fancied they could never take me unawares again. Now, with their red sneer on me, I knew that I had never really believed they would come back, and that I was as defenceless as ever against them. . . . As before, it was the insane irrelevance of their coming that made it so horrible. What the deuce were they after, to leap out at me at such a time? I had lived more or less carelessly in the years since I'd seen them, though my worst indiscretions were not dark enough to invite the searchings of their infernal glare; but at this particular moment I was really in what might have been called a state of grace; and I can't tell you how the fact added to their horror. . . .

"But it's not enough to say they were as bad as before: they were worse. Worse by just so much as I'd learned of life in the interval; by all the damnable implications my wider experience read into them. I saw now what I hadn't seen before: that they were eyes which had grown hideous gradually, which had built up their baseness coral-wise, bit by bit, out of a series of small turpitudes slowly accumulated through the industrious years. Yes—it came to me that what made them so bad was that they'd grown bad so slowly. . . .

"There they hung in the darkness, their swollen lids dropped across the little watery bulbs rolling loose in the orbits, and the puff of flesh making a muddy shadow underneath—and as their stare moved with my movements, there came over me a sense of their tacit complicity, of a deep hidden understanding between us that was worse than the first shock of their strangeness. Not that I understood them; but that they made it so clear that someday I should. . . . Yes, that was the worst part of it, decidedly; and it was the feeling that became stronger each time they came back. . . .

"For they got into the damnable habit of coming back. They reminded me of vampires with a taste for young flesh, they seemed so to gloat over the taste of good conscience. Every night for a month they came to claim their morsel of mine: since I'd made Gilbert happy they simply wouldn't loosen their fangs. The coincidence almost made me hate him, poor lad, fortuitous as I felt it to be. I puzzled over it a good deal, but couldn't find any hint of an explanation except in the chance of his association with Alice Nowell. But then the eyes had let up on me the moment I had abandoned her, so they could hardly be the emissaries of a woman scorned, even if one could have pictured poor Alice charging such spirits to avenge her. That set me thinking, and I began to wonder if they would let up on me if I abandoned Gilbert. The temptation was insidious, and I had to stiffen myself against it; but really, dear boy! he was too charming to be sacrificed to such demons. And so, after all, I never found out what they wanted. . . ."

* III *

The fire crumbled, sending up a flash which threw into relief the narrator's gnarled face under its grey-black stubble. Pressed into the hollow of the chair back, it stood out an instant like an intaglio of yellowish red-veined stone, with spots of enamel for the eyes; then the fire sank and it became once more a dim Rembrandtish blur.

Phil Frenham, sitting in a low chair on the opposite side of the hearth, one long arm propped on the table behind him, one hand supporting his thrown-back head, and his eyes fixed on his old friend's face, had not moved since the tale began. He continued to maintain his silent immobility after Culwin had ceased to speak, and it was I who, with a vague sense of disappointment at the sudden drop of the story, finally asked: "But how long did you keep on seeing them?"

Culwin, so sunk into his chair that he seemed like a heap of his own empty clothes, stirred a little, as if in surprise at my question. He appeared to have half-forgotten what he had been telling us.

"How long? Oh, off and on all that winter. It was infernal. I never got used to them. I grew really ill."

Frenham shifted his attitude, and as he did so his elbow struck against a small mirror in a bronze frame standing on the table behind him. He turned and changed its angle slightly; then he resumed his former attitude, his dark head thrown back on his lifted palm, his eyes intent on Culwin's face. Something in his silent gaze embarrassed me, and as if to divert attention from it I pressed on with another question:

"And you never tried sacrificing Noyes?"

"Oh, no. The fact is I didn't have to. He did it for me, poor boy!"

"Did it for you? How do you mean?"

"He wore me out—wore everybody out. He kept on pouring out his lamentable twaddle, and hawking it up and down the place till he became a thing of terror. I tried to wean him from writing—oh, ever so gently, you understand, by throwing him with agreeable people, giving him a chance to make himself felt, to come to a sense of what he *really* had to give. I'd foreseen this solution from the beginning—felt sure that, once the first ardor of authorship was quenched, he'd drop into his place as a charming parasitic thing, the kind of chronic Cherubino for whom, in old societies, there's always a seat at table, and a shelter behind the ladies' skirts. I saw him take his place as 'the poet': the poet who doesn't write. One knows the type in every drawing room. Living in that way doesn't cost much—I'd worked it all out in my mind, and felt sure that, with a little help, he could manage it for the next few years; and meanwhile he'd be sure to marry. I saw him married to a widow, rather older, with a good cook and a well-run house. And I actually had my eye on the widow. . . . Meanwhile I did everything to help the transition—lent him money to ease his conscience, introduced him to pretty women to make him forget his vows. But nothing would do him: he had but one idea in his beautiful obstinate head. He wanted the laurel and not the rose, and he kept on repeating Gautier's axiom, and battering and filing at his limp prose till he'd spread it out over Lord knows how many hundred pages. Now and then he would send a barrelful to a publisher, and of course it would always come back.

"At first it didn't matter—he thought he was 'misunderstood.' He took the attitudes of genius, and whenever an opus came home he wrote another to keep it company. Then he had a reaction of despair, and accused me of deceiving him, and Lord knows what. I got angry at that, and told him it was he who had deceived himself. He'd come to me determined to write, and I'd done my best to help him. That was the extent of my offence, and I'd done it for his cousin's sake, not his.

"That seemed to strike home, and he didn't answer for a minute. Then he said: 'My time's up and my money's up. What do you think I'd better do?'

" 'I think you'd better not be an ass,' I said.

" 'What do you mean by being an ass?' he asked.

"I took a letter from my desk and held it out to him.

" 'I mean refusing this offer of Mrs. Ellinger's: to be her secretary at a salary of five thousand dollars. There may be a lot more in it than that."

"He flung out his hand with a violence that struck the letter from mine. 'Oh, I know well enough what's in it!' he said, red to the roots of his hair.

" 'And what's the answer, if you know?' I asked.

"He made none at the minute, but turned away slowly to the door. There, with his hand on the threshold, he stopped to say, almost under his breath: 'Then you really think my stuff's no good?'

"I was tired and exasperated, and I laughed. I don't defend my laugh—it was in wretched taste. But I must plead in extenuation that the boy was a fool, and that I'd done my best for him—I really had.

"He went out of the room, shutting the door quietly after him. That afternoon I left for Frascati, where I'd promised to spend the Sunday with some friends. I was glad to escape from Gilbert, and by the same token, as I learned that night, I had also escaped from the eyes. I dropped into the same lethargic sleep that had come to me before when I left off seeing them; and when I woke the next morning in my peaceful room above the ilexes, I felt the utter weariness and deep relief that always followed on that sleep. I put in two blessed nights at Frascati, and when I got back to my rooms in Rome I found that Gilbert had gone. . . . Oh, nothing tragic had happened—the episode never rose to *that*. He'd simply packed his manuscripts and left for America—for his family and the Wall Street desk. He left a decent enough note to tell me of his decision, and behaved altogether, in the circumstances, as little like a fool as it's possible for a fool to behave. . . ."

* IV *

Culwin paused again, and Frenham still sat motionless, the dusky contour of his young head reflected in the mirror at his back.

"And what became of Noyes afterward?" I finally asked, still disquieted by a sense of incompleteness, by the need of some connecting thread between the parallel lines of the tale.

Culwin twitched his shoulders. "Oh, nothing became of him—because he became nothing. There could be no question of 'becoming' about it. He vegetated in an office, I believe, and finally got a clerkship in a consulate, and married drearily in China. I saw him once in Hong Kong, years afterward. He was fat and hadn't shaved. I was told he drank. He didn't recognize me."

"And the eyes?" I asked, after another pause which Frenham's continued silence made oppressive.

Culwin, stroking his chin, blinked at me meditatively through the shadows. "I never saw them after my last talk with Gilbert. Put two and two together if you can. For my part, I haven't found the link."

He rose, his hands in his pockets, and walked stiffly over to the table on which reviving drinks had been set out.

"You must be parched after this dry tale. Here, help yourself, my dear fellow. Here, Phil—" He turned back to the hearth.

Frenham made no response to his host's hospitable summons. He still sat in his low chair without moving, but as Culwin advanced toward him, their eyes met in a long look; after which the young man, turning suddenly, flung his arms across the table behind him, and dropped his face upon them.

Culwin, at the unexpected gesture, stopped short, a flush on his face.

"Phil—what the deuce? Why, have the eyes scared *you?* My dear boy— my dear fellow—I never had such a tribute to my literary ability, never!"

He broke into a chuckle at the thought, and halted on the hearthrug, his hands still in his pockets, gazing down at the youth's bowed head. Then, as Frenham still made no answer, he moved a step or two nearer.

"Cheer up, my dear Phil! It's years since I've seen them—apparently I've done nothing lately bad enough to call them out of chaos. Unless my present evocation of them has made *you* see them; which would be their worst stroke yet!"

His bantering appeal quivered off into an uneasy laugh, and he moved still nearer, bending over Frenham, and laying his gouty hands on the lad's shoulders.

"Phil, my dear boy, really—what's the matter? Why don't you answer? *Have* you seen the eyes?"

Frenham's face was still hidden, and from where I stood behind Culwin I saw the latter, as if under the rebuff of this unaccountable attitude, draw back slowly from his friend. As he did so, the light of the lamp on the table fell full on his congested face, and I caught its reflection in the mirror behind Frenham's head.

Culwin saw the reflection also. He paused, his face level with the mirror, as if scarcely recognizing the countenance in it as his own. But as he looked his expression gradually changed, and for an appreciable space of time he and the image in the glass confronted each other with a glare of slowly gathering hate. Then Culwin let go on Frenham's shoulders, and drew back a step. . . .

Frenham, his face still hidden, did not stir.

XINGU

MRS. BALLINGER is one of the ladies who pursue Culture in bands, as though it were dangerous to meet alone. To this end she had founded the Lunch Club, an association composed of herself and several other indomitable huntresses of erudition. The Lunch Club, after three or four winters of lunching and debate, had acquired such local distinction that the entertainment of distinguished strangers became one of its accepted functions; in recognition of which it duly extended to the celebrated Osric Dane, on the day of her arrival in Hillbridge, an invitation to be present at the next meeting.

The club was to meet at Mrs. Ballinger's. The other members, behind her back, were of one voice in deploring her unwillingness to cede her rights in favor of Mrs. Plinth, whose house made a more impressive setting for the entertainment of celebrities; while, as Mrs. Leveret observed, there was always the picture gallery to fall back on.

Mrs. Plinth made no secret of sharing this view. She had always regarded it as one of her obligations to entertain the Lunch Club's distinguished guests. Mrs. Plinth was almost as proud of her obligations as she was of her picture gallery; she was in fact fond of implying that the one possession implied the other, and that only a woman of her wealth could afford to live up to a standard as high as that which she had set herself. An all-round sense of duty, roughly adaptable to various ends, was, in her opinion, all that Providence exacted of the more humbly stationed; but the power which had predestined Mrs. Plinth to keep a footman clearly intended her to maintain an equally specialized staff of responsibilities. It was the more to be regretted that Mrs. Ballinger, whose obligations to society were bounded by the narrow scope of two parlormaids, should have been so tenacious of the right to entertain Osric Dane.

The question of that lady's reception had for a month past profoundly moved the members of the Lunch Club. It was not that they felt themselves unequal to the task, but that their sense of the opportunity plunged them into the agreeable uncertainty of the lady who weighs the alternatives of a well-stocked wardrobe. If such subsidiary members as Mrs. Leveret were fluttered by the thought of exchanging ideas with the author of *The Wings of Death,* no forebodings disturbed the conscious adequacy of Mrs. Plinth, Mrs. Ballinger and Miss Van Vluyck. *The Wings of Death* had, in fact, at Miss Van Vluyck's suggestion, been chosen as the subject of discussion at the last club meeting, and each member had thus been enabled to express her own opinion or to appropriate whatever sounded well in the comments of the others.

Mrs. Roby alone had abstained from profiting by the opportunity but it was now openly recognized that, as a member of the Lunch Club, Mrs. Roby was a failure. "It all comes," as Miss Van Vluyck put it, "of accepting a woman on a man's estimation." Mrs. Roby, returning to Hillbridge from a prolonged sojourn in exotic lands—the other ladies no longer took the trouble to remember where—had been heralded by the distinguished biologist, Professor Foreland, as the most agreeable woman he had ever met; and the members of the Lunch Club, impressed by an encomium that carried the weight of a diploma, and rashly assuming that the Professor's social sympathies would follow the line of his professional bent, had seized the chance of annexing a biological member. Their disillusionment was complete. At Miss Van Vluyck's first offhand mention of the pterodactyl Mrs. Roby had confusedly murmured: "I know so little about meters—" and after that painful betrayal of incompetence she had prudently withdrawn from further participation in the mental gymnastics of the club.

"I suppose she flattered him," Miss Van Vluyck summed up—"or else it's the way she does her hair."

The dimensions of Miss Van Vluyck's dining room having restricted the membership of the club to six, the nonconductiveness of one member was a serious obstacle to the exchange of ideas, and some wonder had already been expressed that Mrs. Roby should care to live, as it were, on the intellectual bounty of the others. This feeling was increased by the discovery that she had not yet read *The Wings of Death.* She owned to having heard the name of Osric Dane; but that—incredible as it appeared—was the extent of her acquaintance with the celebrated novelist. The ladies could not conceal their surprise; but Mrs. Ballinger, whose pride in the club made her wish to put even Mrs. Roby in the best possible light, gently insinuated that, though she had not had time to acquaint herself with *The Wings of Death,* she must at least be familiar with its equally remarkable predecessor, *The Supreme Instant.*

Mrs. Roby wrinkled her sunny brows in a conscientious effort of memory, as a result of which she recalled that, oh, yes, she *had* seen the book at her brother's, when she was staying with him in Brazil, and had even carried it off to read one day on a boating party; but they had all got to shying things at each other in the boat, and the book had gone overboard, so she had never had the chance—

The picture evoked by this anecdote did not increase Mrs. Roby's credit with the club, and there was a painful pause, which was broken by Mrs. Plinth's remarking: "I can understand that, with all your other pursuits, you should not find much time for reading; but I should have thought you might at least have *got up The Wings of Death* before Osric Dane's arrival."

Mrs. Roby took this rebuke good-humoredly. She had meant, she owned, to glance through the book; but she had been so absorbed in a novel of Trollope's that—

"No one reads Trollope now," Mrs. Ballinger interrupted.

Mrs. Roby looked pained. "I'm only just beginning," she confessed.

"And does he interest you?" Mrs. Plinth inquired.

"He amuses me."

"Amusement," said Mrs. Plinth, "is hardly what I look for in my choice of books."

"Oh, certainly, *The Wings of Death* is not amusing," ventured Mrs. Leveret, whose manner of putting forth an opinion was like that of an obliging salesman with a variety of other styles to submit if his first selection does not suit.

"Was it *meant* to be?" inquired Mrs. Plinth, who was fond of asking questions that she permitted no one but herself to answer. "Assuredly not."

"Assuredly not—that is what I was going to say," assented Mrs. Leveret, hastily rolling up her opinion and reaching for another. "It was meant to—to elevate."

Miss Van Vluyck adjusted her spectacles as though they were the black cap of condemnation. "I hardly see," she interposed, "how a book steeped in the bitterest pessimism can be said to elevate, however much it may instruct."

"I meant, of course, to instruct," said Mrs. Leveret, flurried by the unexpected distinction between two terms which she had supposed to be synonymous. Mrs. Leveret's enjoyment of the Lunch Club was frequently marred by such surprises; and not knowing her own value to the other ladies as a mirror for their mental complacency she was sometimes troubled by a doubt of her worthiness to join in their debates. It was only the fact of having a dull sister who thought her clever that saved her from a sense of hopeless inferiority.

"Do they get married in the end?" Mrs. Roby interposed.

"They—who?" the Lunch Club collectively exclaimed.

"Why, the girl and man. It's a novel, isn't it? I always think that's the one thing that matters. If they're parted it spoils my dinner."

Mrs. Plinth and Mrs. Ballinger exchanged scandalized glances, and the latter said: "I should hardly advise you to read *The Wings of Death* in that spirit. For my part, when there are so many books one *has* to read, I wonder how any one can find time for those that are merely amusing."

"The beautiful part of it," Laura Glyde murmured, "is surely just this—that no one can tell *how The Wings of Death* ends. Osric Dane, overcome by the awful significance of her own meaning, has mercifully veiled it—perhaps even from herself—as Apelles, in representing the sacrifice of Iphigenia, veiled the face of Agamemnon."

"What's that? Is it poetry?" whispered Mrs. Leveret to Mrs. Plinth, who, disdaining a definite reply, said coldly: "You should look it up. I always make it a point to look things up." Her tone added—"Though I might easily have it done for me by the footman."

"I was about to say," Miss Van Vluyck resumed, "that it must always be a question whether a book *can* instruct unless it elevates."

"Oh—" murmured Mrs. Leveret, now feeling herself hopelessly astray.

"I don't know," said Mrs. Ballinger, scenting in Miss Van Vluyck's tone a tendency to depreciate the coveted distinction of entertaining Osric Dane; "I don't know that such a question can seriously be raised as to a book which has attracted more attention among thoughtful people than any novel since *Robert Elsmere*."

"Oh, but don't you see," exclaimed Laura Glyde, "that it's just the dark hopelessness of it all—the wonderful tone scheme of black on black that makes it such an artistic achievement? It reminded me when I read it of Prince Rupert's *manière noire* . . . the book is etched, not painted, yet one feels the color values so intensely. . . .'

"Who is *he?*" Mrs. Leveret whispered to her neighbor. "Someone she's met abroad?"

"The wonderful part of the book," Mrs. Ballinger conceded, "is that it may be looked at from so many points of view. I hear that as a study of determinism Professor Lupton ranks it with *The Data of Ethics*."

"I'm told that Osric Dane spent ten years in preparatory studies before beginning to write it," said Mrs. Plinth. "She looks up everything—verifies everything. It has always been my principle, as you know. Nothing would induce me, now, to put aside a book before I'd finished it, just because I can buy as many more as I want."

"And what do *you* think of *The Wings of Death*?" Mrs. Roby abruptly asked her.

It was the kind of question that might be termed out of order, and the ladies glanced at each other as though disclaiming any share in such a breach of discipline. They all knew there was nothing Mrs. Plinth so much disliked as being asked her opinion of a book. Books were written to read; if one read them what more could be expected? To be questioned in detail regarding the contents of a volume seemed to her as great an outrage as being searched for smuggled laces at the Custom House. The club had always respected this idiosyncrasy of Mrs. Plinth's. Such opinions as she had were imposing and substantial: her mind, like her house, was furnished with monumental "pieces" that were not meant to be disarranged; and it was one of the unwritten rules of the Lunch Club that, within her own province, each member's habits of thought should be respected. The meeting therefore closed with an increased sense, on the part of the other ladies, of Mrs. Roby's hopeless unfitness to be one of them.

* II *

Mrs. Leveret, on the eventful day, arrived early at Mrs. Ballinger's, her volume of *Appropriate Allusions* in her pocket.

It always flustered Mrs. Leveret to be late at the Lunch Club: she liked to collect her thoughts and gather a hint, as the others assembled, of the turn the conversation was likely to take. Today, however, she felt herself completely at a loss; and even the familiar contact of *Appropriate Allusions,* which stuck into her as she sat down, failed to give her any reassurance. It was an admirable little volume, compiled to meet all the social emergencies; so that, whether on the occasion of Anniversaries, joyful or melancholy (as the classification ran), of Banquets, social or municipal, or of Baptisms, Church of England or sectarian, its student need never be at a loss for a pertinent reference. Mrs. Leveret, though she had for years devoutly conned its pages, valued it, however, rather for its moral support than for its practical services; for though in the privacy of her own room she commanded an army of quotations, these invariably deserted her at the critical moment, and the only phrase she retained—*Canst thou draw out leviathan with a hook?*—was one she had never yet found occasion to apply.

Today she felt that even the complete mastery of the volume would hardly have insured her self-possession; for she thought it probable that, even if she *did,* in some miraculous way, remember an Allusion, it would be only to find that Osric Dane used a different volume (Mrs. Leveret was convinced that literary people always carried them), and would consequently not recognize her quotations.

Mrs. Leveret's sense of being adrift was intensified by the appearance of Mrs. Ballinger's drawing room. To a careless eye its aspect was unchanged;

but those acquainted with Mrs. Ballinger's way of arranging her books would instantly have detected the marks of recent perturbation. Mrs. Ballinger's province, as a member of the Lunch Club, was the Book of the Day. On that, whatever it was, from a novel to a treatise on experimental psychology, she was confidently, authoritatively "up." What became of last year's books, or last week's even; what she did with the "subjects" she had previously professed with equal authority; no one had ever yet discovered. Her mind was an hotel where facts came and went like transient lodgers, without leaving their address behind, and frequently without paying for their board. It was Mrs. Ballinger's boast that she was "abreast with the Thought of the Day," and her pride that this advanced position should be expressed by the books on her table. These volumes, frequently renewed, and almost always damp from the press, bore names generally unfamiliar to Mrs. Leveret, and giving her, as she furtively scanned them, a disheartening glimpse of new fields of knowledge to be breathlessly traversed in Mrs. Ballinger's wake. But today a number of maturer-looking volumes were adroitly mingled with the *primeurs* of the press—Karl Marx jostled Professor Bergson, and the *Confessions of St. Augustine* lay beside the last work on "Mendelism"; so that even to Mrs. Leveret's fluttered perceptions it was clear that Mrs. Ballinger didn't in the least know what Osric Dane was likely to talk about, and had taken measures to be prepared for anything. Mrs. Leveret felt like a passenger on an ocean steamer who is told that there is no immediate danger, but that she had better put on her lifebelt.

It was a relief to be roused from these forebodings by Miss Van Vluyck's arrival.

"Well, my dear," the newcomer briskly asked her hostess, "what subjects are we to discuss today?"

Mrs. Ballinger was furtively replacing a volume of Wordsworth by a copy of Verlaine. "I hardly know," she said, somewhat nervously. "Perhaps we had better leave that to circumstances."

"Circumstances?" said Miss Van Vluyck drily. "That means, I suppose, that Laura Glyde will take the floor as usual, and we shall be deluged with literature."

Philanthropy and statistics were Miss Van Vluyck's province, and she resented any tendency to divert their guest's attention from these topics.

Mrs. Plinth at this moment appeared.

"Literature?" she protested in a tone of remonstrance. "But this is perfectly unexpected. I understood we were to talk of Osric Dane's novel."

Mrs. Ballinger winced at the discrimination, but let it pass. "We can hardly make that our chief subject—at least not *too* intentionally," she suggested. "Of course we can let our talk *drift* in that direction; but we ought to have some other topic as an introduction, and that is what I wanted to consult you about. The fact is, we know so little of Osric Dane's tastes and interests that it is difficult to make any special preparation."

"It may be difficult," said Mrs. Plinth with decision, "but it is necessary. I know what that happy-go-lucky principle leads to. As I told one of my nieces the other day, there are certain emergencies for which a lady should always be prepared. It's in shocking taste to wear colors when one pays a visit of condolence, or a last year's dress when there are reports that one's husband is on the wrong side of the market; and so it is with conversation. All I ask is that I should know beforehand what is to be talked about; then I feel sure of being able to say the proper thing."

"I quite agree with you," Mrs. Ballinger assented; "but—"

And at that instant, heralded by the fluttered parlormaid, Osric Dane appeared upon the threshold.

Mrs. Leveret told her sister afterward that she had known at a glance what was coming. She saw that Osric Dane was not going to meet them halfway. That distinguished personage had indeed entered with an air of compulsion not calculated to promote the easy exercise of hospitality. She looked as though she were about to be photographed for a new edition of her books.

The desire to propitiate a divinity is generally in inverse ratio to its responsiveness, and the sense of discouragement produced by Osric Dane's entrance visibly increased the Lunch Club's eagerness to please her. Any lingering idea that she might consider herself under an obligation to her entertainers was at once dispelled by her manner: as Mrs. Leveret said afterward to her sister, she had a way of looking at you that made you feel as if there was something wrong with your hat. This evidence of greatness produced such an immediate impression on the ladies that a shudder of awe ran through them when Mrs. Roby, as their hostess led the great personage into the dining room, turned back to whisper to the others: "What a brute she is!"

The hour about the table did not tend to revise this verdict. It was passed by Osric Dane in the silent deglutition of Mrs. Ballinger's menu, and by the members of the club in the emission of tentative platitudes which their guest seemed to swallow as perfunctorily as the successive courses of the luncheon.

Mrs. Ballinger's reluctance to fix a topic had thrown the club into a mental disarray which increased with the return to the drawing room, where the actual business of discussion was to open. Each lady waited for the other to speak; and there was a general shock of disappointment when their hostess opened the conversation by the painfully commonplace inquiry: "Is this your first visit to Hillbridge?"

Even Mrs. Leveret was conscious that this was a bad beginning; and a vague impulse of deprecation made Miss Glyde interject: "It is a very small place indeed."

Mrs. Plinth bristled. "We have a great many representative people," she said, in the tone of one who speaks for her order.

Osric Dane turned to her. "What do they represent?" she asked.

Mrs. Plinth's constitutional dislike to being questioned was intensified by her sense of unpreparedness; and her reproachful glance passed the question on to Mrs. Ballinger.

"Why," said that lady, glancing in turn at the other members, "as a community I hope it is not too much to say that we stand for culture."

"For art—" Miss Glyde interjected.

"For art and literature," Mrs. Ballinger amended.

"And for sociology, I trust," snapped Miss Van Vluyck.

"We have a standard," said Mrs. Plinth, feeling herself suddenly secure on the vast expanse of a generalization; and Mrs. Leveret, thinking there must be room for more than one on so broad a statement, took courage to murmur: "Oh, certainly; we have a standard."

"The object of our little club," Mrs. Ballinger continued, "is to concentrate the highest tendencies of Hillbridge—to centralize and focus its intellectual effort."

This was felt to be so happy that the ladies drew an almost audible breath of relief.

"We aspire," the president went on, "to be in touch with whatever is highest in art, literature and ethics."

Osric Dane again turned to her. "What ethics?" she asked.

A tremor of apprehension encircled the room. None of the ladies required any preparation to pronounce on a question of morals; but when they were called ethics it was different. The club, when fresh from the *Encyclopedia Britannica,* the *Reader's Handbook* or Smith's *Classical Dictionary,* could deal confidently with any subject; but when taken unawares it had been known to define agnosticism as a heresy of the Early Church and Professor Froude as a distinguished histologist; and such minor members as Mrs. Leveret still secretly regarded ethics as something vaguely pagan.

Even to Mrs. Ballinger, Osric Dane's question was unsettling, and there was a general sense of gratitude when Laura Glyde leaned forward to say, with her most sympathetic accent: "You must excuse us, Mrs. Dane, for not being able, just at present, to talk of anything but *The Wings of Death.*"

"Yes," said Miss Van Vluyck, with a sudden resolve to carry the war into the enemy's camp. "We are so anxious to know the exact purpose you had in mind in writing your wonderful book."

"You will find," Mrs. Plinth interposed, "that we are not superficial readers."

"We are eager to hear from you," Miss Van Vluyck continued, "if the

pessimistic tendency of the book is an expression of your own convictions or—"

"Or merely," Miss Glyde thrust in, "a somber background brushed in to
throw your figures into more vivid relief. *Are* you not primarily plastic?"

"*I* have always maintained," Mrs. Ballinger interposed, "that you represent the purely objective method—"

Osric Dane helped herself critically to coffee. "How do you define
objective?" she then inquired.

There was a flurried pause before Laura Glyde intensely murmured: "In
reading *you* we don't define, we feel."

Osric Dane smiled. "The cerebellum," she remarked, "is not infrequently
the seat of the literary emotions." And she took a second lump of sugar.

The sting that this remark was vaguely felt to conceal was almost
neutralized by the satisfaction of being addressed in such technical language.

"Ah, the cerebellum," said Miss Van Vluyck complacently. "The club
took a course in psychology last winter."

"Which psychology?" asked Osric Dane.

There was an agonizing pause, during which each member of the club
secretly deplored the distressing inefficiency of the others. Only Mrs. Roby
went on placidly sipping her chartreuse. At last Mrs. Ballinger said, with
an attempt at a high tone: "Well, really, you know, it was last year that we
took psychology, and this winter we have been so absorbed in—

She broke off, nervously trying to recall some of the club's discussions; but
her faculties seemed to be paralyzed by the petrifying stare of Osric Dane. What
had the club been absorbed in? Mrs. Ballinger, with a vague purpose of
gaining time, repeated slowly: "We've been so intensely absorbed in—"

Mrs. Roby put down her liqueur glass and drew near the group with a
smile.

"In Xingu?" she gently prompted.

A thrill ran through the other members. They exchanged confused
glances, and then, with one accord, turned a gaze of mingled relief and
interrogation on their rescuer. The expression of each denoted a different
phase of the same emotion. Mrs. Plinth was the first to compose her
features to an air of reassurance: after a moment's hasty adjustment her look
almost implied that it was she who had given the word to Mrs. Ballinger.

"Xingu, of course!" exclaimed the latter with her accustomed promptness, while Miss Van Vluyck and Laura Glyde seemed to be plumbing the
depths of memory, and Mrs. Leveret, feeling apprehensively for *Appropriate
Allusions,* was somehow reassured by the uncomfortable pressure of its bulk
against her person.

Osric Dane's change of countenance was no less striking than that of her
entertainers. She too put down her coffee cup, but with a look of distinct

annoyance; she too wore, for a brief moment, what Mrs. Roby afterward described as the look of feeling for something in the back of her head; and before she could dissemble these momentary signs of weakness, Mrs. Roby, turning to her with a deferential smile, had said: "And we've been so hoping that today you would tell us just what you think of it."

Osric Dane received the homage of the smile as a matter of course; but the accompanying question obviously embarrassed her, and it became clear to her observers that she was not quick at shifting her facial scenery. It was as though her countenance had so long been set in an expression of unchallenged superiority that the muscles had stiffened, and refused to obey her orders.

"Xingu—" she said, as if seeking in her turn to gain time.

Mrs. Roby continued to press her. "Knowing how engrossing the subject is, you will understand how it happens that the club has let everything else go to the wall for the moment. Since we took up Xingu I might almost say—were it not for your books—that nothing else seems to us worth remembering."

Osric Dane's stern features were darkened rather than lit up by an uneasy smile. "I am glad to hear that you make one exception," she gave out between narrowed lips.

"Oh, of course," Mrs. Roby said prettily; "but as you have shown us that—so very naturally!—you don't care to talk of your own things, we really can't let you off from telling us exactly what you think about Xingu; especially," she added, with a still more persuasive smile, "as some people say that one of your last books was saturated with it."

It was an *it,* then—the assurance sped like fire through the parched minds of the other members. In their eagerness to gain the least little clue to Xingu they almost forgot the joy of assisting at the discomfiture of Mrs. Dane.

The latter reddened nervously under her antagonist's challenge. "May I ask," she faltered out, "to which of my books you refer?"

Mrs. Roby did not falter. "That's just what I want you to tell us; because, though I was present, I didn't actually take part."

"Present at what?" Mrs. Dane took her up; and for an instant the trembling members of the Lunch Club thought that the champion Providence had raised up for them had lost a point. But Mrs. Roby explained herself gaily: "At the discussion, of course. And so we're dreadfully anxious to know just how it was that you went into the Xingu."

There was a portentous pause, a silence so big with incalculable dangers that the members with one accord checked the words on their lips, like soldiers dropping their arms to watch a single combat between their leaders. Then Mrs. Dane gave expression to their inmost dread by saying sharply: "Ah—you say *the* Xingu, do you?"

Mrs. Roby smiled undauntedly. "It is a shade pedantic, isn't it? Personally, I always drop the article: but I don't know how the other members feel about it."

The other members looked as though they would willingly have dispensed with this appeal to their opinion, and Mrs. Roby, after a bright glance about the group, went on: "They probably think, as I do, that nothing really matters except the thing itself—except Xingu."

No immediate reply seemed to occur to Mrs. Dane, and Mrs. Ballinger gathered courage to say: "Surely everyone must feel that about Xingu."

Mrs. Plinth came to her support with a heavy murmur of assent, and Laura Glyde sighed out emotionally: "I have known cases where it has changed a whole life."

"It has done me worlds of good," Mrs. Leveret interjected, seeming to herself to remember that she had either taken it or read it the winter before.

"Of course," Mrs. Roby admitted, "the difficulty is that one must give up so much time to it. It's very long."

"I can't imagine," said Miss Van Vluyck, "grudging the time given to such a subject."

"And deep in places," Mrs. Roby pursued; (so then it was a book!) "And it isn't easy to skip."

"I never skip," said Mrs. Plinth dogmatically.

"Ah, it's dangerous to, in Xingu. Even at the start there are places where one can't. One must just wade through."

"I should hardly call it *wading*," said Mrs. Ballinger sarcastically.

Mrs. Roby sent her a look of interest. "Ah—you always found it went swimmingly?"

Mrs. Ballinger hesitated. "Of course there are difficult passages," she conceded.

"Yes; some are not at all clear—even," Mrs. Roby added, "if one is familiar with the original."

"As I suppose you are?" Osric Dane interposed, suddenly fixing her with a look of challenge.

Mrs. Roby met it by a deprecating gesture. "Oh, it's really not difficult up to a certain point; though some of the branches are very little known, and it's almost impossible to get at the source."

"Have you ever tried?" Mrs. Plinth inquired, still distrustful of Mrs. Roby's thoroughness.

Mrs. Roby was silent for a moment; then she replied with lowered lids: "No—but a friend of mine did; a very brilliant man; and he told me it was best for women—not to. . . ."

A shudder ran around the room. Mrs. Leveret coughed so that the parlormaid, who was handing the cigarettes, should not hear; Miss Van Vluyck's face took on a nauseated expression, and Mrs. Plinth looked as if she were passing someone she did not care to bow to. But the most remarkable result of Mrs. Roby's words was the effect they produced on the Lunch Club's distinguished guest. Osric Dane's impassive features suddenly softened to an expression of the warmest human sympathy, and edging her chair toward Mrs. Roby's she asked: "Did he really? And—did you find he was right?"

Mrs. Ballinger, in whom annoyance at Mrs. Roby's unwonted assumption of prominence was beginning to displace gratitude for the aid she had rendered, could not consent to her being allowed, by such dubious means, to monopolize the attention of their guest. If Osric Dane had not enough self-respect to resent Mrs. Roby's flippancy, at least the Lunch Club would do so in the person of its President.

Mrs. Ballinger laid her hand on Mrs. Roby's arm. "We must not forget," she said with a frigid amiability, "that absorbing as Xingu is to *us,* it may be less interesting to—"

"Oh, no, on the contrary, I assure you," Osric Dane intervened.

"—to others," Mrs. Ballinger finished firmly; "and we must not allow our little meeting to end without persuading Mrs. Dane to say a few words to us on a subject which, today, is much more present in all our thoughts. I refer, of course, to *The Wings of Death.*"

The other members, animated by various degrees of the same sentiment, and encouraged by the humanized mien of their redoubtable guest, repeated after Mrs. Ballinger: "Oh, yes, you really *must* talk to us a little about your book."

Osric Dane's expression became as bored, though not as haughty, as when her work had been previously mentioned. But before she could respond to Mrs. Ballinger's request, Mrs. Roby had risen from her seat, and was pulling down her veil over her frivolous nose.

"I'm so sorry," she said, advancing toward her hostess with outstretched hand, "but before Mrs. Dane begins I think I'd better run away. Unluckily, as you know, I haven't read her books, so I should be at a terrible disadvantage among you all, and besides, I've an engagement to play bridge."

If Mrs. Roby had simply pleaded her ignorance of Osric Dane's works as a reason for withdrawing, the Lunch Club, in view of her recent prowess, might have approved such evidence of discretion; but to couple this excuse with the brazen announcement that she was foregoing the privilege for the purpose of joining a bridge party was only one more instance of her deplorable lack of discrimination.

The ladies were disposed, however, to feel that her departure—now that she had performed the sole service she was ever likely to render them— would probably make for greater order and dignity in the impending discussion, besides relieving them of the sense of self-distrust which her presence always mysteriously produced. Mrs. Ballinger therefore restricted herself to a formal murmur of regret, and the other members were just grouping themselves comfortably about Osric Dane when the latter, to their dismay, started up from the sofa on which she had been seated.

"Oh wait—do wait, and I'll go with you!" she called out to Mrs. Roby; and, seizing the hands of the disconcerted members, she administered a series of farewell pressures with the mechanical haste of a railway conductor punching tickets.

"I'm so sorry—I'd quite forgotten—" she flung back at them from the threshold; and as she joined Mrs. Roby, who had turned in surprise at her appeal, the other ladies had the mortification of hearing her say, in a voice which she did not take the pains to lower: "If you'll let me walk a little way with you, I should so like to ask you a few more questions about Xingu. . . ."

* III *

The incident had been so rapid that the door closed on the departing pair before the other members had time to understand what was happening. Then a sense of the indignity put upon them by Osric Dane's unceremonious desertion began to contend with the confused feeling that they had been cheated out of their due without exactly knowing how or why.

There was a silence, during which Mrs. Ballinger, with a perfunctory hand, rearranged the skillfully grouped literature at which her distinguished guest had not so much as glanced; then Miss Van Vluyck tartly pronounced: "Well, I can't say that I consider Osric Dane's departure a great loss."

This confession crystallized the resentment of the other members, and Mrs. Leveret exclaimed: "I do believe she came on purpose to be nasty!"

It was Mrs. Plinth's private opinion that Osric Dane's attitude toward the Lunch Club might have been very different had it welcomed her in the majestic setting of the Plinth drawing rooms; but not liking to reflect on the inadequacy of Mrs. Ballinger's establishment she sought a roundabout satisfaction in deprecating her lack of foresight.

"I said from the first that we ought to have had a subject ready. It's what always happens when you're unprepared. Now if we'd only got up Xingu—"

The slowness of Mrs. Plinth's mental processes was always allowed for by the club; but this instance of it was too much for Mrs. Ballinger's equanimity.

"Xingu!" she scoffed. "Why, it was the fact of our knowing so much more about it than she did—unprepared though we were—that made Osric Dane so furious. I should have thought that was plain enough to everybody!"

This retort impressed even Mrs. Plinth, and Laura Glyde, moved by an impulse of generosity, said: "Yes, we really ought to be grateful to Mrs. Roby for introducing the topic. It may have made Osric Dane furious, but at least it made her civil."

"I am glad we were able to show her," added Miss Van Vluyck, "that a broad and up-to-date culture is not confined to the great intellectual centers."

This increased the satisfaction of the other members, and they began to forget their wrath against Osric Dane in the pleasure of having contributed to her discomfiture.

Miss Van Vluyck thoughtfully rubbed her spectacles. "What surprised me most," she continued, "was that Fanny Roby should be so up on Xingu."

This remark threw a slight chill on the company, but Mrs. Ballinger said with an air of indulgent irony: "Mrs. Roby always has the knack of making a little go a long way; still, we certainly owe her a debt for happening to remember that she'd heard of Xingu." And this was felt by the other members to be a graceful way of canceling once and for all the club's obligation to Mrs. Roby.

Even Mrs. Leveret took courage to speed a timid shaft of irony. "I fancy Osric Dane hardly expected to take a lesson in Xingu at Hillbridge!"

Mrs. Ballinger smiled. "When she asked me what we represented—do you remember?—I wish I'd simply said we represented Xingu!"

All the ladies laughed appreciatively at this sally, except Mrs. Plinth, who said, after a moment's deliberation: "I'm not sure it would have been wise to do so."

Mrs. Ballinger, who was already beginning to feel as if she had launched at Osric Dane the retort which had just occurred to her, turned ironically on Mrs. Plinth. "May I ask why?" she inquired.

Mrs. Plinth looked grave. "Surely," she said, "I understood from Mrs. Roby herself that the subject was one it was as well not to go into too deeply?"

Miss Van Vluyck rejoined with precision: "I think that applied only to an investigation of the origin of the—of the—"; and suddenly she found that her usually accurate memory had failed her. "It's a part of the subject I never studied myself," she concluded.

"Nor I," said Mrs. Ballinger.

Laura Glyde bent toward them with widened eyes. "And yet it seems—doesn't it—the part that is fullest of an esoteric fascination?"

"I don't know on what you base that," said Miss Van Vluyck argumentatively.

"Well, didn't you notice how intensely interested Osric Dane became as soon as she heard what the brilliant foreigner—he *was* a foreigner, wasn't he—had told Mrs. Roby about the origin—the origin of the rite—or whatever you call it?"

Mrs. Plinth looked disapproving, and Mrs. Ballinger visibly wavered. Then she said: "It may not be desirable to touch on the—on that part of the subject in general conversation; but, from the importance it evidently has to a woman of Osric Dane's distinction, I feel as if we ought not to be afraid to discuss it among ourselves—without gloves—though with closed doors, if necessary."

"I'm quite of your opinion," Miss Van Vluyck came briskly to her support; "on condition, that is, that all grossness of language is avoided."

"Oh, I'm sure we shall understand without that," Mrs. Leveret tittered; and Laura Glyde added significantly: "I fancy we can read between the lines," while Mrs. Ballinger rose to assure herself that the doors were really closed.

Mrs. Plinth had not yet given her adhesion. "I hardly see," she began, "what benefit is to be derived from investigating such peculiar customs—"

But Mrs. Ballinger's patience had reached the extreme limit of tension. "This at least," she returned; "that we shall not be placed again in the humiliating position of finding ourselves less up on our own subjects than Fanny Roby!"

Even to Mrs. Plinth this argument was conclusive. She peered furtively about the room and lowered her commanding tones to ask: "Have you got a copy?"

"A—a copy?" stammered Mrs. Ballinger. She was aware that the other members were looking at her expectantly, and that this answer was inadequate, so she supported it by asking another question. "A copy of what?"

Her companions bent their expectant gaze on Mrs. Plinth, who, in turn, appeared less sure of herself than usual. "Why, of—of—the book," she explained.

"What book?" snapped Miss Van Vluyck, almost as sharply as Osric Dane.

Mrs. Ballinger looked at Laura Glyde, whose eyes were interrogatively fixed on Mrs. Leveret. The fact of being deferred to was so new to the latter that it filled her with an insane temerity. "Why, Xingu, of course!" she exclaimed.

A profound silence followed this challenge to the resources of Mrs. Ballinger's library, and the latter, after glancing nervously toward the Books of the Day, returned with dignity: "It's not a thing one cares to leave about."

"I should think *not!*" exclaimed Mrs. Plinth.

"It *is* a book, then?" said Miss Van Vluyck.

This again threw the company into disarray, and Mrs. Ballinger, with an impatient sigh, rejoined: "Why—there *is* a book—naturally. . . ."

"Then why did Miss Glyde call it a religion?"

Laura Glyde started up. "A religion? I never—"

"Yes, you did," Miss Van Vluyck insisted; "you spoke of rites; and Mrs. Plinth said it was a custom."

Miss Glyde was evidently making a desperate effort to recall her statement; but accuracy of detail was not her strongest point. At length she began in a deep murmur: "Surely they used to do something of the kind at the Eleusinian mysteries—"

"Oh—" said Miss Van Vluyck, on the verge of disapproval; and Mrs. Plinth protested: "I understood there was to be no indelicacy!"

Mrs. Ballinger could not control her irritation. "Really, it is too bad that we should not be able to talk the matter over quietly among ourselves. Personally, I think that if one goes into Xingu at all—"

"Oh, so do I!" cried Miss Glyde.

"And I don't see how one can avoid doing so, if one wishes to keep up with the Thought of the Day—"

Mrs. Leveret uttered an exclamation of relief. "There—that's it!" she interposed.

"What's it?" the President took her up.

"Why—it's a—a Thought: I mean a philosophy."

This seemed to bring a certain relief to Mrs. Ballinger and Laura Glyde, but Miss Van Vluyck said: "Excuse me if I tell you that you're all mistaken. Xingu happens to be a language."

"A language!" the Lunch Club cried.

"Certainly. Don't you remember Fanny Roby's saying that there were several branches, and that some were hard to trace? What could that apply to but dialects?"

Mrs. Ballinger could no longer restrain a contemptuous laugh. "Really, if the Lunch Club has reached such a pass that it has to go to Fanny Roby for instruction on a subject like Xingu, it had almost better cease to exist!"

"It's really her fault for not being clearer," Laura Glyde put in.

"Oh, clearness and Fanny Roby!" Mrs. Ballinger shrugged. "I dare say we shall find she was mistaken on almost every point."

"Why not look it up?" said Mrs. Plinth.

As a rule this recurrent suggestion of Mrs. Plinth's was ignored in the heat of discussion, and only resorted to afterward in the privacy of each member's home. But on the present occasion the desire to ascribe their own confusion of thought to the vague and contradictory nature of Mrs. Roby's statements caused the members of the Lunch Club to utter a collective demand for a book of reference.

At this point the production of her treasured volume gave Mrs. Leveret, for a moment, the unusual experience of occupying the center front; but she was not able to hold it long, for *Appropriate Allusions* contained no mention of Xingu.

"Oh, that's not the kind of thing we want!" exclaimed Miss Van Vluyck. She cast a disparaging glance over Mrs. Ballinger's assortment of literature, and added impatiently: "Haven't you any useful books?"

"Of course I have," replied Mrs. Ballinger indignantly; "I keep them in my husband's dressing room."

From this region, after some difficulty and delay, the parlormaid produced the W-Z volume of an *Encyclopedia* and, in deference to the fact that the demand for it had come from Miss Van Vluyck, laid the ponderous tome before her.

There was a moment of painful suspense while Miss Van Vluyck rubbed her spectacles, adjusted them, and turned to Z; and a murmur of surprise when she said: "It isn't here."

"I suppose," said Mrs. Plinth, "it's not fit to be put in a book of reference."

"Oh, nonsense!" exclaimed Mrs. Ballinger. "Try X."

Miss Van Vluyck turned back through the volume, peering short-sightedly up and down the pages, till she came to a stop and remained motionless, like a dog on a point.

"Well, have you found it?" Mrs. Ballinger inquired after a considerable delay.

"Yes. I've found it," said Miss Van Vluyck in a queer voice.

Mrs. Plinth hastily interposed: "I beg you won't read it aloud if there's anything offensive."

Miss Van Vluyck, without answering, continued her silent scrutiny.

"Well, what *is* it?" exclaimed Laura Glyde excitedly.

"*Do* tell us!" urged Mrs. Leveret, feeling that she would have something awful to tell her sister.

Miss Van Vluyck pushed the volume aside and turned slowly toward the expectant group.

"It's a river."

"A *river?*"

"Yes: in Brazil. Isn't that where she's been living?"

"Who? Fanny Roby? Oh, but you must be mistaken. You've been reading the wrong thing," Mrs. Ballinger exclaimed, leaning over her to seize the volume.

"It's the only Xingu in the *Encyclopedia;* and she *has* been living in Brazil," Miss Van Vluyck persisted.

"Yes: her brother has a consulship there," Mrs. Leveret interposed.

"But it's too ridiculous! I—we—why we *all* remember studying Xingu last year—or the year before last," Mrs. Ballinger stammered.

"I thought I did when *you* said so," Laura Glyde avowed.

"*I* said so?" cried Mrs. Ballinger.

"Yes. You said it had crowded everything else out of your mind."

"Well *you* said it had changed your whole life!"

"For that matter Miss Van Vluyck said she had never grudged the time she'd given it."

Mrs. Plinth interposed: "I made it clear that I knew nothing whatever of the original."

Mrs. Ballinger broke off the dispute with a groan. "Oh, what does it all matter if she's been making fools of us? I believe Miss Van Vluyck's right—she was talking of the river all the while!"

"How could she? It's too preposterous," Miss Glyde exclaimed.

"Listen." Miss Van Vluyck had repossessed herself of the *Encyclopedia,* and restored her spectacles to a nose reddened by excitement. " 'The Xingu, one of the principal rivers of Brazil, rises on the plateau of Matto Grosso, and flows in a northerly direction for a length of no less than one-thousand one-hundred and eighteen miles, entering the Amazon near the mouth of the latter river. The upper course of the Xingu is auriferous and fed by numerous branches. Its source was first discovered in 1884 by the German explorer von den Steinen, after a difficult and dangerous expedition through a region inhabited by tribes still in the Stone Age of culture.' "

The ladies received this communication in a state of stupefied silence from which Mrs. Leveret was the first to rally. "She certainly *did* speak of its having branches."

The word seemed to snap the last thread of their incredulity. "And of its great length," gasped Mrs. Ballinger.

"She said it was awfully deep, and you couldn't skip—you just had to wade through," Miss Glyde added.

The idea worked its way more slowly through Mrs. Plinth's compact resistances. "How could there be anything improper about a river?" she inquired.

"Improper?"

"Why, what she said about the source—that it was corrupt?"

"Not corrupt, but hard to get at," Laura Glyde corrected. "Someone who'd been there had told her so. I dare say it was the explorer himself—doesn't it say the expedition was dangerous?"

" 'Difficult and dangerous,' " read Miss Van Vluyck.

Mrs. Ballinger pressed her hands to her throbbing temples. "There's nothing she said that wouldn't apply to a river—to this river!" She swung about excitedly to the other members. "Why, do you remember her telling us that she hadn't read *The Supreme Instant* because she'd taken it on a boating party while she was staying with her brother, and someone had 'shied' it overboard—'shied' of course was her own expression."

The ladies breathlessly signified that the expression had not escaped them.

"Well—and then didn't she tell Osric Dane that one of her books was simply saturated with Xingu? Of course it was, if one of Mrs. Roby's rowdy friends had thrown it into the river!"

This surprising reconstruction of the scene in which they had just paricipated left the members of the Lunch Club inarticulate. At length, Mrs. Plinth, after visibly laboring with the problem, said in a heavy tone: "Osric Dane was taken in too."

Mrs. Leveret took courage at this. "Perhaps that's what Mrs. Roby did it for. She said Osric Dane was a brute, and she may have wanted to give her a lesson."

Miss Van Vluyck frowned. "It was hardly worth-while to do it at our expense."

"At least," said Miss Glyde with a touch of bitterness, "she succeeded in interesting her, which was more than we did."

"What chance had we?" rejoined Mrs. Ballinger. "Mrs. Roby monopolized her from the first. And *that,* I've no doubt, was her purpose—to give Osric Dane a false impression of her own standing in the club. She would hesitate at nothing to attract attention: we all know how she took in poor Professor Foreland."

"She actually makes him give bridge teas every Thursday," Mrs. Leveret piped up.

Laura Glyde struck her hands together. "Why, this is Thursday, and it's *there* she's gone, of course; and taken Osric with her!"

"And they're shricking over us at this moment," said Mrs. Ballinger between her teeth.

This possibility seemed too preposterous to be admitted. "She would hardly dare," said Miss Van Vluyck, "confess the imposture to Osric Dane."

"I'm not so sure: I thought I saw her make a sign as she left. If she hadn't made a sign, why should Osric Dane have rushed out after her?"

"Well, you know, we'd all been telling her how wonderful Xingu was, and she said she wanted to find out more about it," Mrs. Leveret said, with a tardy impulse of justice to the absent.

This reminder, far from mitigating the wrath of the other members, gave it a stronger impetus.

"Yes—and that's exactly what they're both laughing over now," said Laura Glyde ironically.

Mrs. Plinth stood up and gathered her expensive furs about her monumental form. "I have no wish to criticize," she said; "but unless the Lunch

Club can protect its members against the recurrence of such—such unbecoming scenes, I for one—"

"Oh, so do I!" agreed Miss Glyde, rising also.

Miss Van Vluyck closed the *Encyclopedia* and proceeded to button herself into her jacket. "My time is really too valuable—" she began.

"I fancy we are all of one mind," said Mrs. Ballinger, looking searchingly at Mrs. Leveret, who looked at the others.

"I always deprecate anything like a scandal—" Mrs. Plinth continued.

"She has been the cause of one today!" exclaimed Miss Glyde.

Mrs. Leveret moaned: "I don't see how she *could!*" and Miss Van Vluyck said, picking up her notebook: "Some women stop at nothing."

"—But if," Mrs. Plinth took up her argument impressively, "anything of the kind had happened in *my* house" (it never would have, her tone implied), "I should have felt that I owed it to myself either to ask for Mrs. Roby's resignation—or to offer mine."

"Oh, Mrs. Plinth—" gasped the Lunch Club.

"Fortunately for me," Mrs. Plinth continued with an awful magnanimity, "the matter was taken out of my hands by our President's decision that the right to entertain distinguished guests was a privilege vested in her office; and I think the other members will agree that, as she was alone in this opinion, she ought to be alone in deciding on the best way of effacing its—its really deplorable consequences."

A deep silence followed this outbreak of Mrs. Plinth's long-stored resentment.

"I don't see why *I* should be expected to ask her to resign—" Mrs. Ballinger at length began; but Laura Glyde turned back to remind her: "You know she made you say that you'd got on swimmingly in Xingu."

An ill-timed giggle escaped from Mrs. Leveret, and Mrs. Ballinger energetically continued "—But you needn't think for a moment that I'm afraid to!"

The door of the drawing room closed on the retreating backs of the Lunch Club, and the President of that distinguished association, seating herself at her writing table, and pushing away a copy of *The Wings of Death* to make room for her elbow, drew forth a sheet of the club's notepaper, on which she began to write: "My dear Mrs. Roby—"

AUTRES TEMPS . . .

MRS. LIDCOTE, as the huge menacing mass of New York defined itself far off across the waters, shrank back into her corner of the deck and sat listening with a kind of unreasoning terror to the steady onward drive of the screws.

She had set out on the voyage quietly enough—in what she called her "reasonable" mood—but the week at sea had given her too much time to think of things and had left her too long alone with the past.

When she was alone, it was always the past that occupied her. She couldn't get away from it, and she didn't any longer care to. During her long years of exile she had made her terms with it, had learned to accept the fact that it would always be there, huge, obstructing, encumbering, bigger and more dominant than anything the future could ever conjure up. And, at any rate, she was sure of it, she understood it, knew how to reckon with it; she had learned to screen and manage and protect it as one does an afflicted member of one's family.

There had never been any danger of her being allowed to forget the past. It looked out at her from the face of every acquaintance, it appeared suddenly in the eyes of strangers when a word enlightened them: "Yes, *the* Mrs. Lidcote, don't you know?" It had sprung at her the first day out, when, across the dining room, from the captain's table, she had seen Mrs. Lorin Boulger's revolving eyeglass pause and the eye behind it grow as blank as a dropped blind. The next day, of course, the captain had asked: "You know your ambassadress, Mrs. Boulger?" and she had replied that, No, she seldom left Florence, and hadn't been to Rome for more than a day since the Boulgers had been sent to Italy. She was so used to these phrases that it cost her no effort to repeat them. And the captain had promptly changed the subject.

No, she didn't, as a rule, mind the past, because she was used to it and understood it. It was a great concrete fact in her path that she had to walk around every time she moved in any direction. But now, in the light of the unhappy event that had summoned her from Italy,—the sudden unanticipated news of her daughter's divorce from Horace Pursh and remarriage with Wilbour Barkley—the past, her own poor miserable past, started up at her with eyes of accusation, became, to her disordered fancy, like the afflicted relative suddenly breaking away from nurses and keepers and publicly parading the horror and misery she had, all the long years, so patiently screened and secluded.

Yes, there it had stood before her through the agitated weeks since the news had come—during her interminable journey from India, where Leila's letter had overtaken her, and the feverish halt in her apartment in Florence, where she had had to stop and gather up her possessions for a fresh start—there it had stood grinning at her with a new balefulness which seemed to say: "Oh, but you've got to look at me *now,* because I'm not only your own past but Leila's present."

Certainly it was a master stroke of those arch-ironists of the shears and spindle to duplicate her own story in her daughter's. Mrs. Lidcote had always somewhat grimly fancied that, having so signally failed to be of use to Leila in other ways, she would at least serve her as a warning. She had even abstained from defending herself, from making the best of her case, had stoically refused to plead extenuating circumstances, lest Leila's impulsive sympathy should lead to deductions that might react disastrously on her own life. And now that very thing had happened, and Mrs. Lidcote could hear the whole of New York saying with one voice: "Yes, Leila's done just what her mother did. With such an example what could you expect?"

Yet if she had been an example, poor woman, she had been an awful one; she had been, she would have supposed, of more use as a deterrent than a hundred blameless mothers as incentives. For how could anyone who had seen anything of her life in the last eighteen years have had the courage to repeat so disastrous an experiment?

Well, logic in such cases didn't count, example didn't count, nothing probably counted but having the same impulses in the blood; and that was the dark inheritance she had bestowed upon her daughter. Leila hadn't consciously copied her; she had simply "taken after" her, had been a projection of her own long-past rebellion.

Mrs. Lidcote had deplored, when she started, that the "Utopia" was a slow steamer, and would take eight full days to bring her to her unhappy daughter; but now, as the moment of reunion approached, she would willingly have turned the boat about and fled back to the high seas. It was not only because she felt still so unprepared to face what New York had in store for her, but because she needed more time to dispose of what the "Utopia" had already given her. The past was bad enough, but the present and future were worse, because they were less comprehensible, and because, as she grew older, surprises and inconsequences troubled her more than the worst certainties.

There was Mrs. Boulger, for instance. In the light, or rather the darkness, of new developments, it might really be that Mrs. Boulger had not meant to cut her, but had simply failed to recognize her. Mrs. Lidcote had arrived at this hypothesis simply by listening to the conversation of the persons sitting next to her on deck—two lively young women with the latest Paris hats on their heads and the latest New York ideas in them. These ladies, as to whom it would have been impossible for a person with Mrs. Lidcote's old-fashioned categories to determine whether they were married or unmarried, "nice" or "horrid," or any one or other of the definite things which young women, in her youth and her society, were conveniently assumed to be, had revealed a familiarity with the world of New York that, again according to Mrs. Lidcote's traditions, should have implied a recognized place in it. But in the present fluid state of manners what did anything imply except what their hats implied—that no one could tell what was coming next?

They seemed, at any rate, to frequent a group of idle and opulent people who executed the same gestures and revolved on the same pivots as Mrs. Lidcote's daughter and her friends: their Coras, Matties and Mabels seemed at any moment likely to reveal familiar patronymics, and once one of the speakers, summing up a discussion of which Mrs. Lidcote had missed the beginning, had affirmed with headlong confidence: "Leila? Oh, *Leila's* all right."

Could it be *her* Leila, the mother had wondered, with a sharp thrill of apprehension? If only they would mention surnames! But their talk leaped elliptically from allusion to allusion, their unfinished sentences dangled over bottomless pits of conjecture, and they gave their bewildered hearer the impression not so much of talking only of their intimates, as of being intimate with everyone alive.

Her old friend Franklin Ide could have told her, perhaps; but here was the last day of the voyage, and she hadn't yet found courage to ask him. Great as had been the joy of discovering his name on the passenger list and seeing his friendly bearded face in the throng against the taffrail at Cherbourg, she had as yet said nothing to him except, when they had met: "Of course I'm going out to Leila."

She had said nothing to Franklin Ide because she had always instinctively shrunk from taking him into her confidence. She was sure he felt sorry for her, sorrier perhaps than anyone had ever felt; but he had always paid her the supreme tribute of not showing it. His attitude allowed her to imagine that compassion was not the basis of his feeling for her, and it was part of her joy in his friendship that it was the one relation seemingly unconditioned by her state, the only one in which she could think and feel and behave like any other woman.

Now, however, as the problem of New York loomed nearer, she began to regret that she had not spoken, had not at least questioned him about the hints she had gathered on the way. He did not know the two ladies next to her, he did not even, as it chanced, know Mrs. Lorin Boulger; but he knew New York, and New York was the sphinx whose riddle she must read or perish.

Almost as the thought passed through her mind his stooping shoulders and grizzled head detached themselves against the blaze of light in the west, and he sauntered down the empty deck and dropped into the chair at her side.

"You're expecting the Barkleys to meet you, I suppose?" he asked.

It was the first time she had heard any one pronounce her daughter's new name, and it occurred to her that her friend, who was shy and inarticulate, had been trying to say it all the way over and had at last shot it out at her only because he felt it must be now or never.

"I don't know. I cabled, of course. But I believe she's at—they're at—*his* place somewhere."

"Oh, Barkley's; yes, near Lenox, isn't it? But she's sure to come to town to meet you."

He said it so easily and naturally that her own constraint was relieved, and suddenly, before she knew what she meant to do, she had burst out: "She may dislike the idea of seeing people."

Ide, whose absent shortsighted gaze had been fixed on the slowly gliding water, turned in his seat to stare at his companion.

"Who? Leila?" he said with an incredulous laugh.

Mrs. Lidcote flushed to her faded hair and grew pale again. "It took *me* a long time—to get used to it," she said.

His look grew gently commiserating. "I think you'll find"—he paused for a word—"that things are different now—altogether easier."

"That's what I've been wondering—ever since we started." She was determined now to speak. She moved nearer, so that their arms touched, and she could drop her voice to a murmur. "You see, it all came on me in a flash. My going off to India and Siam on that long trip kept me away from letters for weeks at a time; and she didn't want to tell me beforehand—oh, I understand *that,* poor child! You know how good she's always been to me; how she's tried to spare me. And she knew, of course, what a state of horror I'd be in. She knew I'd rush off to her at once and try to stop it. So she never gave me a hint of anything, and she even managed to muzzle Susy Suffern—you know Susy is the one of the family who keeps me informed about things at home. I don't yet see how she prevented Susy's telling me; but she did. And her first letter, the one I got up at Bangkok, simply said the thing was over—the divorce, I mean—and that the very next day she'd—well, I suppose there was no use waiting; and *he* seems to have behaved as well as possible, to have wanted to marry her as much as—"

"Who? Barkley?" he helped her out. "I should say so! Why what do you suppose—" He interrupted himself: "He'll be devoted to her, I assure you."

"Oh, of course; I'm sure he will. He's written me—really beautifully. But it's a terrible strain on a man's devotion. I'm not sure that Leila realizes—"

Ide sounded again his little reassuring laugh. "I'm not sure that you realize. *They're* all right."

It was the very phrase that the young lady in the next seat had applied to the unknown "Leila," and its recurrence on Ide's lips flushed Mrs. Lidcote with fresh courage.

"I wish I knew just what you mean. The two young women next to me—the ones with the wonderful hats—have been talking in the same way."

"What? About Leila?"

"About *a* Leila; I fancied it might be mine. And about society in general. All their friends seem to be divorced; some of them seem to announce their engagements before they get their decree. One of them—*her* name was Mabel—as far as I could make out, her husband found out that she meant to divorce him by noticing that she wore a new engagement ring."

"Well, you see Leila did everything 'regularly,' as the French say," Ide rejoined.

"Yes; but are these people in society? The people my neighbors talk about?"

He shrugged his shoulders. "It would take an arbitration commission a good many sittings to define the boundaries of society nowadays. But at any rate they're in New York; and I assure you you're *not;* you're farther and farther from it."

"But I've been back there several times to see Leila." She hesitated and looked away from him. Then she brought out slowly: "And I've never noticed—the least change—in—in my own case—"

"Oh," he sounded deprecatingly, and she trembled with the fear of having gone too far. But the hour was past when such scruples could restrain her. She must know where she was and where Leila was. "Mrs. Boulger still cuts me," she brought out with an embarrassed laugh.

"Are you sure? You've probably cut *her;* if not now, at least in the past. And in a cut if you're not first you're nowhere. That's what keeps up so many quarrels."

The word roused Mrs. Lidcote to a renewed sense of realities. "But the Purshes," she said—"the Purshes are so strong! There are so many of them, and they all back each other up, just as my husband's family did. I know what it means to have a clan against one. They're stronger than any number of separate friends. The Purshes will *never* forgive Leila for leaving Horace. Why, his mother opposed his marrying her because of—of me. She tried to get Leila to promise that she wouldn't see me when they went to Europe on their honeymoon. And now she'll say it was my example."

Her companion, vaguely stroking his beard, mused a moment upon this; then he asked, with seeming irrelevance, "What did Leila say when you wrote that you were coming?"

"She said it wasn't the least necessary, but that I'd better come, because it was the only way to convince me that it wasn't."

"Well, then, that proves she's not afraid of the Purshes."

She breathed a long sigh of remembrance. "Oh, just at first, you know—one never is."

He laid his hand on hers with a gesture of intelligence and pity. "You'll see, you'll see," he said.

A shadow lengthened down the deck before them, and a steward stood there, proffering a Marconigram.

"Oh, now I shall know!" she exclaimed.

She tore the message open, and then let it fall on her knees, dropping her hands on it in silence.

Ide's inquiry roused her: "It's all right?"

"Oh, quite right. Perfectly. She can't come; but she's sending Susy Suffern. She says Susy will explain." After another silence she added, with a sudden gush of bitterness: "As if I needed any explanation!"

She felt Ide's hesitating glance upon her. "She's in the country?"

"Yes. 'Prevented last moment. Longing for you, expecting you. Love from both.' Don't you *see,* the poor darling, that she couldn't face it?"

"No, I don't." He waited. "Do you mean to go to her immediately?"

"It will be too late to catch a train this evening; but I shall take the first tomorrow morning." She considered a moment. "Perhaps it's better. I need a talk with Susy first. She's to meet me at the dock, and I'll take her straight back to the hotel with me."

As she developed this plan, she had the sense that Ide was still thoughtfully, even gravely, considering her. When she ceased, he remained silent a moment; then he said almost ceremoniously: "If your talk with Miss Suffern doesn't last too late, may I come and see you when it's over? I shall be dining at my club, and I'll call you up at about ten, if I may. I'm off to Chicago on business tomorrow morning, and it would be a satisfaction to know, before I start, that your cousin's been able to reassure you, as I know she will."

He spoke with a shy deliberateness that, even to Mrs. Lidcote's troubled perceptions, sounded a long-silenced note of feeling. Perhaps the breaking down of the barrier of reticence between them had released unsuspected emotions in both. The tone of his appeal moved her curiously and loosened the tight strain of her fears.

"Oh, yes, come—do come," she said, rising. The huge threat of New York was imminent now, dwarfing, under long reaches of embattled masonry, the great deck she stood on and all the little specks of life it carried. One of them, drifting nearer, took the shape of her maid, followed by luggage-laden stewards, and signing to her that it was time to go below. As they descended to the main deck, the throng swept her against Mrs. Lorin Boulger's shoulder, and she heard the ambassadress call out to someone, over the vexed sea of hats: "So sorry! I should have been delighted, but I've promised to spend Sunday with some friends at Lenox."

*   II   *

Susy Suffern's explanation did not end till after ten o'clock, and she had just gone when Franklin Ide, who, complying with an old New York tradition, had caused himself to be preceded by a long white box of roses, was shown into Mrs. Lidcote's sitting room.

He came forward with his shy half-humorous smile and, taking her hand, looked at her for a moment without speaking.

"It's all right," he then pronounced.

Mrs. Lidcote returned his smile. "It's extraordinary. Everything's changed. Even Susy has changed; and you know the extent to which Susy used to represent the old New York. There's no old New York left, it seems. She talked in the most amazing way. She snaps her fingers at the Purshes. She told me—*me,* that every woman had a right to happiness and that self-expression was the highest duty. She accused me of misunderstanding Leila; she said my point of view was conventional! She was bursting with pride at having been in the secret, and wearing a brooch that Wilbour Barkley'd given her!"

Franklin Ide had seated himself in the armchair she had pushed forward for him under the electric chandelier. He threw back his head and laughed. "What did I tell you?"

"Yes; but I can't believe that Susy's not mistaken. Poor dear, she has the habit of lost causes; and she may feel that, having stuck to me, she can do no less than stick to Leila."

"But she didn't—did she—openly defy the world for you? She didn't snap her fingers at the Lidcotes?"

Mrs. Lidcote shook her head, still smiling. "No. It was enough to defy *my* family. It was doubtful at one time if they would tolerate her seeing me, and she almost had to disinfect herself after each visit. I believe that at first my sister-in-law wouldn't let the girls come down when Susy dined with her."

"Well, isn't your cousin's present attitude the best possible proof that times have changed?"

"Yes, yes; I know." She leaned forward from her sofa-corner, fixing her eyes on his thin kindly face, which gleamed on her indistinctly through her tears. "If it's true, it's—it's dazzling. She says Leila's perfectly happy. It's as if an angel had gone about lifting gravestones, and the buried people walked again, and the living didn't shrink from them."

"That's about it," he assented.

She drew a deep breath, and sat looking away from him down the long perspective of lamp-fringed streets over which her windows hung.

"I can understand how happy you must be," he began at length.

She turned to him impetuously. "Yes, yes; I'm happy. But I'm lonely, too—lonelier than ever. I didn't take up much room in the world before; but now—where is there a corner for me? Oh, since I've begun to confess myself, why shouldn't I go on? Telling you this lifts a gravestone from *me!* You see, before this, Leila needed me. She was unhappy, and I knew it, and though we hardly ever talked of it I felt that, in a way, the thought that I'd been through the same thing, and down to the dregs of it, helped her. And her needing me helped *me*. And when the news of her marriage came my first thought was that now she'd need me more than ever, that she'd have no one but me to turn to. Yes, under all my distress there was a fierce joy in that. It was so new and wonderful to feel again that there was one person who wouldn't be able to get on without me! And now what you and Susy tell me seems to have taken my child from me; and just at first that's all I can feel."

"Of course it's all you feel." He looked at her musingly. "Why didn't Leila come to meet you?"

"That was really my fault. You see, I'd cabled that I was not sure of being able to get off on the 'Utopia,' and apparently my second cable was delayed, and when she received it she'd already asked some people over Sunday—one or two of her old friends, Susy says. I'm so glad they should have wanted to go to her at once; but naturally I'd rather have been alone with her."

"You still mean to go, then?"

"Oh, I must. Susy wanted to drag me off to Ridgefield with her over Sunday, and Leila sent me word that of course I might go if I wanted to, and that I was not to think of her; but I know how disappointed she would be. Susy said she was afraid I might be upset at her having people to stay, and that, if I minded, she wouldn't urge me to come. But if *they* don't mind, why should I? And of course, if they're willing to go to Leila it must mean—"

"Of course. I'm glad you recognize that," Franklin Ide exclaimed abruptly. He stood up and went over to her, taking her hand with one of his quick gestures. "There's something I want to say to you," he began—

The next morning, in the train, through all the other contending thoughts in Mrs. Lidcote's mind there ran the warm undercurrent of what Franklin Ide had wanted to say to her.

He had wanted, she knew, to say it once before, when, nearly eight years earlier, the hazard of meeting at the end of a rainy autumn in a deserted Swiss hotel had thrown them for a fortnight into unwonted propinquity. They had walked and talked together, borrowed each other's books and newspapers, spent the long chill evenings over the fire in the dim lamp-light of her little pitch-pine sitting room; and she had been wonderfully comforted by his presence, and hard frozen places in her had melted, and she had known that she would be desperately sorry when he went. And then, just at the end, in his odd indirect way, he had let her see that it rested with her to have him stay. She could still relive the sleepless night she had given to that discovery. It was preposterous, of course, to think of repaying his devotion by accepting such a sacrifice; but how find reasons to convince him? She could not bear to let him think her less touched, less inclined to him than she was: the generosity of his love deserved that she should repay it with the truth. Yet how let him see what she felt, and yet refuse what he offered? How confess to him what had been on her lips when he made the offer: "I've seen what it did to one man; and there must never, never be another"? The tacit ignoring of her past had been the element in which their friendship lived, and she could not suddenly, to him of all men, begin to talk of herself like a guilty woman in a play. Somehow, in the end, she had managed it, had averted a direct explanation, had made him understand that her life was over, that she existed only for her daughter, and that a more definite word from him would have been almost a breach of delicacy. She was so used to behaving as if her life were over! And, at any rate, he had taken her hint, and she had been able to spare her sensitiveness and his. The next year, when he came to Florence to see her, they met again in the old friendly way; and that till now had continued to be the tenor of their intimacy.

And now, suddenly and unexpectedly, he had brought up the question again, directly this time, and in such a form that she could not evade it: putting the renewal of his plea, after so long an interval, on the ground that, on her own showing, her chief argument against it no longer existed.

"You tell me Leila's happy. If she's happy, she doesn't need you—need you, that is, in the same way as before. You wanted, I know, to be always in reach, always free and available if she should suddenly call you to her or take refuge with you. I understood that—I respected it. I didn't urge my case because I saw it was useless. You couldn't, I understand well enough, have felt free to take such happiness as life with me might give you while she was unhappy, and, as you imagined, with no hope of release. Even then I didn't feel as you did about it; I understood better the trend of things here. But ten years ago the change hadn't really come; and I had no way of convincing you that it was coming. Still, I always fancied that Leila might not think her case was closed, and so I chose to think that ours wasn't either. Let me go on thinking so, at any rate, till you've seen her, and confirmed with your own eyes what Susy Suffern tells you."

* III *

All through what Susy Suffern told and retold her during their four-hours' flight to the hills this plea of Ide's kept coming back to Mrs. Lidcote. She did not yet know what she felt as to its bearing on her own fate, but it was something on which her confused thoughts could stay themselves amid the welter of new impressions, and she was inexpressibly glad that he had said what he had, and said it at that particular moment. It helped her to hold fast to her identity in the rush of strange names and new categories that her cousin's talk poured out on her.

With the progress of the journey Miss Suffern's communications grew more and more amazing. She was like a cicerone preparing the mind of an inexperienced traveler for the marvels about to burst on it.

"You won't know Leila. She's had her pearls reset. Sargent's to paint her. Oh, and I was to tell you that she hopes you won't mind being the least bit squeezed over Sunday. The house was built by Wilbour's father, you know, and it's rather old-fashioned—only ten spare bedrooms. Of course that's small for what they mean to do, and she'll show you the new plans they've had made. Their idea is to keep the present house as a wing. She told me to explain—she's so dreadfully sorry not to be able to give you a sitting room just at first. They're thinking of Egypt for next winter, unless, of course, Wilbour gets his appointment. Oh, didn't she write you about that? Why, he wants Rome, you know—the second secretaryship. Or, rather, he wanted England; but Leila insisted that if they went abroad she must be near you. And of course what she says is law. Oh, they quite hope they'll get it. You see Horace's uncle is in the Cabinet—one of the assistant secretaries—and I believe he has a good deal of pull—"

"Horace's uncle? You mean Wilbour's, I suppose," Mrs. Lidcote interjected, with a gasp of which a fraction was given to Miss Suffern's flippant use of the language.

"Wilbour's? No, I don't. I mean Horace's. There's no bad feeling between them, I assure you. Since Horace's engagement was announced —you didn't know Horace was engaged? Why, he's marrying one of Bishop Thorbury's girls: the red-haired one who wrote the novel that everyone's talking about. *This Flesh of Mine.* They're to be married in the cathedral. Of course Horace *can,* because it was Leila who—but, as I say, there's not the *least* feeling, and Horace wrote himself to his uncle about Wilbour."

Mrs. Lidcote's thoughts fled back to what she had said to Ide the day before on the deck of the "Utopia." "I didn't take up much room before, but now where is there a corner for me?" Where indeed in this crowded, topsy-turvy world, with its headlong changes and helter-skelter readjustments, its new tolerances and indifferences and accommodations, was there room for a character fashioned by slower sterner processes and a life broken under their inexorable pressure? And then, in a flash, she viewed the chaos from a new angle, and order seemed to move upon the void. If the old processes were changed, her case was changed with them; she, too, was a part of the general readjustment, a tiny fragment of the new pattern worked out in bolder freer harmonies. Since her daughter had no penalty to pay, was not she herself released by the same stroke? The rich arrears of youth and joy were gone; but was there not time enough left to accumulate new stores of happiness? That, of course, was what Franklin Ide had felt and had meant her to feel. He had seen at once what the change in her daughter's situation would make in her view of her own. It was almost— wondrously enough!—as if Leila's folly had been the means of vindicating hers.

Everything else for the moment faded for Mrs. Lidcote in the glow of her daughter's embrace. It was unnatural, it was almost terrifying, to find herself standing on a strange threshold, under an unknown roof, in a big hall full of pictures, flowers, firelight, and hurrying servants, and in this spacious unfamiliar confusion to discover Leila, bareheaded, laughing, authoritative, with a strange young man jovially echoing her welcome and transmitting her orders; but once Mrs. Lidcote had her child on her breast, and her child's "It's all right, you old darling!" in her ears, every other feeling was lost in the deep sense of well-being that only Leila's hug could give.

The sense was still with her, warming her veins and pleasantly fluttering her heart, as she went up to her room after luncheon. A little constrained by the presence of visitors, and not altogether sorry to defer for a few hours the "long talk" with her daughter for which she somehow felt herself tremulously unready, she had withdrawn, on the plea of fatigue, to the bright luxurious bedroom into which Leila had again and again apologized for having been obliged to squeeze her. The room was bigger and finer than any in her small apartment in Florence; but it was not the standard of affluence implied in her daughter's tone about it that chiefly struck her, nor yet the finish and complexity of its appointments. It was the look it shared with the rest of the house, and with the perspective of the gardens beneath its windows, of being part of an "establishment"—of something solid, avowed, founded on sacraments and precedents and principles. There was nothing about the place, or about Leila and Wilbour, that suggested either passion or peril: their relation seemed as comfortable as their furniture and as respectable as their balance at the bank.

This was, in the whole confusing experience, the thing that confused Mrs. Lidcote most, that gave her at once the deepest feeling of security for Leila and the strongest sense of apprehension for herself. Yes, there was something oppressive in the completeness and compactness of Leila's well-being. Ide had been right: her daughter did not need her. Leila, with her first embrace, had unconsciously attested the fact in the same phrase as Ide himself and as the two young women with the hats. "It's all right, you old darling!" she had said: and her mother sat alone, trying to fit herself into the new scheme of things which such a certainty betokened.

Her first distinct feeling was one of irrational resentment. If such a change was to come, why had it not come sooner? Here was she, a woman not yet old, who had paid with the best years of her life for the theft of the happiness that her daughter's contemporaries were taking as their due. There was no sense, no sequence, in it. She had had what she wanted, but she had had to pay too much for it. She had had to pay the last bitterest price of learning that love has a price: that it is worth so much and no more. She had known the anguish of watching the man she loved discover this first, and of reading the discovery in his eyes. It was a part of her history that she had not trusted herself to think of for a long time past: she always took a big turn about that haunted corner. But now, at the sight of the young man downstairs, so openly and jovially Leila's, she was overwhelmed at the senseless waste of her own adventure, and wrung with the irony of perceiving that the success or failure of the deepest human experiences may hang on a matter of chronology.

Then gradually the thought of Ide returned to her. "I chose to think that our case wasn't closed," he had said. She had been deeply touched by that. To everyone else her case had been closed so long! *Finis* was scrawled all over her. But here was one man who had believed and waited, and what if what he believed in and waited for were coming true? If Leila's "all right" should really foreshadow hers?

As yet, of course, it was impossible to tell. She had fancied, indeed, when she entered the drawing room before luncheon, that a too-sudden hush had fallen on the assembled group of Leila's friends, on the slender vociferous young women and the lounging golf-stockinged young men. They had all received her politely, with the kind of petrified politeness that may be either a tribute to age or a protest at laxity; but to them, of course, she must be an old woman because she was Leila's mother, and in a society so dominated by youth the mere presence of maturity was a constraint.

One of the young girls, however, had presently emerged from the group, and, attaching herself to Mrs. Lidcote, had listened to her with a blue gaze of admiration which gave the older woman a sudden happy consciousness of her long-forgotten social graces. It was agreeable to find herself attracting this young Charlotte Wynn, whose mother had been among her closest friends, and in whom something of the soberness and softness of the earlier manners had survived. But the little colloquy, broken up by the announcement of luncheon, could of course result in nothing more definite than this reminiscent emotion.

No, she could not yet tell how her own case was to be fitted into the new order of things; but there were more people—"older people" Leila had put it—arriving by the afternoon train, and that evening at dinner she would doubtless be able to judge. She began to wonder nervously who the newcomers might be. Probably she would be spared the embarrassment of finding old acquaintances among them; but it was odd that her daughter had mentioned no names.

Leila had proposed that, later in the afternoon, Wilbour should take her mother for a drive: she said she wanted them to have a "nice, quiet talk." But Mrs. Lidcote wished her talk with Leila to come first, and had, moreover, at luncheon, caught stray allusions to an impending tennis match in which her son-in-law was engaged. Her fatigue had been a sufficient pretext for declining the drive, and she had begged Leila to think of her as peacefully resting in her room till such time as they could snatch their quiet moment.

"Before tea, then, you duck!" Leila with a last kiss had decided; and presently Mrs. Lidcote, through her open window, had heard the fresh loud voices of her daughter's visitors chiming across the gardens from the tennis court.

* IV *

Leila had come and gone, and they had had their talk. It had not lasted as long as Mrs. Lidcote wished, for in the middle of it Leila had been summoned to the telephone to receive an important message from town, and had sent word to her mother that she couldn't come back just then, as one of the young ladies had been called away unexpectedly and arrangements had to be made for her departure. But the mother and daughter had had almost an hour together, and Mrs. Lidcote was happy. She had never seen Leila so tender, so solicitous. The only thing that troubled her was the very excess of this solicitude, the exaggerated expression of her daughter's annoyance that their first moments together should have been marred by the presence of strangers.

"Not strangers to me, darling, since they're friends of yours," her mother had assured her.

"Yes; but I know your feeling, you queer wild mother. I know how you've always hated people." (*Hated people!* Had Leila forgotten why?) "And that's why I told Susy that if you preferred to go with her to Ridgefield on Sunday I should perfectly understand, and patiently wait for our good hug. But you didn't really mind them at luncheon, did you, dearest?"

Mrs. Lidcote, at that, had suddenly thrown a startled look at her daughter. "I don't mind things of that kind any longer," she had simply answered.

"But that doesn't console me for having exposed you to the bother of it, for having let you come here when I ought to have *ordered* you off to Ridgefield with Susy. If Susy hadn't been stupid she'd have made you go there with her. I hate to think of you up here all alone."

Again Mrs. Lidcote tried to read something more than a rather obtuse devotion in her daughter's radiant gaze. "I'm glad to have had a rest this afternoon, dear; and later—"

"Oh, yes, later, when all this fuss is over, we'll more than make up for it, shan't we, you precious darling?" And at this point Leila had been summoned to the telephone, leaving Mrs. Lidcote to her conjectures.

These were still floating before her in cloudy uncertainty when Miss Suffern tapped at the door.

"You've come to take me down to tea? I'd forgotten how late it was," Mrs. Lidcote exclaimed.

Miss Suffern, a plump peering little woman, with prim hair and a conciliatory smile, nervously adjusted the pendent bugles of her elaborate black dress. Miss Suffern was always in mourning, and always commemorating the demise of distant relatives by wearing the discarded wardrobe of their next of kin. "It isn't *exactly* mourning," she would say; "but it's the only stitch of black poor Julia had—and of course George was only my mother's step-cousin."

As she came forward Mrs. Lidcote found herself humorously wondering whether she were mourning Horace Pursh's divorce in one of his mother's old black satins.

"Oh, *did* you mean to go down for tea?" Susy Suffern peered at her, a little fluttered. "Leila sent me up to keep you company. She thought it would be cozier for you to stay here. She was afraid you were feeling rather tired."

"I was; but I've had the whole afternoon to rest in. And this wonderful sofa to help me."

"Leila told me to tell you that she'd rush up for a minute before dinner, after everybody had arrived; but the train is always dreadfully late. She's in despair at not giving you a sitting room; she wanted to know if I thought you really minded."

"Of course I don't mind. It's not like Leila to think I should." Mrs. Lidcote drew aside to make way for the housemaid, who appeared in the doorway bearing a table spread with a bewildering variety of tea cakes.

"Leila saw to it herself," Miss Suffern murmured as the door closed. "Her one idea is that you should feel happy here."

It struck Mrs. Lidcote as one more mark of the subverted state of things that her daughter's solicitude should find expression in the multiplicity of sandwiches and the piping hotness of muffins; but then everything that had happened since her arrival seemed to increase her confusion.

The note of a motor horn down the drive gave another turn to her thoughts. "Are those the new arrivals already?" she asked.

"Oh, dear, no; they won't be here till after seven." Miss Suffern craned her head from the window to catch a glimpse of the motor. "It must be Charlotte leaving."

"Was it the little Wynn girl who was called away in a hurry? I hope it's not on account of illness."

"Oh, no; I believe there was some mistake about dates. Her mother telephoned her that she was expected at the Stepleys, at Fishkill, and she had to be rushed over to Albany to catch a train."

Mrs. Lidcote meditated. "I'm sorry. She's a charming young thing. I hoped I should have another talk with her this evening after dinner."

"Yes; it's too bad." Miss Suffern's gaze grew vague. "You *do* look tired, you know," she continued, seating herself at the tea table and preparing to dispense its delicacies. "You must go straight back to your sofa and let me wait on you. The excitement has told on you more than you think, and you mustn't fight against it any longer. Just stay quietly up here and let yourself go. You'll have Leila to yourself on Monday."

Mrs. Lidcote received the teacup which her cousin proffered, but showed no other disposition to obey her injunctions. For a moment she stirred her tea in silence; then she asked: "Is it your idea that I should stay quietly up here till Monday?"

Miss Suffern set down her cup with a gesture so sudden that it endangered an adjacent plate of scones. When she had assured herself of the safety of the scones she looked up with a fluttered laugh. "Perhaps, dear, by tomorrow you'll be feeling differently. The air here, you know—"

"Yes, I know." Mrs. Lidcote bent forward to help herself to a scone. "Who's arriving this evening?" she asked.

Miss Suffern frowned and peered. "You know my wretched head for names. Leila told me—but there are so many—"

"So many? She didn't tell me she expected a big party."

"Oh, not big: but rather outside of her little group. And of course, as it's the first time, she's a little excited at having the older set."

"The older set? Our contemporaries, you mean?"

"Why—yes." Miss Suffern paused as if to gather herself up for a leap. "The Ashton Gileses," she brought out.

"The Ashton Gileses? Really? I shall be glad to see Mary Giles again. It must be eighteen years," said Mrs. Lidcote steadily.

"Yes," Miss Suffern gasped, precipitately refilling her cup.

"The Ashton Gileses; and who else?"

"Well, the Sam Fresbies. But the most important person, of course, is Mrs. Lorin Boulger."

"Mrs. Boulger? Leila didn't tell me she was coming."

"Didn't she? I suppose she forgot everything when she saw you. But the party was got up for Mrs. Boulger. You see, it's very important that she should—well, take a fancy to Leila and Wilbour; his being appointed to Rome virtually depends on it. And you know Leila insists on Rome in order to be near you. So she asked Mary Giles, who's intimate with the Boulgers, if the visit couldn't possibly be arranged; and Mary's cable caught Mrs. Boulger at Cherbourg. She's to be only a fortnight in America; and getting her to come directly here was rather a triumph."

"Yes; I see it was," said Mrs. Lidcote.

"You know, she's rather—rather fussy; and Mary was a little doubtful if—"

"If she would, on account of Leila?" Mrs. Lidcote murmured.

"Well, yes. In her official position. But luckily she's a friend of the Barkleys. And finding the Gileses and Fresbies here will make it all right. The times have changed!" Susy Suffern indulgently summed up.

Mrs. Lidcote smiled. "Yes; a few years ago it would have seemed improbable that I should ever again be dining with Mary Giles and Harriet Fresbie and Mrs. Lorin Boulger."

Miss Suffern did not at the moment seem disposed to enlarge upon this theme; and after an interval of silence Mrs. Lidcote suddenly resumed: "Do they know I'm here, by the way?"

The effect of her question was to produce in Miss Suffern an exaggerated access of peering and frowning. She twitched the tea things about, fingered her bugles, and, looking at the clock, exclaimed amazedly: "Mercy! Is it seven already?"

"Not that it can make any difference, I suppose," Mrs. Lidcote continued. "But did Leila tell them I was coming?"

Miss Suffern looked at her with pain. "Why, you don't suppose, dearest, that Leila would do anything—"

Mrs. Lidcote went on: "For, of course, it's of the first importance, as you say, that Mrs. Lorin Boulger should be favorably impressed, in order that Wilbour may have the best possible chance of getting Rome."

"I *told* Leila you'd feel that, dear. You see, it's actually on *your* account—so that they may get a post near you—that Leila invited Mrs. Boulger."

"Yes, I see that." Mrs. Lidcote, abruptly rising from her seat, turned her eyes to the clock. "But, as you say, it's getting late. Oughtn't we to dress for dinner?"

Miss Suffern, at the suggestion, stood up also, an agitated hand among her bugles. "I do wish I could persuade you to stay up here this evening. I'm sure Leila'd be happier if you would. Really, you're much too tired to come down."

"What nonsense, Susy!" Mrs. Lidcote spoke with a sudden sharpness, her hand stretched to the bell. "When do we dine? At half-past eight? Then I must really send you packing. At my age it takes time to dress."

Miss Suffern, thus projected toward the threshold, lingered there to repeat: "Leila'll never forgive herself if you make an effort you're not up to." But Mrs. Lidcote smiled on her without answering, and the icy light-wave propelled her through the door.

*   *V*   *

Mrs. Lidcote, though she had made the gesture of ringing for her maid, had not done so.

When the door closed, she continued to stand motionless in the middle of her soft spacious room. The fire which had been kindled at twilight danced on the brightness of silver and mirrors and sober gilding; and the sofa toward which she had been urged by Miss Suffern heaped up its cushions in inviting proximity to a table laden with new books and papers. She could not recall having ever been more luxuriously housed, or having ever had so strange a sense of being out alone, under the night, in a wind-beaten plain. She sat down by the fire and thought.

A knock on the door made her lift her head, and she saw her daughter on the threshold. The intricate ordering of Leila's fair hair and the flying folds of her dressing gown showed that she had interrupted her dressing to hasten to her mother; but once in the room she paused a moment, smiling uncertainly, as though she had forgotten the object of her haste.

Mrs. Lidcote rose to her feet. "Time to dress, dearest? Don't scold! I shan't be late."

"To dress?" Leila stood before her with a puzzled look. "Why, I thought, dear—I mean, I hoped you'd decided just to stay here quietly and rest."

Her mother smiled. "But I've been resting all the afternoon!"

"Yes, but—you know you *do* look tired. And when Susy told me just now that you meant to make the effort—"

"You came to stop me?"

"I came to tell you that you needn't feel in the least obliged—"

"Of course. I understand that."

There was a pause during which Leila, vaguely averting herself from her mother's scrutiny, drifted toward the dressing table and began to disturb the symmetry of the brushes and bottles laid out on it. "Do your visitors know that I'm here?" Mrs. Lidcote suddenly went on.

"Do they—of course—why, naturally," Leila rejoined, absorbed in trying to turn the stopper of a salts bottle.

"Then won't they think it odd if I don't appear?"

"Oh, not in the least, dearest. I assure you they'll *all* understand." Leila laid down the bottle and turned back to her mother, her face alight with reassurance.

Mrs. Lidcote stood motionless, her head erect, her smiling eyes on her daughter's. "Will they think it odd if I *do?*"

Leila stopped short, her lips half parted to reply. As she paused, the color stole over her bare neck, swept up to her throat, and burst into flame in her cheeks. Thence it sent its devastating crimson up to her very temples, to the lobes of her ears, to the edges of her eyelids, beating all over her in fiery waves, as if fanned by some imperceptible wind.

Mrs. Lidcote silently watched the conflagration; then she turned away her eyes with a slight laugh. "I only meant that I was afraid it might upset the arrangement of your dinner table if I didn't come down. If you can assure me that it won't, I believe I'll take you at your word and go back to this irresistible sofa." She paused, as if waiting for her daughter to speak; then she held out her arms. "Run off and dress, dearest; and don't have me on your mind." She clasped Leila close, pressing a long kiss on the last afterglow of her subsiding blush. "I do feel the least bit overdone, and if it won't inconvenience you to have me drop out of things, I believe I'll basely take to my bed and stay there till your party scatters. And now run off, or you'll be late; and make my excuses to them all."

* VI *

The Barkleys' visitors had dispersed, and Mrs. Lidcote, completely restored by her two days' rest, found herself, on the following Monday, alone with her children and Miss Suffern.

There was a note of jubilation in the air, for the party had "gone off" so extraordinarily well, and so completely, as it appeared, to the satisfaction of Mrs. Lorin Boulger, that Wilbour's early appointment to Rome was almost to be counted on. So certain did this seem that the prospect of a prompt reunion mitigated the distress with which Leila learned of her mother's decision to return almost immediately to Italy. No one understood this decision; it seemed to Leila absolutely unintelligible that Mrs. Lidcote should not stay on with them till their own fate was fixed, and Wilbour echoed her astonishment.

"Why shouldn't you, as Leila says, wait here till we can all pack up and go together?"

Mrs. Lidcote smiled her gratitude with her refusal. "After all, it's not yet sure that you'll be packing up."

"Oh, you ought to have seen Wilbour with Mrs. Boulger," Leila triumphed.

"No, you ought to have seen Leila with her," Leila's husband exulted.

Miss Suffern enthusiastically appended: "I *do* think inviting Harriet Fresbie was a stroke of genius!"

"Oh, we'll be with you soon," Leila laughed. "So soon that it's really foolish to separate."

But Mrs. Lidcote held out with the quiet firmness which her daughter knew it was useless to oppose. After her long months in India, it was really imperative, she declared, that she should get back to Florence and see what was happening to her little place there; and she had been so comfortable on the "Utopia" that she had a fancy to return by the same ship. There was nothing for it, therefore, but to acquiesce in her decision and keep her with them till the afternoon before the day of the "Utopia's" sailing. This arrangement fitted in with certain projects which, during her two days' seclusion, Mrs. Lidcote had silently matured. It had become to her of the first importance to get away as soon as she could, and the little place in Florence, which held her past in every fold of its curtains and between every page of its books, seemed now to her the one spot where that past would be endurable to look upon.

She was not unhappy during the intervening days. The sight of Leila's well-being, the sense of Leila's tenderness, were, after all, what she had come for; and of these she had had full measure. Leila had never been happier or more tender; and the contemplation of her bliss, and the enjoyment of her affection, were an absorbing occupation for her mother. But they were also a sharp strain on certain overtightened chords, and Mrs. Lidcote, when at last she found herself alone in the New York hotel to which she had returned the night before embarking, had the feeling that she had just escaped with her life from the clutch of a giant hand.

She had refused to let her daughter come to town with her; she had even rejected Susy Suffern's company. She wanted no viaticum but that of her own thoughts; and she let these come to her without shrinking from them as she sat in the same high-hung sitting room in which, just a week before, she and Franklin Ide had had their memorable talk.

She had promised her friend to let him hear from her, but she had not kept her promise. She knew that he had probably come back from Chicago, and that if he learned of her sudden decision to return to Italy it would be impossible for her not to see him before sailing; and as she wished above all things not to see him she had kept silent, intending to send him a letter from the steamer.

There was no reason why she should wait till then to write it. The actual moment was more favorable, and the task, though not agreeable, would at least bridge over an hour of her lonely evening. She went up to the writing table, drew out a sheet of paper and began to write his name. And as she did so, the door opened and he came in.

The words she met him with were the last she could have imagined herself saying when they had parted. "How in the world did you know that I was here?"

He caught her meaning in a flash. "You didn't want me to, then?" He stood looking at her. "I suppose I ought to have taken your silence as meaning that. But I happened to meet Mrs. Wynn, who is stopping here, and she asked me to dine with her and Charlotte, and Charlotte's young man. They told me they'd seen you arriving this afternoon, and I couldn't help coming up."

There was a pause between them, which Mrs. Lidcote at last surprisingly broke with the exclamation: "Ah, she *did* recognize me, then!"

"Recognize you?" He stared. "Why—"

"Oh, I saw she did, though she never moved an eyelid. I saw it by Charlotte's blush. The child has the prettiest blush. I saw that her mother wouldn't let her speak to me."

Ide put down his hat with an impatient laugh. "Hasn't Leila cured you of your delusions?"

She looked at him intently. "Then you don't think Margaret Wynn meant to cut me?"

"I think your ideas are absurd."

She paused for a perceptible moment without taking this up; then she said, at a tangent: "I'm sailing tomorrow early. I meant to write to you—there's the letter I'd begun."

Ide followed her gesture, and then turned his eyes back to her face. "You didn't mean to see me, then, or even to let me know that you were going till you'd left?"

"I felt it would be easier to explain to you in a letter—"

"What in God's name is there to explain?" She made no reply, and he pressed on: "It can't be that you're worried about Leila, for Charlotte Wynn told me she'd been there last week, and there was a big party arriving when she left: Fresbies and Gileses, and Mrs. Lorin Boulger—all the board of examiners! If Leila has passed *that,* she's got her degree."

Mrs. Lidcote had dropped down into a corner of the sofa where she had sat during their talk of the week before. "I was stupid," she began abruptly. "I ought to have gone to Ridgefield with Susy. I didn't see till afterward that I was expected to."

"You were expected to?"

"Yes. Oh, it wasn't Leila's fault. She suffered—poor darling; she was distracted. But she'd asked her party before she knew I was arriving."

"Oh, as to that—" Ide drew a deep breath of relief. "I can understand that it must have been a disappointment not to have you to herself just at first. But, after all, you were among old friends or their children: the Gileses and Fresbies—and little Charlotte Wynn." He paused a moment before the last name, and scrutinized her hesitatingly. "Even if they came at the wrong time, you must have been glad to see them all at Leila's."

She gave him back his look with a faint smile. "I didn't see them."

"You didn't see them?"

"No. That is, excepting little Charlotte Wynn. That child is exquisite. We had a talk before luncheon the day I arrived. But when her mother found out that I was staying in the house she telephoned her to leave immediately, and so I didn't see her again."

The color rushed to Ide's sallow face. "I don't know where you get such ideas!"

She pursued, as if she had not heard him: "Oh, and I saw Mary Giles for a minute too. Susy Suffern brought her up to my room the last evening, after dinner, when all the others were at bridge. She meant it kindly—but it wasn't much use."

"But what were you doing in your room in the evening after dinner?"

"Why, you see, when I found out my mistake in coming,—how embarrassing it was for Leila, I mean—I simply told her I was very tired, and preferred to stay upstairs till the party was over."

Ide, with a groan, struck his hand against the arm of his chair. "I wonder how much of all this you simply imagined!"

"I didn't imagine the fact of Harriet Fresbie's not even asking if she might see me when she knew I was in the house. Nor of Mary Giles's getting Susy, at the eleventh hour, to smuggle her up to my room when the others wouldn't know where she'd gone; nor poor Leila's ghastly fear lest Mrs. Lorin Boulger, for whom the party was given, should guess I was in the house, and prevent her husband's giving Wilbour the second secretaryship because she'd been obliged to spend a night under the same roof with his mother-in-law!"

Ide continued to drum on his chair arm with exasperated fingers. "You don't *know* that any of the acts you describe are due to the causes you suppose."

Mrs. Lidcote paused before replying, as if honestly trying to measure the weight of this argument. Then she said in a low tone: "I know that Leila was in an agony lest I should come down to dinner the first night. And it was for me she was afraid, not for herself. Leila is never afraid for herself."

"But the conclusions you draw are simply preposterous. There are narrow-minded women everywhere, but the women who were at Leila's knew perfectly well that their going there would give her a sort of social sanction, and if they were willing that she should have it, why on earth should they want to withhold it from you?"

"That's what I told myself a week ago, in this very room, after my first talk with Susy Suffern." She lifted a misty smile to his anxious eyes. "That's why I listened to what you said to me the same evening, and why your arguments half-convinced me, and made me think that what had been possible for Leila might not be impossible for me. If the new dispensation had come, why not for me as well as for the others? I can't tell you the flight my imagination took!"

Franklin Ide rose from his seat and crossed the room to a chair near her sofa-corner. "All I cared about was that it seemed—for the moment—to be carrying you toward me," he said.

"I cared about that, too. That's why I meant to go away without seeing you." They gave each other grave look for look. "Because, you see, I was mistaken," she went on. "We were both mistaken. You say it's preposterous that the women who didn't object to accepting Leila's hospitality should have objected to meeting me under her roof. And so it is; but I begin to understand why. It's simply that society is much too busy to revise its own judgments. Probably no one in the house with me stopped to consider that my case and Leila's were identical. They only remembered that I'd done something which, at the time I did it, was condemned by society. My case had been passed on and classified: I'm the woman who has been cut for nearly twenty years. The older people have half-forgotten why, and the younger ones have never really known: it's simply become a tradition to cut me. And traditions that have lost their meaning are the hardest of all to destroy."

Ide sat motionless while she spoke. As she ended, he stood up with a short laugh and walked across the room to the window. Outside, the immense black prospect of New York, strung with its myriad lines of light, stretched away into the smoky edges of the night. He showed it to her with a gesture.

"What do you suppose such words as you've been using—'society,' 'tradition,' and the rest—mean to all the life out there?"

She came and stood by him in the window. "Less than nothing, of course. But you and I are not out there. We're shut up in a little tight round of habit and association, just as we're shut up in this room. Remember, I thought I'd got out of it once; but what really happened was that the other people went out, and left me in the same little room. The only difference was that I was there alone. Oh, I've made it habitable now, I'm used to it; but I've lost any illusions I may have had as to an angel's opening the door."

Ide again laughed impatiently. "Well, if the door won't open, why not let another prisoner in? At least it would be less of a solitude—"

She turned from the dark window back into the vividly lighted room.

"It would be more of a prison. You forget that I know all about that. We're all imprisoned, of course—all of us middling people, who don't carry our freedom in our brains. But we've accommodated ourselves to our different cells, and if we're moved suddenly into the new ones we're likely to find a stone wall where we thought there was thin air, and to knock ourselves senseless against it. I saw a man do that once."

Ide, leaning with folded arms against the window frame, watched her in silence as she moved restlessly about the room, gathering together some scattered books and tossing a handful of torn letters into the paper basket. When she ceased, he rejoined: "All you say is based on preconceived theories. Why didn't you put them to the test by coming down to meet your old friends? Don't you see the inference they would naturally draw from your hiding yourself when they arrived? It looked as though you were afraid of them—or as though you hadn't forgiven them. Either way, you put them in the wrong instead of waiting to let them put you in the right. If Leila had buried herself in a desert do you suppose society would have gone to fetch her out? You say you were afraid for Leila and that she was afraid for you. Don't you see what all these complications of feeling mean? Simply that you were too nervous at the moment to let things happen naturally, just as you're too nervous now to judge them rationally." He paused and turned her eyes to her face. "Don't try to just yet. Give yourself a little more time. Give *me* a little more time. I've always known it would take time."

He moved nearer, and she let him have her hand. With the grave kindness of his face so close above her she felt like a child roused out of frightened dreams and finding a light in the room.

"Perhaps you're right—" she heard herself begin; then something within her clutched her back, and her hand fell away from him.

"I know I'm right: trust me," he urged. "We'll talk of this in Florence soon."

She stood before him, feeling with despair his kindness, his patience and his unreality. Everything he said seemed like a painted gauze let down between herself and the real facts of life; and a sudden desire seized her to tear the gauze into shreds.

She drew back and looked at him with a smile of superficial reassurance. "You *are* right—about not talking any longer now. I'm nervous and tired, and it would do no good. I brood over things too much. As you say, I must try not to shrink from people." She turned away and glanced at the clock. "Why, it's only ten! If I send you off I shall begin to brood again; and if you stay we shall go on talking about the same thing. Why shouldn't we go down and see Margaret Wynn for half an hour?"

She spoke lightly and rapidly, her brilliant eyes on his face. As she watched him, she saw it change, as if her smile had thrown a too vivid light upon it.

"Oh, no—not tonight!" he exclaimed.

"Not tonight? Why, what other night have I, when I'm off at dawn? Besides, I want to show you at once that I mean to be more sensible—that I'm not going to be afraid of people any more. And I should really like another glimpse of little Charlotte." He stood before her, his hand in his beard, with the gesture he had in moments of perplexity. "Come!" she ordered him gaily, turning to the door.

He followed her and laid his hand on her arm. "Don't you think—hadn't you better let me go first and see? They told me they'd had a tiring day at the dressmaker's. I dare say they have gone to bed."

"But you said they'd a young man of Charlotte's dining with them. Surely he wouldn't have left by ten? At any rate, I'll go down with you and see. It takes so long if one sends a servant first." She put him gently aside, and then paused as a new thought struck her. "Or wait; my maid's in the next room. I'll tell her to go and ask if Margaret will receive me. Yes, that's much the best way."

She turned back and went toward the door that led to her bedroom; but before she could open it she felt Ide's quick touch again.

"I believe—I remember now—Charlotte's young man was suggesting that they should all go out—to a music hall or something of the sort. I'm sure—I'm positively sure that you won't find them."

Her hand dropped from the door, his dropped from her arm, and as they drew back and faced each other she saw the blood rise slowly through his sallow skin, redden his neck and ears, encroach upon the edges of his beard, and settle in dull patches under his kind troubled eyes. She had seen the same blush on another face, and the same impulse of compassion she had then felt made her turn her gaze away again.

A knock on the door broke the silence, and a porter put his head into the room.

"It's only just to know how many pieces there'll be to go down to the steamer in the morning."

With the words she felt that the veil of painted gauze was torn in tatters, and that she was moving again among the grim edges of reality.

"Oh, dear," she exclaimed, "I never *can* remember! Wait a minute; I shall have to ask my maid."

She opened her bedroom door and called out: "Annette!"

KERFOL

"YOU OUGHT to buy it," said my host; "it's just the place for a solitary-minded devil like you. And it would be rather worth-while to own the most romantic house in Brittany. The present people are dead broke, and it's going for a song—you ought to buy it."

It was not with the least idea of living up to the character my friend Lanrivain ascribed to me (as a matter of fact, under my unsociable exterior I have always had secret yearnings for domesticity) that I took his hint one autumn afternoon and went to Kerfol. My friend was motoring over to Quimper on business: he dropped me on the way, at a crossroad on a heath, and said: "First turn to the right and second to the left. Then straight ahead till you see an avenue. If you meet any peasants, don't ask your way. They don't understand French, and they would pretend they did and mix you up. I'll be back for you here by sunset—and don't forget the tombs in the chapel."

I followed Lanrivain's directions with the hesitation occasioned by the usual difficulty of remembering whether he had said the first turn to the right and second to the left, or the contrary. If I had met a peasant I should certainly have asked, and probably been sent astray; but I had the desert landscape to myself, and so stumbled on the right turn and walked across the heath till I came to an avenue. It was so unlike any other avenue I have ever seen that I instantly knew it must be *the* avenue. The grey-trunked trees sprang up straight to a great height and then interwove their pale grey branches in a long tunnel through which the autumn light fell faintly. I know most trees by name, but I haven't to this day been able to decide what those trees were. They had the tall curve of elms, the tenuity of poplars, the ashen color of olives under a rainy sky; and they stretched ahead of me for half a mile or more without a break in their arch. If ever I saw an avenue that unmistakably led to something, it was the avenue at Kerfol. My heart beat a little as I began to walk down it.

Presently the trees ended and I came to a fortified gate in a long wall. Between me and the wall was an open space of grass, with other grey avenues radiating from it. Behind the wall were tall slate roofs mossed with silver, a chapel belfry, the top of a keep. A moat filled with wild shrubs and brambles surrounded the place; the drawbridge had been replaced by a stone arch, and the portcullis by an iron gate. I stood for a long time on the hither side of the moat, gazing about me, and letting the influence of the place sink in. I said to myself: "If I wait long enough, the guardian will turn up and show me the tombs—" and I rather hoped he wouldn't turn up too soon.

I sat down on a stone and lit a cigarette. As soon as I had done it, it struck me as a puerile and portentous thing to do, with that great blind house looking down at me, and all the empty avenues converging on me. It may have been the depth of the silence that made me so conscious of my gesture. The squeak of my match sounded as loud as the scraping of a brake, and I almost fancied I heard it fall when I tossed it onto the grass. But there was more than that: a sense of irrelevance, of littleness, of futile bravado, in sitting there puffing my cigarette smoke into the face of such a past.

I knew nothing of the history of Kerfol—I was new to Brittany, and Lanrivain had never mentioned the name to me till the day before—but one couldn't as much as glance at that pile without feeling in it a long accumulation of history. What kind of history I was not prepared to guess: perhaps only that sheer weight of many associated lives and deaths which gives a majesty to all old houses. But the aspect of Kerfol suggested something more—a perspective of stern and cruel memories stretching away, like its own grey avenues, into a blur of darkness.

Certainly no house had ever more completely and finally broken with the present. As it stood there, lifting its proud roofs and gables to the sky, it might have been its own funeral monument. "Tombs in the chapel? The whole place is a tomb!" I reflected. I hoped more and more that the guardian would not come. The details of the place, however striking, would seem trivial compared with its collective impressiveness; and I wanted only to sit there and be penetrated by the weight of its silence.

"It's the very place for you!" Lanrivain had said; and I was overcome by the almost blasphemous frivolity of suggesting to any living being that Kerfol was the place for him. "Is it possible that anyone could *not* see—?" I wondered. I did not finish the thought: what I meant was undefinable. I stood up and wandered toward the gate. I was beginning to want to know more; not to *see* more—I was by now so sure it was not a question of seeing—but to feel more: feel all the place had to communicate. "But to get in one will have to rout out the keeper," I thought reluctantly, and hesitated. Finally I crossed the bridge and tried the iron gate. It yielded, and I walked through the tunnel formed by the thickness of the *chemin de ronde*. At the farther end, a wooden barricade had been laid across the entrance, and beyond it was a court enclosed in noble architecture. The main building faced me; and I now saw that one-half was a mere ruined front, with gaping windows through which the wild growths of the moat and the trees of the park were visible. The rest of the house was still in its robust beauty. One end abutted on the round tower, the other on the small traceried chapel, and in an angle of the building stood a graceful well-head crowned with mossy urns. A few roses grew against the walls, and on an upper windowsill I remember noticing a pot of fuchsias.

My sense of the pressure of the invisible began to yield to my architectural interest. The building was so fine that I felt a desire to explore it for its own sake. I looked about the court, wondering in which corner the guardian lodged. Then I pushed open the barrier and went in. As I did so, a dog barred my way. He was such a remarkably beautiful little dog that for a moment he made me forget the splendid place he was defending. I was not sure of his breed at the time, but have since learned that it was Chinese, and that he was of a rare variety called the "Sleevedog." He was very small and golden brown, with large brown eyes and a ruffled throat: he looked like a large tawny chrysanthemum. I said to myself: "These little beasts always snap and scream, and somebody will be out in a minute."

The little animal stood before me, forbidding, almost menacing: there was anger in his large brown eyes. But he made no sound, he came no nearer. Instead, as I advanced, he gradually fell back, and I noticed that another dog, a vague rough brindled thing, had limped up on a lame leg. "There'll be a hubbub now," I thought; for at the same moment a third dog, a long-haired white mongrel, slipped out of a doorway and joined the others. All three stood looking at me with grave eyes; but not a sound came from them. As I advanced they continued to fall back on muffled paws, still watching me. "At a given point, they'll all charge at my ankles: it's one of the jokes that dogs who live together put up on one," I thought. I was not alarmed, for they were neither large nor formidable. But they let me wander about the court as I pleased, following me at a little distance—always the same distance—and always keeping their eyes on me. Presently I looked across at the ruined façade, and saw that in one of its empty window frames another dog stood: a white pointer with one brown ear. He was an old grave dog, much more experienced than the others; and he seemed to be observing me with a deeper intentness.

"I'll hear from *him*," I said to myself; but he stood in the window frame, against the trees of the park, and continued to watch me without moving. I stared back at him for a time, to see if the sense that he was being watched would not rouse him. Half the width of the court lay between us, and we gazed at each other silently across it. But he did not stir, and at last I turned away. Behind me I found the rest of the pack, with a newcomer added: a small black greyhound with pale agate-colored eyes. He was shivering a little, and his expression was more timid than that of the others. I noticed that he kept a little behind them. And still there was not a sound.

I stood there for fully five minutes, the circle about me—waiting, as they seemed to be waiting. At last I went up to the little golden brown dog and stooped to pat him. As I did so, I heard myself give a nervous laugh. The little dog did not start, or growl, or take his eyes from me—he simply slipped back about a yard, and then paused and continued to look at me. "Oh, hang it!" I exclaimed, and walked across the court toward the well.

As I advanced, the dogs separated and slid away into different corners of the court. I examined the urns on the well, tried a locked door or two, and looked up and down the dumb façade; then I faced about toward the chapel. When I turned I perceived that all the dogs had disappeared except the old pointer, who still watched me from the window. It was rather a relief to be rid of that cloud of witnesses; and I began to look about me for a way to the back of the house. "Perhaps there'll be somebody in the garden," I thought. I found a way across the moat, scrambled over a wall smothered in brambles, and got into the garden. A few lean hydrangeas and geraniums pined in the flower beds, and the ancient house looked down on them indifferently. Its garden side was plainer and severer than the other: the long granite front, with its few windows and steep roof, looked like a fortress prison. I walked around the farther wing, went up some disjointed steps, and entered the deep twilight of a narrow and incredibly old box walk. The walk was just wide enough for one person to slip through, and its branches met overhead. It was like the ghost of a box walk, its lustrous green all turning to the shadowy greyness of the avenues. I walked on and on, the branches hitting me in the face and springing back with a dry rattle; and at length I came out on the grassy top of the *chemin de ronde*. I walked along it to the gate tower, looking down into the court, which was just below me. Not a human being was in sight; and neither were the dogs. I found a flight of steps in the thickness of the wall and went down them; and when I emerged again into the court, there stood the circle of dogs, the golden brown one a little ahead of the others, the black greyhound shivering in the rear.

"Oh, hang it—you uncomfortable beasts, you!" I exclaimed, my voice startling me with a sudden echo. The dogs stood motionless, watching me. I knew by this time that they would not try to prevent my approaching the house, and the knowledge left me free to examine them. I had a feeling that they must be horribly cowed to be so silent and inert. Yet they did not look hungry or ill-treated. Their coats were smooth and they were not thin, except the shivering greyhound. It was more as if they had lived a long time with people who never spoke to them or looked at them: as though the silence of the place had gradually benumbed their busy inquisitive natures. And this strange passivity, this almost human lassitude, seemed to me sadder than the misery of starved and beaten animals. I should have liked to rouse them for a minute, to coax them into a game or a scamper; but the longer I looked into their fixed and weary eyes the more preposterous the idea became. With the windows of that house looking down on us, how could I have imagined such a thing? The dogs knew better: *they* knew what the house would tolerate and what it would not. I even fancied that they knew what was passing through my mind, and pitied me for my frivolity. But even that feeling probably reached them through a thick fog of listlessness. I had an idea that their distance from me was as nothing to my remoteness from them. The impression they produced was that of having in common one memory so deep and dark that nothing that had happened since was worth either a growl or a wag.

"I say," I broke out abruptly, addressing myself to the dumb circle, "do you know what you look like, the whole lot of you? You look as if you'd seen a ghost—that's how you look! I wonder if there *is* a ghost here, and nobody but you left for it to appear to?" The dogs continued to gaze at me without moving. . . .

It was dark when I saw Lanrivain's motor lamps at the crossroads—and I wasn't exactly sorry to see them. I had the sense of having escaped from the loneliest place in the whole world, and of not liking loneliness—to that degree—as much as I had imagined I should. My friend had brought his solicitor back from Quimper for the night, and seated beside a fat and affable stranger I felt no inclination to talk of Kerfol. . . .

But that evening, when Lanrivain and the solicitor were closeted in the study, Madame de Lanrivain began to question me in the drawing room.

"Well—are you going to buy Kerfol?" she asked, tilting up her gay chin from her embroidery.

"I haven't decided yet. The fact is, I couldn't get into the house," I said, as if I had simply postponed my decision, and meant to go back for another look.

"You couldn't get in? Why, what happened? The family are mad to sell the place, and the old guardian has orders—"

"Very likely. But the old guardian wasn't there."

"What a pity! He must have gone to market. But his daughter—?"

"There was nobody about. At least I saw no one."

"How extraordinary! Literally nobody?"

"Nobody but a lot of dogs—a whole pack of them—who seemed to have the place to themselves."

Madame de Lanrivain let the embroidery slip to her knee and folded her hands on it. For several minutes she looked at me thoughtfully.

"A pack of dogs—you *saw* them?"

"Saw them? I saw nothing else!"

"How many?" She dropped her voice a little. "I've always wondered—"

I looked at her with surprise: I had supposed the place to be familiar to her. "Have you never been to Kerfol?" I asked.

"Oh, yes: often. But never on that day."

"What day?"

"I'd quite forgotten—and so had Hervé, I'm sure. If we'd remembered, we never should have sent you today—but then, after all, one doesn't half believe that sort of thing, does one?"

"What sort of thing?" I asked, involuntarily sinking my voice to the level of hers. Inwardly I was thinking: "I *knew* there was something. . . ."

Madame de Lanrivain cleared her throat and produced a reassuring smile. "Didn't Hervé tell you the story of Kerfol? An ancestor of his was mixed up in it. You know every Breton house has its ghost story; and some of them are rather unpleasant."

"Yes—but those dogs?"

"Well, those dogs are the ghosts of Kerfol. At least, the peasants say there's one day in the year when a lot of dogs appear there; and that day the keeper and his daughter go off to Morlaix and get drunk. The women in Brittany drink dreadfully." She stooped to match a silk; then she lifted her charming inquisitive Parisian face. "Did you *really* see a lot of dogs? There isn't one at Kerfol," she said.

* II *

Lanrivain, the next day, hunted out a shabby calf volume from the back of an upper shelf of his library.

"Yes—here it is. What does it call itself? *A History of the Assizes of the Duchy of Brittany. Quimper,* 1702. The book was written about a hundred years later than the Kerfol affair; but I believe the account is transcribed pretty literally from the judicial records. Anyhow, it's queer reading. And there's a Hervé de Lanrivain mixed up in it—not exactly *my* style, as you'll see. But then he's only a collateral. Here, take the book up to bed with you. I don't exactly remember the details; but after you've read it I'll bet anything you'll leave your light burning all night!"

I left my light burning all night, as he had predicted; but it was chiefly because, till near dawn, I was absorbed in my reading. The account of the trial of Anne de Cornault, wife of the lord of Kerfol, was long and closely printed. It was, as my friend had said, probably an almost literal transcription of what took place in the courtroom; and the trial lasted nearly a month. Besides, the type of the book was very bad. . . .

At first I thought of translating the old record. But it is full of wearisome repetitions, and the main lines of the story are forever straying off into side issues. So I have tried to disentangle it, and give it here in a simpler form. At times, however, I have reverted to the text because no other words could have conveyed so exactly the sense of what I felt at Kerfol; and nowhere have I added anything of my own.

* III *

It was in the year 16— that Yves de Cornault, lord of the domain of Kerfol, went to the *pardon* of Locronan to perform his religious duties. He was a rich and powerful noble, then in his sixty-second year, but hale and sturdy, a great horseman and hunter and a pious man. So all his neighbors attested. In appearance he was short and broad, with a swarthy face, legs slightly bowed from the saddle, a hanging nose and broad hands with black hairs on them. He had married young and lost his wife and son soon after, and since then had lived alone at Kerfol. Twice a year he went to Morlaix, where he had a handsome house by the river, and spent a week or ten days there; and occasionally he rode to Rennes on business. Witnesses were found to declare that during these absences he led a life different from the one he was known to lead at Kerfol, where he busied himself with his estate, attended mass daily, and found his only amusement in hunting the wild boar and waterfowl. But these rumors are not particularly relevant, and it is certain that among people of his own class in the neighborhood he passed for a stern and even austere man, observant of his religious obligations, and keeping strictly to himself. There was no talk of any familiarity with the women on his estate, though at that time the nobility were very free with their peasants. Some people said he had never looked at a woman since his wife's death; but such things are hard to prove, and the evidence on this point was not worth much.

Well, in his sixty-second year, Yves de Cornault went to the *pardon* at Locronan, and saw there a young lady of Douarnenez, who had ridden over pillion behind her father to do her duty to the saint. Her name was Anne de Barrigan, and she came of good old Breton stock, but much less great and powerful than that of Yves de Cornault; and her father had squandered his fortune at cards, and lived almost like a peasant in his little granite manor on the moors. . . . I have said I would add nothing of my own to this bald statement of a strange case; but I must interrupt myself here to describe the young lady who rode up to the lych-gate of Locronan at the very moment when the Baron de Cornault was also dismounting there. I take my description from a faded drawing in red crayon, sober and truthful enough to be by a late pupil of the Clouets, which hangs in Lanrivain's study, and is said to be a portrait of Anne de Barrigan. It is unsigned and has no mark of identity but the initials A. B., and the date 16—, the year after her marriage. It represents a young woman with a small oval face, almost pointed, yet wide enough for a full mouth with a tender depression at the corners. The nose is small, and the eyebrows are set rather high, far apart, and as lightly penciled as the eyebrows in a Chinese painting. The forehead is high and serious, and the hair, which one feels to be fine and thick and fair, is drawn off it and lies close like a cap. The eyes are neither large nor small, hazel probably, with a look at once shy and steady. A pair of beautiful long hands are crossed below the lady's breast. . . .

The chaplain of Kerfol, and other witnesses, averred that when the Baron came back from Locronan he jumped from his horse, ordered another to be instantly saddled, called to a young page to come with him, and rode away that same evening to the south. His steward followed the next morning with coffers laden on a pair of pack mules. The following week Yves de Cornault rode back to Kerfol, sent for his vassals and tenants, and told them he was to be married at All Saints to Anne de Barrigan of Douarnenez. And on All Saints' Day the marriage took place.

As to the next few years, the evidence on both sides seems to show that they passed happily for the couple. No one was found to say that Yves de Cornault had been unkind to his wife, and it was plain to all that he was content with his bargain. Indeed, it was admitted by the chaplain and other witnesses for the prosecution that the young lady had a softening influence on her husband, and that he became less exacting with his tenants, less harsh to peasants and dependents, and less subject to the fits of gloomy silence which had darkened his widowhood. As to his wife, the only grievance her champions could call up in her behalf was that Kerfol was a lonely place, and that when her husband was away on business at Rennes or Morlaix—whither she was never taken—she was not allowed so much as to walk in the park unaccompanied. But no one asserted that she was unhappy, though one servant woman said she had surprised her crying, and had heard her say that she was a woman accursed to have no child, and nothing in life to call her own. But that was a natural enough feeling in a wife attached to her husband; and certainly it must have been a great grief to Yves de Cornault that she bore no son. Yet he never made her feel her childlessness as a reproach—she admits this in her evidence—but seemed to try to make her forget it by showering gifts and favors on her. Rich though he was, he had never been openhanded; but nothing was too fine for his wife, in the way of silks or gems or linen, or whatever else she fancied. Every wandering merchant was welcome at Kerfol, and when the master was called away he never came back without bringing his wife a handsome present—something curious and particular—from Morlaix or Rennes or Quimper. One of the waiting women gave, in cross-examination, an interesting list of one year's gifts, which I copy. From Morlaix, a carved ivory junk, with Chinamen at the oars, that a strange sailor had brought back as a votive offering for Notre Dame de la Clarté, above Ploumanac'h; from Quimper, an embroidered gown, worked by the nuns of the Assumption; from Rennes, a silver rose that opened and showed an amber Virgin with a crown of garnets; from Morlaix, again, a length of Damascus velvet shot with gold, bought of a Jew from Syria; and for Michaelmas that same year, from Rennes, a necklet or bracelet of round stones—emeralds and pearls and rubies—strung like beads on a fine gold chain. This was the present that pleased the lady best, the woman said. Later on, as it happened, it was produced at the trial, and appears to have struck the Judges and the public as a curious and valuable jewel.

The very same winter, the Baron absented himself again, this time as far as Bordeaux, and on his return he brought his wife something even odder and prettier than the bracelet. It was a winter evening when he rode up to Kerfol and, walking into the hall, found her sitting by the hearth, her chin on her hand, looking into the fire. He carried a velvet box in his hand and, setting it down, lifted the lid and let out a little golden brown dog.

Anne de Cornault exclaimed with pleasure as the little creature bounded toward her. "Oh, it looks like a bird or a butterfly!" she cried as she picked it up; and the dog put its paws on her shoulders and looked at her with eyes "like a Christian's." After that she would never have it out of her sight, and petted and talked to it as if it had been a child—as indeed it was the nearest thing to a child she was to know. Yves de Cornault was much pleased with his purchase. The dog had been brought to him by a sailor from an East India merchantman, and the sailor had bought it of a pilgrim in a bazaar at Jaffa, who had stolen it from a nobleman's wife in China: a perfectly permissible thing to do, since the pilgrim was a Christian and the nobleman a heathen doomed to hell-fire. Yves de Cornault had paid a long price for the dog, for they were beginning to be in demand at the French court, and the sailor knew he had got hold of a good thing; but Anne's pleasure was so great that, to see her laugh and play with the little animal, her husband would doubtless have given twice the sum.

So far, all the evidence is at one, and the narrative plain sailing; but now the steering becomes difficult. I will try to keep as nearly as possible to Anne's own statements, though toward the end, poor thing. . . .

Well, to go back. The very year after the little brown dog was brought to Kerfol, Yves de Cornault, one winter night, was found dead at the head of a narrow flight of stairs leading down from his wife's rooms to a door opening on the court. It was his wife who found him and gave the alarm, so distracted, poor wretch, with fear and horror—for his blood was all over her—that at first the roused household could not make out what she was saying, and thought she had suddenly gone mad. But there, sure enough, at the top of the stairs lay her husband, stone dead, and head foremost, the blood from his wounds dripping down to the steps below him. He had been dreadfully scratched and gashed about the face and throat, as if with curious pointed weapons; and one of his legs had a deep tear in it which had cut an artery, and probably caused his death. But how did he come there, and who had murdered him?

His wife declared that she had been asleep in her bed, and hearing his cry had rushed out to find him lying on the stairs; but this was immediately questioned. In the first place, it was proved that from her room she could not have heard the struggle on the stairs, owing to the thickness of the walls and the length of the intervening passage; then it was evident that she had not been in bed and asleep, since she was dressed when she roused the house, and her bed had not been slept in. Moreover, the door at the bottom of the stairs was ajar, and it was noticed by the chaplain (an observant man) that the dress she wore was stained with blood about the knees, and that there were traces of small bloodstained hands low down on the staircase walls, so that it was conjectured that she had really been at the postern door when her husband fell and, feeling her way up to him in the darkness on her hands and knees, had been stained by his blood dripping down on her. Of course it was argued on the other side that the blood marks on her dress might have been caused by her kneeling down by her husband when she rushed out of her room; but there was the open door below, and the fact that the finger marks in the staircase all pointed upward.

The accused held to her statement for the first two days, in spite of its improbability; but on the third day word was brought to her that Hervé de Lanrivain, a young nobleman of the neighborhood, had been arrested for complicity in the crime. Two or three witnesses thereupon came forward to say that it was known throughout the country that Lanrivain had formerly been on good terms with the lady of Cornault; but that he had been absent from Brittany for over a year, and people had ceased to associate their names. The witnesses who made this statement were not of a very reputable sort. One was an old herb-gatherer suspected of witchcraft, another a drunken clerk from a neighboring parish, the third a half-witted shepherd who could be made to say anything; and it was clear that the prosecution was not satisfied with its case, and would have liked to find more definite proof of Lanrivain's complicity than the statement of the herb-gatherer, who swore to having seen him climbing the wall of the park on the night of the murder. One way of patching out incomplete proofs in those days was to put some sort of pressure, moral or physical, on the accused person. It is not clear what pressure was put on Anne de Cornault; but on the third day, when she was brought in court, she "appeared weak and wandering," and after being encouraged to collect herself and speak the truth, on her honor and the wounds of her Blessed Redeemer, she confessed that she had in fact gone down the stairs to speak with Hervé de Lanrivain (who denied everything), and had been surprised there by the sound of her husband's fall. That was better; and the prosecution rubbed its hands with satisfaction. The satisfaction increased when various dependents living at Kerfol were induced to say—with apparent sincerity—that during the year or two preceding his death their master had once more grown uncertain and irascible, and subject to the fits of brooding silence which his household had learned to dread before his second marriage. This seemed to show that things had not been going well at Kerfol; though no one could be found to say that there had been any signs of open disagreement between husband and wife.

Anne de Cornault, when questioned as to her reason for going down at night to open the door to Hervé de Lanrivain, made an answer which must have sent a smile around the court. She said it was because she was lonely and wanted to talk with the young man. Was this the only reason? she was asked; and replied: "Yes, by the Cross over your Lordships' heads." "But why at midnight?" the court asked. "Because I could see him in no other way." I can see the exchange of glances across the ermine collars under the Crucifix.

Anne de Cornault, further questioned, said that her married life had been extremely lonely: "desolate" was the word she used. It was true that her husband seldom spoke harshly to her; but there were days when he did not speak at all. It was true that he had never struck or threatened her; but he kept her like a prisoner at Kerfol, and when he rode away to Morlaix or Quimper or Rennes he set so close a watch on her that she could not pick a flower in the garden without having a waiting woman at her heels. "I am no Queen, to need such honors," she once said to him; and he had answered that a man who has a treasure does not leave the key in the lock when he goes out. "Then take me with you," she urged; but to this he said that towns were pernicious places, and young wives better off at their own firesides.

"But what did you want to say to Hervé de Lanrivain?" the court asked; and she answered: "To ask him to take me away."

"Ah—you confess that you went down to him with adulterous thoughts?"

"No."

"Then why did you want him to take you away?"

"Because I was afraid for my life."

"Of whom were you afraid?"

"Of my husband."

"Why were you afraid of your husband?"

"Because he had strangled my little dog."

Another smile must have passed around the courtroom: in days when any nobleman had a right to hang his peasants—and most of them exercised it—pinching a pet animal's windpipe was nothing to make a fuss about.

At this point one of the Judges, who appears to have had a certain sympathy for the accused, suggested that she should be allowed to explain herself in her own way; and she thereupon made the following statement.

The first years of her marriage had been lonely; but her husband had not been unkind to her. If she had had a child she would not have been unhappy; but the days were long, and it rained too much.

It was true that her husband, whenever he went away and left her, brought her a handsome present on his return; but this did not make up for the loneliness. At least nothing had, till he brought her the little brown dog from the East: after that she was much less unhappy. Her husband seemed pleased that she was so fond of the dog; he gave her leave to put her jeweled bracelet around its neck, and to keep it always with her.

One day she had fallen asleep in her room, with the dog at her feet, as his habit was. Her feet were bare and resting on his back. Suddenly she was waked by her husband: he stood beside her, smiling not unkindly.

"You look like my great-grandmother, Juliane de Cornault, lying in the chapel with her feet on a little dog," he said.

The analogy sent a chill through her, but she laughed and answered: "Well, when I am dead you must put me beside her, carved in marble, with my dog at my feet."

"Oho—we'll wait and see," he said, laughing also, but with his black brows close together. "The dog is the emblem of fidelity."

"And do you doubt my right to lie with mine at my feet?"

"When I'm in doubt I find out," he answered. "I am an old man," he added, "and people say I make you lead a lonely life. But I swear you shall have your monument if you earn it."

"And I swear to be faithful," she returned, "if only for the sake of having my little dog at my feet."

Not long afterward he went on business to the Quimper Assizes; and while he was away his aunt, the widow of a great nobleman of the duchy, came to spend a night at Kerfol on her way to the *pardon* of Ste. Barbe. She was a woman of piety and consequence, and much respected by Yves de Cornault, and when she proposed to Anne to go with her to Ste. Barbe no one could object, and even the chaplain declared himself in favor of the pilgrimage. So Anne set out for Ste. Barbe, and there for the first time she talked with Hervé de Lanrivain. He had come once or twice to Kerfol with his father, but she had never before exchanged a dozen words with him. They did not talk for more than five minutes now: it was under the chestnuts, as the procession was coming out of the chapel. He said: "I pity you," and she was surprised, for she had not supposed that anyone thought her an object of pity. He added: "Call for me when you need me," and she smiled a little, but was glad afterward, and thought often of the meeting.

She confessed to having seen him three times afterward: not more. How or where she would not say—one had the impression that she feared to implicate someone. Their meetings had been rare and brief; and at the last he had told her that he was starting the next day for a foreign country, on a mission which was not without peril and might keep him for many months absent. He asked her for a remembrance, and she had none to give him but the collar about the little dog's neck. She was sorry afterward that she had given it, but he was so unhappy at going that she had not had the courage to refuse.

Her husband was away at the time. When he returned a few days later he picked up the animal to pet it, and noticed that its collar was missing. His wife told him that the dog had lost it in the undergrowth of the park, and that she and her maids had hunted a whole day for it. It was true, she explained to the court, that she had made the maids search for the necklet—they all believed the dog had lost it in the park. . . .

Her husband made no comment, and that evening at supper he was in his usual mood, between good and bad: you could never tell which. He talked a good deal, describing what he had seen and done at Rennes; but now and then he stopped and looked hard at her, and when she went to bed she found her little dog strangled on her pillow. The little thing was dead, but still warm; she stooped to lift it, and her distress turned to horror when she discovered that it had been strangled by twisting twice round its throat the necklet she had given to Lanrivain.

The next morning at dawn she buried the dog in the garden, and hid the necklet in her breast. She said nothing to her husband, then or later, and he said nothing to her; but that day he had a peasant hanged for stealing a faggot in the park, and the next day he nearly beat to death a young horse he was breaking.

Winter set in, and the short days passed, and the long nights, one by one; and she heard nothing of Hervé de Lanrivain. It might be that her husband had killed him; or merely that he had been robbed of the necklet. Day after day by the hearth among the spinning maids, night after night alone on her bed, she wondered and trembled. Sometimes at table her husband looked across at her and smiled; and then she felt sure that Lanrivain was dead. She dared not try to get news of him, for she was sure her husband would find out if she did: she had an idea that he could find out anything. Even when a witch woman who was a noted seer, and could show you the whole world in her crystal, came to the castle for a night's shelter, and the maids flocked to her, Anne held back.

The winter was long and black and rainy. One day, in Yves de Cornault's absence, some gypsies came to Kerfol with a troop of performing dogs. Anne bought the smallest and cleverest, a white dog with a feathery coat and one blue and one brown eye. It seemed to have been ill-treated by the gypsies, and clung to her plaintively when she took it from them. That evening her husband came back, and when she went to bed she found the dog strangled on her pillow.

After that she said to herself that she would never have another dog; but one bitter cold evening a poor lean greyhound was found whining at the castle gate, and she took him in and forbade the maids to speak of him to her husband. She hid him in a room that no one went to, smuggled food to him from her own plate, made him a warm bed to lie on and petted him like a child.

Yves de Cornault came home, and the next day she found the greyhound strangled on her pillow. She wept in secret, but said nothing, and resolved that even if she met a dog dying of hunger she would never bring him into the castle; but one day she found a young sheep dog, a brindled puppy with good blue eyes, lying with a broken leg in the snow of the park. Yves de Cornault was at Rennes, and she brought the dog in, warmed and fed it, tied up its leg and hid it in the castle till her husband's return. The day before, she gave it to a peasant woman who lived a long way off, and paid her handsomely to care for it and say nothing; but that night she heard a whining and scratching at her door, and when she opened it the lame puppy, drenched and shivering, jumped up on her with little sobbing barks. She hid him in her bed, and the next morning was about to have him taken back to the peasant woman when she heard her husband ride into the court. She shut the dog in a chest, and went down to receive him. An hour or two later, when she returned to her room, the puppy lay strangled on her pillow. . . .

After that she dared not make a pet of any other dog; and her loneliness became almost unendurable. Sometimes, when she crossed the court of the castle, and thought no one was looking, she stopped to pat the old pointer at the gate. But one day as she was caressing him her husband came out of the chapel; and the next day the old dog was gone. . . .

This curious narrative was not told in one sitting of the court, or received without impatience and incredulous comment. It was plain that the Judges were surprised by its puerility, and that it did not help the accused in eyes of the public. It was an odd tale, certainly; but what did it prove? That Yves de Cornault disliked dogs, and that his wife, to gratify her own fancy, persistently ignored this dislike. As for pleading this trivial disagreement as an excuse for her relations—whatever their nature—with her supposed accomplice, the argument was so absurd that her own lawyer manifestly regretted having let her make use of it, and tried several times to cut short her story. But she went on to the end, with a kind of hypnotized insistence, as though the scenes she evoked were so real to her that she had forgotten where she was and imagined herself to be reliving them.

At length the Judge who had previously shown a certain kindness to her said (leaning forward a little, one may suppose, from his row of dozing colleagues): "Then you would have us believe that you murdered your husband because he would not let you keep a pet dog?"

"I did not murder my husband."

"Who did, then? Hervé de Lanrivain?"

"No."

"Who then? Can you tell us?"

"Yes, I can tell you. The dogs—" At that point she was carried out of the court in a swoon.

It was evident that her lawyer tried to get her to abandon this line of defense. Possibly her explanation, whatever it was, had seemed convincing when she poured it out to him in the heat of their first private colloquy; but now that it was exposed to the cold daylight of judicial scrutiny, and the banter of the town, he was thoroughly ashamed of it, and would have sacrificed her without a scruple to save his professional reputation. But the obstinate Judge—who perhaps, after all, was more inquisitive than kindly—evidently wanted to hear the story out, and she was ordered, the next day, to continue her deposition.

She said that after the disappearance of the old watchdog nothing particular happened for a month or two. Her husband was much as usual: she did not remember any special incident. But one evening a peddler woman came to the castle and was selling trinkets to the maids. She had no heart for trinkets, but she stood looking on while the women made their choice. And then, she did not know how, but the peddler coaxed her into buying for herself a pear-shaped pomander with a strong scent in it—she had once seen something of the kind on a gypsy woman. She had no desire for the pomander, and did not know why she had bought it. The peddler said that whoever wore it had the power to read the future; but she did not really believe that, or care much either. However, she bought the thing and took it up to her room, where she sat turning it about in her hand. Then the strange scent attracted her and she began to wonder what kind of spice was in the box. She opened it and found a grey bean rolled in a strip of paper; and on the paper she saw a sign she knew, and a message from Hervé de Lanrivain, saying that he was at home again and would be at the door in the court that night after the moon had set. . . .

She burned the paper and sat down to think. It was nightfall, and her husband was at home. . . . She had no way of warning Lanrivain, and there was nothing to do but to wait. . . .

At this point I fancy the drowsy courtroom beginning to wake up. Even to the oldest hand on the bench there must have been a certain relish in picturing the feelings of a woman on receiving such a message at nightfall from a man living twenty miles away, to whom she had no means of sending a warning. . . .

She was not a clever woman, I imagine; and as the first result of her cogitation she appears to have made the mistake of being, that evening, too kind to her husband. She could not ply him with wine, according to the traditional expedient, for though he drank heavily at times he had a strong head; and when he drank beyond its strength it was because he chose to, and not because a woman coaxed him. Not his wife, at any rate—she was an old story by now. As I read the case, I fancy there was no feeling for her left in him but the hatred occasioned by his supposed dishonor.

At any rate, she tried to call up her old graces; but early in the evening he complained of pains and fever, and left the hall to go up to the closet where he sometimes slept. His servant carried him a cup of hot wine, and brought back word that he was sleeping and not to be disturbed; and an hour later, when Anne lifted the tapestry and listened at his door, she heard his loud regular breathing. She thought it might be a feint, and stayed a long time barefooted in the passage, her ear to the crack; but the breathing went on too steadily and naturally to be other than that of a man in a sound sleep. She crept back to her room reassured, and stood in the window watching the moon set through the trees of the park. The sky was misty and starless, and after the moon went down the night was black as pitch. She knew the time had come, and stole along the passage, past her husband's door—where she stopped again to listen to his breathing—to the top of the stairs. There she paused a moment, and assured herself that no one was following her; then she began to go down the stairs in the darkness. They were so steep and winding that she had to go very slowly, for fear of stumbling. Her one thought was to get the door unbolted, tell Lanrivain to make his escape, and hasten back to her room. She had tried the bolt earlier in the evening, and managed to put a little grease on it; but nevertheless, when she drew it, it gave a squeak . . . not loud, but it made her heart stop; and the next minute, overhead, she heard a noise. . . .

"What noise?" the prosecution interposed.

"My husband's voice calling out my name and cursing me."

"What did you hear after that?"

"A terrible scream and a fall."

"Where was Hervé de Lanrivain at this time?"

"He was standing outside in the court. I just made him out in the darkness. I told him for God's sake to go, and then I pushed the door shut."

"What did you do next?"

"I stood at the foot of the stairs and listened."

"What did you hear?"

"I heard dogs snarling and panting." (Visible discouragement of the bench, boredom of the public, and exasperation of the lawyer for the defense. Dogs again—! But the inquisitive Judge insisted.)

"What dogs?"

She bent her head and spoke so low that she had to be told to repeat her answer: "I don't know."

"How do you mean—you don't know?"

"I don't know what dogs. . . ."

The Judge again intervened: "Try to tell us exactly what happened. How long did you remain at the foot of the stairs?"

"Only a few minutes."

"And what was going on meanwhile overhead?"

"The dogs kept on snarling and panting. Once or twice he cried out. I think he moaned once. Then he was quiet."

"Then what happened?"

"Then I heard a sound like the noise of a pack when the wolf is thrown to them—gulping and lapping."

(There was a groan of disgust and repulsion through the court, and another attempted intervention by the distracted lawyer. But the inquisitive Judge was still inquisitive.)

"And all the while you did not go up?"

"Yes—I went up then—to drive them off."

"The dogs?"

"Yes."

"Well—?"

"When I got there it was quite dark. I found my husband's flint and steel and struck a spark. I saw him lying there. He was dead."

"And the dogs?"

"The dogs were gone."

"Gone—where to?"

"I don't know. There was no way out—and there were no dogs at Kerfol."

She straightened herself to her full height, threw her arms above her head, and fell down on the stone floor with a long scream. There was a moment of confusion in the courtroom. Someone on the bench was heard to say: "This is clearly a case for the ecclesiastical authorities"—and the prisoner's lawyer doubtless jumped at the suggestion.

After this, the trial loses itself in a maze of cross-questioning and squabbling. Every witness who was called corroborated Anne de Cornault's statement that there were no dogs at Kerfol: had been none for several months. The master of the house had taken a dislike to dogs, there was no denying it. But, on the other hand, at the inquest, there had been long and bitter discussions as to the nature of the dead man's wounds. One of the surgeons called in had spoken of marks that looked like bites. The suggestion of witchcraft was revived, and the opposing lawyers hurled tomes of necromancy at each other.

At last Anne de Cornault was brought back into court—at the insistence of the same Judge—and asked if she knew where the dogs she spoke of could have come from. On the body of her Redeemer she swore that she did not. Then the Judge put his final question: "If the dogs you think you heard had been known to you, do you think you would have recognized them by their barking?"

"Yes."

"Did you recognize them?"

"Yes."

"What dogs do you take them to have been?"

"My dead dogs," she said in a whisper. . . . She was taken out of court, not to reappear there again. There was some kind of ecclesiastical investigation, and the end of the business was that the Judges disagreed with each other, and with the ecclesiastical committee, and that Anne de Cornault was finally handed over to the keeping of her husband's family, who shut her up in the keep of Kerfol, where she is said to have died many years later, a harmless madwoman.

So ends her story. As for that of Hervé de Lanrivain, I had only to apply to his collateral descendant for its subsequent details. The evidence against the young man being insufficient, and his family influence in the duchy considerable, he was set free, and left soon afterward for Paris. He was probably in no mood for a worldly life, and he appears to have come almost immediately under the influence of the famous M. Arnauld d'Andilly and the gentlemen of Port Royal. A year or two later he was received into their Order, and without achieving any particular distinction he followed its good and evil fortunes till his death some twenty years later. Lanrivain showed me a portrait of him by a pupil of Philippe de Champaigne: sad eyes, an impulsive mouth and a narrow brow. Poor Hervé de Lanrivain: it was a grey ending. Yet as I looked at his stiff and sallow effigy, in the dark dress of the Jansenists, I almost found myself envying his fate. After all, in the course of his life two great things had happened to him: he had loved romantically, and he must have talked with Pascal. . . .

THE LONG RUN

The shade of those our days that had no tongue.

IT WAS LAST WINTER, after a twelve years' absence from New York, that I saw again, at one of the Jim Cumnors' dinners, my old friend Halston Merrick.

The Cumnors' house is one of the few where, even after such a lapse of time, one can be sure of finding familiar faces and picking up old threads; where for a moment one can abandon one's self to the illusion that New York humanity is a shade less unstable than its bricks and mortar. And that evening in particular I remember feeling that there could be no pleasanter way of re-entering the confused and careless world to which I was returning than through the quiet softly-lit dining room in which Mrs. Cumnor, with a characteristic sense of my needing to be broken in gradually, had contrived to assemble so many friendly faces.

I was glad to see them all, including the three or four I did not know, or failed to recognize, that had no difficulty in passing as in the tradition and of the group; but I was most of all glad—as I rather wonderingly found—to set eyes again on Halston Merrick.

He and I had been at Harvard together, for one thing, and had shared there curiosities and ardors a little outside the current tendencies: had, on the whole, been more critical than our comrades, and less amenable to the accepted. Then, for the next following years, Merrick had been a vivid and promising figure in young American life. Handsome, careless, and free, he had wandered and tasted and compared. After leaving Harvard he had spent two years at Oxford; then he had accepted a private secretaryship to our Ambassador in England, and had come back from this adventure with a fresh curiosity about public affairs at home, and the conviction that men of his kind should play a larger part in them. This led, first, to his running for a State Senatorship which he failed to get, and ultimately to a few

229

months of intelligent activity in a municipal office. Soon after being deprived of this post by a change of party he had published a small volume of delicate verse, and, a year later, an odd uneven brilliant book on Municipal Government. After that one hardly knew where to look for his next appearance; but chance rather disappointingly solved the problem by killing off his father and placing Halston at the head of the Merrick Iron Foundry at Yonkers.

His friends had gathered that, whenever this regrettable contingency should occur, he meant to dispose of the business and continue his life of free experiment. As often happens in just such cases, however, it was not the moment for a sale, and Merrick had to take over the management of the foundry. Some two years later he had a chance to free himself; but when it came he did not choose to take it. This tame sequel to an inspiriting start was disappointing to some of us, and I was among those disposed to regret Merrick's drop to the level of the prosperous. Then I went away to a big engineering job in China, and from there to Africa, and spent the next twelve years out of sight and sound of New York doings.

During that long interval I heard of no new phase in Merrick's evolution, but this did not surprise me, as I had never expected from him actions resonant enough to cross the globe. All I knew—and this did surprise me—was that he had not married, and that he was still in the iron business. All through those years, however, I never ceased to wish, in certain situations and at certain turns of thought, that Merrick were in reach, that I could tell this or that to Merrick. I had never, in the interval, found any one with just his quickness of perception and just his sureness of response.

After dinner, therefore, we irresistibly drew together. In Mrs. Cumnor's big easy drawing room cigars were allowed, and there was no break in the communion of the sexes; and, this being the case, I ought to have sought a seat beside one of the ladies among whom we were allowed to remain. But, as had generally happened of old when Merrick was in sight, I found myself steering straight for him past all minor ports of call.

There had been no time, before dinner, for more than the barest expression of satisfaction at meeting, and our seats had been at opposite ends of the longish table, so that we got our first real look at each other in the secluded corner to which Mrs. Cumnor's vigilance now directed us.

Merrick was still handsome in his stooping tawny way: handsomer perhaps, with thinnish hair and more lines in his face, than in the young excess of his good looks. He was very glad to see me and conveyed his gladness by the same charming smile; but as soon as we began to talk I felt a change. It was not merely the change that years and experience and altered values bring. There was something more fundamental the matter with Merrick, something dreadful, unforeseen, unaccountable: Merrick had grown conventional and dull.

In the glow of his frank pleasure in seeing me I was ashamed to analyze the nature of the change; but presently our talk began to flag—fancy a talk with Merrick flagging!—and self-deception became impossible as I watched myself handing out platitudes with the gesture of the salesman offering something to a purchaser "equally good." The worst of it was that Merrick—Merrick, who had once felt everything!—didn't seem to feel the lack of spontaneity in my remarks, but hung on them with a harrowing faith in the resuscitating power of our past. It was as if he hugged the empty vessel of our friendship without perceiving that the last drop of its essence was dry.

But after all, I am exaggerating. Through my surprise and disappointment I felt a certain sense of well-being in the mere physical presence of my old friend. I liked looking at the way his dark hair waved away from the forehead, at the tautness of his dry brown cheek, the thoughtful backward tilt of his head, the way his brown eyes mused upon the scene through lowered lids. All the past was in his way of looking and sitting, and I wanted to stay near him, and felt that he wanted me to stay; but the devil of it was that neither of us knew what to talk about.

It was this difficulty which caused me, after a while, since I could not follow Merrick's talk, to follow his eyes in their roaming circuit of the room.

At the moment when our glances joined, his had paused on a lady seated at some distance from our corner. Immersed, at first, in the satisfaction of finding myself again with Merrick, I had been only half aware of this lady, as of one of the few persons present whom I did not know, or had failed to remember. There was nothing in her appearance to challenge my attention or to excite my curiosity, and I don't suppose I should have looked at her again if I had not noticed that my friend was doing so.

She was a woman of about forty-seven, with fair faded hair and a young figure. Her gray dress was handsome but ineffective, and her pale and rather serious face wore a small unvarying smile which might have been pinned on with her ornaments. She was one of the women in whom increasing years show rather what they have taken than what they have bestowed, and only on looking closely did one see that what they had taken must have been good of its kind.

Phil Cumnor and another man were talking to her, and the very intensity of the attention she bestowed on them betrayed the straining of rebellious thoughts. She never let her eyes stray or her smile drop; and at the proper moment I saw she was ready with the proper sentiment.

The party, like most of those that Mrs. Cumnor gathered about her, was not composed of exceptional beings. The people of the old vanished New York set were not exceptional: they were mostly cut on the same convenient and unobtrusive pattern; but they were often exceedingly "nice." And this obsolete quality marked every look and gesture of the lady I was scrutinizing.

While these reflections were passing through my mind I was aware that Merrick's eyes rested still on her. I took a cross-section of his look and found in it neither surprise nor absorption, but only a certain sober pleasure just about at the emotional level of the rest of the room. If he continued to look at her, his expression seemed to say, it was only because, all things considered, there were fewer reasons for looking at anybody else.

This made me wonder what were the reasons for looking at *her;* and as a first step toward enlightenment I said: "I'm sure I've seen the lady over there in gray—"

Merrick detached his eyes and turned them on me with a wondering look.

"Seen her? You know her." He waited. *"Don't* you know her? It's Mrs. Reardon."

I wondered that he should wonder, for I could not remember, in the Cumnor group or elsewhere, having known anyone of the name he mentioned.

"But perhaps," he continued, "you hadn't heard of her marriage? You knew her as Mrs. Trant."

I gave him back his stare. "Not Mrs. Philip Trant?"

"Yes; Mrs. Philip Trant."

"Not Paulina?"

"Yes—Paulina," he said, with a just perceptible delay before the name.

In my surprise I continued to stare at him. He averted his eyes from mine after a moment, and I saw that they had strayed back to her. "You find her so changed?" he asked.

Something in his voice acted as a warning signal, and I tried to reduce my astonishment to less unbecoming proportions. "I don't find that she looks much older."

"No. Only different?" he suggested, as if there were nothing new to him in my perplexity.

"Yes—awfully different."

"I suppose we're all awfully different. To you, I mean—coming from so far?"

"I recognized all the rest of you," I said, hesitating. "And she used to be the one who stood out most."

There was a flash, a wave, a stir of something deep down in his eyes. "Yes," he said. *"That's* the difference."

"I see it is. She—she looks worn down. Soft but blurred, like the figures in that tapestry behind her."

He glanced at her again, as if to test the exactness of my analogy.

"Life wears everybody down," he said.

"Yes—except those it makes more distinct. They're the rare ones, of course; but she *was* rare."

He stood up suddenly, looking old and tired. "I believe I'll be off. I wish you'd come down to my place for Sunday. . . . No, don't shake hands—I want to slide away unawares."

He had backed away to the threshold and was turning the noiseless doorknob. Even Mrs. Cumnor's doorknobs had tact and didn't tell.

"Of course I'll come," I promised warmly. In the last ten minutes he had begun to interest me again.

"All right. Good-bye." Half through the door he paused to add: *"She remembers you. You ought to speak to her."*

"I'm going to. But tell me a little more." I thought I saw a shade of constraint on his face, and did not add as I had meant to: "Tell me—because she interests me—what wore her down?" Instead, I asked: "How soon after Trant's death did she remarry?"

He seemed to make an effort of memory. "It was seven years ago, I think."

"And is Reardon here tonight?"

"Yes; over there, talking to Mrs. Cumnor."

I looked across the broken groupings and saw a large glossy man with straw-colored hair and red face, whose shirt and shoes and complexion seemed all to have received a coat of the same expensive varnish.

As I looked there was a drop in the talk about us, and I heard Mr. Reardon pronounce in a big booming voice: "What I say is: what's the good of disturbing things? Thank the Lord, I'm content with what I've got!"

"Is *that* her husband? What's he like?"

"Oh, the best fellow in the world," said Merrick, going.

* II *

Merrick had a little place at Riverdale, where he went occasionally to be near the Iron Works, and where he hid his weekends when the world was too much with him.

Here, on the following Saturday afternoon I found him awaiting me in a pleasant setting of books and prints and faded parental furniture.

We dined late, and smoked and talked afterward in his book-walled study till the terrier on the hearthrug stood up and yawned for bed. When we took the hint and moved toward the staircase I felt, not that I had found the old Merrick again, but that I was on his track, had come across traces of his passage here and there in the thick jungle that had grown up between us. But I had a feeling that when I finally came on the man himself he might be dead. . . .

As we started upstairs he turned back with one of his abrupt shy movements, and walked into the study.

"Wait a bit!" he called to me.

I waited, and he came out in a moment carrying a limp folio.

"It's typewritten. Will you take a look at it? I've been trying to get to work again," he explained, thrusting the manuscript into my hand.

"What? Poetry, I hope?" I exclaimed.

He shook his head with a gleam of derision. "No—just general considerations. The fruit of fifty years of inexperience."

He showed me to my room and said good night.

The following afternoon we took a long walk inland, across the hills, and I said to Merrick what I could of his book. Unluckily there wasn't much to say. The essays were judicious, polished and cultivated: but they lacked the freshness and audacity of his youthful work. I tried to conceal my opinion behind the usual generalizations, but he broke through these feints with a quick thrust to the heart of my meaning.

"It's worn down—blurred? Like the figures in the Cumnors' tapestry?"

I hesitated. "It's a little too damned resigned," I said.

"Ah," he exclaimed, "so am I. Resigned." He switched the bare brambles by the roadside. "A man can't serve two masters."

"You mean business and literature?"

"No; I mean theory and instinct. The gray tree and the green. You've got to choose which fruit you'll try; and you don't know till afterward which of the two has the dead core."

"How can anybody be sure that only one of them has?"

"I'm sure," said Merrick sharply.

We turned back to the subject of his essays, and I was astonished at the detachment with which he criticized and demolished them. Little by little, as we talked, his old perspective, his old standards came back to him; but with the difference that they no longer seemed like functions of his mind but merely like attitudes assumed or dropped at will. He could still, with an effort, put himself at the angle from which he had formerly seen things;

but it was with the effort of a man climbing mountains after a sedentary life in the plain.

I tried to cut the talk short, but he kept coming back to it with nervous insistence, forcing me into the last retrenchments of hypocrisy, and anticipating the verdict I held back. I perceived that a great deal—immensely more than I could see a reason for—had hung for him on my opinion of his book.

Then, as suddenly, his insistence dropped and, as if ashamed of having forced himself so long on my attention, he began to talk rapidly and uninterestingly of other things.

We were alone again that evening, and after dinner, wishing to efface the impression of the afternoon, and above all to show that I wanted him to talk about himself, I reverted to his work. "You must need an outlet of that sort. When a man's once had it in him, as you have—and when other things begin to dwindle—"

He laughed. "Your theory is that a man ought to be able to return to the Muse as he comes back to his wife after he's ceased to interest other women?"

"No; as he comes back to his wife after the day's work is done." A new thought came to me as I looked at him. "You ought to have had one," I added.

He laughed again. "A wife, you mean? So that there'd have been someone waiting for me even if the Muse decamped?" He went on after a pause: "I've a notion that the kind of woman worth coming back to wouldn't be much more patient than the Muse. But as it happens I never tried—because, for fear they'd chuck me, I put them both out of doors together."

He turned his head and looked past me with a queer expression at the low-paneled door at my back. "Out of that very door they went—the two of 'em, on a rainy night like this: and one stopped and looked back, to see if I wasn't going to call her—and I didn't—and so they both went."

* III *

"The Muse?" (said Merrick, refilling my glass and stooping to pat the terrier as he went back to his chair) "Well, you've met the Muse in the little volume of sonnets you used to like; and you've met the woman too, and you used to like *her;* though you didn't know her when you saw her the other evening. . . .

"No, I won't ask you how she struck you when you talked to her: I know. She struck you like that stuff I gave you to read last night. She's conformed—I've conformed—the mills have caught us and ground us: ground us, oh, exceedingly small!

"But you remember what she was; and that's the reason why I'm telling you this now. . . .

"You may recall that after my father's death I tried to sell the Works. I was impatient to free myself from anything that would keep me tied to New York. I don't dislike my trade, and I've made, in the end, a fairly good thing of it; but industrialism was not, at that time, in the line of my tastes, and I know now that it wasn't what I was meant for. Above all, I wanted to get away, to see new places and rub up against different ideas. I had reached a time of life—the top of the first hill, so to speak—where the distance draws one, and everything in the foreground seems tame and stale. I was sick to death of the particular set of conformities I had grown up among; sick of being a pleasant popular young man with a long line of dinners on my list, and the dead certainty of meeting the same people, or their prototypes, at all of them.

"Well—I failed to sell the Works, and that increased my discontent. I went through moods of cold unsociability, alternating with sudden flushes of curiosity, when I gloated over stray scraps of talk overheard in railway stations and omnibuses, when strange faces that I passed in the street tantalized me with fugitive promises. I wanted to be among things that were unexpected and unknown; and it seemed to me that nobody about me understood in the least what I felt, but that somewhere just out of reach there was someone who *did,* and whom I must find or despair. . . .

"It was just then that, one evening, I saw Mrs. Trant for the first time.

"Yes: I know—you wonder what I mean. I'd known her, of course, as a girl; I'd met her several times after her marriage; and I'd lately been thrown with her, quite intimately and continuously, during a succession of country-house visits. But I had never, as it happened, really *seen* her. . . .

"It was at a dinner at the Cumnors'; and there she was, in front of the very tapestry we saw her against the other evening, with people about her, and her face turned from me, and nothing noticeable or different in her dress or manner; and suddenly she stood out for me against the familiar unimportant background, and for the first time I saw a meaning in the stale phrase of a picture's walking out of its frame. For, after all, most people *are* just that to us: pictures, furniture, the inanimate accessories of our little island area of sensation. And then sometimes one of these graven images moves and throws out live filaments toward us, and the line they make draws us across the world as the moon track seems to draw a boat across the water. . . .

"There she stood; and as this queer sensation came over me I felt that she was looking steadily at me, that her eyes were voluntarily, consciously resting on me with the weight of the very question I was asking.

"I went over and joined her, and she turned and walked with me into the music room. Earlier in the evening someone had been singing, and there were low lights there, and a few couples still sitting in those confidential corners of which Mrs. Cumnor has the art; but we were under no illusion as to the nature of these presences. We knew that they were just painted in, and that the whole of life was in us two, flowing back and forward between us. We talked, of course; we had the attitudes, even the words, of the others: I remember her telling me her plans for the spring and asking me politely about mine! As if there were the least sense in plans, now that this thing had happened!

"When we went back into the drawing room I had said nothing to her that I might not have said to any other woman of the party; but when we shook hands I knew we should meet the next day—and the next. . . .

"That's the way, I take it, that Nature has arranged the beginning of the great enduring loves; and likewise of the little epidermal flurries. And how is a man to know where he is going?

"From the first my feeling for Paulina Trant seemed to me a grave business; but then the Enemy is given to producing that illusion. Many a man—I'm talking of the kind with imagination—has thought he was seeking a soul when all he wanted was a closer view of its tenement. And I tried—honestly tried—to make myself think I was in the latter case. Because, in the first place, I didn't, just then, want a big disturbing influence in my life; and because I didn't want to be a dupe; and because Paulina Trant was not, according to hearsay, the kind of woman for whom it was worth-while to bring up the big batteries. . . .

"But my resistance was only half-hearted. What I really felt—*all* I really felt—was the flood of joy that comes of heightened emotion. She had given me that, and I wanted her to give it to me again. That's as near as I've ever come to analyzing my state in the beginning.

"I knew her story, as no doubt you know it: the current version, I mean. She had been poor and fond of enjoyment, and she had married that pompous stick Philip Trant because she needed a home, and perhaps also because she wanted a little luxury. Queer how we sneer at women for wanting the thing that gives them half their attraction!

"People shook their heads over the marriage, and divided, prematurely, into Philip's partisans and hers: for no one thought it would work. And they were almost disappointed when, after all, it did. She and her wooden consort seemed to get on well enough. There was a ripple, at one time, over her friendship with young Jim Dalham, who was always with her during a summer at Newport and an autumn in Italy; then the talk died out, and she and Trant were seen together, as before, on terms of apparent good fellowship.

"This was the more surprising because, from the first, Paulina had never made the least attempt to change her tone or subdue her colors. In the gray Trant atmosphere she flashed with prismatic fires. She smoked, she talked subversively, she did as she liked and went where she chose, and danced over the Trant prejudices and the Trant principles as if they'd been a ballroom floor; and all without apparent offence to her solemn husband and his cloud of cousins. I believe her frankness and directness struck them dumb. She moved like a kind of primitive Una through the virtuous rout, and never got a finger mark on her freshness.

"One of the finest things about her was the fact that she never, for an instant, used her situation as a means of enhancing her attraction. With a husband like Trant it would have been so easy! He was a man who always saw the small sides of big things. He thought most of life compressible into a set of bylaws and the rest unmentionable; and with his stiff frock-coated and tall-hatted mind, instinctively distrustful of intelligences in another dress, with his arbitrary classification of whatever he didn't understand into 'the kind of thing I don't approve of,' 'the kind of thing that isn't done,' and—deepest depth of all—'the kind of thing I'd rather not discuss,' he lived in bondage to a shadowy moral etiquette of which the complex rites and awful penalties had cast an abiding gloom upon his manner.

"A woman like his wife couldn't have asked a better foil; yet I'm sure she never consciously used his dullness to relieve her brilliancy. She may have felt that the case spoke for itself. But I believe her reserve was rather due to a lively sense of justice, and to the rare habit (you said she was rare) of looking at facts as they are, without any throwing of sentimental lime-lights. She knew Trant could no more help being Trant than she could help being herself—and there was an end of it. I've never known a woman who 'made up' so little mentally. . . .

"Perhaps her very reserve, the fierceness of her implicit rejection of sympathy, exposed her the more to—well, to what happened when we met. She said afterward that it was like having been shut up for months in the hold of a ship, and coming suddenly on deck on a day that was all flying blue and silver. . . .

"I won't try to tell you what she was. It's easier to tell you what her friendship made of me; and I can do that best by adopting her metaphor of the ship. Haven't you, sometimes, at the moment of starting on a journey, some glorious plunge into the unknown, been tripped up by the thought: 'If only one hadn't to come back'? Well, with her one had the sense that one would never have to come back; that the magic ship would always carry one farther. And what an air one breathed on it! And, oh, the wind, and the islands, and the sunsets!

"I said just now 'her friendship'; and I used the word advisedly. Love is deeper than friendship, but friendship is a good deal wider. The beauty of our relation was that it included both dimensions. Our thoughts met as naturally as our eyes: it was almost as if we loved each other because we liked each other. The quality of a love may be tested by the amount of friendship it contains, and in our case there was no dividing line between loving and liking, no disproportion between them, no barrier against which desire beat in vain or from which thought fell back unsatisfied. Ours was a robust passion that could give an open-eyed account of itself, and not a beautiful madness shrinking away from the proof. . . .

"For the first months friendship sufficed us, or rather gave us so much by the way that we were in no hurry to reach what we knew it was leading to. But we were moving there nevertheless, and one day we found ourselves on the borders. It came about through a sudden decision of Trant's to start on a long tour with his wife. We had never foreseen that: he seemed rooted in his New York habits and convinced that the whole social and financial machinery of the metropolis would cease to function if he did not keep an eye on it through the columns of his morning paper, and pronounce judgment on it in the afternoon at his club. But something new had happened to him: he caught a cold, which was followed by a touch of pleurisy, and instantly he perceived the intense interest and importance which ill-health may add to life. He took the fullest advantage of it. A discerning doctor recommended travel in a warm climate; and suddenly, the morning paper, the afternoon club, Fifth Avenue, Wall Street, all the complex phenomena of the metropolis, faded into insignificance, and the rest of the terrestrial globe, from being a mere geographical hypothesis, useful in enabling one to determine the latitude of New York, acquired reality and magnitude as a factor in the convalescence of Mr. Philip Trant.

"His wife was absorbed in preparations for the journey. To move him was like mobilizing an army, and weeks before the date set for their departure it was almost as if she were already gone.

"This foretaste of separation showed us what we were to each other. Yet I was letting her go—and there was no help for it, no way of preventing it. Resistance was as useless as the vain struggles in a nightmare. She was Trant's and not mine: part of his luggage when he traveled as she was part of his household furniture when he stayed at home. . . .

"The day she told me that their passages were taken—it was on a November afternoon, in her drawing room in town—I turned away from her and, going to the window, stood looking out at the torrent of traffic interminably pouring down Fifth Avenue. I watched the senseless machinery of life revolving in the rain and mud, and tried to picture myself performing my small function in it after she had gone from me.

" 'It can't be—it can't be!' I exclaimed.

" 'What can't be?'

"I came back into the room and sat down by her. 'This—this—' I hadn't any words. 'Two weeks!' I said. 'What's two weeks?'

"She answered, vaguely, something about their thinking of Spain for the spring—

" 'Two weeks—two weeks!' I repeated. 'And the months we've lost —the days that belonged to us!'

" 'Yes,' she said, 'I'm thankful it's settled.'

"Our words seemed irrelevant, haphazard. It was as if each were answering a secret voice, and not what the other was saying.

" 'Don't you *feel* anything at all?' I remember bursting out at her. As I asked it the tears were streaming down her face. I felt angry with her, and was almost glad to note that her lids were red and that she didn't cry becomingly. I can't express my sensation to you except by saying that she seemed part of life's huge league against me. And suddenly I thought of an afternoon we had spent together in the country, on a ferny hillside, when we had sat under a beech tree, and her hand had lain palm upward in the moss, close to mine, and I had watched a little black and red beetle creeping over it. . . .

"The bell rang, and we heard the voice of a visitor and the click of an umbrella in the umbrella stand.

"She rose to go into the inner drawing room, and I caught her suddenly by the wrist. 'You understand,' I said, 'that we can't go on like this?'

" 'I understand,' she answered, and moved away to meet her visitor. As I went out I heard her saying in the other room: 'Yes, we're really off on the twelfth.'

* IV *

"I wrote her a long letter that night, and waited two days for a reply.

"On the third day I had a brief line saying that she was going to spend Sunday with some friends who had a place near Riverdale, and that she would arrange to see me while she was there. That was all.

"It was on a Saturday that I received the note and I came out here the same night. The next morning was rainy, and I was in despair, for I had counted on her asking me to take her for a drive or a long walk. It was hopeless to try to say what I had to say to her in the drawing room of a crowded country house. And only eleven days were left!

"I stayed indoors all the morning, fearing to go out lest she should telephone me. But no sign came, and I grew more and more restless and anxious. She was too free and frank for coquetry, but her silence and evasiveness made me feel that, for some reason, she did not wish to hear what she knew I meant to say. Could it be that she was, after all, more conventional, less genuine, than I had thought? I went again and again over the whole maddening round of conjecture; but the only conclusion I could rest in was that, if she loved me as I loved her, she would be as determined as I was to let no obstacle come between us during the days that were left.

"The luncheon hour came and passed, and there was no word from her. I had ordered my trap to be ready, so that I might drive over as soon as she summoned me; but the hours dragged on, the early twilight came, and I sat here in this very chair, or measured up and down, up and down, the length of this very rug—and still there was no message and no letter.

"It had grown quite dark, and I had ordered away, impatiently, the servant who came in with the lamps: I couldn't *bear* any definite sign that the day was over! And I was standing there on the rug, staring at the door, and noticing a bad crack in its panel, when I heard the sound of wheels on the gravel. A word at last, no doubt—a line to explain. . . . I didn't seem to care much for her reasons, and I stood where I was and continued to stare at the door. And suddenly it opened and she came in.

"The servant followed her with a light, and then went out and closed the door. Her face looked pale in lamplight, but her voice was as clear as a bell.

" 'Well,' she said, 'you see I've come.'

"I started toward her with hands outstretched. 'You've come—you've come!' I stammered.

"Yes; it was like her to come in that way—without dissimulation or explanation or excuse. It was like her, if she gave at all, to give not furtively or in haste, but openly, deliberately, without stinting the measure or counting the cost. But her quietness and serenity disconcerted me. She did not look like a woman who has yielded impetuously to an uncontrollable impulse. There was something almost solemn in her face.

"The effect of it stole over me as I looked at her, suddenly subduing the huge flush of gratified longing.

" 'You're here, here, here!' I kept repeating, like a child singing over a happy word.

" 'You said,' she continued, in her grave clear voice, 'that we couldn't go on as we were—'

" 'Ah, it's divine of you!' I held out my arms to her.

"She didn't draw back from them, but her faint smile said, 'Wait,' and lifting her hands she took the pins from her hat, and laid the hat on the table.

"As I saw her dear head bare in the lamplight, with the thick hair waving away from the parting, I forgot everything but the bliss and wonder of her being here—here, in my house, on my hearth—that fourth rose from the corner of the rug is the exact spot where she was standing. . . .

"I drew her to the fire, and made her sit down in the chair you're in, and knelt down by her, and hid my face on her knees. She put her hand on my head, and I was happy to the depths of my soul.

" 'Oh, I forgot—' she exclaimed suddenly. I lifted my head and our eyes met. Hers were smiling.

"She reached out her hand, opened the little bag she had tossed down with her hat, and drew a small object from it. 'I left my trunk at the station. Here's the check. Can you send for it?' she asked.

"Her trunk—she wanted me to send for her trunk! Oh, yes—I see your smile, your 'lucky man!' Only, you see, I didn't love her in that way. I knew she couldn't come to my house without running a big risk of discovery, and my tenderness for her, my impulse to shield her, was stronger, even then, than vanity or desire. Judged from the point of view of those emotions I fell terribly short of my part. I hadn't any of the proper feelings. Such an act of romantic folly was so unlike her that it almost irritated me, and I found myself desperately wondering how I could get her to reconsider her plan without—well, without seeming to want her to.

"It's not the way a novel hero feels; it's probably not the way a man in real life ought to have felt. But it's the way I felt—and she saw it.

"She put her hands on my shoulders and looked at me with deep, deep eyes. 'Then you didn't expect me to stay?' she asked.

"I caught her hands and pressed them to me, stammering out that I hadn't dared to dream. . . .

" 'You thought I'd come—just for an hour?'

" 'How could I dare think more? I adore you, you know, for what you've done! But it would be known if you—if you stayed on. My servants—everybody about here knows you. I've no right to expose you to the risk.' She made no answer, and I went on tenderly: 'Give me, if you will, the next few hours: there's a train that will get you to town by midnight. And then we'll arrange something—in town—where it's safer for you—more easily managed. . . . It's beautiful, it's heavenly of you to have come; but I love you too much—I must take care of you and think for you—'

"I don't suppose it ever took me so long to say so few words, and though they were profoundly sincere they sounded unutterably shallow, irrelevant and grotesque. She made no effort to help me out, but sat silent, listening, with her meditative smile. 'It's my duty, dearest, as a man,' I rambled on. 'The more I love you the more I'm bound—'

" 'Yes; but you don't understand,' she interrupted.

"She rose as she spoke, and I got up also, and we stood and looked at each other.

" 'I haven't come for a night; if you want me I've come for always,' she said.

"Here again, if I give you an honest account of my feelings I shall write myself down as the poor-spirited creature I suppose I am. There wasn't, I swear, at the moment, a grain of selfishness, of personal reluctance, in my feeling. I worshiped every hair of her head—when we were together I was happy, when I was away from her something was gone from every good thing: but I had always looked on our love for each other, our possible relation to each other, as such situations are looked on in what is called society. I had supposed her, for all her freedom and originality, to be just as tacitly subservient to that view as I was: ready to take what she wanted on the terms on which society concedes such taking, and to pay for it by the usual restrictions, concealments and hypocrisies. In short, I supposed that she would 'play the game'—look out for her own safety, and expect me to look out for it. It sounds cheap enough, put that way—but it's the rule we live under, all of us. And the amazement of finding her suddenly outside of it, oblivious of it, unconscious of it, left me, for an awful minute, stammering at her like a graceless dolt. . . . Perhaps it wasn't even a minute; but in it she had gone the whole round of my thoughts.

" 'It's raining,' she said, very low. 'I suppose you can telephone for a trap?'

"There was no irony or resentment in her voice. She walked slowly across the room and paused before the Brangwyn etching over there. 'That's a good impression. *Will* you telephone, please?' she repeated.

"I found my voice again, and with it the power of movement. I followed her and dropped at her feet. 'You can't go like this!' I cried.

"She looked down on me from heights and heights. 'I can't stay like this,' she answered.

"I stood up and we faced each other like antagonists. 'You don't know,' I accused her passionately, 'in the least what you're asking me to ask of you!'

" 'Yes, I do: *everything,*' she breathed.

" 'And it's got to be that or nothing?'

" 'Oh, on both sides,' she reminded me.

" '*Not* on both sides. It's not fair. That's why—'

" 'Why you won't?'

" 'Why I cannot—may not!'

" 'Why you'll take a night and not a life?'

"The taunt, for a woman usually so sure of her aim, fell so short of the mark that its only effect was to increase my conviction of her helplessness. The very intensity of my longing for her made me tremble where she was fearless. I had to protect her first, and think of my own attitude afterward.

"She was too discerning not to see this too. Her face softened, grew inexpressibly appealing, and she dropped again into that chair you're in, leaned forward, and looked up with her grave smile.

" 'You think I'm beside myself—raving? (You're not thinking of yourself, I know.) I'm not: I never was saner. Since I've known you I've often thought this might happen. This thing between us isn't an ordinary thing. If it had been we shouldn't, all these months, have drifted. We should have wanted to skip to the last page—and then throw down the book. We shouldn't have felt we could *trust* the future as we did. We were in no hurry because we knew we shouldn't get tired; and when two people feel that about each other they must live together—or part. I don't see what else they can do. A little trip along the coast won't answer. It's the high seas—or else being tied up to Lethe wharf. And I'm for the high seas, my dear!'

"Think of sitting here—here, in this room, in this chair—and listening to that, and seeing the light on her hair, and hearing the sound of her voice! I don't suppose there ever was a scene just like it. . . .

"She was astounding—inexhaustible; through all my anguish of resistance I found a kind of fierce joy in following her. It was lucidity at white heat: the last sublimation of passion. She might have been an angel arguing a point in the empryrean if she hadn't been, so completely, a woman pleading for her life. . . .

"Her life: that was the thing at stake! She couldn't do with less of it than she was capable of; and a woman's life is inextricably part of the man's she cares for.

"That was why, she argued, she couldn't accept the usual solution: couldn't enter into the only relation that society tolerates between people situated like ourselves. Yes: she knew all the arguments on *that* side: didn't I suppose she'd been over them and over them? She knew (for hadn't she often said it of others?) what is said of the woman who, by throwing in her lot with her lover's, binds him to a lifelong duty which has the irksomeness without the dignity of marriage. Oh, she could talk on that side with the best of them: only she asked me to consider the other—the side of the man and woman who love each other deeply and completely enough to want their lives enlarged, and not diminished, by their love. What, in such a case—she reasoned—must be the inevitable effect of concealing, denying, disowning, the central fact, the motive power of one's existence? She asked me to picture the course of such a love: first working as a fever in the blood, distorting and deflecting everything, making all other interests insipid, all other duties irksome, and then, as the acknowledged claims of life regained their hold, gradually dying—the poor starved passion!—for want of the wholesome necessary food of common living and doings, yet leaving life impoverished by the loss of all it might have been.

" 'I'm not talking, dear—' I see her now, leaning toward me with shining eyes: 'I'm not talking of the people who haven't enough to fill their days, and to whom a little mystery, a little maneuvering, gives an illusion of importance that they can't afford to miss; I'm talking of you and me, with all our tastes and curiosities and activities; and I ask you what our love would become if we had to keep it apart from our lives, like a pretty useless animal that we went to peep at and feed with sweetmeats through its cage?'

"I won't, my dear fellow, go into the other side of our strange duel: the arguments I used were those that most men in my situation would have felt bound to use, and that most women in Paulina's accept instinctively, without even formulating them. The exceptionalness, the significance, of the case lay wholly in the fact that she had formulated them all and then rejected them. . . .

"There was one point I didn't, of course, touch on; and that was the popular conviction (which I confess I shared) that when a man and a woman agree to defy the world together the man really sacrifices much more than the woman. I was not even conscious of thinking of this at the time, though it may have lurked somewhere in the shadow of my scruples for her; but she dragged it out into the daylight and held me face to face with it.

" 'Remember, I'm not attempting to lay down any general rule,' she insisted; 'I'm not theorizing about Man and Woman, I'm talking about you and me. How do I know what's best for the woman in the next house? Very likely she'll bolt when it would have been better for her to stay at home. And it's the same with the man: he'll probably do the wrong thing. It's generally the weak heads that commit follies, when it's the strong ones that ought to: and my point is that you and I are both strong enough to behave like fools if we want to. . . .

" 'Take your own case first—because, in spite of the sentimentalists, it's the man who stands to lose most. You'll have to give up the Iron Works: which you don't much care about—because it won't be particularly agreeable for us to live in New York: which you don't care much about either. But you won't be sacrificing what is called "a career." You made up your mind long ago that your best chance of self-development, and consequently of general usefulness, lay in thinking rather than doing; and, when we first met, you were already planning to sell out your business, and travel and write. Well! Those ambitions are of a kind that won't be harmed by your dropping out of your social setting. On the contrary, such work as you want to do ought to gain by it, because you'll be brought nearer to life-as-it-is, in contrast to life-as-a-visiting-list. . . .'

"She threw back her head with a sudden laugh. 'And the joy of not having any more visits to make! I wonder if you've ever thought of *that?* Just at first, I mean; for society's getting so deplorably lax that, little by little, it will edge up to us—you'll see! I don't want to idealize the situation, dearest, and I won't conceal from you that in time we shall be called on. But, oh, the fun we shall have had in the interval! And then, for the first time we shall be able to dictate our own terms, one of which will be that no bores need apply. Think of being cured of all one's chronic bores! We shall feel as jolly as people do after a successful operation.'

"I don't know why this nonsense sticks in my mind when some of the graver things we said are less distinct. Perhaps it's because of a certain iridescent quality of feeling that made gaiety seem like sunshine through a shower. . . .

" 'You ask me to think of myself?' she went on. 'But the beauty of our being together will be that, for the first time, I shall dare to! Now I have to think of all the tedious trifles I can pack the days with, because I'm afraid—I'm afraid—to hear the voice of the real me, down below, in the windowless underground hole where I keep her. . . .

" 'Remember again, please, it's not Woman, it's Paulina Trant, I'm talking of. The woman in the next house may have all sorts of reasons— honest reasons—for staying there. There may be some one there who needs her badly: for whom the light would go out if she went. Whereas to Philip I've been simply—well, what New York was before he decided to travel: the most important thing in life till he made up his mind to leave it; and now merely the starting place of several lines of steamers. Oh, I didn't have to love you to know that! I only had to live with *him.* . . . If he lost his eyeglasses he'd think it was the fault of the eyeglasses; he'd really feel that the eyeglasses had been careless. And he'd be convinced that no others would suit him quite as well. But at the optician's he'd probably be told that he needed something a little different, and after that he'd feel that the old eye-glasses had never suited him at all, and that *that* was their fault too. . . .'

"At one moment—but I don't recall when—I remember she stood up with one of her quick movements, and came toward me, holding out her arms. 'Oh, my dear, I'm pleading for my life; do you suppose I shall ever want for arguments?' she cried. . . .

"After that, for a bit, nothing much remains with me except a sense of darkness and of conflict. The one spot of daylight in my whirling brain was the conviction that I couldn't—whatever happened—profit by the sudden impulse she had acted on, and allow her to take, in a moment of passion, a decision that was to shape her whole life. I couldn't so much as lift my little finger to keep her with me then, unless I were prepared to accept for her as well as for myself the full consequences of the future she had planned for us. . . .

"Well—there's the point: I wasn't. I felt in her—poor fatuous idiot that I was!—that lack of objective imagination which had always seemed to me to account, at least in part, for many of the so-called heroic qualities in women. When their feelings are involved they simply can't look ahead. Her unfaltering logic notwithstanding, I felt this about Paulina as I listened. She had a specious air of knowing where she was going, but she didn't. She seemed the genius of logic and understanding, but the demon of illusion spoke through her lips. . . .

"I said just now that I hadn't, at the outset, given my own side of the case a thought. It would have been truer to say that I hadn't given it a *separate* thought. But I couldn't think of her without seeing myself as a factor—the chief factor—in her problem, and without recognizing that whatever the experiment made of me, it must fatally, in the end, make of her. If I couldn't carry the thing through she must break down with me: we should have to throw our separate selves into the melting pot of this mad adventure, and be 'one' in a terrible indissoluble completeness of which marriage is only an imperfect counterpart. . . .

"There could be no better proof of her extraordinary power over me, and of the way she had managed to clear the air of sentimental illusion, than the fact that I presently found myself putting this before her with a merciless precision of touch.

" 'If we love each other enough to do a thing like this, we must love each other enough to see just what it is we're going to do.'

"So I invited her to the dissecting table, and I see now the fearless eye with which she approached the cadaver. 'For that's what it is, you know,' she flashed out at me, at the end of my long demonstration. 'It's a dead body, like all the instances and examples and hypothetical cases that ever were! What do you expect to learn from *that?* The first great anatomist was the man who stuck his knife in a heart that was beating; and the only way to find out what doing a thing will be like is to do it!'

"She looked away from me suddenly, as if she were fixing her eyes on some vision on the outer rim of consciousness. 'No: there's one other way,' she exclaimed; 'and that is, *not* to do it! To abstain and refrain; and then see what we become, or what we don't become, in the long run, and to draw our inferences. That's the game that almost everybody about us is playing, I suppose; there's hardly one of the dull people one meets at dinner who hasn't had, just once, the chance of a berth on a ship that was off for the Happy Isles, and hasn't refused it for fear of sticking on a sandbank!

" 'I'm doing my best, you know,' she continued, 'to see the sequel as you see it, as you believe it's your duty to me to see it. I know the instances you're thinking of: the listless couples wearing out their lives in shabby watering places, and hanging on the favor of hotel acquaintances; or the proud quarreling wretches shut up alone in a fine house because they're too good for the only society they can get, and trying to cheat their boredom by squabbling with their tradesmen and spying on their servants. No doubt there are such cases; but I don't recognize either of us in those dismal figures. Why, to do it would be to admit that our life, yours and mine, is in the people about us and not in ourselves; that we're parasites and not self-sustaining creatures; and that the lives we're leading now are so brilliant, full and satisfying that what we should have to give up would surpass even the blessedness of being together!'

"At that stage, I confess, the solid ground of my resistance began to give way under me. It was not that my convictions were shaken, but that she had swept me into a world whose laws were different, where one could reach out in directions that the slave of gravity hasn't pictured. But at the same time my opposition hardened from reason into instinct. I knew it was her voice, and not her logic, that was unsettling me. I knew that if she'd written out her thesis and sent it to me by post I should have made short work of it; and again the part of me which I called by all the finest names: my chivalry, my unselfishness, my superior masculine experience, cried out with one voice: 'You can't let a woman use her graces to her own undoing—you can't, for her own sake, let her eyes convince you when her reasons don't!'

"And then, abruptly, and for the first time, a doubt entered me: a doubt of her perfect moral honesty. I don't know how else to describe my feeling that she wasn't playing fair, that in coming to my house, in throwing herself at my head (I called things by their names), she had perhaps not so much obeyed an irresistible impulse as deeply, deliberately reckoned on the dissolvent effect of her generosity, her rashness and her beauty. . . .

"From the moment that this mean doubt raised its head in me I was once more the creature of all the conventional scruples: I was repeating, before the looking glass of my self-consciousness, all the stereotyped gestures of the 'man of honor.' . . . Oh, the sorry figure I must have cut! You'll understand my dropping the curtain on it as quickly as I can. . . .

"Yet I remember, as I made my point, being struck by its impressiveness. I was suffering and enjoying my own suffering. I told her that, whatever step we decided to take, I owed it to her to insist on its being taken soberly, deliberately—

"('No: it's "advisedly," isn't it? Oh, I was thinking of the Marriage Service,' she interposed with a faint laugh.)

"—That if I accepted, there, on the spot, her headlong beautiful gift of herself, I should feel I had taken an unfair advantage of her, an advantage which she would be justified in reproaching me with afterward; that I was not afraid to tell her this because she was intelligent enough to know that my scruples were the surest proof of the quality of my love; that I refused to owe my happiness to an unconsidered impulse; that we must see each other again, in her own house, in less agitating circumstances, when she had had time to reflect on my words, to study her heart and look into the future. . . .

"The factitious exhilaration produced by uttering these beautiful sentiments did not last very long, as you may imagine. It fell, little by little, under her quiet gaze, a gaze in which there was neither contempt nor irony nor wounded pride, but only a tender wistfulness of interrogation; and I think the acutest point in my suffering was reached when she said, as I ended: 'Oh; yes, of course I understand.'

" 'If only you hadn't come to me here!' I blurted out in the torture of my soul.

"She was on the threshold when I said it, and she turned and laid her hand gently on mine. 'There was no other way,' she said; and at the moment it seemed to me like some hackneyed phrase in a novel that she had used without any sense of its meaning.

"I don't remember what I answered or what more we either of us said. At the end a desperate longing to take her in my arms and keep her with me swept aside everything else, and I went up to her, pleading, stammering, urging I don't know what. . . . But she held me back with a quiet look, and went. I had ordered the carriage, as she asked me to; and my last definite recollection is of watching her drive off in the rain. . . .

"I had her promise that she would see me, two days later, at her house in town, and that we should then have what I called 'a decisive talk'; but I don't think that even at the moment I was the dupe of my phrase. I knew, and she knew, that the end had come. . . .

* V *

"It was about that time (Merrick went on after a long pause) that I definitely decided not to sell the Works, but to stick to my job and conform my life to it.

"I can't describe to you the rage of conformity that possessed me. Poetry, ideas—all the picture-making processes stopped. A kind of dull self-discipline seemed to me the only exercise worthy of a reflecting mind. I *had* to justify my great refusal, and I tried to do it by plunging myself up to the eyes into the very conditions I had been instinctively struggling to get away from. The only possible consolation would have been to find in a life of business routine and social submission such moral compensations as may reward the citizen if they fail the man; but to attain to these I should have had to accept the old delusion that the social and the individual man are two. Now, on the contrary, I found soon enough that I couldn't get one part of my machinery to work effectively while another wanted feeding: and that in rejecting what had seemed to me a negation of action I had made all my action negative.

"The best solution, of course, would have been to fall in love with another woman; but it was long before I could bring myself to wish that this might happen to me. . . . Then, at length, I suddenly and violently desired it; and as such impulses are seldom without some kind of imperfect issue I contrived, a year or two later, to work myself up into the wished-for state. . . . She was a woman in society, and with all the awe of that institution that Paulina lacked. Our relation was consequently one of those unavowed affairs in which triviality is the only alternative to tragedy. Luckily we had, on both sides, risked only as much as prudent people stake in a drawing-room game; and when the match was over I take it that we came out fairly even.

"My gain, at all events, was of an unexpected kind. The adventure had served only to make me understand Paulina's abhorrence of such experiments, and at every turn of the slight intrigue I had felt how exasperating and belittling such a relation was bound to be between two people who, had they been free, would have mated openly. And so from a brief phase of imperfect forgetting I was driven back to a deeper and more understanding remembrance. . . .

"This second incarnation of Paulina was one of the strangest episodes of the whole strange experience. Things she had said during our extraordinary talk, things I had hardly heard at the time, came back to me with singular vividness and a fuller meaning. I hadn't any longer the cold consolation of believing in my own perspicacity: I saw that her insight had been deeper and keener than mine.

"I remember, in particular, starting up in bed one sleepless night as there flashed into my head the meaning of her last words: 'There was no other way'; the phrase I had half-smiled at at the time, as a parrot-like echo of the novel heroine's stock farewell. I had never, up to that moment, wholly understood why Paulina had come to my house that night. I had never been able to make that particular act—which could hardly, in the light of her subsequent conduct, be dismissed as a blind surge of passion— square with my conception of her character. She was at once the most spontaneous and the steadiest-minded woman I had ever known, and the last to wish to owe any advantage to surprise, to unpreparedness, to any play on the spring of sex. The better I came, retrospectively, to know her, the more sure I was of this, and the less intelligible her act appeared. And then, suddenly, after a night of hungry restless thinking, the flash of enlightenment came. She had come to my house, had brought her trunk with her, had thrown herself at my head with all possible violence and publicity, in order to give me a pretext, a loophole, an honorable excuse for doing and saying—why, precisely what I had said and done!

"As the idea came to me it was as if some ironic hand had touched an electric button, and all my fatuous phrases had leapt out on me in fire.

"Of course she had known all along just the kind of thing I should say if I didn't at once open my arms to her; and to save my pride, my dignity, my conception of the figure I was cutting in her eyes, she had recklessly and magnificently provided me with the decentest pretext a man could have for doing a pusillanimous thing. . . .

"With that discovery the whole case took a different aspect. It hurt less to think of Paulina—and yet it hurt more. The tinge of bitterness, of doubt, in my thoughts of her had had a tonic quality. It was harder to go on persuading myself that I had done right as, bit by bit, my theories crumbled under the test of time. Yet, after all, as she herself had said, one could judge of results only in the long run. . . .

"The Trants stayed away for two years; and about a year after they got back, you may remember, Trant was killed in a railway accident. You know Fate's way of untying a knot after everybody has given up tugging at it!

"Well—there I was, completely justified: all my weaknesses turned into merits! I had 'saved' a weak woman from herself, I had kept her to the path of duty, I had spared her the humiliation of scandal and the misery of self-reproach; and now I had only to put out my hand and take my reward.

"I had avoided Paulina since her return, and she had made no effort to see me. But after Trant's death I wrote her a few lines, to which she sent a friendly answer; and when a decent interval had elapsed, and I asked if I might call on her, she answered at once that she would see me.

"I went to her house with the fixed intention of asking her to marry me—and I left it without having done so. Why? I don't know that I can tell you. Perhaps you would have had to sit there opposite her, knowing what I did and feeling as I did, to understand why. She was kind, she was compassionate—I could see she didn't want to make it hard for me. Perhaps she even wanted to make it easy. But there, between us, was the memory of the gesture I hadn't made, forever parodying the one I was attempting! There wasn't a word I could think of that hadn't an echo in it of words of hers I had been deaf to; there wasn't an appeal I could make that didn't mock the appeal I had rejected. I sat there and talked of her husband's death, of her plans, of my sympathy; and I knew she understood; and knowing that, in a way, made it harder. . . . The doorbell rang and the footman came in to ask if she would receive other visitors. She looked at me a moment and said 'Yes,' and I got up and shook hands and went away.

"A few days later she sailed for Europe, and the next time we met she had married Reardon. . . ."

* VI *

It was long past midnight, and the terrier's hints became imperious.

Merrick rose from his chair, pushed back a fallen log and put up the fender. He walked across the room and stared a moment at the Brangwyn etching before which Paulina Trant had paused at a memorable turn of their talk. Then he came back and laid his hand on my shoulder.

"She summed it all up, you know, when she said that one way of finding out whether a risk is worth taking is *not* to take it, and then to see what one becomes in the long run, and draw one's inferences. The long run— well, we've run it, she and I. I know what I've become, but that's nothing to the misery of knowing what she's become. She had to have some kind of life, and she married Reardon. Reardon's a very good fellow in his way; but the worst of it is that it's not her way. . . .

"No: the worst of it is that now she and I meet as friends. We dine at the same houses, we talk about the same people, we play bridge together, and I lend her books. And sometimes Reardon slaps me on the back and says: 'Come in and dine with us, old man! What you want is to be cheered up!' And I go and dine with them, and he tells me how jolly comfortable she makes him, and what an ass I am not to marry; and she presses on me a second helping of *poulet Maryland,* and I smoke one of Reardon's cigars, and at half-past ten I get into my overcoat, and walk back alone to my rooms. . . ."

A Bottle
of Perrier

A TWO DAYS' STRUGGLE over the treacherous trails in a well-in-tentioned but short-winded "flivver," and a ride of two more on a hired mount of unamiable temper, had disposd young Medford, of the American School of Archaeology at Athens, to wonder why his queer English friend, Henry Almodham, had chosen to live in the desert.

Now he understood.

He was leaning against the roof parapet of the old building, half Christian fortress, half Arab palace, which had been Almodham's pretext; or one of them. Below, in an inner court, a little wind, rising as the sun sank, sent through a knot of palms the rainlike rattle so cooling to the pilgrims of the desert. An ancient fig tree, enormous, exuberant, writhed over a whitewashed wellhead, sucking life from what appeared to be the only source of moisture within the walls. Beyond these, on every side, stretched away the mystery of the sands, all golden with promise, all livid with menace, as the sun alternately touched or abandoned them.

Young Medford, somewhat weary after his journey from the coast, and awed by his first intimate sense of the omnipresence of the desert, shivered and drew back. Undoubtedly, for a scholar and a misogynist, it was a wonderful refuge; but one would have to be, incurably, both.

"Let's take a look at the house," Medford said to himself, as if speedy contact with man's handiwork were necessary to his reassurance.

The house, he already knew, was empty save for the quick cosmopolitan manservant, who spoke a sort of palimpsest Cockney lined with Mediterra-nean tongues and desert dialects—English, Italian or Greek, which was he?—and two or three burnoused underlings who, having carried Medford's bags to his room, had relieved the place of their gliding presences. Mr. Almodham, the servant told him, was away; suddenly summoned by a

253

friendly chief to visit some unexplored ruins to the south, he had ridden off at dawn, too hurriedly to write, but leaving messages of excuse and regret. That evening late he might be back, or next morning. Meanwhile Mr. Medford was to make himself at home.

Almodham, as young Medford knew, was always making these archaeological explorations; they had been his ostensible reason for settling in that remote place, and his desultory search had already resulted in the discovery of several early Christian ruins of great interest.

Medford was glad that his host had not stood on ceremony, and rather relieved, on the whole, to have the next few hours to himself. He had had a malarial fever the previous summer, and in spite of his cork helmet he had probably caught a touch of the sun; he felt curiously, helplessly tired, yet deeply content.

And what a place it was to rest in! The silence, the remoteness, the illimitable air! And in the heart of the wilderness green leafage, water, comfort—he had already caught a glimpse of wide wicker chairs under the palms—a humane and welcoming habitation. Yes, he began to understand Almodham. To anyone sick of the Western fret and fever the very walls of this desert fortress exuded peace.

As his foot was on the ladder-like stair leading down from the roof, Medford saw the manservant's head rising toward him. It rose slowly and Medford had time to remark that it was sallow, bald on the top, diagonally dented with a long white scar, and ringed with thick ash-blond hair. Hitherto Medford had noticed only the man's face—youngish, but sallow also—and been chiefly struck by its wearing an odd expression which could best be defined as surprise.

The servant, moving aside, looked up, and Medford perceived that his air of surprise was produced by the fact that his intensely blue eyes were rather wider open than most eyes, and fringed with thick ash-blond lashes; otherwise there was nothing noticeable about him.

"Just to ask—what wine for dinner, sir? Champagne, or—"

"No wine, thanks."

The man's disciplined lips were played over by a faint flicker of deprecation or irony, or both.

"Not any at all, sir?"

Medford smiled back. "It's not out of respect for Prohibition." He was sure that the man, of whatever nationality, would understand that; and he did.

"Oh, I don't suppose, sir—"

"Well, no; but I've been rather seedy, and wine's forbidden."

The servant remained incredulous. "Just a little light Moselle, though, to color the water, sir?"

"No wine at all," said Medford, growing bored. He was still in the stage of convalescence when it is irritating to be argued with about one's dietary. "Oh—what's your name, by the way?" he added, to soften the curtness of his refusal.

"Gosling," said the other unexpectedly, though Medford didn't in the least know what he had expected him to be called.

"You're English, then?"

"Oh, yes, sir."

"You've been in these parts a good many years, though?"

Yes, he had, Gosling said; rather too long for his own liking; and added that he had been born at Malta. "But I know England well too." His deprecating look returned. "I will confess, sir, I'd like to have 'ad a look at Wembley. Mr. Almodham 'ad promised me—but there—" As if to minimize the abandon of this confidence, he followed it up by a ceremonious request for Medford's keys, and an inquiry as to when he would like to dine. Having received a reply, he still lingered, looking more surprised than ever.

"Just a mineral water, then, sir?"

"Oh, yes—anything."

"Shall we say a bottle of Perrier?"

Perrier in the desert! Medford smiled assentingly, surrendered his keys and strolled away.

The house turned out to be smaller than he had imagined, or at least the habitable part of it; for above this towered mighty dilapidated walls of yellow stone, and in their crevices clung plaster chambers, one above the other, cedar beamed, crimson shuttered but crumbling. Out of this jumble of masonry and stucco, Christian and Moslem, the latest tenant of the fortress had chosen a cluster of rooms tucked into an angle of the ancient keep. These apartments opened on the uppermost court, where the palms chattered and the fig tree coiled above the well. On the broken marble pavement, chairs and a low table were grouped, and a few geraniums and blue morning glories had been coaxed to grow between the slabs.

A white-skirted boy with watchful eyes was watering the plants; but at Medford's approach he vanished like a wisp of vapor.

There was something vaporous and insubstantial about the whole scene; even the long arcaded room opening on the court, furnished with saddlebag cushions, divans with gazelle skins and rough indigenous rugs; even the table piled with old *Timeses* and ultra-modern French and English reviews—all seemed, in that clear mocking air, born of the delusion of some desert wayfarer.

A seat under the fig tree invited Medford to doze, and when he woke the hard blue dome above him was gemmed with stars and the night breeze gossiped with the palms.

Rest—beauty—peace. Wise Almodham!

* II *

Wise Almodham! Having carried out—with somewhat disappointing results—the excavation with which an archaeological society had charged him twenty-five years ago, he had lingered on, taken possession of the Crusaders' stronghold, and turned his attention from ancient to medieval remains. But even these investigations, Medford suspected, he prosecuted only at intervals, when the enchantment of his leisure did not lie on him too heavily.

The young American had met Henry Almodham at Luxor the previous winter; had dined with him at old Colonel Swordsley's, on that perfumed starlit terrace above the Nile; and, having somehow awakened the archaeologist's interest, had been invited to look him up in the desert the following year.

They had spent only that one evening together, with old Swordsley blinking at them under memory-laden lids, and two or three charming women from the Winter Palace chattering and exclaiming; but the two men had ridden back to Luxor together in the moonlight, and during that ride Medford fancied he had puzzled out the essential lines of Henry Almodham's character. A nature saturnine yet sentimental; chronic indolence alternating with spurts of highly intelligent activity; gnawing self-distrust soothed by intimate self-appreciation; a craving for complete solitude coupled with the inability to tolerate it for long.

There was more, too, Medford suspected; a dash of Victorian romance, gratified by the setting, the remoteness, the inaccessibility of his retreat, and by being known as *the* Henry Almodham—"the one who lives in a Crusaders' castle, you know"—the gradual imprisonment in a pose assumed in youth, and into which middle age had slowly stiffened; and something deeper, darker, too, perhaps, though the young man doubted that; probably just the fact that living in that particular way had brought healing to an old wound, an old mortification, something which years ago had touched a vital part and left him writhing. Above all, in Almodham's hesitating movements and the dreaming look of his long well-featured brown face with its shock of gray hair, Medford detected an inertia, mental and moral, which life in this castle of romance must have fostered and excused.

"Once here, how easy not to leave!" he mused, sinking deeper into his deep chair.

"Dinner, sir," Gosling announced.

The table stood in an open arch of the living room; shaded candles made a rosy pool in the dusk. Each time he emerged into their light the servant, white jacketed, velvet footed, looked more competent and more surprised than ever. Such dishes, too—the cook also a Maltese? Ah, they were geniuses, these Maltese! Gosling bridled, smiled his acknowledgment, and started to fill the guest's glass with Chablis.

"No wine," said Medford patiently.

"Sorry, sir. But the fact is—"

"You said there was Perrier?"

"Yes, sir; but I find there's none left. It's been awfully hot, and Mr. Almodham has been and drank it all up. The new supply isn't due till next week. We 'ave to depend on the caravans going south."

"No matter. Water, then. I really prefer it."

Gosling's surprise widened to amazement. "Not water, sir? Water—in these parts?"

Medford's irritability stirred again. "Something wrong with your water? Boil it then, can't you? I won't—" He pushed away the half-filled wineglass.

"Oh—boiled? Certainly, sir." The man's voice dropped almost to a whisper. He placed on the table a succulent mess of rice and mutton, and vanished.

Medford leaned back, surrendering himself to the night, the coolness, the ripple of wind in the palms.

One agreeable dish succeeded another. As the last appeared, the diner began to feel the pangs of thirst, and at the same moment a beaker of water was placed at his elbow. "Boiled, sir, and I squeezed a lemon into it."

"Right. I suppose at the end of the summer your water gets a bit muddy?"

"That's it, sir. But you'll find this all right, sir."

Medford tasted. "Better than Perrier." He emptied the glass, leaned back and groped in his pocket. A tray was instantly at his hand with cigars and cigarettes.

"You don't—smoke, sir?"

Medford, for answer, held up his cigar to the man's light. "What do you call this?"

"Oh, just so. I meant the other style." Gosling glanced discreetly at the opium pipes of jade and amber laid out on a low table.

Medford shrugged away the invitation—and wondered. Was that perhaps Almodham's other secret—or one of them? For he began to think there might be many; and all, he was sure, safely stored away behind Gosling's vigilant brow.

"No news yet of Mr. Almodham?"

Gosling was gathering up the dishes with dexterous gestures. For a moment he seemed not to hear. Then—from beyond the candle gleam —"News, sir? There couldn't 'ardly be, could there? There's no wireless in the desert, sir; not like London." His respectful tone tempered the slight irony. "But tomorrow evening ought to see him riding in." Gosling paused, drew nearer, swept one of his swift hands across the table in pursuit of the last crumbs, and added tentatively: "You'll surely be able, sir, to stay till then?"

Medford laughed. The night was too rich in healing; it sank on his spirit like wings. Time vanished, fret and troubles were no more. "Stay? I'll stay a year if I have to!"

"Oh—a year?" Gosling echoed it playfully, gathered up the dessert dishes and was gone.

* III *

Medford had said that he would wait for Almodham a year; but the next morning he found that such arbitrary terms had lost their meaning. There were no time measures in a place like this. The silly face of his watch told its daily tale to emptiness. The wheeling of the constellations over those ruined walls marked only the revolutions of the earth; the spasmodic motions of man meant nothing.

The very fact of being hungry, that stroke of the inward clock, was minimized by the slightness of the sensation—just the ghost of a pang, that might have been quieted by dried fruit and honey. Life had the light monotonous smoothness of eternity.

Toward sunset Medford shook off this queer sense of otherwhereness and climbed to the roof. Across the desert he spied for Almodham. Southward the Mountains of Alabaster hung like a blue veil lined with light. In the west a great column of fire shot up, spraying into plumy cloudlets which turned the sky to a fountain of rose leaves, the sands beneath to gold.

No riders specked them. Medford watched in vain for his absent host till night fell, and the punctual Gosling invited him once more to table.

In the evening Medford absently fingered the ultra-modern reviews

—three months old, and already so stale to the touch—then tossed them aside, flung himself on a divan and dreamed. Almodham must spend a lot of time in dreaming; that was it. Then, just as he felt himself sinking down into torpor, he would be off on one of these dashes across the desert in quest of unknown ruins. Not such a bad life.

Gosling appeared with Turkish coffee in a cup cased in filigree.

"Are there any horses in the stable?" Medford suddenly asked.

"Horses? Only what you might call pack horses, sir. Mr. Almodham has the two best saddle horses with him."

"I was thinking I might ride out to meet him."

Gosling considered. "So you might, sir."

"Do you know which way he went?"

"Not rightly, sir. The Caïd's man was to guide them."

"Them? Who went with him?"

"Just one of our men, sir. They've got the two thoroughbreds. There's a third but he's lame." Gosling paused. "Do you know the trails, sir? Excuse me, but I don't think I ever saw you here before."

"No," Medford acquiesced, "I've never been bere before."

"Oh, then"—Gosling's gesture added: "In that case, even the best thoroughbred wouldn't help you."

"I suppose he may still turn up tonight?"

"Oh, easily, sir. I expect to see you both breakfasting here tomorrow morning," said Gosling cheerfully.

Medford sipped his coffee. "You said you'd never seen me here before. How long have you been here yourself?"

Gosling answered instantly, as though the figures were never long out of his memory: "Eleven years and seven months altogether, sir."

"Nearly twelve years! That's a longish time."

"Yes, it is."

"And I don't suppose you often get away?"

Gosling was moving off with the tray. He halted, turned back, and said with sudden emphasis: "I've never once been away. Not since Mr. Almodham first brought me here."

"Good Lord! Not a single holiday?"

"Not one, sir."

"But Mr. Almodham goes off occasionally. I met him at Luxor last year."

"Just so, sir. But when he's here he needs me for himself; and when he's away he needs me to watch over the others. So you see—"

"Yes, I see. But it must seem to you devilish long."

"It seems long, sir."

"But the others? You mean they're not—wholly trustworthy?"

"Well, sir, they're just Arabs," said Gosling with careless contempt.

"I see. And not a single old reliable among them?"

"The term isn't in their language, sir."

Medford was busy lighting his cigar. When he looked up he found that Gosling still stood a few feet off.

"It wasn't as if it 'adn't been a promise, you know, sir," he said, almost passionately.

"A promise?"

"To let me 'ave my holiday, sir. A promise—agine and agine."

"And the time never came?"

"No, sir. The days just drifted by—"

"Ah. They would, here. Don't sit up for me," Medford added. "I think I shall wait up—wait for Mr. Almodham."

Gosling's stare widened. "Here, sir? Here in the court?"

The young man nodded, and the servant stood still regarding him, turned by the moonlight to a white spectral figure, the unquiet ghost of a patient butler who might have died without his holiday.

"Down here in this court all night, sir? It's a lonely spot. I couldn't 'ear you if you was to call. You're best in bed, sir. The air's bad. You might bring your fever on again."

Medford laughed and stretched himself in his long chair. "Decidedly," he thought, "the fellow needs a change." Aloud he remarked: "Oh, I'm all right. It's you who are nervous, Gosling. When Mr. Almodham comes back I mean to put in a word for you. You shall have your holiday."

Gosling still stood motionless. For a minute he did not speak. "You would, sir, you would?" He gasped it out on a high cracked note, and the last word ran into a laugh—a brief shrill cackle, the laugh of one long unused to such indulgences.

"Thank you, sir. Good night, sir." He was gone.

* IV *

"You do boil my drinking water, always?" Medford questioned, his hand clasping the glass without lifting it.

The tone was amicable, almost confidential; Medford felt that since his rash promise to secure a holiday for Gosling he and Gosling were on terms of real friendship.

"Boil it? Always, sir. Naturally." Gosling spoke with a slight note of reproach, as though Medford's question implied a slur—unconscious, he hoped—on their newly established relation. He scrutinized Medford with his astonished eyes, in which a genuine concern showed itself through the glaze of professional indifference.

"Because, you know, my bath this morning—"

Gosling was in the act of receiving from the hands of a gliding Arab a fragrant dish of *kuskus*. Under his breath he hissed to the native: "You damned aborigine, you, can't you even 'old a dish steady? Ugh!" The Arab vanished before the imprecation, and Gosling, with a calm deliberate hand, set the dish before Medford. "All alike, they are." Fastidiously he wiped a trail of grease from his linen sleeve.

"Because, you know, my bath this morning simply stank," said Medford, plunging fork and spoon into the dish.

"Your bath, sir?" Gosling stressed the word. Astonishment, to the exclusion of all other emotion, again filled his eyes as he rested them on Medford. "Now, I wouldn't 'ave 'ad that 'appen for the world," he said self-reproachfully.

"There's only the one well here, eh? The one in the court?"

Gosling aroused himself from absorbed consideration of the visitor's complaint. "Yes, sir; only the one."

"What sort of a well is it? Where does the water come from?"

"Oh, it's just a cistern, sir. Rain water. There's never been any other here. Not that I ever knew it to fail; but at this season sometimes it does turn queer. Ask any o' them Arabs, sir; they'll tell you. Liars as they are, they won't trouble to lie about that."

Medford was cautiously tasting the water in his glass. "This seems all right," he pronounced.

Sincere satisfaction was depicted on Gosling's countenance. "I seen to its being boiled myself, sir. I always do. I 'ope that Perrier'll turn up tomorrow, sir."

"Oh, tomorrow—" Medford shrugged, taking a second helping. "Tomorrow I may not be here to drink it."

"What—going away, sir?" cried Gosling.

Medford, wheeling round abruptly, caught a new and incomprehensible look in Gosling's eyes. The man had seemed to feel a sort of doglike affection for him; had wanted, Medford could have sworn, to keep him on, persuade him to patience and delay; yet now, Medford could equally have sworn, there was relief in his look, satisfaction, almost, in his voice.

"So soon, sir?"

"Well, this is the fifth day since my arrival. And as there's no news yet of Mr. Almodham, and you say he may very well have forgotten all about my coming—"

"Oh, I don't say that, sir; not forgotten! Only, when one of those old piles of stones takes 'old of him, he does forget about the time, sir. That's what I meant. The days drift by—'e's in a dream. Very likely he thinks you're just due now, sir." A small thin smile sharpened the lusterless gravity of Gosling's features. It was the first time that Medford had seen him smile.

"Oh, I understand. But still—" Medford paused. Through the spell of inertia laid on him by the drowsy place and its easeful comforts his instinct of alertness was struggling back. "It's odd—"

"What's odd?" Gosling echoed unexpectedly, setting the dried dates and figs on the table.

"Everything," said Medford.

He leaned back in his chair and glanced up through the arch at the lofty sky from which noon was pouring down in cataracts of blue and gold. Almodham was out there somewhere under that canopy of fire, perhaps, as the servant said, absorbed in his dream. The land was full of spells.

"Coffee, sir?" Gosling reminded him. Medford took it.

"It's odd that you say you don't trust any of these fellows—these Arabs—and yet that you don't seem to feel worried at Mr. Almodham's being off God knows where, all alone with them."

Gosling received this attentively, impartially; he saw the point. "Well, sir, no—you wouldn't understand. It's the very thing that can't be taught, when to trust 'em and when not. It's 'ow their interests lie, of course, sir; and their religion, as they call it." His contempt was unlimited. "But even to begin to understand why I'm not worried about Mr. Almodham, you'd 'ave to 'ave lived among them, sir, and you'd 'ave to speak their language."

"But I—" Medford began. He pulled himself up short and bent above his coffee.

"Yes, sir?"

"But I've traveled among them more or less."

"Oh, traveled!" Even Gosling's intonation could hardly conciliate respect with derision in his reception of this boast.

"This makes the fifth day, though," Medford continued argumentatively. The midday heat lay heavy even on the shaded side of the court, and the sinews of his will were weakening.

"I can understand, sir, a gentleman like you 'aving other engagements—being pressed for time, as it were," Gosling reasonably conceded.

He cleared the table, committed its freight to a pair of Arab arms that just showed and vanished, and finally took himself off while Medford sank into the divan. A land of dreams. . . .

*   *   *

The afternoon hung over the place like a great velarium of cloth-of-gold stretched across the battlements and drooping down in ever slacker folds upon the heavy-headed palms. When at length the gold turned to violet, and the west to a bow of crystal clasping the dark sands, Medford shook off his sleep and wandered out. But this time, instead of mounting to the roof, he took another direction.

He was surprised to find how little he knew of the place after five days of loitering and waiting. Perhaps this was to be his last evening alone in it. He passed out of the court by a vaulted stone passage which led to another walled enclosure. At his approach two or three Arabs who had been squatting there rose and melted out of sight. It was as if the solid masonry had received them.

Beyond, Medford heard a stamping of hoofs, the stir of a stable at nightfall. He went under another archway and found himself among horses and mules. In the fading light an Arab was rubbing down one of the horses, a powerful young chestnut. He too seemed about to vanish; but Medford caught him by the sleeve.

"Go on with your work," he said in Arabic.

The man, who was young and muscular, with a lean Bedouin face, stopped and looked at him.

"I didn't know your Excellency spoke our language."

"Oh, yes," said Medford.

The man was silent, one hand on the horse's restless neck, the other thrust into his woolen girdle. He and Medford examined each other in the faint light.

"Is that the horse that's lame?" Medford asked.

"Lame?" The Arab's eyes ran down the animal's legs. "Oh, yes; lame," he answered vaguely.

Medford stooped and felt the horse's knees and fetlocks. "He seems pretty fit. Couldn't he carry me for a canter this evening if I felt like it?"

The Arab considered; he was evidently perplexed by the weight of responsibility which the question placed on him.

"Your Excellency would like to go for a ride this evening?"

"Oh, just a fancy. I might or I might not." Medford lit a cigarette and offered one to the groom, whose white teeth flashed his gratification. Over the shared match they drew nearer and the Arab's diffidence seemed to lessen.

"Is this one of Mr. Almodham's own mounts?" Medford asked.

"Yes, sir; it's his favorite," said the groom, his hand passing proudly down the horse's bright shoulder.

"His favorite? Yet he didn't take him on this long expedition?"

The Arab fell silent and stared at the ground.

"Weren't you surprised at that?" Medford queried.

The man's gesture declared that it was not his business to be surprised.

The two remained without speaking while the quick blue night descended.

At length Medford said carelessly: "Where do you suppose your master is at this moment?"

The moon, unperceived in the radiant fall of day, had now suddenly possessed the world, and a broad white beam lay full on the Arab's white smock, his brown face and the turban of camel's hair knotted above it. His agitated eyeballs glistened like jewels.

"If Allah would vouchsafe to let us know!"

"But you suppose he's safe enough, don't you? You don't think it's necessary yet for a party to go out in search of him?"

The Arab appeared to ponder this deeply. The question must have taken him by surprise. He flung a brown arm about the horse's neck and continued to scrutinize the stones of the court.

"When the master is away Mr. Gosling is our master."

"And he doesn't think it necessary?"

The Arab signed: "Not yet."

"But if Mr. Almodham were away much longer—"

The man was again silent, and Medford continued: "You're the head groom, I suppose?"

"Yes, Excellency."

There was another pause. Medford half turned away; then, over his shoulder: "I suppose you know the direction Mr. Almodham took? The place he's gone to?"

"Oh, assuredly, Excellency."

"Then you and I are going to ride after him. Be ready an hour before daylight. Say nothing to anyone. Mr. Gosling or anybody else. We two ought to be able to find him without other help."

The Arab's face was all a responsive flash of eyes and teeth. "Oh, sir, I undertake that you and my master shall meet before tomorrow night. And none shall know of it."

"He's as anxious about Almodham as I am," Medford thought; and a faint shiver ran down his back. "All right. Be ready," he repeated.

He strolled back and found the court empty of life, but fantastically peopled by palms of beaten silver and a white marble fig tree.

"After all," he thought irrelevantly, "I'm glad I didn't tell Gosling that I speak Arabic."

He sat down and waited till Gosling, approaching from the living room, ceremoniously announced for the fifth time that dinner was served.

* V *

Medford sat up in bed with the jerk which resembles no other. Someone was in his room. The fact reached him not by sight or sound—for the moon had set, and the silence of the night was complete—but by a peculiar faint disturbance of the invisible currents that enclose us.

He was awake in an instant, caught up his electric hand lamp and flashed it into two astonished eyes. Gosling stood above the bed.

"Mr. Almodham—he's back?" Medford exclaimed.

"No, sir; he's not back." Gosling spoke in low controlled tones. His extreme self-possession gave Medford a sense of danger—he couldn't say why, or of what nature. He sat upright, looking hard at the man.

"Then what's the matter?"

"Well, sir, you might have told me you talked Arabic"—Gosling's tone was now wistfully reproachful—"before you got 'obnobbing with that Selim. Making randy-voos with 'im by night in the desert."

Medford reached for his matches and lit the candle by the bed. He did not know whether to kick Gosling out of the room or to listen to what the man had to say; but a quick movement of curiosity made him determine on the latter course.

"Such folly! First I thought I'd lock you in. I might 'ave." Gosling drew a key from his pocket and held it up. "Or again I might 'ave let you go. Easier than not. But there was Wembley."

"Wembley?" Medford echoed. He began to think the man was going mad. One might, so conceivably, in that place of postponements and enchantments! He wondered whether Almodham himself were not a little mad—if, indeed, Almodham were still in a world where such a fate is possible.

"Wembley. You promised to get Mr. Almodham to give me an 'oliday—to let me go back to England in time for a look at Wembley. Every man 'as 'is fancies, 'asn't 'e, sir? And that's mine. I've told Mr. Almodham so, agine and agine. He'd never listen, or only make believe to; say: 'We'll see, now, Gosling, we'll see'; and no more 'eard of it. But you was different, sir. You said it, and I knew you meant it—about my 'oliday. So I'm going to lock you in."

Gosling spoke composedly, but with an underthrill of emotion in his queer Mediterranean-Cockney voice.

"Lock me in?"

"Prevent you somehow from going off with that murderer. You don't suppose you'd ever 'ave come back alive from that ride, do you?"

A shiver ran over Medford, as it had the evening before when he had said to himself that the Arab was as anxious as he was about Almodham. He gave a slight laugh.

"I don't know what you're talking about. But you're not going to lock me in."

The effect of this was unexpected. Gosling's face was drawn up into a convulsive grimace and two tears rose to his pale eyelashes and ran down his cheeks.

"You don't trust me, after all," he said plaintively.

Medford leaned on his pillow and considered. Nothing as queer had ever before happened to him. The fellow looked almost ridiculous enough to laugh at; yet his tears were certainly not simulated. Was he weeping for Almodham, already dead, or for Medford, about to be committed to the same grave?

"I should trust you at once," said Medford, "if you'd tell me where your master is."

Gosling's face resumed its usual guarded expression, though the trace of the tears still glittered on it.

"I can't do that, sir."

"Ah, I thought so!"

"Because—'ow do I know?"

Medford thrust a leg out of bed. One hand, under the blanket, lay on his revolver.

"Well, you may go now. Put that key down on the table first. And don't try to do anything to interfere with my plans. If you do I'll shoot you," he added concisely.

"Oh, no, you wouldn't shoot a British subject; it makes such a fuss. Not that I'd care—I've often thought of doing it myself. Sometimes in the sirocco season. That don't scare me. And you shan't go."

Medford was on his feet now, the revolver visible. Gosling eyed it with indifference.

"Then you do know where Mr. Almodham is? And you're determined that I shan't find out?" Medford challenged him.

"Selim's determined," said Gosling, "and all the others are. They all want you out of the way. That's why I've kept 'em to their quarters—done all the waiting on you myself. Now will you stay here? For God's sake, sir! The return caravan is going through to the coast the day after tomorrow. Join it, sir—it's the only safe way! I darsn't let you go with one of our men, not even if you was to swear you'd ride straight for the coast and let this business be."

"This business? What business?"

"This worrying about where Mr. Almodham is, sir. Not that there's anything to worry about. The men all know that. But the plain fact is they've stolen some money from his box, since he's been gone, and if I hadn't winked at it they'd 'ave killed me; and all they want is to get you to ride out after 'im, and put you safe away under a 'eap of sand somewhere off the caravan trails. Easy job. There; that's all, sir. My word it is."

There was a long silence. In the weak candlelight the two men stood considering each other.

Medford's wits began to clear as the sense of peril closed in on him. His mind reached out on all sides into the enfolding mystery, but it was everywhere impenetrable. The odd thing was that, though he did not believe half of what Gosling had told him, the man yet inspired him with a queer sense of confidence as far as their mutual relation was concerned. "He may be lying about Almodham, to hide God knows what; but I don't believe he's lying about Selim."

Medford laid his revolver on the table. "Very well," he said. "I won't ride out to look for Mr. Almodham, since you advise me not to. But I won't leave by the caravan; I'll wait here till he comes back."

He saw Gosling whiten under his sallowness. "Oh, don't do that, sir; I couldn't answer for them if you was to wait. The caravan'll take you to the coast the day after tomorrow as easy as if you was riding in Rotten Row."

"Ah, then you know that Mr. Almodham won't be back by the day after tomorrow?" Medford caught him up.

"I don't know anything, sir."

"Not even where he is now?"

Gosling reflected. "He's been gone too long, sir, for me to know that," he said from the threshold.

The door closed on him.

Medford found sleep unrecoverable. He leaned in his window and watched the stars fade and the dawn break in all its holiness. As the stir of life rose among the ancient walls he marveled at the contrast between that fountain of purity welling up into the heavens and the evil secrets clinging bat-like to the nest of masonry below.

He no longer knew what to believe or whom. Had some enemy of Almodham's lured him into the desert and bought the connivance of his people? Or had the servants had some reason of their own for spiriting him away, and was Gosling possibly telling the truth when he said that the same fate would befall Medford if he refused to leave?

Medford, as the light brightened, felt his energy return. The very impenetrableness of the mystery stimulated him. He would stay, and he would find out the truth.

* VI *

It was always Gosling himself who brought up the water for Medford's bath; but this morning he failed to appear with it, and when he came it was to bring the breakfast tray. Medford noticed that his face was of a pasty pallor, and that his lids were reddened as if with weeping. The contrast was unpleasant, and a dislike for Gosling began to shape itself in the young man's breast.

"My bath?" he queried.

"Well, sir, you complained yesterday of the water—"

"Can't you boil it?"

"I 'ave, sir."

"Well, then—"

Gosling went out sullenly and presently returned with a brass jug. "It's the time of year—we're dying for rain," he grumbled, pouring a scant measure of water into the tub.

Yes, the well must be pretty low, Medford thought. Even boiled, the water had the disagreeable smell that he had noticed the day before, though of course in a slighter degree. But a bath was a necessity in that climate. He splashed the few cupfuls over himself as best as he could.

He spent the day in rather fruitlessly considering his situation. He had hoped the morning would bring counsel, but it brought only courage and resolution, and these were of small use without enlightenment. Suddenly he remembered that the caravan going south from the coast would pass near the castle that afternoon. Gosling had dwelt on the date often enough, for it was the caravan which was to bring the box of Perrier water.

"Well, I'm not sorry for that," Medford reflected, with a slight shrinking of the flesh. Something sick and viscous, half smell, half substance, seemed to have clung to his skin since his morning bath, and the idea of having to drink that water again was nauseating.

But his chief reason for welcoming the caravan was the hope of finding in it some European, or at any rate some native official from the coast, to whom he might confide his anxiety. He hung about, listening and waiting, and then mounted to the roof to gaze northward along the trail. But in the afternoon glow he saw only three Bedouins guiding laden pack mules toward the castle.

As they mounted the steep path he recognized some of Almodham's men, and guessed at once that the southward caravan trail did not actually pass under the walls and that the men had been out to meet it, probably at a small oasis behind some fold of the sand hills. Vexed at his own thoughtlessness in not foreseeing such a possibility, Medford dashed down to the court, hoping the men might have brought back some news of Almodham, though, as the latter had ridden south, he could at best only have crossed the trail by which the caravan had come. Still, even so, someone might know something, some report might have been heard— since everything was always known in the desert.

As Medford reached the court, angry vociferations, and retorts as vehement, rose from the stable yard. He leaned over the wall and listened.

Hitherto nothing had surprised him more than the silence of the place. Gosling must have had a strong arm to subdue the shrill voices of his underlings. Now they had all broken loose, and it was Gosling's own voice—usually so discreet and measured—which dominated them.

Gosling, master of all the desert dialects, was cursing his subordinates in a half dozen.

"And you didn't bring it—and you tell me it wasn't there, and I tell you it was, and that you know it, and that you either left it on a sand heap while you were jawing with some of those slimy fellows from the coast, or else fastened it on to the horse so carelessly that it fell off on the way—and all of you too sleepy to notice. Oh, you sons of females I wouldn't soil my lips by naming! Well, back you go to hunt it up, that's all!"

"By Allah and the tomb of his Prophet, you wrong us unpardonably. There was nothing left at the oasis, nor yet dropped off on the way back. It was not there, and that is the truth in its purity."

"Truth! Purity! You miserable lot of shirks and liars, you—and the gentleman here not touching a drop of anything but water—as you profess to do, you liquor-swilling humbugs!"

Medford drew back from the parapet with a smile of relief. It was nothing but a case of Perrier—the missing case—which had raised the passions of these grown men to the pitch of frenzy! The anti-climax lifted a load from his breast. If Gosling, the calm and self-controlled, could waste his wrath on so slight a hitch in the working of the commissariat, he at least must have a free mind. How absurd this homely incident made Medford's speculations seem!

He was at once touched by Gosling's solicitude, and annoyed that he should have been so duped by the hallucinating fancies of the East.

Almodham was off on his own business; very likely the men knew where and what the business was; and even if they had robbed him in his absence, and quarreled over the spoils, Medford did not see what he could do. It might even be that his eccentric host—with whom, after all, he had had but one evening's acquaintance—repenting of an invitation too rashly given, had ridden away to escape the boredom of entertaining him. As this alternative occurred to Medford it seemed so plausible that he began to wonder if Almodham had not simply withdrawn to some secret suite of that intricate dwelling, and were waiting there for his guest's departure.

So well would this explain Gosling's solicitude to see the visitor off—so completely account for the man's nervous and contradictory behavior—that Medford, smiling at his own obtuseness, hastily resolved to leave on the morrow. Tranquillized by this decision, he lingered about the court till dusk fell, and then, as usual, went up to the roof. But today his eyes, instead of raking the horizon, fastened on the clustering edifice of which, after six days' residence, he knew so little. Aerial chambers, jutting out at capricious angles, baffled him with closely shuttered windows, or here and there with the enigma of painted panes. Behind which window was his host concealed, spying, it might be, at this very moment on the movements of his lingering guest?

The idea that that strange moody man, with his long brown face and shock of white hair, his half-guessed selfishness and tyranny, and his morbid self-absorption, might be actually within a stone's throw, gave Medford, for the first time, a sharp sense of isolation. He felt himself shut out, unwanted—the place, now that he imagined someone might be living in it unknown to him, became lonely, inhospitable, dangerous.

"Fool that I am—he probably expected me to pack up and go as soon as I found he was away!" the young man reflected. Yes; decidedly, he would leave the next morning.

Gosling had not shown himself all the afternoon. When at length, belatedly, he came to set the table, he wore a look of sullen, almost surly, reserve which Medford had not yet seen on his face. He hardly returned the young man's friendly "Hallo—dinner?" and when Medford was seated handed him the first dish in silence. Medford's glass remained unfilled till he touched its brim.

"Oh, there's nothing to drink, sir. The men lost the case of Perrier—or dropped it and smashed the bottles. They say it never came. 'Ow do I know, when they never open their 'eathen lips but to lie?" Gosling burst out with sudden violence.

He set down the dish he was handing, and Medford saw that he had been obliged to do so because his whole body was shaking as if with fever.

"My dear man, what does it matter? You're going to be ill," Medford exclaimed, laying his hand on the servant's arm. But the latter, muttering: "Oh, God, if I'd only 'a' gone for it myself," jerked away and vanished from the room.

Medford sat pondering; it certainly looked as if poor Gosling were on the edge of a breakdown. No wonder, when Medford himself was so oppressed by the uncanniness of the place. Gosling reappeared after an interval, correct, close-lipped, with the dessert and a bottle of white wine. "Sorry, sir."

To pacify him, Medford sipped the wine and then pushed his chair away and returned to the court. He was making for the fig tree by the well when Gosling, slipping ahead, transferred his chair and wicker table to the other end of the court.

"You'll be better here—there'll be a breeze presently," he said. "I'll fetch your coffee."

He disappeared again, and Medford sat gazing up at the pile of masonry and plaster, and wondering whether he had not been moved away from his favorite corner to get him out of—or into?—the angle of vision of the invisible watcher. Gosling, having brought the coffee, went away and Medford sat on.

At length he rose and began to pace up and down as he smoked. The moon was not yet up, and darkness fell solemnly on the ancient walls. Presently the breeze arose and began its secret commerce with the palms.

Medford went back to his seat; but as soon as he had resumed it he fancied that the gaze of his hidden watcher was jealously fixed on the red spark of his cigar. The sensation became increasingly distasteful; he could almost feel Almodham reaching out long ghostly arms from somewhere above him in the darkness. He moved back into the living room, where a shaded light hung from the ceiling; but the room was airless, and finally he went out again and dragged his seat to its old place under the fig tree. From there the windows which he suspected could not command him, and he felt easier, though the corner was out of the breeze and the heavy air seemed tainted with the exhalation of the adjoining well.

"The water must be very low," Medford mused. The smell, though faint, was unpleasant; it smirched the purity of the night. But he felt safer there, somehow, farther from those unseen eyes which seemed mysteriously to have become his enemies.

"If one of the men had knifed me in the desert, I shouldn't wonder if it would have been at Almodham's orders," Medford thought. He drowsed.

When he woke the moon was pushing up its ponderous orange disk above the walls, and the darkness in the court was less dense. He must have slept for an hour or more. The night was delicious, or would have been anywhere but there. Medford felt a shiver of his old fever and remembered that Gosling had warned him that the court was unhealthy at night.

"On account of the well, I suppose. I've been sitting too close to it," he reflected. His head ached, and he fancied that the sweetish foulish smell clung to his face as it had after his bath. He stood up and approached the well to see how much water was left in it. But the moon was not yet high enough to light those depths, and he peered down into blackness.

Suddenly he felt both shoulders gripped from behind and forcibly pressed forward, as if by someone seeking to push him over the edge. An instant later, almost coinciding with his own swift resistance, the push became a strong tug backward, and he swung round to confront Gosling, whose hands immediately dropped from his shoulders.

"I thought you had the fever, sir—I seemed to see you pitching over," the man stammered.

Medford's wits returned. "We must both have it, for I fancied you were pitching me," he said with a laugh.

"Me, sir?" Gosling gasped. "I pulled you back as 'ard as ever—"

"Of course. I know."

"Whatever are you doing here, anyhow, sir? I warned you it was un'ealthy at night," Gosling continued irritably.

Medford leaned against the wellhead and contemplated him. "I believe the whole place is unhealthy."

Gosling was silent. At length he asked: "Aren't you going up to bed, sir?"

"No," said Medford, "I prefer to stay here."

Gosling's face took on an expression of dogged anger. "Well, then, I prefer that you shouldn't."

Medford laughed again. "Why? Because it's the hour when Mr. Almodham comes out to take the air?"

The effect of this question was unexpected. Gosling dropped back a step or two and flung up his hands, pressing them to his lips as if to stifle a low outcry.

"What's the matter?" Medford queried. The man's antics were beginning to get on his nerves.

"Matter?" Gosling still stood away from him, out of the rising slant of moonlight.

"Come! Own up that he's here and have done with it!" cried Medford impatiently.

"Here? What do you mean by 'here'? You 'aven't seen 'im, 'ave you?" Before the words were out of the man's lips he flung up his arms again, stumbled forward and fell in a heap at Medford's feet.

Medford, still leaning against the wellhead, smiled down contemptuously at the stricken wretch. His conjecture had been the right one, then; he had not been Gosling's dupe after all.

"Get up, man. Don't be a fool! It's not your fault if I guessed that Mr. Almodham walks here at night—"

"Walks here!" wailed the other, still cowering.

"Well, doesn't he? He won't kill you for owning up, will he?"

"Kill me? Kill me? I wish I'd killed *you!*" Gosling half got to his feet, his head thrown back in ashen terror. "And I might 'ave, too, so easy! You felt me pushing of you over, didn't you? Coming 'ere spying and sniffing—" His anguish seemed to choke him.

Medford had not changed his position. The very abjectness of the creature at his feet gave him an easy sense of power. But Gosling's last cry had suddenly deflected the course of his speculations. Almodham was here, then; that was certain; but just where was he, and in what shape? A new fear scuttled down Medford's spine.

"So you did want to push me over?" he said. "Why? As the quickest way of joining your master?"

The effect was more immediate than he had foreseen.

Gosling, getting to his feet, stood there bowed and shrunken in the accusing moonlight.

"Oh, God—and I 'ad you 'arf over! You know I did! And then—it was what you said about Wembley. So help me, sir, I felt you meant it, and it 'eld me back." The man's face was again wet with tears, but this time Medford recoiled from them as if they had been drops splashed up by a falling body from the foul waters below.

Medford was silent. He did not know if Gosling were armed or not, but he was no longer afraid; only aghast, and yet shudderingly lucid.

Gosling continued to ramble on half deliriously:

"And if only that Perrier 'ad of come. I don't believe it'd ever 'ave crossed your mind, if only you'd 'ave had your Perrier regular, now would it? But you say 'e walks—and I knew he would! Only—what was I to do with him, with you turning up like that the very day?"

Still Medford did not move.

"And 'im driving me to madness, sir, sheer madness, that same morning. Will you believe it? The very week before you come, I was to sail for England and 'ave my 'oliday, a 'ole month, sir—and I was entitled to six, if there was any justice—a 'ole month in 'Ammersmith, sir, in a cousin's 'ouse, and the chance to see Wembley thoroughly; and then 'e 'eard you was coming, sir, and 'e was bored and lonely 'ere, you understand—'e 'ad to have new excitements provided for 'im or 'e'd go off 'is bat—and when 'e 'eard you were coming, 'e come out of his black mood in a flash and was 'arf crazy with pleasure, and said: 'I'll keep 'im 'ere all winter—a remarkable young man, Gosling—just my kind.' And when I says to him: 'And 'ow about my 'oliday?' he stares at me with those stony eyes of 'is and says: ' 'Oliday? Oh, to be sure; why, next year—we'll see what can be done about it next year.' Next year, sir, as if 'e was doing me a favor! And that's the way it 'ad been for nigh on twelve years.

"But this time, if you 'adn't 'ave come I do believe I'd 'ave got away, for he was getting used to 'aving Selim about 'im and his 'ealth was never better—and, well, I told 'im as much, and 'ow a man 'ad his rights after all, and my youth was going, and me that 'ad served him so well chained up 'ere like 'is watchdog, and always next year and next year—and, well, sir, 'e just laughed, sneering-like, and lit 'is cigarette. 'Oh, Gosling, cut it out,' 'e says.

"He was standing on the very spot where you are now, sir; and he turned to walk into the 'ouse. And it was then I 'it 'im. He was a heavy man, and he fell against the well curb. And just when you were expected any minute—oh, my God!"

Gosling's voice died out in a strangled murmur.

Medford, at his last words, had unvoluntarily shrunk back a few feet. The two men stood in the middle of the court and stared at each other without speaking. The moon, swinging high above the battlements, sent a searching spear of light down into the guilty darkness of the well.

AFTER HOLBEIN

ANSON WARLEY had had his moments of being a rather remarkable man; but they were only intermittent; they recurred at ever-lengthening intervals; and between times he was a small poor creature, chattering with cold inside, in spite of his agreeable and even distinguished exterior.

He had always been perfectly aware of these two sides of himself (which, even in the privacy of his own mind, he contemptuously refused to dub a dual personality); and as the rather remarkable man could take fairly good care of himself, most of Warley's attention was devoted to ministering to the poor wretch who took longer and longer turns at hearing his name, and was more and more insistent in accepting the invitations which New York, for over thirty years, had tirelessly poured out on him. It was in the interest of this lonely fidgety unemployed self that Warley, in his younger days, had frequented the gaudiest restaurants and the most glittering Palace Hotels of two hemispheres, subscribed to the most advanced literary and artistic reviews, bought the pictures of the young painters who were being the most vehemently discussed, missed few of the showiest first nights in New York, London or Paris, sought the company of the men and women—especially the women—most conspicuous in fashion, scandal, or any other form of social notoriety, and thus tried to warm the shivering soul within him at all the passing bonfires of success.

The original Anson Warley had begun by staying at home in his little flat, with his books and his thoughts, when the other poor creature went forth; but gradually—he hardly knew when or how—he had slipped into the way of going too, till finally he made the bitter discovery that he and the creature had become one, except on the increasingly rare occasions when, detaching himself from all casual contingencies, he mounted to the lofty watershed which fed the sources of his scorn. The view from there was vast and glorious, the air was icy but exhilarating; but soon he began to find the place too lonely, and too difficult to get to, especially as the lesser Anson not only refused to go up with him but began to sneer, at first ever so faintly, then with increasing insolence, at this affectation of a taste for the heights.

"What's the use of scrambling up there, anyhow? I could understand it if you brought down anything worth-while—a poem or a picture of your own. But just climbing and staring: what does it lead to? Fellows with the creative gift have got to have their occasional Sinaïs; I can see that. But for a mere looker-on like you, isn't that sort of thing rather a pose? You talk awfully well—brilliantly, even (oh, my dear fellow, no false modesty between you and *me*, please!) But who the devil is there to listen to you, up there among the glaciers? And sometimes, when you come down, I notice that you're rather—well, heavy and tongue-tied. Look out, or they'll stop asking us to dine! And sitting at home every evening—brr! Look here, by the way; if you've got nothing better for tonight, come along with me to Chrissy Torrance's—or the Bob Briggses'—or Princess Kate's; anywhere where there's lots of racket and sparkle, places that people go to in Rollses, and that are smart and hot and overcrowded, and you have to pay a lot—in one way or another—to get in."

Once and again, it is true, Warley still dodged his double and slipped off on a tour to remote uncomfortable places, where there were churches or pictures to be seen, or shut himself up at home for a good bout of reading, or just, in sheer disgust at his companion's platitude, spent an evening with people who were doing or thinking real things. This happened seldomer than of old, however, and more clandestinely; so that at last he used to sneak away to spend two or three days with an archaeologically-minded friend, or an evening with a quiet scholar, as furtively as if he were stealing to a lover's tryst; which, as lovers' trysts were now always kept in the limelight, was after all a fair exchange. But he always felt rather apologetic to the other Warley about these escapades—and, if the truth were known, rather bored and restless before they were over. And in the back of his mind there lurked an increasing dread of missing something hot and noisy and overcrowded when he went off to one of his mountain tops. "After all, that high-brow business has been awfully overdone—now hasn't it?" the little Warley would insinuate, rummaging for his pearl studs, and consulting his flat evening watch as nervously as if it were a railway timetable. "If only we haven't missed something really jolly by all this backing and filling. . . ."

"Oh, you poor creature, you! Always afraid of being left out, aren't you? Well—just for once, to humor you, and because I happen to be feeling rather stale myself. But only to think of a sane man's wanting to go to places just because they're hot and smart and overcrowded!" And off they would dash together. . . .

* II *

All that was long ago. It was years now since there had been two distinct Anson Warleys. The lesser one had made away with the other, done him softly to death without shedding of blood; and only a few people suspected (and they no longer cared) that the pale white-haired man, with the small slim figure, the ironic smile and the perfect evening clothes, whom New York still indefatigably invited, was nothing less than a murderer.

Anson Warley—Anson Warley! No party was complete without Anson Warley. He no longer went abroad now; too stiff in the joints; and there had been two or three slight attacks of dizziness. . . . Nothing to speak of, nothing to think of, even; but somehow one dug one's self into one's comfortable quarters, and felt less and less like moving out of them, except to motor down to Long Island for weekends, or to Newport for a few visits in summer. A trip to the Hot Springs, to get rid of the stiffness, had not helped much, and the ageing Anson Warley (who really, otherwise, felt as young as ever) had developed a growing dislike for the promiscuities of hotel life and the monotony of hotel food.

Yes; he was growing more fastidious as he grew older. A good sign, he thought. Fastidious not only about food and comfort but about people also. It was still a privilege, a distinction, to have him to dine. His old friends were faithful, and the new people fought for him, and often failed to get him; to do so they had to offer very special inducements in the way of cuisine, conversation or beauty. Young beauty; yes, that would do it. He did like to sit and watch a lovely face, and call laughter into lovely eyes. But no dull dinners for *him,* not even if they fed you off gold. As to that he was as firm as the other Warley, the distant aloof one with whom he had—er, well, parted company, oh, quite amicably, a good many years ago. . . .

On the whole, since that parting, life had been much easier and pleasanter; and by the time the little Warley was sixty-three he found himself looking forward with equanimity to an eternity of New York dinners.

Oh, but only at the right houses—always at the right houses; that was understood! The right people—the right setting—the right wines. . . . He smiled a little over his perennial enjoyment of them; said "Nonsense, Filmore," to his devoted tiresome manservant, who was beginning to hint that really, every night, sir, and sometimes a dance afterward, was too much, especially when you kept at it for months on end; and Dr.—

"Oh, damn your doctors!" Warley snapped. He was seldom ill-tempered;

he knew it was foolish and upsetting to lose one's self-control. But Filmore began to be a nuisance, nagging him, preaching at him. As if he himself wasn't the best judge. . . .

Besides, he chose his company. He'd stay at home any time rather than risk a boring evening. Damned rot, what Filmore had said about his going out every night. Not like poor old Mrs. Jaspar, for instance . . . he smiled self-approvingly as he evoked her tottering image. "That's the kind of fool Filmore takes me for," be chuckled, his good humor restored by an analogy that was so much to his advantage.

Poor old Evelina Jaspar! In his youth, and even in his prime, she had been New York's chief entertainer—"leading hostess," the newspapers called her. Her big house in Fifth Avenue had been an entertaining machine. She had lived, breathed, invested and reinvested her millions, to no other end. At first her pretext had been that she had to marry her daughters and amuse her sons; but when sons and daughters had married and left her she had seemed hardly aware of it; she had just gone on entertaining. Hundreds, no, thousands of dinners (on gold plate, of course, and with orchids, and all the delicacies that were out of season), had been served in that vast pompous dining room, which one had only to close one's eyes to transform into a railway buffet for millionaires, at a big junction, before the invention of restaurant trains. . . .

Warley closed his eyes, and did so picture it. He lost himself in amused computation of the annual number of guests, of saddles of mutton, of legs of lamb, of terrapin, canvas backs, magnums of champagne and pyramids of hot-house fruit that must have passed through that room in the last forty years.

And even now, he thought—hadn't one of old Evelina's nieces told him the other day, half bantering, half shivering at the avowal, that the poor old lady, who was gently dying of softening of the brain, still imagined herself to be New York's leading hostess, still sent out invitations (which of course were never delivered), still ordered terrapin, champagne and orchids, and still came down every evening to her great shrouded drawing rooms, with her tiara askew on her purple wig, to receive a stream of imaginary guests?

Rubbish, of course—a macabre pleasantry of the extravagant Nelly Pierce, who had always had her joke at Aunt Evelina's expense. . . . But Warley could not help smiling at the thought that those dull monotonous dinners were still going on in their hostess's clouded imagination. Poor old Evelina, he thought! In a way she was right. There was really no reason why that kind of standardized entertaining should ever cease; a performance so undiscriminating, so undifferentiated, that one could almost imagine, in the hostess' tired brain, all the dinners she had ever given merging into one Gargantuan pyramid of food and drink, with the same faces, perpetually the same faces, gathered stolidly about the same gold plate.

Thank heaven, Anson Warley had never conceived of social values in terms of mass and volume. It was years since he had dined at Mrs. Jaspar's. He even felt that he was not above reproach in that respect. Two or three times, in the past, he had accepted her invitations (always sent out weeks ahead), and then chucked her at the eleventh hour for something more amusing. Finally, to avoid such risks, he had made it a rule always to refuse her dinners. He had even—he remembered—been rather funny about it once, when someone had told him that Mrs. Jaspar couldn't understand . . . was a little hurt . . . said it couldn't be true that he always had another engagement the nights she asked him. . . . *"True?* Is the truth what she wants? All right! Then the next time I get a 'Mrs. Jaspar requests the pleasure' I'll answer it with a 'Mr. Warley declines the boredom.' Think she'll understand that, eh?" And the phrase became a catchword in his little set that winter. " 'Mr. Warley declines the boredom' —good, good, *good!"* "Dear Anson, I do hope you won't decline the boredom of coming to lunch next Sunday to meet the new Hindu Yoghi"—or the new saxophone soloist, or that genius of a mulatto boy who plays Negro spirituals on a toothbrush; and so on and so on. He only hoped poor old Evelina never heard of it. . . .

"Certainly I shall *not* stay at home tonight—why, what's wrong with me?" he snapped, swinging round on Filmore.

The valet's long face grew longer. His way of answering such questions was always to pull out his face; it was his only means of putting any expression into it. He turned away into the bedroom, and Warley sat alone by his library fire. . . . Now what did the man see that was wrong with him, he wondered? He had felt a little confusion that morning, when he was doing his daily sprint around the Park (his exercise was reduced to that!); but it had been only a passing flurry, of which Filmore could of course know nothing. And as soon as it was over his mind had seemed more lucid, his eye keener, than ever; as sometimes (he reflected) the electric light in his library lamps would blaze up too brightly after a break in the current, and he would say to himself, wincing a little at the sudden glare on the page he was reading: "That means that it'll go out again in a minute."

Yes; his mind, at that moment, had been quite piercingly clear and perceptive; his eye had passed with a renovating glitter over every detail of the daily scene. He stood still for a minute under the leafless trees of the Mall, and looking about him with the sudden insight of age, understood that he had reached the time of life when Alps and cathedrals became as transient as flowers.

Everything was fleeting, fleeting . . . yes, that was what had given him the vertigo. The doctors, poor fools, called it the stomach, or high blood pressure; but it was only the dizzy plunge of the sands in the hour glass, the everlasting plunge that emptied one of heart and bowels, like the drop of an elevator from the top floor of a skyscraper.

Certainly, after that moment of revelation, he had felt a little more tired than usual for the rest of the day; the light had flagged in his mind as it sometimes did in his lamps. At Chrissy Torrance's, where he had lunched, they had accused him of being silent, his hostess had said that he looked pale; but he had retorted with a joke, and thrown himself into the talk with a feverish loquacity. It was the only thing to do; for he could not tell all these people at the lunch table that very morning he had arrived at the turn in the path from which mountains look as transient as flowers—and that one after another they would all arrive there too.

He leaned his head back and closed his eyes, but not in sleep. He did not feel sleepy, but keyed up and alert. In the next room he heard Filmore reluctantly, protestingly, laying out his evening clothes. . . . He had no fear about the dinner tonight; a quiet intimate little affair at an old friend's house. Just two or three congenial men, and Elfmann, the pianist (who would probably play), and that lovely Elfrida Flight. The fact that people asked him to dine to meet Elfrida Flight seemed to prove pretty conclusively that he was still in the running! He chuckled softly at Filmore's pessimism, and thought: "Well, after all, I suppose no man seems young to his valet. . . . Time to dress very soon," he thought; and luxuriously postponed getting up out of his chair. . . .

* III *

"She's worse than usual tonight," said the day nurse, laying down the evening paper as her colleague joined her. "Absolutely determined to have her jewels out."

The night nurse, fresh from a long sleep and an afternoon at the movies with a gentleman friend, threw down her fancy bag, tossed off her hat and rumpled up her hair before old Mrs. Jaspar's tall toilet mirror. "Oh, I'll settle that—don't you worry," she said brightly.

"Don't you fret her, though, Miss Cress," said the other, getting wearily out of her chair. "We're very well off here, take it as a whole, and I don't want her pressure rushed up for nothing."

Miss Cress, still looking at herself in the glass, smiled reassuringly at Miss Dunn's pale reflection behind her. She and Miss Dunn got on very well together, and knew on which side their bread was buttered. But at the

end of the day Miss Dunn was always fagged out and fearing the worst.
The patient wasn't as hard to handle as all that. Just let her ring for her old
maid, old Lavinia, and say: "My sapphire velvet tonight, with the diamond
stars"—and Lavinia would know exactly how to manage her.

Miss Dunn had put on her hat and coat, and crammed her knitting, and
the newspaper, into her bag, which, unlike Miss Cress's, was capacious and
shabby; but she still loitered undecided on the threshold. "I could stay
with you till ten as easy as not. . . ." She looked almost reluctantly about
the big high-studded dressing room (everything in the house was high-
studded), with its rich dusky carpet and curtains, and its monumental
dressing table draped with lace and laden with gold-backed brushes and
combs, gold-stoppered toilet bottles, and all the charming paraphernalia of
beauty at her glass. Old Lavinia even renewed every morning the roses and
carnations in the slim crystal vases between the powder boxes and the nail
polishers. Since the family had shut down the hothouses at the uninhabited
country place on the Hudson, Miss Cress suspected that old Lavinia bought
these flowers out of her own pocket.

"Cold out tonight?" queried Miss Dunn from the door.

"Fierce . . . reg'lar blizzard at the corners. Say, shall I lend you my fur
scarf?" Miss Cress, pleased with the memory of her afternoon (they'd be
engaged soon, she thought), and with the drowsy prospect of an evening in
a deep armchair near the warm gleam of the dressing-room fire, was
disposed to kindliness toward that poor thin Dunn girl, who supported her
mother, and her brother's idiot twins. And she wanted Miss Dunn to
notice her new fur.

"My! Isn't it too lovely? No, not for worlds, thank you. . . ." Her hand
on the doorknob, Miss Dunn repeated: "Don't you cross her now," and
was gone.

Lavinia's bell rang furiously, twice; then the door between the dressing
room and Mrs. Jaspar's bedroom opened, and Mrs. Jaspar herself emerged.

"Lavinia!" she called, in a high irritated voice; then, seeing the nurse,
who had slipped into her print dress and starched cap, she added in a lower
tone: "Oh, Miss Lemoine, good evening." Her first nurse, it appeared, had
been called Miss Lemoine; and she gave the same name to all the others,
quite unaware that there had been any changes in the staff.

"I heard talking, and carriages driving up. Have people begun to
arrive?" she asked nervously. "Where is Lavinia? I still have my jewels to
put on."

She stood before the nurse, the same petrifying apparition which always,
at this hour, struck Miss Cress to silence. Mrs. Jaspar was tall; she had
been broad; and her bones remained impressive though the flesh had
withered on them. Lavinia had encased her, as usual, in her low-necked

purple velvet dress, nipped in at the waist in the old-fashioned way, expanding in voluminous folds about the hips and flowing in a long train over the darker velvet of the carpet. Mrs. Jaspar's swollen feet could no longer be pushed into the high-heeled satin slippers which went with the dress; but her skirts were so long and spreading that, by taking short steps, she managed (so Lavinia daily assured her) entirely to conceal the broad round tips of her black orthopedic shoes.

"Your jewels, Mrs. Jaspar? Why, you've got them on," said Miss Cress brightly.

Mrs. Jaspar turned her porphyry-tinted face to Miss Cress, and looked at her with a glassy incredulous gaze. Her eyes, Miss Cress thought, were the worst. . . . She lifted one old hand, veined and knobbed as a raised map, to her elaborate purple-black wig, groped among the puffs and curls and undulations (queer, Miss Cress thought, that it never occurred to her to look into the glass), and after an interval affirmed: "You must be mistaken, my dear. Don't you think you ought to have your eyes examined?"

The door opened again, and a very old woman, so old as to make Mrs. Jaspar appear almost young, hobbled in with sidelong steps. "Excuse me, madam. I was downstairs when the bell rang."

Lavinia had probably always been small and slight; now, beside her towering mistress, she looked a mere feather, a straw. Everything about her had dried, contracted, been volatilized into nothingness, except her watchful gray eyes, in which intelligence and comprehension burned like two fixed stars. "Do excuse me, madam," she repeated.

Mrs. Jaspar looked at her despairingly. "I hear carriages driving up. And Miss Lemoine says I have my jewels on; and I know I haven't."

"With that lovely necklace!" Miss Cress ejaculated.

Mrs. Jaspar's twisted hand rose again, this time to her denuded shoulders, which were as stark and barren as the rock from which the hand might have been broken. She felt and felt, and tears rose in her eyes. . . .

"Why do you lie to me?" she burst out passionately.

Lavinia softly intervened. "Miss Lemoine meant how lovely you'll be when you get the necklace on, madam."

"Diamonds, diamonds," said Mrs. Jaspar with an awful smile.

"Of course, madam."

Mrs. Jaspar sat down at the dressing table, and Lavinia, with eager random hands, began to adjust the *point de Venise* about her mistress' shoulders, and to repair the havoc wrought in the purple-black wig by its wearer's gropings for her tiara.

"Now you do look lovely, madam," she sighed.

Mrs. Jaspar was on her feet again, stiff but incredibly active. ("Like a cat she is," Miss Cress used to relate.) "I do hear carriages—or is it an automobile? The Magraws, I know, have one of those new-fangled auto-mobiles. And now I hear the front door opening. Quick, Lavinia! My fan, my gloves, my handkerchief . . . how often have I got to tell you? I used to have a *perfect* maid—"

Lavinia's eyes brimmed. "That was me, madam," she said, bending to straighten out the folds of the long purple-velvet train. ("To watch the two of 'em," Miss Cress used to tell a circle of appreciative friends, "is a lot better than any circus.")

Mrs. Jaspar paid no attention. She twitched the train out of Lavinia's vacillating hold, swept to the door, and then paused there as if stopped by a jerk of her constricted muscles. "Oh, but my diamonds—you cruel woman, you! You're letting me go down without my diamonds!" Her ruined face puckered up in a grimace like a new-born baby's, and she began to sob despairingly. "Everybody . . . every . . . body's . . . against me . . ." she wept in her powerless misery.

Lavinia helped herself to her feet and tottered across the floor. It was almost more than she could bear to see her mistress in distress. "Madam, madam—if you'll just wait till they're got out of the safe," she entreated.

The woman she saw before her, the woman she was entreating and consoling, was not the old petrified Mrs. Jaspar with porphyry face and wig awry whom Miss Cress stood watching with a smile, but a young proud creature, commanding and splendid in her Paris gown of amber *moiré,* who, years ago, had burst into just such furious sobs because, as she was sweeping down to receive her guests, the doctor had told her that little Grace, with whom she had been playing all the afternoon, had a diphthe-ritic throat, and no one must be allowed to enter. "Everybody's against me, everybody . . ." she sobbed in her fury; and the young Lavinia, stricken by such Olympian anger, had stood speechless, longing to comfort her, and secretly indignant with little Grace and the doctor. . . .

"If you'll just wait, madam, while I go down and ask Munson to open the safe. There's no one come yet, I do assure you. . . ."

Munson was the old butler, the only person who knew the combination of the safe in Mrs. Jaspar's bedroom. Lavinia had once known it too, but now she was no longer able to remember it. The worst of it was that she feared lest Munson, who had been spending the day in the Bronx, might not have returned. Munson was growing old too, and he did sometimes forget about these dinner parties of Mrs. Jaspar's, and then the stupid footman, George, had to announce the names; and you couldn't be sure that Mrs. Jaspar wouldn't notice Munson's absence, and be excited and angry. These dinner party nights were killing old Lavinia, and she did so want to keep alive; she wanted to live long enough to wait on Mrs. Jaspar to the last.

She disappeared, and Miss Cress poked up the fire, and persuaded Mrs. Jaspar to sit down in an armchair and "tell her who was coming." It always amused Mrs. Jaspar to say over the long list of her guests' names, and generally she remembered them fairly well, for they were always the same—the last people, Lavinia and Munson said, who had dined at the house, on the very night before her stroke. With recovered complacency she began, counting over one after another on her ring-laden fingers: "The Italian Ambassador, the Bishop, Mr. and Mrs. Torrington Bligh, Mr. and Mrs. Fred Amesworth, Mr. and Mrs. Mitchell Magraw, Mr. and Mrs. Torrington Bligh. . . ." ("You've said them before," Miss Cress interpolated, getting out her fancy knitting—a necktie for her friend—and beginning to count the stitches.) And Mrs. Jaspar, distressed and bewildered by the interruption, had to repeat over and over: "Torrington Bligh, Torrington Bligh," till the connection was re-established, and she went on again swimmingly with "Mr. and Mrs. Fred Amesworth, Mr. and Mrs. Mitchell Magraw, Miss Laura Ladew, Mr. Harold Ladew, Mr. and Mrs. Benjamin Bronx, Mr. and Mrs. Torrington Bl—no, I mean, Mr. Anson Warley. Yes, Mr. Anson Warley; that's it," she ended complacently.

Miss Cress smiled and interrupted her counting. "No, that's *not* it."

"What do you mean, my dear—not it?"

"Mr. Anson Warley. He's not coming."

Mrs. Jaspar's jaw fell, and she stared at the nurse's coldly smiling face. "Not coming?"

"No. He's not coming. He's not on the list." (That old list! As if Miss Cress didn't know it by heart! Everybody in the house did, except the booby, George, who heard it reeled off every other night by Munson, and who was always stumbling over the names, and having to refer to the written paper.)

"Not on the list?" Mrs. Jaspar gasped.

Miss Cress shook her pretty head.

Signs of uneasiness gathered on Mrs. Jaspar's face and her lip began to tremble. It always amused Miss Cress to give her these little jolts, though she knew Miss Dunn and the doctors didn't approve of her doing so. She knew also that it was against her own interests, and she did try to bear in mind Miss Dunn's oft-repeated admonition about not sending up the patient's blood pressure; but when she was in high spirits, as she was tonight (they would certainly be engaged), it was irresistible to get a rise out of the old lady. And she thought it funny, this new figure unexpectedly appearing among those time-worn guests. ("I wonder what the rest of 'em 'll say to him," she giggled inwardly.)

"No; he's not on the list." Mrs. Jaspar, after pondering deeply, announced the fact with an air of recovered composure.

"That's what I told you," snapped Miss Cress.

"He's not on the list; but he promised me to come. I saw him yesterday," continued Mrs. Jaspar, mysteriously.

"You *saw* him—where?"

She considered. "Last night, at the Fred Amesworths' dance."

"Ah," said Miss Cress, with a little shiver; for she knew that Mrs. Amesworth was dead, and she was the intimate friend of the trained nurse who was keeping alive, by dint of *piqûres* and high frequency, the inarticulate and inanimate Mr. Amesworth. "It's funny," she remarked to Mrs. Jaspar, "that you'd never invited Mr. Warley before."

"No, I hadn't; not for a long time. I believe he felt I'd neglected him; for he came up to me last night, and said he was so sorry he hadn't been able to call. It seems he's been ill, poor fellow. Not as young as he was! So of course I invited him. He was very much gratified."

Mrs. Jaspar smiled at the remembrance of her little triumph; but Miss Cress's attention had wandered, as it always did when the patient became docile and reasonable. She thought: "Where's old Lavinia? I bet she can't find Munson." And she got up and crossed the floor to look into Mrs. Jaspar's bedroom, where the safe was.

There an astonishing sight met her. Munson, as she had expected, was nowhere visible; but Lavinia, on her knees before the safe, was in the act of opening it herself, her twitching hand slowly moving about the mysterious dial.

"Why, I thought you'd forgotten the combination!" Miss Cress exclaimed.

Lavinia turned a startled face over her shoulder. "So I had, Miss. But I've managed to remember it, thank God. I *had* to, you see, because Munson's forgot to come home."

"Oh," said the nurse incredulously ("Old fox," she thought, "I wonder why she's always pretended she'd forgotten it.") For Miss Cress did not know that the age of miracles is not yet past.

Joyous, trembling, her cheeks wet with grateful tears, the little old woman was on her feet again, clutching to her breast the diamond stars, the necklace of solitaires, the tiara, the earrings. One by one she spread them out on the velvet-lined tray in which they always used to be carried from the safe to the dressing room; then, with rambling fingers, she managed to lock the safe again, and put the keys in the drawer where they belonged, while Miss Cress continued to stare at her in amazement. "I don't believe the old witch is as shaky as she makes out," was her reflection as Lavinia passed her, bearing the jewels to the dressing room where Mrs. Jaspar, lost in pleasant memories, was still computing: "The Italian Ambassador, the Bishop, the Torrington Blighs, the Mitchell Magraws, the Fred Amesworths. . . ."

Mrs. Jaspar was allowed to go down to the drawing room alone on dinner party evenings because it would have mortified her too much to receive her guests with a maid or a nurse at her elbow; but Miss Cress and Lavinia always leaned over the stair rail to watch her descent, and make sure it was accomplished in safety.

"She do look lovely yet, when all her diamonds is on," Lavinia sighed, her purblind eyes bedewed with memories, as the bedizened wig and purple velvet disappeared at the last bend of the stairs. Miss Cress, with a shrug, turned back to the fire and picked up her knitting, while Lavinia set about the slow ritual of tidying up her mistress' room. From below they heard the sound of George's stentorian monologue: "Mr. and Mrs. Torrington Bligh, Mr. and Mrs. Mitchell Magraw . . . Mr. Ladew, Miss Laura Ladew. . . ."

* IV *

Anson Warley, who had always prided himself on his equable temper, was conscious of being on edge that evening. But it was an irritability which did not frighten him (in spite of what those doctors always said about the importance of keeping calm) because he knew it was due merely to the unusual lucidity of his mind. He was in fact feeling uncommonly well, his brain clear and all his perceptions so alert that he could positively hear the thoughts passing through his manservant's mind on the other side of the door, as Filmore grudgingly laid out the evening clothes.

Smiling at the man's obstinacy, he thought: "I shall have to tell them tonight that Filmore thinks I'm no longer fit to go into society." It was always pleasant to hear the incredulous laugh with which his younger friends received any allusion to his supposed senility. "What, *you?* Well, that's a good one!" And he thought it was, himself.

And then, the moment he was in his bedroom, dressing, the sight of Filmore made him lose his temper again. "No; *not* those studs, confound it. The black onyx ones—haven't I told you a hundred times? Lost them, I suppose? Sent them to the wash again in a soiled shirt? That it?" He laughed nervously, and sitting down before his dressing table began to brush back his hair in short angry strokes.

"Above all," he shouted out suddenly, "don't stand there staring at me as if you were watching to see exactly at what minute to telephone for the undertaker!"

"The under—? Oh, sir!" gasped Filmore.

"The—the—damn it, are you *deaf* too? Who said undertaker? I said *taxi;* can't you hear what I say?"

"You want me to call a taxi, sir?"

"No; I don't. I've already told you so. I'm going to walk." Warley straightened his tie, rose and held out his arms toward his dress coat.

"It's bitter cold, sir; better let me call a taxi all the same."

Warley gave a short laugh. "Out with it, now! What you'd really like to suggest is that I should telephone to say I can't dine out. You'd scramble me some eggs instead, eh?"

"I wish you would stay in, sir. There's eggs in the house."

"My overcoat," snapped Warley.

"Or else let me call a taxi; now do, sir."

Warley slipped his arms into his overcoat, tapped his chest to see if his watch (the thin evening watch) and his notecase were in their proper pockets, turned back to put a dash of lavender on his handkerchief, and walked with stiff quick steps toward the front door of his flat.

Filmore, abashed, preceded him to ring for the lift; and then, as it quivered upward through the long shaft, said again: "It's a bitter cold night, sir; and you've had a good deal of exercise today."

Warley leveled a contemptuous glance at him. "Dare say that's why I'm feeling so fit," he retorted as he entered the lift.

It *was* bitter cold; the icy air hit him in the chest when he stepped out of the overheated building, and he halted on the doorstep and took a long breath. "Filmore's missed his vocation; ought to be nurse to a paralytic," he thought. "He'd love to have to wheel me about in a chair."

After the first shock of the biting air he began to find it exhilarating, and walked along at a good pace, dragging one leg ever so little after the other. (The *masseur* had promised him that he'd soon be rid of that stiffness.) Yes—decidedly a fellow like himself ought to have a younger valet; a more cheerful one, anyhow. He felt like a young'un himself this evening; as he turned into Fifth Avenue he rather wished he could meet someone he knew, some man who'd say afterward at his club: "Warley? Why, I saw him sprinting up Fifth Avenue the other night like a two-year-old; that night it was four or five below. . . ." He needed a good counter-irritant for Filmore's gloom. "Always have young people about you," he thought as he walked along; and at the words his mind turned to Elfrida Flight, next to whom he would soon be sitting in a warm pleasantly lit dining room—*where?*

It came as abruptly as that: the gap in his memory. He pulled up at it as if his advance had been checked by a chasm in the pavement at his feet. Where the dickens was he going to dine? And with whom was he going to dine? God! But things didn't happen in that way; a sound strong man didn't suddenly have to stop in the middle of the street and ask himself where he was going to dine. . . .

"Perfect in mind, body and understanding." The old legal phrase bobbed up inconsequently into his thoughts. Less than two minutes ago he had answered in every particular to that description; what was he now? He put his hand to his forehead, which was bursting; then he lifted his hat and let the cold air blow for a while over his overheated temples. It was queer, how hot he'd got, walking. Fact was, he'd been sprinting along at a damned good pace. In future he must try to remember not to hurry. . . . Hang it—one more thing to remember! . . . Well, but what was all the fuss about? Of course, as people got older their memories were subject to these momentary lapses; he'd noticed it often enough among his contemporaries. And, brisk and alert though he still was, it wouldn't do to imagine himself totally exempt from human ills. . . .

Where was it he was dining? Why, somewhere farther up Fifth Avenue; he was perfectly sure of that. With that lovely . . . that lovely. . . . No; better not make any effort for the moment. Just keep calm, and stroll slowly along. When he came to the right street corner of course he'd spot it; and then everything would be perfectly clear again. He walked on, more deliberately, trying to empty his mind of all thoughts. "Above all," he said to himself, "don't worry."

He tried to beguile his nervousness by thinking of amusing things. "Decline the boredom—" He thought he might get off that joke tonight. "Mrs. Jaspar requests the pleasure—Mr. Warley declines the boredom." Not so bad, really; and he had an idea he'd never told it to the people . . . what in hell *was* their name? . . . the people he was on his way to dine with . . . *Mrs. Jaspar requests the pleasure.* Poor old Mrs. Jaspar; again it occurred to him that he hadn't always been very civil to her in old times. When everybody's running after a fellow it's pardonable now and then to chuck a boring dinner at the last minute; but all the same, as one grew older one understood better how an unintentional slight of that sort might cause offense, cause even pain. And he hated to cause people pain. . . . He thought perhaps he'd better call on Mrs. Jaspar some afternoon. She'd be surprised! Or ring her up, poor old girl, and propose himself, just informally, for dinner. One dull evening wouldn't kill him—and how pleased she'd be! Yes—he thought decidedly . . . when he got to be her age, he could imagine how much he'd like it if somebody still in the running should ring him up unexpectedly and say—

He stopped, and looked up, slowly, wonderingly, at the wide illuminated façade of the house he was approaching. Queer coincidence—it was the Jaspar house. And all lit up; for a dinner evidently. And that was queerer yet; almost uncanny; for here he was, in front of the door, as the clock struck a quarter past eight; and of course—he remembered it quite clearly now—it was just here, it was with Mrs. Jaspar, that he was dining

. . . Those little lapses of memory never lasted more than a second or two. How right he'd been not to let himself worry. He pressed his hand on the doorbell.

"God," he thought, as the double doors swung open, "but it's good to get in out of the cold."

* V *

In that hushed sonorous house the sound of the doorbell was as loud to the two women upstairs as if it had been rung in the next room.

Miss Cress raised her head in surprise, and Lavinia dropped Mrs. Jaspar's other false set (the more comfortable one) with a clatter on the marble washstand. She stumbled across the dressing room, and hastened out to the landing. With Munson absent, there was no knowing how George might muddle things. . . .

Miss Cress joined her. "Who is it?" she whispered excitedly. Below, they heard the sound of a hat and a walking stick being laid down on the big marble-topped table in the hall, and then George's stentorian drone: "Mr. Anson Warley."

"It is—it *is!* I can see him—a gentleman in evening clothes," Miss Cress whispered, hanging over the stair rail.

"Good gracious—mercy me! And Munson not here! Oh, whatever, whatever shall we do?" Lavinia was trembling so violently that she had to clutch the stair rail to prevent herself from falling. Miss Cress thought, with her cold lucidity: "She's a good deal sicker than the old woman."

"What shall we do, Miss Cress? That fool of a George—he's showing him in! Who could have thought it?" Miss Cress knew the images that were whirling through Lavinia's brain: the vision of Mrs. Jaspar's having another stroke at the sight of this mysterious intruder, of Mr. Anson Warley's seeing her there, in her impotence and her abasement, of the family's being summoned, and rushing in to exclaim, to question, to be horrified and furious—and all because poor old Munson's memory was going, like his mistress', like Lavinia's, and because he had forgotten that it was one of the *dinner nights.* Oh, misery! . . . The tears were running down Lavinia's cheeks, and Miss Cress knew she was thinking: "If the daughters send him off— and they will—where's he going to, old and deaf as he is, and all his people dead? Oh, if only he can hold on till she dies, and get his pension. . . ."

Lavinia recovered herself with one of her supreme efforts. "Miss Cress, we must go down at once, at once! Something dreadful's going to happen. . . ." She began to totter toward the little velvet-lined lift in the corner of the landing.

Miss Cress took pity on her. "Come along," she said. "But nothing dreadful's going to happen. You'll see."

"Oh, thank you, Miss Cress. But the shock—the awful shock to her—of seeing that strange gentleman walk in."

"Not a bit of it." Miss Cress laughed as she stepped into the lift. "He's not a stranger. She's expecting him."

"Expecting him? Expecting Mr. Warley?"

"Sure she is. She told me so just now. She says she invited him yesterday."

"But, Miss Cress, what are you thinking of? Invite him—how? When you know she can't write nor telephone?"

"Well, she says she saw him; she saw him last night at a dance."

"Oh, God," murmured Lavinia, covering her eyes with her hands.

"At a dance at the Fred Amesworths'—that's what she said," Miss Cress pursued, feeling the same little shiver run down her back as when Mrs. Jaspar had made the statement to her.

"The Amesworths—oh, not the Amesworths?" Lavinia echoed, shivering too. She dropped her hands from her face, and followed Miss Cress out of the lift. Her expression had become less anguished, and the nurse wondered why. In reality, she was thinking, in a sort of dreary beatitude: "But if she's suddenly got as much worse as this, she'll go before me, after all, my poor lady, and I'll be able to see to it that she's properly laid out and dressed, and nobody but Lavinia's hands'll touch her."

"You'll see—if she was expecting him, as she says, it won't give her a shock, anyhow. Only, how did *he* know?" Miss Cress whispered, with an acuter renewal of her shiver. She followed Lavinia with muffled steps down the passage to the pantry, and from there the two women stole into the dining room, and placed themselves noiselessly at its farther end, behind the tall Coromandel screen through the cracks of which they could peep into the empty room.

The long table was set, as Mrs. Jaspar always insisted that it should be on these occasions; but old Munson not having returned, the gold plate (which his mistress also insisted on) had not been got out, and all down the table, as Lavinia saw with horror, George had laid the coarse blue-and-white plates from the servants' hall. The electric wall lights were on, and the candles lit in the branching Sèvres candelabra—so much at least had been done. But the flowers in the great central dish of Rose Dubarry porcelain, and in the smaller dishes which accompanied it—the flowers, oh shame, had been forgotten! They were no longer real flowers; the family had long since suppressed that expense; and no wonder, for Mrs. Jaspar always insisted on orchids. But Grace, the youngest daughter, who was the kindest, had hit on the clever device of arranging three beautiful clusters of artificial orchids and maidenhair, which had only to be lifted from their shelf in the pantry and set in the dishes—only, of course, that imbecile footman had forgotten, or had not known where to find them. And, oh, horror, realizing his oversight too late, no doubt, to appeal to Lavinia, he had taken some old newspapers and bunched them up into something that he probably thought resembled a bouquet, and crammed one into each of the priceless Rose Dubarry dishes.

Lavinia clutched at Miss Cress's arm. "Oh, look—look what he's done; I shall die of the shame of it. . . . Oh, Miss, hadn't we better slip around to the drawing room and try to coax my poor lady upstairs again, afore she ever notices?"

Miss Cress, peering through the crack of the screen, could hardly suppress a giggle. For at that moment the double doors of the dining room were thrown open, and George, shuffling about in a baggy livery inherited from a long-departed predecessor of more commanding build, bawled out in his loud singsong: "Dinner is served, madam."

"Oh, it's too late," moaned Lavinia. Miss Cress signed to her to keep silent, and the two watchers glued their eyes to their respective cracks of the screen.

What they saw, far off down the vista of empty drawing rooms, and after an interval during which (as Lavinia knew) the imaginary guests were supposed to file in and take their seats, was the entrance, at the end of the ghostly cortège, of a very old woman, still tall and towering, on the arm of a man somewhat smaller than herself, with a fixed smile on a darkly pink face, and a slim erect figure clad in perfect evening clothes, who advanced with short measured steps, profiting (Miss Cress noticed) by the support of the arm he was supposed to sustain. "Well—I never!" was the nurse's inward comment.

The couple continued to advance, with rigid smiles and eyes staring straight ahead. Neither turned to the other, neither spoke. All their attention was concentrated on the immense, the almost unachievable effort of reaching that point, halfway down the long dinner table, opposite the big Dubarry dish, where George was drawing back a gilt armchair for Mrs. Jaspar. At last they reached it, and Mrs. Jaspar seated herself, and waved a stony hand to Mr. Warley. "On my right." He gave a little bow, like the bend of a jointed doll, and with infinite precaution let himself down into his chair. Beads of perspiration were standing on his forehead, and Miss Cress saw him draw out his handkerchief and wipe them stealthily away. He then turned his head somewhat stiffly toward his hostess.

"Beautiful flowers," he said, with great precision and perfect gravity, waving his hand toward the bunched-up newspaper in the bowl of Sèvres.

Mrs. Jaspar received the tribute with complacency. "So glad . . . orchids . . . from High Lawn . . . every morning," she simpered.

"Marvelous," Mr. Warley completed.

"I always say to the Bishop . . . ," Mrs. Jaspar continued.

"Ha—of course," Mr. Warley warmly assented.

"Not that I don't think . . ."

"Ha—rather!"

George had reappeared from the pantry with a blue crockery dish of mashed potatoes. This he handed in turn to one after another of the imaginary guests, and finally presented to Mrs. Jaspar and her right-hand neighbor.

They both helped themselves cautiously, and Mrs. Jaspar addressed an arch smile to Mr. Warley. " 'Nother month—no more oysters."

"Ha—no more!"

George, with a bottle of Apollinaris wrapped in a napkin, was saying to each guest in turn: "Perrier-Jouet, '95." (He had picked that up, thought Miss Cress, from hearing old Munson repeat it so often.)

"Hang it—well, then just a sip," murmured Mr. Warley.

"Old times," bantered Mrs. Jaspar; and the two turned to each other and bowed their heads and touched glasses.

"I often tell Mrs. Amesworth . . . ," Mrs. Jaspar continued, bending to an imaginary presence across the table.

"Ha—*ha!*" Mr. Warley approved.

George reappeared and slowly encircled the table with a dish of spinach. After the spinach the Apollinaris also went the rounds again, announced successively as Château Lafite, '74, and "the old Newbold Madeira." Each time that George approached his glass, Mr. Warley made a feint of lifting a defensive hand, and then smiled and yielded. "Might as well—hanged for a sheep . . . ," he remarked gaily; and Mrs. Jaspar giggled.

Finally a dish of Malaga grapes and apples was handed. Mrs. Jaspar, now growing perceptibly languid, and nodding with more and more effort at Mr. Warley's pleasantries, transferred a bunch of grapes to her plate, but nibbled only two or three. "Tired," she said suddenly, in a whimper like a child's; and she rose, lifting herself up by the arms of her chair, and leaning over to catch the eye of an invisible lady, presumably Mrs. Amesworth, seated opposite to her. Mr. Warley was on his feet too, supporting himself by resting one hand on the table in a jaunty attitude. Mrs. Jaspar waved to him to be reseated. "Join us—after cigars," she smilingly ordained; and with a great and concentrated effort he bowed to her as she passed toward the double doors which George was throwing open. Slowly, majestically, the purple-velvet train disappeared down the long enfilade of illuminated rooms, and the last door closed behind her.

"Well, I do believe she's enjoyed it!" chuckled Miss Cress, taking Lavinia by the arm to help her back to the hall. Lavinia, for weeping, could not answer.

* VI *

Anson Warley found himself in the hall again, getting into his fur-lined overcoat. He remembered suddenly thinking that the rooms had been intensely overheated, and that all the other guests had talked very loud and laughed inordinately. "Very good talk though, I must say," he had to acknowledge.

In the hall, as he got his arms into his coat (rather a job, too, after that Perrier-Jouet) he remembered saying to somebody (perhaps it was to the old butler): "Slipping off early—going on; 'nother engagement," and thinking to himself the while that when he got out into the fresh air again he would certainly remember where the other engagement was. He smiled a little while the servant, who seemed a clumsy fellow, fumbled with the fastening of the door. "And Filmore, who thought I wasn't even well enough to dine out! Damned ass! What would he say if he knew I was going on?"

The door opened, and with an immense sense of exhilaration Mr. Warley issued forth from the house and drew in a first deep breath of night air. He heard the door closed and bolted behind him, and continued to stand motionless on the step, expanding his chest, and drinking in the icy draught.

" 'Spose it's about the last house where they give you Perrier-Jouet, '95," he thought; and then: "Never heard better talk either. . . ."

He smiled again with satisfaction at the memory of the wine and the wit. Then he took a step forward, to where a moment before the pavement had been—and where now there was nothing.

MR. JONES

LADY JANE LYNKE was unlike other people: when she heard that she had inherited Bells, the beautiful old place which had belonged to the Lynkes of Thudeney for something like six hundred years, the fancy took her to go and see it unannounced. She was staying at a friend's nearby, in Kent, and the next morning she borrowed a motor and slipped away alone to Thudeney-Blazes, the adjacent village.

It was a lustrous motionless day. Autumn bloom lay on the Sussex downs, on the heavy trees of the weald, on streams moving indolently, far off across the marshes. Farther still, Dungeness, a fitful streak, floated on an immaterial sea which was perhaps, after all, only sky.

In the softness Thudeney-Blazes slept: a few aged houses bowed about a duck pond, a silvery spire, orchards thick with dew. Did Thudeney-Blazes ever wake?

Lady Jane left the motor to the care of the geese on a miniature common, pushed open a white gate into a field (the griffoned portals being padlocked), and struck across the park toward a group of carved chimney stacks. No one seemed aware of her.

In a dip of the land, the long low house, its ripe brick masonry overhanging a moat deeply sunk about its roots, resembled an aged cedar spreading immemorial red branches. Lady Jane held her breath and gazed.

A silence distilled from years of solitude lay on lawns and gardens. No one had lived at Bells since the last Lord Thudeney, then a penniless younger son, had forsaken it sixty years before to seek his fortune in Canada. And before that, he and his widowed mother, distant poor relations, were housed in one of the lodges, and the great place, even in their day, had been as mute and solitary as the family vault.

Lady Jane, daughter of another branch, to which an earldom and considerable possessions had accrued, had never seen Bells, hardly heard its name. A succession of deaths, and the whim of an old man she had never known, now made her heir to all this beauty; and as she stood and looked she was glad she had come to it from so far, from impressions so remote and different. "It would be dreadful to be used to it—to be thinking already about the state of the roof, or the cost of a heating system."

Till this her thirty-fifth year, Lady Jane had led an active, independent and decided life. One of several daughters, moderately but sufficiently provided for, she had gone early from home, lived in London lodgings, traveled in tropic lands, spent studious summers in Spain and Italy, and written two or three brisk business-like little books about cities usually dealt with sentimentally. And now, just back from a summer in the south of France, she stood ankle-deep in wet bracken, and gazed at Bells lying there under a September sun that looked like moonlight.

"I shall never leave it!" she ejaculated, her heart swelling as if she had taken the vow to a lover.

She ran down the last slope of the park and entered the faded formality of gardens with clipped yews as ornate as architecture, and holly hedges as solid as walls. Adjoining the house rose a low deep-buttressed chapel. Its door was ajar, and she thought this of good augury: her forebears were waiting for her. In the porch she remarked fly-blown notices of services, an umbrella stand, a disheveled door mat: no doubt the chapel served as the village church. The thought gave her a sense of warmth and neighborliness. Across the damp flags of the chancel, monuments and brasses showed through a traceried screen. She examined them curiously. Some hailed her with vocal memories, others whispered out of the remote and the unknown: it was a shame to know so little about her own family. But neither Crofts nor Lynkes had ever greatly distinguished themselves; they had gathered substance simply by holding on to what they had, and slowly accumulating privileges and acres. "Mostly by clever marriages," Lady Jane thought with a faint contempt.

At that moment her eyes lit on one of the less ornate monuments: a plain sarcophagus of gray marble niched in the wall and surmounted by the bust of a young man with a fine arrogant head, a Byronic throat and tossed-back curls.

"Peregrine Vincent Theobald Lynke, Baron Clouds, fifteenth Viscount Thudeney of Bells, Lord of the Manors of Thudeney, Thudeney-Blazes, Upper Lynke, Lynke-Linnet—" so it ran, with the usual tedious enumeration of honors, titles, court and county offices, ending with: "Born on May 1st, 1790, perished of the plague at Aleppo in 1828." And underneath, in small cramped characters, as if crowded as an afterthought into an insufficient space: "Also His Wife."

That was all. No names, dates, honors, epithets, for the Viscountess Thudeney. Did she too die of the plague at Aleppo? Or did the "also" imply her actual presence in the sarcophagus which her husband's pride had no doubt prepared for his own last sleep, little guessing that some Syrian drain was to receive him? Lady Jane racked her memory in vain. All she knew was that the death without issue of this Lord Thudeney had caused the property to revert to the Croft-Lynkes, and so, in the end, brought her to the chancel step where, shyly, she knelt a moment, vowing to the dead to carry on their trust.

She passed on to the entrance court, and stood at last at the door of her new home, a blunt tweed figure in heavy mud-stained shoes. She felt as intrusive as a tripper, and her hand hesitated on the doorbell. "I ought to have brought someone with me," she thought; an odd admission on the part of a young woman who, when she was doing her books of travel, had prided herself on forcing single-handed the most closely guarded doors. But those other places, as she looked back, seemed easy and accessible compared to Bells.

She rang, and a tinkle answered, carried on by a flurried echo which seemed to ask what in the world was happening. Lady Jane, through the nearest window, caught the spectral vista of a long room with shrouded furniture. She could not see its farther end, but she had the feeling that someone stationed there might very well be seeing her.

"Just at first," she thought, "I shall have to invite people here—to take the chill off."

She rang again, and the tinkle again prolonged itself; but no one came.

At last she reflected that the caretakers probably lived at the back of the house, and pushing open a door in the courtyard wall she worked her way around to what seemed a stable yard. Against the purple brick sprawled a neglected magnolia, bearing one late flower as big as a planet. Lady Jane rang at a door marked "Service." This bell, though also languid, had a wake-fuller sound, as if it were more used to being rung, and still knew what was likely to follow; and after a delay during which Lady Jane again had the sense of being peered at—from above, through a lowered blind—a bolt shot, and a woman looked out. She was youngish, unhealthy, respectable and frightened; and she blinked at Lady Jane like someone waking out of sleep.

"Oh," said Lady Jane—"do you think I might visit the house?"

"The house?"

"I'm staying near here—I'm interested in old houses. Mightn't I take a look?"

The young woman drew back. "The house isn't shown."

"Oh, but not to—not to—" Jane weighed the case. "You see," she explained, "I know some of the family: the Northumberland branch."

"You're related, madam?"

"Well—distantly, yes." It was exactly what she had not meant to say; but there seemed no other way.

The woman twisted her apron strings in perlexity.

"Come, you know," Lady Jane urged, producing half-a-crown. The woman turned pale.

"I couldn't, madam; not without asking." It was clear that she was sorely tempted.

"Well, ask, won't you?" Lady Jane pressed the tip into a hesitating hand. The young woman shut the door and vanished. She was away so long that the visitor concluded her half-crown had been pocketed, and there was an end; and she began to be angry with herself, which was more often her habit than to be so with others.

"Well, for a fool, Jane, you're a complete one," she grumbled.

A returning footstep, listless, reluctant—the tread of one who was not going to let her in. It began to be rather comic.

The door opened, and the young woman said in her dull singsong: "Mr. Jones says that no one is allowed to visit the house."

She and Lady Jane looked at each other for a moment, and Lady Jane read the apprehension in the other's eyes.

"Mr. Jones? Oh?—Yes; of course, keep it. . . ." She waved away the woman's hand.

"Thank you, madam." The door closed again, and Lady Jane stood and gazed up at the inexorable face of her own home.

* II *

"But you didn't get in? You actually came back without so much as a peep?"

Her story was received, that evening at dinner, with mingled mirth and incredulity.

"But, my dear! You mean to say you asked to see the house, and they wouldn't let you? *Who* wouldn't?" Lady Jane's hostess insisted.

"Mr. Jones."

"Mr. Jones?"

"He said no one was allowed to visit it."

"Who on earth is Mr. Jones?"

"The caretaker, I suppose. I didn't see him."

"Didn't see him either? But I never heard such nonsense! Why in the world didn't you insist?"

"Yes; why didn't you?" they all chorused; and she could only answer, a little lamely: "I think I was afraid."

"Afraid? *You,* darling?" There was fresh hilarity. "Of Mr. Jones?"

"I suppose so." She joined in the laugh, yet she knew it was true: she had been afraid.

Edward Stramer, the novelist, an old friend of her family, had been listening with an air of abstraction, his eyes on his empty coffee cup. Suddenly, as the mistress of the house pushed back her chair, he looked across the table at Lady Jane. "It's odd: I've just remembered something. Once, when I was a youngster, I tried to see Bells; over thirty years ago it must have been." He glanced at his host. "Your mother drove me over. And we were not let in."

There was a certain flatness in this conclusion, and someone remarked that Bells had always been known as harder to get into than any other house thereabouts.

"Yes," said Stramer; "but the point is that we were refused in exactly the same words. Mr. Jones said no one was allowed to visit the house."

"Ah—he was in possession already? Thirty years ago? Unsociable fellow, Jones. Well, Jane, you've got a good watchdog."

They moved to the drawing room, and the talk drifted to other topics. But Stramer came and sat down beside Lady Jane. "It is queer, though, that at such a distance of time we should have been given exactly the same answer."

She glanced up at him curiously. "Yes; and you didn't try to force your way in either?"

"Oh, no: it was not possible."

"So I felt," she agreed.

"Well, next week, my dear, I hope we shall see it all, in spite of Mr. Jones," their hostess intervened, catching their last words as she moved toward the piano.

"I wonder if we shall see Mr. Jones," said Stramer.

* III *

Bells was not nearly as large as it looked; like many old houses it was very narrow, and but one story high, with servants' rooms in the low attics, and much space wasted in crooked passages and superfluous stairs. If she closed the great salon, Jane thought, she might live there comfortably with the small staff which was the most she could afford. It was a relief to find the place less important than she had feared.

For already, in that first hour of arrival, she had decided to give up everything else for Bells. Her previous plans and ambitions—except such as might fit in with living there—had fallen from her like a discarded garment, and things she had hardly thought about, or had shrugged away with the hasty subversiveness of youth, were already laying quiet hands on her; all the lives from which her life had issued, with what they bore of example or admonishment. The very shabbiness of the house moved her more than splendors, made it, after its long abandonment, seem full of the careless daily coming and going of people long dead, people to whom it had not been a museum, or a page of history, but cradle, nursery, home, and sometimes, no doubt, a prison. If those marble lips in the chapel could speak! If she could hear some of their comments on the old house which had spread its silent shelter over their sins and sorrows, their follies and submissions! A long tale, to which she was about to add another chapter, subdued and humdrum beside some of those earlier annals, yet probably freer and more varied than the unchronicled lives of the great-aunts and great-grandmothers buried there so completely that they must hardly have known when they passed from their beds to their graves. "Piled up like dead leaves," Jane thought, "layers and layers of them, to preserve something forever budding underneath."

Well, all these piled-up lives had at least preserved the old house in its integrity; and that was worth-while. She was satisfied to carry on such a trust.

She sat in the garden looking up at those rosy walls, iridescent with damp and age. She decided which windows should be hers, which rooms given to the friends from Kent who were motoring over, Stramer among them, for a modest housewarming; then she got up and went in.

The hour had come for domestic questions; for she had arrived alone, unsupported even by the old family housemaid her mother had offered her. She preferred to start afresh, convinced that her small household could be staffed from the neighborhood. Mrs. Clemm, the rosy-cheeked old person who had curtsied her across the threshold, would doubtless know.

Mrs. Clemm, summoned to the library, curtsied again. She wore black silk, gathered and spreading as to skirt, flat and perpendicular as to bodice. On her glossy false front was a black lace cap with ribbons which had faded from violet to ash-color, and a heavy watch chain descended from the lava brooch under her crochet collar. Her small round face rested on the collar like a red apple on a white plate: neat, smooth, circular, with a pursed-up mouth, eyes like black seeds, and round ruddy cheeks with the skin so taut that one had to look close to see that it was as wrinkled as a piece of old crackly.

Mrs. Clemm was sure there would be no trouble about servants. She herself could do a little cooking: though her hand might be a bit out. But there was her niece to help; and she was quite of her ladyship's opinion, that there was no need to get in strangers. They were mostly a poor lot;

and besides, they might not take to Bells. There were persons who didn't. Mrs. Clemm smiled a sharp little smile, like the scratch of a pin, as she added that she hoped her ladyship wouldn't be one of them.

As for under-servants . . . well, a boy, perhaps? She had a great-nephew she might send for. But about women—under-housemaids—if her ladyship thought they couldn't manage as they were; well, she really didn't know. Thudeney-Blazes? Oh, she didn't think so. . . . There was more dead than living at Thudeney-Blazes . . . everyone was leaving there . . . or in the church yard . . . one house after another being shut . . . death was everwhere, wasn't it, my lady? Mrs. Clemm said it with another of her short sharp smiles, which provoked the appearance of a frosty dimple.

"But my niece Georgiana is a hard worker, my lady; her that let you in the other day. . . ."

"That didn't," Lady Jane corrected.

"Oh, my lady, it was too unfortunate. If only your ladyship had have said . . . poor Georgiana had ought to have seen; but she never *did* have her wits about her, not for answering the door."

"But she was only obeying orders. She went to ask Mr. Jones."

Mrs. Clemm was silent. Her small hands, wrinkled and resolute, fumbled with the folds of her apron, and her quick eyes made the circuit of the room and then came back to Lady Jane's.

"Just so, my lady; but, as I told her, she'd ought to have known—"

"And who is Mr. Jones?"

Mrs. Clemm's smile snapped out again, deprecating, respectful. "Well, my lady, he's more dead than living, too . . . if I may say so," was her surprising answer.

"Is he? I'm sorry to hear that; but who is he?"

"Well, my lady, he's . . . he's my great-uncle, as it were . . . my grandmother's own brother, as you might say."

"Ah; I see." Lady Jane considered her with growing curiosity. "He must have reached a great age, then."

"Yes, my lady; he has that. Though I'm not," Mrs. Clemm added, the dimple showing, "as old myself as your ladyship might suppose. Living at Bells all these years has been ageing to me; it would be to anybody."

"I suppose so. And yet," Lady Jane continued, "Mr. Jones has survived; has stood it well—as you certainly have?"

"Oh, not as well as I have," Mrs. Clemm interjected, as if resentful of the comparison.

"At any rate, he still mounts guard; mounts it as well as he did thirty years ago."

"Thirty years ago?" Mrs. Clemm echoed, her hands dropping from her apron to her sides.

"Wasn't he here thirty years ago?"

"Oh, yes, my lady, certainly; he's never once been away that I know of."

"What a wonderful record! And what exactly are his duties?"

Mrs. Clemm paused again, her hands still motionless in the folds of her skirt. Lady Jane noticed that the fingers were tightly clenched, as if to check an involuntary gesture.

"He began as pantry boy; then footman; then butler, my lady; but it's hard to say, isn't it, what an old servant's duties are, when he's stayed on in the same house so many years?"

"Yes; and that house always empty."

"Just so, my lady. Everything came to depend on him; one thing after another. His late lordship thought the world of him."

"His late lordship? But he was never here! He spent all his life in Canada."

Mrs. Clemm seemed slightly disconcerted. "Certainly, my lady." (Her voice said: "Who are you, to set me right as to the chronicles of Bells?") "But by letter, my lady; I can show you the letters. And there was his lordship before, the sixteenth Viscount. He *did* come here once."

"Ah, did he?" Lady Jane was embarrassed to find how little she knew of them all. She rose from her seat. "They were lucky, all these absentees, to have some one to watch over their interests so faithfully. I should like to see Mr. Jones—to thank him. Will you take me to him now?"

"Now?" Mrs. Clemm moved back a step or two; Lady Jane fancied her cheeks paled a little under their ruddy varnish. "Oh, not today, my lady."

"Why? Isn't he well enough?"

"Not nearly. He's between life and death, as it were," Mrs. Clemm repeated, as if the phrase were the nearest approach she could find to a definition of Mr. Jones's state.

"He wouldn't even know who I was?"

Mrs. Clemm considered a moment. "I don't say *that,* my lady;" her tone implied that to do so might appear disrespectful. "He'd know you, my lady; but you wouldn't know *him.*" She broke off and added hastily: "I mean, for what he is: he's in no state for you to see him."

"He's so very ill? Poor man! And is everything possible being done?"

"Oh, everything; and more too, my lady. But perhaps," Mrs. Clemm suggested, with a clink of keys, "this would be a good time for your ladyship to take a look about the house. If your ladyship has no objection, I should like to begin with the linen."

* IV *

"And Mr. Jones?" Stramer queried, a few days later, as they sat, Lady Jane and the party from Kent, about an improvised tea table in a recess of one of the great holly hedges.

The day was as hushed and warm as that on which she had first come to Bells, and Lady Jane looked up with a smile of ownership at the old walls which seemed to smile back, the windows which now looked at her with friendly eyes.

"Mr. Jones? Who's Mr. Jones?" the others asked; only Stramer recalled their former talk.

Lady Jane hesitated. "Mr. Jones is my invisible guardian; or rather, the guardian of Bells."

They remembered then. "Invisible? You don't mean to say you haven't seen him yet?"

"Not yet; perhaps I never shall. He's very old—and very ill, I'm afraid."

"And he still rules here?"

"Oh, absolutely. The fact is," Lady Jane added, "I believe he's the only person left who really knows all about Bells."

"Jane, my *dear!* That big shrub over there against the wall! I verily believe it's *Templetonia retusa.* It *is!* Did any one ever hear of its standing an English winter?" Gardeners all, they dashed off towards the shrub in its sheltered angle. "I shall certainly try it on a south wall at Dipway," cried the hostess from Kent.

Tea over, they moved on to inspect the house. The short autumn day was drawing to a close; but the party had been able to come only for an afternoon, instead of staying over the weekend, and having lingered so long in the gardens they had only time, indoors, to puzzle out what they could through the shadows. Perhaps, Lady Jane thought, it was the best hour to see a house like Bells, so long abandoned, and not yet warmed into new life.

The fire she had had lit in the salon sent its radiance to meet them, giving the great room an air of expectancy and welcome. The portraits, the Italian cabinets, the shabby armchairs and rugs, all looked as if life had but lately left them; and Lady Jane said to herself: "Perhaps Mrs. Clemm is right in advising me to live here and close the blue parlor."

"My dear, what a fine room! Pity it faces north. Of course you'll have to shut it in winter. It would cost a fortune to heat."

Lady Jane hesitated. "I don't know: I *had* meant to. But there seems to be no other. . . ."

"No other? In all this house?" They laughed; and one of the visitors, going ahead and crossing a paneled anteroom, cried out: "But here! A delicious room; windows south—yes, and west. The warmest of the house. This is perfect."

They followed, and the blue room echoed with exclamations. "Those charming curtains with the parrots . . . and the blue of that petit point fire screen! But, Jane, of course you must live here. Look at this citron wood desk!"

Lady Jane stood on the threshold. "It seems that the chimney smokes hopelessly."

"Hopelessly? Nonsense! Have you consulted anybody? I'll send you a wonderful man. . . ."

"Besides, if you put in one of those one-pipe heaters. . . . At Dipway. . . ."

Stramer was looking over Lady Jane's shoulder. "What does Mr. Jones say about it?"

"He says no one has ever been able to use this room; not for ages. It was the housekeeper who told me. She's his great-niece, and seems simply to transmit his oracles."

Stramer shrugged. "Well, he's lived at Bells longer than you have. Perhaps he's right."

"How absurd!" one of the ladies cried. "The housekeeper and Mr. Jones probably spend their evenings here, and don't want to be disturbed. Look—ashes on the hearth! What did I tell you?"

Lady Jane echoed the laugh as they turned away. They had still to see the library, damp and dilapidated, the paneled dining room, the breakfast parlor, and such bedrooms as had any old furniture left; not many, for the late lords of Bells, at one time or another, had evidently sold most of its removable treasures.

When the visitors came down their motors were waiting. A lamp had been placed in the hall, but the rooms beyond were lit only by the broad clear band of western sky showing through uncurtained casements. On the doorstep one of the ladies exclaimed that she had lost her handbag—no, she remembered; she had laid it on the desk in the blue room. Which way was the blue room?

"I'll get it," Jane said, turning back. She heard Stramer following. He asked if he should bring the lamp.

"Oh, no; I can see."

She crossed the threshold of the blue room, guided by the light from its western window; then she stopped. Some one was in the room already; she felt rather than saw another presence. Stramer, behind her, paused also; he did not speak or move. What she saw, or thought she saw, was simply an old man with bent shoulders turning away from the citron wood desk.

Almost before she had received the impression there was no one there; only the slightest stir of the needlework curtain over the farther door. She heard no step or other sound.

"There's the bag," she said, as if the act of speaking, and saying something obvious, were a relief.

In the hall her glance crossed Stramer's, but failed to find there the reflection of what her own had registered.

He shook hands, smiling. "Well, good-bye. I commit you to Mr. Jones's care; only don't let him say that *you're* not shown to visitors."

She smiled: "Come back and try," and then shivered a little as the lights of the last motor vanished beyond the great black hedges.

* V *

Lady Jane had exulted in her resolve to keep Bells to herself till she and the old house should have had time to make friends. But after a few days she recalled the uneasy feeling which had come over her as she stood on the threshold after her first tentative ring. Yes; she had been right in thinking she would have to have people about her to take the chill off. The house was too old, too mysterious, too much withdrawn into its own secret past, for her poor little present to fit into it without uneasiness.

But it was not a time of year when, among Lady Jane's friends, it was easy to find people free. Her own family were all in the north, and impossible to dislodge. One of her sisters, when invited, simply sent her back a list of shooting dates; and her mother wrote: "Why not come to us? What can you have to do all alone in that empty house at this time of year? Next summer we're all coming."

Having tried one or two friends with the same result, Lady Jane bethought her of Stramer. He was finishing a novel, she knew, and at such times he liked to settle down somewhere in the country where he could be sure of not being disturbed. Bells was a perfect asylum, and though it was probable that some other friend had anticipated her, and provided the requisite seclusion, Lady Jane decided to invite him. "Do bring your work and stay till it's finished—and don't be in a hurry to finish. I promise that no one shall bother you—" and she added, half-nervously: "Not even Mr. Jones." As she wrote she felt an absurd impulse to blot the words out. "He might not like it," she thought; and the "he" did not refer to Stramer.

Was the solitude already making her superstitious? She thrust the letter into an envelope, and carried it herself to the post office at Thudeney-Blazes. Two days later a wire from Stramer announced his arrival.

* * *

He came on a cold stormy afternoon, just before dinner, and as they went up to dress Lady Jane called after him: "We shall sit in the blue parlor this evening." The housemaid Georgiana was crossing the passage with hot water for the visitor. She stopped and cast a vacant glance at Lady Jane. The latter met it, and said carelessly: "You hear, Georgiana? The fire in the blue parlor."

While Lady Jane was dressing she heard a knock, and saw Mrs. Clemm's round face just inside the door, like a red apple on a garden wall.

"Is there anything wrong about the salon, my lady? Georgiana understood—"

"That I want the fire in the blue parlor. Yes. What's wrong with the salon is that one freezes there."

"But the chimney smokes in the blue parlor."

"Well, we'll give it a trial, and if it does I'll send for someone to arrange it."

"Nothing can be done, my lady. Everything has been tried, and—"

Lady Jane swung about suddenly. She had heard Stramer singing a cheerful hunting song in a cracked voice, in his dressing room at the other end of the corridor.

"That will do, Mrs. Clemm. I want the fire in the blue parlor."

"Yes, my lady." The door closed on the housekeeper.

"So you decided on the salon after all?" Stramer said, as Lady Jane led the way there after their brief repast.

"Yes: I hope you won't be frozen. Mr. Jones swears that the chimney in the blue parlor isn't safe; so, until I can fetch the mason over from Strawbridge—"

"Oh, I see." Stramer drew up to the blaze in the great fireplace. "We're very well off here; though heating this room is going to be ruinous. Meanwhile, I note that Mr. Jones still rules."

Lady Jane gave a slight laugh.

"Tell me," Stramer continued, as she bent over the mixing of the Turkish coffee, "what is there about him? I'm getting curious."

Lady Jane laughed again, and heard the embarrassment in her laugh. "So am I."

"Why—you don't mean to say you haven't seen him yet?"

"No. He's still too ill."

"What's the matter with him? What does the doctor say?"

"He won't see the doctor."

"But look here—if things take a worse turn—I don't know; but mightn't you be held to have been negligent?"

"What can I do? Mrs. Clemm says he has a doctor who treats him by correspondence. I don't see that I can interfere."

"Isn't there someone beside Mrs. Clemm whom you can consult?"

She considered: certainly, as yet, she had not made much effort to get into relation with her neighbors. "I expected the vicar to call. But I've inquired: there's no vicar any longer at Thudeney-Blazes. A curate comes from Strawbridge every other Sunday. And the one who comes now is new: nobody about the place seems to know him."

"But I thought the chapel here was in use? It looked so when you showed it to us the other day."

"I thought so too. It used to be the parish church of Lynke-Linnet and Lower-Lynke; but it seems that was years ago. The parishioners objected to coming so far; and there weren't enough of them. Mrs. Clemm says that nearly everybody has died off or left. It's the same at Thudeney-Blazes."

Stramer glanced about the great room, with its circle of warmth and light by the hearth, and the sullen shadows huddled at its farther end, as if hungrily listening. "With this emptiness at the center, life was bound to cease gradually on the outskirts."

Lady Jane followed his glance. "Yes; it's all wrong. I must try to wake the place up."

"Why not open it to the public? Have a visitors' day?"

She thought a moment. In itself the suggestion was distasteful; she could imagine few things that would bore her more. Yet to do so might be a duty, a first step toward re-establishing relations between the lifeless house and its neighborhood. Secretly, she felt that even the coming and going of indifferent unknown people would help to take the chill from those rooms, to brush from their walls the dust of too-heavy memories.

"Who's that?" asked Stramer. Lady Jane started in spite of herself, and glanced over her shoulder; but he was only looking past her at a portrait which a dart of flame from the hearth had momentarily called from its obscurity.

"That's a Lady Thudeney." She got up and went toward the picture with a lamp. "Might be an Opie, don't you think? It's a strange face, under the smirk of the period."

Stramer took the lamp and held it up. The portrait was that of a young woman in a short-waisted muslin gown caught beneath the breast by a cameo. Between clusters of beribboned curls a long fair oval looked out dumbly, inexpressively, in a stare of frozen beauty. "It's as if the house had been too empty even then," Lady Jane murmured. "I wonder which she was? Oh, I know: it must be *'Also His Wife.'* "

Stramer stared.

"It's the only name on her monument. The wife of Peregrine Vincent Theobald, who perished of the plague at Aleppo in 1828. Perhaps she was very fond of him, and this was painted when she was an inconsolable widow."

"They didn't dress like that as late as 1828." Stramer holding the lamp closer, deciphered the inscription on the border of the lady's India scarf; *Juliana, Viscountess Thudeney, 1818.* "She must have been inconsolable before his death, then."

Lady Jane smiled. "Let's hope she grew less so after it."

Stramer passed the lamp across the canvas. "Do you see where she was painted? In the blue parlor. Look: the old paneling; and she's leaning on the citron wood desk. They evidently used the room in winter then." The lamp paused on the background of the picture: a window framing snow-laden paths and hedges in icy perspective.

"Curious," Stramer said—"and rather melancholy: to be painted against that wintry desolation. I wish you could find out more about her. Have you dipped into your archives?"

"No. Mr. Jones—"

"He won't allow that either?"

"Yes; but he's lost the key of the muniment room. Mrs. Clemm has been trying to get a locksmith."

"Surely the neighborhood can still produce one?"

"There *was* one at Thudeney-Blazes; but he died the week before I came."

"Of course!"

"Of course?"

"Well, in Mrs. Clemm's hands keys get lost, chimneys smoke, locksmiths die. . . ." Stramer stood, light in hand, looking down the shadowy length of the salon. "I say, let's go and see what's happening now in the blue parlor."

Lady Jane laughed: a laugh seemed easy with another voice near by to echo it. "Let's—"

She followed him out of the salon, across the hall in which a single candle burned on a far-off table, and past the stairway yawning like a black funnel above them. In the doorway of the blue parlor Stramer paused. "Now, then, Mr. Jones!"

It was stupid, but Lady Jane's heart gave a jerk: she hoped the challenge would not evoke the shadowy figure she had half seen that other day.

"Lord, it's cold!" Stramer stood looking about him. "Those ashes are still on the hearth. Well, it's all very queer." He crossed over to the citron wood desk. "There's where she sat for her picture—and in this very armchair—look!"

"Oh, don't!" Lady Jane exclaimed. The words slipped out unawares.

"Don't—what?"

"Try those drawers—" she wanted to reply; for his hand was stretched toward the desk.

"I'm frozen; I think I'm starting a cold. Do come away," she grumbled, backing toward the door.

Stramer lighted her out without comment. As the lamplight slid along the walls Lady Jane fancied that the needlework curtain over the farther door stirred as it had that other day. But it may have been the wind rising outside. . . .

The salon seemed like home when they got back to it.

"There *is* no Mr. Jones!"

Stramer proclaimed it triumphantly when they met the next morning. Lady Jane had motored off early to Strawbridge in quest of a mason and a locksmith. The quest had taken longer than she had expected, for everybody in Strawbridge was busy on jobs nearer by, and unaccustomed to the idea of going to Bells, with which the town seemed to have had no communication within living memory. The younger workmen did not even know where the place was, and the best Lady Jane could do was to coax a locksmith's apprentice to come with her, on the understanding that he would be driven back to the nearest station as soon as his job was over. As for the mason, he had merely taken note of her request, and promised half-heartedly to send somebody when he could. "Rather off our beat, though."

She returned, discouraged and somewhat weary, as Stramer was coming downstairs after his morning's work.

"No Mr. Jones?" she echoed.

"Not a trace! I've been trying the old Glamis experiment—situating his room by its window. Luckily the house is smaller. . . ."

Lady Jane smiled. "Is this what you call locking yourself up with your work?"

"I can't work: that's the trouble. Not till this is settled. Bells is a fidgety place."

"Yes," she agreed.

"Well, I wasn't going to be beaten; so I went to try to find the head gardener."

"But there isn't—"

"No. Mrs. Clemm told me. The head gardener died last year. That woman positively glows with life whenever she announces a death. Have you noticed?"

Yes: Lady Jane had.

"Well—I said to myself that if there wasn't a head-gardener there must be an underling; at least one. I'd seen somebody in the distance, raking leaves, and I ran him down. Of course he'd never seen Mr. Jones."

"You mean that poor old half-blind Jacob? He couldn't see anybody."

"Perhaps not. At any rate, he told me that Mr. Jones wouldn't let the leaves be buried for leaf mold—I forget why. Mr. Jones's authority extends even to the gardens."

"Yet you say he doesn't exist!"

"Wait. Jacob is half blind, but he's been here for years, and knows more about the place than you'd think. I got him talking about the house, and I pointed to one window after another, and he told me each time whose the room was, or had been. But he couldn't situate Mr. —Jones."

"I beg your ladyship's pardon—" Mrs. Clemm was on the threshold, cheeks shining, skirt rustling, her eyes like drills. "The locksmith your ladyship brought back; I understand it was for the lock of the muniment room—"

"Well?"

"He's lost one of his tools, and can't do anything without it. So he's gone. The butcher's boy gave him a lift back."

Lady Jane caught Stramer's faint chuckle. She stood and stared at Mrs. Clemm, and Mrs. Clemm stared back, deferential but unflinching.

"Gone? Very well; I'll motor after him."

"Oh, my lady, it's too late. The butcher's boy had his motorcycle. . . . Besides, what could he do?"

"Break the lock," exclaimed Lady Jane, exasperated.

"Oh, my lady—" Mrs. Clemm's intonation marked the most respectful incredulity. She waited another moment, and then withdrew, while Lady Jane and Stramer considered each other.

"But this is absurd," Lady Jane declared when they had lunched, waited on, as usual, by the flustered Georgiana. "I'll break in that door myself, if I have to.—Be careful please, Georgiana," she added; "I was speaking of doors, not dishes." For Georgiana had let fall with a crash the dish she was removing from the table. She gathered up the pieces in her tremulous fingers, and vanished. Jane and Stramer returned to the salon.

"Queer!" the novelist commented.

"Yes." Lady Jane, facing the door, started slightly. Mrs. Clemm was there again; but this time subdued, unrustling, bathed in that odd pallor which enclosed but seemed unable to penetrate the solid crimson of her cheeks.

"I beg pardon, my lady. The key is found." Her hand, as she held it out, trembled like Georgiana's.

* VI *

"It's not here," Stramer announced, a couple of hours later.

"What isn't?" Lady Jane queried, looking up from a heap of disordered papers. Her eyes blinked at him through the fog of yellow dust raised by her manipulations.

"The clue.— I've got all the 1800 to 1840 papers here; and there's a gap."

She moved over to the table above which he was bending. "A gap?"

"A big one. Nothing between 1815 and 1835. No mention of Peregrine or of Juliana."

They looked at each other across the tossed papers, and suddenly Stramer exclaimed: "Someone has been here before us—just lately."

Lady Jane stared, incredulous, and then followed the direction of his downward pointing hand.

"Do you wear flat heelless shoes?" he questioned. "And of that size? Even my feet are too small to fit into those footprints. Luckily there wasn't time to sweep the floor!"

Lady Jane felt a slight chill, a chill of a different and more inward quality than the shock of stuffy coldness which had met them as they entered the unaired attic set apart for the storing of the Thudeney archives.

"But how absurd! Of course when Mrs. Clemm found we were coming up she came—or sent someone—to open the shutters."

"That's not Mrs. Clemm's foot, or the other woman's. She must have sent a man—an old man with a shaky uncertain step. Look how it wanders."

"Mr. Jones, then!" said Lady Jane, half impatiently.

"Mr. Jones. And he got what he wanted, and put it—where?"

"Ah, *that*—! I'm freezing, you know; let's give this up for the present." She rose, and Stramer followed her without protest; the muniment room was really untenable.

"I must catalogue all this stuff someday, I suppose," Lady Jane continued, as they went down the stairs. "But meanwhile, what do you say to a good tramp, to get the dust out of our lungs?"

He agreed, and turned back to his room to get some letters he wanted to post at Thudeney-Blazes.

Lady Jane went down alone. It was a fine afternoon, and the sun, which had made the dust clouds of the muniment room so dazzling, sent a long shaft through the west window of the blue parlor, and across the floor of the hall.

Certainly Georgiana kept the oak floors remarkably well; considering how much else she had to do, it was surp—

Lady Jane stopped as if an unseen hand had jerked her violently back. On the smooth parquet before her she had caught the trace of dusty footprints—the prints of broad-soled heelless shoes—making for the blue parlor and crossing its threshold. She stood still with the same inward shiver that she had felt upstairs; then, avoiding the footprints, she too stole very softly toward the blue parlor, pushed the door wider, and saw, in the long dazzle of autumn light, as if translucid, edged with the glitter, an old man at the desk.

"Mr. Jones."

A step came up behind her: Mrs. Clemm with the post bag. "You called, my lady?"

"I . . . yes. . . ."

When she turned back to the desk there was no one there.

She faced about on the housekeeper. "Who was that?"

"Where, my lady?"

Lady Jane, without answering, moved toward the needlework curtain, in which she had detected the same faint tremor as before. "Where does that door go to—behind the curtain?"

"Nowhere, my lady. I mean; there is no door."

Mrs. Clemm had followed; her step sounded quick and assured. She lifted up the curtain with a firm hand. Behind it was a rectangle of roughly plastered wall, where an opening had visibly been bricked up.

"When was that done?"

"The wall built up? I couldn't say. I've never known it otherwise," replied the housekeeper.

The two women stood for an instant measuring each other with level eyes; then the housekeeper's were slowly lowered, and she let the curtain fall from her hand. "There are a great many things in old houses that nobody knows about," she said.

"There shall be as few as possible in mine," said Lady Jane.

"My lady!" The housekeeper stepped quickly in front of her. "My lady, what are you doing?" she gasped.

Lady Jane had turned back to the desk at which she had just seen—or fancied she had seen—the bending figure of Mr. Jones.

"I am going to look through these drawers," she said.

The housekeeper still stood in pale immobility between her and the desk. "No, my lady—no. You won't do that."

"Because—?"

Mrs. Clemm crumpled up her black silk apron with a despairing gesture. "Because—if you *will* have it—that's where Mr. Jones keeps his private papers. I know he'd oughtn't to. . . ."

"Ah—then it was Mr. Jones I saw here?"

The housekeeper's arms sank to her sides and her mouth hung open on an unspoken word. "You *saw* him?" The question came out in a confused whisper; and before Lady Jane could answer, Mrs. Clemm's arms rose again, stretched before her face as if to fend off a blaze of intolerable light, or some forbidden sight she had long since disciplined herself not to see. Thus screening her eyes she hurried across the hall to the door of the servants' wing.

Lady Jane stood for a moment looking after her; then, with a slightly shaking hand, she opened the desk and hurriedly took out from it all the papers—a small bundle—that it contained. With them she passed back into the salon.

As she entered it her eye was caught by the portrait of the melancholy lady in the short-waisted gown whom she and Stramer had christened "Also His Wife." The lady's eyes, usually so empty of all awareness save of her own frozen beauty, seemed suddenly waking to an anguished participation in the scene.

"Fudge!" muttered Lady Jane, shaking off the spectral suggestion as she turned to meet Stramer on the threshold.

* VIII *

The missing papers were all there. Stramer and she spread them out hurriedly on a table and at once proceeded to gloat over their find. Not a particularly important one, indeed; in the long history of the Lynkes and Crofts it took up hardly more space than the little handful of documents did, in actual bulk, among the stacks of the muniment room. But the fact that these papers filled a gap in the chronicles of the house, and situated the sad-faced beauty as veritably the wife of the Peregrine Vincent Theobald Lynke who had "perished of the plague at Aleppo in 1828"—this was a discovery sufficiently exciting to whet amateur appetites, and to put out of Lady Jane's mind the strange incident which had attended the opening of the cabinet.

For a while she and Stramer sat silently and methodically going through their respective piles of correspondence; but presently Lady Jane, after glancing over one of the yellowing pages, uttered a startled exclamation.

"How strange! Mr. Jones again—always Mr. Jones!"

Stramer looked up from the papers he was sorting. "You too? I've got a lot of letters here addressed to a Mr. Jones by Peregrine Vincent, who seems to have been always disporting himself abroad, and chronically in want of money. Gambling debts, apparently . . . ah and women . . . a dirty record altogether. . . ."

"Yes? My letter is not written to a Mr. Jones; but it's about one. Listen."
Lady Jane began to read. " 'Bells, February 20th, 1826. . . .' (It's from
poor 'Also His Wife' to her husband.) 'My dear Lord, Acknowledging as I
ever do the burden of the sad impediment which denies me the happiness
of being more frequently in your company, I yet fail to conceive how
anything in my state obliges that close seclusion in which Mr. Jones
persists—and by your express orders, so he declares—in confining me.
Surely, my lord, had you found it possible to spend more time with me
since the day of our marriage, you would yourself have seen it to be
unnecessary to put this restraint upon me. It is true, alas, that my unhappy
infirmity denies me the happiness to speak with you, or to hear the accents
of the voice I should love above all others could it but reach me; but, my
dear husband, I would have you consider that my mind is in no way
affected by this obstacle, but goes out to you, as my heart does, in a
perpetual eagerness of attention, and that to sit in this great house
alone, day after day, month after month, deprived of your company,
and debarred also from any intercourse but that of the servants you
have chosen to put about me, is a fate more cruel than I deserve
and more painful than I can bear. I have entreated Mr. Jones, since
he seems all-powerful with you, to represent this to you, and to transmit
this my last request—for should I fail I am resolved to make no other—
that you should consent to my making the acquaintance of a few of
your friends and neighbors, among whom I cannot but think there
must be some kind hearts that would take pity on my unhappy situation, and afford me such companionship as would give me more courage
to bear your continual absence. . . .' "

Lady Jane folded up the letter. "Deaf and dumb—ah, poor creature!
That explains the look—"

"And this explains the marriage," Stramer continued, unfolding a stiff
parchment document. "Here are the Viscountess Thudeney's marriage
settlements. She appears to have been a Miss Portallo, daughter of Obadiah
Portallo Esqre, of Purflew Castle, Caermarthenshire, and Bombay House,
Twickenham, East India merchant, senior member of the banking house of
Portallo and Prest—and so on and so on. And the figures run up into
hundreds of thousands."

"It's rather ghastly—putting the two things together. All the millions
and—imprisonment in the blue parlor. I suppose her Viscount had to have
the money, and was ashamed to have it known how he had got it . . . ."
Lady Jane shivered. "Think of it—day after day, winter after winter, year
after year . . . speechless, soundless, alone . . . under Mr. Jones's guardian-
ship. Let me see: what year were they married?"

"In 1817."

"And only a year later that portrait was painted. And she had the frozen look already."

Stramer mused: "Yes; it's grim enough. But the strangest figure in the whole case is still—Mr. Jones."

"Mr. Jones—yes. Her keeper," Lady Jane mused. "I suppose he must have been this one's ancestor. The office seems to have been hereditary at Bells."

"Well—I don't know."

Stramer's voice was so odd that Lady Jane looked up at him with a stare of surprise. "What if it were the same one?" suggested Stramer with a queer smile.

"The same?" Lady Jane laughed. "You're not good at figures are you? If poor Lady Thudeney's Mr. Jones were alive now he'd be—"

"I didn't say ours was alive now," said Stramer.

"Oh—why, what . . . ?" she faltered.

But Stramer did not answer; his eyes had been arrested by the precipitate opening of the door behind his hostess, and the entry of Georgiana, a livid, dishevelled Georgiana, more than usually bereft of her faculties, and gasping out something inarticulate.

"Oh, my lady—it's my aunt—she won't answer me," Georgiana stammered in a voice of terror.

Lady Jane uttered an impatient exclamation. "Answer you? Why—what do you want her to answer?"

"Only whether she's alive, my lady," said Georgiana with streaming eyes.

Lady Jane continued to look at her severely. "Alive? Alive? Why on earth shouldn't she be?"

"She might as well be dead—by the way she just lies there."

"Your aunt dead? I saw her alive enough in the blue parlor half an hour ago," Lady Jane returned. She was growing rather blasé with regard to Georgiana's panics; but suddenly she felt this to be of a different nature from any of the others. "Where is it your aunt's lying?"

"In her own bedroom, on her bed," the other wailed, "and won't say why."

Lady Jane got to her feet, pushing aside the heaped-up papers, and hastening to the door with Stramer in her wake.

As they went up the stairs she realized that she had seen the housekeeper's bedroom only once, on the day of her first obligatory round of inspection, when she had taken possession of Bells. She did not even remember very clearly where it was, but followed Georgiana down the passage and through a door which communicated, rather surprisingly, with a narrow walled-in staircase that was unfamiliar to her. At its top she and

Stramer found themselves on a small landing upon which two doors opened. Through the confusion of her mind Lady Jane noticed that these rooms, with their special staircase leading down to what had always been called his lordship's suite, must obviously have been occupied by his lordship's confidential servants. In one of them, presumably, had been lodged the original Mr. Jones, the Mr. Jones of the yellow letters, the letters purloined by Lady Jane. As she crossed the threshold, Lady Jane remembered the housekeeper's attempt to prevent her touching the contents of the desk.

Mrs. Clemm's room, like herself, was neat, glossy and extremely cold. Only Mrs. Clemm herself was no longer like Mrs. Clemm. The red-apple glaze had barely faded from her cheeks, and not a lock was disarranged in the unnatural luster of her false front; even her cap ribbons hung symmetrically along either cheek. But death had happened to her, and had made her into someone else. At first glance it was impossible to say if the unspeakable horror in her wide open eyes were only the reflection of that change, or of the agent by whom it had come. Lady Jane, shuddering, paused a moment while Stramer went up to the bed.

"Her hand is warm still—but no pulse." He glanced about the room. "A glass anywhere?" The cowering Georgiana took a hand glass from the neat chest of drawers, and Stramer held it over the housekeeper's drawn-back lip. . . .

"She's dead," he pronounced.

"Oh, poor thing! But how—?" Lady Jane drew near, and was kneeling down, taking the inanimate hand in hers, when Stramer touched her on the arm, and then silently raised a finger of warning. Georgiana was crouching in the farther corner of the room, her face buried in her lifted arms.

"Look here," Stramer whispered. He pointed to Mrs. Clemm's throat, and Lady Jane, bending over, distinctly saw a circle of red marks on it—the marks of recent bruises. She looked again into the awful eyes.

"She's been strangled," Stramer whispered.

Lady Jane, with a shiver of fear, drew down the housekeeper's lids. Georgiana, her face hidden, was still sobbing convulsively in the corner. There seemed, in the air of the cold orderly room, something that forbade wonderment and silenced conjecture. Lady Jane and Stramer stood and looked at each other without speaking. At length Stramer crossed over to Georgiana, and touched her on the shoulder. She appeared unaware of the touch, and he grasped her shoulder and shook it. "Where is Mr. Jones?" he asked.

The girl looked up, her face blurred and distorted with weeping, her eyes dilated as if with the vision of some latent terror. "Oh, sir, she's not really dead, is she?"

Stramer repeated his question in a loud authoritative tone; and slowly she echoed it in a scarce-heard whisper. "Mr. Jones—?"

"Get up, my girl, and send him here to us at once, or tell us where to find him."

Georgiana, moved by the old habit of obedience, struggled to her feet and stood unsteadily, her heaving shoulders braced against the wall. Stramer asked her sharply if she had not heard what he had said.

"Oh, poor thing, she's so upset—" Lady Jane intervened compassionately. "Tell me, Georgiana: where shall we find Mr. Jones?"

The girl turned to her with eyes as fixed as the dead woman's. "You won't find him anywhere," she slowly said.

"Why not?"

"Because he's not here."

"Not here? Where is he, then?" Stramer broke in.

Georgiana did not seem to notice the interruption. She continued to stare at Lady Jane with Mrs. Clemm's awful eyes. "He's in his grave in the churchyard—these years and years he is. Long before ever I was born . . . my aunt hadn't ever seen him herself, not since she was a tiny child. . . . That's the terror of it . . . that's why she always had to do what he told her to . . . because you couldn't ever answer him back. . . ." Her horrified gaze turned from Lady Jane to the stony face and fast-glazing pupils of the dead woman. "You hadn't ought to have meddled with his papers, my lady. . . . That's what he's punished her for. . . . When it came to those papers he wouldn't ever listen to human reason . . . he wouldn't. . . ." Then, flinging her arms above her head, Georgiana straightened herself to her full height before falling in a swoon at Stramer's feet.

POMEGRANATE
SEED

CHARLOTTE ASHBY paused on her doorstep. Dark had descended on the brilliancy of the March afternoon, and the grinding rasping street life of the city was at its highest. She turned her back on it, standing for a moment in the old-fashioned, marble-flagged vestibule before she inserted her key in the lock. The sash curtains drawn across the panes of the inner door softened the light within to a warm blur through which no details showed. It was the hour when, in the first months of her marriage to Kenneth Ashby, she had most liked to return to that quiet house in a street long since deserted by business and fashion. The contrast between the soulless roar of New York, its devouring blaze of lights, the oppression of its congested traffic, congested houses, lives, minds and this veiled sanctuary she called home, always stirred her profoundly. In the very heart of the hurricane she had found her tiny islet—or thought she had. And now, in the last months, everything was changed, and she always wavered on the doorstep and had to force herself to enter.

While she stood there she called up the scene within: the hall hung with old prints, the ladder-like stairs, and on the left her husband's long shabby library, full of books and pipes and worn armchairs inviting to meditation. How she had loved that room! Then, upstairs, her own drawing room, in which, since the death of Kenneth's first wife, neither furniture nor hangings had been changed, because there had never been money enough, but which Charlotte had made her own by moving furniture about and adding more books, another lamp, a table for the new reviews. Even on the occasion of her only visit to the first Mrs. Ashby—a distant, self-centered woman, whom she had known very slightly—she had looked about her with an innocent envy, feeling it to be exactly the drawing room she would have liked for herself; and now for more than a year it had been hers to deal with as she chose—the room to which she hastened back at dusk on winter days, where she sat reading by the fire, or answering notes at the pleasant roomy desk, or going over her step-children's copybooks, till she heard her husband's step.

Sometimes friends dropped in; sometimes—oftener—she was alone; and she liked that best, since it was another way of being with Kenneth, thinking over what he had said when they parted in the morning, imagining what he would say when he sprang up the stairs, found her by herself and caught her to him.

Now, instead of this, she thought of one thing only—the letter she might or might not find on the hall table. Until she had made sure whether or not it was there, her mind had no room for anything else. The letter was always the same—a square grayish envelope with "Kenneth Ashby, Esquire," written on it in bold but faint characters. From the first it had struck Charlotte as peculiar that anyone who wrote such a firm hand should trace the letters so lightly; the address was always written as though there were not enough ink in the pen, or the writer's wrist were too weak to bear upon it. Another curious thing was that, in spite of its masculine curves, the writing was so visibly feminine. Some hands are sexless, some masculine, at first glance; the writing on the gray envelope, for all its strength and assurance, was without doubt a woman's. The envelope never bore anything but the recipient's name; no stamp, no address. The letter was presumably delivered by hand—but by whose? No doubt it was slipped into the letter box, whence the parlormaid, when she closed the shutters and lit the lights, probably extracted it. At any rate, it was always in the evening, after dark, that Charlotte saw it lying there. She thought of the letter in the singular, as "it," because, though there had been several since her marriage—seven, to be exact—they were so alike in appearance that they had become merged in one another in her mind, become one letter, become "it."

The first had come the day after their return from their honeymoon—a journey prolonged to the West Indies, from which they had returned to New York after an absence of more than two months. Reentering the house with her husband, late on that first evening—they had dined at his mother's—she had seen, alone on the hall table, the gray envelope. Her eye fell on it before Kenneth's, and her first thought was: "Why, I've seen that writing before"; but where she could not recall. The memory was just definite enough for her to identify the script whenever it looked up at her faintly from the same pale envelope; but on that first day she would have thought no more of the letter if, when her husband's glance lit on it, she had not chanced to be looking at him. It all happened in a flash—his seeing the letter, putting out his hand for it, raising it to his shortsighted eyes to decipher the faint writing, and then abruptly withdrawing the arm he had slipped through Charlotte's, and moving away to the hanging light, his back turned to her. She had waited—waited for a sound, an exclamation; waited for him to open the letter; but he had slipped it into his pocket without a word and followed her into the library. And there they had sat down by the fire and lit their cigarettes, and he had remained silent, his head thrown back broodingly against the armchair, his eyes fixed on the hearth, and presently had passed his hand over his forehead and said: "Wasn't it unusually hot at my mother's tonight? I've got a splitting head. Mind if I take myself off to bed?"

That was the first time. Since then Charlotte had never been present when he had received the letter. It usually came before he got home from his office, and she had to go upstairs and leave it lying there. But even if she had not seen it, she would have known it had come by the change in his face when he joined her—which, on those evenings, he seldom did before they met for dinner. Evidently, whatever the letter contained, he wanted to be by himself to deal with it; and when he reappeared he looked years older, looked emptied of life and courage, and hardly conscious of her presence. Sometimes he was silent for the rest of the evening; and if he spoke, it was usually to hint some criticism of her household arrangements, suggest some change in the domestic administration, to ask, a little nervously, if she didn't think Joyce's nursery governess was rather young and flighty, or if she herself always saw to it that Peter—whose throat was delicate—was properly wrapped up when he went to school. At such times Charlotte would remember the friendly warnings she had received when she became engaged to Kenneth Ashby: "Marrying a heartbroken widower! Isn't that rather risky? You know Elsie Ashby absolutely dominated him"; and how she had jokingly replied: "He may be glad of a little liberty for a change." And in this respect she had been right. She had needed no one to tell her, during the first months, that her husband was perfectly happy with her. When they came back from their protracted honeymoon the same friends said: "What have you done to Kenneth? He looks twenty years younger"; and this time she answered with careless joy: "I suppose I've got him out of his groove."

But what she noticed after the gray letters began to come was not so much his nervous tentative faultfinding—which always seemed to be uttered against his will—as the look in his eyes when he joined her after receiving one of the letters. The look was not unloving, not even indifferent; it was the look of a man who had been so far away from ordinary events that when he returns to familiar things they seem strange. She minded that more than the faultfinding.

Though she had been sure from the first that the handwriting on the gray envelope was a woman's, it was long before she associated the mysterious letters with any sentimental secret. She was too sure of her husband's love, too confident of filling his life, for such an idea to occur to her. It seemed far more likely that the letters—which certainly did not appear to cause him any sentimental pleasure—were addressed to the busy lawyer than to the private person. Probably they were from some tiresome client—women, he had often hold her, were nearly always tiresome as clients—who did not want her letters opened by his secretary and therefore had them carried to his house. Yes; but in that case the unknown female must be unusually troublesome, judging from the effect her letters produced. Then again, though his professional discretion was exemplary, it was odd that he had never uttered an impatient comment, never remarked to Charlotte, in a moment of expansion, that there was a nuisance of a woman who kept badgering him about a case that had gone against her. He had made more than one semiconfidence of the kind—of course without giving names or details; but concerning this mysterious correspondent his lips were sealed.

There was another possibility: what is euphemistically called an "old entanglement." Charlotte Ashby was a sophisticated woman. She had few illusions about the intricacies of the human heart; she knew that there were often old entanglements. But when she had married Kenneth Ashby, her friends, instead of hinting at such a possibility, had said: "You've got your work cut out for you. Marrying a Don Juan is a sinecure to it. Kenneth's never looked at another woman since he first saw Elsie Corder. During all the years of their marriage he was more like an unhappy lover than a comfortably contented husband. He'll never let you move an armchair or change the place of a lamp; and whatever you venture to do, he'll mentally compare with what Elsie would have done in your place."

Except for an occasional nervous mistrust as to her ability to manage the children—a mistrust gradually dispelled by her good humor and the children's obvious fondness for her—none of these forebodings had come true. The desolate widower, of whom his nearest friends said that only his absorbing professional interests had kept him from suicide after his first wife's death, had fallen in love, two years later, with Charlotte Gorse, and after an impetuous wooing had married her and carried her off on a tropical honeymoon. And ever since he had been as tender and lover-like as during those first radiant weeks. Before asking her to marry him he had spoken to her frankly of his great love for his first wife and his despair after her sudden death; but even then he had assumed no stricken attitude, or implied that life offered no possibility of renewal. He had been perfectly simple and natural, and had confessed to Charlotte that from the beginning he had hoped the future held new gifts for him. And when, after their marriage, they returned to the house where his twelve years with his first wife had been spent, he had told Charlotte at once that he was sorry he couldn't afford to do the place over for her, but that he knew every woman had her own views about furniture and all sorts of household arrangements a man would never notice, and had begged her to make any changes she saw fit without bothering to consult him. As a result, she made as few as possible; but his way of beginning their new life in the old setting was so frank and unembarrassed that it put her immediately at her ease, and she was almost sorry to find that the portrait of Elsie Ashby, which used to hang over the desk in his library, had been transferred in their absence to the children's nursery. Knowing herself to be the indirect cause of this banishment, she spoke of it to her husband; but he answered: "Oh, I thought they ought to grow up with her looking down on them." The answer moved Charlotte, and satisfied her; and as time went by she had to confess that she felt more at home in her house, more at ease and in confidence with her husband, since that long coldly beautiful face on the library wall no longer followed her with guarded eyes. It was as if Kenneth's love had penetrated to the secret she hardly acknowledged to her own heart—her passionate need to feel herself the sovereign even of his past.

With all this stored-up happiness to sustain her, it was curious that she had lately found herself yielding to a nervous apprehension. But there the apprehension was; and on this particular afternoon—perhaps because she was more tired than usual, or because of the trouble of finding a new cook or, for some other ridiculously trivial reason, moral or physical—she found herself unable to react against the feeling. Latchkey in hand, she looked back down the silent street to the whirl and illumination of the great thoroughfare beyond, and up at the sky already aflare with the city's nocturnal life. "Outside there," she thought, "skyscrapers, advertizements, telephones, wireless, airplanes, movies, motors, and all the rest of the twentieth century; and on the other side of the door something I can't explain, can't relate to them. Something as old as the world, as mysterious as life. . . . Nonsense! What am I worrying about? There hasn't been a letter for three months now—not since the day we came back from the country after Christmas. . . . Queer that they always seem to come after our holidays! . . . Why should I imagine there's going to be one tonight!"

No reason why, but that was the worst of it—one of the worst!—that there were days when she would stand there cold and shivering with the premonition of something inexplicable, intolerable, to be faced on the other side of the curtained panes; and when she opened the door and went in, there would be nothing; and on other days when she felt the same premonitory chill, it was justified by the sight of the gray envelope. So that ever since the last had come she had taken to feeling cold and premonitory every evening, because she never opened the door without thinking the letter might be there.

Well, she'd had enough of it: that was certain. She couldn't go on like that. If her husband turned white and had a headache on the days when the letter came, he seemed to recover afterward; but she couldn't. With her the strain had become chronic, and the reason was not far to seek. Her husband knew from whom the letter came and what was in it; he was prepared beforehand for whatever he had to deal with, and master of the situation, however bad; whereas she was shut out in the dark with her conjectures.

"I can't stand it! I can't stand it another day!" she exclaimed aloud, as she put her key in the lock. She turned the key and went in; and there, on the table, lay the letter.

* II *

She was almost glad of the sight. It seemed to justify everything, to put a seal of definiteness on the whole blurred business. A letter for her husband; a letter from a woman—no doubt another vulgar case of "old entanglement." What a fool she had been ever to doubt it, to rack her brains for less obvious explanations! She took up the envelope with a steady contemptuous hand, looked closely at the faint letters, held it against the light and just discerned the outline of the folded sheet within. She knew that now she would have no peace till she found out what was written on that sheet.

Her husband had not come in; he seldom got back from his office before half-past six or seven, and it was not yet six. She would have time to take the letter up to the drawing room, hold it over the tea kettle which at that hour always simmered by the fire in expectation of her return, solve the mystery and replace the letter where she had found it. No one would be the wiser, and her gnawing uncertainty would be over. The alternative, of course, was to question her husband; but to do that seemed even more diificult. She weighed the letter between thumb and finger, looked at it again under the light, started up the stairs with the envelope—and came down again and laid it on the table.

"No, I evidently can't," she said, disappointed.

What should she do, then? She couldn't go up alone to that warm welcoming room, pour out her tea, look over her correspondence, glance at a book or review—not with that letter lying below and the knowledge that in a little while her husband would come in, open it and turn into the library alone, as he always did on the days when the gray envelope came.

Suddenly she decided. She would wait in the library and see for herself; see what happened between him and the letter when they thought themselves unobserved. She wondered the idea had never occurred to her before. By leaving the door ajar and sitting in the corner behind it, she could watch him unseen. . . . Well, then, she would watch him! She drew a chair into the corner, sat down, her eyes on the crack, and waited.

As far as she could remember, it was the first time she had ever tried to surprise another person's secret, but she was conscious of no compunction. She simply felt as if she were fighting her way through a stifling fog that she must at all costs get out of.

At length she heard Kenneth's latchkey and jumped up. The impulse to rush out and meet him had nearly made her forget why she was there; but she remembered in time and sat down again. From her post she covered the whole range of his movements—saw him enter the hall, draw the key from the door and take off his hat and overcoat. Then he turned to throw his gloves on the hall table, and at that moment he saw the envelope. The light was full on his face, and what Charlotte first noted there was a look of surprise. Evidently he had not expected the letter—had not thought of the possibility of its being there that day. But though he had not expected it, now that he saw it he knew well enough what it contained. He did not open it immediately, but stood motionless, the color slowly ebbing from his face. Apparently he could not make up his mind to touch it; but at length he put out his hand, opened the envelope, and moved with it to the light. In doing so he turned his back on Charlotte, and she saw only his bent head and slightly stooping shoulders. Apparently all the writing was on one page, for he did not turn the sheet but continued to stare at it for so long that he must have reread it a dozen times—or so it seemed to the woman breathlessly watching him. At length she saw him move; he raised the letter still closer to his eyes, as though he had not fully deciphered it. Then he lowered his head, and she saw his lips touch the sheet.

"Kenneth!" she exclaimed, and went on out into the hall.

The letter clutched in his hand, her husband turned and looked at her. "Where were you?" he said, in a low bewildered voice, like a man waked out of his sleep.

"In the library, waiting for you." She tried to steady her voice: "What's the matter! What's in that letter? You look ghastly."

Her agitation seemed to calm him, and he instantly put the envelope into his pocket with a slight laugh. "Ghastly? I'm sorry. I've had a hard day in the office—one or two complicated cases. I look dog-tired, I suppose."

"You didn't look tired when you came in. It was only when you opened that letter—"

He had followed her into the library, and they stood gazing at each other. Charlotte noticed how quickly he had regained his self-control; his profession had trained him to rapid mastery of face and voice. She saw at once that she would be at a disadvantage in any attempt to surprise his secret, but at the same moment she lost all desire to maneuver, to trick him into betraying anything he wanted to conceal. Her wish was still to penetrate the mystery, but only that she might help him to bear the burden it implied. "Even if it *is* another woman," she thought.

"Kenneth," she said, her heart beating excitedly, "I waited here on purpose to see you come in. I wanted to watch you while you opened that letter."

His face, which had paled, turned to dark red; then it paled again. "That letter? Why especially that letter?"

"Because I've noticed that whenever one of those letters comes it seems to have such a strange effect on you."

A line of anger she had never seen before came out between his eyes, and she said to herself: "The upper part of his face is too narrow; this is the first time I ever noticed it."

She heard him continue, in the cool and faintly ironic tone of the prosecuting lawyer making a point: "Ah, so you're in the habit of watching people open their letters when they don't know you're there?"

"Not in the habit. I never did such a thing before. But I had to find out what she writes to you, at regular intervals, in those gray envelopes."

He weighed this for a moment; then: "The intervals have not been regular," he said.

"Oh, I dare say you've kept a better account of the dates than I have," she retorted, her magnanimity vanishing at his tone. "All I know is that every time that woman writes to you—"

"Why do you assume it's a woman?"

"It's a woman's writing. Do you deny it?"

He smiled. "No, I don't deny it. I asked only because the writing is generally supposed to look more like a man's."

Charlotte passed this over impatiently. "And this woman—what does she write to you about?"

Again he seemed to consider a moment. "About business."

"Legal business?"

"In a way, yes. Business in general."

"You look after her affairs for her?"

"Yes."

"You've looked after them for a long time?"

"Yes. A very long time."

"Kenneth, dearest, won't you tell me who she is?"

"No. I can't." He paused, and brought out, as if with a certain hesitation: "Professional secrecy."

The blood rushed from Charlotte's heart to her temples. "Don't say that—don't!"

"Why not?"

"Because I saw you kiss the letter."

The effect of the words was so disconcerting that she instantly repented having spoken them. Her husband, who had submitted to her cross-questioning with a sort of contemptuous composure, as though he were humoring an unreasonable child, turned on her a face of terror and distress. For a minute he seemed unable to speak; then, collecting himself, with an effort, he stammered out: "The writing is very faint; you must have seen me holding the letter close to my eyes to try to decipher it."

"No; I saw you kissing it." He was silent. "Didn't I see you kissing it?"

He sank back into indifference. "Perhaps."

"Kenneth! You stand there and say that—to me?"

"What possible difference can it make to you? The letter is on business, as I told you. Do you suppose I'd lie about it? The writer is a very old friend whom I haven't seen for a long time."

"Men don't kiss business letters, even from women who are very old friends, unless they have been their lovers, and still regret them."

He shrugged his shoulders slightly and turned away, as if he considered the discussion at an end and were faintly disgusted at the turn it had taken.

"Kenneth!" Charlotte moved toward him and caught hold of his arm.

He paused with a look of weariness and laid his hand over hers. "Won't you believe me?" he asked gently.

"How can I? I've watched these letters come to you—for months now they've been coming. Ever since we came back from the West Indies—one of them greeted me the very day we arrived. And after each one of them I see their mysterious effect on you, I see you disturbed, unhappy, as if someone were trying to estrange you from me."

"No, dear; not that. Never!"

She drew back and looked at him with passionate entreaty. "Well, then, prove it to me, darling. It's so easy!"

He forced a smile. "It's not easy to prove anything to a woman who's once taken an idea into her head."

"You've only got to show me the letter."

His hand slipped from hers and he drew back and shook his head.

"You won't?"

"I can't."

"Then the woman who wrote it is your mistress."

"No, dear. No."

"Not now, perhaps. I suppose she's trying to get you back, and you're struggling, out of pity for me. My poor Kenneth!"

"I swear to you she never was my mistress."

Charlotte felt the tears rushing to her eyes. "Ah, that's worse, then —that's hopeless! The prudent ones are the kind that keep their hold on a man. We all know that." She lifted her hands and hid her face in them.

Her husband remained silent; he offered neither consolation nor denial, and at length, wiping away her tears, she raised her eyes almost timidly to his.

"Kenneth, think! We've been married such a short time. Imagine what you're making me suffer. You say you can't show me this letter. You refuse even to explain it."

"I've told you the letter is on business. I will swear to that too."

"A man will swear to anything to screen a woman. If you want me to believe you, at least tell me her name. If you'll do that, I promise you I won't ask to see the letter."

There was a long interval of suspense, during which she felt her heart beating against her ribs in quick admonitory knocks, as if warning her of the danger she was incurring.

"I can't," he said at length.

"Not even her name?"

"No."

"You can't tell me anything more?"

"No."

Again a pause; this time they seemed both to have reached the end of their arguments and to be helplessly facing each other across a baffling waste of incomprehension.

Charlotte stood breathing rapidly, her hands against her breast. She felt as if she had run a hard race and missed the goal. She had meant to move her husband and had succeeded only in irritating him; and this error of reckoning seemed to change him into a stranger, a mysterious incomprehensible being whom no argument or entreaty of hers could reach. The curious thing was that she was aware in him of no hostility or even impatience, but only of a remoteness, an inaccessibility, far more difficult to overcome. She felt herself excluded, ignored, blotted out of his life. But after a moment or two, looking at him more calmly, she saw that he was suffering as much as she was. His distant guarded face was drawn with pain; the coming of the gray envelope, though it always cast a shadow, had never marked him as deeply as this discussion with his wife.

Charlotte took heart; perhaps, after all, she had not spent her last shaft. She drew nearer and once more laid her hand on his arm. "Poor Kenneth! If you knew how sorry I am for you—"

She thought he winced slightly at this expression of sympathy, but he took her hand and pressed it.

"I can think of nothing worse than to be incapable of loving long," she continued, "to feel the beauty of a great love and to be too unstable to bear its burden."

He turned on her a look of wistful reproach. "Oh, don't say that of me. Unstable!"

She felt herself at last on the right tack, and her voice trembled with excitement as she went on: "Then what about me and this other woman? Haven't you already forgotten Elsie twice within a year?"

She seldom pronounced his first wife's name; it did not come naturally to her tongue. She flung it out now as if she were flinging some dangerous explosive into the open space between them, and drew back a step, waiting to hear the mine go off.

Her husband did not move; his expression grew sadder, but showed no resentment. "I have never forgotten Elsie," he said.

Charlotte could not repress a faint laugh. "Then, you poor dear, between the three of us—"

"There are not—" he began; and then broke off and put his hand to his forehead.

"Not what?"

"I'm sorry; I don't believe I know what I'm saying. I've got a blinding headache." He looked wan and furrowed enough for the statement to be true, but she was exasperated by his evasion.

"Ah, yes; the gray envelope headache!"

She saw the surprise in his eyes. "I'd forgotten how closely I've been watched," he said coldly. "If you'll excuse me, I think I'll go up and try an hour in the dark, to see if I can get rid of this neuralgia."

She wavered; then she said, with desperate resolution: "I'm sorry your head aches. But before you go I want to say that sooner or later this question must be settled between us. Someone is trying to separate us, and I don't care what it costs me to find out who it is." She looked him steadily in the eyes. "If it costs me your love, I don't care! If I can't have your confidence I don't want anything from you."

He still looked at her wistfully. "Give me time."

"Time for what? It's only a word to say."

"Time to show you that you haven't lost my love or my confidence."

"Well, I'm waiting."

He turned toward the door, and then glanced back hesitatingly. "Oh, do wait, my love," he said, and went out of the room.

She heard his tired step on the stairs and the closing of his bedroom door above. Then she dropped into a chair and buried her face in her folded arms. Her first movement was one of compunction; she seemed to herself to have been hard, unhuman, unimaginative. "Think of telling him that I didn't care if my insistence cost me his love! The lying rubbish!" She started up to follow him and unsay the meaningless words. But she was checked by a reflection. He had had his way, after all; he had eluded all attacks on his secret, and now he was shut up alone in his room, reading that other woman's letter.

* III *

She was still reflecting on this when the surprised parlormaid came in and found her. No, Charlotte said, she wasn't going to dress for dinner; Mr. Ashby didn't want to dine. He was very tired and had gone up to his room to rest; later she would have something brought on a tray to the drawing room. She mounted the stairs to her bedroom. Her dinner dress was lying on the bed, and at the sight the quiet routine of her daily life took hold of her and she began to feel as if the strange talk she had just had with her husband must have taken place in another world, between two beings who were not Charlotte Gorse and Kenneth Ashby, but phantoms projected by her fevered imagination. She recalled the year since her marriage—her husband's constant devotion; his persistent, almost too insistent tenderness; the feeling he had given her at times of being too eagerly dependent on her, too searchingly close to her, as if there were not air enough between her soul and his. It seemed preposterous, as she recalled all this, that a few moments ago she should have been accusing him of an intrigue with another woman! But, then, what—

Again she was moved by the impulse to go up to him, beg his pardon and try to laugh away the misunderstanding. But she was restrained by the fear of forcing herself upon his privacy. He was troubled and unhappy, oppressed by some grief or fear; and he had shown her that he wanted to fight out his battle alone. It would be wiser, as well as more generous, to respect his wish. Only, how strange, how unbearable, to be there, in the next room to his, and feel herself at the other end of the world! In her nervous agitation she almost regretted not having had the courage to open the letter and put it back on the hall table before he came in. At least she would have known what his secret was, and the bogy might have been laid. For she was beginning now to think of the mystery as something conscious, malevolent: a secret persecution before which he quailed, yet from which he could not free himself. Once or twice in his evasive eyes she thought she had detected a desire for help, an impulse of confession, instantly restrained and suppressed. It was as if he felt she could have helped him if she had known, and yet had been unable to tell her!

There flashed through her mind the idea of going to his mother. She was very fond of old Mrs. Ashby, a firm-fleshed clear-eyed old lady, with an astringent bluntness of speech which responded to the forthright and simple in Charlotte's own nature. There had been a tacit bond between them ever since the day when Mrs. Ashby Senior, coming to lunch for the first time with her new daughter-in-law, had been received by Charlotte downstairs in the library, and glancing up at the empty wall above her son's desk, had remarked laconically: "Elsie gone, eh?" adding, at Charlotte's murmured explanation: "Nonsense. Don't have her back. Two's company." Charlotte, at this reading of her thoughts, could hardly refrain from exchanging a smile of complicity with her mother-in-law; and it seemed to her now that Mrs. Ashby's almost uncanny directess might pierce to the core of this new mystery. But here again she hesitated, for the idea almost suggested a betrayal. What right had she to call in anyone, even so close a relation, to surprise a secret which her husband was trying to keep from her? "Perhaps, by and by, he'll talk to his mother of his own accord," she thought, and then ended: "But what does it matter? He and I must settle it between us."

She was still brooding over the problem when there was a knock on the door and her husband came in. He was dressed for dinner and seemed surprised to see her sitting there, with her evening dress lying unheeded on the bed.

"Aren't you coming down?"

"I thought you were not well and had gone to bed," she faltered.

He forced a smile. "I'm not particularly well, but we'd better go down." His face, though still drawn, looked calmer than when he had fled upstairs an hour earlier.

"There it is; he knows what's in the letter and has fought his battle out again, whatever it is," she reflected, "while I'm still in darkness." She rang and gave a hurried order that dinner should be served as soon as possible—just a short meal, whatever could be got ready quickly, as both she and Mr. Ashby were rather tired and not very hungry.

Dinner was announced, and they sat down to it. At first neither seemed able to find a word to say; then Ashby began to make conversation with an assumption of ease that was more oppressive than his silence. "How tired he is! How terribly overtired!" Charlotte said to herself, pursuing her own thoughts while he rambled on about municipal politics, aviation, an exhibition of modern French painting, the health of an old aunt and the installing of the automatic telephone. "Good heavens, how tired he is!"

When they dined alone they usually went into the library after dinner, and Charlotte curled herself up on the divan with her knitting while he settled down in his armchair under the lamp and lit a pipe. But this evening, by tacit agreement, they avoided the room in which their strange talk had taken place, and went up to Charlotte's drawing room.

They sat down near the fire, and Charlotte said: "Your pipe?" after he had put down his hardly tasted coffee.

He shook his head. "No, not tonight."

"You must go to bed early; you look terribly tired. I'm sure they overwork you at the office."

"I suppose we all overwork at times."

She rose and stood before him with sudden resolution. "Well, I'm not going to have you use up your strength slaving in that way. It's absurd. I can see you're ill." She bent over him and laid her hand on his forehead. "My poor old Kenneth. Prepare to be taken away soon on a long holiday."

He looked up at her, startled. "A holiday?"

"Certainly. Didn't you know I was going to carry you off at Easter? We're going to start in a fortnight on a month's voyage to somewhere or other. On any one of the big cruising steamers." She paused and bent closer, touching his forehead with her lips. "I'm tired, too, Kenneth."

He seemed to pay no heed to her last words, but sat, his hands on his knees, his head drawn back a little from her caress, and looked up at her with a stare of apprehension. "Again? My dear, we can't; I can't possibly go away."

"I don't know why you say 'again,' Kenneth; we haven't taken a real holiday this year."

"At Christmas we spend a week with the children in the country."

"Yes, but this time I mean away from the children, from servants, from the house. From everything that's familiar and fatiguing. Your mother will love to have Joyce and Peter with her."

He frowned and slowly shook his head. "No, dear; I can't leave them with my mother."

"Why, Kenneth, how absurd! She adores them. You didn't hesitate to leave them with her for over two months when we went to the West Indies."

He drew a deep breath and stood up uneasily. "That was different."

"Different? Why?"

"I mean, at that time I didn't realize—" He broke off as if to choose his words and then went on: "My mother adores the children, as you say. But she isn't always very judicious. Grandmothers always spoil children. And sometimes she talks before them without thinking." He turned to his wife with an almost pitiful gesture of entreaty. "Don't ask me to, dear."

Charlotte mused. It was true that the elder Mrs. Ashby had a fearless tongue, but she was the last woman in the world to say or hint anything before her grandchildren at which the most scrupulous parent could take offense. Charlotte looked at her husband in perplexity.

"I don't understand."

He continued to turn on her the same troubled and entreating gaze. "Don't try to," he muttered.

"Not try to?"

"Not now—not yet." He put up his hands and pressed them against his temples. "Can't you see that there's no use in insisting? I can't go away, no matter how much I might want to."

Charlotte still scrutinized him gravely. "The question is, *do* you want to?"

He returned her gaze for a moment; then his lips began to tremble, and he said, hardly above his breath: "I want—anything you want."

"And yet—"

"Don't ask me. I can't leave—I can't!"

"You mean that you can't go away out of reach of those letters!"

Her husband had been standing before her in an uneasy half-hesitating attitude; now he turned abruptly away and walked once or twice up and down the length of the room, his head bent, his eyes fixed on the carpet.

Charlotte felt her resentfulness rising with her fears. "It's that," she persisted. "Why not admit it? You can't live without them."

He continued his troubled pacing of the room; then he stopped short, dropped into a chair and covered his face with his hands. From the shaking of his shoulders, Charlotte saw that he was weeping. She had never seen a man cry, except her father after her mother's death, when she was a little girl; and she remembered still how the sight had frightened her. She was frightened now; she felt that her husband was being dragged away from her into some mysterious bondage, and that she must use up her last atom of strength in the struggle for his freedom, and for hers.

"Kenneth—Kenneth!" she pleaded, kneeling down beside him. "Won't you listen to me? Won't you try to see what I'm suffering? I'm not unreasonable, darling, really not. I don't suppose I should ever have noticed the letters if it hadn't been for their effect on you. It's not my way to pry into other people's affairs; and even if the effect had been different —yes, yes, listen to me—if I'd seen that the letters made you happy, that you were watching eagerly for them, counting the days between their coming, that you wanted them, that they gave you something I haven't known how to give—why, Kenneth, I don't say I shouldn't have suffered from that, too; but it would have been in a different way, and I should have had the courage to hide what I felt, and the hope that someday you'd come to feel about me as you did about the writer of the letters. But what I can't bear is to see how you dread them, how they make you suffer, and yet how you can't live without them and won't go away lest you should miss one during your absence. Or perhaps," she added, her voice breaking into a cry of accusation—"perhaps it's because she's actually forbidden you to leave. Kenneth, you must answer me! Is that the reason? Is it because she's forbidden you that you won't go away with me?"

She continued to kneel at his side, and raising her hands, she drew his gently down. She was ashamed of her persistence, ashamed of uncovering that baffled disordered face, yet resolved that no such scruples should arrest her. His eyes were lowered, the muscles of his face quivered; she was making him suffer even more than she suffered herself. Yet this no longer restrained her.

"Kenneth, is it that? She won't let us go away together?"

Still he did not speak or turn his eyes to her; and a sense of defeat swept over her. After all, she thought, the struggle was a losing one. "You needn't answer. I see I'm right," she said.

Suddenly, as she rose, he turned and drew her down again. His hands caught hers and pressed them so tightly that she felt her rings cutting into her flesh. There was something frightened, convulsive in his hold; it was the clutch of a man who felt himself slipping over a precipice. He was staring up at her now as if salvation lay in the face she bent above him. "Of course we'll go away together. We'll go wherever you want," he said in a low confused voice; and putting his arm about her, he drew her close and pressed his lips on hers.

* IV *

Charlotte had said to herself: "I shall sleep tonight," but instead she sat before her fire into the small hours, listening for any sound that came from her husband's room. But he, at any rate, seemed to be resting after the tumult of the evening. Once or twice she stole to the door and in the faint light that came in from the street through his open window she saw him stretched out in heavy sleep—the sleep of weakness and exhaustion. "He's ill," she thought—"he's undoubtedly ill. And it's not overwork; it's this mysterious persecution."

She drew a breath of relief. She had fought through the weary fight and the victory was hers—at least for the moment. If only they could have started at once—started for anywhere! She knew it would be useless to ask him to leave before the holidays; and meanwhile the secret influence—as to which she was still so completely in the dark—would continue to work against her, and she would have to renew the struggle day after day till they started on their journey. But after that everything would be different. If once she could get her husband away under other skies, and all to herself, she never doubted her power to release him from the evil spell he was under. Lulled to quiet by the thought, she too slept at last.

When she woke, it was long past her usual hour, and she sat up in bed surprised and vexed at having overslept herself. She always liked to be down to share her husband's breakfast by the library fire; but a glance at the clock made it clear that he must have started long since for his office. To make sure, she jumped out of bed and went into his room, but it was empty. No doubt he had looked in on her before leaving, seen that she still slept, and gone downstairs without disturbing her; and their relations were sufficiently lover-like for her to regret having missed their morning hour.

She rang and asked if Mr. Ashby had already gone. Yes, nearly an hour ago, the maid said. He had given orders that Mrs. Ashby should not be waked and that the children should not come to her till she sent for them. . . . Yes, he had gone up to the nursery himself to give the order. All this sounded usual enough, and Charlotte hardly knew why she asked: "And did Mr. Ashby leave no other message?"

Yes, the maid said, he did; she was so sorry she'd forgotten. He'd told her, just as he was leaving, to say to Mrs. Ashby that he was going to see about their passages, and would she please be ready to sail tomorrow?

Charlotte echoed the woman's "Tomorrow," and sat staring at her incredulously. "Tomorrow—you're sure he said to sail tomorrow?"

"Oh, ever so sure, ma'am. I don't know how I could have forgotten to mention it."

"Well, it doesn't matter. Draw my bath, please." Charlotte sprang up, dashed through her dressing, and caught herself singing at her image in the glass as she sat brushing her hair. It made her feel young again to have scored such a victory. The other woman vanished to a speck on the horizon, as this one, who ruled the foreground, smiled back at the reflection of her lips and eyes. He loved her, then—he loved her as passionately as ever. He had divined what she had suffered, had understood that their happiness depended on their getting away at once, and finding each other again after yesterday's desperate groping in the fog. The nature of the influence that had come between them did not much matter to Charlotte now; she had faced the phantom and dispelled it. "Courage—that's the secret! If only people who are in love weren't always so afraid of risking their happiness by looking it in the eyes." As she brushed back her light abundant hair it waved electrically above her head, like the palms of victory. Ah, well, some women knew how to manage men, and some didn't—and only the fair— she gaily paraphrased—deserve the brave! Certainly she was looking very pretty.

The morning danced along like a cockleshell on a bright sea—such a sea as they would soon be speeding over. She ordered a particularly good dinner, saw the children off to their classes, had her trunks brought down, consulted with the maid about getting out summer clothes—for of course they would be heading for heat and sunshine—and wondered if she oughtn't to take Kenneth's flannel suits out of camphor. "But how absurd," she reflected, "that I don't yet know where we're going!" She looked at the clock, saw that it was close on noon, and decided to call him up at his office. There was a slight delay; then she heard his secretary's voice saying that Mr. Ashby had looked in for a moment early, and left again almost immediately. . . . Oh, very well; Charlotte would ring up later. How soon was he likely to be back? The secretary answered that she couldn't tell; all they knew in the office was that when he left he had said he was in a hurry because he had to go out of town.

Out of town! Charlotte hung up the receiver and sat blankly gazing into new darkness. Why had he gone out of town? And where had he gone? And of all days, why should he have chosen the eve of their suddenly planned departure? She felt a faint shiver of apprehension. Of course he had gone to see that woman—no doubt to get her permission to leave. He was as completely in bondage as that; and Charlotte had been fatuous enough to see the palms of victory on her forehead. She burst into a laugh and, walking across the room, sat down again before her mirror. What a different face she saw! The smile on her pale lips seemed to mock the rosy vision of the other Charlotte. But gradually her color crept back. After all, she had a right to claim the victory, since her husband was doing what she wanted, not what the other woman exacted of him. It was natural enough, in view of his abrupt decision to leave the next day, that he should have arrangements to make, business matters to wind up; it was not even necessary to suppose that his mysterious trip was a visit to the writer of the letters. He might simply have gone to see a client who lived out of town. Of course they would not tell Charlotte at the office; the secretary had hesitated before imparting even such meager information as the fact of Mr. Ashby's absence. Meanwhile she would go on with her joyful preparations, content to learn later in the day to what particular island of the blest she was to be carried.

The hours wore on, or rather were swept forward on a rush of eager preparations. At last the entrance of the maid who came to draw the curtains roused Charlotte from her labors, and she saw to her surprise that the clock marked five. And she did not yet know where they were going the next day! She rang up her husband's office and was told that Mr. Ashby had not been there since the early morning. She asked for his partner, but the partner could add nothing to her information, for he himself, his suburban train having been behind time, had reached the office after Ashby had come and gone. Charlotte stood perplexed; then she decided to telephone to her mother-in-law. Of course Kenneth, on the eve of a month's absence, must have gone to see his mother. The mere fact that the children—in spite of his vague objections—would certainly have to be left with old Mrs. Ashby, made it obvious that he would have all sorts of matters to decide with her. At another time Charlotte might have felt a little hurt at being excluded from their conference, but nothing mattered now but that she had won the day, that her husband was still hers and not another woman's. Gaily she called up Mrs. Ashby, heard her friendly voice, and began: "Well, did Kenneth's news surprise you? What do you think of our elopement?"

Almost instantly, before Mrs. Ashby could answer, Charlotte knew what her reply would be. Mrs. Ashby had not seen her son, she had had no word from him and did not know what her daughter-in-law meant. Charlotte stood silent in the intensity of her surprise. "But then, where *has* he been?" she thought. Then, recovering herself, she explained their sudden decision to Mrs. Ashby, and in doing so, gradually regained her own self-confidence, her conviction that nothing could ever again come between Kenneth and herself. Mrs. Ashby took the news calmly and approvingly. She, too, had thought that Kenneth looked worried and overtired, and she agreed with her daughter-in-law that in such cases change was the surest remedy. "I'm always so glad when he gets away. Elsie hated traveling; she was always finding pretexts to prevent his going anywhere. With you, thank goodness, it's different." Nor was Mrs. Ashby surprised at his not having had time to let her know of his departure. He must have been in a rush from the moment the decision was taken; but no doubt he'd drop in before dinner. Five minutes' talk was really all they needed. "I hope you'll gradually cure Kenneth of his mania for going over and over a question that could be settled in a dozen words. He never used to be like that, and if he carried the habit into his professional work he'd soon lose all his clients. . . . Yes, do come in for a minute, dear, if you have time; no doubt he'll turn up while you're here." The tonic ring of Mrs. Ashby's voice echoed on reassuringly in the silent room while Charlotte continued her preparations.

Toward seven the telephone rang, and she darted to it. Now she would know! But it was only from the conscientious secretary, to say that Mr. Ashby hadn't been back, or sent any word, and before the office closed she thought she ought to let Mrs. Ashby know. "Oh, that's all right. Thanks a lot!" Charlotte called out cheerfully, and hung up the receiver with a trembling hand. But perhaps by this time, she reflected, he was at his mother's. She shut her drawers and cupboards, put on her hat and coat and called up to the nursery that she was going out for a minute to see the children's grandmother.

Mrs. Ashby lived nearby, and during her brief walk through the cold spring dusk Charlotte imagined that every advancing figure was her husband's. But she did not meet him on the way, and when she entered the house she found her mother-in-law alone. Kenneth had neither telephoned nor come. Old Mrs. Ashby sat by her bright fire, her knitting needles flashing steadily through her active old hands, and her mere bodily presence gave reassurance to Charlotte. Yes, it was certainly odd that Kenneth had gone off for the whole day without letting any of them know; but, after all, it was to be expected. A busy lawyer held so many threads in his hands that any sudden change of plan would oblige him to make all sorts of unforeseen arrangements and adjustments. He might have gone to see some client in the suburbs and been detained there; his mother remembered his telling her that he had charge of the legal business of a queer old recluse somewhere in New Jersey, who was immensely rich but too mean to have a telephone. Very likely Kenneth had been stranded there.

But Charlotte felt her nervousness gaining on her. When Mrs. Ashby asked her at what hour they were sailing the next day and she had to say she didn't know—that Kenneth had simply sent her word he was going to take their passages—the uttering of the words again brought home to her the strangeness of the situation. Even Mrs. Ashby conceded that it was odd; but she immediately added that it only showed what a rush he was in.

"But, mother, it's nearly eight o'clock! He must realize that I've got to know when we're starting tomorrow."

"Oh, the boat probably doesn't sail till evening. Sometimes they have to wait till midnight for the tide. Kenneth's probably counting on that. After all, he has a level head."

Charlotte stood up. "It's not that. Something has happened to him."

Mrs. Ashby took off her spectacles and rolled up her knitting. "If you begin to let yourself imagine things—"

"Aren't you in the least anxious?"

"I never am till I have to be. I wish you'd ring for dinner, my dear. You'll stay and dine? He's sure to drop in here on his way home."

Charlotte called up her own house. No, the maid said, Mr. Ashby hadn't come in and hadn't telephoned. She would tell him as soon as he came that Mrs. Ashby was dining at his mother's. Charlotte followed her mother-in-law into the dining room and sat with parched throat before her empty plate, while Mrs. Ashby dealt calmly and efficiently with a short but carefully prepared repast. "You'd better eat something, child, or you'll be as bad as Kenneth. . . . Yes, a little more asparagus, please, Jane."

She insisted on Charlotte's drinking a glass of sherry and nibbling a bit of toast; then they returned to the drawing room, where the fire had been made up, and the cushions in Mrs. Ashby's armchair shaken out and smoothed. How safe and familiar it all looked; and out there, somewhere in the uncertainty and mystery of the night, lurked the answer to the two women's conjectures, like an indistinguishable figure prowling on the threshold.

At last Charlotte got up and said: "I'd better go back. At this hour Kenneth will certainly go straight home."

Mrs. Ashby smiled indulgently. "It's not very late, my dear. It doesn't take two sparrows long to dine."

"It's after nine." Charlotte bent down to kiss her. "The fact is, I can't keep still."

Mrs. Ashby pushed aside her work and rested her two hands on the arms of her chair. "I'm going with you," she said, helping herself up.

Charlotte protested that it was too late, that it was not necessary, that she would call up as soon as Kenneth came in, but Mrs. Ashby had already rung for her maid. She was slightly lame, and stood resting on her stick while her wraps were brought. "If Mr. Kenneth turns up, tell him he'll find me at his own house," she instructed the maid as the two women got into the taxi which had been summoned. During the short drive Charlotte gave thanks that she was not returning home alone. There was something warm and substantial in the mere fact of Mrs. Ashby's nearness, something that corresponded with the clearness of her eyes and the texture of her fresh firm complexion. As the taxi drew up she laid her hand encouragingly on Charlotte's. "You'll see; there'll be a message."

The door opened at Charlotte's ring and the two entered. Charlotte's heart beat excitedly; the stimulus of her mother-in-law's confidence was beginning to flow through her veins.

"You'll see—you'll see," Mrs. Ashby repeated.

The maid who opened the door said no, Mr. Ashby had not come in, and there had been no message from him.

"You're sure the telephone's not out of order?" his mother suggested; and the maid said, well, it certainly wasn't half an hour ago; but she'd just go and ring up to make sure. She disappeared, and Charlotte turned to take off her hat and cloak. As she did so her eyes lit on the hall table, and there lay a gray envelope, her husband's name faintly traced on it. "Oh!" she cried out, suddenly aware that for the first time in months she had entered her house without wondering if one of the gray letters would be there.

"What is it, my dear?" Mrs. Ashby asked with a glance of surprise.

Charlotte did not answer. She took up the envelope and stood staring at it as if she could force her gaze to penetrate to what was within. Then an idea occurred to her. She turned and held out the envelope to her mother-in-law.

"Do you know that writing?" she asked.

Mrs. Ashby took the letter. She had to feel with her other hand for her eyeglasses, and when she had adjusted them she lifted the envelope to the light. "Why!" she exclaimed; and then stopped. Charlotte noticed that the letter shook in her usually firm hand. "But this is addressed to Kenneth," Mrs. Ashby said at length, in a low voice. Her tone seemed to imply that she felt her daughter-in-law's question to be slightly indiscreet.

"Yes, but no matter," Charlotte spoke with sudden decision. "I want to know—do you know the writing?"

Mrs. Ashby handed back the letter. "No," she said distinctly.

The two women had turned into the library. Charlotte switched on the electric light and shut the door. She still held the envelope in her hand.

"I'm going to open it," she announced.

She caught her mother-in-law's startled glance. "But, dearest—a letter not addressed to you? My dear, you can't!"

"As if I cared about that—now!" She continued to look intently at Mrs. Ashby. "This letter may tell me where Kenneth is."

Mrs. Ashby's glossy bloom was effaced by a quick pallor; her firm cheeks seemed to shrink and wither. "Why should it? What makes you believe—It can't possibly—"

Charlotte held her eyes steadily on that altered face. "Ah, then you *do* know the writing?" she flashed back.

"Know the writing? How should I? With all my son's correspondents. . . . What I do know is—" Mrs. Ashby broke off and looked at her daughter-in-law entreatingly, almost timidly.

Charlotte caught her by the wrist. "Mother! What do you know? Tell me! You must!"

"That I don't believe any good ever came of a woman's opening her husband's letters behind his back."

The words sounded to Charlotte's irritated ears as flat as a phrase culled from a book of moral axioms. She laughed impatiently and dropped her mother-in-law's wrist. "Is that all? No good can come of this letter, opened or unopened. I know that well enough. But whatever ill comes, I mean to find out what's in it." Her hands had been trembling as they held the envelope, but now they grew firm, and her voice also. She still gazed intently at Mrs. Ashby. "This is the ninth letter addressed in the same hand that has come for Kenneth since we've been married. Always these same gray envelopes. I've kept count of them because after each one he has been like a man who has had some dreadful shock. It takes him hours to shake off their effect. I've told him so. I've told him I must know from whom they come, because I can see they're killing him. He won't answer my questions; he says he can't tell me anything about the letters; but last night he promised to go away with me—to get away from them."

Mrs. Ashby, with shaking steps, had gone to one of the armchairs and sat down in it, her head drooping forward on her breast. "Ah," she murmured.

"So now you understand—"

"Did he tell you it was to get away from them?"

"He said, to get away—to get away. He was sobbing so that he could hardly speak. But I told him I knew that was why."

"And what did he say?"

"He took me in his arms and said he'd go wherever I wanted."

"Ah, thank God!" said Mrs. Ashby. There was a silence, during which she continued to sit with bowed head, and eyes averted from her daughter-in-law. At last she looked up and spoke. "Are you sure there have been as many as nine?"

"Perfectly. This is the ninth. I've kept count."

"And he has absolutely refused to explain?"

"Absolutely."

Mrs. Ashby spoke through pale contracted lips. "When did they begin to come? Do you remember?"

Charlotte laughed again. "Remember? The first one came the night we got back from our honeymoon."

"All that time?" Mrs. Ashby lifted her head and spoke with sudden energy. "Then—yes, open it."

The words were so unexpected that Charlotte felt the blood in her temples, and her hands began to tremble again. She tried to slip her finger under the flap of the envelope, but it was so tightly stuck that she had to hunt on her husband's writing table for his ivory letter opener. As she pushed about the familiar objects his own hands had so lately touched, they sent through her the icy chill emanating from the little personal effects of someone newly dead. In the deep silence of the room the tearing of the paper as she slit the envelope sounded like a human cry. She drew out the sheet and carried it to the lamp.

"Well?" Mrs. Ashby asked below her breath.

Charlotte did not move or answer. She was bending over the page with wrinkled brows, holding it nearer and nearer to the light. Her sight must be blurred, or else dazzled by the reflection of the lamplight on the smooth surface of the paper, for, strain her eyes as she would, she could discern only a few faint strokes, so faint and faltering as to be nearly undecipherable.

"I can't make it out," she said.

"What do you mean, dear?"

"The writing's too indistinct. . . . Wait."

She went back to the table and, sitting down close to Kenneth's reading lamp, slipped the letter under a magnifying glass. All this time she was aware that her mother-in-law was watching her intently.

"Well?" Mrs. Ashby breathed.

"Well, it's no clearer. I can't read it."

"You mean the paper is an absolute blank?"

"No, not quite. There is writing on it. I can make out something like 'mine'—oh, and 'come.' It might be 'come.' "

Mrs. Ashby stood up abruptly. Her face was even paler than before. She advanced to the table and, resting her two hands on it, drew a deep breath. "Let me see," she said, as if forcing herself to a hateful effort.

Charlotte felt the contagion of her whiteness. "She knows," she thought. She pushed the letter across the table. Her mother-in-law lowered her head over it in silence, but without touching it with her pale wrinkled hands.

Charlotte stood watching her as she herself, when she had tried to read the letter, had been watched by Mrs. Ashby. The latter fumbled for her glasses, held them to her eyes, and bent still closer to the outspread page, in order, as it seemed, to avoid touching it. The light of the lamp fell directly on her old face, and Charlotte reflected what depths of the unknown may lurk under the clearest and most candid lineaments. She had never seen her mother-in-law's features express any but simple and sound emotions—cordiality, amusement, a kindly sympathy; now and again a flash of wholesome anger. Now they seemed to wear a look of fear and hatred, of incredulous dismay and almost cringing defiance. It was as if the spirits warring within her had distorted her face to their own likeness. At length she raised her head. "I can't—I can't," she said in a voice of childish distress.

"You can't make it out either?"

She shook her head, and Charlotte saw two tears roll down her cheeks.

"Familiar as the writing is to you?" Charlotte insisted with twitching lips.

Mrs. Ashby did not take up the challenge. "I can make out nothing —nothing."

"But you do know the writing?"

Mrs. Ashby lifted her head timidly; her anxious eyes stole with a glance of apprehension around the quiet familiar room. "How can I tell? I was startled at first. . . ."

"Startled by the resemblance?"

"Well, I thought—"

"You'd better say it out, mother! You knew at once it was *her* writing?"

"Oh, wait, my dear—wait."

"Wait for what?"

Mrs. Ashby looked up; her eyes, traveling slowly past Charlotte, were lifted to the blank wall behind her son's writing table.

Charlotte, following the glance, burst into a shrill laugh of accusation. "I needn't wait any longer! You've answered me now! You're looking straight at the wall where her picture used to hang!"

Mrs. Ashby lifted her hand with a murmur of warning. "Sh-h."

"Oh, you needn't imagine that anything can ever frighten me again!" Charlotte cried.

Her mother-in-law still leaned against the table. Her lips moved plaintively. "But we're going mad—we're both going mad. We both know such things are impossible."

Her daughter-in-law looked at her with a pitying stare. "I've known for a long time now that everything was possible."

"Even this?"

"Yes, exactly this."

"But this letter—after all, there's nothing in this letter—"

"Perhaps there would be to him. How can I tell? I remember his saying to me once that if you were used to a handwriting the faintest stroke of it became legible. Now I see what he meant. He *was* used to it."

"But the few strokes that I can make out are so pale. No one could possibly read that letter."

Charlotte laughed again. "I suppose everything's pale about a ghost," she said stridently.

"Oh, my child—my child—don't say it!"

"Why shouldn't I say it, when even the bare walls cry it out? What difference does it make if her letters are illegible to you and me? If even you can see her face on that blank wall, why shouldn't he read her writing on this blank paper? Don't you see that she's everywhere in this house, and the closer to him because to everyone else she's become invisible?" Charlotte dropped into a chair and covered her face with her hands. A turmoil of sobbing shook her from head to foot. At length a touch on her shoulder made her look up, and she saw her mother-in-law bending over her. Mrs. Ashby's face seemed to have grown still smaller and more wasted, but it had resumed its usual quiet look. Through all her tossing anguish, Charlotte felt the impact of that resolute spirit.

"Tomorrow—tomorrow. You'll see. There'll be some explanation tomorrow."

Charlotte cut her short. "An explanation? Who's going to give it, I wonder?"

Mrs. Ashby drew back and straightened herself heroically. "Kenneth himself will," she cried out in a strong voice. Charlotte said nothing, and the old woman went on: "But meanwhile we must act; we must notify the police. Now, without a moment's delay. We must do everything —everything."

Charlotte stood up slowly and stiffly; her joints felt as cramped as an old woman's. "Exactly as if we thought it could do any good to do anything?"

Resolutely Mrs. Ashby cried: "Yes!" and Charlotte went up to the telephone and unhooked the receiver.

ROMAN FEVER

FROM THE TABLE at which they had been lunching two American ladies of ripe but well-cared-for middle age moved across the lofty terrace of the Roman restaurant and, leaning on its parapet, looked first at each other, and then down on the outspread glories of the Palatine and the Forum, with the same expression of vague but benevolent approval.

As they leaned there a girlish voice echoed up gaily from the stairs leading to the court below. "Well, come along, then," it cried, not to them but to an invisible companion, "and let's leave the young things to their knitting"; and a voice as fresh laughed back: "Oh, look here, Babs, not actually *knitting*—" "Well, I mean figuratively," rejoined the first. "After all, we haven't left our poor parents much else to do. . . ." and at that point the turn of the stairs engulfed the dialogue.

The two ladies looked at each other again, this time with a tinge of smiling embarrassment, and the smaller and paler one shook her head and colored slightly.

"Barbara!" she murmured, sending an unheard rebuke after the mocking voice in the stairway.

The other lady, who was fuller, and higher in color, with a small determined nose supported by vigorous black eyebrows, gave a good-humored laugh. "That's what our daughters think of us!"

Her companion replied by a deprecating gesture. "Not of us individually. We must remember that. It's just the collective modern idea of Mothers. And you see—" Half-guiltily she drew from her handsomely mounted black hand-bag a twist of crimson silk run through by two fine knitting needles. "One never knows," she murmured. "The new system has certainly given us a good deal of time to kill; and sometimes I get tired just looking—even at this." Her gesture was now addressed to the stupendous scene at their feet.

The dark lady laughed again, and they both relapsed upon the view, contemplating it in silence, with a sort of diffused serenity which might have been borrowed from the spring effulgence of the Roman skies. The luncheon hour was long past, and the two had their end of the vast terrace to themselves. At its opposite extremity a few groups, detained by a lingering look at the outspread city, were gathering up guidebooks and fumbling for tips. The last of them scattered, and the two ladies were alone on the air-washed height.

"Well, I don't see why we shouldn't just stay here," said Mrs. Slade, the lady of the high color and energetic brows. Two derelict basket chairs stood near, and she pushed them into the angle of the parapet, and settled herself in one, her gaze upon the Palatine. "After all, it's still the most beautiful view in the world."

"It always will be, to me," assented her friend Mrs. Ansley, with so slight a stress on the "me" that Mrs. Slade, though she noticed it, wondered if it were not merely accidental, like the random underlinings of old-fashioned letter writers.

"Grace Ansley was always old-fashioned," she thought; and added aloud, with a retrospective smile: "It's a view we've both been familiar with for a good many years. When we first met here we were younger than our girls are now. You remember?"

"Oh, yes, I remember," murmured Mrs. Ansley, with the same undefinable stress. "There's that headwaiter wondering," she interpolated. She was evidently far less sure than her companion of herself and of her rights in the world.

"I'll cure him of wondering," said Mrs. Slade, stretching her hand toward a bag as discreetly opulent-looking as Mrs. Ansley's. Signing to the headwaiter, she explained that she and her friend were old lovers of Rome, and would like to spend the end of the afternoon looking down on the view—that is, if it did not disturb the service? The headwaiter, bowing over her gratuity, assured her that the ladies were most welcome, and would be still more so if they would condescend to remain for dinner. A full-moon night, they would remember. . . .

Mrs. Slade's black brows drew together, as though references to the moon were out of place and even unwelcome. But she smiled away her frown as the headwaiter retreated. "Well, why not? We might do worse. There's no knowing, I suppose, when the girls will be back. Do you even know back from *where*? I don't!"

Mrs. Ansley again colored slightly. "I think those young Italian aviators we met at the Embassy invited them to fly to Tarquinia for tea. I suppose they'll want to wait and fly back by moonlight."

"Moonlight—moonlight! What a part it still plays. Do you suppose they're as sentimental as we were?"

"I've come to the conclusion that I don't in the least know what they are," said Mrs. Ansley. "And perhaps we didn't know much more about each other."

"No; perhaps we didn't."

Her friend gave her a shy glance. "I never should have supposed you were sentimental, Alida."

"Well, perhaps I wasn't." Mrs. Slade drew her lids together in retrospect; and for a few moments the two ladies, who had been intimate since childhood, reflected how little they knew each other. Each one, of course, had a label ready to attach to the other's name; Mrs. Delphin Slade, for instance, would have told herself, or anyone who asked her, that Mrs. Horace Ansley, twenty-five years ago, had been exquisitely lovely—no, you wouldn't believe it, would you? . . . though, of course, still charming, distinguished. . . . Well, as a girl she had been exquisite; far more beautiful than her daughter Barbara, though certainly Babs, according to the new standards at any rate, was more effective—had more *edge,* as they say. Funny where she got it, with those two nullities as parents. Yes; Horace Ansley was—well, just the duplicate of his wife. Museum specimens of old New York. Good-looking, irreproachable, exemplary. Mrs. Slade and Mrs. Ansley had lived opposite each other—actually as well as figuratively—for years. When the drawing-room curtains in No. 20 East 73rd Street were renewed, No. 23, across the way, was always aware of it. And of all the movings, buyings, travels, anniversaries, illnesses—the tame chronicle of an estimable pair. Little of it escaped Mrs. Slade. But she had grown bored with it by the time her husband made his big *coup* in Wall Street, and when they bought in upper Park Avenue had already begun to think: "I'd rather live opposite a speakeasy for a change; at least one might see it raided." The idea of seeing Grace raided was so amusing that (before the move) she launched it at a woman's lunch. It made a hit, and went the rounds—she sometimes wondered if it had crossed the street, and reached Mrs. Ansley. She hoped not, but didn't much mind. Those were the days when respectability was at a discount, and it did the irreproachable no harm to laugh at them a little.

A few years later, and not many months apart, both ladies lost their husbands. There was an appropriate exchange of wreaths and condolences, and a brief renewal of intimacy in the half-shadow of their mourning; and now, after another interval, they had run across each other in Rome, at the same hotel, each of them the modest appendage of a salient daughter. The similarity of their lot had again drawn them together, lending itself to mild jokes, and the mutual confession that, if in old days it must have been tiring to "keep up" with daughters, it was now, at times, a little dull not to.

No doubt, Mrs. Slade reflected, she felt her unemployment more than poor Grace ever would. It was a big drop from being the wife of Delphin Slade to being his widow. She had always regarded herself (with a certain conjugal pride) as his equal in social gifts, as contributing her full share to the making of the exceptional couple they were: but the difference after his death was irremediable. As the wife of the famous corporation lawyer, always with an international case or two on hand, every day brought its exciting and unexpected obligation: the impromptu entertaining of eminent colleagues from abroad, the hurried dashes on legal business to London, Paris or Rome, where the entertaining was so handsomely reciprocated; the amusement of hearing in her wake: "What, that handsome woman with the good clothes and the eyes is Mrs. Slade—*the* Slade's wife? Really? Generally the wives of celebrities are such frumps."

Yes; being *the* Slade's widow was a dullish business after that. In living up to such a husband all her faculties had been engaged; now she had only her daughter to live up to, for the son who seemed to have inherited his father's gifts had died suddenly in boyhood. She had fought through that agony because her husband was there, to be helped and to help; now, after the father's death, the thought of the boy had become unbearable. There was nothing left but to mother her daughter; and dear Jenny was such a perfect daughter that she needed no excessive mothering. "Now with Babs Ansley I don't know that I *should* be so quiet," Mrs. Slade sometimes half-enviously reflected; but Jenny, who was younger than her brilliant friend, was that rare accident, an extremely pretty girl who somehow made youth and prettiness seem as safe as their absence. It was all perplexing—and to Mrs. Slade a little boring. She wished that Jenny would fall in love—with the wrong man, even; that she might have to be watched, out-maneuvered, rescued. And instead, it was Jenny who watched her mother, kept her out of drafts, made sure that she had taken her tonic. . . .

Mrs. Ansley was much less articulate than her friend, and her mental portrait of Mrs. Slade was slighter, and drawn with fainter touches. "Alida Slade's awfully brilliant; but not as brilliant as she thinks," would have summed it up; though she would have added, for the enlightenment of strangers, that Mrs. Slade had been an extremely dashing girl; much more so than her daughter, who was pretty, of course, and clever in a way, but had none of her mother's—well, "vividness," someone had once called it. Mrs. Ansley would take up current words like this, and cite them in quotation marks, as unheard-of audacities. No; Jenny was not like her mother. Sometimes Mrs. Ansley thought Alida Slade was disappointed; on the whole she had had a sad life. Full of failures and mistakes; Mrs. Ansley had always been rather sorry for her. . . .

So these two ladies visualized each other, each through the wrong end of her little telescope.

* II *

For a long time they continued to sit side by side without speaking. It seemed as though, to both, there was a relief in laying down their somewhat futile activities in the presence of the vast Memento Mori which faced them. Mrs. Slade sat quite still, her eyes fixed on the golden slope of the Palace of the Caesars, and after a while Mrs. Ansley ceased to fidget with her bag, and she too sank into meditation. Like many intimate friends, the two ladies had never before had occasion to be silent together, and Mrs. Ansley was slightly embarrassed by what seemed, after so many years, a new stage in their intimacy, and one with which she did not yet know how to deal.

Suddenly the air was full of that deep clangor of bells which periodically covers Rome with a roof of silver. Mrs. Slade glanced at her wristwatch. "Five o'clock already," she said, as though surprised.

Mrs. Ansley suggested interrogatively: "There's bridge at the Embassy at five." For a long time Mrs. Slade did not answer. She appeared to be lost in contemplation, and Mrs. Ansley thought the remark had escaped her. But after a while she said, as if speaking out of a dream: "Bridge, did you say? Not unless you want to. . . . But I don't think I will, you know."

"Oh, no," Mrs. Ansley hastened to assure her. "I don't care to at all. It's so lovely here; and so full of old memories, as you say." She settled herself in her chair, and almost furtively drew forth her knitting. Mrs. Slade took sideway note of this activity, but her own beautifully cared-for hands remained motionless on her knee.

"I was just thinking," she said slowly, "what different things Rome stands for to each generation of travelers. To our grandmothers, Roman fever; to our mothers, sentimental dangers—how we used to be guarded! —to our daughters, no more dangers than the middle of Main Street. They don't know it—but how much they're missing!"

The long golden light was beginning to pale, and Mrs. Ansley lifted her knitting a little closer to her eyes. "Yes; how we were guarded!"

"I always used to think," Mrs. Slade continued, "that our mothers had a much more difficult job than our grandmothers. When Roman fever stalked the streets it must have been comparatively easy to gather in the girls at the danger hour; but when you and I were young, with such beauty calling us, and the spice of disobedience thrown in, and no worse risk than catching cold during the cool hour after sunset, the mothers used to be put to it to keep us in—didn't they?"

She turned again toward Mrs. Ansley, but the latter had reached a delicate point in her knitting. "One, two, three—slip two; yes, they must have been," she assented, without looking up.

Mrs. Slade's eyes rested on her with a deepened attention. "She can knit—in the face of *this!* How like her. . . ."

Mrs. Slade leaned back, brooding, her eyes ranging from the ruins which faced her to the long green hollow of the Forum, the fading glow of the church fronts beyond it, and the outlying immensity of the Colosseum. Suddenly she thought: "It's all very well to say that our girls have done away with sentiment and moonlight. But if Babs Ansley isn't out to catch that young aviator—the one who's a Marchese—then I don't know anything. And Jenny has no chance beside her. I know that too. I wonder if that's why Grace Ansley likes the two girls to go everywhere together? My poor Jenny as a foil—!" Mrs. Slade gave a hardly audible laugh, and at the sound Mrs. Ansley dropped her knitting.

"Yes—?"

"I—oh, nothing. I was only thinking how your Babs carries everything before her. That Campolieri boy is one of the best matches in Rome. Don't look so innocent, my dear—you know he is. And I was wondering, ever so respectfully, you understand . . . wondering how two such exemplary characters as you and Horace had managed to produce anything quite so dynamic." Mrs. Slade laughed again, with a touch of asperity.

Mrs. Ansley's hands lay inert across her needles. She looked straight out at the great accumulated wreckage of passion and splendor at her feet. But her small profile was almost expressionless. At length she said: "I think you overrate Babs, my dear."

Mrs. Slade's tone grew easier. "No; I don't. I appreciate her. And perhaps envy you. Oh, my girl's perfect; if I were a chronic invalid I'd—well, I think I'd rather be in Jenny's hands. There must be times . . . but there! I always wanted a brilliant daughter . . . and never quite understood why I got an angel instead."

Mrs. Ansley echoed her laugh in a faint murmur. "Babs is an angel too."

"Of course—of course! But she's got rainbow wings. Well, they're wandering by the sea with their young men; and here we sit . . . and it all brings back the past a little too acutely."

Mrs. Ansley had resumed her knitting. One might almost have imagined (if one had known her less well, Mrs. Slade reflected) that, for her also, too many memories rose from the lengthening shadows of those august ruins. But no; she was simply absorbed in her work. What was there for her to worry about? She knew that Babs would almost certainly come back engaged to the extremely eligible Campolieri. "And she'll sell the New York house, and settle down near them in Rome, and never be in their way . . . she's much too tactful. But she'll have an excellent cook, and just the right people in for bridge and cocktails . . . and a perfectly peaceful old age among her grandchildren."

Mrs. Slade broke off this prophetic flight with a recoil of self-disgust. There was no one of whom she had less right to think unkindly than of Grace Ansley. Would she never cure herself of envying her? Perhaps she had begun too long ago.

She stood up and leaned against the parapet, filling her troubled eyes with the tranquilizing magic of the hour. But instead of tranquilizing her the sight seemed to increase her exasperation. Her gaze turned toward the Colosseum. Already its golden flank was drowned in purple shadow, and above it the sky curved crystal clear, without light or color. It was the moment when afternoon and evening hang balanced in mid-heaven.

Mrs. Slade turned back and laid her hand on her friend's arm. The gesture was so abrupt that Mrs. Ansley looked up, startled.

"The sun's set. You're not afraid, my dear?"

"Afraid—?"

"Of Roman fever or pneumonia? I remember how ill you were that winter. As a girl you had a very delicate throat, hadn't you?"

"Oh, we're all right up here. Down below, in the Forum, it does get deathly cold, all of a sudden . . . but not here."

"Ah, of course you know because you had to be so careful." Mrs. Slade turned back to the parapet. She thought: "I must make one more effort not to hate her." Aloud she said: "Whenever I look at the Forum from up here, I remember that story about a great-aunt of yours, wasn't she? A dreadfully wicked great-aunt?"

"Oh, yes; great-aunt Harriet. The one who was supposed to have sent her young sister out to the Forum after sunset to gather a night-blooming flower for her album. All our great-aunts and grandmothers used to have albums of dried flowers."

Mrs. Slade nodded. "But she really sent her because they were in love with the same man—"

"Well, that was the family tradition. They said Aunt Harriet confessed it years afterward. At any rate, the poor little sister caught the fever and died. Mother used to frighten us with the story when we were children."

"And you frightened *me* with it, that winter when you and I were here as girls. The winter I was engaged to Delphin."

Mrs. Ansley gave a faint laugh. "Oh, did I? Really frightened you? I don't believe you're easily frightened."

"Not often; but I was then. I was easily frightened because I was too happy. I wonder if you know what that means?"

"I—yes . . ." Mrs. Ansley faltered.

"Well, I suppose that was why the story of your wicked aunt made such an impression on me. And I thought: 'There's no more Roman fever, but the Forum is deathly cold after sunset—especially after a hot day. And the Colosseum's even colder and damper'."

"The Colosseum—?"

"Yes. It wasn't easy to get in, after the gates were locked for the night. Far from easy. Still, in those days it could be managed; it *was* managed, often. Lovers met there who couldn't meet elsewhere. You knew that?"

"I—I dare say. I don't remember."

"You don't remember? You don't remember going to visit some ruins or other one evening, just after dark, and catching a bad chill? You were supposed to have gone to see the moon rise. People always said that expedition was what caused your illness."

There was a moment's silence; then Mrs. Ansley rejoined: "Did they? It was all so long ago."

"Yes. And you got well again—so it didn't matter. But I suppose it struck your friends—the reason given for your illness, I mean—because everybody knew you were so prudent on account of your throat, and your mother took such care of you. . . . You *had* been out late sight-seeing, hadn't you, that night?"

"Perhaps I had. The most prudent girls aren't always prudent. What made you think of it now?"

Mrs. Slade seemed to have no answer ready. But after a moment she broke out: "Because I simply can't bear it any longer!"

Mrs. Ansley lifted her head quickly. Her eyes were wide and very pale. "Can't bear what?"

"Why—your not knowing that I've always known why you went."

"Why I went—?"

"Yes. You think I'm bluffing, don't you? Well, you went to meet the man I was engaged to—and I can repeat every word of the letter that took you there."

While Mrs. Slade spoke Mrs. Ansley had risen unsteadily to her feet. Her bag, her knitting and gloves, slid in a panic-stricken heap to the ground. She looked at Mrs. Slade as though she were looking at a ghost.

"No, no—don't," she faltered out.

"Why not? Listen, if you don't believe me. 'My one darling, things can't go on like this. I must see you alone. Come to the Colosseum immediately after dark tomorrow. There will be somebody to let you in. No one whom you need fear will suspect'—but perhaps you've forgotten what the letter said?"

Mrs. Ansley met the challenge with an unexpected composure. Steadying herself against the chair she looked at her friend, and replied: "No; I know it by heart too."

"And the signature? 'Only *your* D.S.' Was that it? I'm right, am I? That was the letter that took you out that evening after dark?"

Mrs. Ansley was still looking at her. It seemed to Mrs. Slade that a slow struggle was going on behind the voluntarily controlled mask of her small quiet face. "I shouldn't have thought she had herself so well in hand," Mrs. Slade reflected, almost resentfully. But at this moment Mrs. Ansley spoke. "I don't know how you knew. I burnt that letter at once."

"Yes; you would, naturally—you're so prudent!" The sneer was open now. "And if you burnt the letter you're wondering how on earth I know what was in it. That's it, isn't it?"

Mrs. Slade waited, but Mrs. Ansley did not speak.

"Well, my dear, I know what was in that letter because I wrote it!"

"You wrote it?"

"Yes."

The two women stood for a minute staring at each other in the last golden light. Then Mrs. Ansley dropped back into her chair. "Oh," she murmured, and covered her face with her hands.

Mrs. Slade waited nervously for another word or movement. None came, and at length she broke out: "I horrify you."

Mrs. Ansley's hands dropped to her knee. The face they uncovered was streaked with tears. "I wasn't thinking of you. I was thinking—it was the only letter I ever had from him!"

"And I wrote it. Yes; I wrote it! But I was the girl he was engaged to. Did you happen to remember that?"

Mrs. Ansley's head drooped again. "I'm not trying to excuse myself . . . I remembered. . . ."

"And still you went?"

"Still I went."

Mrs. Slade stood looking down on the small bowed figure at her side. The flame of her wrath had already sunk, and she wondered why she had ever thought there would be any satisfaction in inflicting so purposeless a wound on her friend. But she had to justify herself.

"You do understand? I'd found out—and I hated you, hated you. I knew you were in love with Delphin—and I was afraid; afraid of you, of your quiet ways, your sweetness . . . your . . . well, I wanted you out of the way, that's all. Just for a few weeks; just till I was sure of him. So in a blind fury I wrote that letter . . . I don't know why I'm telling you now."

"I suppose," said Mrs. Ansley slowly, "it's because you've always gone on hating me."

"Perhaps. Or because I wanted to get the whole thing off my mind." She paused. "I'm glad you destroyed the letter. Of course I never thought you'd die."

Mrs. Ansley relapsed into silence, and Mrs. Slade, leaning above her, was conscious of a strange sense of isolation, of being cut off from the warm current of human communion. "You think me a monster!"

"I don't know. . . . It was the only letter I had, and you say he didn't write it?"

"Ah, how you care for him still!"

"I cared for that memory," said Mrs. Ansley.

Mrs. Slade continued to look down on her. She seemed physically reduced by the blow—as if, when she got up, the wind might scatter her like a puff of dust. Mrs. Slade's jealousy suddenly leapt up again at the sight. All these years the woman had been living on that letter. How she must have loved him, to treasure the mere memory of its ashes! The letter of the man her friend was engaged to. Wasn't it she who was the monster?

"You tried your best to get him away from me, didn't you? But you failed; and I kept him. That's all."

"Yes. That's all."

"I wish now I hadn't told you. I'd no idea you'd feel about it as you do; I thought you'd be amused. It all happened so long ago, as you say; and you must do me the justice to remember that I had no reason to think you'd ever taken it seriously. How could I, when you were married to Horace Ansley two months afterward? As soon as you could get out of bed your mother rushed you off to Florence and married you. People were rather surprised—they wondered at its being done so quickly; but I thought I knew. I had an idea you did it out of *pique*—to be able to say you'd got ahead of Delphin and me. Girls have such silly reasons for doing the most serious things. And your marrying so soon convinced me that you'd never really cared."

"Yes. I suppose it would," Mrs. Ansley assented.

The clear heaven overhead was emptied of all its gold. Dusk spread over it, abruptly darkening the Seven Hills. Here and there lights began to twinkle through the foliage at their feet. Steps were coming and going on the deserted terrace—waiters looking out of the doorway at the head of the stairs, then reappearing with trays and napkins and flasks of wine. Tables were moved, chairs straightened. A feeble string of electric lights flickered out. Some vases of faded flowers were carried away, and brought back replenished. A stout lady in a dust coat suddenly appeared, asking in broken Italian if anyone had seen the elastic band which held together her tattered Baedeker. She poked with her stick under the table at which she had lunched, the waiters assisting.

The corner where Mrs. Slade and Mrs. Ansley sat was still shadowy and deserted. For a long time neither of them spoke. At length Mrs. Slade began again: "I suppose I did it as a sort of joke—"

"A joke?"

"Well, girls are ferocious sometimes, you know. Girls in love especially. And I remember laughing to myself all that evening at the idea that you were waiting around there in the dark, dodging out of sight, listening for every sound, trying to get in— Of course I was upset when I heard you were so ill afterward."

Mrs. Ansley had not moved for a long time. But now she turned slowly toward her companion. "But I didn't wait. He'd arranged everything. He was there. We were let in at once," she said.

Mrs. Slade sprang up from her leaning position. "Delphin there? They let you in?—Ah, now you're lying!" she burst out with violence.

Mrs. Ansley's voice grew clearer, and full of surprise. "But of course he was there. Naturally he came—"

"Came? How did he know he'd find you there? You must be raving!"

Mrs. Ansley hesitated, as though reflecting. "But I answered the letter. I told him I'd be there. So he came."

Mrs. Slade flung her hands up to her face. "Oh, God—you answered! I never thought of your answering. . . ."

"It's odd you never thought of it, if you wrote the letter."

"Yes. I was blind with rage."

Mrs. Ansley rose, and drew her fur scarf about her. "It is cold here. We'd better go . . . I'm sorry for you," she said, as she clasped the fur about her throat.

The unexpected words sent a pang through Mrs. Slade. "Yes; we'd better go." She gathered up her bag and cloak. "I don't know why you should be sorry for me," she muttered.

Mrs. Ansley stood looking away from her toward the dusky secret mass of the Colosseum. "Well—because I didn't have to wait that night."

Mrs. Slade gave an unquiet laugh. "Yes; I was beaten there. But I oughtn't to begrudge it to you, I suppose. At the end of all these years. After all, I had everything; I had him for twenty-five years. And you had nothing but that one letter that he didn't write."

Mrs. Ansley was again silent. At length she turned toward the door of the terrace. She took a step, and turned back, facing her companion.

"I had Barbara," she said, and began to move ahead of Mrs. Slade toward the stairway.

DURATION

THE PASSAGE in his sister's letter most perplexing to Henly Warbeck
was that in which she expressed her satisfaction that the date of his sailing
from Lima would land him in Boston in good time for Cousin Martha
Little's birthday.

Puzzle as he would, the returning Bostonian could get no light on it.
"Why," he thought, after a third rereading, "I didn't suppose Martha
Little had ever *had* a birthday since the first one!"

Nothing on the fairly flat horizon of Henly Warbeck's youth had been
more lacking in relief than the figure of his father's spinster cousin, Martha
Little; and now, returning home after many years in distant and exotic
lands (during which, however, contact by correspondence had never been
long interrupted), Warbeck could not imagine what change in either
Martha Little's character or in that of Boston could have thrust her into
even momentary prominence.

Even in his own large family connection, where, to his impatient youth,
insignificance seemed endemic, Martha Little had always been the most
effaced, contourless, colorless. Nor had any accidental advantage ever lifted
her out of her congenital twilight: neither money, nor a bad temper, nor a
knack with her clothes, nor any of those happy hazards—chance meetings
with interesting people, the whim of a rich relation, the luck of ministering in a street accident to somebody with money to bequeath—which
occasionally raise the most mediocre above their level. As far as Warbeck
knew, Martha Little's insignificance had been unbroken, and accepted from
the outset, by herself and all the family, as the medium she was fated to
live in: as a person with weak eyes has to live with the blinds down, and be
groped for by stumbling visitors.

The result had been that visitors were few; that Martha was more and more forgotten, or remembered only when she could temporarily replace a nursery governess on holiday, or "amuse" some fidgety child getting over an infantile malady. Then the family took it for granted that she would step into the breach; but when the governess came back, or the child recovered, she disappeared, and was again immediately forgotten.

Once only, as far as Warbeck knew, had she overstepped the line thus drawn for her; but that was so long ago that the occasion had already become a legend in his boyhood. It was when old Mrs. Warbeck, Henly's grandmother, gave the famous ball at which her eldest granddaughter came out; the ball discussed for weeks beforehand and months afterward from Chestnut Street to Bay State Road, not because there was anything exceptional about it (save perhaps its massive "handsomeness"), but simply because old Mrs. Warbeck had never given a ball before, and Boston had never supposed she ever would give one, and there had been hardly three months' time in which to get used to the idea that she was really going to—at last!

All this, naturally, had been agitating, not to say upsetting, to Beacon Street and Commonwealth Avenue, and absorbing to the whole immense Warbeck connection; the innumerable Pepperels, Sturlisses and Syngletons, the Graysons, Wrigglesworths and Perches—even to those remote and negligible Littles whose name gave so accurate a measure of their tribal standing. And to that ball there had been a question of asking, not of course *all* the Littles—that would have been really out of proportion—but two or three younger specimens of the tribe, whom circumstances had happened to bring into closer contact with the Warbeck group.

"And then," one of the married daughters had suggested toward the end of the consultation, "there's Martha Little—"

"*Martha?*" old Mrs. Warbeck echoed, incredulous and ironic, as much as to say: "The name's a slip of the tongue, of course; but whom *did* you mean, my dear, when you said 'Martha'?"

But the married daughter had continued, though more doubtfully: "Well, mother, Martha does sometimes help us out of our difficulties. Last winter, you remember, when Maggie's baby had the chicken pox . . . and then, taking Sara's Charlotte three times a week to her drawing class . . . and you know, as you invite her to stay with you at Milton every summer when we're at the seaside. . . ."

"Ah, you regard that as helping you out of a difficulty?" Mrs. Warbeck drily interposed.

"No, mother, not a difficulty, of course. But it does make us feel so *safe* to know that Martha's with you. And when she hears of the ball she might expect—"

"Expect to *come?*" questioned Mrs. Warbeck.

"Oh, no—how absurd! Only to be invited. . . ." the daughters chorused in reply.

"She'd like to show the invitation at her boardinghouse. . . ."

"She hasn't many pleasures, poor thing. . . ."

"Well, but," the old lady insisted, sticking to her point, "if I did invite her, would she come?"

"To a ball? What an idea!" Martha Little at a ball! Daughters and daughters-in-law laughed. It was really too absurd. But they all had their little debts to settle with Martha Little, and the opportunity was too good to be missed. On the strength of their joint assurances that no risk could possibly be incurred, old Mrs. Warbeck sent the invitation.

The night of the ball came; and so did Martha Little. She was among the first to arrive, and she stayed till the last candle was blown out. The entertainment remained for many years memorable in the annals of Beacon Street, and also in the Warbeck family history, since it was the occasion of Sara's eldest engaging herself to the second of Jake Wrigglesworth's boys (now, Warbeck reflected, himself a grizzled grandparent), and of Phil Syngleton's falling in love with the second Grayson girl; but beyond and above these events towered the formidable fact of Martha Little's one glaring indelicacy. Like Mrs. Warbeck's ball, it was never repeated. Martha retired once more into the twilight in which she belonged, emerging from it, as of old, only when some service was to be rendered somewhere in the many-branched family connection. But the episode of the ball remained fresh in every memory. Martha Little had been invited—*and she had come!* Henly Warbeck, as a little boy, had often heard his aunts describe her appearance: the prim black silk, the antiquated seed pearls and lace mittens, the obvious "front," more tightly crimped than usual; how she had pranced up the illuminated stairs, an absurd velvet reticule over her wrist, greeted her mighty kinswoman on the landing, and complacently mingled with the jeweled and feathered throng under the wax candles of the many chandeliers, while Mrs. Warbeck muttered to her daughters in a withering aside: *"I never should have thought it of Martha Little!"*

The escapade had done Martha Little more harm than good. The following summer Mrs. Warbeck had chosen one of her own granddaughters to keep her company at Milton when the family went to the seaside. It was hoped that this would make Martha realize her fatal error; and it did. And though the following year, at the urgent suggestion of the granddaughter chosen to replace her, she was received back into grace, and had what she called her "lovely summer outing" at Milton, there was certainly a shade of difference in her subsequent treatment. The younger granddaughters especially resented the fact that old Mrs. Warbeck had decided never to give another ball; and the old lady was fond of repeating (before Martha Little) that no, really, she couldn't; the family connection was *too large*—she hadn't room for them all. When the girls wanted to dance, their mothers must hire a public room; at her age Mrs. Warbeck couldn't be subjected to the fatigue, and the—the overcrowding.

Martha Little took the hint. As the grandchildren grew up and married, her services were probably less often required, and by the time that Henly Warbeck had graduated from the Harvard Law School, and begun his life of distant wanderings, she had vanished into a still deeper twilight. Only once or twice, when some member of the tribe had run across Henly abroad, had Martha's name been mentioned. "Oh, she's as dull as Martha Little," one contemptuous cousin had said of somebody; and the last mention of her had been when Warbeck's sister, Mrs. Pepperel—the one to whom he was now returning—had mentioned, years ago, that a remote Grayson cousin, of the Frostingham branch, had bequeathed to Martha his little house at Frostingham—"so that now she's off our minds." And out of our memories, the speaker might have added; for though Frostingham is only a few miles from Boston it was not likely that many visitors would find their way to Martha Little's door.

No; the allusion in this letter of Mrs. Pepperel's remained cryptic to the returning traveler. As the train approached Boston, he pulled it from his pocket, and reread it again. "Luckily you'll get here in good time for Martha Little's birthday," Mrs. Pepperel said.

The train was slowing down. "Frosting*ham*," the conductor shouted, stressing the last syllable in the old Boston way. "Thank heaven," Warbeck thought, "nothing ever really changes in Boston!"

A newsboy came through the Pullman with the evening papers. Warbeck unfolded one and read on the first page: "Frostingham preparing to celebrate Miss Martha Little's hundredth birthday." And underneath: "Frostingham's most distinguished centenarian chats with representative of *Transcript*." But the train was slowing down again—and here was Boston. Warbeck thrust the paper into his suitcase, bewildered yet half-understanding. Where else in the world but in Boston would the fact of having lived to be a hundred lift even a Martha Little into the limelight? Ah, no; Boston forgot nothing, altered nothing. With a swelling heart the penitent exile sprang out, and was folded to the breasts of a long line of Warbecks and Pepperels, all of whom congratulated him on having arrived from the ends of the earth in time for Martha Little's birthday.

* II *

That night after dinner, Warbeck leaned back at ease in the pleasant dining room of the old Pepperel house in Chestnut Street. The Copley portraits looked down familiarly from the walls, the old Pepperel Madeira circulated about the table. (In New York, thought Warbeck, Copleys and Madeiras, if there had been any, would both have been sold long since.)

The atmosphere was warm to the returning wanderer. It was pleasant to see about him the animated replicas of the Copleys on the walls, and to listen again to the local intonations, with the funny stress on the last syllable. His unmarried Pepperel nieces were fresh and good-looking; and the youngest, Lyddy, judging from her photograph, conspicuously handsome. But Lyddy was not there. Cousin Martha, Mrs. Pepperel explained with a certain pride, was so fond of Lyddy that the girl had to be constantly with her; and since the preparations for the hundredth birthday had begun, Lyddy had been virtually a prisoner at Frostingham. "Martha wouldn't even let her off to come and dine with you tonight; she says she's too nervous and excited to be left without Lyddy. Lyddy is my most self-sacrificing child," Mrs. Pepperel added complacently. One of the younger daughters laughed.

"Cousin Martha says she's going to leave Lyddy her seed pearls!"

"Priscilla—!" her mother rebuked her.

"Well, mother, they *are* beauties."

"I should say they were," Mrs. Pepperel bridled. "The old Wrigglesworth seed pearls—simply priceless. Martha's been offered anything for them! All I can say is, if my child gets them, she's deserved it."

Warbeck reflected. "Were they the funny old ornaments that everybody laughed at when Martha wore them at Grandma Warbeck's famous ball?"

His sister wrinkled her brows. "That wonderful ball of Grandma's? Did Martha wear them there, I wonder—all those centuries ago? I suppose then that nobody appreciated them," she murmured.

Warbeck felt as if he were in a dream in which everything happens upside down. He was listening to his sister's familiar kind of family anecdote, told in familiar words and in a familiar setting; but the Family Tyrant, once named with mingled awe and pride, was no longer the all-powerful Grandma Warbeck of his childhood, but her effaced imperceptible victim, Martha Little. Warbeck listened sympathetically, yet he felt an underlying constraint. His sister obviously thought he lacked interest in the Frostingham celebrations, and even her husband, whose mental processes were so slow and subterranean that they never altered his motionless countenance, was heard to mutter: "Well, I don't suppose many families can produce a brace of centenarians in one year."

"A brace—?" Warbeck laughed, while the nieces giggled, and their mother looked suddenly grave.

"You know, Grayson, I've never approved of the Perches forcing themselves in." She turned to Warbeck. "You've been away so long that you won't understand; but I do think it shows a lack of delicacy in the Perches."

"Why, what have they done?" Warbeck asked, while the nieces' giggles grew uncontrollable.

"Dragged an old Perch great-uncle out of goodness knows where, on the pretext that *he's* a hundred too. Of course we never heard a word of it till your aunts and I decided to do something appropriate about Martha Little. And how do we know he *is* a hundred?"

"Sara!" her husband interjected.

"Well, I think we ought to have asked for an affidavit before a notary. Crowding in at the eleventh hour! Why, Syngleton Perch doesn't even live in Massachusetts. Why don't they have *their* centenary in Rhode Island? Because they know nobody'd go to it—that's why!"

"Sara, the excitement's been too much for you," said Mr. Pepperel judicially.

"Well, I believe it will be, if this sort of thing goes on. Girls, are you sure there are programs enough? Come—we'd better go up to the drawing room and go over the list again." She turned affectionately to her brother. "It'll make all the difference to Martha, your being here. She was so excited when she heard you were coming. You've got to sit on the platform next to her—or next but one. Of course she must be between the Senator and the Bishop. Syngleton Perch wanted to crowd into the third place; but it's yours, Martha says; and of course when Martha says a thing, that settles it!"

"Medes and Persians," muttered Mr. Pepperel, with a wink which did not displace his features; but his wife interposed: "Grayson, you know I hate your saying disrespectful things about Martha!"

Warbeck went to bed full of plans for the next day: old friends to be looked up, the museums to be seen, and a tramp out on the Mill Dam, down the throat of a rousing Boston east wind. But these invigorating plans were shattered by an early message from Frostingham. Cousin Martha Little expected Warbeck to come and see her; he was to lunch early and be at Frostingham at two sharp. And he must not fail to be punctual, for before her afternoon nap Cousin Martha was to have a last fitting of her dress for the ceremony.

"You'd think it was her wedding dress!" Warbeck ventured jocosely; but Mrs. Pepperel received the remark without a smile. "Martha is *very* wonderful," she murmured; and her brother acquiesced: "She must be."

At two sharp his car drew up before the little old Grayson house. On the way out to Frostingham the morning papers had shown him photographs of its pilastered front, and a small figure leaning on a stick between the elaborate door lights. "Two Relics of an Historic Past," the headline ran.

Warbeck, guided by the radiant Lyddy, was led into a small square parlor furnished with the traditional Copleys and mahogany. He perceived that old Grayson's dingy little house had been an unsuspected treasury of family relics; and enthroned among them sat the supreme relic, the Crown Jewel of the clan.

"You don't recognize your Cousin Martha!" shrilled a small reedy voice, and a mummied hand shot out of its lace ruffles with a slight upward tilt which Warbeck took as hint to salute it. The hand tasted like an old brown glove that had been kept in a sandalwood box.

"Of course I know you, Cousin Martha. You're not changed the least little bit!"

She lifted from her ruffles a small mottled face like a fruit just changing into a seed pod. Her expression was obviously resentful. "Not changed? Then you haven't noticed the new way I do my hair?"

The challenge disconcerted Warbeck. "Well, you know, it's a long time since we met—going on for thirty years," he bantered.

"Thirty years?" She wrinkled her brows. "When I was as young as that I suppose I still wore a pompadour!"

When she was as young—as seventy! Warbeck felt like a gawky schoolboy. He was at a loss what to say next; but the radiant Lyddy gave him his clue. "Cousin Martha was so delighted when she heard you were coming all the way from Peru on purpose for her birthday." Her eyes met his with such a look of liquid candor that he saw she believed in the legend herself.

"Well, I don't suppose many of the family have come from farther off than I have," he boasted hypocritically.

Miss Little tilted up her chin again. "Did you fly?" she snapped; and without waiting for his answer: "I'm going to fly this summer. I wanted to go up before my birthday; it would have looked well in the papers. But the weather's been too unsettled."

It would have looked well in the papers! Warbeck listened to her, stupefied. Was it the old Martha Little speaking? There was something changed in Boston, after all. But she began to glance nervously toward the door. "Lyddy, I think I heard the bell."

"I'll go and see, Cousin Martha."

Miss Little sank back into her cushions with a satisfied smile. "These reporters—!"

"Ah—you think it's an interview?"

She pursed up her unsteady slit of a mouth. "As if I hadn't told them everything already! It's all coming out in the papers tomorrow. Haven't touched wine or black coffee for forty years. . . . Light massage every morning; very light supper at six. . . . I cleaned out the canary's cage myself everyday till last December. . . . Oh, and I *love* my Sunday sermon on the wireless. . . . But they won't leave a poor old woman in peace. 'Miss

Little, won't you give us your views on President Coolidge—or on com-
panionate marriage?' I suppose this one wants to force himself in for the
rehearsal."

"The rehearsal?"

She pursed up her mouth again. "Sara Pepperel didn't tell you? Such
featherheads, all those Pepperels! Even Lyddy—though she's a good
child. . . . I'm to try on my dress at three; and after that, just a little
informal preparation for the ceremony. The Frostingham Selectmen are to
present me with a cane . . . a gold-headed cane with an inscription . . .
Lyddy!" Her thread of a voice rose in a sudden angry pipe.

Lyddy thrust in a flushed and anxious face. "Oh, Cousin Martha—"

"Well, *is* it a reporter? What paper? Tell him, if he'll promise to sit
perfectly quiet. . . ."

"It's not a reporter, Cousin Martha. It's—it's Cousin Syngleton Perch.
He says he wants to pay you his respects: and he thinks he ought to take
part in the rehearsal. Now please don't excite yourself, Cousin Martha!"

"Excite myself, child? Syngleton Perch can't steal my birthday, can he?
If he chooses to assist at it—after all, the Perches are our own people; his
mother was a Wrigglesworth." Miss Little drew herself up by the arms of
her chair. "Show your cousin Syngleton in, my dear."

On the threshold a middle-aged motherly voice said, rather loudly: "This
way, Uncle Syngleton. You won't take my arm? Well, then put your stick
there; so—this way; careful. . . ." and there tottered in, projected forward by a
series of jaunty jerks, and the arm of his unseen guide, a small old gentleman
in a short pea jacket, with a round withered head buried in layers of woolen
scarf, and eyes hidden behind a huge pair of black spectacles.

"Where's my old friend Martha Little? Now, then, Marty, don't you try and
hide youself away from young Syngleton. Ah, there she is! I see her!" Cousin
Syngleton rattled out in a succession of parrot-like ejaculations, as his elderly
Antigone and the young Lyddy steered him cautiously toward Miss Little's
throne.

From it she critically observed the approach of the rival centenarian; and as
he reached her side, and stretched out his smartly-gloved hand, she dropped
hers into it with a faint laugh. "Well, you really *are* a hundred, Syngleton
Perch; there's no doubt about that," she said in her high chirp. "And I wonder
whether you haven't postponed your anniversary a year or two?" she added
with a caustic touch, and a tilt of her chin toward Warbeck.

* III *

Transporting centenarians from one floor to another was no doubt a delicate
business, for the vigilant Lyddy had staged the trying-on of the ceremonial

dress in the dining room, where the rehearsal was also to take place. Miss Little withdrew, and Cousin Syngleton Perch's watchful relative, having installed him in an armchair facing Warbeck's as carefully as if she had been balancing a basket of eggs on a picket fence, slipped off with an apologetic smile to assist at the trying-on. "I know you'll take care of him, Cousin Henly," she murmured in a last appeal; and added, bending to Warbeck's ear: "Please remember he's a little deaf; and don't let him get too excited talking about his love affairs."

Uncle Syngleton, wedged in tightly with cushions, and sustained by a footstool, peered doubtfully at Warbeck as the latter held out his cigarette case. "Tobacco? Well . . . look here, young man, what paper do you represent?" he asked, his knotty old hand yearningly poised above the coveted cigarette.

Warbeek explained in a loud voice that he was not a journalist, but a member of the family; but Mr. Perch shook his head incredulously. "That's what they all say; worming themselves in everywhere. Plain truth is, I never saw you before, nor you me. But see here; we may have to wait an hour while that young charmer gets into her party togs, and I don't know's I can hold out that long without a puff of tobacco." He shot a wrinkled smile at Warbeck. "Time was when I'd'a been in there myself, assisting at the dish-abille." (He pronounced the first syllable *dish*.) A look of caution replaced his confidential smirk. "Well, young man, I suppose what you want is my receipt for keeping hale and hearty up to the century line. But there's nothing new about it: it's just the golden rule of good behavior that our mothers taught us in the nursery. No wine, no tobacco, no wom— Well," he broke off, with a yearning smile at the cigarette case, "I don't mind if I do. Got a light, young gentleman? Though if I *was* to assist at an undressing, I don't say," he added meditatively, "that it'd be Martha Little's I'd choose. I remember her when she warn't over thirty—too much like a hygienic cigarette even then, for my fancy. Denicotinized, I call her. Well, I like the unexpurgated style better." He held out his twitching hand to Warbeck's lighter, and inserted a cigarette between his purplish lips. "Some punch in that! Only don't you give me away, will you? Not in the papers, I mean. Remember old Syngleton Perch's slogan: 'Live straight and you'll live long. No wine, no tobacco, no wom—' " Again he broke off, and thumped his crumpled fist excitedly against the chair arm. "Damn it, sire, I never *can* finish that lie, somehow! Old Syngleton a vestal? Not if I know anything about him!"

The door opened, and Lyddy and the motherly Antigone showed their flushed faces. "Now then, Uncle Syngleton—all ready!"

They were too much engrossed to notice Warbeck, but he saw that his help was welcome, for extricating Syngleton from his armchair was like hooking up a broken cork which, at each prod, slips down farther into the neck of the bottle. Once on his legs he goose-stepped valiantly forward; but until he had been balanced on them he tended to fold up at the very moment when his supporters thought they could prudently release him.

The transit accomplished, Warbeck found himself in a room from which the dining table had been removed to make way for an improvised platform supporting a row of armchairs. In the central armchair Martha Little, small and hieratic, sat enthroned. About her billowed the rich folds of a silvery shot-silk, and the Wrigglesworth seed pearls hung over her hollow chest and depended from her dusky withered ears. A row of people sat facing her, at the opposite end of the room, and Warbeck noticed that two or three already had their pens in leash above open notebooks. A strange young woman of fashionable silhouette was stooping over the shot-silk draperies and ruffling them with a professional touch. "Isn't she too old-world for anything? Just the Martha Washington note: isn't it lovely, with her pearls? Please note: *The Wrigglesworth pearls,* Miss Lusky," she recommended to a zealous reportress with suspended pen.

"Now, whatever you do, don't shake me!" snapped the shot-silk divinity, as Syngleton and his supporters neared the platform. ("It's the powder in her hair she's nervous about," Lyddy whispered to Warbeck.)

The business of raising the co-divinity to her side was at once ticklish and laborious, for Mr. Perch resented feminine assistance in the presence of strange men, and Warbeck, even with the bungling support of one of the journalists, found it difficult to get his centenarian relative hoisted to the platform. Any attempt to lift him caused his legs to shoot upward, and to steady and direct this levitating tendency required an experience in which both assistants were lacking.

"*There!*" his household Antigone intervened, seizing one ankle while Lyddy clutched the other; and thus ballasted Syngleton Perch recovered his powers of self-direction and made for the armchair on Miss Little's right. At his approach she uttered a shrill cry and tried to raise herself from her seat.

"No, no! This is the Bishop's!" she protested, defending the chair with her mittened hand.

"Oh, my—there go all the folds of her skirt," wailed the dressmaker from the background.

Syngleton Perch stood on the platform and his bullet head grew purple. "Can't stand—got to sit down or keep going," he snapped.

Martha Little subsided majestically among her disordered folds. "Well— keep going!" she decreed.

"Oh, Cousin Martha," Lyddy murmured.

"Well, what of Cousin Martha? It's *my* rehearsal, isn't it?" the lady retorted, like a child whimpering for a toy.

"Cousin Martha—Cousin *Martha!*" Lyddy whispered, while Syngleton, with flickering legs, protested: "Don't I belong anywhere in this show?" and Warbeck caught Lyddy's warning murmur: "Don't forget, Cousin Martha, *his mother was a Wrigglesworth!*"

As if by magic Miss Little's exasperation gave way to a resigned grimace. "*He* says so," she muttered sulkily; but the appeal to the great ancestral name had not been in vain, and she suffered her rival to be established in the armchair just beyond the Bishop's, while his guide, hovering over his shoulder, announced to the journalists: "Mr. Syngleton Perch, of South Perch, Rhode Island, whose hundredth birthday will be celebrated with that of his cousin Miss Little tomorrow—"

"H'm—*tomorrow!*" Miss Little suddenly exclaimed, again attempting to rise from her throne; while Syngleton's staccato began to unroll the automatic phrase: "I suppose you young men all want to know my receipt for keeping hale and hearty up to the century line. Well, there's nothing new about it: it's just the golden rule . . . the . . . what the devil's *that?*" he broke off with a jerk of his chin toward the door.

Warbeck saw that an object had been handed into the room by a maid, and was being passed from hand to hand up to the platform. "Oh," Lyddy exclaimed breathlessly, "of course! It's the ebony cane! The Selectmen have sent it up for Cousin Martha to try today, so that she'll be sure it was just right for her to lean on when she walks out of the Town Hall tomorrow after the ceremony. Look what a beauty it is—you'll let these gentlemen look at it, won't you, Cousin Martha?"

"If they can look at me I suppose they can look at my cane," said Miss Little imperially, while the commemorative stick was passed about the room amid admiring exclamations, and attempts to decipher its laudatory inscription. " 'Offered to Frostingham's most beloved and distinguished citizen, Martha Wrigglesworth Little, in commemoration of the hundredth anniversary of her birth, by her friends the Mayor and Selectmen' . . . very suitable, very interesting," an elderly cousin read aloud with proper emotion, while Mr. Perch was heard to inquire anxiously: "Isn't there anything about me on that cane?" and his companion reassured him: "Of course South Perch means to offer you one of your very own when we go home."

Finally the coveted object was restored to Miss Little, who, straightening herself with a supreme effort, sat resting both hands on the gold crutch while Lyddy hailed the approach of imaginary dignitaries with the successive announcements: "The Bishop—the Mayor. . . . But no, they'd better be seated before you arrive, hadn't they, Cousin Martha? And exactly *when* is the cane to be presented? Oh, well, we'll settle all the details tomorrow . . . the main thing now is the stepping down from the platform and walking out of the Hall, isn't it? Miss Lusky, careful, please. . . . Gentlemen, will you all move your chairs back? . . . Uncle Henly," she appealed to Warbeck, "perhaps you'll be kind enough to act as Mayor, and give your arm to Cousin Martha? Ready, Cousin Martha? So—"

But as she was about to raise Miss Little from her seat, and hook her securely onto Warbeck's arm, a cry between a sob and an expletive burst from the purple lips of Cousin Syngleton.

"Why can't I be the Mayor—ain't I got any rights in this damned show?" he burst out passionately, his legs jerking upward as he attempted to raise himself on his elbows.

His Antigone intervened with a reproachful murmur. "Why, Uncle Syngleton, what in the world are you thinking of? You can't act as anybody but *yourself* tomorrow! But I'm going to be the Bishop now, and give you my arm—there, like this. . . ."

Miss Little, who had just gained her feet, pressed heavily on Warbeck's arm in her effort to jerk around toward Mr. Perch. "Oh, he's going to take the Bishop's arm, is he? Well, the Bishop had better look out, or he'll take his seat too," she chuckled ironically.

Cousin Syngleton turned a deeper purple. "Oh, I'll take his seat too, will I? Well, why not? Isn't this my anniversary as much as it is yours, Martha Little? I suppose you think I'd better follow after you and carry your train, eh?"

Miss Little drew herself up to a height that seemed to overshadow everyone around her. Warbeck felt her shaking on his arm like a withered leaf, but her lips were dangerously merry.

"No; I think you'd better push the Mayor out of the way and give *me* your arm, Syngleton Perch," she flung back gaily.

"Well, why not?" Mr. Perch rejoined, his innocent smile meeting her perfidious one; and some one among the lookers-on was imprudent enough to exclaim: "Oh, wouldn't that be too lovely!"

"Oh, Uncle Syngleton," Lyddy appealed to him—"do you really suppose you *could?*"

"Could—could—could, young woman? Who says I can't, I'd like to know?" Uncle Syngleton sputtered, his arms and legs gyrating vehemently toward Miss Little, who now stood quite still on Warbeck's arm, the cane sustaining her, and her fixed smile seeming to invite her rival's approach.

"An interesting experiment," Warbeck heard someone mutter in the background, and Miss Little's head turned in the direction of the speaker. "This is only a rehearsal," she declared incisively.

She remained motionless and untrembling while the Antigone and Lyddy guided Cousin Syngleton precariously toward her; but just as Warbeck thought she was about to detach her hand from his arm, and transfer her frail weight to Mr. Perch's, she made an unexpected movement. Its immediate result—Warbeck could never say how—was to shoot forward the famous ebony stick which her abrupt gesture (was it unconsciously?) drove directly into the path of Uncle Syngleton. In another instant—but one instant too late for rescue—Warbeck saw the stick entangled in the old man's wavering feet, and beheld him shoot wildly upward, and then fall over with a crash. Everyone in the room gathered about with agitated questions and exclamations, struggling to lift him to his feet; only Miss Little continued to stand apart, her countenance unmoved, her aged fingers still imbedded in Warbeck's arm.

The old man, prone and purple, was being cautiously lifted down from tbe platform while the bewildered spectators parted, awe-struck, to make way for his frightened bearers. Warbeck followed their movements with alarm; then he turned anxiously toward the frail figure on his arm. How would she bear the shock, he asked himself, with a leap of the imagination which seemed to lay her also prone at his feet. But she stood upright, unmoved, and Warbeck met her resolute eyes with a start, and saw in their depths a century of slow revenge.

"Oh, Cousin Martha—Cousin *Martha,*" he breathed, in a whisper of mingled terror and admiration. . . .

"Well, what? I told you it was only a rehearsal," said Martha Little, with her ancient smile.

ALL SOULS'

❧

QUEER AND INEXPLICABLE as the business was, on the surface it appeared fairly simple—at the time, at least; but with the passing of years, and owing to there not having been a single witness of what happened except Sara Clayburn herself, the stories about it have become so exaggerated, and often so ridiculously inaccurate, that it seems necessary that someone connected with the affair, though not actually present—I repeat that when it happened my cousin was (or thought she was) quite alone in her house—should record the few facts actually known.

In those days I was often at Whitegates (as the place had always been called)—I was there, in fact, not long before, and almost immediately after, the strange happenings of those thirty-six hours. Jim Clayburn and his widow were both my cousins, and because of that, and of my intimacy with them, both families think I am more likely than anybody else to be able to get at the facts, as far as they can be called facts, and as anybody can get at them. So I have written down, as clearly as I could, the gist of the various talks I had with cousin Sara, when she could be got to talk—it wasn't often—about what occurred during that mysterious weekend.

I read the other day in a book by a fashionable essayist that ghosts went out when electric light came in. What nonsense! The writer, though he is fond of dabbling, in a literary way, in the supernatural, hasn't even reached the threshold of his subject. As between turreted castles patrolled by headless victims with clanking chains, and the comfortable surburban house with a refrigerator and central heating where you feel, as soon as you're in it, *that there's something wrong*, give me the latter for sending a

366

chill down the spine! And, by the way, haven't you noticed that it's generally not the high-strung and imaginative who see ghosts, but the calm matter-of-fact people who don't believe in them, and are sure they wouldn't mind if they did see one? Well, that was the case with Sara Clayburn and her house. The house, in spite of its age—it was built, I believe, about 1780—was open, airy, high-ceilinged, with electricity, central heating and all the modern appliances: and its mistress was—well, very much like her house. And, anyhow, this isn't exactly a ghost story and I've dragged in the analogy only as a way of showing you what kind of woman my cousin was, and how unlikely it would have seemed that what happened at Whitegates should have happened just there—or to her.

When Jim Clayburn died the family all thought that, as the couple had no children, his widow would give up Whitegates and move either to New York or Boston—for being of good Colonial stock, with many relatives and friends, she would have found a place ready for her in either. But Sally Clayburn seldom did what other people expected, and in this case she did exactly the contrary; she stayed at Whitegates.

"What, turn my back on the old house—tear up all the family roots, and go and hang myself up in a bird-cage flat in one of those new skyscrapers in Lexington Avenue, with a bunch of chickweed and a cuttle-fish to replace my good Connecticut mutton? No, thank you. Here I belong, and here I stay till my executors hand the place over to Jim's next-of-kin—that stupid fat Presley boy. . . . Well, don't let's talk about him. But I tell you what—I'll keep him out of here as long as I can." And she did—for being still in the early fifties when her husband died, and a muscular, rsolute figure of a woman, she was more than a match for the fat Presley boy, and attended his funeral a few years ago, in correct mourning, with a faint smile under her veil.

Whitegates was a pleasant hospitable-looking house, on a height over-looking the stately windings of the Connecticut River; but it was five or six miles from Norrington, the nearest town, and its situation would certainly have seemed remote and lonely to modern servants. Luckily, however, Sara Clayburn had inherited from her mother-in-law two or three old stand-bys who seemed as much a part of the family tradition as the roof they lived under; and I never heard of her having any trouble in her domestic arrangements.

The house, in Colonial days, had been foursquare, with four spacious rooms on the ground floor, an oak-floored hall dividing them, the usual kitchen extension at the back, and a good attic under the roof. But Jim's grandparents, when interest in the "Colonial" began to revive, in the early eighties, had added two wings, at right angles to the south front, so that the old "circle" before the front door became a grassy court, enclosed on three sides, with a big elm in the middle. Thus the house was turned into a roomy dwelling, in which the last three generations of Clayburns had exercised a large hospitality; but the architect had respected the character of the old house, and the enlargement made it more comfortable without lessening its simplicity. There was a lot of land about it, and Jim Clayburn, like his fathers before him, farmed it, not without profit, and played a considerable and respected part in state politics. The Clayburns were always spoken of as a "good influence" in the county, and the townspeople were glad when they learned that Sara did not mean to desert the place— "though it must be lonesome, winters, living all alone up there atop of that hill"—they remarked as the days shortened, and the first snow began to pile up under the quadruple row of elms along the common.

Well, if I've given you a sufficiently clear idea of Whitegates and the Clayburns—who shared with their old house a sort of reassuring orderliness and dignity—I'll efface myself, and tell the tale, not in my cousin's words, for they were too confused and fragmentary, but as I built it up gradually out of her half-avowals and nervous reticences. If the thing happened at all—and I must leave you to judge of that—I think it must have happened in this way. . . .

* I *

The morning had been bitter, with a driving sleet—though it was only the last day of October—but after lunch a watery sun showed for a while through banked-up woolly clouds, and tempted Sara Clayburn out. She was an energetic walker, and given, at that season, to tramping three or four miles along the valley road, and coming back by way of Shaker's wood. She had made her usual round, and was following the main drive to the house when she overtook a plainly-dressed woman walking in the same direction. If the scene had not been so lonely—the way to Whitegates at the end of an autumn day was not a frequented one—Mrs. Clayburn might not have paid any attention to the woman, for she was in no way noticeable; but when she caught up with the intruder my cousin was surprised to find that she was a stranger—for the mistress of Whitegates prided herself on knowing, at least by sight, most of her country neighbors. It was almost dark, and the woman's face was hardly visible, but Mrs. Clayburn told me she recalled her as middle-aged, plain and rather pale.

Mrs. Clayburn greeted her, and then added: "You're going to the house?"

"Yes, ma'am," the woman answered, in a voice that the Connecticut Valley in old days would have called "foreign," but that would have been unnoticed by ears used to the modern multiplicity of tongues. "No, I couldn't say where she came from," Sara always said. "What struck me as queer was that I didn't know her."

She asked the woman, politely, what she wanted, and the woman answered: "Only to see one of the girls." The answer was natural enough, and Mrs. Clayburn nodded and turned off from the drive to the lower part of the gardens, so that she saw no more of the visitor then or afterward. And, in fact, a half hour later something happened which put the stranger entirely out of her mind. The brisk and light-footed Mrs. Clayburn, as she approached the house, slipped on a frozen puddle, turned her ankle and lay suddenly helpless.

Price, the butler, and Agnes, the dour old Scottish maid whom Sara had inherited from her mother-in-law, of course knew exactly what to do. In no time they had their mistress stretched out on a lounge, and Dr. Selgrove had been called up from Norrington. When he arrived, he ordered Mrs. Clayburn to bed, did the necessary examining and bandaging, and shook his head over her ankle, which he feared was fractured. He thought, however, that if she would swear not to get up, or even shift the position of her leg, he could spare her the discomfort of putting it in plaster. Mrs. Clayburn agreed, the more promptly as the doctor warned her that any rash movement would prolong her immobility. Her quick imperious nature made the prospect trying, and she was annoyed with herself for having been so clumsy. But the mischief was done, and she immediately thought what an opportunity she would have for going over her accounts and catching up with her correspondence. So she settled down resignedly in her bed.

"And you won't miss much, you know, if you have to stay there a few days. It's beginning to snow, and it looks as if we were in for a good spell of it," the doctor remarked, glancing through the window as he gathered up his implements. "Well, we don't often get snow here as early as this; but winter's got to begin sometime," he concluded philosophically. At the door he stopped to add: "You don't want me to send up a nurse from Norrington? Not to nurse you, you know; there's nothing much to do till I see you again. But this is a pretty lonely place when the snow begins, and I thought maybe—"

Sara Clayburn laughed. "Lonely? With my old servants? You forget how many winters I've spent here alone with them. Two of them were with me in my mother-in-law's time."

"That's so," Dr. Selgrove agreed. "You're a good deal luckier than most people, that way. Well, let me see; this is Saturday. We'll have to let the inflammation go down before we can X-ray you. Monday morning, first thing, I'll be here with the X-ray man. If you want me sooner, call me up." And he was gone.

* II *

The foot at first, had not been very painful; but toward the small hours Mrs. Clayburn began to suffer. She was a bad patient, like most healthy and active people. Not being used to pain she did not know how to bear it, and the hours of wakefulness and immobility seemed endless. Agnes, before leaving her, had made everything as comfortable as possible. She had put a jug of lemonade within reach, and had even (Mrs. Clayburn thought it odd afterward) insisted on bringing in a tray with sandwiches and a thermos of tea. "In case you're hungry in the night, madam."

"Thank you; but I'm never hungry in the night. And I certainly shan't be tonight—only thirsty. I think I'm feverish."

"Well, there's the lemonade, madam."

"That will do. Take the other things away, please." (Sara had always hated the sight of unwanted food "messing about" in her room.)

"Very well, madam. Only you might—"

"Please take it away," Mrs. Clayburn repeated irritably.

"Very good, madam." But as Agnes went out, her mistress heard her set the tray down softly on a table behind the screen which shut off the door.

"Obstinate old goose!" she thought, rather touched by the old woman's insistence.

Sleep, once it had gone, would not return, and the long black hours moved more and more slowly. How late the dawn came in November! "If only I could move my leg," she grumbled.

She lay still and strained her ears for the first steps of the servants. Whitegates was an early house, its mistress setting the example; it would surely not be long now before one of the women came. She was tempted to ring for Agnes, but refrained. The woman had been up late, and this was Sunday morning, when the household was always allowed a little extra time. Mrs. Clayburn reflected restlessly: "I was a fool not to let her leave the tea beside the bed, as she wanted to. I wonder if I could get up and get it?" But she remembered the doctor's warning, and dared not move. Anything rather than risk prolonging her imprisonment. . . .

Ah, there was the stable clock striking. How loud it sounded in the snowy stillness! One—two—three—four—five. . . .

What? Only five? Three hours and a quarter more before she could hope to hear the door handle turned. . . . After a while she dozed off again, uncomfortably.

Another sound aroused her. Again the stable clock. She listened. But the room was still in deep darkness, and only six strokes fell. . . . She thought of reciting something to put her to sleep; but she seldom read poetry, and being naturally a good sleeper, she could not remember any of the usual devices against insomnia. The whole of her leg felt like lead now. The bandages had grown terribly tight—her ankle must have swollen. . . . She lay staring at the dark windows, watching for the first glimmer of dawn. At last she saw a pale filter of daylight through the shutters. One by one the objects between the bed and the window recovered first their outline, then their bulk, and seemed to be stealthily regrouping themselves, after goodness knows what secret displacements during the night. Who that has lived in an old house could possibly believe that the furniture in it stays still all night? Mrs. Clayburn almost fancied she saw one little slender-legged table slipping hastily back into its place.

"It knows Agnes is coming, and it's afraid," she thought whimsically. Her bad night must have made her imaginative for such nonsense as that about the furniture had never occurred to her before. . . .

At length, after hours more, as it seemed, the stable clock struck eight. Only another quarter of an hour. She watched the hand moving slowly across the face of the little clock beside her bed . . . ten minutes . . . five . . . only five! Agnes was as punctual as destiny . . . in two minutes now she would come. The two minutes passed, and she did not come. Poor Agnes—she had looked pale and tired the night before. She had overslept herself, no doubt—or perhaps she felt ill, and would send the housemaid to replace her. Mrs. Clayburn waited.

She waited half an hour; then she reached up to the bell at the head of the bed. Poor old Agnes—her mistress felt guilty about waking her. But Agnes did not appear—and after a considerable interval Mrs. Clayburn, now with a certain impatience, rang again. She rang once; twice; three times—but still no one came.

Once more she waited; then she said to herself: "There must be something wrong with the electricity." Well—she could find out by switching on the bed lamp at her elbow (how admirably the room was equipped with every practical appliance!). She switched it on—but no light came. Electric current cut off; and it was Sunday, and nothing could be done about it till the next morning. Unless it turned out to be just a burnt-out fuse, which Price could remedy. Well, in a moment now some one would surely come to her door.

It was nine o'clock before she admitted to herself that something uncommonly strange must have happened in the house. She began to feel a nervous apprehension; but she was not the woman to encourage it. If only she had had the telephone put in her room, instead of out on the landing! She measured mentally the distance to be traveled, remembered Dr. Selgrove's admonition, and wondered if her broken ankle would carry her there. She dreaded the prospect of being put in plaster, but she had to get to the telephone, whatever happened.

She wrapped herself in her dressing gown, found a walking stick, and, resting heavily on it, dragged herself to the door. In her bedroom the careful Agnes had closed and fastened the shutters, so that it was not much lighter there than at dawn; but outside in the corridor the cold whiteness of the snowy morning seemed almost reassuring. Mysterious things—dreadful things—were associated with darkness; and here was the wholesome prosaic daylight come again to banish them. Mrs. Clayburn looked about her and listened. Silence. A deep nocturnal silence in that day-lit house, in which five people were presumably coming and going about their work. It was certainly strange. . . . She looked out of the window, hoping to see someone crossing the court or coming along the drive. But no one was in sight, and the snow seemed to have the place to itself: a quiet steady snow. It was still falling, with a business-like regularity, muffling the outer world in layers on layers of thick white velvet, and intensifying the silence within. A noiseless world—were people so sure that absence of noise was what they wanted? Let them first try a lonely country house in a November snowstorm!

She dragged herself along the passage to the telephone. When she unhooked the receiver she noticed that her hand trembled.

She rang up the pantry—no answer. She rang again. Silence—more silence! It seemed to be piling itself up like the snow on the roof and in the gutters. Silence. How many people that she knew had any idea what silence was—and how loud it sounded when you really listened to it?

Again she waited: then she rang up "Central." No answer. She tried three times. After that she tried the pantry again. . . . The telephone was cut off, then; like the electric current. Who was at work downstairs, isolating her thus from the world? Her heart began to hammer. Luckily there was a chair near the telephone, and she sat down to recover her strength—or was it her courage?

Agnes and the housemaid slept in the nearest wing. She would certainly get as far as that when she had pulled herself together. Had she the courage—? Yes, of course she had. She had always been regarded as a plucky woman; and had so regarded herself. But this silence—

It occurred to her that by looking from the window of a neighboring bathroom she could see the kitchen chimney. There ought to be smoke coming from it at that hour; and if there were she thought she would be less afraid to go on. She got as far as the bathroom and looking through the window saw that no smoke came from the chimney. Her sense of loneliness grew more acute. Whatever had happened belowstairs must have happened before the morning's work had begun. The cook had not had time to light the fire, the other servants had not yet begun their round. She sank down on the nearest chair, struggling against her fears. What next would she discover if she carried on her investigations?

The pain in her ankle made progress difficult; but she was aware of it now only as an obstacle to haste. No matter what it cost her in physical suffering, she must find out what was happening belowstairs—or had happened. But first she would go to the maid's room. And if that were empty—well, somehow she would have to get herself downstairs.

She limped along the passage, and on the way steadied herself by resting her hand on a radiator. It was stone-cold. Yet in that well-ordered house in winter the central heating, though damped down at night, was never allowed to go out, and by eight in the morning a mellow warmth pervaded the rooms. The icy chill of the pipes startled her. It was the chauffeur who looked after the heating—so he too was involved in the mystery, whatever it was, as well as the house servants. But this only deepened the problem.

* III *

At Agnes's door Mrs. Clayburn paused and knocked. She expected no answer, and there was none. She opened the door and went in. The room was dark and very cold. She went to the window and flung back the shutters; then she looked slowly around, vaguely apprehensive of what she might see. The room was empty but what frightened her was not so much its emptiness as its air of scrupulous and undisturbed order. There was no sign of anyone having lately dressed in it—or undressed the night before. And the bed had not been slept in.

Mrs. Clayburn leaned against the wall for a moment; then she crossed the floor and opened the cupboard. That was where Agnes kept her dresses; and the dresses were there, neatly hanging in a row. On the shelf above were Agnes's few and unfashionable hats, rearrangements of her mistress's old ones. Mrs. Clayburn, who knew them all, looked at the shelf, and saw that one was missing. And so was also the warm winter coat she had given to Agnes the previous winter.

The woman was out, then; had gone out, no doubt, the night before, since the bed was unslept in, the dressing and washing appliances untouched. Agnes, who never set foot out of the house after dark, who despised the movies as much as she did the wireless, and could never be persuaded that a little innocent amusement was a necessary element in life, had deserted the house on a snowy winter night, while her mistress lay upstairs, suffering and helpless! Why had she gone, and where had she gone? When she was undressing Mrs. Clayburn the night before, taking her orders, trying to make her more comfortable, was she already planning this mysterious nocturnal escape? Or had something—the mysterious and dreadful Something for the clue of which Mrs. Clayburn was still groping—occurred later in the evening, sending the maid downstairs and out of doors into the bitter night? Perhaps one of the men at the garage—where the chauffeur and gardener lived—had been suddenly taken ill, and someone had run up to the house for Agnes. Yes—that must be the explanation. . . . Yet how much it left unexplained.

Next to Agnes's room was the linen room; beyond that was the housemaid's door. Mrs. Clayburn went to it and knocked. "Mary!" No one answered, and she went in. The room was in the same immaculate order as her maid's, and here too the bed was unslept in, and there were no signs of dressing or undressing. The two women had no doubt gone out together—gone where?

More and more the cold unanswering silence of the house weighed down on Mrs. Clayburn. She had never thought of it as a big house, but now, in this snowy winter light, it seemed immense, and full of ominous corners around which one dared not look.

Beyond the housemaid's room were the back stairs. It was the nearest way down, and every step that Mrs. Clayburn took was increasingly painful; but she decided to walk slowly back, the whole length of the passage, and go down by the front stairs. She did not know why she did this; but she felt that at the moment she was past reasoning, and had better obey her instinct.

More than once she had explored the ground floor alone in the small hours, in search of unwonted midnight noises; but now it was not the idea of noises that frightened her, but that inexorable and hostile silence, the sense that the house had retained in full daylight its nocturnal mystery, and was watching her as she was watching it; that in entering those empty orderly rooms she might be disturbing some unseen confabulation on which beings of flesh-and-blood had better not intrude.

The broad oak stairs were beautifully polished, and so slippery that she had to cling to the rail and let herself down tread by tread. And as she descended, the silence descended with her—heavier, denser, more absolute. She seemed to feel its steps just behind her, softly keeping time with hers. It had a quality she had never been aware of in any other silence, as though it were not merely an absence of sound, a thin barrier between the ear and the surging murmur of life just beyond, but an impenetrable substance made out of the world-wide cessation of all life and all movement.

Yes, that was what laid a chill on her: the feeling that there was no limit to this silence, no outer margin, nothing beyond it. By this time she had reached the foot of the stairs and was limping across the hall to the drawing room. Whatever she found there, she was sure, would be mute and lifeless; but what would it be? The bodies of her dead servants, mown down by some homicidal maniac? And what if it were her turn next—if he were waiting for her behind the heavy curtains of the room she was about to enter? Well, she must find out—she must face whatever lay in wait. Not impelled by bravery—the last drop of courage had oozed out of her—but because anything, anything was better than to remain shut up in that snowbound house without knowing whether she was alone in it or not, "I must find that out, I must find that out," she repeated to herself in a sort of meaningless sing-song.

The cold outer light flooded the drawing room. The shutters had not been closed, nor the curtains drawn. She looked about her. The room was empty, and every chair in its usual place. Her armchair was pushed up by the chimney, and the cold hearth was piled with the ashes of the fire at which she had warmed herself before starting on her ill-fated walk. Even her empty coffee cup stood on a table near the armchair. It was evident that the servants had not been in the room since she had left it the day before after luncheon. And suddenly the conviction entered into her that, as she found the drawing room, so she would find the rest of the house; cold, orderly—and empty. She would find nothing, she would find no one. She no longer felt any dread of ordinary human dangers lurking in those dumb spaces ahead of her. She knew she was utterly alone under her own roof. She sat down to rest her aching ankle, and looked slowly about her.

There were the other rooms to be visited, and she was determined to go through them all—but she knew in advance that they would give no answer to her question. She knew it, seemingly, from the quality of the silence which enveloped her. There was no break, no thinnest crack in it anywhere. It had the cold continuity of the snow which was still falling steadily outside.

She had no idea how long she waited before nerving herself to continue her inspection. She no longer felt the pain in her ankle, but was only conscious that she must not bear her weight on it, and therefore moved very slowly, supporting herself on each piece of furniture in her path. On the ground floor no shutter had been closed, no curtain drawn, and she progressed without difficulty from room to room: the library, her morning room, the dining room. In each of them, every piece of furniture was in its usual place. In the dining room, the table had been laid for her dinner of the previous evening, and the candelabra, with candles unlit, stood reflected in the dark mahogany. She was not the kind of woman to nibble a poached egg on a tray when she was alone, but always came down to the dining room, and had what she called a civilized meal.

The back premises remained to be visited. From the dining room she entered the pantry, and there too everything was in irreproachable order. She opened the door and looked down the back passage with its neat linoleum floor covering. The deep silence accompanied her; she still felt it moving watchfully at her side, as though she were its prisoner and it might throw itself upon her if she attempted to escape. She limped on toward the kitchen. That of course would be empty too, and immaculate. But she must see it.

She leaned a minute in the embrasure of a window in the passage. "It's like the 'Mary Celeste'—a 'Mary Celeste' on *terra firma*," she thought, recalling the unsolved sea mystery of her childhood. "No one ever knew what happened on board the 'Mary Celeste.' And perhaps no one will ever know what has happened here. Even I shan't know."

At the thought her latent fear seemed to take on a new quality. It was like an icy liquid running through every vein, and lying in a pool about her heart. She understood now that she had never before known what fear was, and that most of the people she had met had probably never known either. For this sensation was something quite different. . . .

It absorbed her so completely that she was not aware how long she remained leaning there. But suddenly a new impulse pushed her forward, and she walked on toward the scullery. She went there first because there was a service slide in the wall, through which she might peep into the kitchen without being seen; and some indefinable instinct told her that the kitchen held the clue to the mystery. She still felt strongly that whatever had happened in the house must have its source and center in the kitchen.

In the scullery, as she had expected, everything was clean and tidy. Whatever had happened, no one in the house appeared to have been taken by surprise; there was nowhere any sign of confusion or disorder. "It looks as if they'd known beforehand, and put everything straight," she thought. She glanced at the wall facing the door, and saw that the slide was open. And then, as she was approaching it, the silence was broken. A voice was speaking in the kitchen—a man's voice, low but emphatic, and which she had never heard before.

She stood still, cold with fear. But this fear was again a different one. Her previous terrors had been speculative, conjectural, a ghostly emanation of the surrounding silence. This was a plain everyday dread of evildoers. Oh, God, why had she not remembered her husband's revolver, which ever since his death had lain in a drawer in her room?

She turned to retreat across the smooth slippery floor but halfway her stick slipped from her, and crashed down on the tiles. The noise seemed to echo on and on through the emptiness, and she stood still, aghast. Now that she had betrayed her presence, flight was useless. Whoever was beyond the kitchen door would be upon her in a second. . . .

But to her astonishment the voice went on speaking. It was as though neither the speaker nor his listeners had heard her. The invisible stranger spoke so low that she could not make out what he was saying, but the tone was passionately earnest, almost threatening. The next moment she realized that he was speaking in a foreign language, a language unknown to her. Once more her terror was surmounted by the urgent desire to know what was going on, so close to her yet unseen. She crept to the slide, peered cautiously through into the kitchen, and saw that it was as orderly and empty as the other rooms. But in the middle of the carefully scoured table stood a portable wireless, and the voice she heard came out of it. . . .

She must have fainted then, she supposed; at any rate she felt so weak and dizzy that her memory of what next happened remained indistinct. But in the course of time she groped her way back to the pantry, and there found a bottle of spirits—brandy or whisky, she could not remember which. She found a glass, poured herself a stiff drink, and while it was flushing through her veins, managed, she never knew with how many shuddering delays, to drag herself through the deserted ground floor, up the stairs, and down the corridor to her own room. There, apparently, she fell across the threshold, again unconscious. . . .

When she came to, she remembered, her first care had been to lock herself in; then to recover her husband's revolver. It was not loaded, but she found some cartridges, and succeeded in loading it. Then she remembered that Agnes, on leaving her the evening before, had refused to carry away the tray with the tea and sandwiches, and she fell on them with a sudden hunger. She recalled also noticing that a flask of brandy had been put beside the thermos, and being vaguely surprised. Agnes's departure, then, had been deliberately planned, and she had known that her mistress, who never touched spirits, might have need of a stimulant before she returned. Mrs. Clayburn poured some of the brandy into her tea, and swallowed it greedily.

After that (she told me later) she remembered that she had managed to start a fire in her grate, and after warming herself, had got back into her bed, piling on it all the coverings she could find. The afternoon passed in a haze of pain, out of which there emerged now and then a dim shape of fear—the fear that she might lie there alone and untended till she died of cold, and of the terror of her solitude. For she was sure by this time that the house was empty—completely empty, from garret to cellar. She knew it was so, she could not tell why; but again she felt that it must be because of the peculiar quality of the silence—the silence which had dogged her steps wherever she went, and was now folded down on her like a pall. She was sure that the nearness of any other human being, however dumb and secret, would have made a faint crack in the texture of that silence, flawed it as a sheet of glass is flawed by a pebble thrown against it. . . .

* IV *

"Is that easier?" the doctor asked, lifting himself from bending over her ankle. He shook his head disapprovingly. "Looks to me as if you'd dis-obeyed orders—eh? Been moving about, haven't you? And I guess Dr. Selgrove told you to keep quiet till he saw you again, didn't he?"

The speaker was a stranger, whom Mrs. Clayburn knew only by name. Her own doctor had been called away that morning to the bedside of an old patient in Baltimore, and had asked this young man, who was beginning to be known at Norrington, to replace him. The newcomer was shy, and somewhat familiar, as the shy often are, and Mrs. Clayburn decided that she did not much like him. But before she could convey this by the tone of her reply (and she was past mistress of the shades of disapproval) she heard Agnes speaking—yes, Agnes, the same, the usual Agnes, standing behind the doctor, neat and stern-looking as ever. "Mrs. Clayburn must have got up and walked about in the night instead of ringing for me, as she'd ought to," Agnes intervened severely.

This was too much! In spite of the pain, which was now exquisite, Mrs. Clayburn laughed. "Ringing for you? How could I, with the electricity cut off?"

"The electricity cut off?" Agnes's surprise was masterly. "Why, when was it cut off?" She pressed her finger on the bell beside the bed, and the call tinkled through the quiet room. "I tried that bell before I left you last night, madam, because if there'd been anything wrong with it I'd have come and slept in the dressing room sooner than leave you here alone."

Mrs. Clayburn lay speechless, staring up at her. "Last night? But last night I was all alone in the house."

Agnes's firm features did not alter. She folded her hands resignedly across her trim apron. "Perhaps the pain's made you a little confused, madam." She looked at the doctor, who nodded.

"The pain in your foot must have been pretty bad," he said.

"It was," Mrs. Clayburn replied. "But it was nothing to the horror of being left alone in this empty house since the day before yesterday, with the heat and the electricity cut off, and the telephone not working."

The doctor was looking at her in evident wonder. Agnes's sallow face flushed slightly, but only as if in indignation at an unjust charge. "But, madam, I made up your fire with my own hands last night—and look, it's smoldering still. I was getting ready to start it again just now, when the doctor came."

"That's so. She was down on her knees before it," the doctor corroborated.

Again Mrs. Clayburn laughed. Ingeniously as the tissue of lies was being woven about her, she felt she could still break through it. "I made up the fire myself yesterday—there was no one else to do it," she said, addressing the doctor, but keeping her eyes on her maid. "I got up twice to put on more coal, because the house was like a sepulcher. The central heating must have been out since Saturday afternoon."

At this incredible statement Agnes's face expressed only a polite distress; but the new doctor was evidently embarrassed at being drawn into an unintelligible controversy with which he had no time to deal. He said he had brought the X-ray photographer with him, but that the ankle was too much swollen to be photographed at present. He asked Mrs. Clayburn to excuse his haste, as he had all Dr. Selgrove's patients to visit besides his own, and promised to come back that evening to decide whether she could be X-rayed then, and whether, as he evidently feared, the ankle would have to be put in plaster. Then, handing his prescriptions to Agnes, he departed.

Mrs. Clayburn spent a feverish and suffering day. She did not feel well enough to carry on the discussion with Agnes; she did not ask to see the other servants. She grew drowsy, and understood that her mind was confused with fever. Agnes and the housemaid waited on her as attentively as usual, and by the time the doctor returned in the evening her temperature had fallen; but she decided not to speak of what was on her mind until Dr. Selgrove reappeared. He was to be back the following evening; and the new doctor preferred to wait for him before deciding to put the ankle in plaster—though he feared this was now inevitable.

* V *

That afternoon Mrs. Clayburn had me summoned by telephone, and I arrived at Whitegates the following day. My cousin, who looked pale and nervous, merely pointed to her foot, which had been put in plaster, and thanked me for coming to keep her company. She explained that Dr. Selgrove had been taken suddenly ill in Baltimore, and would not be back for several days, but that the young man who replaced him seemed fairly competent. She made no allusion to the strange incidents I have set down, but I felt at once that she had received a shock which her accident, however painful, could not explain.

Finally, one evening, she told me the story of her strange weekend, as it had presented itself to her unusually clear and accurate mind, and as I have recorded it above. She did not tell me this till several weeks after my arrival; but she was still upstairs at the time, and obliged to divide her days between her bed and a lounge. During those endless intervening weeks, she told me, she had thought the whole matter over: and though the events of the mysterious thirty-six hours were still vivid to her, they had already lost something of their haunting terror, and she had finally decided not to reopen the question with Agnes, or to touch on it in speaking to the other servants. Dr. Selgrove's illness had been not only serious but prolonged. He had not yet returned, and it was reported that as soon as he was well enough he would go on a West Indian cruise, and not resume his practice at Norrington till the spring. Dr. Selgrove, as my cousin was perfectly aware, was the only person who could prove that thirty-six hours had elapsed between his visit and that of his successor; and the latter, a shy young man, burdened by the heavy additional practice suddenly thrown on his shoulders, told me (when I risked a little private talk with him) that in the haste of Dr. Selgrove's departure the only instructions he had given about Mrs. Clayburn were summed up in the brief memorandum: "Broken ankle. Have X-rayed."

Knowing my cousin's authoritative character, I was surprised at her decision not to speak to the servants of what had happened; but on thinking it over I concluded she was right. They were all exactly as they had been before that unexplained episode: efficient, devoted, respectful and respectable. She was dependent on them and felt at home with them, and she evidently preferred to put the whole matter out of her mind, as far as she could. She was absolutely certain that something strange had happened in her house, and I was more than ever convinced that she had received a shock which the accident of a broken ankle was not sufficient to account for; but in the end I agreed that nothing was to be gained by cross-questioning the servants or the new doctor.

I was at Whitegates off and on that winter and during the following summer, and when I went home to New York for good early in October I left my cousin in her old health and spirits. Dr. Selgrove had been ordered to Switzerland for the summer, and this further postponement of his return to his practice seemed to have put the happenings of the strange weekend out of her mind. Her life was going on as peacefully and normally as usual, and I left her without anxiety, and indeed without a thought of the mystery, which was now nearly a year old.

I was living then in a small flat in New York by myself, and I had hardly settled into it when, very late one evening—on the last day of October—I heard my bell ring. As it was my maid's evening out, and I was alone, I went to the door myself, and on the threshold, to my amazement, I saw Sara Clayburn. She was wrapped in a fur cloak, with a hat drawn down over her forehead, and a face so pale and haggard that I saw something dreadful must have happened to her. "Sara," I gasped, not knowing what I was saying, "where in the world have you come from at this hour?"

"From Whitegates. I missed the last train and came by car." She came in and sat down on the bench near the door. I saw that she could hardly stand, and sat down beside her, putting my arm about her. "For heaven's sake, tell me what's happened."

She looked at me without seeming to see me. "I telephoned to Nixon's and hired a car. It took me five hours and a quarter to get here." She looked about her. "Can you take me in for the night? I've left my luggage downstairs."

"For as many nights as you like. But you look so ill—"

She shook her head. "No; I'm not ill. I'm only frightened—deathly frightened," she repeated in a whisper.

Her voice was so strange, and the hands I was pressing between mine were so cold, that I drew her to her feet and led her straight to my little guest room. My flat was in an old-fashioned building, not many stories high, and I was on more human terms with the staff than is possible in one of the modern Babels. I telephoned down to have my cousin's bags brought up, and meanwhile I filled a hot water bottle, warmed the bed, and got her into it as quickly as I could. I had never seen her as unquestioning and submissive, and that alarmed me even more than her pallor. She was not the woman to let herself be undressed and put to bed like a baby; but she submitted without a word, as though aware that she had reached the end of her tether.

"It's good to be here," she said in a quieter tone, as I tucked her up and smoothed the pillows. "Don't leave me yet, will you—not just yet."

"I'm not going to leave you for more than a minute—just to get you a cup of tea," I reassured her; and she lay still. I left the door open, so that she could hear me stirring about in the little pantry across the passage, and when I brought her the tea she swallowed it gratefully, and a little color came into her face. I sat with her in silence for some time; but at last she began: "You see it's exactly a year—"

I should have preferred to have her put off till the next morning whatever she had to tell me; but I saw from her burning eyes that she was determined to rid her mind of what was burdening it, and that until she had done so it would be useless to proffer the sleeping draft I had ready.

"A year since what?" I asked stupidly, not yet associating her precipitate arrival with the mysterious occurrences of the previous year at Whitegates.

She looked at me in surprise. "A year since I met that woman. Don't you remember—the strange woman who was coming up the drive the afternoon when I broke my ankle? I didn't think of it at the time, but it was on All Souls' eve that I met her."

Yes, I said, I remembered that it was.

"Well—and this is All Souls' eve, isn't it? I'm not as good as you are on Church dates, but I thought it was."

"Yes. This is All Souls' eve."

"I thought so. . . . Well, this afternoon I went out for my usual walk. I'd been writing letters, and paying bills, and didn't start till late; not till it was nearly dusk. But it was a lovely clear evening. And as I got near the gate, there was the woman coming in—the same woman . . . going toward the house. . . ."

I pressed my cousin's hand, which was hot and feverish now. "If it was dusk, could you be perfectly sure it was the same woman?" I asked.

"Oh, perfectly sure, the evening was so clear. I knew her and she knew me; and I could see she was angry at meeting me. I stopped her and asked: 'Where are you going?' just as I had asked her last year. And she said, in the same queer half-foreign voice: 'Only to see one of the girls', as she had before. Then I felt angry all of a sudden, and I said: 'You shan't set foot in my house again. Do you hear me? I order you to leave.' And she laughed; yes, she laughed—very low, but distinctly. By that time it had got quite dark, as if a sudden storm was sweeping up over the sky, so that though she was so near me I could hardly see her. We were standing by the clump of hemlocks at the turn of the drive, and as I went up to her, furious at her impertinence, she passed behind the hemlocks, and when I followed her she wasn't there. . . . No; I swear to you she wasn't there. . . . And in the darkness I hurried back to the house, afraid that she would slip by me and get there first. And the queer thing was that as I reached the door the black cloud vanished, and there was the transparent twilight again. In the house everything seemed as usual, and the servants were busy about their work; but I couldn't get it out of my head that the woman, under the shadow of that cloud, had somehow got there before me." She paused for breath, and began again. "In the hall I stopped at the telephone and rang up Nixon, and told him to send me a car at once to go to New York, with a man he knew to drive me. And Nixon came with the car himself. . . ."

Her head sank back on the pillow and she looked at me like a frightened child. "It was good of Nixon," she said.

"Yes; it was very good of him. But when they saw you leaving—the servants, I mean. . . ."

"Yes. Well, when I got upstairs to my room I rang for Agnes. She came, looking just as cool and quiet as usual. And when I told her I was starting for New York in half an hour—I said it was on account of a sudden business call—well, then her presence of mind failed her for the first time. She forgot to look surprised, she even forgot to make an objection—and you know what an objector Agnes is. And as I watched her I could see a little secret spark of relief in her eyes, though she was so on her guard. And she just said: 'Very well, madam,' and asked me what I wanted to take with me. Just as if I were in the habit of dashing off to New York after dark on an autumn night to meet a business engagement! No, she made a mistake not to show any surprise—and not even to ask me why I didn't take my own car. And her losing her head in that way frightened me more than anything else. For I saw she was so thankful I was going that she hardly dared speak, for fear she should betray herself, or I should change my mind."

After that Mrs. Clayburn lay a long while silent, breathing less unrestfully; and at last she closed her eyes, as though she felt more at ease now that she had spoken, and wanted to sleep. As I got up quietly to leave her, she turned her head a little and murmured: "I shall never go back to Whitegates again." Then she shut her eyes and I saw that she was falling asleep.

I have set down above, I hope without omitting anything essential, the record of my cousin's strange experience as she told it to me. Of what happened at Whitegates that is all I can personally vouch for. The rest—and of course there is a rest—is pure conjecture; and I give it only as such.

My cousin's maid, Agnes, was from the isle of Skye, and the Hebrides, as everyone knows, are full of the supernatural—whether in the shape of ghostly presences, or the almost ghostlier sense of unseen watchers peopling the long nights of those stormy solitudes. My cousin, at any rate, always regarded Agnes as the—perhaps unconscious, at any rate irresponsible— channel through which communications from the other side of the veil reached the submissive household at Whitegates. Though Agnes had been with Mrs. Clayburn for a long time without any peculiar incident revealing this affinity with the unknown forces, the power to communicate with them may all the while have been latent in the woman, only awaiting a kindred touch; and that touch may have been given by the unknown visitor whom my cousin, two years in succession, had met coming up the drive at Whitegates on the eve of All Souls'. Certainly the date bears out my hypothesis; for I suppose that, even in this unimaginative age, a few people still remember that All Souls' eve is the night when the dead can walk—and when, by the same token, other spirits, piteous or malevolent, are also freed from the restrictions which secure the earth to the living on the other days of the year.

If the recurrence of this date is more than a coincidence—and for my part I think it is—then I take it that the strange woman who twice came up the drive at Whitegates on All Souls' eve was either a "fetch," or else, more probably, and more alarmingly, a living woman inhabited by a witch. The history of witchcraft, as is well known, abounds in such cases, and such a messenger might well have been delegated by the powers who rule in these matters to summon Agnes and her fellow servants to a midnight "Coven" in some neighboring solitude. To learn what happens at Covens, and the reason of the irresistible fascination they exercise over the timorous and superstitious, one need only address oneself to the immense body of literature dealing with these mysterious rites. Anyone who has once felt the faintest curiosity to assist at a Coven apparently soon finds the curiosity increase to desire, the desire to an uncontrollable longing, which, when the opportunity presents itself, breaks down all inhibitions; for those who have once taken part in a Coven will move heaven and earth to take part again.

Such is my—conjectural—explanation of the strange happenings at Whitegates. My cousin always said she could not believe that incidents which might fit into the desolate landscape of the Hebrides could occur in the cheerful and populous Connecticut Valley; but if she did not believe, she at least feared—such moral paradoxes are not uncommon—and though she insisted that there must be some natural explanation of the mystery, she never returned to investigate it.

"No, no," she said with a little shiver, whenever I touched on the subject of her going back to Whitegates, "I don't want ever to risk seeing that woman again. . . ." And she never went back.

A Complete List
of the Stories
# of Edith Wharton

Early Uncollected Stories
(1891–1896)

Mrs. Manstey's View
The Fullness of Life
That Good May Come
The Lamp of Psyche
The Valley of Childish Things, and
    Other Emblems

The Greater Inclination   (1899)

The Muse's Tragedy
A Journey
The Pelican
Souls Belated
A Coward
The Twilight of the God
A Cup of Cold Water
The Portrait

Early Uncollected Stories   (1900)

April Showers
Friends
The Line of Least Resistance

Crucial Instances   (1901)

The Duchess at Prayer
The Angel at the Grave
The Recovery
Copy
The Rembrandt
The Moving Finger
The Confessional

The Descent of Man   (1904)

The Descent of Man
The Mission of Jane
The Other Two
The Quicksand
The Dilettante
The Reckoning
Expiation
The Lady's Maid's Bell
A Venetian Night's Entertainment

Uncollected Stories   (1904–1908)

The Letter
The House of the Dead Hand
The Introducers
Les Metteurs en Scène

The Hermit and the Wild Woman
   (1908)

   The Hermit and the Wild Woman
   The Last Asset
   In Trust
   The Pretext
   The Verdict
   The Potboiler
   The Best Man

Tales of Men and Ghosts   (1910)

   The Bolted Door
   His Father's Son
   The Daunt Diana
   The Debt
   Full Circle
   The Legend
   The Eyes
   The Blond Beast
   Afterward
   The Letters

Xingu   (1916)

   Xingu
   Coming Home
   Autres Temps . . .
   Kerfol
   The Long Run
   The Triumph of Night
   The Choice

Uncollected Story   (1919)

   Writing a War Story

Here and Beyond   (1926)

   Miss Mary Pask
   The Young Gentlemen
   Bewitched
   The Seed of the Faith
   The Temperate Zone
   Velvet Ear Pads

Certain People   (1930)

   Atrophy
   A Bottle of Perrier
   After Holbein
   Dieu d'Amour
   The Refugees
   Mr. Jones

Human Nature   (1933)

   Her Son
   The Day of the Funeral
   A Glimpse
   Joy in the House
   Diagnosis

The World Over   (1936)

   Charm Incorporated
   Pomegranate Seed
   Permanent Wave
   Confession
   Roman Fever
   The Looking Glass
   Duration

From *Ghosts*   (1937)

   All Souls'

NOTES

Most of the information about the first publication of these stories is taken from *Edith Wharton: An Annotated Secondary Bibliography*, by Kristin O. Lauer and Margaret P. Murray (Garland, 1990). I owe an immense debt of gratitude to this voluminous work.

1. "A Journey." Written in the late autumn of 1898. Not published in magazine form.

2. "The Pelican." Written in March 1898; published in *Scribner's Magazine* in November of the same year.
   A late-medieval legend describes the pelican (which was also a symbol of Christ) as feeding her young with her own blood.

3. "Souls Belated." Written in the summer of 1898. Not published in magazine form.

4. "The Descent of Man." Published in *Scribner's*, 1909.

5. "The Mission of Jane." Published in *Harper's Magazine* in December 1902.

6. "The Other Two." Published in *Collier's*, February 13, 1904.

7. "The Dilettante." Published in *Harper's*, December 1903.

8. "The Lady's Maid's Bell." Published in *Scribner's*, November 1902. Edith Wharton's first ghost story.

9. "The Legend." Published in *Scribner's*, March 1910. On the relation between the protagonist of this story, John Pellerin, and Henry James, see EW to Morton Fullerton, March 19, 1910 (*The Letters of Edith Wharton*, edited by R.W.B. Lewis and Nancy Lewis, 1988: pp. 201–202)

10. "The Eyes." Published in *Scribner's,* June 1910.

11. "Xingu." *Scribner's,* December 1911. Edith Wharton's interest in the river Xingu, which flows north into the Amazon in north central Brazil, probably derived from Henry James and the latter's reminiscings about his brother William. In 1865 William took part in a Brazilian zoological expedition under the leadership of the great Swiss-born naturalist Louis Agassiz. In the fall of that year, William with the others journeyed up the Amazon on a river steamer, the trip being broken at the mouth of the Xingu, two hundred and fifty miles inland. From here William wrote home to say that amid the beauties of the Xingu area (spelling it Shingu, correctly, after the Indian tribe which gave the region its name), he was at last beginning to enjoy the whole experience. In 1911, when Edith Wharton was writing "Xingu," Henry James was making preparations for his autobiographical volumes, the second of which, *Notes of a Son and Brother,* makes mention of William's Brazilian adventure and the special richness of his letters about it.

12. "Autres Temps . . ." Published as "Other Times, Other Manners" in the *Century Magazine,* July 1911.

      The real-life domestic drama on which this story is based took place in Boston, rather than New York, and involved the family of Francis Lee Higginson. The latter was a member of the prestigious Higginson clan that included Henry Lee Higginson, banker and founder of the Boston Symphony Orchestra, and Thomas Wentworth Higginson of Civil War and later of literary distinction.

      In 1890 Higginson's wife, the mother of his numerous children and a woman in her mid-thirties, ran off with another and somewhat younger man. Higginson offered her divorce on very severe terms, but Mrs. Higginson set up house openly with her lover in Paris without waiting for the decree. The two were married a little later.

      The rest of the real-life story has been told in some detail by A. Alvarez in the enthralling fourth chapter of his book *Life After Marriage* (1982). In New York in the 1970s, Alvarez came to know the granddaughter—whom he calls Emily—of the original Mrs. Higginson, the model for Edith Wharton's Mrs. Lidcote, and whom he calls Charlotte. From Emily he learns that unlike Edith Wharton's Leila, Charlotte's children were entirely on their father's side. "When Charlotte, after years of penance and exile, mustered the courage to return to the States, they allowed her to visit them [only] furtively: in a limousine with drawn blinds when her grand-children were out of the house." They never forgave their mother for the humiliations they suffered at school and elsewhere because of her behavior. When in 1940, half a century after the scandalous event, the family decided it was time to patch things up, they sent Charlotte a cable to the boat which was transporting her to America: "Welcome home." Charlotte, as Alvarez tells the story, read the cable, had a heart attack, and died within the hour.

As Emily talked to Alvarez over tea in New York on a winter afternoon, she explained what she had learned about her mother's violence of feeling toward *her* mother. "I understand that her shame was not social at all; it was sexual. That was the true effect of Grandmother Charlotte's recklessness. However cunningly they wrapped it up, the whole family was in a state of sexual shock . . . and thereafter their lives were controlled by a muted terror of sex."

Emily quotes to Alvarez a phrase from Edith Wharton's tale, referring to Mrs. Lidcote's belief that she had bestowed a "dark inheritance upon her daughter." Paraphrasing, Alvarez adds: "Unlike Leila, Emily's mother coped with her 'dark inheritance' by denying the impulses in her blood and concentrating on decorum. But that in no way lessened her private sense of doom."

"Edith Wharton got it wrong," Emily says. "Poor Charlotte: the real curse was not hers, it was my mother's overpowering sense of sin."

13. "Kerfol." Published in *Scribner's,* March 1916. This story may have been written some years earlier, and held back for some reason. Soon after the appearance of *Xingu,* the volume that contained the story "Kerfol," and in response to a word of praise about it from her friend Gaillard Lapsley, Edith Wharton wrote (December 21, 1916): "I'm awfully glad you like the book . . . but I don't deserve all the coruscating things you say about it. *All* the stories except Coming Home [a tale set in German-occupied France] were written before the war!"

14. "The Long Run." Published in the *Atlantic Monthly,* February 1912.

15. "A Bottle of Perrier." Published as "A Bottle of Evian" in the *Saturday Evening Post,* March 27, 1926.

This story, as Bernard Berenson testified in consternation, was written in a single day.

Wembley. The place outside of London (at this time) that was the site of a famous exhibition, in part a display of British imperial glory, in 1924.

"A Bottle of Perrier" contains what is perhaps Edith Wharton's most secretive storytelling performance. One has to reread with care to determine just what has happened and is now happening. It is no doubt a tribute to the author's skillful maneuverings that, although the first nine pages are hopelessly out of order in the 1968 two-volume *Collected Short Stories of Edith Wharton,* no reader in the twenty-two years since that publication has (to this editor's knowledge) ever commented on the fact. The proper sequence of the first nine pages is: 511-512-513-518-515-514-517-516-519; after that, the pagination is correct.

16. "After Holbein." Published in the *Saturday Evening Post,* May 5, 1928.

The portrait of Mrs. Jaspar, greeting scores of imaginary guests in her senile last years, is taken from Mrs. William Backhouse Astor, self-declared as *the* Mrs. Astor, leader and part founder of the social elite known as "the 400." The former Caroline Schermerhorn, Mrs. Astor was a first cousin of Edith Wharton's father, George Frederic Jones, and a first cousin once removed of Edith herself.

17. "Mr. Jones." Published in the *Ladies' Home Journal,* April 1928.

18. "Pomegranate Seed." Published in the *Saturday Evening Post,* April 25, 1931.
    On the mythological origins of the title, see the Introduction.

19. "Roman Fever." Published in *Liberty,* November 10, 1934.

20. "Duration." This story was taken and paid for by the *Woman's Home Companion,* after Edith Wharton had revised the ending at the editor's request. The editor, Gertrude Lane, then wrote Edith Wharton's agent Rutger B. Jewett, in September 1933, to say that the magazine was unable to publish it— apparently because, though "Duration" is in fact almost pure zany comedy, it was misread at *Woman's Home Companion* as a stiff and gloomy tale about very old age. The magazine's readers, in this Depression time, were thought to want to read only escapist fiction.

    "I was so much taken aback by Miss Lane's communication that I did not know what to say," Edith Wharton wrote Jewett in late October. "When I think of my position as a writer I am really staggered at the insolence of her letter, and if it were possible to make any one of that kind understand what she had done, I should not be sorry to do so."

    The story was not published in magazine form.

21. "All Souls'." This story was finished and sent to Edith Wharton's agent (now James Pinker) in February 1937, and published later that year in the collection called *Ghosts.*

    There is a certain confusion or inconsistency in Edith Wharton's dating of the events she associates with All Souls'. She herself observed the feast correctly on November 2. But in her poem of 1909 the dead are said to see and hear and respond on All Souls' *Night;* whereas in the story of 1937, it is on All Souls' *Eve* that the dead are believed to walk.

    The matter is made murkier by the strange woman approaching the house, two years running, on "the last day of October." Mrs. Clayburn and her niece agree (page 382) that October 31 is All Souls' eve, and the niece is even said to be "good . . . on Church dates". In fact of course All Souls' eve is November 1. Precision in the dating of religious rituals was not unimportant for Edith Wharton, though here for once she somehow slipped up.